MISCHIEVOUS MALAMUTE MYSTERY SERIES — BOOKS 1-3

HARLEY CHRISTENSEN

OTHER BOOKS BY HARLEY

Mischievous Malamute Mystery Series
Book 1 ~ Gemini Rising
Book 2 ~ Beyond Revenge
Book 3 ~ Blood of Gemini
Book 4 ~ Deadly Current
Book 5 ~ COMING SOON!

Six Seasons Suspense Series
Book 1 ~ First Fall
Book 2 ~ Winter Storm

GEMINI RISING

Mischievous Malamute Mystery Series Book 1

PROLOGUE

Life is funny sometimes.

You go through it believing you are a plain old Joe, or Jane, living a normal, mundane existence.

You work.

You pay bills.

You walk your dog.

You eat.

You sleep.

The point being, you get up every day and do it all over again, because nothing out of the ordinary ever really happens.

Right?

Here's the kicker: Once in a while Life throws in a bit of mischief—kind of like the snarky little brother you wish you could permanently lock in his room, rather than those few cherished times you've gotten away with when Mom wasn't looking —only much, much worse. And because you're expecting the same old same old, you're flabbergasted when Life punches you in the gut.

As you crumble to the ground, gasping for air, you might have that notorious *ah-ha* moment. You know the one I mean. The one where you come to the realization the experience was your wake-up call—a reminder you're alive and in control of your destiny—and to make the most of it.

The cynic in me thinks it's Life's not-so-funny way of reminding you who's really in control—the punch line being—you only *think* you are.

CHAPTER ONE

Shortly after 4 a.m. on Tuesday, I woke to a start, realizing it was garbage day and I'd forgotten to set mine out. Again. It was late November and though it doesn't get that cold in this part of the Southwest—certainly not like other parts of the country—the Saltillo tile was chilly on my feet as I jumped out of bed. Nicoh, my ninety-eight pound Alaskan Malamute—still on top of the bed and ever the helpful one—peered at me from under the blankets and pillows he managed to steal during the night, before returning to whatever doggie dreams he'd been having.

Ugh. Someday I'd get my bed back. Today wasn't going to be that day. The city's garbage collection truck would arrive in ten minutes, so I grabbed the trash bag from the kitchen and opened the door. It was still dark outside but the moon hung lazily in the sky, providing a single source of light as I moved through the backyard and out the iron gate that led to the alley where I shared a dumpster with my neighbors.

Except for the occasional hum of a passing car on the nearby street, it was silent. With my free hand, I wiped the sleep from my eyes and cursed myself again before tossing the lid of the dumpster, which as usual, was sticky and nasty. Just wonderful. I firmly grabbed the trash bag with both hands to toss it in but stopped short when I noticed the smudgy reddish-brown imprint my hand left against the starkness of the white bag. I started to look more closely when a putrid metallic stench filled the air, forcing me to focus my attention on the open dumpster.

I swallowed hard and tried not to breathe in too deeply as I looked over the edge, expecting to find a package of rotten meat or at most, a dead animal. I gasped in disbelief and shock at the horrific scene before me.

A girl's thin frame, clad only in a hot pink tank top and jeans, nestled among the trash bags and lawn trimmings. Her bare arms —flung above her head as if celebrating a touchdown—were a sharp contrast to her legs, which were bent in awkward, unnatural angles beneath her.

Disturbing as her body was, her face told an even more vicious and sinister tale. No, there was no celebration. Someone had made sure of that when they erased whatever smile she'd had —the wrinkle her nose made as she laughed, the twinkle that glistened in her eyes—replacing it with a death mask of pulverized flesh and bone, rendering her faceless. Unrecognizable. Blood congealed in her hair, likely once long and lush, now matted and tangled into oblivion.

Though sickened at the sight, an immense sadness came over me—who could be so cruel, so hateful—to end her life so violently? I clenched my fists as sadness turned to anger.

The blaring horn of the garbage truck disrupted my thoughts. I dropped the forgotten trash bag as I swirled to face it and waved my arms frantically at the driver, who looked at me through his hazy window with disgust. I was clearly messing with his schedule. I ignored the profanities he barked in my direction and continued to flap my arms, begging him to stop.

"Sir, please call 911!" I yelled. "There's a body in the dumpster!"

The worker pulled the brake on his truck, jumped out and joined me at the dumpster, probably doubting my sanity. After a whiff and an unexpected eyeful, he turned away and vomited loudly against my neighbor's retaining wall. Several seconds later he coughed, pulled out his cell phone and called 911.

Finally, he addressed me, "Hon, you seriously could've warned me."

I shook my head and for once, held my tongue.

CHAPTER TWO

Detective Jonah Ramirez stepped out of the cruiser and checked his watch. 4:45 a.m. Man, did it ever get it any easier? he wondered to himself. After sixteen years on the job—eleven of them in Homicide—he knew the answer. Over time, he tried to put the names and faces behind him, letting them blend into one another until they became less and less distinct. Still, the memories haunted him. Drove him. He shrugged as he surveyed the scene unfolding in the alley.

The crime scene unit had been dispatched shortly after the 911 call at 4:07 a.m., so Robert Jabawski and his team were in the midst of their investigation.

"Whatcha got for me, Jabba?" Ramirez asked as he reached the lead technician, calling the man by his nickname.

The stout tech grimaced as he came up from bent knees—an old football injury, he always claimed—pushing thick black-framed glasses to the top of his head before squinting at Ramirez.

"Nice of you to finally show up, Detective," he quipped. "You bring me any coffee or are you just here to block my light?"

Ramirez chuckled, then handed his old friend the usual offering: a venti-sized Starbucks Pike Place Roast with six Splenda packets and a splash of half-and-half. Jabawski sniffed the contents and nodded in approval.

"We've got ourselves a female victim—no identification— with extensive trauma to the face and head. Damage was inflicted elsewhere, but her body made its way into the dumpster before she expired."

"A beating?" Ramirez questioned.

Jabawski nodded. "Yeah, it's looking that way. There was a significant amount of rage driving this perp. Girl's got no face left. Here, see for yourself." The tech moved a few feet to where two members of his team were working.

Death filled his nostrils as Ramirez followed Jabawski to the dumpster. Though he'd grown accustomed to her pungent fragrance over the years, it was Death's indiscriminate vicious- ness that set him on edge. As the techs continued to work, he leaned in to observe her current reaping. Jabawski had been right, Death had been brutal—savage even—as she snatched the girl's life into her rakish clutches. Triumphant, no doubt, as she claimed her victory, despite the means with which she obtained it. He knew it was her way. Death—like Life—didn't play fair. Ramirez shook his head in frustration and turned his attention back to Jabawski.

"Anything to work with yet?" he asked.

"We're still collecting, but it's not promising," Jabawski replied somberly. "We're working with a dumpster and an alley, not exactly a CSU's dream."

"Witnesses?" Ramirez prompted.

"Nope. The owner of the house directly behind us found the victim while taking her trash out. Her name is Arianna Jackson. City's trash guy arrived within a minute or two after that. She waved him down and got him to call 911. Anyway, he's over by his truck. Despite having chucked his morning McMuffin all over the wall, he has quite a mouth on him. Ms. Jackson is with your guys in her backyard." Jabawski thumbed over his left shoulder.

As Ramirez started in that direction, Jabawski called after him, laughing, "Watch out for the big bad wolf, he's got a mouth on him, too."

Everything was moving in slow motion. Or at least it appeared to be. Police officers and crime scene technicians swarmed like worker bees from the hive, scouting out their surroundings meticulously, in hope of finding even the most minuscule of clues.

I'd spoken to several officers and carefully detailed my actions before finding the body. One officer eventually allowed me to retrieve Nicoh, who had awoken from his doggie slumber and—not one to be left out—had gone into full howl mode. Not pretty given the hour.

Unfortunately, it also hadn't done much to detract the small crowd of onlookers congregating at the alley's entrance. Now that I was safely in his sights, his piercing howls subsided, though there were still the occasional whoo-whoos as techs and officers passed. If anybody was going to get the last word, it would be Nicoh.

While we waited, I offered the crime scene techs shoe prints, fingerprints and paw prints for exclusionary purposes, along with a couple other items I thought might be useful, including a list of neighbors.

At first, they indulged me, but after a short while, most resorted to a tight smile, a nod of the head or a pat on the back before politely asking me to return to my backyard to wait for Detective Ramirez, the lead investigator on the case, to arrive.

With nothing left to do, I resorted to flicking paint chips off the weathered bench where I sat. Nicoh grumbled in disgust—

hopefully at the situation and not my choice of tasks—before sighing and placing his large head on his paws.

We carried on like this for a bit until a dark figure strode purposefully through the back gate. I had to keep from gasping audibly as I took in the tall, imposing stranger. Wavy black hair framed tanned skin, a strong, chiseled jaw and piercing green eyes. Though dressed in faded jeans, worn cowboy boots and a semi-pressed button-down shirt, his demeanor indicated he was the man in charge. His expression gave nothing away but I knew he was sizing us up, analyzing us in his cop-like way.

"Alaskan Malamute?" he asked.

"Very good, Detective Ramirez. Most people assume he's a Siberian Husky or wolf-hybrid, but Nicoh's 100 percent Malamute," I replied. "All ninety-eight pounds of him."

Nicoh sat up straighter and whoo-whoo'd with delight because of course, any conversation he was the subject of had to be a good one, right? Some protector, I mused.

"You know who I am." It was more of a statement than a question, though Ramirez arched an eyebrow in mock surprise.

"Well, I've been interviewed by most everyone here, excluding the media, of course," I subconsciously snarled out the word "media," which ignited a flicker of amusement in Ramirez's eyes. "Anyway, several of the officers mentioned you were the lead detective, noted I would need to speak with you and told me that my animal and I would need to sit quietly and wait until you arrived on the scene," I paraphrased the actual conversations, but was sure Ramirez caught the sarcasm. "So, now that you are here, how can I help you, Detective?"

* * *

Ramirez hadn't been sure what to make of Jabawski's last

comment, but as he entered the gate leading into Arianna Jackson's backyard, two things struck him.

First was the large canine. Surrounded by a dark mask, its eyes reflected off the lights, giving them an eerie, copper cast. It bore a strong, muscular body with a bushy, curly tail, draped carelessly along its back as it rose to acknowledge his arrival. Its pointed, megaphone-like ears jutted forward. If not mistaken, it was an Alaskan Malamute—not a breed he'd often seen in a city like Phoenix.

The second thing he noticed was the woman the dog pressed himself against protectively. She wore an oversized crimson Henley, black running pants and ASICS with fluorescent yellow shoelaces. Her long dark hair was pulled into a high ponytail on the back of her head. Angled bangs shaded her eyes, though Ramirez could tell they were bright blue, with a fleck of something he couldn't quite make out, given the distance between them. Whatever it was, it was striking. She wore no makeup but had a healthy flush to her cheeks. While tall and slender, her composed manner indicated she could handle both herself and that big dog, if needed.

She wasn't rude but seemed eager to proceed, so he dispensed with the small talk and got down to business. As he questioned her, he found her direct and to the point, with a great deal of confidence and control. Her eyes met his with each response, her voice never wavering as she detailed her steps. A cool customer for someone who had stumbled upon a body in her dumpster, he noted. It didn't mean she was immune to it, just that she'd tucked it away until prepared to deal with it. He'd seen it before—she didn't want to lose control in front of him. She was a tough one, for sure.

After they finished their discussion, he offered to call someone to come and stay with her or to take her elsewhere. As he'd expected, she politely thanked him for his offer but declined.

He gave her his card, told her he'd be in touch and scratched Nicoh behind the ears as he turned to leave.

Violet, like a brewing storm, he decided—that was the color of the flecks in her eyes.

Detective Ramirez quickly put me at ease as he questioned me and for the first time in a long while, I found another person's company strangely comforting. In fact, I didn't relish the thought of him leaving, but holding him hostage with my feminine wiles wasn't an option, considering the circumstances.

I kicked myself. Seriously? Thoughts like that were so unlike me, I must have been suffering from exhaustion. I sighed to myself and let Ramirez go before I made a complete idiot out of myself. Well, almost.

"One last question?" I asked.

Ramirez looked at me intently. "Shoot."

"You got a first name, Detective?" Eck, I mentally winced at my obviousness.

Ramirez broke into a small smile. "Jonah. Good night, Ms. Jackson."

"AJ," I countered.

"Good night, AJ." And with that, he strode out of the gate, just as easily as he'd come in.

Nicoh peered at me—a glint of mischief in his eyes—and for a moment, I thought he was going to follow. I know how you feel, buddy, I thought. I know how you feel.

CHAPTER THREE

He stood on the fringe of the crowd, smirking to himself as he eavesdropped on their whispered speculations about what had transpired in the alley. If they only knew.

Fools.

The task had been completed. Not to his satisfaction, of course, but completed. One more detail lingered. After years of waiting, it would soon be finished.

For now, he needed to focus on the end goal—obtain the final piece of the puzzle and destroy anyone who got in his way.

CHAPTER FOUR

Getting back to normal—uh yeah, good luck with that. After finding the body, I tried my best, but something was off. Several days later, as Nicoh and I walked to the park, I reflected on what bothered me. True, the incident had been a shocker. It wasn't as though I'd seen many dead bodies before, certainly not ones mutilated so barbarically. I shuddered, the image forever tattooed in my memory.

As unpleasant as it had been, that wasn't it. It was almost as though I'd missed something, something I'd seen and not registered. I kicked myself, my eyes had been trained better than that. As a freelance photographer, I was familiar with visualizing subject matter from multiple angles and perspectives. Yet this time, it eluded me. Maybe it was something I hadn't seen? A feeling, perhaps?

I continued to rehash the events of that morning and was so engrossed I nearly ran Nicoh head-on into the Greyhound trio—Molly, Maxine and Maybelline. Fortunately, I adjusted my step just in time and nodded to their owner—a man whose name I'll admit I don't remember. He nodded in return while the dogs did their usual sniff-and-wag bit.

Nicoh straightened his stance more than usual—head and ears held high, chest thrust forward—perhaps to compensate for my clumsiness, but certainly not for the affections of the elegant trio. Nope, he had his eye on a she-devil named Pandora, a silver and white Keeshond that lived around the corner with a retired lawyer. Sadly, I didn't remember his name either, but Pandora managed to find her way into our yard to visit on occasion, so her lawyer and I knew each other by dog and yard. Our little neighborhood was funny that way.

Situated in east Phoenix on the borders of Scottsdale and Paradise Valley, we were nestled into an area that was older than most, but where the homes and yards were well-maintained, despite their age. Citrus trees and date palms lined the streets, providing a canopy from the blistering Arizona sun without blocking the view of the surrounding mountains. A once highly-coveted neighborhood among the up-and-coming and affluent, the attraction of newer, cookie-cutter neighborhoods farther north had lured residents away over the past ten to fifteen years. While lacking personality, these newer neighborhoods provided many conveniences—high-end outdoor malls, restaurants, theaters, etc.—within a stone's throw in every direction, converting the congested neighborhoods into mini cities, which appealed to the masses.

A few diehards, like my parents, stayed on in the old neighborhood, meticulously caring for and upgrading their lovely Ranch-style home with its sprawling yard and manicured gardens until they died unexpectedly two years ago. The house had been left to me—their only child. I could not afford such a house on my freelance earnings alone, but my parents had paid cash for it and then set aside a monthly stipend for maintenance and updates, which was also willed to me. I couldn't bear to part with it yet. It was the house they loved so much, where I'd grown-up and created many incredible memories. The memories and the house were all I had left of my parents. A lump grew in my throat as I thought of them. Missed them.

I was jerked to the present by my companion's annoyed whoo-whoos. We had reached the park. No distractions while on his time, Nicoh reminded me. *Doggie translation:* Time to get down to business.

CHAPTER FIVE

Ramirez felt uneasy as he approached the house. He had initially liked the spunky gal. Maybe a bit too much. True, she had been annoyingly abrupt at their first meeting, but he'd also found her direct and brutally honest—traits he admired. Absently, he shook his head. Even though experience and an ever-increasing mound of concrete evidence told him what he was about to do was just, the task gave him no pleasure. He exhaled deeply as he knocked on the front door.

Nicoh and I had returned from our nightly jaunt around the neighborhood when there was a knock on the door. Strange that the person wouldn't ring the doorbell, I thought. Nicoh simply huffed at the interruption. It was dinnertime, after all. Some guard dog, I grumbled. So glad someone had his priorities straight. My thoughts on Nicoh's questionable qualities ceased as I opened the door to a grim-faced detective.

"Oh, good evening, Detective Ramirez." I surprised myself by managing to sound half way put-together, though inside I felt anything but.

"Good evening, Ms. Jackson," the Homicide detective replied evenly, though I noticed he was shifting uneasily from one foot to the other. Uh-oh, I thought. This can't be good.

"Please, call me AJ," I reminded him. "I assume you are here about the case? Do you have more questions for me? Have there been any new developments? Has the poor girl been identified? Has her family been notified? Are there any leads?" Ok, I'll admit it, perhaps babbling nonstop and getting to the point should be mutually exclusive.

Ramirez suppressed a smile when AJ fired-off a series of questions the moment he'd said hello. She had been much the same way the morning she'd found the girl in the dumpster. A casual observer would have thought her a calm, cool and collected customer, undaunted by the tragic circumstances that surrounded her. He had the benefit of training and experience, however, and knew the type well. It was a front, a shell she created to keep everything and everyone at an arm's length when the world around her was out of control. By presenting the tough exterior, she was able to retain some semblance of that control, even if it was only of herself and her emotions.

She had proven his point when she declined his offer to call a friend or family member to join her that morning. Even before he'd asked, he'd known she would turn him down. In fact, she seemed to have anticipated the offer when she quickly but graciously declined, as though purposely willing him to move on, to focus his attention elsewhere. Anywhere, but on her.

He forced his thoughts back to the present and to the matter at hand. Given her nature, she would expect directness, he decided.

"Actually, yes, there have been developments, AJ," he began.

"We have identified the victim but not notified the next-of-kin because there are none. We have no suspects—a few persons-of-interest, at most and at this point, only theories on the motive," he paused, but she looked at him expectantly, so he pressed on. "The victim has been identified as Victoria Winestone, a commercial real estate agent from Los Angeles. Does the name sound familiar to you?"

"No, I don't believe so," she responded firmly, though he could feel a cloud of unease surround her. "Should it?"

He ignored her question and continued, "I'd like to show you a couple of pictures. One is a copy of Ms. Winestone's California driver's license, taken a few years ago, and the other is from her LinkedIn profile, which is more recent."

Ramirez removed the pictures from the worn file folder he'd been holding. He placed each photo in front of her, studying her as she peered with interest, first at one, then the other. After a few moments, her expression transformed from one of curiosity to another of surprise and confusion, her mouth forming a tiny "o."

"As you can see, AJ, the resemblance is quite remarkable." Though she didn't reply, he moved on. "We compared Ms. Winestone's fingerprints to the ones you had on file from your freelance work with the County. Again, the similarities were remarkable. Finally, we compared Ms. Winestone's DNA to the sample you graciously provided at the crime scene," Ramirez paused to catch his breath, collect his thoughts and make sure AJ was still with him. She was, though her expression hadn't changed.

He delivered the rest, the part he had been dreading since his arrival, "The thing is, AJ, the DNA samples matched. In fact, they were *exact* matches." Ramirez placed a hand firmly on her arm. "Having said that, I have to ask you again. Are you sure you have never met this woman—murdered feet away from your home—who, by all accounts, was your identical twin sister?"

* * *

I gasped at his words, my mind reeling as I attempted to register their meaning. Though her hair was several shades lighter—a honey blonde compared to my reddish-brown—the girl in the pictures did bear a striking resemblance. Her eyes were the same crystal blue, speckled with a hint of violet. A quirk of a smile played on the left-hand side of her mouth, turning it up ever so slightly, as though amused by something only she was aware of. Perhaps an inside joke meant solely for her? I, too, had that quirk.

I scoffed. What Detective Ramirez was suggesting was beyond ridiculous. A twin? An identical twin, at that? It wasn't even possible. I was an only child. If my parents had still been alive, they would have found the conversation laughable.

Still, the fact remained. A girl had been murdered. Brutally. Her face bashed in, her body broken and disposed of like trash in my alley. How could this have happened? And why?

Suddenly, the ground felt as though it was shifting as nausea set in and bile threatened the base of my throat. Oh, no—I was not going to faint. Or hurl. Or cry. Or burst into some other crazy display of emotions. I squeezed my hands into fists and clutched them at my side, waiting for the feelings to subside. I knew I was being silly. Reactions like this were normal and probably expected, especially given the circumstances. They just weren't *my* normal.

Yet somehow, I knew from that moment on, normal was going to be a thing of the past.

Nicoh grumbled quietly, as if in agreement.

CHAPTER SIX

After that revelation, "no" was all I could manage, as a significant amount of brain-freeze had developed.

"There's more," Ramirez said. This time he would not meet my gaze.

"What?" I squeaked.

"Two years ago, your parents, Richard and Eileen Jackson perished when their plane crashed while in transit from Albuquerque to Colorado Springs."

I shuddered at the memory but added, "Yes, along with their pilot, Phil Stevens."

"According to the official report," Ramirez nodded toward the thickly-bound document he was holding, "all three passengers were accounted for and identified by their dental records. The investigator ruled the cause of the crash as engine failure, which was consistent with the pilot's final communication. In the end, it was considered an untimely, albeit tragic accident and the investigation was subsequently closed." This was not news to me, so I simply nodded in agreement.

"A couple of days ago, I was in Starbucks getting my morning brew when I was approached by two men who introduced themselves as private investigators from Los Angeles. Although I was skeptical, they indicated they had some information to offer. Typically with PIs, it's the other way around, so I decided to hear them out.

"They were searching for a client of theirs who had recently gone missing after heading to Phoenix. That client was Victoria Winestone. Unfortunately, I had to break the news about her death.

"As it turned out, Victoria had hired them six months earlier to quietly look into your parent's accident—everything from the events leading up to the crash to the investigation that followed." Ramirez stopped briefly to let this sink in.

Frankly, I was dumbfounded. "Why would this girl go to the trouble of hiring PIs to investigate an accidental plane crash? More importantly, why was she even interested in my family in the first place?"

"According to the PIs, Victoria was convinced the crash was not accidental. She felt bigger forces were at play. Forces that not only affected your family but hers as well. The thing is, Victoria's parents recently died, too," he said solemnly.

"Wow, that is awful, though I still don't see the correlation…"

When I didn't finish my thought, Ramirez completed it for me, "I know it's not going to make any sense, but there was a correlation, a connection between all of you. Victoria had proof of it. Proof you were her sister. Proof you were both adopted." He paused to look at me and for a moment, I wondered what he saw: fear, disbelief, horror?

Whatever it was, he let pass and continued on, though his voice had grown quiet, "The PIs indicated Victoria had known about you and the adoption for some time but weren't sure why she hadn't made contact. They were surprised when she suddenly left them a voicemail, indicating her plans to travel to Arizona, for you. It was the last time they heard from her. The next day, she was dead."

CHAPTER SEVEN

My head was spinning. Had I fallen asleep or been knocked unconscious, left to fend for myself in some sort of bizarro alternate reality? Or, better yet, perhaps I was being punk'd? I was sure Ramirez thought I had lost my marbles as I swiveled my head from side to side, searching for the hidden cameras. Finding none, I took a deep breath and opted to stare at the worn tread on my tennis shoes while I mulled things over.

"Are you ok, AJ?" Ramirez asked, concern filling his voice.

After a moment, I looked up at him and nodded absently. "In the last twenty minutes, I've found out"—I held my fingers up as I counted—"that *one*: the girl brutally murdered a few hundred feet away from where we are standing was not only my sister but my dead twin sister; *two*: I was adopted, and *three*: according to this dead twin sister, my parent's deaths were not the result of an unfortunate cosmic accident, but of some evil force out there killing adoptive parents." I laughed, perhaps a bit too harshly. "Seriously? This has all the makings of a bad Lifetime movie. Now that you've shared, what is it you expect me to do with all this information, Detective?"

Ramirez nodded in understanding. He had entered her world,

basically dumped all over it and then offered nothing in return but confusion and drama. She had every right to question him. He owed her. It was time to come clean.

"Shortly after Victoria's body was identified, the local FBI swooped in, debriefed us, rounded up all pertinent files and told us they would take it from there. So officially, we're off the case." I started to say something, but he held up his hand. "To make matters worse, every single time those guys take over one of our cases, it conveniently gets filed into their black hole of bureaucracy. In the meantime, any leads there might have been will go cold.

Unfortunately, this also means Victoria Winestone will end up a statistic—another nameless victim whose justice will never come—and that does not sit right with me. Not one bit." Ramirez became quiet for a moment, his eyes haunted, before turning to face me.

"I took a huge risk coming here and telling you all of this, but I had a gut feeling about you—one that told me you would want to know more and the opportunity to do more."

I shook my head in disbelief and nearly laughed at the absurdity of that comment.

"What is it you think I can do, Detective? I am nobody. A photographer with a dog who has bad manners and even worse breath. None of that qualifies me for the starring role as Nancy Drew."

Ramirez chuckled. "Dog-related behavioral and hygiene issues aside, you've got a lot more going for you than you think. Plus, you've got two PIs at your disposal."

At my furrowed brow, he quickly added, "Don't worry. They don't have your name yet—and I won't pass it along until you agree—but they're more than ready to get back to work on this. I'll admit, while they aren't saints, they are decent, hard-working guys—guys who don't like it when their client gets herself killed on their watch. They want to make this right, AJ, and I fully believe you can trust them to do it."

"But what if your bosses or the FBI find out? Surely they'll realize the information about Victoria's identity was leaked from somewhere?"

"I will deal with it as it comes."

He provided me with the PIs particulars, scratching Nicoh behind the ears before turning to leave. As he pulled the door behind him, he looked at me, his gaze intense.

"AJ?"

"Yeah?"

"Watch your back. My gut also tells me this is far from over."

"Is your gut ever wrong, Detective?"

"Good or bad, there's a first time for everything."

CHAPTER EIGHT

My brain was still swimming from Ramirez's visit when the front door opened and my best friend, Leah Campbell, popped her head in. Despite the concern crinkling at the corners of her eyes and mouth, I smiled at the sight of her. Tired of the Sunshine Barbie nickname her co-workers at the newspaper had bestowed upon her, Leah recently rebelled by lopping off her long shimmering locks in favor of a shorter, spiky cut—which still made her adorable, but gave her more of an edgy, precocious appearance. Think Meg Ryan in *Addicted to Love*.

She offered me one of the iced lattes she was holding, then slipped a doggie treat from her pocket and tossed it into the air. Nicoh inhaled it without chewing, all while giving her one of his famous I-almost-had-to-wait looks. I took a long sip of my beverage before nodding in satisfaction and then proceeded to fill her in on my conversation with Ramirez. She said nothing until I finished, though her usually perky features were grim as she listened intently.

"You ok?" she asked after a long moment, self-consciously attempting to tuck a stray spike behind her ear, only to have it errantly jut in the opposite direction. "It's a lot to digest for anyone, Ajax. Even you."

She used the nickname she had given me years earlier. Not that I liked being compared to cleaning products but she had a point—despite my sometimes outwardly abrasive and direct nature, I always managed to get the job done.

I shrugged. I certainly didn't feel like I was living up to my nickname today. I turned to the kitchen counter, where I had spread out the notes for my next photo assignment—a failed attempt at distracting myself from the day's events.

"What's this?" Leah asked, eyeing me carefully. "I thought you were going to take a couple of days off?"

"I was, but wallowing in self-pity doesn't pay the bills or feed this gluttonous beast." I scratched Nicoh behind his massive, downy-soft ears and was rewarded with a low whoo-whoo of approval.

"Besides," I continued, "Charlie basically threatened me if I didn't get the shots of his new Tempe Town Lake condo done." I waved to the paperwork in front of me. "Apparently, he has a deadline for another hoity-toity magazine."

Ahh…Charlie Wilson. My client. Born with a titanium spoon in his mouth. The spoiled grandson of a software magnate. Never worked a day in his life, but notorious for throwing very public, Oscar award-winning—or at the very least, Daytime Emmy award-winning—tantrums. And, to keep up appearances, the tantrums surfaced daily—sometimes even hourly—though thankfully, I hadn't had the displeasure of being on the receiving end. Yet. I wasn't inclined to make this the first time, either.

I should have been grateful Charlie had chosen me as his photographer. Of course, he had only done so because he felt we had history, if you could call attending the same high school history.

Our working relationship started at a party we both attended after returning from college—me from UCLA and Charlie from Harvard. While rekindling said history, Charlie generously offered to throw some work my way.

Charlie turned out to be more demanding and difficult than all my other clients combined, but his jobs not only paid the bulk of my bills, they provided me with the word-of-mouth needed to get my business off the ground.

At the time, I was appreciative, as I had recently started my freelance photography business, aptly named Mischievous Malamute after a few photoshoot mishaps featuring my canine companion. Thankfully, it had never been more than a couple misplaced dinner rolls or uprooted props, but it was still embarrassing. In the end, naming the business after my companion seemed appropriate—not only as a warning to future clients but a reminder to myself to keep him in check while on location.

I sighed and returned my attention to Leah, who was still focused intently on me. She knew, just as I did, Charlie's project provided a temporary distraction. I'd have to deal with Ramirez's news sooner or later. Knowing me as she did, she decided sooner was better and jumped in head-first.

"What do you want to do, Ajax? And, more importantly, what can I do to help?"

CHAPTER NINE

After much debate, Leah and I agreed—actually, Leah decided and I agreed—it couldn't hurt to meet the private investigators to get their take on the situation.

Using the business card Ramirez left, I made an appointment with Stanton Investigations of L.A. The administrative assistant, Anna Goodwin, told me Abe and Elijah Stanton were still in Phoenix awaiting my call and would meet me at Starbucks the next morning. I'd never dealt with PIs before, so Leah offered to be my backup in case things "got rough." Her words, not mine. I agreed though I got the distinct impression she was hoping a pair of Thomas Magnums would show up in a red Ferrari.

Leah, Nicoh—my backup-backup—and I arrived at Starbucks the following morning fifteen minutes early. Nicoh and I selected a corner seat on the covered outdoor patio while Leah grabbed beverages and snacks. I scoped the area but didn't see any PI-types lurking, so I settled for nervously picking the corners of my notepad. I doubted I would be able to calm down enough to take any notes, but as a reporter, Leah felt it was crucial to carry props. Of course, I'd forced her to leave the tape recorder at home, so she settled for a small notepad like mine.

We also decided against divulging her occupation. I needed to get information out of these guys, not send them running.

Leah came out a short time later, laden with caffeinated beverages and goodies. I grumbled I wasn't going to be able to eat, to which Leah smartly replied Nicoh would be more than happy to help me. Did I mention she'd already bought him his own maple scone? No wonder he was so incorrigible. And stocky. I was too nervous to chastise her, so I nibbled on the corner of my blueberry scone before Nicoh had the chance to claim it.

Minutes later, two ex-football player types entered the patio. Our PIs had arrived. Abe and Elijah Stanton were clearly brothers, both standing over 6 feet 3 inches, clad in black leather jackets, jeans and wayfarers, with the same angular features and sky-blue eyes. That was where the similarity ended.

Abe wore his tawny hair shorter with gelled spikes on the top —that whole Brad Pitt bedhead look guys claim they don't spend hours in front of the mirror perfecting—a black t-shirt and black Doc Marten boots.

While Elijah's hair fell to his shoulders in messy sun-bleached waves, the rest of him was anything but, with his immaculately-pressed button-down shirt that matched his eyes and expensive-looking loafers. Though I put them both in their early-to-mid thirties, it was up in the air as to which brother was the eldest. I looked over at Leah—who'd gone from an annoyingly tidy scone-eater to drooling mouth-breather—and kicked her as I rose from the table to greet them.

Fortunately, Leah collected herself as introductions were made and Nicoh gave them his sniff of approval. Though both stole glances at me when they thought I wasn't looking—likely due to my resemblance to Victoria—Elijah quickly started things off, indicating their intention to keep the meeting informal by outlining the information they'd gathered at Victoria's request and answering questions that surfaced as a result.

I was too antsy to tackle the tough stuff up front, so I asked them to give us a bit of background on themselves. I wasn't sure what I expected, but it wasn't their unabridged life history.

The Stanton brothers were born and raised in Salinas, California by a Highway Patrol officer and a high school history teacher. Like their father—a former college athlete—both excelled in football and were awarded full athletic scholarships, Abe first to the University of Southern California and Elijah two years later to my alma mater, UCLA. That cleared up my older vs. younger brother question.

Abe graduated with honors with a degree in Criminal Justice and immediately signed up for the Los Angeles Police Academy. After graduating from the academy six months later, he spent his requisite time on Metro patrol assignments, before competing for and being promoted to Police Detective.

Elijah, meanwhile, also graduated with honors with degrees in both Law and Business Administration but unlike his brother, struggled for direction for the first time in his life. Working as a clerk and research assistant in a top L.A. law firm had been interesting—and paid the bills—but didn't inspire the passion in him he dreamed it would. He wasn't afraid of hard work, and did enjoy the research, but couldn't see himself becoming a barrister for the next forty years.

Around the same time, Abe had begun to fester over the never-ending stream of bureaucratic red tape he encountered on a daily basis. No matter how tirelessly he worked, his efforts were routinely quashed for political reasons. After a particularly difficult period, he came to the overwhelming realization that unless he made a change, he would forever face the inability to make the type of difference he envisioned.

The brothers had each reached crossroads. Both wanted to affect change and be in control of how they went about it. Even if they only managed to do in small pieces over time, it was better than being at the mercy of people with ulterior motives, standing by going through the motions or worse yet, doing nothing. After much discussion, they combined the best of their skills—Elijah's knowledge of criminal justice and law enforcement and Abe's of law, business and research—and started a private investigation firm.

Starting small, they got leads from their former workplaces—including Elijah's law firm—and built their business on delivering thorough, consistent results in a professional, honest and timely manner.

The strong work ethic they'd learned from their parents, coupled with their tenacity and drive served them well. Within a short time, they had a steady flow of work—solely due to word of mouth—and their business thrived.

They splurged by opening a small office and hiring Anna, a former co-worker of Elijah's, to handle all scheduling and billing and more frequently, to assist with research. It was a win-win situation, Anna loved the autonomy the brothers gave her to run the operation and they were free to work out in the field.

Meanwhile, Dad and Mom—now retired—couldn't have been more proud of their sons. Of course, both expressed concern over their sons being more than 300 miles from home, though Abe and Elijah suspected both were making noise to cover their excitement. They would no longer need to make excuses for the additional trips to L.A.—their dad for his sporting events and mom for the surplus of shopping venues. We all laughed at the subterfuge.

I enjoyed Abe and Elijah's sharing of their background so much, I'd almost forgotten the purpose of the meeting. I said almost.

"So, how did you come to be here in Phoenix?" I asked.

"Way to be a buzz-kill, Ajax," Leah growled, loud enough for Abe and Elijah to hear.

Eyebrows lifted at my nickname, but Abe replied, "As Detective Ramirez mentioned, Victoria was our client. Two weeks ago, she left a voicemail indicating she was heading to Phoenix. It was the last time we heard from her. When she didn't respond to any of our phone calls or texts, we hopped in the car. After we arrived, we stopped at the police precinct down in Central Phoenix, introduced ourselves as PIs and showed them Victoria's picture.

"Ramirez must have been vigilant in circulating the details of the case—something about a bottle of thirty-year-old single malt —because no sooner had the words left our mouths, the desk sergeant supplied us with Ramirez's contact information, height, weight, shoe size, favorite flavor of ice cream…" We all chuckled in unison.

Elijah continued, "We were also able to find out Ramirez got his caffeine fix around the same time each morning," he glanced around, "at this Starbucks. So we took the opportunity to catch up with him.

"Of course, we still hadn't received confirmation Victoria was dead—the chatty Cathy desk sergeant hadn't managed to divulge that bit of information—though we already suspected something was up. I mean, if a Homicide detective is trading $1200 bottles of scotch for information, it can't be good.

"Anyway, Ramirez was suspicious at first, but once we gave him the condensed version of our background"—he paused to smile at me as I realized I had erroneously made the comment about their life history out loud—"and shared our connection to Victoria, he told us of her murder." Elijah looked away and Abe bowed his head, quietly studying his folded hands.

"I'm so sorry," I murmured, "she was more than a client—"

"She was a *client*," Abe snarked, taking me by surprise.

"I'm sorry. I didn't mean to imply…" I stammered, as Leah shot me a terse look that told me to shut up.

"No apologies necessary, AJ," Elijah said, his voice quiet. "What my brother means is Victoria was our client first. Working

on a case like this, for as long as we have, you get to know someone, especially when she puts as much in as she gets. It's hard not
to care. So, yes, though we worked side by side as professionals,
Victoria was more than our client. She'd become our friend."

"How did Victoria find you in the first place?" Leah asked,
quickly shifting the subject.

"We'd taken on several projects for Platinum International,
the real estate firm where she was employed, and though she
never worked with her directly, she was familiar with our work,"
Elijah replied.

"Yeah, surprised the heck out of us." Abe smiled at the
memory. "She was the first client who actually made an appointment to meet us at our office. We hadn't physically been there in
months—Anna keeps things running smoothly—so we raced
there to make sure everything was still in order. Of course,
Victoria arrived ahead of us, and she and Anna were chatting
away like old friends, in our meticulously-organized and taste-
fully-decorated office. And there sat Anna, with a coy, knowing
smile."

"She knew what the two of you were up to," I commented
with a light chuckle.

Abe, obviously no longer peeved at me, laughed. "She knew
we'd come rushing to fix things, which meant we owed her a big
fat raise for doubting her abilities."

"Lesson learned?" Leah teased.

They both laughed and nodded before Elijah turned the
conversation back to their meeting with Ramirez.

"Anyway, Ramirez seemed like a good guy—and though he
told us he'd been removed from the case earlier that morning—
we thought perhaps he could help.

"Ramirez might have mentioned this, but when Victoria first
hired us six months ago, it was to look into your parent's plane
crash." I nodded, so he continued, "Victoria's story started before

that, with the death of her parents, Joseph and Susan Winestone. You may have heard of them?"

We shook our heads. "No? Well, they made their fortune designing and building some of the most elite golf courses and resorts in the world—from California to Florida and Hawaii in the USA—to Australia, Scotland, Spain, etc."

"Oh my, yes! I remember them now," Leah exclaimed. "In fact, when they scouted locations in Arizona five years ago—" I kicked her hard before she inadvertently divulged she was a reporter. "Uh, I saw them being interviewed on the local news." I smiled at her sweetly, to which she pinched me under the table. I didn't dare look but was pretty sure she'd drawn blood.

If Abe or Elijah noticed our little squabble, they didn't let on. Abe continued where his brother had left off, "Anyway, the Winestones were taking the new Jag out for a spin along the Pacific Coast Highway. At one point during their trip, between Malibu and Santa Monica, the car veered, crashed through the divider and tumbled down the embankment, killing them both instantly."

"According to witnesses, the driver—Susan Winestone— never hit the brakes, nor appeared to be speeding. The crash investigators indicated the condition of that portion of the road had been good at the time of the accident—no potholes, dips, etc. —and the weather had been dry and clear. Technicians later confirmed the vehicle had no apparent defects.

"When Mrs. Winestone's autopsy results were released, there were no indications of heart attack or stroke, and her blood work showed no signs she'd been impaired by drugs or alcohol."

Abe took a deep breath and nodded at his brother, who continued, "However, that wasn't the only thing her blood confirmed. It held another secret, as did Joseph Winestone's. Her mother's blood type was O and her father's type B, but Victoria's was type AB, meaning they didn't match. Joseph and Susan Winestone couldn't have been her birth parents."

"My blood type is AB, too," I whispered. Leah gave my hand a quick squeeze but motioned for Elijah to continue.

"Victoria was devastated, not only had she tragically lost her parents, but possibly her identity, as well. They had obviously not meant for her to find out she'd been adopted. Being the way she was, Victoria didn't fault them for it. She simply believed they'd had their reasons and the best of intentions. Nevertheless, once she knew, she was determined to find out more about her background.

"Having been an only child, she had no other family to confide in, so she turned to her parent's oldest friend, Sir Edward Harrington. Though he was known as Sir Edward to everyone else, Victoria insisted upon calling him Sir Harry from the time she was a toddler, despite her parent's opposition.

"Anyway, upon their deaths, Sir Edward received a key from Joseph Winestone to a safety deposit box at a bank near his residence in London. The letter that accompanied the key was written in Mr. Winestone's handwriting and instructed Sir Edward to review the contents and make his own decision with regard to their handling. He immediately called Victoria and encouraged her to come to London."

"Did Sir Edward know about Victoria's adoption beforehand?" I asked.

"That's a good question. Victoria asked him the same thing." Abe smiled. "Though the Winestones never directly discussed it with him, he guessed an adoption had taken place. They were very public people, and though there were months they would hunker down to work on a project, a pregnancy would not have gone unnoticed. No one said a word when little Victoria was finally spotted in public. Perhaps because of the era, or perhaps, like Sir Edward, people were happy the couple had something other than work to occupy their lives. As strange as it sounds, the adoption never came up."

"Perhaps the wealthy do live charmed lives," Leah remarked as I excused myself so I could take Nicoh for a quick walk. Poor baby hadn't gotten much attention since introductions were made and had been dancing on the tips of his paws for at least fifteen minutes. He finished his business, and after I gave him some well-deserved scratches, we headed back to join the others.

Preoccupied with the conversation, I hadn't realized how much the patio had filled in. We now had company on both sides: a couple bickering over wedding invites on the left and a guy wearing an Arizona Diamondbacks hat on the right similar to one my dad once owned, listening to his iPod while reading the paper.

I realized Abe and Elijah were laughing at Leah's stories of our good old days in high school, so I quickly sat down and gave her the look, which made them laugh even harder. Great. That was the last time she was going to borrow my vintage 1950s cat-eye sunglasses, which coincidentally, were currently perched on top of her head. Would anyone notice if I suddenly snatched them?

Once the chuckles finally subsided and I decided to leave the sunglasses alone, I nodded at Elijah to continue.

"Victoria went to London to meet Sir Edward. Before opening the safety deposit box, he let her read the letter, in which Joseph Winestone came clean about the adoption. He and his wife had intended to have children, but work encompassed their lives. By the time they felt they could make a go of it, it was too late. Determined to have a family, they did the next best thing. They adopted.

"According to the letter, the box contained the documentation relating to the adoption and as promised, an overwhelming pile of paper was enclosed. The adoption had been arranged through the Sterling Joy Agency, a Chicago-based firm. Neither Sir Edward nor Victoria was familiar with the laws relating to adoptions, but it seemed the Winestones collected every tidbit of information they could find on the birth parents, including age, appearance, education, occupation, current relationship, reason for the adoption, etc., which is how they found out both were deceased.

The birth mother had died of complications following child-birth and the father…passed, a short time later." Elijah swallowed hard. Clearly, something bothered him about that but before I could ask, he went on, "Fortunately, they had the foresight to make arrangements with an agency in the event of their deaths—likely because they had no living family—otherwise their children would have become wards of the state.

"Anyway, Victoria also found out about you. Under a section titled 'Other Children Born to Birth Parents', there was a single listing: 'Female, one-month of age, born at the University of Chicago Medical Center'. Same birth location as was listed for Victoria, as well as her age at the time of her birth.

"This intrigued both Victoria and Sir Edward. Why hadn't her parents adopted both children? They had wanted a family—this would have been the perfect solution. They found the answer further down in the papers.

Once the Winestones learned of the second child—you—they immediately contacted the agency. Though the agency sympa-thized, they claimed the birth parents had explicitly stated under no circumstances were the children to be adopted together. And, based upon the letters exchanged between Sterling Joy and the Winestones, it also became quite clear the agency had been paid handsomely to honor the birth parent's last wishes."

"That is strange," Leah commented, before looking to me to gauge my reaction to this news. I wasn't sure what my face showed, but I was astonished.

"There was one final surprise waiting on the bottom of the security deposit box. Five documents were bound together, almost symbolically. They included Victoria's current birth certificate, her original birth certificate, your original birth certificate, your current birth certificate and your parent's address." My address.

"Oh, my gosh," I gasped as I looked at Leah, flabbergasted, "that is totally insane. Do you think they contacted my parents— that my parents knew?"

"We don't know, AJ," Abe replied quietly, "and with the players deceased, I'm not sure we'll ever know. It was this information, however, that prompted Victoria to search for you. And, it was at the beginning of this search she learned of your parent's tragic accident. That's when she hired us."

Leah murmured absently, "Perhaps there's another safety deposit box lurking around somewhere? One with more clues?"

"We'd thought of that too. It's certainly something we can pursue," Elijah replied, "but first, there's a bit more we need to tell you."

"Are you serious?" Leah squawked a bit too loudly, which made Nicoh moan like a moose.

I couldn't blame him, I wanted to moan like a moose myself —this conversation was becoming more and more like the one with Ramirez. Abe and Elijah both apologized, but I told them to continue, so Abe picked up where Elijah had left off.

"When Victoria got back from London, she went to her parent's house to check on things. On the answering machine, there was a message from someone at the dealership where her mother had purchased her Jaguar, apologizing for the mix-up and confirming she still wanted the original car. Victoria lost it."

"What rock had this guy been living under?" Leah snarked.

"Victoria said she gave him an earful," Abe replied. "The manager apologized profusely. He returned from a cruise vacation and wasn't exactly sure how it happened, but in his absence, the assistant manager had delivered her mother's custom-designed car to another client. Rather than disappoint that client, who had already fallen in love with the car, he immediately called Victoria's mother to confess his oversight. As gracious as ever, she let the assistant manager off the hook and agreed to take the car until another could be ordered."

"So, the car she was driving when the accident occurred wasn't the car she should have been driving?" I asked.

"Nope," Abe continued, "but that wasn't the end of it."

"Of course not," I retorted, perhaps a bit too sarcastically, "why would it be?"

"What raised the red flags—and frankly, still raises the hair on the back our necks—was when Victoria asked to speak with the assistant manager."

"The manager had already fired him?" Leah asked.

"He probably should have been fired, but no, it didn't go down quite that way," Abe replied. "He disappeared."

"Well, perhaps that's not such a loss," I countered.

"No, probably not," Abe agreed, "but when he went missing, so did all the other client's paperwork."

"As if that weren't a flaming red flag," Leah mused. This situation just kept getting better and better.

"So, is that something you'd still be willing to look into?" I asked, not even remotely familiar with the private investigator protocol, considering Victoria had originally hired them.

"Absolutely," Abe and Elijah said at the same time. Unless I was mistaken, they almost seemed relieved I had asked. Perhaps my affirmation meant they had passed some sort of imaginary test?

"Well, I'm sure your brains are mush by now, we've covered so much stuff today." Elijah smiled warmly. "Maybe now would be a good time to discuss where we go from here, if that's what you'd like?"

Though I was pretty sure he was asking me, Leah nearly swooned as she burst out, "We definitely like." I rewarded her by smacking her arm, which drew chuckles from Abe and Elijah and a serious unhappy-face from Leah.

"Yeah, I think so," I replied as Leah feigned rubbing her injured limb, "but I'm not sure how we do this. Do we divide and conquer, or do you guys prefer to work solo?"

"Heck, no, we'll take any help we can get, plus, we've got Anna too, who has pretty much already made this case her mission in life," Abe commented.

"Wow," was all I could muster. Victoria must have had as profound of an effect on Anna as she had on Abe and Elijah. In my opinion, they all seemed pretty loyal to the cause.

"So, if you are cool with it, here's what we thought some of the next steps—or action items as we call them—could be," Elijah said.

"Oooh, I like action items," Leah cooed but toned her oozing enthusiasm down once she caught a glimpse of my I-will-smack-you-again look.

"As I was saying," Elijah stifled another laugh, obviously enjoying our banter, "if you wouldn't be opposed to it, it would be helpful if you could find out some more information about the adoption, about your biological parents, their backgrounds, etc. We'll have Anna send you the documents Victoria brought back from the London safety deposit box."

At my questioning look, he continued, "Victoria would have wanted you to have them. I know she would." Elijah turned to his brother, who nodded in agreement.

I nodded back. "I can definitely do that. Plus, as the adoptee, it would probably be easier for me to obtain the information, without raising a ruckus."

"Yeah, we'd prefer it if you limited the ruckus-raising. We wouldn't want it to result in a brew-ha-ha, after all," Abe teased. "Anyway, while you look into that, we'll try to find out more about the dealership's missing assistant manager and the client who took possession of Mrs. Winestone's Jag.

"In addition, we'll be tracking down whatever information Victoria found that led her to believe your parent's plane crash was not an accident," Elijah said. I had almost forgotten about the cryptic voicemail Victoria had left Abe and Elijah. Her last voicemail.

"She believed 'bigger forces were at play' that affected all of us," I repeated from memory, my voice barely a whisper.

Elijah nodded. "We're not stopping until we determine what those forces might be. Whatever they are, they killed Victoria."

* * *

"Well, there's good news and bad news." Leah sighed as we walked to the parking lot several minutes later.

"Bad news first, as always," I told her, though I wasn't sure I was prepared for anymore.

"The bad news is they didn't pull up in a red Ferrari." She pouted, confirming my previous suspicions about the dual *Magnum, PI* fantasy. Stupefied, I could only shake my head.

"But, the good news is—it was black!" She squealed with delight.

More proof that the more things change, the more they stay the same. With the month I'd had so far, I guess I should have taken comfort in that.

CHAPTER TEN

He sat with his back to them. Arizona Diamondbacks baseball hat pulled low, eyes covered by dark aviator sunglasses.

Their conversation barely amused him.

Amateurs.

What did intrigue him was the girl. She was a dead ringer for the other one. Perhaps she would be just as feisty.

He could hardly wait to find out.

CHAPTER ELEVEN

After meeting with Abe and Elijah, all I wanted to do was take a nap. My brain hurt and I needed to put it into neutral for a while. Unfortunately, I had Charlie's project to complete, preferably before he burst a gasket. I always carried photo equipment in the back of my Mini Cooper, so I dropped Leah off at her office and headed over to his condo in Tempe.

I wasn't sure if his intention for showcasing the condo in the local home decor magazine was to sell it or to show it off—it was always a bit of a toss-up with Charlie—but my guess was the latter. Either way, the deadline for the winter edition was fast approaching, which had him chomping at the bit.

The editor offered to send one of her staff photographers over, but for as much of a braggart as Charlie was, he despised having people touch his stuff. After rebuking the idea of using one of the magazine's photographers—huffily exclaiming he had one of his own—Charlie promptly texted me and demanded I contact the editor as soon as possible, or else.

I did but found myself apologizing to her for half an hour for Charlie's rudeness before she agreed to send me the magazine's specs. I continued to grovel and was granted three days to submit the photos, though I knew the deadline was at least twenty days out. Deciding not to press my luck, I thanked her profusely and hung up, feeling about as well-received as a piece of gum on the bottom of her Jimmy Choos.

Thankfully, I was on the short of list of people he considered worthy of granting entry to his condo, though I was convinced his preference was to have me suit up like the forensics team on CSI. Fortunately, he settled for powder- and latex-free gloves and elasticized, non-static booties. Yeah, don't even get me started. Of course, I was required to leave Nicoh with the doorman, who always had a few extra doggie treats handy.

Sufficiently geared up, I was ready to go in. The condo had an open floor plan—reminiscent of the lofts you might see in Manhattan—and was designed in an ultra-modern industrial style —lots of steel and glass. Charlie furnished it with more steel and glass, using only black, gray and an occasional splash of white to accent the space. It was kind of cool, in a very sterile, antiseptic way. Case in point, his floor was definitely cleaner than any plate in my house.

I was grateful Charlie couldn't be present while I worked. His personal assistant, Arch, was there in his place to hawk-eye my every move. I actually preferred him to Charlie and found him fairly harmless, though I was pretty sure I spotted him snapping pictures of me with his iPhone. Whatever—I could deal with Arch.

I took several shots on both levels of the condo—the natural lighting was awesome—and was able to capture what I needed within a couple of hours. I packed my gear and shouted goodbye to Arch, though I knew he was lurking somewhere nearby. I collected Nicoh from the doorman, who had been receiving the royal treatment in my absence. Still, he trotted happily to the Mini and jumped into the passenger seat.

As we drove home, I suddenly realized how tired I was. Typically, Leah mused at my Energizer-bunny intensity, but the events of the day had drained me, both physically and emotionally. My mind hadn't gotten the signal, there was so much to contemplate.

I decided to wait for the package from Abe and Elijah's assistant, Anna, to begin my part of the research. Instead, I called Ramirez to give him an update, though I knew he wasn't anticipating one. He must have been expecting another call because he answered on the first ring, but seemed genuinely pleased to hear from me and listened quietly as I filled him in on the meeting with Abe and Elijah.

Only when I finished did he speak, "How are you, AJ?"

"I don't know. I've got a lot to digest and yet, I just want to sleep. Unfortunately, my mind won't let me."

"I'm sorry, perhaps I shouldn't have pushed you?"

"Hey, Victoria died trying to make contact with me. I owe it to her to figure this out, to finish it, whatever *it* is."

Ramirez was silent for a moment then quietly said, "I'm here for you, AJ, day or night."

"Thanks, Detective."

"Jonah, please call me Jonah."

"Thanks, Jonah. Have a good night."

"You're welcome, AJ. Sleep well."

I appreciated the sentiment but doubted rest would come anytime soon. And yet, I was out as soon as my head hit the pillow.

CHAPTER TWELVE

The documentation from the safety deposit box arrived promptly at 10 a.m. via Federal Express. Anna called less than a minute after I signed for the package to confirm it had arrived. I told her it had and thanked her for her promptness in sending it.

"Have Abe and Elijah made it back to L.A.?" I asked.

"Not yet, but I expect them this afternoon," Anna replied.

"Please, thank them again for me. I truly appreciate everything."

"Thank you, for agreeing to help. We all liked Victoria and hope that while getting you some much-needed answers, we'll also get her the justice she deserves."

"I hope I can find something that will help. By the way, my friend Leah has also offered to assist if she can. I probably should have mentioned it yesterday, but she's a reporter, so she has some resources and connections that might be useful."

Anna's laugh tinkled into the phone, a pleasant, carefree sound. "We're well aware of Ms. Campbell's profession. And please, thank her for us. We may need to utilize some of those resources in the future."

Despite being busted, I decided to play it cool. "Uh, great. I'll let her know," I stammered, making Anna laugh again. Being cool under pressure was so underrated.

"And AJ, I'm a resource, too, should you need one."

"Thanks, Anna, I appreciate it. I have a feeling I'm going to need all the help I can get."

"Just remember, we are always here for you, AJ." I truly believed she meant it.

We said our goodbyes and hung up. Even though I was left sitting with the FedEx envelope, thanks to Anna's call, I didn't feel so alone.

I still wasn't sure I was up for the task at hand, but with Charlie's photos already e-mailed to the magazine, Nicoh snoring soundly on his doggie pillow in the living room and a full caramel sauce latte sitting in front of me, I'd run out of reasons to procrastinate. Unceremoniously, I opened the FedEx box from Anna.

On the top of the stack, she had left a note indicating all documents from the safety deposit box were present and ordered by date. I wondered if they'd been like that or if Anna had arranged them for efficiency. Either way, I was appreciative. Just looking at the size of the stack was daunting enough, without having to organize it as well. It was official—Anna was my new second best friend.

Following Anna's letter was Joseph Winestone's letter to Sir Edward. It matched what Elijah had mentioned the previous day. Winestone had come clean to his old friend about the adoption and the supporting documents contained within the safety deposit box.

Four to five reams of adoption-related legalese comprised the bulk of the documentation. I waded through it, though I needed an interpreter—and a stronger beverage—to understand it all. I did make note of the pertinent stuff I found: the address and phone numbers of 1) the primary contact at the Sterling Joy Agency, Mrs.

Mavis Baumgardner, 2) the Winestone's lawyer, Mr. Jonathan Silverton and 3) the contact at the University of Chicago Medical Center, Cheryl Earley. After nearly thirty years, I wondered how current this information was going to be. My guess was not very.

Next was a document titled "Non-identifying Information." Interesting, considering while it didn't provide names of the birth parents, etc., it certainly seemed to provide a lot of other personal information. In fact, it was more information than most people probably knew about me. I read through it anyway, to see if anything stood out.

Non-identifying Information

Age: Father—35; Mother—34

Race: Both—Caucasian

Religion: Unknown

Ethnic background: Unknown

General description: Father—6 feet 2 inches, 210 pounds, black-brown hair, dark-blue eyes; Mother—5 feet 10 inches, 130 pounds, reddish-brown hair, blue-gray eyes

Education: Both—Post-graduate; Father—PhD

Occupation: Father—Scientist; Mother—Researcher

Hobbies: Unknown

Interests: Unknown

Talents: Both—multilingual; specific languages unknown

Relationship between birth parents (*Married, Single, Separated, Divorced*): Unknown

Birth grandparents: Deceased/Unknown

Current status/Reason given for adoption: Birth parents deceased

Actual birthplace and date of adoptee:

University of Chicago Medical Center, Chicago, Illinois; June 19

Age of adoptee at time of adoption: Two months

Existence and age of other children born to birth parents: One; Girl—Two months

Current status of other children: Unknown

That was it for the non-identifying information. Next was a letter from Joseph Winestone to Mavis Baumgardner, requesting additional information about the parents' deaths, as well as an updated status of the other baby girl.

Mrs. Baumgardner must have initially elected not to respond in writing because the following pages were handwritten notes— perhaps by Mr. Winestone—detailing a conversation between Mrs. Baumgardner, Jonathan Silverton and the Winestones that addressed the previous letter.

The notes were consistent with the information Elijah had supplied the previous day regarding the arrangements made by the biological parents and the subsequent passing of the mother following childbirth. And then, the bombshell Elijah hadn't shared.

According to the notes, the father committed suicide shortly after his twin girls were born and the mother of his children had died. My heart ached as my eyes filled with tears. I dropped the papers, hugged my knees and rocked back and forth.

Sufficiently subdued, I returned to my task. Mrs. Baumgardner had chosen not to share any more information regarding the suicide, though perhaps no one had asked. Would that have been considered tacky? If so, I would have flunked in the social etiquette arena, but then I didn't feel so crummy because I knew Leah would have too.

For now, I appreciated a reprieve from the details, but it was information we'd have to follow up on regardless. I made a mental note to add that to the list later, on Leah's side. I understood why Elijah had hesitated yesterday and silently thanked him for his compassion.

According to Mr. Winestone's notes, Mrs. Baumgardner

indicated the birth parents had made it abundantly clear that under no circumstances were the children to be adopted together. Though the Winestones were clearly disappointed, Mrs. Baumgardner refused to be pressed further on the topic. There wasn't much merit in the rest of their conversation, though Mr. Winestone did make a note to follow up on the girl at a later date.

Sure enough, immediately following Mr. Winestone's hand-written notes were a slew of letters, both to and from Mrs. Baumgardner that continued to breach the subject. She remained unrelenting—under no circumstances would she violate the agreement the agency had made with the birth parents. In her final letter, however, she did assure the Winestones the other baby girl had found a loving home, though she shared no more than that. In my book, the whole thing felt off somehow.

Finally, I reached the birth certificates—the documents I dreaded, and yet longed to see. I was glad Abe and Elijah had prepared me for this, but my stomach was still filled with butterflies.

I carefully lifted Victoria's most-recent birth certificate out and found mine directly beneath. Though both contained facts I already knew, I was shaking. Where the heck had the Winestones gotten this information? I shuddered, considering the possibilities. Next was a plain piece of typing paper, which contained nothing but my parent's Phoenix address, now my home. Though I'd been told it was here, I had hoped for some note, some comment or indication of how it had made its way into the Winestone's possession. If it had secrets to tell—which I was sure it did—it wasn't sharing.

I knew the final two pieces of paper contained the most important information—perhaps more important than anything I would read again. I took a deep breath and grasped a certificate in each hand. As I held them side-by-side, I read the names of the birth parents I would never know: Father—Martin Alexander Singer; Mother—Alison Marie Anders.

I then proceeded to read the name of each child. Ella Marie Singer was born at 2:15:30 a.m. on June 19. Victoria had been my older sister by a minute and a half, I realized as I glanced at the other certificate. Arianna Elena Singer had been born at 2:17:00 a.m. on the same day. The butterflies turned to outright queasiness as I absorbed the fact my parents—Richard and Eileen Jackson— had kept all but the surname I'd been given at birth. How much more had they known, I wondered? And, had it played a role in their deaths? Victoria thought it had, and she'd only begun to unravel the secrets.

Well, big sister, I thought as I gently placed our birth certificates back into the box. It's high time we finished what you started.

CHAPTER THIRTEEN

I was jacked-up and ready to roll. I decided to start my action items by contacting the individuals and organizations involved with the adoption. First on my list was Mavis Baumgardner of the Sterling Joy Agency. I used the phone number from the documentation in the Winestone's safety deposit box and received a "number is no longer in service" recording, so I called directory assistance. There was no listing under the Sterling Joy Agency, Mavis Baumgardner or any Baumgardner, for that matter, in Chicago or any of the surrounding areas. Perhaps they moved out of the state? It wouldn't be all that surprising, considering it had been almost thirty years.

I searched the Internet, and while there was no listing or website for the agency, I did find a tidbit in a twenty-five-year-old business journal-type article that read "...Maxwell Baumgardner and his wife, Mavis, founders of the Sterling Joy Agency, have decided to close their doors after years of service to the community. When interviewed, Mr. Baumgardner indicated the decision had been based on the desire to spend more time with family and to pursue other opportunities."

I wondered what those "other opportunities" might have been, so I continued my search. Two hours later, I had nothing. Nada. It appeared as though the Baumgardners had fallen off the face of the earth. I said appeared, not had. I had one more trick up my sleeve—a crack-shot newspaper reporter and researcher extraordinaire—my BFF, Leah. I started a to-do list for her. Generous of me, I know. Seriously, the girl lives for the stuff.

Next on my list was Jonathan Silverton, the Winestone's former lawyer. This time, the number worked, however, I awkwardly learned he had passed a few years earlier after suffering a massive stroke. His widow, Jeannie, was remarkably pleasant, and though I was somewhat vague about my reason for calling, seemed happy to have a distraction from her shows.

She had heard about the Winestone's accident on the national news and apologized for my loss. Ok, I *might* have told her I was Victoria's sister, but she drew her own conclusion about my relationship to the Winestones.

According to Mrs. Silverton, her husband had been in private practice for the better part of his career, though she made no mention of the Sterling Joy Agency. I asked if she knew what had become of his case files, and she said no. I believed her. She was probably one of those wives who had no idea what their husbands did during the day and didn't care to know, just as long as they came home for dinner. Now, I'm not saying there's anything wrong with that, it just wouldn't work for me. *Disclaimer:* This is solely the opinion of a single woman in her late twenties—please feel free to draw your own conclusions.

Anyway, as it was clearly a dead-end, I thanked the nice lady for her time, and we said our goodbyes. It wasn't all for nothing. I did come up with some nice to-dos for Anna's list. Yup, still spreading the generosity.

Before contacting the University of Chicago Medical Center, I did some quick research. Cheryl Earley had been an administrator at the time Victoria and I were born. Turns out, she still was, but nowadays, she was a little higher up on the food chain.

Unfortunately, in my experience, the higher up you are, the more assistants there are between you and Jill Public, aka me. As expected, it took me quite a few transfers to get to the point where I was granted access to Ms. Earley's voicemail.

Imagine my surprise when Cheryl Earley picked up. Avoiding the crazy, sordid details, I stuck with the basics and told Ms. Earley I was trying to track down information surrounding my adoption—that my sister and I had been born at UCMC almost thirty years earlier and both of our parents had died a short time later, resulting in our adoptions with a local agency. I was about to go on, but she stopped me dead in my tracks.

"Oh my goodness," she whispered, "you're one of the twins."

"You know about me?" I croaked. "About my family?"

"I could hardly forget. I had recently been promoted to my first administrator position. You and your sister had been born prematurely—by a couple of weeks if I remember correctly—but you were both healthy. And your mother, she was doing great. Then, all of a sudden, she wasn't. She went so fast. They couldn't save her..." she trailed off. "I'm sorry. I shouldn't be telling you this."

"No, no...please, it's why I called." I told her of my adoptive parent's deaths, Victoria's—then Ella—parent's deaths and finally, about Victoria's murder.

I waited for her response. And waited. Then, I realized I'd made a colossal error in judgment. I was convinced she was going to hang up on me.

Instead, she surprised me. "Arianna, I'm so sorry, for all the loss you've had to endure. If only things could have been different. It's almost as though your mother's death set off a chain reaction that would follow you for the rest of your life." I would later reflect on the truth of that statement. "What can I do to help?"

"I'm still trying to get my head around all of this. I've run into nothing but brick walls so far, but perhaps you can help me find out more information about my birth parents—any documents, records, etc. that might still exist. Anything, no matter how insignificant it seems, could lead to something."

"Please dear, call me Cheryl. I think I can help. Records dating back that far are archived at an understaffed, off-site facility. It's going to take some time, but I might have a way to cut through some of the bureaucratic red tape. Here's what we'll do—give me your e-mail address."

After I rattled off my email, she continued, "I'm going to e-mail you the standard medical record request form. Just fill out the basic parts and e-mail it back to me, along with a copy of your current birth certificate and driver's license. Once I've got it, I'll fill in all the nitty-gritty details—with the appropriate codes—so you get anything and everything related to your parents. Believe me, when I'm done, if one of your birth parents broke a foot and had it casted here when they were twelve-years-old, you'll know about it." I chuckled.

"Anyway, I know the director over there. He owes me a favor. I'll call and give him a heads-up, then send a messenger to place the request and your documents right into his hands. When his people are done, I'll have him do the same back to me, and I'll ship it to you overnight. Will that work, Arianna?"

"Heck, yes. Th-thank you," I stammered, before attempting to collect my wits. "A couple of questions, though?"

Cheryl laughed. "Shoot."

"Don't take this the wrong way, Cheryl, but why are you helping me? Aren't you risking a lot?"

Again, she laughed, but perhaps a bit more tersely. "Call me jaded. Or perhaps I've become too complacent over the years, but it's been a long time since I've had the opportunity to the right thing for the right reasons. And this feels right. Plus, you caught me on a good day." It was my turn to chuckle.

"Whatever the reasons, thank you, again. This means a lot to me."

"I know it does. You said a 'couple' of questions?"

"Oh yeah, please call me AJ? All of my friends do."

"Certainly, AJ. I'd like to hear how this turns out."

As promised, I had an e-mail from Cheryl waiting in my Inbox shortly after the call ended. I quickly filled out the section she'd highlighted, scanned my birth certificate and driver's license and e-mailed them back with another quick thank you.

I know I should have been ecstatic following the call with Cheryl —a part of me was—but I also worried it would lead to more questions. What is it they say about not looking a gift horse in the mouth? Perhaps said horse should just kick my butt now and be done with it.

While I'd been talking to Cheryl, Anna had emailed Sir Edward Harrington's home and cell phone numbers and indicated she'd given him a head's up—he would be expecting my call—so I kept it to the basics, leaving him enough of a message on his cell to elicit a return call.

After that, I took a couple of minutes to jot down a few to-do items I'd conjured up for Anna, Leah and myself throughout the day. I decided to wait until I heard back from Sir Edward before touching base with them regarding these items, just in case I needed to add a few more.

LEAH

Maxwell & Mavis Baumgardner / Sterling Joy Agency
   Question: What happened to the Sterling Joy Agency?

Question: What "other opportunities" did the Baumgardners have in mind?

Question: What became of the couple?

Martin Singer / Bio dad

Question: Are there other details surrounding his suicide?

ANNA

Jonathan Silverton / Winestone's lawyer

Question: What happened to Silverton's files once he retired?

Question: Who are the Winestone's other lawyers?

Question: Did the other lawyers know about Silverton?

Question: Did Silverton procure the birth certificates and/or my parent's address at the Winestone's request (provided they did not come from the Baumgardners)?

AJ

Sir Edward Harrington / Winestone family friend

Question: Did he know Jonathan Silverton?

Question: Did the Winestones know my parents?

Cheryl Earley / UCMC Administrator

Awaiting records on Martin Singer and Alison Anders / bio parents

Other

Question: Did the birth certificates and/or my parent's address come from the Baumgardners, despite Mrs. Baumgardner's resolve to the contrary (provided they did not come from Silverton)?

Once completed, I reviewed my to-do items and chuckled as I flashed on a quote from Nero Wolfe to Archie Goodwin, "...I didn't say this [exercise] *would* be useful, only that it *could* be useful..."

At this point, I could only hope Abe, Elijah and Anna were faring better.

CHAPTER FOURTEEN

Meanwhile, Abe and Elijah were wondering the same thing about AJ.

They had returned to L.A. the previous day, ready to hit the ground running. Unfortunately, the only things they managed to hit in the past several hours were a series of brick walls.

Victoria had been convinced the Jackson's plane crash was not accidental. They learned from working long, hard hours with her she didn't jump to conclusions easily—quite the opposite, in fact —and oh, so stubborn, that one. She routinely drove them crazy with her don't-tell-me-prove-it-to-me attitude. And yet, the day before she was killed, she'd been so certain, despite the fact they had previously gone over and over the official report, talked to the crash investigator, looked at the crash site and found nothing. What had changed her mind?

While she had likely memorized the contents of the report, Abe and Elijah agreed it couldn't have been the source of her new evidence. Anna had locked their only copy in the safe weeks ago, and Victoria hadn't asked her to retrieve it or make copies. They all agreed she would have done so, had it contained the linchpin they'd spent months searching for. As simple as an explanation as that seemed, it was her nature. She simply wouldn't have made the comment without having evidence to support it. They'd already searched her condo and had come up empty.

That left Winslow Clark, the crash investigator. Surely, she must have contacted him and asked him to confirm some nugget of information? Their disappointment mounted when he said no, not only had he not talked to Victoria, he hadn't seen her since the three of them had met him at the crash site several months earlier. He didn't ask about her, and they didn't offer—no need to voluntarily put her death out there—so once they had their answer, they thanked Clark for his time and hung up.

Too frustrated to think straight, they headed back to the office to touch base with Anna. She was not only an amazing admin, she got them back on track when they went off the rails. Yup, right now they needed a strong dose of Anna.

Anna was delighted to see them again, too. She knew the Phoenix trip had taken its toll—especially after learning of Victoria's death—but she had also seen grief and anger turn into something else—a mission. It had become personal. For all of them. She smiled warmly as they bounded through the door, like two schoolboys fresh off the playground. They scooped her up into a big bear hug and spun her around, laughing as they ignored her feigned pleas about wrinkling her outfit. Finally, Abe put her back on her feet, but not before Elijah mock-mussed her hair.

"Touch the locks and you're done, buster," she growled, though there was a gleam of mischief in her eyes. She made a display of smoothing the wrinkles out of the black long sleeve cotton blouse she'd paired with rolled-up boyfriend jeans and ballet flats, but a grin peeked out from under the long raven hair that had fallen over her face during their horseplay.

Abe and Elijah laughed heartily. Though she was drop-dead gorgeous—easily passing as a sibling of Angie Everhart's—and as sweet as they come, she could definitely throw-down when she needed to. Growing up with five older brothers would do that to a girl. Plus, they'd seen her in action at a couple of her martial arts classes. Anna wasn't a gal you'd want to mess with in a dark alley, much less a well-lit one. Of course, she'd lay you out flat, then apologize by baking you fudge brownies later. Still, they were glad Anna was on their side.

"Any word from AJ?" Elijah asked her.

"Yeah, in fact, we've spoken on the phone, as well as e-mailed back and forth a few times. She's busy tracking down leads at the hospital and adoption agency and is also hoping to speak personally with Jonathan Silverton and Sir Edward," Anna replied. "Oh, and she fessed-up about her friend Leah." They all laughed, before she added, "Anyway, I like her. She's got spunk and isn't afraid to speak her mind."

"Kind of like you, huh? Like two beans on a stalk," Abe chuckled as he went into the kitchenette to fill his water bottle.

"That's two peas in a pod, smart guy!" Anna shouted at him.

"Thanks for proving my point," he shouted back, laughing.

Elijah took his brother's absence to lean in and whisper, "I think Abe has a little crush on AJ."

"Really?" Anna replied, crooking her eyebrow. Elijah nodded and put a finger to his lips as Abe returned.

"What are you two whispering about?" he asked, eyeing them both suspiciously. "You know my birthday isn't until next month, though if you wanted to start shopping now, there's a sweeeet Jag—"

"Stop right there," Anna teased, "you'll ruin the big surprise." Roars of laughter filled the office.

Once the last of the chuckles subsided, Elijah turned the conversation back to the case, "Speaking of Jags, we should follow up with the dealership manager about his missing employee."

"And the missing paperwork," Abe added.

"Let me go grab his number out of the file, and we'll conference him," Elijah said.

As he strode into the other office, Abe turned to Anna and murmured, "I think Elijah has a crush on AJ."

"You don't say?" Anna deadpanned.

As Elijah came back, file in hand, Abe gave her a sly wink, to which she returned a quick nod. His secret was safe with her.

Oblivious to their collusion, Elijah sat down and dialed the dealership's number. The receptionist transferred the call directly to the manager, who picked up on the first ring.

"Jaguar of Malibu, Paul Switzer at your service. Today is the day—don't just dream it—drive it!"

He deflated a bit when Elijah introduced himself as a PI—most likely after mentally calculating the probability of a sale—but allowed Elijah to continue.

"My brother, Abe, and my associate, Anna are also on the call with us," he paused as they said quick hellos. "Victoria Winestone hired us several months ago on another matter. It has recently come to our attention, however, the situation with her mother's car might be related to this matter, so we're hoping you would entertain a few questions?"

"I have already explained everything to Victoria," Switzer huffed, "as well as to the police. Three times."

"If you wouldn't mind telling us, just once, we'd greatly appreciate it," Anna added in her most sultry voice. Perhaps a feminine touch would inspire cooperation? It did. Abe and Elijah rolled their eyes as Anna smirked.

"This 'situation,' as you so kindly phrased it, started when I won the dealership's yearly raffle for a European cruise. First time in twenty years I could take the wife on a real vacation. And this happens. Worse cluster in my entire career and it goes down the minute I walk out of the dealership." His frustration oozed through the phone.

"My now-former assistant manager, Tanner Dolby, was supposed to be in charge during my absence. Ms. Winestone's car was delivered on a truck, along with four others, as scheduled. Her car was the only one that had been a custom job. You know—special wheels, tires, leather, etc.—the works. The color was the same as one of the other four, but even then, you'd have to be a complete idiot to confuse the two, which Dolby managed to do.

"Dolby delivered Mrs. Winestone's car to another customer, Frederick Glass, before realizing his mistake. He claimed to have called Glass back immediately, but Glass rebuffed him, indicating his wife had already fallen in love with her new car. Under no circumstances was he prepared to disappoint her because of Dolby's oversight.

"Rather than get me involved, Dolby contacted Mrs. Winestone himself and played the sympathy card, appealing to her good nature. She was legendary for it, but he took advantage of her generosity as a means of covering for his mistake. It disgusts me to think about it, especially considering I will never get a chance to make it right with her," he sighed, his former employee's manipulation obviously weighed heavily on his conscience.

"Anyway, Dolby convinced Mrs. Winestone to take Glass' Jag temporarily—still a remarkable piece of machinery, just not what she'd ordered and paid for—while he ordered another customized car. I can't believe she went for it. It had taken months to get the car in, not to mention the weeks she'd already put into carefully selecting the customizations. Once she agreed, he probably figured the problem was solved, and he was off the hook."

"So he confessed when you got back and *then* bailed?" Abe asked.

Switzer laughed harshly. "Nope, I didn't even get the courtesy. He bolted the day Mrs. Winestone took delivery of the car—originally Glass' car—and never came back. My sales manager didn't have the good sense to call me while it was going down, so I got hit with everything my first day back from vacation. Let's just say, the only one I plan on taking in the future is called retirement."

"Victoria mentioned that when Dolby went missing, Glass' paperwork did too?" Elijah asked.

"Ha, I wish it was only the paperwork. Dolby not only allegedly removed or destroyed the relevant physical documentation but the electronic stuff, as well. And, believe me, it wasn't like you see on *CSI* or *Law & Order* when they are able to retrieve traces of the deleted documents after twenty minutes. In this real-life scenario, the hard drive was g-o-n-e, as in Dolby swapped it out with a new one and took it with him. Allegedly, of course.

"Anyway, I haven't even told you the best part yet. After Dolby skipped out, Mrs. Winestone's custom car went missing. And Frederick Glass? Well, he never existed."

Abe, Elijah, and Anna looked at one another. Something wasn't adding up. "Seems like a pretty elaborate plan just to steal a car," Anna commented, to no one in particular. "Why the cover-up? Why not just take Mrs. Winestone's car and go? Unless..." she paused as they all mentally finished her thought. Dolby needed to get the other car into Mrs. Winestone's hands. They were silent as they pondered the possibilities.

It was Switzer who finally spoke, changing the subject. "Say, you guys mind doing me a favor? Would you let Victoria know she left her sunglasses here? I would have mailed them, but I don't know where she lives."

"Wait, Victoria was there?" Anna stuttered as Abe and Elijah's eyes widened in surprise. "When was this?"

"Um, a couple of weeks ago," Switzer replied. "I needed her to come down and finalize some paperwork pertaining to her mother's car, for insurance purposes and things of that nature."

"We always assumed she had only called you," Abe

commented, looking at Anna and his brother, who both nodded in return.

"Well, she did call me, but that was on a previous occasion, after my new assistant manager left a message on her parent's machine about her mother's car. He's not from around here and, unfortunately, wasn't aware they'd been killed several months prior.

"Anyway, on the day she was here, I had to leave her for a couple of minutes while I dealt with a crisis in the service department. When I came back, she was gone. The receptionist, Bonnie, said Victoria literally ran out the door, indicating something urgent had come up, and she was sorry, but she had to leave. Bonnie also said if she hadn't known better, she would have thought Victoria had seen a ghost."

Abe, Elijah, and Anna could do nothing but look at each other, open-mouthed, as Switzer dropped that bombshell.

"Anyway, it must have been something important, because she left some pretty nice Dolce & Gabbana sunglasses behind."

Important indeed.

CHAPTER FIFTEEN

As they looked at one another, an executive decision was made. Elijah gently told Switzer of Victoria's untimely and very recent death. He was quiet for so long, they weren't sure if he had abandoned them altogether.

His voice was somber when he spoke, "I can't believe it." Again, he went silent.

"The thing is, Paul," Abe said, calling the man by his first name, "Victoria was on to something before she was killed. It's a long, convoluted story, but in her last voicemail, she said she had proof her family member's deaths hadn't been accidental," he paused to look at Elijah and Anna.

They nodded, realizing he was being purposely vague with Switzer—throwing out enough rope for him to grasp—without being completely untruthful or divulging too much. They both nodded and made gestures with their hands for him to proceed.

"We had worked together for months, coming up with a lot of facts and theories, but no concrete proof, like you mentioned before. Then suddenly, she meets with you and walks—no, runs —out with what might have been the needle in the haystack, because right after that, she left us that ominous last voicemail.

The next day, she was found…murdered. You get what I'm saying here, Paul?"

Switzer let out a low whistle before replying, "I do, and I get that you're giving me enough to read between the lines." When there was a pregnant pause on the other end, he chuckled. "I may sell cars for a living, but I'm no dolt. I'm good at reading people and situations, even over the phone." That garnered him a collective chuckle. "However," he continued, "I'm not sure what you are asking of me. I mean, if you want to come down and look around, all you need to do is ask."

Anna was the one to breach the silence from their side of the line, "Paul, have you ever considered a job in private investigation?"

An ear-splitting collection of male laughter erupted before he responded, "If I do, I'll let you know." More laughter followed. "So, when can I expect you?" Switzer asked.

"We'll be there in an hour and a half," Elijah responded.

"And guys?" Switzer said. "Make sure you bring back-up."

Abe and Elijah grinned at Anna, who sweetly replied, "Honey, I'll be there."

Still chuckling, they signed-off and piled into Anna's massive SUV. Abe and Elijah speculated loudly as to how she managed to park the thing, to which she tartly replied, "Oh my, I think I accidentally ran over one of your 'toys' while scootching into my parking space this morning. Thought the Ferrari was a speed bump. Sorry, my bad." At their looks of horror, she giggled slyly. Still, they might have been a little bit afraid. Yeah, just a little.

Their kidding continued all the way to Malibu, which made for a quick trip as they pulled into the parking lot of the dealership. Switzer must have been watching for them, because a little round man who could have passed for Hercule Poirot's double, sans the curly-tips on the mustache, was at Anna's door before she had finished parking.

"Holy crap," he exclaimed, "with all the money you've spent buying gas for this tank, you could have bought one of these." He pointed to the sparkling new Jaguars that spanned the front of the lot.

"Yeah, and I could have had a V-8, too," Anna retorted.

"I like this gal," the little man replied as he stuck out a beefy hand. "I'm Paul Switzer. You must be Anna."

She took his hand. "Good guess, now I'm convinced you were meant for PI work." They all laughed as introductions were officially made.

"So, how do you want to do this?" Switzer asked.

"Why don't we walk through your conversation with Victoria. Where you were, what you did," Abe suggested.

"That's easy," Switzer said as he escorted them into the dealership. They nodded at the receptionist at the entrance of the showroom—who must have been Bonnie—before moving into a spacious glass office behind her desk. Nice, if you were into the whole fishbowl theme.

"We were in here until I left to deal with the service issue."

"Did anyone stop by during that time?" Elijah asked.

"No, no one. All the salespeople were with customers."

"What about the service people? You said there was an issue?" Abe added.

"The service manager called me from his office. He didn't stop by."

"What about when you left?" Anna asked.

"I checked with Bonnie, and she said, no, there was no one. And as you can see, from the position of her desk"—it was literally at the entrance of the dealership—"nobody's getting by her without her seeing them. And before you ask, she didn't go on break that entire time.

"Also, not that she was being nosy or anything, but Bonnie

didn't see her take any phone calls. In fact, she said she never saw her pull out a cell, even to check text messages."

"That definitely sounds like Victoria," Elijah commented. "She wasn't one to obsessively check for messages. And she never sent texts."

He turned to his brother and Anna, who were both looking intently at the wall outside Switzer's office.

"What is that?" he asked Switzer as he joined them.

"Oh, that's our employee bulletin board. We post employee accolades, upcoming activities and contests, photos from holiday parties, stuff like that. In fact, you two are looking at the photos from last year's Christmas party. Pretty random stuff, but a fun time for friends and family."

Random was right—there were photos of adults and children of all shapes and sizes eating, dancing, singing or playing games.

"What was here?" Anna asked, pointing to a section of the collage where the construction paper backing peeked through, exposing a small piece of transparent tape.

"Wow, I don't know. Looks like someone pulled one of the photos down." Switzer squinted, then turned to his receptionist and asked her to join them. The young petite blonde shuffled over, wringing her hands, clearly fearing the worst.

"Bonnie, can you tell me if something was here?" Switzer asked her as he pointed at the empty section.

"I can't tell you what that picture was of or who was in it, but I'm sure there used to be one there." She looked at us earnestly, wringing her hands even more feverishly, before adding, "That girl, Victoria, was looking at them right before she left, though I can't say if she took anything with her."

Abe, Elijah and Anna quickly looked at one another. It wasn't much, but it was something.

Anna gently touched the girl on the shoulder. "Hi Bonnie, I'm Anna. We appreciate your help and your honesty. I was wondering, do you happen to know who shot the photographs for the party?" Relief filled the girl's eyes as she realized she wasn't in trouble.

Bonnie nodded. "Well, we all did. It's the same way we do it at all the parties, Mr. Switzer. There are tables with disposable cameras everywhere so anybody can take pictures any time they want."

"Are there negative of these pictures somewhere, Bonnie?" Switzer asked.

"Negatives, sir?" She blinked. "I don't know about that. I'm pretty sure everything is digital. You know, like on a CD?"

Bonnie wasn't trying to offend her boss, she was way too sweet to be rude like that, and young. Abe and Elijah tried to keep from grinning while Anna elbowed them both in the ribs, mouthing for them to stop.

"Um, Bonnie, how many of these cameras would you estimate there were at the party?" Abe asked.

"Five hundred," she replied promptly, "with twenty-seven pictures each. I know because I'm the one who ordered them."

"Wow, that's over 13,000 photos, assuming they all turned out and all the cameras were used." Elijah whistled.

"I currently have all the images on my desktop. I could copy them onto a thumb drive if that would be helpful?" Bonnie offered politely. "Of course, only if it's ok with you, Mr. Switzer?"

"Yes, Bonnie, that would be more than ok. It would be helpful, wouldn't it?" he asked as he turned to the others.

"Absolutely, thank you, Bonnie," Anna replied.

"It will take me awhile, but if you want to grab some late lunch or something, I should have them ready by the time you get back," Bonnie added thoughtfully.

"That's a great idea—best one I've heard all day," Elijah agreed, as his stomach growled loudly.

They asked Switzer if he wanted to join them but the dealership manager graciously waved them off, citing issues that needed his attention. They headed to a nearby chain restaurant, but elected not to discuss the events of the day.

"We've got the whole ride home for that," Abe commented. "No sense giving ourselves indigestion." Anna and Elijah nodded in the affirmative.

As promised, Bonnie had a thumb drive waiting for them upon their return. Before heading back to L.A., they popped their heads into Switzer's office to thank him and say their goodbyes. They also had one final question, something that occurred to them on their way back to the dealership.

"You don't happen to have a picture of Dolby do you?" Abe asked him.

"You know, the police asked me that too. Unfortunately, I don't. Or at least nothing useful. We took a copy of his driver's license when we hired him, but the picture is so grainy, it could be anyone, including my mother-in-law."

"Gotcha, just thought we'd ask," Elijah said. "Thanks for everything, Paul."

"You betcha. I'd love it if you guys would keep in touch and let me know how this thing works out. Of course, if you're ever in the market for a Jag, or want to trade in that tank"—he thumbed at Anna's SUV—"for something classy."

"Gee, Paul, you really know the way to a girl's heart," Anna replied sarcastically.

Always the salesman, Switzer winked and blew her a kiss.

CHAPTER SIXTEEN

It was the following afternoon before I heard back from Sir Edward. He apologized profusely, indicating he had inadvertently let the battery in his cell phone die and hadn't noticed it until that morning.

Heck, I could hardly be upset with him—who hadn't done that? That was until he made a follow-up comment about firing the assistant who had failed to keep his phone fully charged. At my pregnant pause, he burst into laughter.

"I seem to have pulled one over on you, Ms. Jackson," he chortled in a heavy English accent. "I'm sorry. Sometimes I can be quite a naughty old devil."

I laughed lightly. "So your cell phone-charging assistant's job is safe for another day?"

"It'll have to be. Otherwise, I'd be firing myself every other day. I have no assistant to manage my cell or for any other task or any family, for that matter, now the Victoria is gone," he remarked somberly.

"I'm sorry, but losing Joseph and Susan was devastating enough. When I lost Victoria so soon after, it nearly killed me." I heard him gasp. "Oh goodness, please forgive me for my choice of words." A heart-wrenching sob escaped over the connection.

"Sir Edward, I'm the one who should be apologizing. I was so focused on my own agenda it hadn't occurred to me to think about what you must be going through. How you must feel. I'm sorry, please forgive me." It was true. I had forged ahead like a crazed bull, annihilating everything in my path. In doing so, I had exposed feelings he had not yet had time to digest, or heal. I had hurt this man. I felt like a complete and utter jerk.

He only allowed me to wallow in self-pity for a moment. Though sniffling, he quietly said, "No, you don't understand. Receiving your call, hearing your voice…was the most comforting thing I've experienced since Victoria died."

My heart ached as I recognized the voice of loneliness and abandonment. Like me, he had lost his family, his connection to the very thing that binds us to this earth—the thing that grounds us and makes us feel like a part of something—something that has meaning. When I had reached out to him, I had done so for my own selfish reasons, and yet this man had still found in me a kindred spirit. It was at that moment that I realized Sir Edward and I needed one another to gain some semblance of that lost connection.

I put my questions aside for the time-being, and we talked. I told him about growing up in Arizona with my parents, about family vacations, going off to college and my triumphant return home. We talked about my career and laughed over stories of my clients. And, as a dog-lover himself, he was delighted to hear about my adventures with Nicoh.

In turn, he told me about Victoria and her parents and how doting they were, despite their busy schedules. As a child, they took her everywhere they went, immersing her in new cultures and languages and anything else that sparked her interest. He quickly pointed out that while she had grown-up privileged,

Victoria was never spoiled or self-involved. Instead, she was caring and compassionate, taking nothing for granted. She was also fiercely independent. When it came time for her to start thinking about colleges, she refused to allow her parents to influence the admission boards, and was accepted to Columbia University on her own hard work and merit, where she earned a degree in Biomedical Sciences.

Talking about Victoria seemed to lift Sir Edward's spirits, invigorating him. Pride radiated from him as he told story after story. Though they weren't related by blood, he loved her like the daughter he had never had. Their powerful relationship continued from the time she was a toddler, through the awful teen years and as she had entered adulthood. Now reveling in the memories he had collected, he realized he too, had meant the world to her. I felt honored to be able to share that moment with him. Using the back of my hand, I wiped the tears from my cheeks and barely managed to stifle a sniffle before my nose started running. I heard sounds on the other end of the line that led me to believe Sir Edward wasn't faring much better, but neither of us made a comment to that effect.

I had planned on leaving my questions for another call—it certainly didn't seem appropriate to address them now—so I was surprised when Sir Edward asked me to elaborate. I could tell he wasn't simply being polite, so I proceeded.

"I know Jonathan Silverton handled Victoria's adoption for the Winestones. Prior to that, did you know him? Or, did he perform any other services after-the-fact for the Winestones or their company?"

"I had never heard of him until Victoria and I read the contents of the safety deposit box. It did come as somewhat of a surprise because I knew almost all the lawyers they kept on retainer. I used many of them myself, and played a round of two of golf with the rest," he chuckled, before continuing, "but no,

I'm not aware of Joseph or Susan utilizing his services for any other purpose."

"It is so strange," I commented, "his widow didn't mention adoptions being his specialty. If anything, he seems to have been more of a generalist which is curious, because the Winestones had a bevy of lawyers at their disposal. Finding a generalist would have been easy work.

"Besides, Silverton seemed like a random choice for such an important set of circumstances. I didn't know the Winestones—so correct me if am wrong—but from what I've heard about them, it didn't seem as though they would leave something like that to chance."

"You are absolutely correct, they wouldn't have. Having children had always been important to them. If they believed it to be their only opportunity, they wouldn't have subjected themselves to that great of a risk," Sir Edward replied. "There had to have been a valid reason for Silverton's involvement."

"I agree. I wish I could track down Maxwell and Mavis Baumgardner. It seems as though they would be able to shed some light on some of these questions. Perhaps Silverton was their contact, or hired at their suggestion," I mused.

"That's an interesting thought," Sir Edward replied. "Hope this isn't too personal, but you never came across any documents relating to your adoption in your parent's papers, did you?"

"Definitely not too personal," I responded, appreciative of his consideration. "No, not a shred, though I'm not giving up yet. That does bring me to the other question I had for you—is there a possibility the Winestones knew my parents?"

"Arianna, at this point, we can safely assume anything is possible. I can't say I ever recall coming across your parent's names. At least not until Victoria and I found your current birth certificate," he paused for a moment. "Now there's a thought.

What if Silverton was their adoption lawyer, too?" he pondered out loud.

"That would be a very convenient coincidence," I replied. "I've got to see if Leah can track the Baumgardners down. The more we talk about it, the more I believe they are crucial to solving this puzzle."

"Great minds…" Sir Edward started, to which I finished, "think alike."

"They most certainly do, my dear." He chuckled. "I've thoroughly enjoyed, and appreciated our conversation. If I may be so bold to say, I believe I've made a new friend today, though at the same time, I feel like I've known you forever."

"You may indeed be so bold." I laughed. "I too, very much enjoyed and appreciated our conversation, but Sir Edward?" I added, in my best English accent. "If we are to be friends—new or old—you must simply call me AJ."

"Well, turnabout is fair play, my dear. If I must call you AJ, you must call me Sir Harry in return." I was both stunned and touched by his proposition.

"Are you sure?" I managed to stutter. "I thought…only Victoria…"

He cut me off before I could finish. "It's what she would have wanted, AJ. If she was here, she would tell you the same."

I stifled a sob and whispered, "Ok, Sir Harry, but just so you know, you're stuck with me now."

He laughed in a way I knew we'd made a pact. A pinky-swear of sorts.

"AJ, love, I wouldn't have it any other way."

CHAPTER SEVENTEEN

It was late by the time I signed-off with Sir Harry, but I wanted to touch base with Leah and Anna. I knew Leah would still be at the newspaper, so I called her first and filled her in on my activities up to that point—coming up empty in my attempt to locate the Baumgardners and after speaking with Silverton's widow, playing wait-and-see with the information Cheryl Earley said she would collect from the UCMC archive and finally, about generating more questions than answers in my conversation with Sir Harry. Once finished, I had even more mixed feelings about my accomplishments than when I started. For my efforts, had I made any progress?

Surprisingly, Leah reacted more positively than I would have expected. "Wow, you've actually gotten quite a bit of legwork done, Ajax." When I made a noise that indicated I was giving her the scrunchy-face over the phone, she added, "Just because you don't have tangible evidence yet, doesn't mean your efforts were for nothing. It's like that onion analogy, you've got to peel back the layers gradually to see what's underneath. To get to the good stuff. It takes patience, determination, perseverance—" At my groan, she stopped. "What?"

"Isn't this dialogue hijacked from the speech your editor gave at last year's journalism awards party?"

"Not that I remember," she groused.

"Well, I do, because you made me fill in as your date when Boytoy Bobby bailed on you at the last minute. Besides, I think your editor filched it from some macho-high-tech-superhero-spy-action flick."

"Is that even an official genre?" Leah quipped. "Because I'm pretty sure Jason Statham, Vin Diesel and Dwayne Johnson would beg to differ."

"Ok, ok, I'm throwing in the towel on this round. You win. I get what you are saying about the onion. I did some initial work that might not have led us to much yet, but if we keep digging we're bound to find what? A tastier piece of onion?"

"That's the spirit." She giggled. "Now, as your researcher extraordinaire aka BFF, how can I assist?

I gave her a run-down of what I had in mind, taken from the list I had created for her:

Maxwell & Mavis Baumgardner / Sterling Joy Agency

Question: What happened to the Sterling Joy Agency?

Question: What "other opportunities" did the Baumgardners have in mind?

Question: What became of the couple?

Martin Singer / Bio dad

Question: Are there other details surrounding his suicide?

"It's a good start. Just be prepared, the answers will likely lead to more questions," she said when I finished. "In the meantime, what are your plans while you wait for the records from UCMC?"

"I'm going to dig through my parent's papers again, and see if I can find any references to the Winestones or to Silverton, to see if there were any prior relationships there. It's probably too much to expect to find any adoption-specific information among their stuff at this point—I've been through it all a zillion times already—but I'd love to know how the Winestones came into possession of my birth certificates, as well as my parent's address."

"My money is on Silverton or the Baumgardners," Leah said.

"I would tend to agree, but until we track down Silverton's files or the Baumgardners themselves."

"Gotcha—I'll get going on this, but I've got to tell you, you're gonna owe me big time when this is all said and done," she added.

"Let me guess," I replied, thinking of her recent analogy, "onion rings?"

"You got it, girl. Extra crispy with a trough of ranch dressing." Seriously, the girl had a one-track mind.

* * *

My conversation with Anna went a bit more smoothly. Thankfully, no onion analogies were involved. Of course, Anna hadn't put up with me for the better part of her life, either.

I gave her the same rundown of my activities I'd given Leah and afterward, she filled me in on what she, Abe and Elijah had been accomplished.

When she told me about the thumb drive they'd brought back from the dealership, I asked, "Is it possible the missing assistant manager, Tanner Dolby, could be in those photos?"

"That's an interesting thought," Anna admitted. "I could ask Switzer if Dolby worked at the dealership at the time of the

Christmas party. If so, perhaps he would allow Bonnie to look through the photos during her downtime to help us identify him."

"Certainly worth a call. It would be nice to know whether Dolby was involved somehow," I replied. "With everything else that's gone down, it seems unlikely he was in it only to steal a high-priced luxury car."

"I like the way your mind works," she replied appreciatively. "Not to change the subject, but you mentioned some items regarding Silverton you wanted to track down?"

"Yeah, after talking with Sir Harry, we both agreed Silverton was an odd choice for handling Victoria's adoption. Way too random—and risky—for people like the Winestones. Which made us wonder, who recommended him? The Baumgardners? Was he some sort of package deal? If so, did my parents use him too?

"I'd also like to know if Silverton procured the birth certificates and my parent's address for the Winestones, assuming they were not from the Baumgardners. Anyway, I know I'm throwing a lot of miscellaneous stuff out there."

"No, this is all good. It would be huge if Leah caught a lead on the Baumgardners. In the meantime, we can definitely hit the Silverton angle. I have a positive feeling that sometime soon, one of these threads is going to start unraveling."

"I totally agree. Again, thank you, Anna. Please say hi to Abe and Elijah for me."

"Will do," she replied. "Oh, and AJ? You made quite an impression on Sir Edward, for him to ask you to call him Sir Harry."

Though she couldn't see me, I was blushing deeply. "Um, we did get along fairly well, but I don't know about an impression."

"Oh, AJ," she laughed, "you don't fool me. I wasn't *asking* you if you had made an impression on Sir Edward, I was *telling* you that you had."

"Wh-what?" I stuttered, my face on fire at this point. I was sure she could tell, but before I could ponder that any further, she replied, laughing even harder.

"Who do you think he called after the two of you hung up? He wanted to thank me personally for giving you his number. He told me your conversation both inspired and invigorated him. In fact, he's convinced if anyone is going to figure this whole thing out, it's going to be you. So, go Team AJ!"

I wondered, could severe blushing cause second-degree burns?

CHAPTER EIGHTEEN

I awoke the next morning with a sense of anticipation and purpose. Despite the fact we hadn't gleaned much information up to this point, I was convinced we were on the right track, and once we toppled that first hurdle, there would be no stopping us.

I reflected on the events of the past several weeks as Nicoh and I walked briskly through the neighborhood. I was so deep in thought I failed to see my next-door neighbor, Suzy Kemp, waving as we passed her house. Nicoh, however, was on full alert —Suzy typically had snacks in her pocket—and suddenly stopped short, forcing the lead to strain between us. Suzy chuckled as I gasped in surprise, barely catching myself before I face-planted into her ocotillos.

"I'm so sorry, dear. I didn't mean to alarm you." She patted Nicoh on the head and reached into her treasure trove, better known as the snack pocket, as his tail thwapped wildly on the ground. As usual, he was oblivious to the fact he'd nearly graced me with multiple face-piercings—compliments of the ocotillos— in his lust of the elusive Suzy snack.

"It's ok, Suze, it's not your fault." I glared at Nicoh. "I was distracted, though it also appears we both need training."

Suzy laughed. "You were pretty focused. I called out a few times and flopped my hands about like a crazy chicken, but only Nicoh seemed amused."

It was my turn to laugh. "I'm sure your crazy chicken routine was quite entertaining, but I have a sneaking suspicion it was the never-ending supply of snacks you keep in your pocket that drew his attention."

"Oh, that reminds me, I meant to give you this." She reached into the non-snack pocket of her hoody, pulled out a small white envelope and handed it to me.

"As you might remember, I was out of town visiting my sister for the past several weeks." At my nod, she continued, "I had my mail held at the post office and didn't have time to go down and pick it up until now. Anyway, looks like they inadvertently put this in my box." I briefly looked at the envelope. I didn't recognize the handwriting, and there was no return address, though it had been postmarked in Phoenix a few weeks earlier.

"Thanks, Suze, probably an exclusive offer to refinance, or better yet, I've won an all-expenses-paid trip to the Bahamas."

"Well now, perhaps I should take that back?" Suzy teased.

"Weren't you just out of town?" I teased back.

"Honey, did I fail to mention I was with my sister? I believe I've earned that vacation."

We both laughed as I thanked her and we headed home. A FedEx package was waiting on the front step when we got there. It couldn't be the information from Cheryl Earley at UCMC already, could it? I could barely contain my excitement as I hustled Nicoh into the house and threw everything on the counter. After a deep breath, I ripped the box open and whooped at the top of my lungs. It was from Cheryl.

My hands shook as I read the note she had enclosed, which simply read: *AJ—it was truly a pleasure talking to you earlier this week. Enclosed are the documents we discussed. I hope they help you find what you are looking for. Keep in touch—Cheryl.*

Before delving into the contents, I gave her a quick call, and upon receiving her voicemail, left her my thanks. I then called Leah and shared my good news.

"I'll be over in ten," she squealed.

"Really? Are you sure?"

"Are you kidding? This could be more exciting than a Duran Duran reunion tour." I shuddered. Depending upon whose mouth it was coming out of, an exclamation like that could go either way. Fortunately, Leah had been my best friend since we were six, so it was definitely leaning toward the positive.

As promised, she arrived with two minutes to spare, though I hated thinking how many laws she'd broken along the way, especially considering her office was at least twenty minutes from my house, without traffic. I could only stare as she bustled through the door, two Starbucks in hand. My estimate of roadway violations increased two-fold.

"Where is it?" she blurted out as she plunked a beverage in front of me.

"Holy crap, Leah—are you sure you haven't already had enough caffeine?" I began to feel a bit of remorse for her co-workers.

"Sorry, sorry." She dabbed at the liquid she'd slopped on the counter. "I'm really excited!"

"Hmm, I couldn't tell."

"Aren't you excited?"

"Yeah, though I'm not sure it necessitated defying the laws of motion."

"Well, I do," she huffed, but then laughed. "Let's get this show on the road—no pun intended."

We grabbed the FedEx box and settled on my living room floor. Nicoh thought it was some sort of game, so he situated himself in the middle of the action, which meant across both our laps. Did I mention Nicoh is not a lap dog?

Anyway, working around said canine, we pulled the documents out and reviewed them one-by-one as Leah took notes. There wasn't as much in the box as I would have anticipated coming from an organization like UCMC, but it was still a pretty healthy-sized stack. Enough to take us through the end of the afternoon, anyway.

During that time, we managed to weed through enough standardized hospital forms to uphold my conviction of a child-free existence. If Leah had been on the fence about wanting children, she wasn't by the time we managed to make it halfway through the stack. It wasn't all for nothing, however.

We located the requisite medical insurance forms, which contained employment information that would be useful. Martin Avery Singer, MD/Ph.D., was a Geneticist, employed by GenTech. Alison Marie Anders was employed as a Research Assistant of Developmental Biology, Gene Expression and Histopathology at Alcore Ltd.

Crazy titles aside, one thing was for sure, I found it hard to believe two extremely left-brained individuals—scientists, to boot —managed to produce a severely right-brained photographer. I mean, seriously? If I remembered correctly, Victoria's undergraduate degree from Columbia had been in Biomedical Sciences, so one out of two wasn't bad.

Leah immediately noticed the same thing and commented, "Gosh, if it wasn't for you, they would have had the ideal gene pool."

"Sensitive, Leah, real sensitive," I replied sarcastically.

"Sorry, that was bad." In all honesty, her words hadn't offended me. I simply had to take the opportunity to yank her chain when the occasion presented itself.

"There's the soap, should you feel so inclined." I pointed to the pump container on the counter.

"Perhaps I should pace myself," she retorted. "In the meantime, should I add GenTech and Alcore to my research, to find out what they do and what, specifically, your bios did for them?"

"Bios?" I asked.

"Yeah, I figured we could come up with a shortened version of biological parents—a sort of code—to reference them," she replied.

"Ahh, gotcha. Bios works for me, but are you sure you haven't already got enough on your plate? I mean, we haven't even breached this pile yet." I gestured to the plethora of documents in front of us.

"No worries, it might actually help me in researching Martin's suicide. Might give me another angle, too."

We moved on to the medical history forms, which, for our current exercise, contained nothing of merit. Next was the mass of legal documents—living will, things of that nature—you could literally hear the trees crying.

I was glazing over when Leah commented, "I don't understand most of this mumbo-jumbo, but have you noticed what all these documents have told us so far?"

"Do tell," I responded, eager for even a remote break.

"Even though Martin Singer and Alison Anders claimed one another as beneficiaries, they weren't married, nor did they reside in the same location."

"So they conceived out of wedlock. Big whoopee." I had noticed that too, so my response came out a bit more snarky than I'd meant it to.

"I think it's interesting. Could be something there." She pouted.

I'd hurt her feelings. "No, you are absolutely right. It could tie into the bigger picture. What if they worked for competing companies or something?"

"Exactly." She brightened at the thought.

The legal documentation also included final requests and wills, which is where things got interesting. Martin and Alison had included a legal document that expressed their wishes in the event they both passed. In that document, the Sterling Joy Agency would serve as guardian to any living minor children of the couple upon death.

As we read through it, I asked, "Do you think this is the standard procedure, to give something like this to the hospital?"

"I don't know. Maybe they provided it because neither had family," she replied as she wrote on her notepad. I nodded, and we continued reading through the pages, which from both of our expressions, were above both of our legalese-comprehension levels. The last page was signed by Martin and Alison; the Sterling Joy Agency representative, Mavis Baumgardner; a witness named Sophie Allen and finally, the lawyer, Jonathan Silverton.

We looked at one another for a long moment before Leah broke the silence, "Silverton seems to keep popping up all over the place, doesn't he?"

"You've got that right," I responded. "I hope Anna can track down some more info for us because there was definitely something fishy going on with him ...and the Baumgardners."

"No doubt."

"No doubt, indeed."

We made our way through the rest of the legal documents without finding anything that sparked our interest. Next were Alison's medical records, charts, etc. while she had been admitted, which I allowed Leah to review. Apparently, reading medical records was a skill she'd picked up during her reporting assignments. Uh, yeah. Let's just leave it at that.

According to Leah—who paraphrased the documents—Alison

had arrived at the hospital late on June 18 with contractions and gave birth to twin girls in the wee hours of June 19. As they were several weeks premature, the twins were placed in intensive care, but were doing fine. Though exhausted, Alison was also resting comfortably. Three hours after giving birth, she complained of chest pains. Minutes later, she went into cardiac arrest, but the hospital staff was unable to revive her. Alison was officially declared dead three and a half hours after she had given birth to her daughters. Someone had noted the father was not present when she had expired. A signed death certificate was enclosed, in which the cause of death was listed as heart failure. End of story. Like I said, Leah had been paraphrasing. I was certain she had done so for my benefit.

We looked at the next set of documents, which included the twins' medical charts, progress reports, etc. as they stayed on in the hospital. Pretty much what you'd expect until we reached the release forms. The documents indicated a change of guardianship had occurred during their stay. As per the request of Martin and Alison, the Sterling Joy Agency had taken guardianship of the twins, as both parents were deceased at the time. Enclosed was a second death certificate bearing Martin's name. The official cause of death was listed as suicide by drowning, dated five days prior to the change of guardianship. Martin Singer had taken his life less than two weeks after the birth of his daughters and the death of the mother of his children.

While the situation seemed to become more disturbing and confusing with each document we read, something in particular had been nagging at me.

"When Alison arrived at the hospital, she couldn't have known she would be giving birth prematurely—the contractions had come on quickly, without warning—yet she and Martin had all the adoption documentation ready to go. It's almost like they already knew they wouldn't be alive to care for their children."

Leah shrugged in response, as though there was nothing that would have surprised her.

We continued sifting through the last of the items in the box. At this point, it was mostly notes and follow-up documentation—cover-your-booty type of stuff. One thing that caught my eye was the billing statement. Even with today's prices, you could have bought a house and furnished it with the amount that had been due. However, the most intriguing thing about the bill wasn't the total. It was that Martin's company, GenTech, had paid the balance in full.

When I pointed it out to Leah, the look on her face spoke volumes. Maybe there was something left that could surprise her after all.

CHAPTER NINETEEN

Leah was called back to the office. How she was able to be absent from her job for extended periods of time was beyond me. When I asked, all I got in response was a mumbled "external research." I sighed. Leah was a big girl and could handle herself.

I looked at the little pig pen we'd made in the middle of the living room floor and decided I'd better get the papers cleaned up before Nicoh went tromping across them. He was currently dozing beyond the periphery of the mess. He'd had a hard afternoon—napping—after all. I marveled at how he could manage to sleep so much. Honestly, I was a bit jealous.

As I reorganized, I found the Sterling Joy guardianship documentation, which made me think—not once had I seen a reference to Martin and Alison's request. The one where Victoria and I were to be adopted by separate parties. In fact, we only had the Baumgardner's word for it.

I plopped the repacked FedEx box on the counter, the envelope from Suzy catching my eye. In my excitement over Cheryl's delivery, I'd forgotten all about it. I looked at the handwritten address again, only this time I noticed the sender's error. It was addressed using my name, but the street number was off by one house—no wonder it had erroneously been delivered to Suzy. Perhaps I was getting that trip to the Bahamas after all, I chuckled as I ripped the flap.

The envelope contained a single photo of several unfamiliar faces enjoying themselves at what appeared to be a holiday party. There wasn't anything written on the back, though the photo lab had graciously stamped their proprietary information in multiple places. I laughed, it appeared the envelope had been meant for Suzy all along. Surely these people were her friends or family. I picked up my cell phone to call her when it rang. Leah's exuberant voice filled my ear as I answered.

"You were right," she cheered, nearly bursting my eardrum in the process, "GenTech and Alcore were competitors. Both were into genetic engineering. You know, messing around with genes by introducing new DNA?"

"Uh, yeah, how very Wikipedia of you. Anyway, assuming I understand that, go on," I urged.

"Well, remember how scientists cloned that sheep back in the late 1990s?"

"Vaguely," I replied, seriously hoping this wasn't going to be a science lesson. It hadn't been one of my stronger subjects.

"GenTech and Alcore were involved in genetic mutation long before that—specifically with regards to cloning—only they bypassed Mary's little lamb and went directly to Mary."

"Are you telling me they were able to clone humans nearly thirty years ago? Almost fifteen years before the sheep was cloned?" Now things were getting interesting.

"More like attempting to clone humans, but yes, they definitely preceded the sheep. Anyway, GenTech and Alcore were both privately funded, sometimes by the same benefactors. This created a hugely adversarial relationship between the two companies," Leah explained.

"Whoever led the human cloning race received the bulk of the funds," I added.

"Exactly," she confirmed. "Of course, even back then, cloning was controversial, so they concealed their efforts behind other projects—the ones promoted to the public. Again, the more progress a company made, the greater the assistance they received from the benefactors."

"Where do Martin Singer and Alison Anders play into this?" I asked.

"Martin was one of five scientists on the human cloning project at GenTech and Alison was the lead researcher on the same project at Alcore," she replied.

"Wow, that's a serious conflict of interest—which explains why they couldn't come out as a couple—it was probably outlined in their contracts, in triplicate. Both of them could have been terminated if their respective companies had found out about their relationship."

"Interesting choice of words," Leah mused. "Perhaps they had to give up their first-born children and then they were terminated."

"Oh, my gosh, Leah—do you know what you are suggesting?" I growled at her.

"Calm down, it's not like it hadn't occurred to you."

"True," I bristled, my voice several pitches calmer. "I hadn't said it out loud though—that Martin's and Alison's deaths were related to the adoptions."

"Well, I apologize for being insensitive," she said sincerely, "but now that it's out there, here's the real question—were you and Victoria adopted through Sterling Joy because your bios were both dead? Or, did your bios already have to be dead in order for you to be adopted?

"While I'm on a roll, let me add more food for thought. I also researched Martin's suicide. According to witnesses, he walked off the Skyway Bridge on the morning of July 1 during rush hour." She paused to allow me to reflect on the fact Martin Singer had taken his life by jumping off a bridge.

"Though his body was never recovered, based upon the eyewitness' accounts, the location where he went in and the condition of the water, he was officially declared dead and a death certificate subsequently issued. No note was ever found in his apartment or at the lab."

Leah paused again, before adding, "You know, he could have simply been distraught over Alison's death and overwhelmed by the prospect of raising twins alone. Of course, no one would have known about either because he and Alison had been careful to keep their lives separate."

"Someone knew. GenTech footed Alison's hospital bill," I reminded her.

"Yeah, there's that," she replied.

"So, what happened to the project after Martin's death?" I asked.

"Interestingly, it immediately fizzled, but not only for GenTech. Within a month, Alcore went out of business altogether. They had essentially put too many eggs in one basket. No pun intended. GenTech, on the other hand, elected to put their focus elsewhere, claiming the timing wasn't right for human cloning. They are still in the game today, mostly doing medical research, stuff of that nature, but they are nowhere near the industry giant they once were."

"It's almost as though the opportunity slipped through their fingers thirty years ago," I reflected. "Kind of coincidental, don't you think?"

"I guess it depends. Do you believe in coincidences?"

CHAPTER TWENTY

After talking with Leah, I decided to check in with Abe, Elijah and Anna to see how things were going on their end and at the same time, fill them in on what Leah and I had discovered. I hadn't had a chance to find out how she'd gotten that last bit of research so quickly. Leah likely would have claimed trade secrets, which I could have easily gotten her to divulge with a batch of my white chocolate macadamia nut cookies, but perhaps it was better to let sleeping dogs lie.

Anna put me on speakerphone and I began by telling them the medical records from UCMC had arrived, which elicited raucous cheers.

"Nice work, AJ," Elijah exclaimed.

"Cheryl Earley is the one we should be throwing a parade for," I chuckled at their enthusiasm, "but if you like that, then you'll like what Leah and I found *in* the documents."

I proceeded to tell them everything we'd learned, from the guardianship document to the details of Alison's medical records. From there, I explained how Martin and Alison had worked for competing genetics firms while managing to keep their relationship secret, how both companies were involved in human cloning projects that were privately funded by similar benefactors and how the projects fizzled, and the money dried up after Martin and Alison had died, ultimately, putting one out of business while forcing the other to pursue alternate projects. And finally, how Martin's company footed Alison's entire hospital bill.

"Wow, you got all of that—from medical records?" Abe asked.

"Well, from that and the research Leah managed to scrounge up afterward," I replied.

"Shoot, that girl works fast. Maybe we should offer her a job?" Elijah said, only halfway joking.

"After this, she might need one. I'm not exactly sure how she's getting the info, but her editor is going to catch on sooner or later."

"For the sake of this case, let's hope it's later," Abe added. "But after that, let her know we'd like to talk."

I laughed. "I'm sure she'll appreciate that."

"In the meantime," Anna gracefully shifted gears, "we should fill you in on what we've discovered the past couple of days."

"Absolutely, let's do it," I replied, thoroughly excited to hear what they'd learned. I wished Leah was on the call. She would have loved this. I mentally kicked myself for failing to think of that earlier, but made a note for the next time.

"Actually, your research filled in one of our blanks," Elijah began. "When we dug into Sterling Joy's background, we found they were owned by a genetics firm by the name of GenTech. At the time, it didn't mean much, but when you told us they were Martin Singer's employer, a piece of the puzzle fell into place."

"GenTech owned the Sterling Joy Agency?" I asked as another thought rumbled around in my brain. "Wait…that means GenTech undoubtedly would have already known about Martin and Alison's relationship before Victoria and I were born."

"It certainly appears that way, doesn't it?" Abe agreed, then pressed forward, "We also believe Silverton was Sterling Joy's inside man. We aren't completely sure how the whole thing worked, but he typically served as the lawyer for both sides of the adoption. We think the Baumgardners recommended him and encouraged the adoptive parents to utilize his services as a means of ensuring the adoption went smoothly. If this was the case, the Baumgardners essentially used the adoptive parents' insecurities —knowing they wouldn't risk losing the opportunity to have a child—to successfully cover their own bases."

"What about Silverton's other clients?" I asked, still reeling from what I'd heard.

"Regardless of what the man told his wife, we couldn't find any," Abe responded.

"So, what happened to the Baumgardners?"

"They disappeared into thin air. We haven't found a trace of them since they closed the agency. We think Silverton's files went wherever they did," Elijah said.

"So much for pursuing those other opportunities," I commented. "Speaking of the Baumgardners, the other thing that bothers me is their claim Martin and Alison requested separate adoptions, yet there's nothing in the documentation substantiating it."

"It wouldn't surprise me in the least if the Baumgardners made it up," Elijah responded. "Not to be insensitive, but maybe it was more profitable for them to secure adoptions for two different parties, rather than being saddled with a two-for-one deal?"

"Perhaps," I replied, but something told me whatever the Baumgardner's reasoning, it hadn't been isolated to greed.

"Changing the subject to another, slightly less-illuminating topic," Anna piped up, "we are still working our way through the

Christmas party photos from the dealership, trying to identify who or what caused Victoria to bolt.

"After you suggested it, I asked Switzer if the missing assistant manager, Dolby, had worked at the dealership at the time the photos were taken. Switzer confirmed he had and agreed to have Bonnie run through the images on her computer to see if anyone had captured Dolby in any of the holiday shots.

"So far, we haven't found anything useful yet—it's taking a while to get through all 13,000 pictures—but I appreciate your insight."

"Hey, no problem," I replied, "I appreciate you letting me know. I can't imagine having to look through that many photos. Even my own." They all laughed.

"Speaking of photos, you reminded me of one that was delivered to my neighbor by accident. Well, actually, I think it was delivered to me by accident." I proceeded to tell them how Suzy had received an envelope addressed to my name but to her street number.

"When I opened, I found a single photo of a bunch of people I don't know at what looks like a holiday party. There was no return address on the envelope and no notation on the back of the picture other than the proprietary information from the photo lab. Anyway, I think it was actually meant for Suzy." I laughed, noticing the lack of response from the other end of the line.

Anna broke the silence, "AJ, is there a photo number or a jpeg reference next to that proprietary information?"

I knew what she was talking about, but hadn't looked that closely at it the first time. I went to the counter, pulled the photo from the envelope and flipped it over. "Yeah, there's a jpeg reference, it's labeled as IMG 011120.jpg. Does that mean something to you?"

"Maybe," I heard fingers clicking on a keyboard, "describe what you see." I did as she asked, describing everything down to the silly lighted bow ties several of the guys were sporting. Now that I look more closely, I realized the photo was unmistakably of an office party, not a family gathering.

Suddenly, the sound of clicking fingers was replaced by a collective gasp.

CHAPTER TWENTY-ONE

"What is it?" I asked as my heart thudded against my chest.

"We recognize one of the people in this photo," Abe replied, a tremor in his usually-steady voice.

"It can't be. It makes no sense. Why would he…" Elijah's voice trailed off.

"What? What can't be?" I asked nervously.

Ignoring my queries, Abe spoke to either Elijah or Anna, "Let's get Bonnie on the line and have her pull up that photo. Get Switzer involved if you have to."

"What's going on?" I asked again, a little more loudly and forcefully than I had intended. Blame it on the nerves.

"Hang on, AJ, Anna's calling the dealership," Abe replied.

I sat tight and strained to hear Anna as she spoke to Bonnie, but I all I could hear was mumbling. Minutes passed, and I started squirming like a kindergartener anxious for recess.

Finally, the mumbles faded, and Anna's voice came in crystal clear, though there was a hint of shakiness to it, "Both Bonnie and Switzer confirmed it. The person in the photo is Tanner Dolby."

"Unbelievable!" Elijah's voice raged with fury.

Abe's voice matched his brother's, "Bloody hell, there's no

way—no possible way!" I was sure I heard something break on the other end of the connection.

"I…I don't understand," I stuttered, struggling to keep from sounding whiney.

A moment passed before Anna spoke, her voice calmer than either Abe's or Elijah's, but still troubled, "After she saw it, Bonnie was almost positive it was the same photo that had been on the employee bulletin board—the one that went missing after Victoria was there." Tightness began to fill my chest as I waited for her to continue, though I knew where this conversation was heading. "It's the same picture you are holding right now."

"So you think Victoria took the photo from the dealership and then sent it to me after she got to Phoenix?" I thought of the postmark from a few weeks earlier. The timeframe did fit with her arrival from L.A., but why send it to me? Something else was troubling me.

"This makes no sense. I thought you had never met Tanner Dolby?"

"We hadn't…met him as Dolby," Abe replied, his voice tense. "When we the met the man in the photo, he introduced himself to us a Winslow Clark." The name sounded familiar, but I had read so many documents the past several days that when my mind panned through its index, it came back with a big fat goose egg.

"Clark handled the investigation of your parent's plane crash," Elijah reminded me after my extended silence.

I quietly considered what he was saying: the crash investigator and the missing dealership manager were the same person. The other shoe had dropped.

"Tanner Dolby *was* Winslow Clark." Though my voice was barely a whisper, I was sure they heard me, loud and clear.

CHAPTER TWENTY-TWO

"It appears that way, otherwise Dolby was Clark's twin. And frankly, that would be too much of a coincidence," Abe replied. I winced at the thought. Way too much of a coincidence.

I looked at the photo in my hands, at the faces smiling back at me. "Which one is he?" I asked.

"Third from the right," Elijah offered tersely.

Winslow Clark/Tanner Dolby was surprisingly attractive—a pretty-boy type you'd expect to see in a Calvin Klein ad—with artfully-tousled surfer hair and deep-blue eyes that crinkled ever-so-slightly at the corners when he smiled. His teeth were brilliantly white—of the toothpaste commercial variety—which annoyingly, only enhanced his chiseled good looks. I pegged him for my age, but he could have easily gone five years either way. The only flaw in his appearance was the noticeably burnt-out lights on that ridiculous bow tie, and even they curiously added to his magnetism. For as attractive as he might have been, however, Clark/Dolby—or whatever his name currently was—gave me the willies.

"You all knew Victoria, do you find it interesting she would have inadvertently gotten my address wrong on something she believed to be so important?" I asked, after shaking off the unsettling, icky vibe I got from looking at the photo.

Anna replied without hesitation, "Knowing Victoria, she probably intentionally sent the photo to your neighbor, to make sure you got it."

"Especially if she felt she was being followed, or was in danger," Abe added.

"Or was concerned that AJ might be," Elijah thought aloud.

"But why," I asked, "why this picture?"

"It's the one thing that links Clark…Dolby to both the Winestones and your parents," Abe explained. "It's too much of a coincidence that the same person—posing in two entirely different roles—could have been associated with the Winestone's car crash and your parent's plane crash. This was Victoria's proof he was not only tied to both but was involved as well."

I thought for a moment. "Ok, I see where you are going with this, but the Winestones knew Dolby from the dealership, whereas Clark was an investigator on my parent's plane crash after-the-fact. He never actually met my parents," I pointed out.

"True. But who else could do a better job of covering up their handiwork than the person investigating the scene?" Elijah countered. "If he's even a real investigator."

"You're thinking what? That he was in the perfect position to monkey with my parent's plane and the Winestone's car? Without leaving a trace of evidence?" I asked incredulously, though the longer it rattled around in my brain, the more it made sense.

"At this point, anything is possible," Elijah replied. I heard a muffled agreement from Abe, but nothing from Anna.

Something occurred to me. "Wait—didn't you guys talk to Clark? To see if Victoria had followed up with him."

"Yeah, he said he hadn't heard from her since the three of us had met with him," Elijah said.

Abruptly, Anna came on the line. "Well, that confirms it.

While you three were talking, I popped into the other office and tried Clark's number. It's been disconnected."

I froze, "What would you have done if he had answered?"

"Don't worry, I was fully prepared to play the bar floozy and give him a sad little but-I-don't-understand-he-gave-me-this-number song and dance," she chuckled lightly. "Plus, the phone I used is blocked."

"Our girl Anna, both brains and beauty," Abe teased.

"Obviously," she replied sarcastically.

Though I typically would have appreciated their repartee, my head was swimming. Whoever had killed Victoria had done so viciously, publicly and without a hint of remorse. Had Clark/Dolby left a trail of bodies—masked as accidents, deaths by natural cause or suicide, or as people who had appeared to have fallen off the grid? Considering that, I made a mental inventory of possible victims—no matter how far-fetched—that included my parents, the pilot of my parent's plane, Victoria's parents, Jonathan Silverton and of course, Victoria.

If Clark/Dolby was a cold-blooded killer, one thing became apparent as I contemplated my list. If you followed his sick progression, a name was conspicuously missing. Mine. I may not have figured out his end game, but I had a bad feeling about his next move.

Once again, I stared at the photo. Could that enigmatic smile belong to a sadistic killer? I blanched—people had asked the same thing about Ted Bundy.

CHAPTER TWENTY-THREE

Abe, Anna, Elijah and I decided to take a breather and regroup in the morning. In the meantime, I needed to get some fresh air. Perhaps I was naive. I'd seen his handiwork firsthand when I'd found Victoria and should have been scared out of my gourd. Clark/Dolby—if he truly was the killer—wouldn't have hesitated to kill me on the spot. Instead, I was fuming and felt an overwhelming need to vent. So after coaxing Leah into taking a dinner break, I packed a sleepy Nicoh into the Mini and headed to her office.

Silly me, with all my bravado, I failed to check my surroundings as I pulled onto Camelback Road. Had I elected to do so, I would have noticed the white Toyota Camry matching me, turn for turn. We all know what they say about hindsight.

Twenty minutes later, I secured a spot in the parking structure next to the building where Leah's newspaper office was located. As I got out, I was careful to note the level number and section color of the spot I had selected—can you say directionally-challenged? Since we were only three levels up, I opted for the stairs, which didn't win me any points with Nicoh. Finally, we emerged onto the street.

I couldn't take Nicoh into the building, so we waited for Leah in the building's outdoor courtyard and marveled at the skyscraper of glass before us. It should have been peaceful—with the manicured landscaping, beautiful sculptures and luxurious seating—but I was so antsy I could barely sit still. Uncharacteristically, I snapped at Nicoh when he started to sniff some nearby bougainvilleas that bordered the courtyard. His feelings were hurt, so he sat with his back to me, refusing to acknowledge my presence. Great—nothing like a passive-aggressive canine—he'd make me pay for it later.

Leah had warned me she wouldn't be down for a bit, so I took the opportunity to contact Jim Pearce, my parent's former lawyer and friend. I knew he worked late and though I didn't anticipate obtaining anything substantial from him, I needed to keep busy. As expected, he was still in the office and answered on the first ring.

"Hi Jim, it's AJ."

"AJ, how are you doing? It's been awhile—is everything ok? Is there an issue with the house?" Fatherly concern filled his voice.

"No, no, nothing like that. Everything is fine with the house. However, there's something else I wanted to talk to you about. Do you have a minute?"

"Of course, honey, what's going on?"

"Well, this is probably a conversation that is better suited in person, but I'm meeting Leah in a few minutes and well, time is of the essence."

"I understand. Just tell me, what is it?"

"Well, um, there's no easy way to say this, but I recently found out I was adopted," I said bluntly.

"I see," his tone indicated he had known, but I needed further confirmation.

"Did you know?" I asked gently. "I'm not trying to put you on the spot here, Jim. I'm looking for some specifics about the adoption and hope you can help.

I heard a deep sigh on the other end before he responded, "I did, but after-the-fact." He then told me a story that sounded eerily similar to the one Sir Harry had told about a busy, working couple who found out too late in life they couldn't have children, so they decided to adopt. And, like the Winestones, my parents were very private about the details, but one day, there I was. He hadn't been involved in the adoption, nor did my parents speak of it until several years later.

"Your father only briefly mentioned the adoption once, and at the time, he was strangely agitated. The lawyer he and your mother had used for the adoption—someone the agency had highly recommended—had sent him some documents related to the adoption he found troubling. Just sent them out-of-the-blue. Nearly thirty years later. He hadn't told your mother about the documents, for fear they would upset her, but realized he would need to come clean with both of you at some point. I never got the opportunity to bring it up again. They died in the plane crash a week later."

He paused briefly, but I remained silent, allowing his words to register. "After they were gone, I wasn't sure it was my place to tell you. I didn't want to cast a shadow over your memories of them. I'm so, so sorry, AJ."

"Jim, I understand. And I don't blame you. My parents had their reasons. I...I'm sure they were doing what they thought was best at the time. I loved...love...them unconditionally. Nothing will ever change that." I fought back a sob as a single tear escaped down my cheek.

"Thank you for understanding, AJ," Jim sighed.

"Thank you, Jim, for your honesty," I replied sincerely. "Out of curiosity, did my father happen to mention the name of the adoption lawyer?"

"Hmm, if memory serves, it was Silver-something," Jim recalled.

"Silverton?" I asked hopefully.

"Yes, that's it. Silverton," he confirmed.

Bingo. Another piece of the puzzle slid into place.

I saw Leah coming out of the front entrance, so I thanked Jim, told him we would meet for lunch soon and said my goodbyes.

"Hey, what's up?" Leah plopped down on the chair next to mine and scruffed Nicoh's ears before slipping him a cookie.

"Besides the fact you are turning my dog into a chunky monkey?" I sniped as I gave her the evil eye, which as usual, she waved off. I decided to tell her about my call to Jim before proceeding on to the details of my conversation with Abe, Elijah and Anna. The way she had scrunched up her face and plucked at the spiky wisps jutting from her head told me she was miffed about not receiving an invite to the latter.

"I know that look, Leah. You've already helped me immensely. Plus, you can't keep ducking out of work."

"Don't worry about it. I've got it under control. My work is getting done, despite my extracurricular activities. Next time, I want in. Or else." Based upon previous experience, such veiled threats usually resulted in adding an extra five pounds to my dog's already enormous physique.

Adequately chastised, I told her about GenTech's ownership of the Sterling Joy Agency, which garnered me an intrigued "oooooh," how Silverton was servicing both sides of the adoption —as Jim had confirmed was the case in my adoption—and finally, of the Clark/Dolby connection. Leah was as floored as the rest of us had been, then horrified when I added in my theory about his list of victims.

"Oh my, AJ, if you are right, do you think that sicko left Victoria's mutilated body for you to find on purpose? You know, a way of putting you on notice?"

I shuddered. "I have no idea. I mean, maybe I'm getting us both worked up by drawing conclusions where there are none. What if Victoria's murder was an isolated incident?"

"Come on, AJ," Leah threw her hands up as she launched off her seat, "do you really believe that?"

I didn't, but the alternative was terrifying. "No. I don't. However, whether Clark/Dolby is our guy, we're missing a key piece of the puzzle."

"Explain." She had calmed down significantly but still stood rigidly, hands on hips, facing me.

"If you look at all the breadcrumbs we've collected so far, from the accidents, to the people that have gone MIA, to Victoria's murder," I paused to look at her earnestly, "all roads eventually lead us back to Alcore and GenTech."

"Six-degrees of separation," she murmured.

I absently nodded. "We've got to go back to the beginning. Find people who either knew about or were involved in the feud between Alcore and GenTech. People who worked with either Martin or Alison."

"Easier said than done," Leah said as she began tormenting her hair again.

"Even for a hotshot reporter like yourself?" I teased.

"As if." She pretended to pout. "I've got connections."

"Top-secret   you'd-have-to-kill-me-if-you-told-me-type connections?

"You know it. Give me until morning?" I stood as she turned to head back up to her office.

"Absolutely. And Leah?"

"Yeah?" she paused, looking at me.

"Thanks for everything." I moved forward and gave her a quick hug.

She hugged me back, even tighter. "Anytime, Ajax, anytime."

Even with the courtyard lights on, it was still dark, so I

watched until I saw her head bob into the building, then nudged Nicoh with my foot.

"You ready to go, buddy?"

He grumbled in response and took his time stretching as he got up, pausing to sniff the bougainvilleas I had scolded him about earlier. This time, I pretended not to notice and instead took a moment to survey my surroundings. The lights must have been playing tricks on me. For a moment, I thought I saw something in the shadows off to the side of the building, but when I squinted, it was gone. I shivered, then chuckled to myself. I needed to get a grip. The past few weeks were messing with my head.

We made our way back to the parking structure and up the three flights of stairs to our level, now less than halfway full, because of the hour. I reached into my bag to pull out my keys, and once again thought I sensed movement in the shadows. Rather than appease my curiosity, I listened to hairs on the back of my neck and hustled Nicoh to the vehicle. Once we were safely locked-in, strapped-in and the vehicle was revved-up, I quickly peered from side-to-side and front-to-back. Boogeyman-free, I shifted into drive and got the heck out of Dodge.

My senses were still working overtime, so I glanced in my rearview mirror more frequently than I normally would have, which is how I spotted him. He exited the parking structure in a white Toyota approximately twenty seconds after I had. At first, I just figured it was paranoia and took an alternate route home to prove it to myself, opting to weave through a myriad of neighborhoods instead of traveling the main streets. My heart dropped. At every turn, he was there, lurking 200-300 feet behind. I'd watched enough Burn Notice episodes to realize this was not a loose tail, especially after my seventh right-hand turn.

Thoroughly freaked-out, I did the only thing I could think of at that moment. I called Ramirez.

CHAPTER TWENTY-FOUR

Ramirez wasn't on duty when I called, but fortunately, he was nearby and directed me to his location. Of all places, he was at Starbucks. At night. Guy must need to get his coffee buzz on at all hours. I mentally slapped myself—who was I to judge? Right now, I was in dire need of his assistance and thanks to his late-night caffeine therapy session, he was able to come to my aid. A shout out to baristas working late everywhere.

As I pulled into the parking lot and eased into the first available space, the Toyota passed. Though the driver didn't look in my direction, I caught a glimpse of something familiar. An Arizona Diamondbacks hat. I know, you're probably thinking, duh, you're in Phoenix—it'd be pretty common to see people wearing the home team's swag—and you'd be right.

This hat was distinctive, though, a piece of memorabilia from the 1998 inaugural season. At the time, only one hundred bearing the design had been made. I knew this because Leah's dad, a well-known sportscaster at the time, helped me procure one for my dad's fortieth birthday. On the inside, it had the imprint: #40 of 100. Leah's dad had Andy Benes, a pitcher at the time, sign the bill of the hat, along with owner Jerry Colangelo and manager Buck

Showalter. It was my dad's favorite hat. So much so, he wore it all through my high school and college years. He was wearing it the last time I hugged him goodbye—as he and my mother rushed out the door to catch their flight to Albuquerque, where they would catch another small commuter flight to Colorado Springs. Within twenty-four hours, they would both be gone.

I hadn't seen a hat like it since. That was until I'd met with Abe and Elijah a few days earlier. At this very Starbucks, in fact. The man sitting alone at the table behind us had been wearing a similar hat, though I hadn't thought about it much at the time. We'd been having a pretty heavy conversation, and I had been glad to escape it for a few minutes while Nicoh did his business. Had the man been eavesdropping? Could it have been Clark/Dolby? I thought back to the photo of the man known as Dolby and shook my head. I hadn't been able to see much with the way he had positioned himself at the table, his hat pulled low. However, now that I'd seen a similar man and hat in the span of a few days, I was taking nothing to chance. I jumped when Ramirez lightly tapped on the window.

"Sorry," he murmured when I opened the door to get out, "I didn't mean to startle you. Are you ok?"

"No, it's not your fault, I was distracted. And yeah, I'm ok now, thanks. Just a bit of a disconcerting ride over. Did you see him?" I glanced toward the street, but the Toyota was long gone.

"I did." He looked at me carefully, as though I was going to crack right before his eyes. Wow, did I look that frazzled? *Note to self:* Immediately consult mirror after indulging in Mr. Toad's Wild Ride, especially when a hunky guy is involved.

"California plates—was able to get a number. I'm not expecting much, but I'll run it through the system, see what pops up."

"Good. Thanks. You have a minute? I'd better fill you in on a few things." When Ramirez nodded, I collected Nicoh and the three of us headed to the same patio table where Abe, Elijah, Leah and I had sat. I plopped into the chair, suddenly weary. The adrenaline had worn off, and the day's events were finally catching up with me. I needed to pull it together long enough to get Ramirez up to speed.

I'm not sure what I expected, but when I finished, his steely gaze fixed on me, his lips drawn into a tight, thin line. My eyes popped—was he angry with me?

I opened my mouth to speak, but he put his hand up and quietly uttered, "AJ, I'm sorry. I should have never pushed you into getting involved."

I started to protest and once again, his hand rose to stop me. "You are in over your heads. All of you."

Perhaps I was too tired at this point to control my emotions because his condescending tone made me snap. "Yeah? Well, I may be in over my head, Detective, but please do tell, what have you and your FBI pals come up with so far?" I snarled, sarcastically emphasizing "Detective."

"Darn it AJ," he growled, "you're going to get yourself killed."

"As opposed to getting myself killed waiting around?" I spat, undeterred by his outburst. "A killer is out there and if you think I'm going to sit by and take things as they come, or wait for someone to save the day, you are sorely mistaken."

"You seem to have needed saving this evening, AJ," Ramirez snarked, but once he witnessed the fury burning in my eyes, I knew he regretted the words the minute they'd escaped. Given my mood, I wasn't about to let him off the hook.

"My mistake. One I won't be making again." I tugged on Nicoh's leash, and for once, he didn't dawdle as I hustled him toward the car. After a few steps, I turned on my heel and faced

Ramirez, who stood stoically, hands on hips, an indecipherable expression on his face.

"And just to be clear—your apology is not accepted. If you gave me that information expecting a different result, you severely underestimated the girl you thought me to be," I hissed.

"Furthermore, this may be too much for your ego to absorb, but I don't need anyone coming to my rescue. My nickname is Ajax for a reason. You'd do well to remember that in the future, Detective." I left him standing there as I marched purposefully to the Mini, and after quickly situating Nicoh and myself, sped out of the parking lot.

Had I spared a look back in Ramirez's direction, I would have seen the slightest hint of a smirk playing on his lips.

CHAPTER TWENTY-FIVE

I grumbled as the alarm chirped happily. Morning arrived too soon, following a stress-filled day and sleepless night. Adding to the irritation was the persistent beep echoing from my cell phone, conveniently out of reach across the room on the dresser. I negotiated my way around Nicoh, who had once again monopolized the majority of the bed and was currently running joyously in his uninterrupted sleep. No doubt dreaming of the elusive Pandora. If only my life were that simple.

I sighed as I looked at my phone, then immediately wished I had stayed in bed. Ramirez had left me a message. Great. Maybe he'd gotten a clue and decided to apologize for real this time. Realistically, the odds of that were about as likely as Nicoh sleeping on his own doggie bed. I queued up the voicemail and prepared for the worst.

Ramirez's message was brief, "Got a match on the plate. The Toyota is registered to Tanner Adam Dolby of Santa Monica, California. Do with it what you will, AJ." Ignoring the curt delivery, I focused on the message itself.

I needed to contact Abe and Elijah ASAP, but before I could finish that thought, my phone rang to the sound of Leah's ringtone, Duran Duran's *Notorious*. As soon as I answered, she blurted, "Wait 'til you hear what I've got for you!" At my silence, her excitement dimmed. "What's wrong?"

I told her about my mad dash through the streets of Phoenix, meeting with Ramirez at Starbucks—including a play-by-play of our tiff—and his follow-up call this morning.

"So we have confirmation Dolby is in town, stalking you, waiting for the perfect moment to swoop in and—"

"Stop," I gritted out through clenched teeth, "this is my life, not one of your stupid articles."

"Whoa—someone got up on the wrong side of the bed. Don't you dare snark at me, Arianna Jackson." Immediately, I regretted my snottiness and started to apologize when she added, "Don't forget I know what you looked like before you had braces and have the pictures to prove it." After a moment, we both burst out laughing.

"I'm sorry, Leah. I'm being a total jerk."

"Yes, you are, but that's what I'm here for, to de-jerkify you when you need it. You are fortunate I'm always on my best behavior and never in need of such services in return." Again, laughter filled both sides of the connection. "Clark/Dolby-related issues aside, do you want to hear why I called?"

"Absolutely," I replied.

"I have a friend at the *Chicago Tribune* who owes me a favor," she began.

"Wait, what friend?" I asked, suddenly suspicious and dreading her response.

"Michael Rafferty," she briskly replied. I groaned. Michael had been Leah's college boyfriend. They had dated for a year until he moved on to greener pastures, meaning the busty editor of the school paper. In an attempt to mend Leah's broken heart, we had both gained five pounds indulging in chocolate Oreo cookie ice cream. Michael eventually regretted his fling with the editor, who hadn't given him the choice stories he had hoped his association with her would garner, and tried to make amends with Leah. Though she'd repeatedly rebuffed his apologies, he'd pop out of the woodwork every few years in an effort to rekindle the relationship. To date, I thought she had succeeded in warding him off.

"I can hear the gears working in that melon of yours, AJ," she warned. "Just for the record, I'm not giving Rafferty the time of day. He owes me a favor. As a colleague. Which I'm cashing in. For you. So thank me and let's get on with it."

"Thank you, Leah," I replied sincerely. "I do appreciate your assistance."

"As you should," she teased. "Anywhoo, I gave Michael the bare minimum—nothing involving you or Victoria—said I was looking for information on Alcore and GenTech, their ongoing feud, the demise of Alcore, etc. I made it clear I wanted the behind-the-scenes goods, not the stuff edited for public consumption.

"Anyway, Rafferty did one better. He found us someone who had first-hand knowledge, a former bureau chief by the name of Mort Daniels. And this is where it gets good. Turns out, Daniels retired back in the 1990s and moved to sunny Ahwatukee, Arizona."

"No way. I can't believe we'd get that lucky."

"I know. That's not even the best part. Rafferty contacted Daniels and set up a meeting. Daniels wanted time to pull some of his old notes, but he's able to see us in a couple of hours."

"That's awesome. Rafferty must want to get back into your good graces," I remarked.

"Don't you worry, missy." Leah chuckled mischievously. "Like I said, he owes me."

"Whatever, I appreciate it. You want me to swing by and pick you up?" I asked.

"Yeah, see ya in a few," she chirped happily as she hung up.

I looked at the clock. My call to Abe and Elijah would have to wait.

Nicoh and I picked Leah up at her condo forty-five minutes later and headed to Daniels' home in the Ahwatukee Foothills. The ride was unusually quiet, as both of us deep in thought. I can't speak for Leah, but I was also more than a little anxious about our impending meeting. Fortunately, before the anxiety manifested into a full-blown panic attack, we arrived at our destination.

Daniels lived in a gated community filled with carefully-maintained custom-built homes. His house was located at the back of a cul-de-sac and was spacious without being pretentious. He greeted us as we pulled into his turnaround driveway, a smiling man of tall stature and slight build. I pegged him for late 60s or early 70s, but there was a twinkle in his eye that led me to believe he was as spry as a man half his age.

After introductions were made, he gestured for us to join him in the backyard for iced tea. We ooo'd and ahh'd at the enchanting landscape. Flowers and plants of various species and colors intermingled artfully along the cobblestone pathway, which lead to an outdoor seating area filled with lush chairs in richly-colored fabrics. A small natural stone waterfall cascaded gently into the koi pond below, producing a soothing background rhythm for the already serene surroundings.

"Lovely," I murmured as Leah nodded, her eyes wide as they roamed over every detail.

"Thank you," Daniels beamed, "it's always nice to hear one's handiwork is appreciated."

"You did all of this?" Leah asked, using both arms to gesture toward the landscape the surrounded us.

"Sure did." He chuckled. "Of course, it was dumb luck. When I moved in, it was nothing but dirt back here. And bugs. Lots of 'em. What was meant to be a quick stop at Home Depot to pick up some insecticide turned into a two-year project," he paused as both of us gawked at him, open-mouthed. "Anyway, long story short, I found something to keep myself busy during retirement."

We all laughed as he motioned for us to sit. He poured tall glasses of iced tea while we made small talk, discussing items such as landscaping in the desert and our black thumbs. Ours, not his. Once we were all situated—even Nicoh had his own water bowl with ice cubes—Daniels got down to business.

"Michael told me you were looking for some background information on Alcore and GenTech from back in the day?" When we both nodded, he continued, "Well, you're in luck. Those two happen to have been pet projects of mine." He pulled a large file box from around the side of his chair and removed the lid. Inside were dozens of folders, neatly arranged by month and year.

"Michael also said you had already done some initial research. Don't hesitate to let me know if I'm rehashing familiar territory." He smiled at us warmly as he absently rubbed Nicoh behind the ears.

"As you are likely aware, Alcore and GenTech were fierce competitors in the field of genetic engineering, often battling for funding from the same sources. Though both companies had other projects, these sources were primarily interested in the human cloning aspect of the science."

"And where the money goes, the project focus goes as well," Leah added.

"Exactly," Daniels continued, "and with the money also came protection. Not only was genetic mutation controversial, even the mere thought of human replication moved the science into an entirely different arena. One with moral and ethical consequences. Alcore's and GenTech's benefactors carried the clout to shelter them from the pandemonium that would have ensued had government and religious sectors got involved."

"What was going on at Alcore and GenTech?" I asked, hoping

I hadn't disrupted our host's train of thought. If I had, he didn't let on.

"According to my source—"

"Your source?" Leah inquired, though as a reporter herself, she knew what his response would be.

"To this day, I have not divulged his identity, though I can confirm he had intimate knowledge of the day-to-day operations at GenTech and was familiar with Alcore's as well. For today's purposes, we shall call him X. Please pardon the cliché." He chuckled.

"Anyway, according to X, both companies were attempting to replicate a human life—a child—by isolating non-reproductive cells from the mother. Once they had removed these donor cells, their nuclei would be transferred to a host cell. Though the scientist's methods were radically different at each company, the host cell in each scenario was chemically altered to the point it behaved like one generated during the union of female egg and a male sperm. The resulting host cell contained all the DNA necessary to develop into a human child. Once the host cell evolved into an embryo, it was implanted back into the mother and carried to a full term.

"In natural reproduction, half of a child's DNA comes from the mother and the other half from the father. With cloning, the DNA comes entirely from one source: the mother. The resulting child is a genetic replica of that source."

"Wow—that could make for an interesting family dinner, say if a mother gives birth to a daughter," I thought aloud.

"Ugh, can you say daddy issues?" Leah added. "And what about the mother-daughter relationship—could you imagine getting into an argument with yourself?"

Daniels watched us, obviously amused by our banter, but when he spoke again, his tone was serious. "And therein lies some of the ethical concerns with regards to human cloning." We both nodded in agreement, though we could certainly think of others.

"So, how many mothers were involved in the experiment?" I asked, moving the conversation away from the unsettling ethical dilemmas the subject brought to mind.

"GenTech had six mothers come to full term, and while Alcore had twice as many volunteers in their program, none of them made it through the entire gestation period."

"After all of that, there were only six offspring?" Leah asked, a perplexed expression crossing her face.

Daniels sighed, scratching his head. "Well, that's where things got a little fuzzy. A little grayer, perhaps. Each mother was actually implanted with two embryos. X said GenTech wanted to pad the odds, to ensure at least one made it to term. That was one of the reasons, anyway."

"Meaning if they did come to term, the mother would have had twins?" I asked.

Daniels nodded. "It's sketchy whether all came to term—even X wasn't sure—but yes, had they all survived, there would have been twelve children. Six sets of twins. All girls." We all took a moment to reflect on that tidbit.

Leah broke the awkward silence. "You said 'one of the reasons' GenTech implanted two embryos—what was another?"

His friendly demeanor immediately turned to one filled with disgust and distaste. "There were rumors—that not even X could fully substantiate—GenTech was also creating the twin as a means of providing 'spare parts,' for lack of better phrasing."

"Oh my," I whispered as I looked to Leah, her eyes wide and mouth opened in shock.

"There were other rumors, too, that painted darker pictures of their intentions." Daniels shook his head, sickened. "I can't even begin to bring myself to utter the words."

"Don't," Leah said gently. "What I don't understand is how

the mothers would knowingly subject themselves or their unborn children to that possibility?"

"They didn't know," Daniels replied. "I'm not sure about Alcore, but prior to the cell extraction, GenTech required the mothers to sign an agreement relinquishing all rights to any child born as a result of their participation in the program. They used the awkward family dynamic you mentioned as their BS rationale. Of course, after considering the alternatives, the mothers quickly acquiesced. Plus, they were handsomely rewarded for their cooperation.

"But GenTech didn't stop there when it came to getting the mother's consent. They also guaranteed the children would be adopted separately, to parents in different states. This limited the possibility the mother or any of her other non-program children would come into contact with the cloned child during their lifetimes. That time clock started the moment she gave birth."

Something clicked into place as Daniels spoke, but I wasn't sure exactly what.

"How come you never ran the story?" Leah asked, changing the subject.

"By the time I was able to collect all of this," he motioned toward the file box, "the benefactors had lost their footing—too many hands in the pot—and the Feds, as well other public and private sectors were rapidly closing in. As a result, their purse strings tightened, forcing GenTech to return their focus to the other—pre-cloning—projects and Alcore to close altogether.

"Despite the shift, I continued tracking GenTech, but many of those involved in the project were quickly transitioned out. Others couldn't or wouldn't talk, or they conveniently disappeared. No one wanted that cat coming out of the bag, so keeping it quiet from that point forward wasn't an issue."

"Unless you were a newspaperman," Leah added.

Daniels' head bobbed in agreement. "Unless you were a news-paperman."

"So, out of curiosity, did the cloning program ever have a name?" I asked.

He nodded, chuckling. "I could never decide if the GenTech scientists who named it did so out of total madness or pure genius. Anyway, in the early days of the project, they simply referred to it as Gemini."

The astrological sign of the twins.

With all that I had heard today, my money was on the prior —madness.

CHAPTER TWENTY-SIX

Daniels looked at us intently, as if making a decision about something important. Finally, he spoke, "I'm hoping you will entertain a question in return?" At our nods he continued, "After all these years, why are you really interested in Alcore and GenTech?" I looked at Leah, and she bobbed her head in the affirmative—we could trust Daniels with the truth.

"My interest lies with Martin Singer, a former scientist at GenTech and Alison Anders, a researcher at Alcore. I recently learned they were my birth parents," I paused before Leah and I proceeded to give him the *Reader's Digest* version of the past several weeks. When we were finished, he was unnervingly quiet for a long while.

"Interesting. That definitely changes things." He reached forward and dug through his file box, extracting a single photo. "I thought you looked oddly familiar."

He handed me an 8" x 10" photo of a group of roughly thirty men and women in stark white lab coats—the only splash of color provided by the orange and blue Alcore logo on the left breast pocket. Several individuals had crossed arms, with serious faces. This certainly wasn't one of your school photos where someone makes a ridiculous face or forms rabbit ears with their fingers behind the teacher's head. These people looked annoyed, as if posing for the photo had been an unnecessary distraction in their busy day—an impediment to the progression of their important work.

"This was the team involved in Alcore's cloning project," Daniels offered, pointing to a single face in the group.

Leah and I squinted at the woman he had indicated. "Whoa, that's creepy," Leah whispered as I sucked in a shallow breath. A mirror image of my own face stared back.

My birth mother, Alison Anders.

"I see the resemblance, but you recognized me from this?" I gestured toward the one-inch orb that was Alison's face. Daniels laughed heartily, a deep rumbling sound.

"No dear, I had the honor of seeing her in person, plus the benefit of a photographic memory." He tapped his temple. "I've got pictures from GenTech too, of Martin Singer, but you certainly favor your mother. I assume your sister did too?"

I shuddered as I thought of the last time—the only time—I had ever seen Victoria in the flesh. I didn't want to remember her that way, yet the vision was forever embedded in my memory. I forced it down, and thought back to the photos Ramirez had brought me of her twinkling eyes and smiling face. Finally, I nodded at Daniels.

"I'm so sorry, dear, I didn't mean to—" I put a hand up to stop him.

"It's ok. I'm trying to get my head around all of this." I chuckled lightly, sadly. "Half the time I don't know what to think or feel." Leah rubbed my shoulder as Daniels looked at me, his eyes filled with compassion.

"I was sorry to hear Martin and Alison had passed. I doubt anyone knew they were involved with one another. X certainly didn't mention it," he added, thoughtfully.

"Given the sensitivity of the projects they were working on, not to mention the ongoing hostility between their companies, I'm sure they would have both been terminated had their affair come to light. Besides, it would have been a violation of both of their employment contracts.

"No, I'm quite sure no one was wise to their liaison. And, the proximity of their deaths didn't set off any alarms either. There was too much else going on at the time," he paused, remembering the past.

"Earlier, you said 'that definitely changes things'—what did you mean?" Leah asked.

"Please, don't get me wrong. When we were talking before, I wasn't leaving things out to purposely deceive you, I didn't think they were relevant to your research at the time. Now that I know the whole story, they may be pertinent.

"When the benefactors pulled their money, forcing the cloning projects to be terminated, and Alcore to close, it was rumored Martin Singer had gone into the GenTech lab and removed all the formulas and procedures required to develop the clones so they couldn't be reproduced—or misused—in the future.

"The same week, after Alcore had let everyone go, their cloning lab suddenly went up in flames. It was blamed on faulty wiring, but interestingly enough, it was the only area in the entire building that sustained any damage."

"Surely no one thought Martin had orchestrated that little mishap, too?" I queried.

"Nothing could be substantiated, but X said there was speculation. Now that I know of the connection between Martin and Alison though—" Leah abruptly cut Daniels off, surprising the older man.

"Come on—you are not seriously considering the notion Alison provided Martin with the means to sneak into enemy territory, undetected, so he could destroy the lab?" I tended to agree with her, the idea seemed rather outlandish. "Let's not forget she died before the projects ended and Alcore closed."

Quickly overcoming his surprise at Leah's outburst, Daniels chuckled. "Just thinking out loud, my dear, forgive an old, rambling mind."

I spared a look to Leah, neither of us was buying it. After divulging all that he had, why hold back now?

"So, after Martin committed suicide, the formulas were never found?"

"No, to this day, the formulas and procedures have never been found. Whatever secrets he held went with him. When he died, effectively, so did the project," Daniels added, his face unreadable.

"Convenient, don't you think?" Leah commented.

Convenient, I silently agreed, but for who?

"Then why is there a killer still out there?" I asked of no one, in particular.

It was Daniels who replied, "Now that's the million-dollar question, isn't it?"

CHAPTER TWENTY-SEVEN

Daniels waved goodbye to the girls as they pulled out of his drive-way. Once they were safely out of sight, he pulled a disposable cell phone from his trousers and dialed the number he'd only used on two other occasions, nearly thirty years earlier.

After all that time, the same crisp voice answered on the third ring. Always on the third ring.

"How much did they know?" the voice inquired, emphasizing each word in an almost painful, unyielding way.

"Enough," Daniels replied, "they knew enough."

"He won't be pleased," the voice replied, the tone unchanged.

"No, I expect he won't," Daniels said in return.

This time, there was no reply, only a deafening silence on the other end of the connection.

CHAPTER TWENTY-EIGHT

We were on the outskirts of Daniels' neighborhood when Leah turned to me. "Super nice man—kind of lonely in a sweet way— but something was definitely up."

I nodded. "Do you think we should have held off telling him why we really wanted to talk to him?"

"No way. Telling him got us that last little nugget on Martin. And these." She shook the envelope containing photos of the former Alcore and GenTech employees Daniels had lent us. "Besides, he's probably harmless."

She had a point, though I wasn't sure I totally agreed with her on the last one. Honestly, I didn't know why. Chalk it up to a gut thing. I momentarily put it on the back burner, electing to focus instead on our conversation with Daniels.

"Pretty crazy stuff going on at Alcore and GenTech back in the day, huh? Can you believe they were actually replicating humans thirty years ago?"

"I know. Can you imagine what those formulas could have morphed into if scientists had been improving upon them over the years?" She scrunched up her face.

"I know. I wish I could simply look at the benefits associated with that project, but when Daniels mentioned the whole spare parts bit, I nearly barfed." I blanched at the thought. "Certainly makes you stop and think twice, doesn't it?"

"This may be taking it to the extreme, but what if someone had developed an entire army of clones—the perfect soldiers—to serve as the ultimate wartime killing machines? Yeesh, think of what could have happened had those formulas gotten into the wrong hands."

"Sounds like the plot of a campy sci-fi horror flick to me, and fortunately, that was not the case."

"Yeah, thanks to Martin, but what do you think happened to the children who came out of the Gemini project?"

"Hard to say. If they truly were adopted, as Daniels suggested, then we can only hope they are leading happy, normal lives." Leah looked at me, a bit sadly and nodded.

"But his reference to the adoption agreements, you realize what that means, right?"

I nodded, having already considered the idea. "We've got yet another thread to tie the Sterling Joy Agency to GenTech. Though he didn't name them specifically, we already knew GenTech owned them, probably for that very purpose." Ugh. It seemed so all-in-the-family. Double ugh—no pun intended.

"Yeah, I noticed Daniels didn't go into too many details on that particular subject."

"Me too. In thinking over the conversation, he was pretty careful—giving us bits he wanted us to know, leaving others out —but why? What would be his motivation? It wasn't as though you were going to run away with his pet story after all these years and publish it yourself." I snorted. I truly didn't believe that was Daniels' rationale.

We were so deep into our conversation, we arrived at Leah's office before we both knew it. Considering the amount of time we had spent with Daniels, we agreed it would be better if I dropped her off at work and then picked her up later. I watched her as she got out the Mini, collected her things and gave Nicoh a hug and some scratches.

"Thanks, Leah," I said earnestly. "I appreciate you contacting Rafferty. The interview with Daniels was definitely worth it."

"My pleasure, Ajax. I'd do anything for you." She patted the side of the car. "I'll give you a call when I'm ready to take off for the night. In the meantime, have fun perusing the Alcore/GenTech I'm-too-serious-to-be-sexy glamour shots." She giggled and bounded off in the direction of her office building.

I was still laughing when I pulled into my own driveway. That was until I realized I hadn't called Abe and Elijah about Clark/Dolby yet. Crap. Any messages? Nope. Good. I tried their office, and when Anna picked up, she put me on hold while she called Abe's cell, returning momentarily, once she has us all connected.

Elijah called out, "How're things in Phoenix, AJ?"

"Interesting, to say the least," I said, my tone serious as I proceeded to tell them about the tail the previous night, my suspicions it had been Clark/Dolby and finally, Ramirez's confirmation this morning the car was registered to Dolby.

I could hear one, if not both, of the guys start to comment, but I pressed on and told them of the morning Leah and I had spent with Mort Daniels, including our after-commentary and analysis. I wrapped up, letting them know the photos Daniels had given me were next on my agenda. Finally, I expelled a deep breath.

Anna spoke first, "Um, AJ? I think you might have blown someone's gasket. A couple gaskets, actually."

"Wh…what?" I stuttered, but before she could respond, the floodgates opened and two enraged brothers came tumbling out.

For several minutes, they both read me the riot act. I won't go into the back and forth dialogue, but it was certainly colorful and went along the lines of a classic *Dick and Jane* book. The basic plot of this particular story being stupid girl doesn't think, stupid girl acts carelessly, stupid girl gets into trouble, stupid girl gets dead. Oh no, poor stupid girl. Redundant and annoying, isn't it?

After the riot act came the directive.

"So, Ms. Jackson," Abe seethed as I silently reflected on the fact we had gone back to using formal names. "Abe and I are currently en route to Phoenix. You are to stay put—that means in your house, with Nicoh nearby—until we arrive. We can discuss future logistics at that time, but under no circumstances are you to go anywhere, alone or otherwise, until we knock on your front door."

Perhaps I'd had too many Wheaties this morning. Usually, I knew better than to open my pie-hole while the tiger was pacing. "But—" I started.

"Shut it!" Abe growled, immediately cutting me off, though the angry temperature of his voice had reduced significantly since the aforementioned butt-chewing.

I'd never had older brothers, but I was guessing this was what it must be like. What a treat. My deepest sympathies go out to all the little sisters in the world.

"So, are we all on the same page?" Elijah asked once his brother had finished, though he wasn't really asking. "You will remain where you are until you see our beady little eyes staring back through your peephole. Is that clear?"

I mumbled a curt "yes," hoping when they arrived six hours later, I would finally be allowed to come out of the corner and take my dunce hat off.

CHAPTER TWENTY-NINE

After my illuminating call with the Stanton brothers, I powered my cell phone off. I needed time to think. Good thing I had at least six hours on my hands.

Did I take Abe and Elijah seriously? You betcha. Don't get me wrong, despite their good looks, those boys could be pretty darn intimidating. They did have some valid points—I hadn't been particularly careful the past few days—and besides, it wasn't going to kill me to cool my jets for a while.

I settled on the couch and proceeded to sift through the photos Daniels had supplied while Nicoh placed his large head on my feet. I opted to look through the Alcore photos first, which included many of the same people as the one he had shown us earlier, in similar poses. Perhaps it had been an attempt at a public relations photo-op?

I had hoped for a more detailed shot of Alison Anders, but the angle and distance were consistent from one photo to the next. Still, I was drawn to her face. It was like looking at a time-warped version of myself. Although her mouth was serious, her eyes were warm, the same shade of blue, with a hint of violet. Her soft reddish-brown hair, though styled more simply than was typical for the era—it was the 1980s, after all—cascaded over her shoulder in a long ponytail. No-nonsense bangs framed her heart-shaped face. I shuddered, the resemblance was downright eerie.

My thoughts drifted to the woman I'd known to be my mother, who had raised and nurtured me, given me unconditional love. While there had been several similarities—it was the woman in the photo who had given me life.

I lingered on that for a moment. Had Alison survived, would she have loved me as equally? My eyes drifted to her left hand. It was pressed, almost protectively, against the base of her ribcage, right above her tummy, exposing the small swell I'd missed before. Even with her roomy lab coat, it was obvious she was pregnant. I looked again into her eyes and found my answer.

I shuffled through the rest of the photos, wishing Daniels had provided a date and some names to identify the members of the Alcore team. My wish was partially granted when I flipped to the last photo in the stack. Someone had neatly typed the name of each person in order of appearance and row on a sticker affixed to the back of the photo. I glanced through them and not surprisingly, only recognized Alison's name. There was still no date, but Alison and her baby bump made the timeframe a bit more definitive.

I moved to the GenTech photos, which differed from Alcore's in that they were of smaller groups of three to four people, all at work in what appeared to be various locations of the lab. Working on the Gemini project, perhaps? This time, each photo was labeled with a date and the names of the people in the image. I panned through several, searching the names, looking for one in particular.

I was about halfway through the pile when I found it—a photo of Martin Singer. The photographer had captured three-quarters of his face. He was ruggedly-handsome, with dark eyes and sharp, angular features that would have made him look severe, had it not been for the mop of wavy brown hair that brushed the base of his neck, giving him a boyish, playful look.

Based on his facial expression, he was deep in conversation with the man to his right, who was looking—no, glaring—directly into the camera, as if annoyed by its presence.

Taking in the man's features, I gasped—not because his stare seemed to bore through me—because he looked eerily similar to someone else I had seen recently, also in a photograph. My heart clenched as I checked the name on the back of the photo. I double-checked. The label identified the man as Theodore Winslow. Coincidence? Definitely not.

There was no doubt in my mind Theodore Winslow was Winslow Clark's/Tanner Dolby's father.

My mind started racing. Daniels had said only mothers had been cloned, resulting in female offspring. Had he been misinformed? Or lying? Was it possible GenTech had progressed further on the Gemini project than originally thought?

I wondered who had taken the photos. There was no signature or copyright on the back. Convenient. Could it have been Daniels' mysterious Mr. X? There were so many pieces to the puzzle strewn about, yet I had a sneaking suspicion we were closer than we thought. I pulled out a stack of index cards and started writing the items we had learned to this point.

It had started with Alcore and GenTech. Both had initiated controversial human cloning projects, funded by the same sources. GenTech had reportedly progressed more quickly, producing several successful offspring while Alcore had struggled, yielding none. GenTech was quick to conceal their results—possibly to retain their competitive advantage over Alcore—by severing the connection between the mother and children shortly after birth, using the pretense of a secure adoption.

Enter the Sterling Joy Agency—owned by GenTech—managed and operated by the conveniently missing Maxwell and

Mavis Baumgardner. Sterling Joy appeared to exist for the sole purpose of unloading Gemini's offspring. By separating the twins, then adopting them to parents in different states, they were able to assist GenTech in concealing the project's secrets.

In doing so, the Baumgardners retained Jonathan Silverton as their lawyer to oversee both sides of the adoption and serve as liaison for the agency. Silverton seemed to work exclusively for Sterling Joy, as no other clients were ever identified. That being the case, he was likely at the forefront of the interactions between GenTech and Sterling Joy and could easily have been singled out as the scapegoat if and when crap hit the fan.

I wondered if Silverton had gone to his grave feeling remorse for his involvement, essentially off-loading cloned babies for GenTech, spreading them throughout the country to childless, unknowing couples. Had he been alive, I would have asked him.

If he had felt remorse, had he forwarded the birth certificates and other documents on to the Winestones? I tended to think he had. I also believed he had sent the same documents to my parents, the ones that had upset my dad shortly before he and my mother perished in the plane crash.

Had those last repentant acts also made him a liability? If so, had his stroke been induced—made to look like an accident—as a means of averting a repeat performance? I realized I had identi-fied far more questions than answers, all of which would need to be given some more thought. In the meantime, I returned my attention to GenTech.

GenTech employed Martin Singer, one of five scientists, on the Gemini project. Martin had an affair with Alison Anders, a researcher for the competition, on a similar, less successful cloning project. Although Daniels said X never spoke of their involvement or even indicated anyone had ever been the wiser, someone at GenTech had known enough to pay for Alison's medical bills after her death. Paid, despite the fact Martin had allegedly removed the formulas and destroyed the Alcore lab once the project had been terminated. Yeah, right.

If that weren't crazy enough, there were the events surrounding our births. Before Alison went into premature labor, she and Martin happened to make arrangements with the Sterling Joy Agency in the event they both unexpectedly died? Arrangements—as in separate adoptions—which also happened to be the status quo for GenTech at the time. Conveniently, both Alison and Martin passed within days of one another, and the adoptions went off without a hitch. I shook my head. Something didn't sit right with me. A lot of things, if truth be told.

There was also the recent discovery of Theodore Winslow, who—after seeing the father-son similarities—was likely Clark's/ Dolby's father. Winslow, also a scientist, worked side-by-side with Martin at GenTech. What was the state of their relationship? I wondered. Not to be cliché, but they say a picture is worth a thousand words, and if the pictures I had seen were any indication, it was tumultuous at best.

Had Winslow used the project to produce his own clones? Had Martin felt the need to remove the formulas and procedures from GenTech because of people like Winslow? Finally, had Winslow sought revenge against Martin by turning his son into a manipulator and cold-blooded killer?

I was contemplating the validity of that theory when the doorbell rang, forcing Nicoh into his grumbly guard dog mode. I looked at my watch. Abe and Elijah had made good time. I rose, squinted through the peephole and after taking in their stern looks, mentally prepared myself for a continuation of the morning's butt-chewing as I opened the door.

"Why is your cell phone off?" Abe growled before I had an opportunity to speak. Though Nicoh was familiar with Abe and his brother, he was wary of the tone and quickly moved his body protectively between us.

I scruffed Nicoh ears gently, ignoring the question. "Well. Hello. To. You. Too. You two made good time. Won't you please come in?" My voice remained calm. Pleasant.

Elijah huffed out something that sounded like "hi" and pushed passed his brother, apparently taking me up on my offer. Nicoh and I moved to the side as he entered. Abe scowled but muttered his own greeting and followed.

"I turned my cell phone off so I could think. After the reaming you two gave me earlier, I took some time—" I had prepared a little mea culpa speech, but Abe put his hand up to stop me, his expression softening, and when he spoke, it was not the incensed tone I had anticipated. It was one of concern.

"We're sorry, AJ. We were worried when we couldn't get a hold of you. After everything that has happened…" he looked down at his feet, unable to finish his thought. A moment passed before Elijah completed it for him, his voice uncharacteristically shaky.

"What my brother is trying to say is we care about you. We don't want you getting hurt on our watch." Abe looked up for only a moment to affirm what his brother has said, then sullenly resumed staring downward.

Understanding washed over me. They were unable to contact Victoria that last day. In their race to reach me, they feared history had repeated itself.

"Ohhh, I'm so sorry. I didn't think." I choked back a sob, awkwardly balling my fists at my side. Now I was the one left staring at my shoes.

Abe shocked me when he pulled me into a tight hug, a motion which almost forced tears to spring freely from my already dampened eyes. He released me and Elijah followed suit, enclosing me in a massive bear hug. At this point, all three of us sported red-rimmed, dewy eyes, which thankfully, none of us was quick to point out.

Once we had all recovered from our moment, Elijah was the first to speak, "AJ, we've got some news. Anna called us while we were on the road. She heard from Paul Switzer at the Jaguar dealership over in Malibu." He let out a deep breath before proceeding, "Tanner Dolby is dead. His body was found in a ravine near Big Bear by a couple of hikers. The condition of the body was pretty degraded, but the medical examiner's office was able to make an identification based on dental records. Anyway, they estimate he'd been dead at least eight months."

"Before the Winestone's accident," I said quietly, positive the colored had drained from my face.

He nodded. "And before the falsified mix-up with Mrs. Winestone's Jag."

"How did he die?" I asked.

"Undetermined. Could have been anything from exposure to a fall. There wasn't enough left."

I shook my head. "It doesn't matter. I'm pretty sure he left this world with help from his twin brother, Winslow Clark."

CHAPTER THIRTY

I showed Abe and Elijah the photos Daniels had supplied, including the one of Martin Singer and Theodore Winslow, then shared the conclusions I had drawn, adding in the one I had formulated about Tanner Dolby and Winslow Clark being twins, rather than the same person. It was the only way he could have been in two places at the same time. One was dead in a ravine while the other worked at the Jaguar dealership in Malibu. Actually, if you added in his stint as a crash site investigator, that would make it three. Regardless, the former Clark/Dolby, now Clark, had been a very busy, very bad boy.

When I finished, Abe excused himself, stepping outside. "Let me give Anna a quick update. She's still trying to track down a co-worker of either Martin's or Alison's and this information could be useful."

"Pretty sketchy, huh?" I asked Elijah.

"I wouldn't say that," he replied, "though it would be helpful to know more about Martin's working relationship with Winslow."

"I could give Daniels a call, see if X had mentioned anything specifically?" I shrugged.

"Worth a shot," Elijah agreed.

Several messages awaited me as I powered my cell phone on. "How many times did you two call me, anyway?"

Elijah grinned at me sheepishly. "Uh, maybe a couple?"

I laughed while I dialed the number Daniels had supplied during our visit. The older gentleman picked up on the first ring, and once greetings were exchanged, I asked him about the GenTech scientists. Abe came in the front door and tucked his cell into his pocket as I hung up with Daniels.

"Everything cool?" I asked.

He gave me a quick thumbs-up, indicating Anna was good to go.

"So, I called Daniels while you were outside and asked him if X had ever mentioned the working relationships among the scientists at GenTech, and he literally burst out laughing. He asked if I meant the ongoing feud between Theodore Winslow and Martin Singer."

"Interesting," Abe commented as Elijah nodded.

"Their relationship was contentious, at best. X told Daniels the two were often seen in heated arguments and while it didn't turn physical, it caused a great deal of tension for the entire Gemini team."

"Any idea what fueled it?" Elijah asked as he settled on the couch, Nicoh nestled comfortably at his feet.

"Egos?" Abe offered.

"Indirectly, yeah. Martin felt Winslow was pushing the project farther and farther into moral and ethical gray areas. You know, the kind that makes you feel squishy just thinking about them?"

Both Abe and Elijah both shook their heads in the affirmative. Abe made himself at home on the other end of the couch, opposite his brother, while I paced.

"Martin tried to rein Winslow in and even attempted to get the other team members involved, but Winslow was the lead scientist, which gave him a great deal of authority and control over the project. Most were afraid he'd boot them off the project or make it difficult to move to another if they challenged him, so he was basically allowed to do as he pleased."

"Jerk-wad," Abe grunted.

"Major jerk-wad," I corrected. "Regardless, Martin remained diligent in his efforts to keep Winslow under control and remained a thorn in his side until the project was dismantled."

"Martin wasn't afraid Winslow would oust him?" Elijah asked.

I shook my head. "Winslow may have been the lead but Martin had a sharper mind. He needed Martin. Unfortunately, from what X told Daniels, he used Martin as well, taking Martin's formulas and tweaking them to fit his own purposes, which tended toward the—"

"Squishy gray areas?" Abe finished my sentence.

"The squishy gray areas," I agreed. "Anyway, I'm guessing Winslow was pretty bent when Martin snatched the formulas and project procedures."

"Bent enough for revenge," Elijah stated, more than asked.

We all looked at one another. It was definite possibility. But after thirty years?

I remembered I hadn't listened to my messages and quickly dialed my voicemail as I went to the kitchen for beverages. There were eleven waiting for me. Eleven? I glanced back at the two and smiled.

Both were working hard to be Nicoh's favorite. Abe was giving him belly-scratches while Elijah mussed his face and ears. Delighted whoo-whoos filled the air as Nicoh reveled in the extra attention.

The first three messages were from Abe and Elijah, clearly not happy campers. The fourth was from Leah, about four hours earlier, letting me know she would be working late on a story and would catch a ride home with her editor. Her editor? Ok, that was weird. I continued to listen to rest of the messages. All were from Abe or Elijah. The content, more of the same. I shook my head. They were persistent, I'd give them that. I was about to send a snarky comment to that effect in their direction when my phone rang.

By the time I finished the call, I had dropped the phone on the floor and collapsed to my knees. My body shook as Abe and Elijah rushed to my side.

"It was Leah's editor," I whispered, barely able to form the words. "He wanted to know when he could expect to see her today. He said he knew we were working on a side project and if she didn't want to jeopardize her current job, she needed to check in ASAP."

I took a deep breath and upon noting their confused expressions, added, "I dropped Leah off in front of her office building over six hours ago. One of the messages was from her, a couple of hours later, telling me she was working late and wouldn't need me to pick her up after all," I choked out the last words, a sob threatening to break free. "She said she was getting a ride with her editor. *That* editor."

Abe and Elijah moved to the floor with me, a brother flanking each side.

"AJ—" Elijah started, rubbing my arm tenderly.

I didn't give him a chance to finish, "He has her, doesn't he? Clark has her."

I looked at them both earnestly, but regardless of the response, I knew it was true. Leah told me as much in her message. She wouldn't ask her editor for a favor, much less catch a ride with him. Ever. Period. She knew I'd known that and used it as a means to let me know something was awry.

"We need to call Detective Ramirez," I said firmly, without waiting for a response.

"Agreed. I'll handle it." Abe patted my hand as he rose from his squatted position and moved into the kitchen, already dialing.

"He'll need an update," Elijah called after his brother.

An update, meaning from the time Ramirez called to confirm the identification of Tanner Dolby's car to the discovery of his body in Big Bear. It was a call I was glad I wasn't making. Best to let them talk ex-cop to cop. Regardless, I had a feeling Abe would be earning his keep on that one.

Elijah looked at me for a long moment, and I realized he was still holding my arm, almost as though his grasp was keeping me upright. Perhaps it was. Finally, he spoke, his tone quiet, but even. Confident.

"We'll get her back AJ, I promise."

Before I had a chance to respond, my cell phone rang. Fortunately, it still worked after I had dropped in on the hardwood floor.

"It's Leah's number!" I exclaimed, tilting the screen so Elijah could see.

He nodded. "Put it on speakerphone."

I did, and at his second nod, answered it, "Leah?" I heard a mechanical click on the other end.

"Arianna? It's me. I don't have much time."

It was a recording. Though her voice echoed over the speakerphone, she sounded so small, so alone. My heart clenched for my best friend.

"He wants to make a trade. You…for me. My office building…the thirty-first floor in one hour. The key card for the elevator is in your mailbox. Don't bring the cops. And don't be late."

The recording ended and so did the call. I couldn't do anything but stare at the phone lying in my outstretched palm.

"She must be so scared," I uttered, barely a whisper, my heart breaking into a million pieces.

Had he hurt her? Or worse? I hadn't heard Abe come back in. He gently took the phone from my hand, and for the second time that afternoon, pulled me into a hug.

"It'll be ok, AJ. She'll be ok. I promise." Both brothers had given me their word in as many minutes.

As I pulled away, I looked each of them in the eye. "I'm going to hold you to that. Both of you." Pulling myself together for Leah's sake, I asked, "Now, how are we going to do this?"

Twenty minutes later, we had formulated a plan and were en route to Leah's office building. Ok, it wasn't much of a plan because Clark held all the cards, but it was something. I was glad to have it, as well as Abe and Elijah on my side.

I knew Clark had purposely selected the thirty-first floor because the top ten floors in Leah's office building were currently empty. Number thirty-one was smack-dab in the middle of the empty floors, meaning there would be no traffic coming or going and no neighbors above or below.

I hated to think how he had managed to secure a key card or when he had slipped it into my mailbox. The mere thought of him being that close to me—ugh. I needed to stop that type of thinking and focus on the plan.

Abe and Elijah would accompany Nicoh and me as far as Clark would allow. Leah had specified no cops and perhaps we had taken liberties with that statement, but for the time being, that didn't rule out everyone else. I'd much rather have them cooling their jets on the elevator than thirty-plus floors out of reach.

Ramirez would have an undercover team waiting at a safe distance, but since we'd decided not to risk wearing any special gadgets Clark might find, they'd be flying blind, waiting only on signals from Abe or Elijah. Yeah, like I said, not much of a plan. It wasn't something I could control, or worry about. I'd let the rest of them do that. For now, all I could think about was Leah.

I was surprisingly calm as the four of us entered Leah's office building, my mind clear. Even Nicoh stood at attention, his head held high, despite being tethered to my side. Abe and Elijah were equally stoic, clad in all black ensembles, one flanking us on each side. From the hostile, almost frightening expressions each wore, I was glad they were on my team.

Clark had selected a time of day where the hustle and bustle of the workday had long subsided and we moved easily through the lobby to the bank of elevators that would take us to the thirty-first floor. As the massive doors slid shut, I caught a glimpse of a figure lingering next to the faux palm trees that lined the hallway. Our eyes connected as the gap disappeared and the elevator began its ascent.

Ramirez.

It lasted seconds, but the ride to the thirty-first floor felt like an eternity.

"You sure you're ready to do this?" Abe asked, his tone was one I would have expected him to reserve for a comrade heading into battle, not for a hysterical photographer with knocking knees and sweaty palms.

I gave him a curt nod. Sure, why not? I thought to myself. I was ready. I did this kind of thing every day, between picking up dog doo and dealing with self-important, entitled clients like Charlie. Oh yeah, here it was, on my daily to-do list: rescue best friend from maniacal killer. Easy peasy. Rah. Go, team. I blew out a deep breath as the elevator slid to a halt, then inserted the key card Clark had supplied. The doors screeched opened, resembling fingernails on a chalkboard. Fitting—in a Freddy Kruger sort of way.

We peered around as we edged out of the elevator and found nothing but a hallway leading to the left. A sharp voice boomed over the intercom, nearly piercing my eardrums, "Ms. Jackson. I need you to throw that key card as far down the hallway as possible. No girly throws, please." I tossed the card as requested and it landed about fifty feet ahead of where we stood.

"Very good, Ms. Jackson. I guess lugging all that camera equipment around does a body good." Obnoxious. "Your arm candy can step back into the elevator. Their job is done here. They may return to the lobby and tell Detective Ramirez to get his men out of the building while making sure they do the same. In the meantime, I need you and your canine to move slowly down the hall."

Great. I glanced one last time at Abe and Elijah and gave them a single head nod. Their faces were stony and expressions unreadable as they moved onto the elevator and the doors closed. I waited until I heard it descend before advancing slowly down the hall.

I reached the end before I heard the voice again. This time, it was almost conversational, the frosty tone gone, "Ah, finally, we are alone. Please turn right. You will see a series of concrete posts immediately to your left. Select one and secure the canine's lead to it. I'll wait." How considerate, I thought snarkily as I turned into an expansive, unfinished room.

The floor hadn't been built-out yet, so all the beams, wiring and fluorescent lighting remained exposed. I saw the concrete posts the voice had referenced and made a show of looping Nicoh's lead around it twice before tying it off.

His warm eyes bore into mine, pleading as I took his big head in my hands and whispered, "I love you, Nic, be a good boy while I get Leah."

He started to howl when I moved away, so I stretched out a hand, touching it gently to his nose.

"It's ok, baby." He tilted his head, obviously not satisfied, but ceased nonetheless.

"Oh my, what a well-behaved pet. One can certainly appreciate that." The voice laughed, sarcastically." Jerk-wad. "You'll be happy to know your bodyguards complied—handsome couple, by the way—and your cop friend and his donut-eating buddies have officially left the building."

More laughter. Grating. No one likes a comedian who laughs at his own jokes.

"It's a lovely evening, Ms. Jackson. Please join us on the veranda."

Veranda? Give me a break. I moved through the open space, thankful the lights were on as I made my way to the opposite side of the floor, where I assumed the patio was located.

As promised, Winslow Clark waited for me in the broad entrance that led to the outdoor patio, looking like he had walked straight off the pages of *GQ*. His sun-bleached hair was slicked back off his tanned face, exposing his piercing blue eyes and too-too polished teeth, visible through his fabricated smile. He was dressed to the hilt in what looked to be an Armani suit of exceptional cut, a crisp white button-down dress shirt underneath. Shoes were of the Italian variety, with a high gloss sheen I could have probably seen my reflection in.

"You like the suit?" He preened, waving his hand in a downward motion. "I borrowed it from my brother when he graciously lent me his identity. Guy had great taste, but his choice of professions? Commission-only? In this economy? You've got to be kidding. Besides, who wants to stand around talking about a Jaguar all day? Totally overrated. All the fun is in driving it." More boisterous, annoying laughter.

I ignored Clark's attempt at banter. "Where. Is. Leah?"

"Oh come on, Arianna. You're no fun. Leah said you'd be fun. Now I'm not so sure."

I seriously doubted Leah had said anything of the sort. He stepped backward onto the patio and nudged something with his foot. There was a built-in planter in the way so I couldn't determine what *it* was, though I had a bad feeling.

"Hmm. Looks like Leah's not going to be any fun for a bit, either."

Gasping, I stepped forward slightly—just out of Clark's reach —so I could get a better look. I could almost make out Leah's crumpled form at the base of the planter. She wasn't moving.

"What did you do to her? Is she…is she…"

"Relax, Arianna. Take a load off. She's fine. I gave her a little something to help her…mellow out," he said, laughing at his own little joke. Irritating. "Girl was giving me a raging headache with all that talking. How do you deal with it?"

"I manage fine," I replied dryly. "Are you sure she's ok?"

"Arianna, I'm hurt." He pretended to pout, pulling his lips into a tight frown. "I said she was fine, and she is. She'll be back in the Land of Chatty Cathy in a while."

More laughter. I gritted my teeth. Even under normal circum- stances—those being the ones where he wasn't planning on killing me—this guy would get on my nerves. Give him a big fuzzy microphone and you'd have the epitome of a cheesy 1970s game show host. Seriously. It was all I could do not to punch him in the throat. A sudden burst of adrenaline made me decide I would do so later, given the opportunity. For now, I had to keep him talking. So far, so good.

Clark blathered on, "Moreover, we had a deal. A trade is a trade. And it wouldn't be fair if I reneged on my part before we even started, now would it?"

Ah, now we were getting somewhere. "If that is the case, surely you won't mind if I move Leah to the elevator and send her on her merry way? Now that I'm here, that is."

"I would mind, actually. We're getting to know one another and here you are, already making up new rules. Arianna, have I mistakenly given you the impression I would be open to negotiat- ing?" his tone steeled, ever-so-slightly, but enough to let me know I had hit a nerve.

I put on the best remorseful expression I could muster. "My apologies, I didn't mean to imply—"

"Ah, Arianna, I see we are going to get along just fine," he chuckled, "but you simply must call me Clark. Like Clark Kent. I'm dashing, like Superman, aren't I?" My gag reflexes engaged two-fold.

"Is Clark you're given name?" I asked sincerely, ignoring his question. It was likely rhetorical, anyhow.

"It is indeed. Given to me by my father, Theodore Winslow, to whom you've recently become acquainted." At my surprised look —I was truly—he threw his head back and laughed. "Don't be so surprised. I know about all the mischief you and the lovely Leah have been stirring up the past few weeks. Just between you and me, liked her hair better the other way. This screams retro-Meg Ryan. *So* not a good look on her.

"But I digress. Before you ask, yes, my father raised me, if you could call it that. He was truly brilliant, but a bit of a one-trick pony," he babbled. "GenTech, specifically, the Gemini project, was his life. Thanks to *your* father, Martin Singer, my father's work was nearly destroyed."

He leaned against the wall, reminiscing. Obviously, he'd heard the story from his father many times over the years.

"Is your father still alive?" I asked quietly, prompting him to continue, to keep him talking.

"He is, but the loss of Gemini consumed him. Ate at him. Reduced him to nothing but a shell of the man he once was. Even exacting revenge failed to fill the void he felt. That he still feels."

"Revenge?" I was pretty sure I knew what he was referencing, but wanted him…needed him to spell it out.

"Come on, Arianna," Clark shook his head, "I thought you were smarter than this, that you and your chum here had at least the basics figured out." He rolled his eyes at my apologetic shrug but continued, "He killed Alison Anders, of course. To get back at Martin."

I had been prepared for this admission, but mentally shuddered at his cool, nonchalant delivery. I needed to keep my emotions in check for the duration. I was sure there would be more revelations to come. For the time being, however, Clark was engrossed in his tale and oblivious to my discomfort.

"The duplicity of their affair enraged him. Not that he cared they had one, but that they thought they could get away with it. Martin judged and chastised my father for years, calling him immoral and self-righteous. And yet, in the end, Martin was no better. He manipulated the project for his own personal gain while accusing my father of doing the same. My father simply couldn't take it any longer, he had to do something. He developed a plan that would take cunning and patience. However, to reap the rewards, he could wait.

"Once he learned Alison was pregnant, he kept tabs on them, educating himself on their every habit and routine. Alison's premature contractions were his doing—he was a doctor, after all —so slipping the right concoction into her herbal tea while she lunched with friends was easy work for him. It just took a bit of creativity.

"After she went into labor and had given birth to you and your sister, he made a quick trip to the hospital to administer a healthy dose of happy juice to the new mother. Before anyone knew what had happened, it was bye, bye, Alison." Clark sounded so proud, so enamored of his father, I wanted to vomit. I palmed my fists at my sides. Keep it together, I thought to myself.

"Despite having pulled one over on Martin—who was devastated by Alison's death—his revenge was short-lived. GenTech lost its funding and pulled the plug on Gemini. It wouldn't have been so bad, had Martin not subsequently destroyed or taken everything pertaining to the project. Once again, my father had to act. And quickly. He even coerced the Baumgardners and their lawyer, Silverton, into fabricating the adoption paperwork he would later slip into the hospital files. All that remained was taking care of Martin."

"He killed Martin, too?" I asked, my tone casting doubt. Tread carefully, I told myself.

Unaffected, he nodded. "Only after he had given Martin every opportunity to come clean, to tell him where the formulas were. Martin refused, of course, so father had to help him see the error of his ways. I'm sure Martin had plenty of time to contemplate that during his trip off the Skyway Bridge. No pun intended." He smirked and though I hadn't flinched, added, "Oops. Too soon? Sorry, my bad." Internally, I barely managed to contain myself, though my face remained a blank slate.

Nonplussed, Clark continued, "Anyway, with Martin out of the picture, the Baumgardners stepped in to stake their claim, as was their legal and dutiful right, and presto, little Victoria and Arianna got new lives." He threw his hands up, as if announcing we'd won a prize, not lost our birth parents.

I ignored him. "So why'd he go to all the trouble of fabricating the documentation? Why take the risk? Why not kill us?"

"All great questions, Arianna. I'm so glad your brain has decided to join us. From the look on your face the past several minutes, I wasn't sure you possessed one." What a jerk. "It was mostly curiosity and convenience, at first. And as it turns out, the best decision he ever made."

"What happened to the Baumgardners?" I asked.

"Dead. That witness, Sophie Allen, too," he responded lightly, as though I had asked him whether he took cream or sugar in his coffee. "Father planted a few false stories to make it seem as though they had abandoned the adoption business to pursue other opportunities, things of that nature."

"So, their deaths…were your father's doing?" Clark nodded,

before adding, "Of course, once I was old enough, I helped him out when I could. You know, first with the lawyer, Silverton. Old fool was on borrowed time, anyway. A bad heart and all. I helped ease him into the next life once he started getting sentimental about the old days, sending copies of stuff he shouldn't have to your parents and the Winestones. Of course, I had to clean up that mess, too."

I took a deep breath, readying myself for whatever Clark was about to dish out. I knew it would be bad. Keep him talking a little longer, I thought. Just a little longer...

"Do you realize how hard it is to make a plane crash look accidental?" He grinned, clearly enjoying himself, then continued without waiting for a response. "I had no idea. I won't go into all the gory details, but once it was done? What a rush. Love your pop's D-backs hat, by the way. It's one of my all-time favs," he paused to wink while I tempered my emotions, my heart thudding heavily against my chest.

"Though it wasn't as fun, it did make the Winestone's car accident that much easier, less of an impact and all that, but you take what you can get. Tanner, of course, was the easiest to deal with."

By this point, my fingernails had cut into my palms, making them bleed but still, I had to keep it together. I looked at Leah's prone body for strength and proceeded.

"You...killed your own brother?"

"Yup, gave him a bit of a helping hand while he was out hiking near Big Bear. Boy, was he surprised to see me. It was almost as though he had seen a ghost." He laughed raucously, as I thought back to what Bonnie had told Abe, Elijah and Anna about Victoria the day she had taken the photo from the dealership.

"Anyway, we were brothers by blood only. It's not like we grew up together or anything. He went the Sterling Joy route." As if that explained everything away.

"I never met Tanner-boy until the day he met his maker. Guy was a tool, a real waste of space. My father would have been insulted to know that had come out of his gene pool. It was my duty to handle it before Father could find out."

"What about Frederick Glass, the guy who took ownership of Mrs. Winestone's Jag?"

"At your service," he chortled. "Clever, huh? And just for the record, the Winestone's car was sweeeet. I was actually sorry I had to leave it sitting in that to-remain-unnamed location. Let's just say I'm sure the locals took good care of that fine piece of machinery."

I glanced at Leah again, who still appeared to be unconscious. I prayed that he had only drugged her and that after all of this, she'd be ok. With that in mind, I proceeded with the question I had wanted to ask Clark from the beginning.

"Why Victoria? Why did you kill my sister? Was she getting too close?"

His reaction was not at all what I had expected. "Too close?" He burst out laughing. Loudly. Harshly. Gloating. "Don't you get it? You and Victoria *were* the key all along. Martin gave you both a gift. And thanks to you, *my father's* work—Gemini—will rise again."

Whatever he had anticipated my reaction might be after that announcement, it was not a blank stare. He threw his hands up, thoroughly exasperated.

"You still don't get it, do you?"

I shrugged. "What gift?"

He huffed, still piqued by my underwhelmed response.

"It was two actually. Two gifts. The first is your very existence. Proof of Gemini. Proof of its success." He slapped his hand against his leg after each sentence for emphasis.

"Proof of my father's success," I carefully corrected, purposely stepping into dangerous territory, "but no matter, the question remains, if it was such a gift, then why kill Victoria? Why threaten to kill me?"

Either oblivious to or choosing to ignore the slight I had made to his father, he snickered. "Because of the second gift, of course. In those early years, my father was so blinded by rage he overlooked the bigger picture.

"Martin may have taken the formulas, but he would never have destroyed them. He would have kept them safe. In a place that was logical. Logical to a scientist. He would have kept them with the daughters who were born out of his work." He bobbed his head with excitement.

"My father realized Martin had made only one visit to the hospital after Alison died. During that visit, he injected each of you with a chip that contained one-half of the formulas. That way, someone—that someone being me—would have to get to each of you in order to get the whole enchilada." He grinned as he dug into his pocket. "In fact, here's the one I beat out of Victoria." He held up something that looked to be no bigger than a rubber pencil eraser, tossed it into the air and caught it easily before putting it back into his right trouser pocket.

I thought about Victoria's face the night I had found her in my dumpster, and though I was completely shocked and repulsed by his revelation, it was time to turn the tables on this little production before he did the same to me.

"It took your father thirty years to figure *that* out?" I threw my head back and laughed heartily, throwing in an obnoxious snort for good measure.

As I had anticipated, the temperature of the room shifted. Clark's eyes went cold. Wild. His smile morphed into a contemptuous sneer. Suddenly, several things seemed to happen all at once. Clark pulled a vicious-looking knife from his waistband and lunged in my direction. I charged at Clark's weak side, arms up protectively, ready to defend. What can I say, never bring a girl to a knife fight.

Nicoh charged around the corner and barreled into Clark's midsection, knocking both him and the knife to the ground. Leah scrambled from her prone position, a rock from the planter in hand, and conked the sweet spot on Clark's melon.

While I was pretty sure Nicoh had successfully knocked Clark out with his maneuver, this was a situation where it was definitely better to be safe than sorry, so we found an extension cord and hog-tied him to one of the concrete posts.

Leah might have also kicked him a couple of extra times to make sure he was out. He was. Sweaty and exhausted, both mentally and physically, we sat on the floor and hugged Nicoh, who panted with delight.

Neither of us spoke for a long moment until Leah broke the silence, "I'm not sure where Nicoh learned those moves, but it certainly wasn't from the Brazilian Butt Lift workout videos you've been watching."

We both laughed shakily, just as the cavalry burst in. Ramirez and his guys led the pack, followed closely by Abe and Elijah. Worried expressions quickly turned to surprise as they surveyed the scene. Don't quote me, but I was pretty sure I heard a "bad ass" from one of Ramirez's team members.

True to form, Leah and I looked at one another before turning to the lot of them. "What took you so long?" we both asked, drawing chuckles from the team.

Only Ramirez failed to crack a smile. Instead, he stepped forward until the toes of his boots were touching mine—I was wearing Chuck Taylor's, but you get the picture—and he was looking squarely into my eyes.

"What took you so long?" he grumbled after a long moment.

I gave Leah a sideways glance, and she did the same.

Ramirez's stern expression broke as he erupted into laughter. The whole room followed suit.

"You saw that?" I chirped as quietly as I could. More laughter filled the room as Ramirez nodded.

"And heard it, too. We had guys on the roof of that building." He pointed to the adjacent office building. "Guys on the roof of this building. Mics in the ceiling of the floor below—"

"I get it. I get it. You saw. You heard," I interjected.

"And we acted," Leah clarified.

"Risky maneuver," Ramirez countered.

"But effective." She was still pumped up and ready to take on anyone who dared give her guff.

Ironically, Clark chose that moment to regain consciousness. Before he had a chance to struggle, however, Leah marched over and kicked him solidly in the gut.

"I happen to like my hair, you ass."

CHAPTER THIRTY-ONE

A couple of days later, Ramirez, Abe, Elijah, Leah, Nicoh and I were sitting at Starbucks. Would you have expected us to be somewhere else? Even Anna had driven over from L.A. and after meeting her in person, both Leah and I proclaimed her as our new BFF. The guys gave us the requisite eye rolls in response. All was good in the world.

After hog-tying Clark, the FBI had swooped in, taken over and whisked him away to parts unknown. Ramirez muttered something about jurisdiction, but I had a feeling it was a lot more than that.

Clark's father, Theodore, had been located in Virginia Beach and taken into custody, though the FBI hadn't been particularly forthcoming about what would become of either of them. One thing was for sure, both would have a lot of 'splaining to do. I hoped, at a minimum, they'd be cooling their jets for a long, long time, in a very secure location.

All of us had gone rounds with the FBI, for all the good it did. They were still skeptical about the Gemini project, as well as the whole GenTech/Sterling Joy angle, though my gut tells me they knew more than they let on.

In the meantime, I filled both Cheryl Earley and Sir Harry in, as promised. Abe, Elijah and Anna also let Switzer know what had happened to Tanner Dolby. He hadn't hired a bad guy after all. Dolby just had the misfortune of being in the wrong place at the wrong time. Well, that and being born into a bad gene pool. Anyway, they never did find Mrs. Winestone's car.

As for the children of the Gemini project—where they ended up was anyone's guess. Without the benefit of the Baumgardner's documentation, it could take months, if not years, to track them all down. Besides, there were other ramifications associated with springing that jack-in-the-box.

I still didn't have answers to all of my own questions, either. For now, I was completely content sipping an icy latte with friends and, of course, celebrating Nicoh's new hero status. He had, after all, saved our bacon and was currently reaping the rewards, as scratches were plentiful and scones were in full supply. A favor, though? Let's keep that bacon comment to ourselves. I wouldn't want him assuming he could break into full-howl mode every time he wanted a few dozen pieces—cooked extra crispy—added to his nightly food bowl. I was cringing at the thought when Leah's voice brought me back to the present.

"So, are you really a clone? It would certainly explain a lot," she teased.

I nodded. "It isn't conclusive yet, but it's looking like Martin and Alison combined their knowledge and resources for the benefit of their own side project, for a lack of better words. The tests I had run yesterday will positively confirm one way or the other. I need to sit tight and wait for a few weeks until the results come back."

"If they come back positive, does that mean Martin wasn't your real father, after all?" Elijah asked. "Rather, he was the father of the invention, so to speak?"

"Not necessarily. While the Gemini project isolated cells

solely from the mother, X recently told Daniels that Martin and Alison had developed a way to introduce a few of the father's cells during the chemical alteration phase. If this was indeed the case, the resulting offspring would still retain all the physical characteristics of the mother but could also take on other characteristics of the father."

"So the children would still physically look exactly like the mother, but could take on say…the father's knack for science or math?" Abe asked.

"Yeah, something like that," I laughed.

"Is that how Theodore Winslow created Tanner Dolby and Winslow Clark?" Anna questioned.

"X said Winslow morphed many of Martin's formulas to create his own special hybrid offspring. He basically wanted to replicate himself," I replied seriously. "All he needed was a surrogate."

"Wow, what an ego." Abe shook his head. "But what happened to the surrogate?"

"I doubt we will ever know," I replied.

"You think we can trust X's word?" Elijah asked. "And who is he or she, anyway?"

It was Leah who responded, "We don't know for sure but so far, X has been right on the mark."

Everyone groaned.

Several caffeinated beverages and much reminiscing later…

Ramirez needed to leave to start his shift, so I offered to walk him to his car. He had been noticeably quiet all afternoon, despite the fact I had apologized repeatedly for my previous bad behavior. I wondered if he would ever forgive me and was about to ask him as much when he surprised me by bending over and placing a gentle kiss on my cheek. I stuttered, struggling to find the appropriate words and when I finally mustered the nerve to look up, found him chuckling softly.

"Looks like I finally figured out a way to get the last word in, Ajax."

He winked as he got into his cruiser and drove off. After a moment, the left-hand side of my mouth quirked into a small smile.

"Game on, Detective. Game on."

* * *

Everyone at the table had watched in amused silence as the scene between AJ and Ramirez played out.

While AJ stood in the parking lot, watching Ramirez drive away, Anna leaned over to Abe and Elijah, raised her finger to her lips and whispered, "I think Ramirez has a crush on AJ."

At their flabbergasted expressions, she and Leah turned to one another and pretended to clink their Starbucks cups in a mock toast before bursting into uncontrollable giggles. AJ joined them, and soon the entire table bubbled with laughter.

All was good in the world, indeed.

EPILOGUE

Leah went to my appointment with me. Even though I was only having a standard MRI procedure done, I was still scared to death and needed my best friend there to hold my hand. She did so as long as she was permitted and even then, talked the technician into letting her stay in the observation room for the duration. Despite having to stay in one place longer than I had at any other time in my life, I made it through with flying colors.

The radiologist confirmed I had a chip, no bigger than a pencil eraser, embedded in the soft tissue directly behind my left ear. Though I strongly suspect she mistook it for an electronic identification marker, she made no comment, and I offered nothing in return. I had received the answer I had gone there looking for.

Leah continued to baby me as we left the office, insisting I stay put while she got the car from the parking garage and pulled around to get me. After seeing her use her powers of persuasion on the technician, I quickly conceded, electing to sit on a small concrete bench in front of the medical complex.

While I waited, I slipped the chip from my pocket and let it sit in the center of my palm. Victoria died trying to keep me safe, because of it. If and when I had its partner removed, decisions would need to be made. I closed my hand. For now, I would keep it—keep them—safe.

When I glanced up, a figure stood directly across the street, facing me. Smiling. From a distance, the features looked vaguely familiar and once I squinted, giving them detail, there was a hint of recognition.

Leah pulled to the curb, distracting me. I smiled warmly at my friend, and as I approached the car, a burst of wind blew loose strands of hair into my face. In the moment it took to brush them away, the figure was gone, leaving nothing but an imprint on my mind. I joined Leah in the car, and soon after I rested my head against the seat, found myself dozing.

During my slumber, the figure reappeared. Still smiling, he stepped across the street until he stood directly before me. As we faced one another, he extended his hand, palm upward so that I might grasp it with my own.

"Hello, Arianna. It's nice to finally meet you," he said as I took his hand, his smile broadening.

"Hello, Martin."

~ The End ~

BEYOND REVENGE

Mischievous Malamute Mystery Series Book 2

CHAPTER ONE

Mr. Sandman was mocking me. If the night sweats and night-mares hadn't been the proof I needed, whacking my head on the nightstand after a particularly restless episode should have clued me in. I rubbed the knot that formed, convinced it was an exercise devilishly crafted to test my patience and likely, my sanity. Grumpy, I mentally added "Minion of Hell" to the sandman's epitaph as I struggled to untangle myself from the remnants of a tortured slumber.

Finally free from the destruction that had once resembled a bed, I plopped my feet on the floor. The coolness nipped at my toes as I glanced back at my bedmate, who managed to snore contently after successfully stealing the better part of the blankets. His tongue wiggled rhythmically as he exhaled, a sign he was having good doggie dreams. I really had to stop sharing my bed with a ninety-eight pound Alaskan Malamute.

Tomorrow, I sighed.

I padded down the hall, drawn toward the light emanating from the kitchen, which usually meant Leah was still up working on an assignment. After our last adventure, Leah Campbell, my best friend and now roommate, had thrown in the towel at her newspaper gig for a life of freelance writing and researching. She had no trouble drumming up work, but felt the transition necessitated a change in address.

I peered into the kitchen. My hunch was right, Leah *had* been up working on an assignment—as verified by the mass of paper strewn across every available surface—but apparently, at some point her brain had given in to other ideas. Leah was now sprawled face down—in all her drooling glory—on top of the kitchen island. I was pretty sure there was a stove under there somewhere. *Comfy?* I thought to myself. Every few seconds, she muttered something that sounded eerily like "brownies," though it could have been "bunnies." Regardless, she was obviously stressed about the project at hand.

I removed a spiral binder from beneath her head, hoping she'd thank me for it later, despite the enchanting imprint it left on her check. She was lucky I didn't have my camera handy. Nah, I wouldn't do that to her, though it was fun to jangle her chain every once in a while.

"Yoohoo, Sleeping Beauty, your prince has arrived and is about to storm the castle to avenge your honor. Lest he see his betrothed drooling or he might choose to run off with the witty best friend."

"Shut it…off…" was the muttered response, followed by a colorful variation of "go away."

"Perhaps he'll be so overcome with appreciation of my stunning features, we'll end up running off to Vegas to meet Elvis at The Little White Chapel?"

"Don't care…sleeping here…"

"Ok then, an early morning smooch from Nicoh?"

"That beast so much as breathes in my direction, I'll withhold snacks, indefinitely," Leah mumbled as she opened one eye to glare at me. "Seriously? Can't a girl take a nap around this place without being harassed, or threatened with doggie breath?"

"Tough assignment?" I asked as I began collecting the hand-written notes that had fallen to the floor.

"Tough assignment, tough night," she replied. "Have been doing research all night for the Dynamic Duo."

I nodded. Several of her freelance projects had been contracted by Abe and Elijah Stanton, two brothers who ran a private investigations firm in Los Angeles. We had met them through their involvement with my sister's case a few months earlier. After Leah left the newspaper, they had hired her to research a few of their other cases. Currently, she was embroiled in the details surrounding a seven-year-old missing person's case.

"Starting to look like this gal purposely left a bad situation. Hard to make her reappear when she's worked so hard to escape in the first place." A hint of sadness filled her voice as she yawned.

"What will you do?"

Leah shrugged. "I was hired to do research, which I did. The rest is up to Abe and Elijah."

I handed her the notes I had collected and squeezed her arm. "It's all you can do, Leah. It's in their hands now. You know they'll do the right thing."

She nodded, absently pulling on the short tufts of blond hair that framed her face. While her eyes were puffy and the binder imprint still graced her cheek, I marveled at how she managed to look so good at this time of day. It was her quick wit and smart mouth that usually got her into trouble, though I had a sneaking suspicion she'd caught the attention of the older Stanton brother, Abe, whether she realized it or not. Leah yawned again while glancing at the clock, and after noting the early hour, frowned as she looked at me squarely.

"Still having the dreams," she commented. I nodded, though it hadn't been a question. Leah bowed her head in a quick acknowledgment.

"You ready for tonight?" This time I shrugged. Honestly, I wasn't sure.

We had been recruited by Charlie Wilson, an old high school friend, to help with the condominium-warming party he was throwing at his penthouse that evening. I was using the term "friend" a bit freely, as neither Leah nor I were in Charlie's social circle. We were more or less unpaid help, performing menial tasks, though Charlie insisted it was our particular talents he was interested in procuring for the party.

Charlie was also a frequent client of my photography services, a business I'd aptly named Mischievous Malamute after a few innocent episodes involving Nicoh during some of my earlier assignments. Misbehaved companion aside, Charlie had recruited me for my photographer's eye—as he'd phrased it—requesting my presence during setup to ensure the party's look and feel met with his exacting standards.

He claimed he wanted Leah on hand at the party for her contacts at the paper and within the community, with the hope she could nudge details of the festivities into the appropriate society pages, and into the right ears.

In reality, Charlie needed our help because he was short-handed after firing his personal assistant. Now persona non grata, Arch Underwood had reportedly been booted from the penthouse after having the audacity to don attire that clashed with his surroundings and apparently, Charlie's sensibility. From my experience Charlie favored steel, black or white—meaning any splash of color, or anything denim, not only offended him, it got his blood percolating. Therefore, for his crimes against all things monochromatic, Arch was promptly ejected, leaving Charlie without his minion.

I wasn't Arch's replacement—I did have my own business with my own clients, after all—but every time I was around Charlie, people managed to assume I was his new Girl Friday. I was convinced Charlie had something to do with that, the irony being I wasn't exactly color-coded to his standards, either. Why I was elected to help him with his party was beyond me.

In case you were wondering, my name is Arianna Jackson. My friends call me AJ, or Ajax if I'm being particularly precocious. I'm a twenty-something freelance photographer who, as I briefly mentioned, lives with my ex-reporter best female friend, Leah. Of course, there's also my best canine friend, Nicoh, who possesses marginal manners and an extreme attitude—the dog, not the girl. We reside in the desert setting of Phoenix, Arizona in a home that belonged to my parents before their deaths in a plane crash a few years prior. Until recently, we believed the crash had been a tragic accident. That was until I found my twin sister—a sibling I hadn't previously known existed—violently murdered. My life had changed forever in that moment, replaced by a series of long-buried secrets—the kind of secrets only the dead could reveal. Well, the dead and a couple of murderous wackadoos, as it turned out.

Long story short, both our adoptive parents had been murdered, along with several other innocent people. All because of a very deadly secret that started with our biological parents, who had been the first to perish trying to protect it. As it turned out, Victoria and I were that secret. When Victoria put the pieces together and tried to warn me, she was rewarded with death. Now I'm the sole protector of the secret—the one who holds the key. Literally.

I know I should take solace in the fact the murderers were apprehended and incarcerated, but I don't. I can't. My very existence poses a threat. So while I try to live my life in spite of this challenge, it manages to creep into my thoughts on occasion and more frequently, into my dreams. Fortunately, my days are filled with enough distractions to prevent me from obsessing over them —the most recent of which happens to be named Charlie.

I shook my head in the negative to Leah's question—no one would ever be prepared for one of his shindigs, or for Charlie.

I would soon come to fully appreciate the irony of that.

* * *

Nicoh emerged, suddenly aware he had been missing the action in the kitchen and a possible snacking opportunity, his piercing whoo-whoos notifying us he was awake and in immediate need of attention. Had it not been for his soft brown eyes, almost mega-phone-like ears and endearing smile, it would have been annoy-ing. Somehow, I think the little stinker knew this about himself and used it to its full advantage. Like I said, he's a stinker. But I love him. And, considering my not-so-much of a relationship with a certain homicide detective by the name of Ramirez, Nicoh was *the* man in my life. Granted, some people might consider the non-human members of their households—canines, felines, bovines, etc.—to be mere pets, Nicoh was anything but. He was my companion, my confidante and sometimes, even my hero. As a bonus, he never judged me when I ate too many fries, left the house wearing the clothes I'd slept in or failed to brush my teeth. I couldn't very well complain, could I? He was mostly—if I over-looked the late night cover-stealing and occasional doggie-breath—the perfect pal.

And while Leah is pretty darn good, Nicoh is a natural born jerk-o-meter. If Nicoh doesn't like a guy, they tend to scurry away, man-parts covered. Yes, scurry. Perhaps the honker on an Alaskan Malamute should be registered as a lethal weapon. Go on—look it up if you don't believe me. I'll wait.

That being said, Nicoh and his nozzle were presently on the prowl for one thing and one thing alone. Breakfast. It was still early, so Leah and I hadn't eaten yet. Nicoh wasn't convinced and placed his massive head on the counter to investigate. After rooting around in Leah's notes for a few seconds, he sniffed in disgust and proceeded to look for errant crumbs on the kitchen floor.

"Uh, those were my papers that your dog just boogered on," Leah groused, her brow furrowed.

"He did not booger on anything," I huffed in response, though a smirk played at the corner of my mouth.

"You'd think with all that training he's had, he'd have better manners," she retorted, her own smile forming as she swatted Nicoh's curly tail. Nicoh rewarded her by swooping in and licking her from the crown of her tousled head to the bottom of her perky face.

"Ack!" she cried in mock horror, hopping off the counter and running down the hall to her room.

I laughed at her hasty retreat and smiled at Nicoh, who swished his tailed wildly from side to side in delight before whoo-whooing again, a reminder that he had still not received his requisite nourishment. After all, who was I to make the big beast wait?

An hour later, Nicoh had been properly fed, I had showered and collected the items needed for my trip to Charlie's. Before leaving, I paused to knock on Leah's door, but upon noting the absence of Duran Duran or The Beastie Boys blaring from beneath the threshold, assumed she had decided to sleep in her bed for a change and left her alone. We hopped in my old Mini Cooper and headed to the Tempe Town Lake condominium where Charlie lived and was holding his party.

It was early and traffic was still light, a refreshing change from the usual bumper-to-bumper of rush hour, so we made good time. With Arch no longer in the picture, I figured he'd be short-handed and appreciate my early arrival. As expected, Stuart

Klein, the jovial doorman waved us through. Nicoh and I were frequent visitors, though I suspected Nicoh was his favorite.

Upon exiting the elevator that deposited us into Charlie's penthouse, I stopped short. Arch was back at his post, a small desk Charlie had installed in the entryway just outside the elevator. His gaze was steely as we stepped into his territory, lips curled in distaste. Despite his cool appraisal, I found myself stifling a chuckle. As usual, his facial expressions managed to look as though someone had spiked his latte with vinegar.

He was, however, always fastidiously dressed and today was no exception, though his current ensemble was more toned-down than usual and consisted of a gray silk shirt, matching tie and black slacks. Even his perfectly-gelled hairstyle appeared to have less product applied. Maybe I should have been concerned about his mental state but upon further reflection, the absence of color led me to believe he was merely attempting to work his way back into Charlie's good graces. At least his attire complimented the surroundings, meaning a global crisis had been temporarily averted.

Suddenly self-conscious, I looked down at my own clothing—boot-cut jeans, purple Chuck Taylor high-tops and a black Eddie Bauer Henley covered by a worn leather jacket—and wondered if Charlie would oust me for my inability to blend in with his environment. I chewed my lip as I noticed even Nicoh had me beat on that one, with his natural white, black and silver coat. Considering I was sporting my usual style, or lack thereof, perhaps Charlie had viewed Nicoh as my best accessory all along? I shrugged. There was nothing I could do about it now. Instead, I bit the bullet and attempted to make nice with Charlie's assistant.

"Hey Arch, it's great to see you."

Arch sniffed after taking in my appearance again and glanced disdainfully in Nicoh's direction before responding, "AJ, of all days you'd make Charlie wait on you, today is not that day." He pointed toward the atrium, then turned on his heel and marched off in the direction of the kitchen. Nice to know Arch hadn't changed much during his sabbatical.

Officially dismissed, I pulled Nicoh's mat from my bag and placed it in the area Charlie had designated "for the animal." Nicoh huffed as he grumpily climbed on and situated himself in the center. Once I was sure he was sufficiently comfortable, I scratched him behind the ears before making my way through the spacious penthouse—a study of glass and steel—with its luxurious open floor plan and modern industrial style. Charlie was strict with his color scheme, using only black and gray with an occasional white accent. The atrium was no different.

Charlie stood in the center of the seamless glass encapsulation —like a priceless treasure on display—though his current expression ruined that vision. A scowl formed as he perused the list on the iPad he clutched. I paused at the entrance, taking him in. He was tall and muscular yet lean, and impeccably dressed in a handsomely-tailored charcoal Armani suit and crisp white dress shirt that remained open at the neck. I was surprised by this last detail —Charlie was rarely without a tie—it was as casual as I had seen him since high school. His Berluti's tapped impatiently as he read. He was model attractive, a cross between Matt Bomer and Ian Somerhalder—though there had been speculation in the tabloids that the two actors had actually been separated at birth—with dark hair, striking gray-blue eyes, a strong angular jaw and cheekbones most women would die for. He was a sight, indeed.

Unfortunately, once he opened his mouth, the illusion was destroyed. Even with all his pretty-boy features, Charlie's personality and demeanor made him a less-than-likable human being. I wished I could say it was due to his privileged upbringing, but I had known his parents since we were children and they were everything he was not—kind, respectful, honest and above all else —generous.

Even Charlie's grandfather, a self-made software magnate and source of the family's substantial wealth and stature, had been a humble and gracious individual. Long after his passing, the senior Wilson had continued to leave his mark on our community through various charitable foundations. None of that had rubbed off on Charlie. Though he was smart and savvy, attending Harvard Business School and graduating with honors, he used all his privileges for his own arrogant, selfish gain.

A successful entrepreneur, he used his vast wealth to ruth-lessly "collect" things and often took what others had acquired. When he was unable to do so to his liking, he simply one-upped them by obtaining something he felt was better than they had to offer. In the rare situations where he was unable to get what he wanted, he would throw legendary temper tantrums. And then, he'd get even.

Today, Charlie was in a wicked mood and just short of one of his tantrums. I noted his expression had grown a few shades blacker upon my arrival. On careful approach, I realized he had been reviewing the guest list, which I'd helped compile.

"What. Is. This?" he shouted, shaking the iPad at me.

For a moment, I was convinced his eyes would pop right out of his head. I chastised myself for thinking that might have been a blessing, if not so gruesome, as I gently removed the tablet from his clutches and glanced at the offending screen. It was *a* guest list, it just wasn't *the* guest list he and I had so painstakingly developed over the course of an entire weekend.

At the time, I remembered thinking he wouldn't be able to handle the intrusion of so many people in his home, but we managed to create a list of sixty-five close friends and business associates he claimed he felt comfortable with—meaning people who could actually stand to be in Charlie's presence for several hours and vice-versa. Before I had a chance to respond, he continued to rant, stabbing names on the list with his finger.

"*That* woman uses a self-tanner. I don't want that deposited all over my furniture." He wiped his brow feverishly from some imaginary perspiration before stabbing at another name. "*He* has the audacity to wear knock-off Gucci's, with tassels. Seriously, AJ, even in this economy, I just can't have it. And this guy—well, you dated him, so you are well aware—is a l-o-s-e-r." After squinting at the name beneath his manicured nail, I couldn't disagree, I had dated the loser back when we were in high school but again, Charlie didn't pause long enough for me to respond.

"Please explain, AJ, after all I have done for you, why have you chosen now to do this to me? Did you think I wouldn't notice this was not the guest list we discussed? That I would tolerate such…such disloyalty?" Though he was breathless, he was mid-boil, so there was no stopping him. "I just cannot believe you—of all people—would go behind my back and send out unapproved invites…to these…people. Are you…are you…trying to ruin me?" Finally, he paused for a moment, but not before delivering the final blow. "I fired Arch for lesser offenses," he spat, tossing the iPod to the ground and stomping his foot.

It took everything in me not to snicker at his outburst. He was as red as a grape tomato and as ridiculous-looking as a petulant child used to getting his way. Instead, I patiently waited for the blustering to subside before attempting to respond. After fifteen years, I had plenty of practice dealing with Charlie's outbursts and learned early on that laughing out loud—no matter how warranted it might be—was a bad idea. So I waited. And waited. And once Charlie appeared sufficiently calm—it typically took between three and five and half minutes, depending upon the circumstances—I finally spoke.

"Good morning, Charlie. Like the suit. While I have not had a chance to fully examine the list you are referencing, from the brief glimpse I did get, *that* is not the list you and I compiled and agreed upon, nor is it the one I sent the invitations from. If you would, quickly look at the dates. You will notice that—according to the date and time stamp on the document—the individuals you referenced were added days *after* you and I last met. Furthermore, I have not seen you or the list since that date." I ended on that note, thinking it seemed as though Arch might be getting a bit of revenge on Charlie for terminating his employment and then hiring him back in time to assist with the party.

I decided to let Charlie draw his own conclusions, which he did, considering the rate at which his face transformed into a menacing grimace. Before stalking off to find Arch, he barked out a few directions about the setup. I blew out a long breath, thinking I was off the hook, when he surprised me by spinning on his heel and looking me over from top to bottom. His mouth took a severe downward turn as he reached my worn purple Chucks.

"Make sure you and Leah dress appropriately this evening. It's called a White Party for a reason. I expect you to be dressed as though you were one of the guests." His eyes narrowed, warning me not to test him. Before I had the chance to weigh my options, he was gone.

* * *

Charlie had reluctantly decided to allow guests to have access to the entire penthouse during the party, though the atrium would serve as the focal point for the gathering. Considering my colorful comments about serving the other white meat—in an effort to stick with the whole white theme, of course—had been met with a look of repugnance only Charlie could muster, I wasn't surprised when he relegated me to overseeing the party's decor in lieu of assisting with the catering selections. Therefore, my task this morning was to make sure white touches were tastefully integrated into the existing surroundings as we'd previously discussed.

I was reminded of the party planning meeting, when Charlie had felt it necessary to inform me that "tasteful" did not include papier-mâché streamers, posterboard signs or balloons. Since that also ruled out clowns and face-painting, I had jokingly asked if ice sculptures would be acceptable, to which Charlie had tersely replied that was "so five years ago." Not to mention, completely unrealistic given the desert heat, though at the time, I doubted it had crossed Charlie's mind. It was about keeping up with the Jones', after all, or in this case, the Charlies.

In the end, it turned out that Charlie's main priority was to ensure the room photographed well. Having designed several of my own backdrops, using lighting, a few faux structures and gauzy materials, I was able to fabricate an environment that warmed the steel and glass by incorporating a light, airy feel, giving it an open and inviting ambiance, without making it look like a boudoir.

Several hours later, I realized I had managed to avoid a check-up visit from either Charlie or Arch. Surely Charlie didn't actually trust me, did he? Since my assigned tasks had been completed, I wasn't about to sit around pontificating, so I gathered my belongings and proceeded toward kitchen, where I could hear Arch yelling at the catering staff. I glanced around the corner, where a dozen workers scurried back and forth like crazed mice at Arch's direction, and noted that Charlie was nowhere to be found.

Sensing a break in Arch's diatribe, I quickly announced my presence before he resumed. His head swiveled ever so slightly upon hearing my voice, though he refused to make eye contact. Ignoring the slight, I gave him a quick update and indicated I would return in a few hours—prior to the start of the party and the arrival of the first round of guests—to photograph the penthouse. I also confirmed Leah would be in attendance to work the crowd and obtain choice tidbits to feed to the society rags, as Charlie had requested. Arch begrudgingly nodded, but did not offer Charlie's whereabouts.

Noting the time, I quickly collected Nicoh and drove home, hoping Leah had gotten her requisite hours of sleep. Anything less would result in a troublesome night and would most certainly get us both booted out of Charlie's party.

One could only hope.

CHAPTER TWO

Less than two hours later, Leah and I were dressed and back at Charlie's building. Before leaving, Nicoh had gotten his fill of scratches and snacks but was still miffed about being left behind. He demonstrated his irritation by positioning himself just within our line-of-sight as we exited, his backside facing us while he grumbled at some inanimate object in the opposite direction. Did I mention Alaskan Malamutes could also be moody and stubborn?

Not that I blamed him. If we could have opted-out of Charlie's party, we would have. We were both extremely uncomfortable in our appropriate—and very white—party attire, though Leah managed to look classy in her short, fitted cocktail dress and heels. Tiny rhinestone barrettes kept her cropped locks in place and framed her face, giving her an angelic halo effect.

I sighed as I tugged at my own ensemble, selected solely for the ease it allowed when lugging camera equipment around—tailored slacks with a matching suit jacket over a silk camisole, paired with short and strappy but still sensible sandals. I pulled my long dark hair into a high ponytail, leaving my bangs to hang freely. The only accent I afforded myself was on the lapel of my jacket, a circular diamond pin that had been my mother's.

"Stop fussing," Leah chastised as she drove, "you look fine." I fought the childish urge to stick my tongue out and instead pursed my lips in defiance, making her chuckle. "Someone's been spending too much time with Nicoh." This time we both laughed.

The rest of the trip was quiet. We had been friends long enough we no longer felt the need to fill the void with mundane chatter, though we were also aware the other had things to ponder.

Charlie was waiting for us as we entered the penthouse. We were ahead of schedule, but he operated on a different time zone than the rest of the modern world—the Charlie zone—where you were either always too early or too late, depending upon the circumstances. And Charlie's mood.

Before he spoke, he gave us both the once-over. While waiting for his approval, I returned the favor and checked out his duds. It was amazing me how a guy could pull off a completely white outfit, but Charlie managed to do so amazingly. His hair was carefully slicked back, adding to the effect, and suddenly I wondered if I was there to photograph the penthouse, or its owner?

Upon closer inspection, the only visible imperfections were the tiny black bags under his eyes. Thinking back to that morning, I hadn't recalled seeing them, though I'd been distracted by the incident with the invite list. Interesting, I thought to myself. It wasn't like Charlie to show physical signs of stress or fatigue. Oh sure, he demanded perfection—take this White Party, for example —but in the end, it was more to satisfy himself than to ensure the pleasure of others. No, obtaining the adoration of others was just the icing on the top of the Charlie cake. So what could be festering in that pretty little mind of his?

He might have been preoccupied, but he was also full of surprises. "You both look...satisfactory." Leah and I stole a glance at one another. Was that a compliment? From Charlie? Now I was convinced something was off, especially when he added, "You did a nice job with the atrium, AJ. It is quite lovely."

Before either of us could respond, Charlie strode toward kitchen, calling over his shoulder as he went, "We've got limited time before the guests start arriving. AJ, I suggest you start doing whatever it is you do. And you"—he shot a glance at Leah —"help her until you are needed elsewhere."

Now *that* was the Charlie I knew and loathed.

I had photographed Charlie's penthouse on several occasions —for magazine spreads, publicity ops and things of that nature— so I made quick work of setting up my equipment, as I was familiar with the type of images he required. Leah assisted me as needed, but otherwise sat quietly off to the side and watched—a little too quietly for Leah.

"Want to talk about it?" I asked, referring to the assignment that was most likely consuming her thoughts. "You've been awfully quiet since you handed your research off to Abe and Elijah."

She tilted her head and nodded, indicating she was still thinking. "I know they hired me to do research—that I'm not investigating—but I think the gal disappeared for a reason and either doesn't want to be found, or—" her voice drifted off, her eyes sad.

"Or?" I gently prompted.

"Or can't be found." She sighed, brushing invisible bangs out of her eyes, before clasping her hands together tightly.

"You think she might be dead, then?"

"Yeah," her head bounced in agreement, "nothing in the research corroborates it, but…"

"But your gut says otherwise." Leah's hunches were often on the mark. Sadly, in this case, it would mean the parent's hope of finding their daughter alive, that she might one day come home, would be shattered.

I did my best to console my friend. "Either way, however this turns out, you have to know that Abe and Elijah will find her. They won't stop looking until they can provide the family some closure. You know that, right?" I knew my words offered little comfort, but I still wanted her to know she'd done all she could and Abe and Elijah would do the same.

Leah looked at me and nodded, her eyes brimming with tears. Finally, a small smile emerged. I hugged her gently—trying to avoid mussing her pretty dress—though she squeezed my hand in return, while wiping away an errant drop of moisture that had made its escape.

Leah started to speak just as Arch made his first appearance of the night, interrupting our moment and thankfully, our gloomy moods. I barely contained a giggle as I snuck a glance at Leah, realizing a moment too late I should have avoided doing so, because her perplexed expression made the situation even more hilarious as she repeatedly looked him over from head to toe. Arch was a condensed version of his boss, down to the last stitch. Even the gelled hair and spray tan had been cloned. But where Charlie had looked like...Charlie, Arch looked...well, let's just say it wasn't a good look.

Arch's eyes slivered as he took in our reception, aware we were working hard not to erupt with laughter.

He spoke, his tone clipped, "Charlie wants you"—looking in Leah's direction without making eye contact—"in the entry way. Now. You"—he swiveled his bobble head toward me—"need to wrap it up. The guests are arriving." On that note, he marched, very much like Charlie, right out of the atrium.

"Wow," was all Leah could muster before both of us broke out into shudders of raucous laughter. "Can you say twin-sy?" She started to laugh again but suddenly, her eyes grew wide and both hands flew to her mouth. "Oh...oh my...I'm so sorry AJ...I didn't mean..." I cut her off with a wave of my hand.

"It's ok." Reveling in the moment, she'd forgotten that I had once been a twin. "You should find Charlie before he and Arch have matching hissies." I looked at her, my smile genuine. She returned the smile, quickly squeezing my hand before leaving.

I worked in silence, tearing down the equipment before placing it in the spare closet as Charlie had instructed. I could hear several unfamiliar voices and realized Arch hadn't been exaggerating about guests arriving. Since Charlie had Leah off somewhere doing who knows what, I was on my own to smile and make polite small talk.

To his credit, Charlie had been wise to integrate Leah into the crowd. His parties were notorious for socializing, deal-brokering and of course, being seen. As a reporter, she had a knack for getting people to tell her the most interesting tidbits and though it wasn't her style to use the juicier morsels to further her career, it typically made for exciting popcorn nights.

I stood off to the edge of the atrium and took in the swarm of partygoers. Everyone dressed to impress in their finest white attire, which from my vantage point, made for an intriguing, if not outlandish scene. I'll openly admit I'm certainly no fashionista. My preferences tend to run toward the more classic styles as opposed to the latest, trendy ones favored this evening.

Just then, a statuesque chestnut-haired beauty glided toward Charlie, her movements effortless, as though her feet weren't touching the ground. I recognized her as one of his former girl-friends, Morgan Thompson. They surreptitiously air-kissed before engaging into mindless chatter. I was tall, but Morgan made me look puny. Her entrance made every head turn. Women sneered with envy while the men gawked with more lust than admiration. Her exotic beauty and physique were sure to make even the most breathtaking Victoria's Secret models feel self-conscious. And, as if her rocking bod and gorgeous features weren't devastating enough, the girl also had some serious brains to boot.

As a partner in a highly prestigious San Francisco law firm, Morgan was the whole package. How Charlie had managed to let her slip away was beyond me, though I suspected he brought more drama to a relationship than most girls were willing to accommodate, much less a catch like Morgan.

Like I said, she was a smart chick.

I was so engrossed watching the two interact, I belatedly realized another couple was heading my direction: Parker Harris and Natalie Ingram. I blanched inwardly, praying they would move beyond me. I was too late to stop, drop and roll right under one of Charlie's leather sofas, so I braced myself for the incoming assault.

Parker was one of Charlie's closest and oldest friends—as friends went in Charlie's realm—and Natalie was his girlfriend. We had all attended the same high school—Charlie, Parker, Leah and I—Natalie included, though she'd been a year behind the rest of us. Her brother, Greg, had been in our class and was the third spoke in Charlie and Parker's wheel when they all headed off to Harvard, though personally, I had always found him to be far too normal and way too nice to hang out with the other two. I never got their dynamic. And sadly, I never would.

A few years earlier, Greg had taken his own life. His death surprised everyone, including his two best friends. It was rumored he had been distraught over some failed business deals, but nothing substantial came out of it and neither Charlie nor Parker could lend any credence to the claim. In time, for everyone but Greg, life moved on.

An interesting side-effect of Greg's death came when Parker and Natalie starting dating. It was another union I would never understand. While Parker was competitive and often manipulative, Natalie was sweet and caring. Don't get me wrong, she was certainly no pushover and like Morgan, had brains to spare. Natalie, however, avoided the corporate workplace after graduating from the University of California at Berkeley, dedicating herself instead to charity work and causes that helped promote a better way of life for those who were less fortunate.

So no, I didn't understand her attraction to Parker. She was way too classy to put up with someone so self-involved. Perhaps the relationship allowed her a means of hanging on to a remnant of her brother's life? If that was the case, in my opinion, there were certainly far better ways of going about it.

As they approached, her honey-gold hair draped over her shoulders and down her back as though it were a silky shawl. She was the most tastefully dressed of this evening's attendees and could have passed for a modern day Audrey Hepburn in her white variation of the little black cocktail dress.

I bit my lip, tasting blood when I turned my gaze from Natalie to Parker and realized that, like Arch, he was dressed in exactly the same manner as Charlie. Except for his hairstyle, the twinsies had become triplets. While Charlie and Arch had chosen a slick coif for the evening's festivities, Parker retained his usual perfected bedhead look. Rather than proceeding to make hamburger of my lip, I kept my snickering at bay by reflecting on the similarities between the two friends.

Parker was tall, lean, and modestly handsome and like his pal, Charlie, once his mouth opened, all admiration quickly fell away. But if anyone could exceed Charlie's haughty, self-important demeanor, it was Parker.

"Ariel," he chirped.

Even though we had known each other for years, he purposefully slighted me at any given opportunity, erroneously calling me by one name or the other. I could only assume he'd been watching *The Little Mermaid* before the party. Natalie looked embarrassed and quietly corrected him, though they were standing close enough I heard the exchange.

He shushed her before continuing, his words slurring with

drink, "I heard you were attempting to fill Arch's shoes after he was ousted from his stoop."

Natalie gave me an apologetic glance. Parker was in one of his more antagonistic moods and trying to bait me into an argument. Under other circumstances, I would have welcomed it. Tonight, I was technically on duty, so I complimented Natalie on her lovely dress instead.

Leah must have sensed the incoming attack—or had just seen Parker's beeline in my direction—because suddenly she was at my side, giving Parker a whole new focus, which unfortunately was directed right at her chest.

"Natalie! Parker!" she exclaimed with as much enthusiasm as she could muster. "It's so great to see you. Natalie, hon, you look divine. Doesn't she, Parker?" she gritted out in an attempt to divert his attention back to his girlfriend, who reddened as he continued to ogle my friend.

Leah was having none of it. "You look good, too, Parker. In fact, you and Charlie could be twinsies. Did you two call each other to coordinate? And was that before or after he called Arch?" She giggled slyly as she casually pointed to where Arch was talking animatedly to several of Charlie's guests.

Natalie let a giggle of her own slip as she took in Parker's exasperated look. It was obvious neither she nor Parker had known Arch had been reinstated as Charlie's assistant, much less known he'd be present this evening. His being dressed similarly to Charlie was like adding sprinkles to a platter filled with cupcakes.

Parker attempted to redeem himself, his eyes finally detaching themselves from Leah's breasts. "Lulu, you wouldn't know taste if it—"

Natalie interrupted him before he was able to finish that thought, "Parker, we should say hello to the congressman." She smiled as she not-so-gently tugged his arm and used the bulk of her small frame to propel him forward.

Parker obliged but muttered something under his breath that I won't repeat. As they departed, Natalie shot us a quick wink over her right shoulder. I marveled at her diplomacy and her ability to successfully avert a nasty altercation within the first hour of the party. The girl definitely had more grit than I'd initially given her credit for.

"Thanks for the save, who knows what would have come out of my mouth," I admitted ruefully as I turned to Leah.

"I know," she laughed, clearly pleased, "it was almost a shame to stop you. He deserved whatever it was you were going to unleash on him. I just don't get what Natalie sees in him. Dating Parker takes her IQ down a few digits in my book." I nodded but Natalie's actions as of late had me wondering.

I directed my attention back to my friend. "What the heck have you been up to?"

"Charlie's had me working the room like I was a hooker down on Van Buren Street." Ugh, and here I'd thought I'd had a rough night thus far. "He wanted me to make nicey-nice with a few of his new investor buddies, but that didn't include complimentary grabs of my front or backside, so I moved on. Anyway, I just got done talking to our newest congressman, Bob Fenton. Interesting fellow." She nodded toward a short, cherubic-looking kid clinking martini glasses with Parker, while laughing at something that had been said.

"Uh, *he's* a congressman?" I gasped. "What is he, like twelve?"

Leah chuckled. "Something like that. He's actually got some fresh ideas and a lot of positive energy. I'll be interested to see how he does in the months to come."

I nodded absently, not interested in discussing the new

congressman's political ambitions, as something distinctly more intriguing had caught my eye. Leah stopped to follow my gaze.

Natalie continued talking to Congressman Fenton as Parker turned to catch Charlie's attention before he left the room. Hearing Parker call out, Charlie attempted to retreat in the opposite direction. Parker, however, anticipated the move, hastily stepping close enough to latch onto Charlie's arm. The sounds of the party drowned out their brief conversation, but body language left nothing to the imagination. Charlie barely glanced at his friend, anger flaring in his eyes as he snatched his arm away, leaving Parker to scowl. As quickly as Charlie's anger manifested, it was gone the instant he began talking to the next partygoer.

Natalie also witnessed the interaction and as Parker's outstretched hand turned into a fist, ended her conversation with the congressman and moved to grasp it in almost a dance-like motion, forcing his attention away from Charlie and onto her. Parker rolled her into his arms, smiling tightly as he kissed her forehead, though his eyes remained on his friend. Natalie touched his chin, then ushered him out of the atrium. If Charlie sensed their departure, he made no visible acknowledgment. Obviously something was up between the two besties, though I doubted anyone else had seen the altercation.

It was the first and only interesting point for the remainder of the evening. We didn't see Parker or Natalie again, which actually wasn't all that unusual, given the size of the penthouse and the sheer volume of the people milling about. Everyone seemed to be enjoying themselves, though it likely had more to do with the heavy handed bartender mixing drinks than anything else. Fortunately, due to the limited parking surrounding the building, many of the guests had already planned to take taxis both to and from the party, hopefully ensuring everyone made it home safely.

In the meantime, Leah and I sipped club soda as she introduced me to several partygoers, which included Congressman

Fenton, former State Senator Davis Conrad, a few local musicians, an aspiring L.A. fashion consultant and the architect who designed the building. Though I wasn't surprised Leah knew them, it was shocking Charlie had so many famous friends.

Speaking of Charlie, we finally ran into him again in the wee hours of the morning, as the party was winding down and were pleasantly surprised when he announced we were free to leave. I was curious about his sudden graciousness but didn't wait around, being way too familiar with his propensity for changing his mind.

Leah and I spent the ride home quietly thinking about the altercation between Charlie and Parker, though neither of us mentioned it. Something about the evening had been bothering me, but the minute we arrived home and I freed a few of the covers from beneath Nicoh's snoring form, that train went right on down the tracks just as soon as my head hit the pillow.

CHAPTER THREE

Despite exhaustion, the nightmares continued to plague me. Images flickered like an old black and white film reel, each frame more horrific than the last. Had there been even a splash of color, it would have been red. Crimson. The fear was unbearable, though some invisible force stifled my screams. Death presented himself, tall and imposing. Except for his face, masked by the shadows, I could distinguish every detail about him, down to the stitching on his jacket. I reached out in an attempt to wipe away the haze that concealed his features, but his identity was not for to me to know. "Not this time," came the whisper, just as a chill riveted my body, waking me.

I cursed the buzzing in my head as my eyes adjusted to the sun peeking through the blinds. I was still groggy from sleep, so it took me a moment to register the annoyance as an incoming text message on my cell phone, which I had carelessly placed beside my pillow when I had fallen into bed. Thanks to my fitful slumber, it was now buried—under Nicoh. I wrinkled my nose in disgust as a carefully extracted it, noting it was covered with drool.

I had only received one text message during the short time I had been home, from an unavailable source. *ITS TIME ARIANNA* was all it said. *Time for what?* I wondered. Time to get up, brush my teeth and start working? I didn't need a reminder for that. My curiosity about the message dissolved when Leah burst into my room, her hair wild and eyes raccoony, a side-effect of the previous night's makeup.

Before I had a chance to make a snarky comment, she breathlessly cried out "Parker is missing!" before flopping down on the corner of the bed—the only space available—given that Nicoh was still monopolizing the majority of the queen-sized mattress. She looked at me, her eyes wide and nearly as crazy as the tangled spikes sprouting out of her head.

"What do you mean he's 'missing'?"

Before she could answer, Nicoh let out a disgusted snort before jumping off the bed—apparently we weren't respecting his beauty sleep—leaving us in search of a quieter, less crowded resting place.

"Natalie went to check on Parker this morning and when she noticed his car was gone, figured he'd taken a taxi home from the party. After ringing the doorbell several times and receiving no response, she let herself in with her key. There was no indication that he'd slept in his bed or even made it home. She then called Charlie, who discovered that Parker's Audi was still parked several blocks from his building—it had actually been ticketed. After checking around with some of Parker's other friends and having no luck, she decided to contact the Tempe Police Department to report him missing."

"Let me get this straight. Natalie and Parker came to the party —separately?"

Leah nodded. "Natalie was at a charity event before the party, so they agreed to meet at Charlie's. In fact, she arrived before

Parker and ended up waiting for him in the foyer so they could ride the elevator up together."

"And when they left?"

"Parker called Natalie a cab, they said their goodbyes and she left. That was the last time she saw him."

"What about Charlie? Did Parker go back up to the party?"

"No, Charlie never saw Parker again that night. Claims he never saw him after—well, after that altercation we witnessed—though he describes it a bit differently. The doorman also said Parker never went back into the building. Of course, they haven't checked the security cameras or anything like that yet to confirm it."

"Security cameras of the building's entrance?"

"Yes, those too, but Charlie had cameras installed inside the penthouse before the party."

Cameras *inside* the penthouse? That was news to me, though not all that surprising, given Charlie's disposition. I was more surprised he hadn't installed them during the initial construction of the building, considering he owned it. Then again, perhaps Charlie decided to have them installed because of Arch's return, in case Arch decided to retaliate for being fired in the first place. Now *that* sounded more like the Charlie we all knew and endured. Something else occurred to me.

"How exactly did you get all this information, anyway?"

Leah shrugged. "Except for the part about the penthouse cameras, which Charlie accidentally let slip the other day, a friend at the Tempe Police Department clued me in on the rest. He remembered I'd gone to school with Parker and knew I'd been at the same party last night, so he called after Natalie reported him missing."

"What friend is this?"

"Just someone I met back when I was still working the crime beat at the paper. He might have developed a bit of a crush on me

—the feeling wasn't mutual—but he still feeds me info now and then."

"Hmm, must have been more than a crush." I wiggled my eyebrows suggestively but Leah snorted. "How do we know Parker didn't just ditch Natalie so he could hit one of the nearby clubs? He's probably sleeping off a hangover at some random chick's place. No disrespect to Natalie, but Parker *is* Parker."

"At this point, no one knows anything for sure, but in the meantime…" she paused, scrunching her face in preparation for my reaction, "Natalie wants us to form a search party."

"A what? You have got to be kidding me."

Leah shook her head. "Somehow Natalie managed to convince Charlie it was a good idea and something to do while we wait for TPD to do their thing. She probably pulled the Parker-would-do-the-same-if-the-situation-was-reversed card, though given the display last night, I'd be surprised if Charlie would fall for that alone. Anyway, she wants us to start looking around the area for clues or anything that could lead to Parker's whereabouts, at least until the police get more involved."

"Hold up." I raised a hand. "What is this 'we' and 'us' business? Parker's not even our friend. We don't know his habits." Nor did I want to.

"The thing is…" Leah sighed, "Natalie asked for our help. She called me, filled me in on a few details my TPD friend hadn't provided and I ended up feeling kinda bad for her. It's just a few hours and the least we can do to ease her mind."

I nodded, Natalie was a sweet girl. I hated to think what she was going through. I was going to be angry when Parker finally showed up and shattered whatever illusion she had about their relationship.

"And if we end up finding out Parker was on a bender, or out conjugating irregular verbs with some other gal?"

"Then we let the chips fall," Leah replied solemnly.

"Promise?"

"Promise. And one more thing?"

"What?" I asked cautiously.

Leah squirmed, something that was uncharacteristic for her. *Uh oh,* I thought. "Um, Charlie suggested you bring 'the dog' with you—his phrase, not mine." I could only assume Charlie had conveniently mistaken Nicoh, an Alaskan Malamute, with a Bloodhound.

I shook my head—it was going to be a long day.

We joined Charlie, Arch and Natalie outside the building an hour later. Nicoh ignored Charlie and Arch but immediately took to Natalie, sticking his nose into parts unknown in an effort to get acquainted. I swear, sometimes having an Alaskan Malamute can be so embarrassing.

"Nicoh!" I cried, horrified I had failed to get a handle on him before he managed to insinuate himself onto the new girl. Fortunately, Natalie laughed as she bent down to scratch Nicoh's ears, nuzzling his face with her own.

"It's ok. We had Labrador Retrievers growing up—they were mostly Greg's dogs—but they preferred my bed at night, so I'm used to the intrusion."

Relieved by her response, though still appalled by Nicoh's behavior, I chuckled. "Yeah, I know how that goes."

She nodded and laughed, flipping Nicoh's tail. Excited to have a new playmate, Nicoh scrunched down on his front legs—his behind still wagging in the air—before leaping onto all fours and whisking himself into a series of circles in an attempt to catch his tail. Soon, he had Leah, Natalie and me laughing, causing him to whoo-whoo with delight. Charlie, meanwhile, tapped his foot impatiently while Arch looked bored. Not satisfied with getting attention from only half the crowd, Nicoh attempted the feat again, this time a little too close for the guys' comfort, as they quickly shuffled to put some distance between themselves and the frenzied canine.

I stifled a chuckle. "No worries, guys. Nicoh only goes after things he finds interesting." The looks I received told me they were clearly not amused.

For a moment, the distraction almost made us forget the reason we had gathered at this unforgivable hour of the morning. We hadn't even had a chance to get our caffeinated kickstarter yet.

As if reading my mind, Natalie moved to a tray that had been sitting behind us on a retaining wall and carefully lifted out delicious-smelling coffee beverages, handing each of us one. Ah, liquid gold, I thought as I happily drank in the elixir, nodding my approval to Leah. Natalie was definitely a keeper.

Once everyone was satisfactorily charged, Leah turned to Charlie, "So what's the plan, Stan? Where is everybody?"

At his open-mouthed, surprised look, Natalie quickly stepped in, "Um, this is it. We are the search party. I couldn't get a hold of any of Parker's other friends, so we're it."

Charlie pursed his lips while Arch scoffed—this had clearly been Natalie's idea—and while neither of them thought Parker was missing, they didn't want to have to tell Natalie their suspicions about his current location. I shook my head at him to confirm he would keep his mouth shut. When he glared in return, Leah drew a line across her throat in warning and received a nasty look of her own.

Oblivious to the unspoken conversation among the rest of us, Natalie prattled on, "It's probably better if we start small anyway. At least it will be easier to coordinate our efforts, until the police get involved. I was thinking Charlie and Arch could walk the grounds surrounding the building, then the area where his car was parked."

"Where is Parker's car?" Leah asked.

"We had to move it," Natalie replied. "The City of Tempe was about to tow it, so Charlie, Arch and I took care of it before you arrived. There wasn't anything out of the ordinary in it," she added, before continuing with her plan.

"While the guys go in that direction, I thought the three of us... oh, sorry Nicoh," she smiled down at her new friend, his body resting across her feet, "make that four of us, could walk along the portion of the lake that borders the building." She pointed in the direction she had referenced, just 500 feet from where we were currently standing.

Charlie snorted in amusement. "You think Parker...what? Decided to go for a little late night dip in Tempe Town Lake?"

I grimaced at the nastiness in his tone. He was on the brink of putting the kibosh on the whole outing, meaning he was also on the verge of telling Natalie his thoughts on the whereabouts of her missing boyfriend.

Before he had a chance to continue, I quickly stepped in, "Natalie's right. Perhaps Parker wanted to clear his head before going home, so he took a brief walk along the pathway. Your bartender was pouring some pretty stiff drinks, Charlie."

To my relief, everyone nodded in agreement—except Charlie, of course—it seemed plausible.

"She's right," Leah added. "I saw Parker order about a half dozen gin and tonics...and that was early on in the evening."

Natalie sighed, clearly disappointed Parker had been seen imbibing so heavily at the White Party, but I could see my diversion had worked. The focus was now off Charlie's big mouth. "Actually, it was five—five gin and tonics—though all were pretty light on the tonic."

"Whatever," Charlie grumbled, rolling his eyes, "can we get

this show on the road?" Without waiting for an answer, he stalked in the direction of where I assumed Parker's car had been located. Arch shot a glance in our direction, his expression undecipherable, before faithfully scooting off after his boss.

Leah clapped her hands. "Shall we, girls…and pooch?"

The four of us proceeded in the direction of the lake's walking path. It was starting to get warm, so I was glad everyone had chosen the appropriate attire for the outing.

Once we reached the pathway, Natalie piped up, "I think we should split up. You two could maybe take Nicoh and head west on the path, toward Tempe Beach Park and I'll head east toward Scottsdale Road, though I probably won't go quite that far. If we could just find…anything…" her voice trailed off as her eyes filled with tears.

I looked to Leah for assistance. Perhaps it would be better to tell her what everyone was thinking—that Parker was probably sleeping off a bender somewhere? Wouldn't it be more humane than putting her through all this agony?

Before either of us could respond, Natalie wiped her eyes and smiled thinly. "Anyway, does the divide and conquer plan work for the two of you?"

We gave her the thumbs up and she marched east, but not before giving us a quick wave and a confident nod of the head.

As Leah, Nicoh and I started west—not exactly sure what we were looking for—I reflected on Natalie varied temperaments. "She seems younger than she is, don't you think? Fragile at times, stronger at others."

"Yeah," Leah replied, "I think Greg's death affects her more than most people realize. Greg was her big brother. Her rock. Her protector. Professionally, she appears strong, especially when it comes to her philanthropic endeavors, but in her personal life— just look how she's latched onto her brother's best friend," she commented, mirroring my own thoughts. "Who, by the way, is totally not right for her."

I agreed with her and said as much, "Natalie definitely deserves a lot better. Do you think she is trying to hold onto whatever memory is left of her brother?"

Leah nodded. "Seems like a pretty tortuous way of going about it, if you ask me."

We walked for a distance in silence, still not sure what we were doing, but out of concern for Natalie, we proceeded to look for clues indicating Parker had drifted this way. Eww, poor choice of words, though I'll admit, I did find myself peering into the lake, just to be sure. The three of us continued to walk the path, stopping occasionally to let Nicoh sniff. A lot of people brought their dogs along this route, so there were plenty of scents to keep him entertained. I doubt we had gotten more than a mile when my cell phone starting ringing—Natalie.

She was breathless, her usually soft voice coming across the connection in a half-screech, "I think I found something! Can you...can you come back?"

"Stay put," I commanded, though—silly me—I doubted she would go running off, "we're on our way." Again, unnecessary, though hopefully knowing we were coming would prevent her from completely losing it.

By jogging we were able to reach her more quickly than we would have had we walked, but looking at her face once we arrived, it had clearly seemed like an eternity from her perspective. I surveyed the surroundings, noting Natalie had made it farther east than I would have imagined. She stood rigidly, hugging herself with both arms, her eyes wild. In her hot pink running ensemble, she looked like a piece of bubblegum, ready to explode.

She shakily pointed to her finding. It was a white tie, much like the one many of the men, including Arch, Charlie and Parker, had been sporting the prior evening. Now smudged with dirt and grime and hopelessly crinkled, it trailed limply down the embankment.

While Leah and I peered at it, Natalie nervously uttered, "There's more."

She pointed, this time a few feet down from where we were standing. A man's white Berluti shoe sat on the edge of the dirt pathway, threatening to tumble into the crisp lake water. Like the tie, it was filthy and scuffed, though I knew the prior evening, it had been new.

Natalie rooted around in her large designer bag—an odd choice given the occasion—in an attempt to muffle the sniffles she had been fighting. As she finally extracted a tissue, they turned to guttural, heart-wrenching sobs. Leah and I quickly moved in to console her.

"They're his!" she cried, her voice filled with despair as she leaned her tiny frame into us.

I nodded to Leah—it was time to call the police. We, too, could not deny that Parker could have worn the tie and shoe the previous night. It was too much of a coincidence, especially considering neither Charlie nor Arch would have ambled along this pathway under any circumstances, much less after the party. No, unless there had been another partygoer wearing the same items, they likely belonged to Parker.

Leah stepped away to make the call, while Natalie clutched me tightly. Even Nicoh could sense the gravity of the situation and whoo-whoo'd quietly as I firmly held his lead to prevent him from sniffing the evidence.

A few moments later Leah returned to tell us the police would be sending a team out to our location shortly. "They'd like us to stay put and refrain from touching anything. You didn't, did you, Natalie?" The girl's eye widened as she shook her head from side to side. "While we wait for TPD to arrive then, I should probably call Charlie."

When they joined us a short while later, Charlie and Arch had found nothing of merit in their search for Parker, though given the enormous cones each was carrying, it was obvious they had managed to locate a new gelato shop. At our disgusted expressions, Charlie merely shrugged and indicated that technically, the shop had been in the vicinity of where Parker's car had been parked.

Leah and I shook our heads while Natalie—in a strange twist —threw herself into Charlie's arms. Apparently, his side adventure didn't bother her. The unexpected embrace, however, caught Charlie off-guard, forcing him to quickly adjust his balance. Seeing Charlie's attempt to maneuver triple scoops would have been comical had the circumstances not been so serious. Instead, he quickly shoved the cone at Arch while throwing him a frosty warning. I suspected Arch already knew better than to drop Charlie's treat, even though he had his own triple threat to contend with. I shook my head, wondering if these two possessed the capacity to understand the gravity of the situation. If it meant having to put their own needs aside for the sake of Parker's, then I highly doubted it.

Charlie managed to look interested as Natalie animatedly retraced her steps and pointed at her findings. Once finished, she crumpled against him and started to sniffle into his shirt. Charlie hastily moved her away, making it appear as though he wanted to look at her as he spoke. Knowing better, I glanced at Leah, who mouthed "silk."

To my surprise, he spoke to her into the softest, gentlest voice I had ever heard him use, "You will have to tell all of this to the police when they arrive."

If he had thought this would keep the girl from ruining his shirt, his plan backfired as she gripped him even more closely and openly sobbed. This time, Charlie looked as though he too, wanted to cry.

Fortunately, two black and white patrol units rolled up, saving us from having to witness that particular display. A pair of officers exited each cruiser—one male team and one male and female —the latter approached us as the prior surveyed the scene.

While Natalie relayed her story to the female officer, her male counterpart asked Leah and me to do the same. I rolled my eyes when Leah's flirtatious streak reared its ugly head as she told the officer his outfit looked cute. Ladies—for future reference— never, ever refer to a man's clothing as an "outfit" or "cute." I'm warning you—just don't do it.

Before the officer could arrest her, I stepped in with my own responses, which seemed to mollify the situation as he loosened his stance, even bending down to give Nicoh a healthy round of scratches. He then surprised me by asking if Nicoh had ever had any police dog training. I told him no, not to my knowledge, though some of Nicoh's previous background was unknown. I went on to tell him Nicoh certainly didn't retain any of the training I had taken him to, which likely had more to do with owner error than Nicoh's ability. The officer laughed, noting that he had previously had a canine partner.

Of course, Leah couldn't resist the chance to pipe up. "I'll bet your partner was the better driver."

Having finally gotten the attention off her flirtations, I winced, convinced there were handcuffs in both of our futures if she didn't let up soon. Thankfully, the officer chuckled this time.

"Is this enough evidence to consider Parker a missing person? His girlfriend, Natalie"—I gestured in the direction where Natalie was still talking to the female officer—"can verify he was wearing a similar tie and pair of shoes last night, while Charlie and Arch can confirm the two items aren't theirs, since they were all wearing the same attire last night." The officer was vague in his response but took the information down before excusing himself.

A short time later, a crime scene unit arrived and technicians began collecting evidence from the area cordoned off by the two male officers. It was a little too reminiscent of the scene in my alley a few months earlier, when I had discovered a body in my dumpster, who as it later turned out, belonged to my sister. At least there wasn't a body today, I shuddered. Though I was no fan of Parker's, I held out hope he would make an appearance soon.

The hours that followed were a blur. The effects of the coffee had long worn off and now adrenaline kept me in an upright position. Even Nicoh napped at my side, a few snores escaping every so often. Only he could sleep so soundly in the middle of such commotion, I thought, a bit jealously. Finally, one of the officers told us we were free to go, indicating we would be contacted if there were additional questions. I wondered if perhaps they too thought Parker was sleeping off a hangover somewhere.

Leah and I said goodbye to Charlie and Arch and confirmed they would keep an eye on Natalie as she traipsed after the investigators, begging for information. Though the female officer had done a good job of appeasing the girl, it was all she could do to keep Natalie from insinuating herself into their investigation.

"Maybe now is a good time to contact Ramirez?" Leah suggested.

Overhearing her, the female officer suddenly turned. "Ramirez? As in Phoenix Homicide Detective Jonah Ramirez?"

"Yeah, he's a friend of ours. You know him?" Leah replied.

I swore the officer nearly licked her lips. "Oh yeah, I know him," her voice was lustful as she returned to her duties, leaving us to stare after her. My eyes shot daggers at her back until Nicoh whimpered quietly, forcing Leah to tug my sleeve. I realized I had been gripping the scruff of his neck a little too fiercely.

"Sorry," I mumbled to both of them, glancing over my

shoulder one last time in the officer's direction. "For a minute, I thought I was going to have to take her." As I turned to join my friend, I was pretty sure I heard a muffled giggle escape from behind me.

I grimaced and wished the day could just be over already.

CHAPTER FOUR

Of course, my genie failed me and my wish never came true. Despite the pleasant weather we had during our impromptu search, the clouds rapidly rolled in from the west and threatened the official search party's efforts, which was well under way by the time we departed. We took turns calling the police department for updates, but nothing more had been found. After several hours of combing the area surrounding the lake for clues, divers had been sent into the lake. Everyone was still holding out hope Parker would return on his own but as time passed, it became less and less likely.

Against our pleas, Natalie insisted upon camping out at his house to wait, refusing offers to keep her company. In many ways, she was more resilient than we had initially given her credit for, now that the shock of Parker's disappearance had become more of a reality. Still, Leah and I felt a certain amount of protectiveness toward her, knowing that somewhere beneath her current tough girl facade, the fragile one still remained.

I wasn't familiar with the requirements for searching a man-made body of water such as Tempe Town Lake with inflatable dams at either end, but as it turned out, it wasn't much easier than doing so in a natural body of water. Dirt, sediment and other various odds and ends still shifted and moved with the current, often serving as barriers to the diver's efforts. Of course, the constant threat of the impending monsoon didn't help the weather. We'd had an unusually wet spring as well, which was good for ensuring the summer months would have enough moisture to withstand a tempestuous fire season, but bad for locating clues within a muck-filled basin.

The days were gray and at any given moment, light quickly dissolved into darkness, ending the day's search efforts. In the meantime, Leah and I kept ourselves occupied with work. She juggled a few freelance article requests with her research for Abe and Elijah while I shuttled between photo shoots.

Fortunately, my contracts were for inside work, which wasn't always the case. I also got to test some tasty snacks from the new tapas restaurant on 5th Avenue in Old Town Scottsdale whose owner had hired me to shoot their interior and several menu items for use on their website and in local magazines.

My next photo shoot was at a West Phoenix resort and casino that had recently renovated and needed new marketing materials for an upcoming advertising campaign, followed by a third for a gallery association in Central Phoenix. Each project was interesting in its own right and would certainly be useful for obtaining future work, but my mind wandered as I obsessed about Parker.

Three days later, the storm finally broke free. The sky turned blacker than night and wind taunted the trees, whipping them back and forth like matchsticks. Lightning filled the sky, the tips lashing out and crackling before touching down in fiery anger. Thunder followed its belligerent friend, booming and bellowing in lightning's wake. Then came the rain. The first drops teased the ground as if testing its surface. Growing impatient, it spilled in rivulets, panes of water drenching anything within reach. The wind provided an additional burst of energy and the elements mingled in their theatrical dance. Roads became impassable due to fallen trees and surface streets transitioned from running streams to treacherous, overflowing roadways. The monsoon was upon us. Despite its baffling interplay, it also provided something more—movement. Movement of objects that had been lodged, stagnant and stymied without the benefit of the natural ebb and flow, now brought forth from their silent slumber. Murky water cleared the path as branches and debris broke free from their watery graves.

Parker Harris became one of these objects. His body, now a contorted, bloated mass, had been tangled in the disarray, remaining at the lake's mercy until the storm released him from his temporary resting place. When the storm passed and the divers were able to resume their search, they found him lodged against an embankment, just east of where we had ended our own search.

Using her press credentials and TPD source, Leah had managed to work her way onto the scene at the lake and was gathering details here and there while whispering them to me via cell phone. We both knew the body retrieved from the lake was Parker's, even though the Maricopa County Medical Examiner's Office would officially confirm his identity after conducting their own investigation and medical examination. For us, the facts surrounding his disappearance made the truth inevitable.

None of Charlie's other party guests had gone missing and according to the scuttlebutt at scene, the body was still partially-clothed in a white dress shirt, white suit pants and one very white, very expensive-looking dress shoe. It had yet to be identified as a mate to the Berluti Natalie had found, but it was quite a coincidence.

Leah also gathered other details that weren't so expected. Rumblings about trauma and unusual wound patterns were tossed about, but to her frustration—as verified by the variety of new curse words she uttered in my ear—nothing would be confirmed until the Medical Examiner's inquest.

Our conversation was interrupted by an incoming text message, likely from Charlie, so I placed her on hold while I read it. *IM COMING* was all it said. Again, the sender was unavailable. With the drama surrounding Parker's disappearance, I had completely forgotten about the previous text. Was it from the same person? I shrugged, though it was annoying, the message was probably harmless. I returned to my conversation with Leah and found her cussing me out.

"What the heck, Leah?"

"Err…oh good, you're back! I'm totally freaking out here and was about to pull every hair out of my head!"

"What hair?" I quipped.

"I'm being serious here, Ajax!" That got my attention. "When they were hauling the body out of the lake, one of the technicians slipped and the stretcher slid sideways," she paused to catch her breath, "causing the tarp to shift, exposing—"

"Ewww, I don't want to hear this!"

Leah quickly interjected, "No, it only slipped a little, off one foot. There was no shoe or sock, and that's when I saw it!"

"What? What did you see?"

I heard her expel a deep breath. "Despite being all…all bloaty, there was a scar," she paused a moment to let out another extended breath. "It started at the left side of the ankle and ran in a jagged pattern across the foot, ending at the big toe."

I gasped. I had seen a marking just as Leah described, years earlier. First, in its fresh, bloodied wound state and again, months later when it had healed into an ugly, fleshy scar. In fact, I had been present when the jerk it belonged to had gotten handsy with a particularly spunky little blonde. After his ungentlemanly attempts at pawing her lady parts, she had swiftly—and quite impressively—dispatched a red stiletto into his sandaled foot. The perpetrator had howled like a wounded moose and after removing his offensive mitts, attempted to free his foot from the spiky heel still embedded in the soft tissue. The sudden movement ripped and tore the skin in a jagged motion, all the way down to the big piggy toe. The would-be perpetrator had limped away, humiliated, after receiving the penance he deserved for his unwelcomed, unsavory actions.

Over the years, the recollections of the incident became increasingly grandiose, as tales tend to do. Every detail, every nuance was more animated from one telling to the next, until its notoriety became so far-reaching people began telling me about the perky little blonde who had bruised more than the ego of the well-known playboy. She had scarred him—permanently.

Looking back, I had enjoyed that particular memory. Now, I would have done anything to erase the image of the day Leah had left her mark on Parker Harris.

CHAPTER FIVE

We didn't need an autopsy to confirm the body was Parker's. We did, however, need answers about how he had died and more importantly, ended up in the lake. If not for Parker, then for the people he'd left behind. Like Natalie.

She had several of her own connections and was likely aware a body had been found. Not wanting her to be alone in Parker's house, Leah picked me up after leaving the scene so we could check on her. On our way, we debated about divulging our suspicions. We didn't have definitive DNA proof but the scar was, in our minds, almost proof enough. Besides, it would be weeks before the Medical Examiner's report was released and forcing her to wait any longer might be too much, considering her fluctuating emotional state.

As we approached the towering Spanish-style villa where Parker had lived, Natalie threw the door open, as though expecting our arrival, and hugged us both fiercely. When she finally pulled away, her eyes were red from extensive crying and she seemed thinner than I remembered her being. Clearly, Parker's disappearance was taking its toll.

After guiding us through the maze of a house, she selected a room with the most comfortable couches and once settled, we gently told her what Leah had witnessed, bracing for an eruption of emotion. To our surprise, several moments of silence later, the waterworks still hadn't broken through. I spared a glance at Leah, but my friend's expression told me she had no more idea than I did. Finally, Natalie slowly lifted her head, her eyes free of tears, and simply nodded.

"Thank you for caring enough to tell me the truth. Based upon your description, I think it's him, too. At least now I know." She sighed, then rose from her seated position and gestured toward the door. "I don't mean to seem rude, or unappreciative, but I'd like to be alone now. I need to remember Greg as he was. When I last saw him." On that note, she shuffled out of the room and down the hall, leaving us both wide-eyed and somewhat stupefied.

"She just said—" Before Leah could continue, I quickly put my finger to my lips and motioned to the door. She nodded, taking my cue as we quietly let ourselves out.

Safely out of earshot, she excitedly whispered, "Natalie called Parker by her brother's name!"

I nodded. "She must be in shock. Did you notice how she didn't show any emotion when we told her about the scar?"

"I know it, and after all that huggy-feely crap with Charlie the other day, too! What the heck was that all about? And now, she's got nothing?"

"I'm more concerned about leaving her alone in that house than I am about her emotions being all over the map."

"I don't feel great about leaving her either, but she asked us to let her have some time to herself. Perhaps we should do as she asks, then check on her later?" Leah suggested.

I agreed and as we made our way to her car, I glanced back at Parker's house, my thoughts of the girl suffering inside. Something told me Natalie was battling more than the shock of losing Parker. His death had likely resurrected the demons of her past.

Something I was all too familiar with. It made me wonder how any of us managed to survive, how we got through each day and got up to tackle the next. As we pulled away, I looked at Leah and thought of Nicoh, and had my answer. My thoughts returned to Natalie—who or what would be hers?

Only time would tell. I hoped she could hold out for that long, before the demons destroyed her forever.

On our way home, Leah surprised me by asking if I had planned on calling Ramirez. Ah, Jonah Ramirez—tall, dark and a mystery in and of himself. The homicide detective and I had gotten acquainted when my sister had been murdered several months earlier, but once the case had been closed—meaning the perps had been handed off to the FBI—the detective and I had developed a friendship of sorts. The kind where we'd had several lunches and dinners together, gone on a few day trips to Sedona, Oak Creek Canyon and Tucson with Nicoh and even attended a few local art and music festivals. But aside from a few moon-hanging kisses, I wasn't exactly sure where we stood.

I got the distinct impression he liked me. I definitely liked him and though I hadn't quite managed to make a fool out of myself yet, had planted a few of my own jaw-dropping smooches on him. Anyway, I was pretty sure he knew I liked him, too.

Still, there were times he seemed to be filled with sadness and even a bit of regret, which led me to believe perhaps he wasn't quite over a former lady love, though she hadn't been the topic of conversation to date. As confusing as that made things, I enjoyed his company and let him take the lead, going at a pace he felt comfortable. I wasn't going anywhere and well, he was certainly worth the wait, however long that might be.

Leah snapped me out of my reverie, "So, you are going to call him to see what he can find out, right?"

"I suppose." I sighed. Though Ramirez had been helpful to us in the past, I didn't want to appear desperate for attention, either.

"Stop stressing. Ramirez totally likes you. He just needs to work through some issues. He'll come around, just continue to give him time, like you've been doing. You'll see." She looked fairly satisfied with herself, her pep-talk complete.

I wondered what had brought that on. "What? What is it you know?" I demanded, surprising her with my sharp tone.

She tried acting nonchalant, realizing she had said too much. "My TPD source might have provided me with a few juicy nuggets about our hottie detective." She shrugged, her tone non-committal.

"Spill," I gritted out, agitated she had been holding out on me.

"Whoa, Cujo." She groaned after taking in my expression.

"Still waiting…" I replied tersely.

"All right, all right." She put a hand up in surrender before continuing, "I wasn't going to say anything until I had a chance to do a bit more snooping, but now that you've asked me so nicely, I guess I can 'spill.' All I ask in return is that you abstain from shooting the messenger." It was my turn to groan, she was clearly enjoying this. What I had done to deserve such torture, I wasn't quite sure.

"You remember Serena Fenton, the gal we met the other night at Charlie's party?" she finally asked, chewing absently on a nail.

"Tall, leggy thing, weighs in at about 120? Perfect skin with even more perfect flowing locks? Basically, a dead ringer for Charlize Theron?"

She nodded and focused more intently on the poor nail before answering, "You forgot to mention the part about her being married to Congressman Fenton."

"Well," I mock-scoffed, "I thought that part was a given.

Yeah, clearly I remember meeting Serena Fenton. What about her?"

"She's Ramirez's ex," she replied dryly.

"She's whaaat?" Given the look I received, I realized I might have yelled a little too loudly. "He was married to her?"

"Not married, though I have it on good authority they were a couple for a number of years." I put my head in my hands. "If it makes you feel any better, she left Ramirez for Congressman Bob."

"Oh yeah, loads," I replied sarcastically.

"Of course, he wasn't a congressman back then, but there had been rumblings of political aspirations." She prattled on about his rise in the ranks, but I had stopped listening. Ramirez might no longer be on Serena's radar, she was most definitely still messing with his. "Anyway, rumor has it our young congressman's wife aspired to bigger and better stature, mansions, cars…things she would never get out of a relationship—"

"With a cop," I finished. And no, it didn't make me feel any better. "That's kinda shallow and a pretty awful thing to do to someone like Ramirez."

Leah nodded. "I hope it helps to explain a few things. It isn't about you, AJ," she paused. "Well actually, it is. My source said you were the first gal our boy has taken a shine to since Serena. His words, not mine."

"Wait a minute—how does your TPD source know so much about Ramirez's love life, anyway?"

"Giving away my trade secrets should cost you something," she teased, until I threw another threatening glance her way. "Ok, ok. He plays poker with him every Tuesday night."

Ah, the Tuesday night poker game. Huh. And here I thought guys just drank beer and smoked cigars. Who knew they talked about feelings too? Somehow, I highly doubted Ramirez went out of his way to share his with the group, though perhaps Leah's source was keeping tabs for other reasons, or other persons? I put that thought out of my head for the time-being. I had enough other stuff on my plate without my overactive imagination putting its big fat foot into it, too.

I waited until I knew Ramirez was on his dinner break to place the call. I was uncharacteristically nervous, though any conversation with the detective gave me butterflies, had me weak in the knees and all that other good stuff. These were, however, a different kind of nerves—ones derived from having knowledge I wasn't supposed to have. Even though the conversation I would be having with him had no bearing on his former love life, I felt as though I wore that knowledge like a "Hello, my name is Obvious" badge. He was a detective, and from my experience, a pretty darn good one.

I sighed as I scrolled through my phone's contact list, chuckling when I found his name. Leah had apparently commandeered my phone at some point and added a photo to Ramirez's contact info. Funny girl—her selection was Clint Eastwood as Dirty Harry. Laughing, I quickly moved to the letter "S" and sure enough, she had added photos for both Stanton brothers. For Abe —the brother I was sure had a crush on her—she had inserted her personal favorite, a photo of Tom Selleck as Magnum, P.I. and for Elijah, selected her second favorite detective, Matt Houston a la Lee Horsely. I had pegged him as a Mike Hammer type, but whatever. I bit the proverbial bullet and scrolled back to Dirty Harry.

Just my luck, Ramirez picked up on the first ring. His husky voice filled the connection, "AJ, to what do I owe the pleasure? Are you coming over to share my dinner with me? I made a couple of peanut butter and pickle sandwiches. Your favorite." I sighed, indeed it was.

I'd introduced Ramirez to my childhood vice a few months ago. Initially, he'd been disgusted by the odd coupling, but after a sizable amount of persuasion on my part, he gave in and after one glorious bite, called me a genius. In retrospect, he might have been referring to the sandwich. More importantly, the majority of his meals from that day forward consisted of two PB and pickle delights, though honestly, I wondered how he managed the second alone.

"Um, thanks, but I kind of had a long day and I need to get some stuff done here." I was totally flubbing it but if he noticed, he didn't make any mention, so I quickly filled him in on the events of the day.

He was silent for a moment before responding, "So, I take it you want me to talk to my TPD buddies about the investigation and see if anything can be done to speed the process along?"

"Well, I'm not sure about speeding the process along, but yeah, if you could see what you can find out, that would be helpful. It would mean a lot."

I knew my response sounded a bit canned. Darn it, the knowledge of his former relationship with Serena Fenton was making me act goofy. If he noticed my distraction, I was thankful he didn't press me for details. I certainly wasn't prepared to breech that subject. Someday maybe, or would I? I put myself in his shoes for a moment. What would Ramirez do?

He would wait, I decided. And because I cared about him, I would to do the same. It was settled—I would allow him to share the details of his past if and when he was ready. In the meantime, I'd just have to suck it up and get over this discomfort I was feeling. No sense making a mountain out of a mole hill, or whatever it was my dad used to say. I realized Ramirez had been talking during my pontification and had paused, either awaiting a response, or realizing I hadn't been paying attention.

Silly me, I decided to play it off with a stellar, "Um yeah, that would be great."

Ramirez chuckled. I imagined him on the other end, shaking his head, his eyes crinkling with amusement. "I was just saying dinner would be lonely without you, but that I would see what I could find out from TPD."

Something about the way he said it made me wonder about that second sandwich. Had he always packed it, in case I joined him? Nah, that couldn't be possible, could it? Perhaps Detective Jonah Ramirez wasn't such a mystery after all.

Maybe I hadn't been looking at the right clues.

CHAPTER SIX

A few days later…

It was a refreshingly cool spring day, so Nicoh and I elected to sit out in the covered backyard patio. As we nestled on one of the overstuffed outdoor wicker couches, Nicoh dozed, snoring quietly as his head rested carelessly on my thigh. I looked down at him, absently stroking his velvety ear—a bit envious of his ability to transition to a relaxed state. Physically, I felt as though I could be equally content, but mentally I was all over the place. I processed the events of the past few days—work, Charlie's party, Parker's sudden absence, the search and recovery of his body—even Leah's news about Ramirez's ex rattled around in my head.

I sighed. Nope, there was definitely no way I could join Nicoh in a nap, no matter how enticing I found the gentle rhythms of his breathing and paws drumming against the couch as he chased the elusive Pandora. I stifled a yawn, if I could be that…that…

I was so deep in thought I hadn't heard Ramirez calling my name. I looked up, squinting in the direction of his voice. His lips moved silently, his usually even gaze wild, as he repeated the same word over and over. I realized his arms were pinned with barbs and chains, shredding his clothing and piercing his tender skin. If he was in pain, he refused to allow me to witness his suffering. Instead, he continued to cast desperate glances at me... no...behind me. When I moved to assist him, he immediately shook his head from side to side. Suddenly, there was pressure against my throat, crushing my windpipe. I struggled for breath, the lack of oxygen making me fuzzy. As I lost focus, I caught a hazy glimpse of Ramirez struggling to free himself and realized I had been mistaken, he hadn't been uttering a word. It had been a name. Death.

I woke—my scream silent as I bolted upright, knocking Nicoh from my lap. He moaned sleepily, readjusting himself so that his head rested on a sofa cushion. Once comfortable, he emitted a guttural snore, oblivious to my ghastly dream. I wasn't sure how I'd managed to fall asleep and was glad the beep of my cell phone had woken me.

The afternoon had turned to night since we had ventured to the patio and the air drew a chill, forcing me to wrap my arms around myself as I pulled the phone from my pocket. I hadn't realized how warm Nicoh's head had been until his retreat to the other side of the couch. Sighing, I looked at phone's tiny screen, confused by the cryptic text message: *YOU CANT ESCAPE WHO YOU ARE ARIANNA.* Again, the number was unavailable. Taking everything else into consideration, this was getting just plain weird. Perhaps I would need to ask Ramirez for advice but seriously, who could it be? It was funny how the dreams were starting to coincide with the messages. I shrugged it off and shifted from the couch, being careful not to disturb the snoring beast again after the hard day he'd had.

As I shuffled inside, I wondered when Leah would be home and if she'd had any luck tracking down her TPD contact like she'd planned. As if her ears had been burning, my phone rang and sure enough, the ringtone was hers.

"I was just thinking about you, girl. Were your spidey senses working overtime, or what?" I paused before adding, "By the way, where the heck are you?" There was a lot of shuffling before she responded. Only it wasn't Leah.

Instead, a male voice chirped in my ear, "Arianna, it's been awhile." Given the crackly feedback, I recognized it as a recording. The voice was also vaguely familiar.

"Just wanted you to know, the time has come. You can't escape who, or what, you are." A quick laugh filled the connection before the recording ended and the call disconnected.

Though the words mirrored the text messages, what disturbed me even more was the caller's laugh. It's almost conversational quality caught me off-guard, forcing me back to a time when Leah had been kidnapped and nearly killed. It had been months earlier, but events were still clear in my mind, as was the voice of her captor—the same voice from the recording.

Winslow Clark.

Panic built as I struggled to rationalize the situation. I had been assured both Clark and his father, Theodore Winslow, were locked away in secured FBI facilities. It had to be a farce. He was under constant surveillance, in a psychiatric ward. How would he have gotten a hold of my best friend's cell number, or her phone, or her?

The exercise in rationalization clearly failing, I gritted my teeth and dialed Ramirez's number while several dozen thoughts, combined with a few colorful adjectives, ran through my mind. Impatiently, I counted the rings and contemplated leaving a voice-mail message when he answered.

Unlike our earlier conversation, his voice was clipped, "AJ, twice in one day."

Sensing he was in the middle of something important, I

quickly told him about the text messages and recorded call from Leah's number, saving my suspicions regarding the caller's identity for last.

When Ramirez responded, his voice was only a hint more congenial. "Why am I just now hearing about this?" Ok, perhaps the congenial tone had been wishful thinking on my part.

"Err..." Not my most profound, snappy response to date. "Well, at first I figured it was a joke and—"

"After that?" Ramirez demanded.

"After that, it just seemed silly...err...I guess...I guess I didn't want to seem needy."

Ramirez sighed. This time, his voice softened, "AJ, you are anything but needy. Sometimes I wish...I wish you needed me more. I'm sorry if I gave you that impression. Or made you feel like you couldn't come to me." He paused for a moment, his voice returning to its steely predecessor, "I'll see what I can find out about Clark and his father and at the very least, make sure they are where they're supposed to be. I'll also try to determine what permissions they've been granted for phone calls and visitors. In the meantime, contact Leah, though I'm sure she is fine. The caller probably cloned her phone. Err—hang on a second." There were muffled voices in the background before he placed me on mute.

He returned a few minutes later. "Sorry about that. One of the other detectives had some information, about Parker Harris. I'll share it with you, knowing you'll turn around and share it with Leah, but I'm warning you, if this ends up in the media, regardless of whether her name is associated with it..." He didn't finish the thought, leaving me to draw my own conclusions. If he'd been going for effect, it worked. I swore under my breath.

Apparently satisfied, Ramirez continued, "The Medical Examiner's Office has tentatively identified the body pulled from Tempe Town Lake as Parker Harris." I exhaled, Leah and I had been right. "Based upon the condition of the body, the ME confirmed he was dead before he went into the water."

"Wait, what do you mean 'condition of the body'?"

"Without getting too Patricia Cornwell on you, as you always say, Harris sustained significant internal injuries. Meaning there was no way he made it into the lake on his own—he was already dead."

"I don't understand," my voice came out as a croak. "Are you saying someone *dumped* Parker into the lake?"

"Someone not only dumped him into the lake, that person—or persons—may have also inflicted his injuries, or been present when they occurred."

"Someone...killed Parker...on purpose?" I stuttered. "As in foul play?" I certainly hadn't seen that puck coming down the pipe.

"Harris was definitely killed, then dumped. He didn't drown. Someone threw him in the lake, after the fact."

"But...but it could have...could have been an accident, right? Parker could have accidentally died and then...and then..." I struggled to make the pieces fit an alternative ending, "whoever found him...I don't know, freaked out and dumped his body... because they were afraid?"

"No, AJ. There were clear signs of a struggle—elsewhere. It's likely he was knocked out or somehow incapacitated to the point he could no longer defend himself, then killed. There was no accident about it. He was killed. Murdered." Ramirez paused but not nearly long enough for my mind to fully process it all.

"Harris was likely dumped in an attempt to mask the cause of death, by someone smart enough to realize the body would get tangled up, weighed down or at the very least, hidden from view. Of course, they also risked the possibility the lake would be dredged or drained but by that point, the body would have decomposed, making the cause of death difficult, if not impossible, to identify. Smart, but not smart enough to realize a storm was on the horizon. All the cunning in the world is no match for Mother Nature."

Again, voices murmured in the background on Ramirez's end. This time, however, he didn't mute the conversation and when he returned, something in his tone had changed.

"AJ, there's more," he sighed and was quiet for a moment, "TPD arrested one suspect and are questioning a second person of interest."

I groaned. I hated that phrase and Ramirez knew it. Weren't all people, in some respect, interesting?

Ramirez ignored me. "They've arrested Charlie Wilson—"

"What? That's ridiculous. Charlie might be the biggest pain in the you-know-what since Scrappy Doo joined Scooby and the gang, but he certainly wouldn't scuffle with anyone, much less kill them. What did they think his motive was—Parker's revolting fashion sense? And the murder weapon—a tube of overly-priced hair product?" I laughed, sounding a bit like a crazed circus clown after an hour with an audience filled with rambunctious five-year-olds.

"Not exactly…" Ramirez replied slowly, almost cautiously, "but there's still more." I rolled my eyes. Wasn't there always? "The person they are currently questioning…is Leah."

CHAPTER SEVEN

I was out the door before Ramirez could utter another syllable, spouting a few choice words that would have made my mother's toes curl in horror and was probably quite a sight as I marched into the Tempe Police Department, fists curled, hair flying, armed with an Alaskan Malamute.

The desk sergeant held up a hand in an attempt to cite some police regulation—something about animals not being allowed in government buildings unless being utilized in a service capacity—while I announced my intentions to find Leah and strode purposefully down the hallway. I got as far as the double doors leading who knew where before he gruffly grabbed my arm. Not liking the physicality of the gesture, Nicoh growled in warning and the sergeant's eyes widened in surprise. Before the situation escalated, I raised my hands in surrender. I'd be no help to Leah if I got locked up right alongside her. The officer nodded and released his steely grip. That was gonna leave a mark, I thought dryly, though admittedly, it was my own fault. I had acted in haste and apologized to the officer. Satisfied I was no longer in mortal danger, Nicoh grumbled before sitting on his haunches, carefully placing his large frame directly between us, just in case.

The officer shook his head, his face stern as he informed me had I bothered to listen, I would have been able to see Leah once the detectives were finished talking to her. *Oops...way to muck that up, AJ*, I muttered to myself, expecting to be escorted to the sidewalk. Instead, he pointed to a row of plastic chairs lining the wall before returning to his desk.

A few minutes later, another officer, this one in plain clothes, emerged from the double doors I had attempted and failed to breach. He was tall like Ramirez but had the build of a heavyweight boxer with a roadmap of scars on his face to match. Given his size, I hated to see the other guy. His black hair was cropped short, military-style, making his broad features even more distinctive. His eyes were as dark as his hair and though I was sure he could have put my evil eye to shame—according to Leah, mine was pretty darn good—his gaze was thoughtful as he gave us each the once-over. After a long moment, he nodded at the desk sergeant before ushering us through the doors and down a long, sterile hallway with a half a dozen windowless doors on either side. He wasn't much of a talker, so we moved silently until he stopped at the third door on the left. Nicoh let out a low rumble as we entered and after giving him a hard look, the officer finally broke his silence.

"You know, the dog isn't supposed to be in here, Ms. Jackson,"

"Please call me AJ. And yes, Officer, the err...desk sergeant out front indicated as much. I'm used to taking Nicoh everywhere and honestly, wasn't thinking clearly when I came here. I assure you he is well-behaved and will be no trouble." I shot Nicoh a look of warning but he ignored me, electing to sniff the corners of the room. Like I said, he's well-behaved.

The officer nodded, gesturing to the table and chairs positioned in the center of the room. "It's Detective—Detective Jeremiah Vargas. I thought you and your sidekick would be more comfortable in here while Leah is finishing up."

"Nicoh is hardly a sidekick," I huffed, though there was no real anger behind it. I was more curious about the detective's casual reference to my best friend and said as much.

Vargas chuckled at my pursed lips. "*Ms. Campbell* and I have worked together on several occasions, bridging the gap between the media and police relations, that sort of thing." He shrugged as though it was common knowledge. It was not. "I've also been assigned to the Harris case." Ah, so this was Leah's contact within the Tempe Police Department—the one who also played poker with Ramirez. Her being brought in for questioning would make for interesting shop talk next Tuesday night.

"Have you seen her? Is she ok? And, just for the record, you guys are out of your confounded minds if you think she had anything to do with Parker's death. I mean, no disrespect, but what were you thinking, hauling her in as a person of interest?" I finished my spouting with an emphatic use of finger quotes.

Vargas shook his head, barely able to refrain from erupting in laughter. It was, after all, a serious matter. "Ramirez said you were a spitfire."

I blushed at the mention of Ramirez, but wasn't about to be deterred. "You said she was being questioned, yet you are here. When can I see her?"

"To answer your questions, yes I have seen her and she is fine. And, for the record, we did not haul her in. She came in on her own accord, after I mentioned her name had come up during the investigation. Besides, she was present when the body was recovered from the lake. My partner is currently interviewing her and should be about finished, so if you don't mind hanging tight, I'll leave you two here and bring her back when we've wrapped things up. Are you good with that, AJ?"

"She's not a suspect then?"

Vargas shook his head. "If she is as forthcoming as she typically tends to be, then she'll be free to go as soon as the interview is finished."

"What about Charlie? There's no way he had anything to do with any of this either. Surely, you can see that?" This time, Vargas said nothing, so I changed tactics. "What about the murder weapon or whatever it was that was used to kill Parker before his body was dumped into Tempe Town Lake?"

His brow rose ever-so-slightly as I belatedly clamped my mouth shut. In true AJ form, I had said too much and probably gotten Ramirez into trouble in the process. Vargas' top lip twitched—I made a mental note to mention that to Ramirez, as it could be handy tip for poker night—but instead of pressing me, he departed, his tall frame barely dodging the door jamb as he passed.

I took the opportunity to look around the room. At first, it looked like any other conference room, but upon closer inspection I realized the table was bolted to the concrete floor. The walls, painted a lovely puce, were barren except for two opaque windows, which I could only assume were two-way mirrors. An interrogation room. Just great, AJ, now what have you gotten yourself into? Any more "sharing" and I'd end up in a cell with Charlie. Self-consciously, I glanced at the two-way and wondered if anyone was looking back. Detective Vargas thought we'd be more comfortable in here? Right.

Twenty minutes and several furtive glances at the mirror later, the door burst open and a blond blur flew in and nearly knocked me over, hugging me fiercely. Awkwardly, I attempted to stand and hug her back, but nearly dumped us both onto the floor in the process. Leah chuckled lightly as we broke our embrace.

I immediately noticed how tired and uncharacteristically pale she looked. Bags were visible under her bloodshot, red-rimmed eyes. From the way it stuck out in tangled clumps, it was apparent she had also been running her hands through her usually spiky hair—unless she'd stopped to run backward through a wind tunnel before making her way to the police station. Either way, I hoped she wouldn't catch her reflection in the two-way.

"You ok?" I asked, before making a slight gesture toward the mirrors.

She nodded. "I'm fine for now. Let's get out of here before they change their minds and I have to update my Facebook status from single to incarcerated."

I collected Nicoh, currently sporting an impressive bored look which, in case you weren't aware, involves sprawling on his side in an effort to take up as much real estate as possible, while emitting an equally large puddle of drool. The three of us made haste and retreated from the police station, waving briefly at the desk sergeant who grunted in return. Once we had cleared the threshold, I looked at Leah.

"What about Charlie? We can't just leave him here."

Leah shook her head and wearily replied, "They are still questioning him and from what I've heard, he's not going anywhere anytime soon."

"Maybe they'll at least allow visitors when they are done? I doubt he's faring well." I shuddered at the thought of Charlie Wilson, in jail.

"There's nothing we can do for him here. Let's just go home and I'll fill you in."

"Ok, I guess we'll meet you at home, then."

"Just one thing?" she asked as she unlocked the door to her SUV.

"Yeah?"

"Make some margaritas when you get there. Actually, you'd better make a pitcher."

* * *

Leah looked a bit better after a shower and a few applications of a good hair detangler. The tiredness that surrounded her eyes was still visible, but she beamed when she spied the snacks I had prepared: green chili salsa, guacamole, flour chips from Aunt Chilada's and of course, a pitcher of fresh-squeezed lime margaritas.

"Mmm," she crooned, stuffing a guacamole-laden chip into her mouth while I liberally poured the elixir into Ball jars I had frozen for such an occasion. "This hits the spot."

I took a healthy sip of my own beverage and nodded. "Good stuff."

"Indeed," was her only response as we munched in silence for several minutes.

"So," I put some distance between myself and the food, "I met your…friend, Detective Vargas."

"Jere?" Leah mumbled through a mouthful of chips and salsa. "Yeah, he's a good guy."

"Right….*Jere*. How come this is the first I'm hearing about him?"

She shrugged, pretending to analyze the flakiness of her chip. "There's nothing to tell. He's been a good source of info for me in the past and helped me run down a few details on occasion, while I've ensured nuggets were placed in the paper when needed. Stuff like that."

"Huh." I wasn't totally buying whatever she was attempting to sell, but had more pressing items on my mind. "So what happened? Why did they think you had information about Parker's murder?"

"I know, right? You can imagine my surprise when I showed up to ask Vargas some questions and he informs me I'm at the top of his list of people to question. Me!" She threw her hands up in exasperation.

"But why?" I asked, equally perplexed.

"Because they found an unidentified earring at the scene—meaning it wasn't attached to an ear at the time—and our pal Charlie was gracious enough to let the cops know he'd seen me wearing a pair just like them at his party," she huffed. "Anyway, *that* is how I came to be one of TPD's main persons of interest, after Charlie, of course."

"Wow, I hadn't even realized you'd lost an earring that night." I thought back to the party and our drive home.

"Crap, me either. They were cheap and pinching my ears, so I took them off and threw them in my bag. I never gave them another thought and until Vargas and his partner showed me the evidence bag, had no idea one had fallen out."

"Or made its way to the scene—which was where, by the way? Are we still talking about the area of the lake where Natalie found the tie and shoe, or where Parker was pulled out?"

"Neither, actually. As it turns out, Parker did *not* just accidentally fall into the lake after an evening of drinks at Charlie's party." Though Ramirez had relayed similar information, I shuddered as she blew out a deep breath. "The current theory is some altercation took place that either rendered Parker unconscious or incapacitated him to the point he was no longer a threat. Once he was out of commission..." She shook her head, unable to continue.

When she spoke again, her voice was barely a whisper, "It appears he took a series of blows to the mid-section, which damaged several vital organs and caused him to eventually bleed-out internally."

"They can't think Charlie would do that to Parker...to anyone...with his fists."

"Not his fists," she replied, her voice even quieter, "with his 1959 Cadillac Eldorado."

"Big Bess?" I screeched, causing Nicoh to howl. "They believe Charlie hit Parker—or ran over him—with his car?"

"Err, more like gouged him repeatedly, with her hurking tail-fins while Parker was pinned between the car and the wall." I gasped, mainly out of horror, but partially out of disgust. "Anyway, it appears it all went down in Charlie's parking garage, which is now considered the primary crime scene and lucky me, also where my earring was found."

I groaned, thrusting my face into my hands. This was worse than a bad remake of *Christine*. "This is just so awful. And I don't mean to seem juvenile, but gross. Please tell me they're sure Parker was unconscious?"

She shook her head. "Incapacitated for sure, but they don't know if he was completely unconscious when the impact occurred...if they ever will."

"Just awful," I murmured. I'd never been a fan of Parker's, but no one—not even Parker—deserved to die like that. "It would take someone pretty bent to concoct something sick like that. Charlie's a twerp, but he's not twisted. Struggling with Parker or even incapacitating him would be out of character, but to use Big Bess to *kill* him? No way. Charlie loves that car in an 'it's ok to love your car but don't loooove your car' sort of way." I shook my head.

If you happen to be knowledgeable about classic cars, you're likely familiar with the 1959 Eldorado. She's one big bad beast, all chrome and metal and definitive of an era long past. Not swank and trendy like Charlie's usual baubles. No, Big Bess was definitely not flashy enough to suit Charlie's usual needs.

Charlie liked his clothes, his penthouse, his possessions—even his daily driver, a sporty new Aston Martin something or other—but he *loved* Big Bess, probably as much as he loved himself. Don't ask me why. Charlie liked the latest and greatest toys but when it came to this car, for whatever reason, she broke his mold of perfection.

I'd often wondered if his beloved grandfather had once owned one, causing Charlie to lust after it as a means of emulating the famous man. I shrugged, whatever his rationale, once he'd found his Eldorado, he had to have her.

Big Bess—former name unknown—had been a California girl all her life, meaning she was free of the elements brought into play by harsher climates. She'd been owned by the widow of the man who had originally purchased her in 1959. Since that time, she'd only been driven 328 miles and spent the rest of her days in a climate-controlled garage—Big Bess, not the widow.

Charlie paid a lot of pretty pennies for her. The day she arrived in Arizona, Charlie had been uncharacteristically childlike and filled with pride. As they unloaded her from the transport, he'd carefully shammied her fin to fin, top to bottom. It was the only time I'd seen him show such emotion, which was how I knew Charlie would never risk damaging her, no matter how angry he was with Parker. Perhaps that sounds cruel—weighing the importance of a car over that of a human life—but that was Charlie.

"So did Big Bess show any signs of—"

"Damage?" Leah finished, which was probably a good thing, considering my mind had drifted toward something more gory, as in Parker goo. Yucko. "Neither a dent nor a scratch—that car is a tank. Besides, the killer wiped her down pretty well after he did the deed." I grimaced at Leah's choice of words, the margaritas were definitely kicking in. "But once the crime scene techs got done, they were able to find trace evidence."

"Trace, as in belonging to Parker?" I couldn't help but formulate a visual.

"Um, yeah…fabric, skin, blood…you know…trace."

"Well, thanks for that, Ms. CSI Tempe. I get what trace is, but can you honestly tell me they believe Charlie would actually risk A, ruining a perfectly good manicure by knocking Parker wonky; B, messing up a designer suit—no matter how white or ugly—and

C, destroying his beloved car? And, let's not forget, he'd still had to have the wherewithal to clean up after himself before dumping Parker in the lake?"

Leah looked at me evenly. "Not in a million years."

"Exactly, which is why this is so ridiculous. Even if you forget the bad stuff—like Parker being dead—and crawl into Charlie's world for a minute, there's no way he would risk having a bunch of sweaty crime lab techs man-handle his car."

"True, but for the record, I'm not sure he knows about that, so on the off-chance we talk to him in the near future, hold off on bringing it up. As it is, I hear he's not doing so hot."

I scoffed, "Not doing so hot? Of course he's not doing so hot. He's just been arrested. For murder."

"Well, I heard he's lost it a couple of times."

"Lost it, as in he had a tantrum?"

"No, it was more like a mental break. From what I was told, he started acting out while riding in the back of the police car—complaining about hand sanitizer and the tragedy of faux leather."

"Uh, that's not exactly a mental break. That's Charlie."

She shook her head. "It wasn't just that. It quickly escalated to ranting and by the time they processed him, he was so incoherent, a specialist had to be brought in to confirm he didn't need to be hospitalized. The ranting eventually stopped, but he clammed up altogether."

"As you and I both know, Charlie's used to being the center of attention—good or bad—but he's typically also able to control the situation. Not so in this case." Leah nodded in agreement. "So, before he stopped talking, he obviously had no issue identifying your earring. How did you manage to talk your way out of that one, anyway?"

Leah laughed, but was not smiling as she did so. "Yeah, that. I just told them what I told you. I thought I had thrown them both into my purse at the party. At some point, one of them must have

fallen out and someone, maybe Parker's killer, picked it up and…
I don't know…used it as a diversion at the crime scene? Anyway,
several witnesses corroborated seeing us leave the party, so for the
time-being the earring is considered circumstantial evidence.
They may have more questions for me as the investigation
progresses, though," she shook her head in frustration.

"So don't leave town, the country, yada yada? Guess that
means the all-expenses-paid trip to Hawaii is out."

"Pretty much, though Vargas knows where to find me if he
needs me." She smirked. "As for Charlie, besides the earring bit,
they've gotten squat out of him."

"Typical Charlie, so frustrating. Doesn't he realize the longer
he holds out, the longer he's going to be sitting in a six by eight as
suspect numero uno?" I was thoroughly exasperated. "Surely his
lawyer can convince him it's in his best interest—as an innocent
party—to be as forthcoming as possible, as soon as possible?"

At the mention of a lawyer, Leah scrunched her nose. "Yeah,
about that—Charlie's refused counsel so far." I groaned, slapping
my forehead. She tapped her chin thoughtfully. "But I'm willing
to bet he'd chat with an old friend."

CHAPTER EIGHT

Through her contact at TPD, now known as Detective Jeremiah "Jere" Vargas, Leah was able to work her magic, enabling me to have a brief conversation with Charlie the following morning. Whether Charlie would see me or not was an entirely different story, one that I would tackle later. Leah'd had her fill of police hospitality and quickly opted-out of this excursion. Someone had to stay behind and keep the surly Alaskan Malamute company, she insisted, leaving me to wonder which of us had actually drawn the shorter straw.

When I arrived at the police station the next morning, Vargas was nowhere to be found, but had made arrangements with the desk sergeant on duty, a wiry woman in her late 40s with an iron handshake and expression that revealed nothing.

"Detective Vargas said you'd want to see Charlie Wilson," though she worked hard to mask it, her voice hinted at a slight accent, West Virginia, perhaps?

She gave me an appraising glance. "You do realize that Mr. Wilson has been arrested for murder?" The way she drew out the word "murder" indicated she thought I was too naive to know what I was getting myself into. She hesitated for a moment, expecting me to bolt after learning I'd made a wrong turn on the way to meet with my accountant.

I gritted my teeth. "Yes, I'm here to see my friend, Charlie Wilson."

The sergeant sniffed at my curt response but said nothing as she made a quick phone called in a muttered tone. Once done, she looked at me squarely, her jaw set and stance rigid.

"Very well, then. One of the detectives will be up to collect you momentarily."

Despite being dismissed with a nod in the direction of my favorite plastic chairs, I elected to remain standing. Call it my stubborn side. Sensing the sergeant's eyes burning into the back of my head, I turned to level my own glare. She immediately averted her steely gaze and internally, I reveled in the small win. That was until I realized her focus had actually been directed toward a sturdy-looking officer emerging from the hallway. I was glad I'd held out on that victory dance.

"Ms. Jackson? I'm Detective Sanchez," his voice boomed but was friendly as he extended a beefy hand. I returned the gesture and took the opportunity to marvel at his sausage-like fingers as they clasped mine, thankful I hadn't brought Nicoh, who would have been salivating while looking around for deli mustard. Eww. The handshake itself—once you got over its resemblance to meat —was surprisingly soft, yet firm. Nothing like the death grip the desk sergeant had wielded.

"Mr. Wilson has agreed to see you, but before I take you over to the other building to see him, I'd like to cover a few of our ground rules. I see you managed to leave your canine at home this time around, which is a good start."

I blew out a long breath. Apparently, I was making quite a name for myself around here. Not good. Sanchez took in my expression and chuckled, outlining the visitor protocol as we

exited one building and entered the adjacent, presumably the jail.
If he was curious about my visit, he made no indication.

"Are you one of the investigating officers on Parker Harris'
case?" I was careful not to reference Charlie or murder in the
same sentence. Sanchez nodded but did not elaborate. "So, you
really think you've got enough evidence to move forward?" I
prompted.

Sanchez was a little less friendly this time around. "Charlie
Wilson wouldn't be sitting in that cell if we didn't, Ms. Jackson."

Thankfully, we had arrived at our destination: a small room,
about half the size of the one in the other building. Like the other,
it was devoid of sunlight or windows and armored with two-way
mirrors. The fluorescent lighting was severe, making the drab
interior look even more putrid. A worn steel table was positioned
in the center of the room, with picnic style benches on either side.
All were bolted to the floor in a not so picnic-like way. Someone
had graced the top of the table with several slurs I will not repeat.
Let's just say that during childhood, my mouth had its share of
run-ins with Borax. A few of the more colorful phrases even made
me blush, which is saying a lot, given my familiarity with the
powdered soap.

Sanchez seemed amused by my discomfort and pointed to one
of the benches, etched with drawings that mirrored the sentiments
on the tabletop. I pretended to ignore them and sat, hoping to
position myself in a way that would allow privacy from the
mirrors, but the setup of the room prevented me from doing so. I
glanced around and scowled, realizing Sanchez had slipped out.
After a few minutes he returned, with Charlie in tow.

It was as bad as I had expected. Charlie's once-pressed chinos
were crinkled and dingy with dirt and grime. His button-down
shirt was not tucked and showed significant signs of perspiration;
his usual handmade Italian leather shoes replaced with canvas
slip-ons. Except for the obvious wear and tear, I would have

sworn he was channeling his inner *Miami Vice*. Charlie himself told a less Don Johnson-like story. His typically gelled locks hung limply, covering his eyes and trailing down his cheekbones, now flanked with shadows. His pouty lips formed a thin line as he plunked onto the bench opposite of mine, not appearing to care where the mirrors were positioned. He'd obviously spent a great deal of time in this room.

"Well, at least you got to keep the digs. You know how orange washes you out and tends to make you look…chunky," I attempted to lighten the mood and obvious humiliation Charlie was feeling.

His lips formed a tiny smile. "For now, it seems. Though, it is kind of ironic I'd be allergic to prison couture."

"Huh. I didn't know a doctor's note would work in this situation. That's good to know."

This time, the laugh reached his eyes. "You know me well, AJ, better than most."

Sanchez cleared his throat, reminding us of his presence. "You have thirty minutes. I suggest you make the most of them," he turned to leave, glancing back as he reached the door, "and yes, Ms. Jackson, I'll be watching."

Charlie spoke once Sanchez made his exit, "In case you were wondering, I didn't do it." He eyed me slowly, gauging my reaction.

"Which part of 'it' are you referencing?" I crossed my arms and stared at him evenly.

Charlie blanched, clearly expecting me to take him at his word. Perhaps a part of me did, but I wasn't a complete dolt. Before I gave him the confirmation he needed, he owed me some darn good answers.

After a long moment, he nodded. "First, I didn't have a physical altercation with Parker on that night, or any night. Regardless of what you think about my character, I don't believe in violence as a resolution, no matter the problem. Second, I did not lure him to the parking garage under any circumstances, much less to render him unconscious, as indicated by my first point. Third, I would not and did not impale him with the fins of my car. Fourth, I did not have anything to do with dumping him into Tempe Town Lake. And last, I do not know, nor did I conspire with the individual or individuals who did." He snarled out the last bit, perhaps not only for my benefit but for that of Detective Sanchez and any other law enforcement type lurking behind the mirror. After brushing hair from his eyes, he snarkily added, in true Charlie form, "It's not my style."

"Um, yeah, I got that," I replied in a low tone, my lips barely moving, "but given your current situation, how can you so easily dismiss the fact your best friend was brutally murdered and then dumped like he was nothing more than yesterday's trash? Especially considering you are now suspect numero uno?" The last part came out in a growl and I was sure to our friends behind the glass, I sounded a little crazed. I didn't care. My message was for one person. "Don't be such a nitwit, Charlie! Wake up and smell the Starbucks!"

Given his raised brow and sour expression, Charlie had heard me loud and clear. For once, he wouldn't be able to throw a tantrum or bully his way out, not when someone had orchestrated the situation so beautifully he'd come out looking like the perfect primary suspect.

Charlie finally conceded, "I agree. My attitude has been a bit…vexatious, given the circumstances. But I want to impress upon you, I do take the situation seriously." In an uncharacteristic, self-conscious gesture he ran his hands through his hair. "Perhaps initially…my ego…did not allow me to fully comprehend the ramifications. But after giving it some thought, I've realized a few things about myself. I guess what I'm trying to tell you, is while I had nothing to do with Parker's death directly, there are things from the past—decisions I made, actions I could have taken but didn't—that were just as damaging."

"I'm not sure I'm completely following you."

Charlie nodded, leaning his forearms on his thighs. "As you know, Parker and I went way back, along with Greg. All of us had privileged upbringings and were from well-respected families, so it was natural for us to hang out in high school, head off to Harvard together and things like that. We had access to anything and everything, which made us arrogant. Given our money, status and combined inherent business acumen—as we used to like to think of it—we thought we were a force to be reckoned with. What we didn't take into account was our individual egos. We were in a constant state of one-upping the other and even that was never enough.

"Until recently, I hadn't considered Greg wasn't like Parker. Or me. Not really. He was a good friend. A loyal friend, and far more trusting than Parker and I deserved. We'd take risks—and I mean *huge* risks—and there would be Greg, trying to rationalize things, trying to reason with us, doing anything he could think of to get us to come down off our high horses.

"Looking back, I think we actually enjoyed torturing him with all our elaborate plans and schemes, sometimes literally bullying him into joining our fun. For a long time, things typically worked out in our favor, so we'd tease him mercilessly about his cautiousness. Then came the times things didn't go our way. Still, Parker and I played with money like we'd printed it ourselves.

"I won't go into all the boring details, but for years making money off other people's investments was child's play to us. They made money. We made money. Everybody was happy. Then, a few years ago, Parker took things a step further. Both Greg and I had reservations about complicating our money-making formula, but by that point Parker's ego was even more inflated than my own.

"He'd resort to sneaking around behind our backs if it suited him. Our formula didn't require too many rules, but that one was a deal-breaker. Undaunted, he took unnecessary risks, often based upon a whim or whatever interested him at that moment. In his mind, it was a shortcut to the formula and had the potential for yielding bigger gains. More often than not, however, his off-formula risks resulted in disaster.

"During one of Parker's whims, he dabbled with a large amount of money Greg had earmarked from a group of investors setting up a foundation to fund several local hospices and critical care treatment facilities. All were privately-funded, relying on external sources—like the investment group—for the livelihood of their programs and services, as well as for future research and development. The market unexpectedly turned south and thanks to Parker, the money Greg had raised was gone, leaving nothing for the facilities and no returns for the investors. Parker was off to his next venture while Greg scrambled to recoup the money. Though he salvaged what he could— even using his own money—many of the facilities were either forced to limit services or eliminate others. And, of course, there was the blowback from the investors themselves. Greg was devastated, though Parker had been the one to facilitate the deed. As a group, it wasn't one of our finest moments," Charlie paused to catch his breath.

I realized I could have taken that moment to absolve him by telling him it would all be ok, but I refused to lie to him, or to myself. In truth, I was angry. Seething, actually. And though I fought to keep my face a blank slate, it took everything in me not to turn my back on him and walk out of that room and his life. It was either that or punch him in the throat. I preferred the latter, followed by the prior, and was giving it some serious thought when Charlie interjected.

"That wasn't even the worst part. Parker laughed when he

found out. Laughed. He figured if anything, it would teach Greg to keep his money to himself and not waste it on charity cases."

"What did *you* do?" I managed to grit out, surprising Charlie.

"That's the point, isn't it? I didn't *do* anything." He focused on his hands, as though eye contact with me would be too painful. "I did nothing to stop Parker. And nothing to help Greg."

Something finally clicked into place. "That's why Greg killed himself, isn't it?" Charlie's silence only accelerated my growing fury.

"He's dead because of your stupid…games, your insurmountable egos and your inability to show some spine. You allowed your friend—one of your best friends—to suffer, alone." Charlie flinched at the harshness of my reprimand, but I wasn't in the mood to be merciful.

"Greg couldn't deal with the guilt. And still, you did nothing to ease his pain. No kind words. No show of support. Nothing. He felt he had no other way out. That's it, isn't it?" By this point, my fingernails were digging into my palms. I refused to look at Charlie, fearful I would punch him after all. In the end, I decided a swift sock to the throat was better than he deserved.

As if reading my mind, Charlie spoke, his voice barely a whisper, "So you think I deserve this." It was not a question and for a long while, I did not give him the benefit of a response.

I was still seething when I finally did speak, but my blood had cooled to a somewhat more rational level, "You know what they say about karma, Charlie. So yes, in some ways, you made your own bed. You are a crappy friend and an even worse judge of character. I do not, however, think you deserve to be set up for Parker's murder, any more than I think he deserved to be killed and dumped like garbage. He was an awful, despicable human being, but that doesn't give someone the right to be judge, jury and executioner. No human gets that hook. By putting his blood on their hands, they've only succeeded in taking on his burden themselves. Killing Parker didn't right a wrong. It just created two wrongs."

Charlie nodded, whether he agreed I wasn't sure, though I hoped he'd taken some of what I'd said to heart. I certainly wasn't going to ease up on him, but I needed to change the direction of the conversation, as time was ticking away,

"So, what caused you and Parker to be at odds during the White Party?" I shrugged when he raised his eyebrows. "I saw the daggers you were shooting at him, not to mention your body language. Anyone who knows you even a smidgen realized something was off between the two of you."

"I wasn't aware I was being that obvious." He sighed as he picked invisible fuzz from his trousers. "Parker had done it again. He'd been taking liberties with funds that weren't his, hedging bets, losing millions. As before, Parker took no responsibility, nor could he be bothered with the consequences incurred by others."

"Oh no," I groaned, "who was affected this time, more investors with privately-funded recipients?"

Charlie shook his head. "It's not something I'm willing to discuss yet. I'm sure there will be rumblings in the media before long, though I'm hoping there will be a resolution for the absentee funds and perhaps even another backer." I tried pressing him but he simply raised a hand before continuing, "Like I said, if it's meant to come out, it will soon enough. No offense, but I don't need your best friend pushing things along."

"Really, Charlie?" My temper flared at his insinuation, especially when Leah wasn't present to defend herself. "So it's ok to have a crack reporter at your disposal when it's convenient, when it benefits you directly, but when it comes to something that actually matters to someone else—"

"No, AJ, that is not what I meant," he gritted out, his own emotions rising. "It's just…better for the parties involved to keep things under wraps for the time-being. Got it?"

I shook my head. I did not understand, nor did I buy it. With Charlie, it was never that simple. He was withholding pertinent details, for reasons other than the ones he was intent on convincing me of. Why was that?

It was clear he wasn't going to budge on the subject, so I shifted the conversation, "So, based upon what you've told me, Parker could have had a sizable list of haters. Anyone you like for president of that club?"

"No, Detective Jackson, I couldn't even begin to narrow down that list." I didn't appreciate his sarcasm but managed to keep a snarky retort from escaping. "And murder?" He shook his head. "I don't see anyone, no matter what list they're on, going to that extreme."

"Desperate times breed desperate measures, Charlie."

"True statement, but I'd hardly fit into that category."

"And yet, here you sit."

"Harsh, AJ, harsh. But again, true," he conceded. "Still, I can't believe someone would be spiteful enough to kill him, much less go to the effort of framing me while doing it." Charlie appeared surprised, if not miffed. Clearly, it hadn't occurred to him he might be considered as unseemly of a character as Parker had been. Given the current situation and his new accommodations, I decided it wasn't the best time to rub salt in the wound.

"So, do you have an alibi?"

Charlie frowned, shaking his head from side to side. He studied the two-way before responding, his tone low, "Not one that can be validated. Unfortunately, the security cameras show me exiting the building shortly before Parker was attacked."

"What about the cameras inside the parking garage?"

"They weren't on."

"Isn't that a bit of a coincidence?"

Charlie's pressed his lips together in a tight line. "Not really."

"Seriously, *that's* all you've got?" My voice raised an octave.

I hadn't meant it to, but we were talking about murder charges. Argh, sometimes I wanted to strangle him myself.

"It wasn't a coincidence because I was the one who took them offline."

I groaned and knocked my head against the table. The icy steel of its structure did nothing to tamper the burn of frustration. "Charlie Wilson. Why. Would. You. Do. That? What were you thinking? Weren't you concerned about the lack of security?"

He shrugged. "I own the building, so I can do whatever I want, whenever I want." As if that was an acceptable answer. I popped my head up and gave him my best evil eye, letting him know as much.

"I was making some…adjustments in the parking garage I didn't want to have recorded. I wasn't finished by the time the party started, so I left the cameras off."

I couldn't read his expression, but my gut told me that he was lying, again. Charlie didn't make adjustments to anything himself, he had people for that. So what would have been so important he'd needed to turn those cameras off?

"Big Bess needed to be fixed?" I tossed out.

The question threw him. "Huh?"

"The adjustments you were making in the parking garage, they were on Big Bess?"

"Oh, yeah, um, new door locks." New door locks? Riiight. Now Charlie was a mechanic?

"Interesting." Charlie noted my sarcastic response, but continued to scrutinize the invisible fuzz on his pants. "So, where did you go after the party? Did anyone see you?"

He blew out a deep breath, still refusing to make eye contact. "I decided the clean up could wait until later, so I let you, Leah, Arch, the caterers and the rest of the staff leave. Basically, I just wanted to get some fresh air. I had a few cocktails at the party after seeing Parker, so I went for a walk to clear my mind. I did so on occasion but honestly, not that often.

"After the party, I found myself heading down to the lake, toward the walking path. It was quiet, given the hour, which provided me the solace I sought. Of course, it was also dark out so in the areas where the pathway was unlit, I tripped probably a half a dozen times." He chuckled to himself. "It was my own fault for asking the bartender for such a liberal pour. Anyway, despite the darkness—and my clumsiness—I kept walking, until I'd lost all track of time. It's funny, at the time I was pleased I never crossed paths with another person. Now, not so much."

I muffled a curse, but noting the amused look Charlie was giving me, realized I had not been successful in keeping the sailor to myself. My Borax days long over, I made a mental note to run to Costco. If this conversation was any indication, it looked like I'd soon need a generous supply.

"Which direction did you walk along the lake?"

"Um, east toward Scottsdale Road. Like I said, I don't walk the pathway very often. I prefer Tempe Beach Park or just going to the gym."

Of course he did. Charlie had dedicated an entire floor in his building to a state-of-the-art workout room for himself and the other residents. And yet, he'd chosen that night to go for a walk along the lake—in the direction and roughly around the time Parker had been dumped—possibly even passed the same location where his body had been recovered.

He had also conveniently disarmed the security cameras that would have captured the events in the parking garage that night—cameras that would have eliminated him as a suspect and identified Parker's killer in the process. One thing was for sure, Charlie had worked himself into a real cluster, if not the perfect setup.

"I heard they towed my car to their facility." He nodded toward the two-way as I pursed my lips. Leave it to Charlie to be concerned about possessions at a time like this. "Do you think they will at least attempt to be careful with her?"

Honestly, I didn't know.

"They are professionals, not a bunch of hooligans hauling her off to their seedy chop shop. Short answer is yes, I think the police will do what is necessary to retrieve the evidence they need in a respectful and cautious manner." It was the best response I could offer him given the circumstances. For whatever it was worth, Charlie seemed to appreciate that.

Looking at my watch, I realized our time was nearly up. I mentally kicked myself for not getting more from Charlie, though there were some details he'd purposely kept close to the vest. Some pretty important ones, I feared. As if reading my mind, the door opened and Detective Sanchez's massive presence filled its frame.

"Time's up, Wilson. Hope you two had a nice chat."

I smirked. He would know.

I turned to Charlie, disappointed any last minute questions had eluded me and noticed he'd carefully tucked his emotions away as he returned to his stiff, unreadable demeanor that resembled a figure in the House of Wax. Perhaps this was how Charlie survived the world of the six foot by eight foot cell, by letting his thoughts and feelings slide away. I wondered if Human Charlie would return on my next visit, or if he would even make it that long.

As Sanchez and another officer led him out, Charlie paused briefly. "I appreciate you coming, AJ. When the chips finally fall, it's good to know who your friends are and who'll be there to help you pick up the pieces." A flicker of Human Charlie flashed in his eyes, gone just as quickly as he disappeared through the doorway. I felt a pang of sadness, mixed with curiosity. Were we indeed, friends?

Sanchez returned a moment later. "He's right, you know. You

are a good friend. Doesn't seem a guy like Wilson would have many, so you can imagine my surprise when not one, but two of you showed up."

"What?" I blinked. "Two of us? Leah hasn't seen Charlie yet."

"Not Ms. Campbell. Natalie Ingram, the deceased's girl-friend." You could have blown me over. "She was here yesterday and insisted on being the first to see him after we were done with him." He shook his head. "It's an interesting dynamic those two have."

Sanchez didn't elaborate, leaving me to wonder why Charlie hadn't mentioned it. I thought about our conversation, having to drag crumbs out of him and the odd shifts in personality. Had Charlie fed me the details I'd wanted? Or the ones he wanted me to believe? Had the new, more humane Charlie been real, or simply created for my benefit?

Perhaps I had never known Charlie Wilson at all.

CHAPTER NINE

As they shuffled him back to his luxury suite, he realized he was fortunate to have friends like AJ. He was also painfully aware he hadn't always been the greatest friend in return. Heck, who was he kidding? He'd never been a decent friend, much less a good one. Did he even know how? People who were kind and selfless like AJ and Leah seemed to and still they befriended him, even given his shortcomings in that department. He hadn't ever taken others into consideration. People were disposable commodities who lived and breathed to cater to his needs, not beings with feelings, thoughts and needs of their own. No, he'd never been a true friend. AJ was more of one than he deserved.

He plopped onto the threadbare cot—one that probably had never seen better days—and was rewarded with creaky springs that irritatingly jabbed him in the backside. He sighed, it was another reminder he was not a guest but a ward of his accommodations.

The first reality check emerged as he was unceremoniously collected from his penthouse, stuffed into the back of an ancient and extremely pungent smelling police cruiser and escorted to the station. As they rode in stuffy, unairconditioned silence, beads of sweat quickly turned to drips, stinging his eyes as they continued their journey over his cheeks and onto the thighs of his Armani slacks. Given their smug profiles, the detectives appeared to be enjoying his growing discomfort.

Charlie sniffed, crinkling his nose as he tried to identify the source of the stench permeating the cracked, well-used interior—a cross between a men's locker room and the dance clubs Parker liked to frequent in Scottsdale. He managed to refrain from cringing as he continued to examine his surroundings, which were devoid of any personalization. The only extravagance he observed was the hot pink air fresheners—some hideous floral combo—that failed miserably at keeping the odors at bay. Though the cruiser had been recently vacuumed, as evident by the lines in the plucky-looking carpet and was free from trash or debris, he could see the dirt and grime—*wait, was that mold?*—and some other gunk infesting the crevices of the seats and window sills. Best not to touch anything more than necessary, and even those body parts might need a Brillo later. To date, it had been the longest ten minutes of his life. He hoped it wouldn't be the first of many.

Back in his cell, Charlie shuddered at the memory. The irony was not lost on him. The car ride had been just that—the first of many of the longest minutes of his existence. He was disgusted by his own vanity—that the fear of others knowing he'd been arrested superseded that of what the police thought he'd done. Well, his selfishness had certainly caught up with him two-fold, hadn't it?

It was the reason he'd spent the better part of the day marveling at the fact people like AJ existed. They were so different from him and from Parker. They actually cared when he was in trouble or hurting. He wondered if he would have done the same had the situation been reversed, and shrugged, already knowing the answer. It was a futile, senseless exercise.

Still, AJ had come. It didn't matter if she believed in his innocence. Or did it? He surprised himself—yes, it did. It definitely mattered what AJ thought. After digesting their conversation, he realized he hadn't done much to help himself in that arena. Still, she'd left knowing he was innocent...of killing Parker, at least. As for his complicity in other matters—he was no fool—he'd seen the judgment in her eyes, no matter how hard she'd fought to mask it. She was only human, after all.

Again, he chuckled briefly at the irony, becoming somber as he reflected on how poorly he'd treated her over the years. No matter how decent and generous she had been, he'd taken and never asked what he could do in return. She'd stuck around because of who and how she was. He felt something odd when he was around her, other than the annoyance she spurned in him—admiration, perhaps? She was a determined soul, with insurmountable resolve and loyalty...fierce loyalty. For a moment, he felt something new. Shame. He had desperately wanted to break down and ask her for help.

He put his head in his sweating palms when it hit him—AJ was already helping him, whether she realized it or not.

I arrived home, feeling no better than I'd left though admittedly, no worse, either. I'd gotten the opportunity to visit with Charlie, which had been my intention—only now, I had far more questions than answers. It had been surprising to learn to Natalie had not only gone to see him at the jail, but insisted on being the first in line to do so. Had she been there to deem his innocence? Or guilt?

I was mulling things over when Leah entered the kitchen, carrying a jar of chunky peanut butter in one hand and a bag of plain M&M's in the other, with Nicoh in close pursuit. One glance at his nose told me that she'd been sharing her snack with him, but it was Leah's wide-eyed expression that confirmed it.

Apparently, my BFF had been so engrossed in snackapaloosa, she hadn't heard me enter the house. Feeding a large canine can be so distracting and noisy. Realizing she was busted, she gave up trying to hide the evidence, instead making an animated show of screwing the lid back on the half-empty jar.

"You seriously didn't—" I pointed at the bag she had placed on the counter.

"I'm not a complete dunce. Of course I didn't feed him the M&M's," she scoffed, noticing my gaze had moved to the peanut butter, "and no, I did not allow him to eat directly out of the jar. I put a smidge on his nose to stop the howling. I swear my ears were starting to bleed."

"Well, I'm happy to know I won't need to run out and purchase a people-only jar, aside from the one we already reserve for people who double-dip or allow crumbs to get mixed in, that is."

"Eww, I hate that," Leah replied.

"Totally gross. So, did the peanut butter on the nose trick actually work?"

"Yup, Nicoh was so busy lapping at it, he forgot his reason for being noisy in the first place."

"You mean nosy, don't you?" As expected, our abrupt laughter caused Nicoh to resume his howling.

"How'd the visit with Charlie go?" she asked after we managed to get him calmed back down, though no further peanut butter was traumatized in the process.

"It was interesting, to say the least." I filled her in on our conversation and how Sanchez revealed I hadn't been Charlie's only visitor.

"Wow, Natalie must have connections or something. Charlie was tied up—quite literally—until you and I left yesterday. She must have someone on the inside keeping her up to date."

"Someone like Vargas, wouldn't you say?"

"Maybe…" Absently, I reached into the bag of M&M's while Leah proceeded to pluck the brown ones out. When she placed them on the counter, I tilted my head in Nicoh's direction, noting the saliva dripping in anticipation as he focused on the movement of our hands. And of course, the unattended M&M's. Leah sighed and scooped the stray morsels back into the bag, while Nicoh grumbled.

"It wasn't Vargas, though. I'm pretty sure he's never met Natalie."

"Oh?" I raised my eyebrows.

"Argh, get your mind out of the M&M's bag. Just so you know, it came up when I asked him about the guests who'd attended Charlie's White Party—whether any of them had any prior run-ins with the law. The answer was no, other than a few drunk and disorderlies, no assault, battery—"

"Or murder."

"Not one of them."

"So, what do you make of Natalie visiting Charlie then?"

"Not sure. Like you said, maybe she needed her own confirmation whether Charlie could have killed Parker. Prior to that, I would have guessed the thought wouldn't have occurred to her, especially not after the way she glommed onto him at the lake."

I nodded my head. "That was odd. Even Charlie appeared to think so. You remember the look on his face? Certainly didn't seem like they had much interaction before that. In fact, the only thing they had in common was Parker. Well, and Greg, I guess."

"I wonder if she knew about their business challenges. You would think if she had, she would've made a point of staying as far away from the two of them—especially Parker—as she could."

"Yeah, but you know what they say—keep your friends close…" I didn't need to finish that thought—there was only way to know for sure—we had to go to the source.

* * *

After a quick phone call, we learned Natalie was volunteering at one of the long term care facilities near Old Town Scottsdale that afternoon. She eagerly agreed to meet us at Los Olivos after her shift, a nearby family-owned Mexican restaurant and one of our local favorites. In addition to being a well-known historical landmark, they had the most delicious fresh-squeezed lime margaritas this side of the border. Don't get me wrong—Leah and I weren't trying to get the goods out of Natalie by plying her with alcohol, we simply figured a refreshing beverage couldn't hurt.

Just to be sure, we tested the pitcher Manuel had graciously brought out as we munched on chips, salsa and hot sauce while waiting in the outdoor patio area. As if on cue, our snacking prompted Nicoh to moan like a belligerent moose as he showcased his displeasure for the other diners. We received several understanding nods, since many of them were also accompanied by their canine companions. Thankfully, Natalie arrived before he started in on the full-blown howling, forcing them to change their minds.

"Hey ladies!" She placed a supersized Hermes bag on a seat of its own before carefully sitting in the chair next to it. I handed her a margarita, which she drained in one noisy gulp.

"Delicious!" she exclaimed, pushing her glass forward for a refill. Leah complied and gave me a quick glance, neither of us sure whether we should be impressed, or frightened.

Noting our bewildered expressions, Natalie blushed. "Sorry... rough day. We lost one of our residents today. Chalk it up to being emotionally drained." She studied the ice cubes in her margarita while pushing the lime around with her thumb.

"We are truly sorry, Natalie," Leah replied, while I nodded. "Your day must have been long all around—I'm sure you've heard about Charlie, too?"

"Yeah, I visited him at the jail. It was awful." She shuddered. "I don't care what the police think they have on him, there's no way he killed Parker, or had anything to do with the whole messy incident." Messy incident? That was an interesting way to phrase it, like Charlie had been accused of spilling red wine on Parker's white suit. Natalie inhaled before taking another large swig of margarita. At this rate, we'd need to get her a separate pitcher.

I made a mental note to grab her car keys before pressing her on her last comment. "You seem pretty sure about Charlie's innocence."

Natalie wagged her finger at me and snickered. "Pah-leeze! It's totally not Charlie's style, nor would it have occurred to him. Now Parker, on the other hand, wouldn't have hesitated to elimi-nate anyone or anything in his way." She drained her glass and shakily reached for the pitcher. It slid precariously close to the edge of the table and would have made its way onto the ground had I not managed to catch it. Rather than putting it back, I nonchalantly scooted it to the opposite side of the table and made a show of moving the chips and salsa into its place, hoping it would encourage her to eat a few.

While I maneuvered bowls, Leah kept the conversation moving forward, "What do you think Charlie and Parker were having a row about the night of the White Party?"

I stifled a snort. That was Leah for you—no sense beating around the bush when you can just cut it down. And, another reason I was the photographer and she was the reporter—I did all my work behind the scenes while she preferred being front and center and in your face. She was darn good at it too. Like pit bull good.

An indescribable expression passed over Natalie's pert face as she smoothed her immaculate pantsuit with one hand, gripping the margarita glass with the other. "Oh, you know how those two were. I'm sure Parker had his mitts on something Charlie wanted."

"Is that what Charlie told you?" I kept my tone even, careful not to push her.

"Charlie didn't tell me squat. Parker either"—she giggled —"before he died, of course." She nervously clinked her ice cubes.

Before Natalie requested another refill, Leah distracted her, "So this had nothing to with the money Parker lost?"

I glanced at her. Risky, Leah, very risky. She raised a finger behind the table to let me know she knew what she was doing. It certainly ignited something. Natalie's death grip turned to white knuckles as anger flared, but vanished as she carefully tucked it away with the rest of her emotions.

"I wouldn't know anything about that," she replied flatly, still obsessed with torturing those poor ice cubes. "It was between Charlie and Parker—only Charlie and Parker. Parker never shared the specifics of his business dealings with me and I never asked. Our relationship worked best that way."

It sounded like a relationship of convenience more than one of love or respect. Not that it surprised me, anything more would have been inconvenient for Parker. No wonder Natalie seemed all over the charts when it came to coping with her boyfriend's death.

She changed the subject before we could ask her additional questions about their relationship. "On a cheerier note, I was able to raise enough money this past month to add new rehabilitation and counseling services at a few of the facilities."

As Natalie prattled on, we listened with interest. It was truly inspiring to hear about the work she was doing. I noticed the more engrossed we were, the more she animated she became. Clearly, she was proud of what she'd accomplished and loved to receive praise. I seriously doubted Parker had provided her with much positive reinforcement, which explained why she so eagerly ate up any attention she was given.

Speaking of eating, both Leah and I noticed how little she'd had, given the amount of liquor she'd imbibed. It was curious, I hadn't seen her drink any more while we talked, but somehow she'd managed to put away almost another entire pitcher. A solid liquid diet wasn't great for anyone, especially not a tiny little thing like Natalie. I was about to suggest some other appetizer or food options but she glanced at her watch and suddenly launched out of her seat.

"Oh, I've gotta jet. I have plans this evening."

Quickly thanking us, she collected her massive handbag—which made her look like a six-year-old after raiding her mother's closet—blew a few air kisses and started to leave when I called after her, "Hey, Nat—why don't you hold up for a sec? We'll pay our tab and share a taxi with you."

She waved a hand at me. "Thanks, but I've already got a ride. You didn't actually think I'd risk ending up like Parker, did you?" She giggled, giving us a quick wink as she departed.

Once she was at a safe distance, Leah slid from her seat and ventured after our tipsy friend. She returned moments later, frowning.

"What?"

"Well, Natalie's designated driver picked her up." An odd expression crossed her face. "Driving a blue Audi R8." Parker's car.

"One more thing—the driver was female." I gave her a long look. Parker had no female relatives. In fact, there wasn't anyone who should have been driving his car. Leah nodded in return, having come to the same conclusion. I looked longingly at the empty margarita pitcher. Like Alice, down the rabbit hole we would go.

CHAPTER TEN

Leah hadn't seen more than a wisp of the driver's auburn hair as Natalie hopped into the Audi and the two hightailed it out of there. Fortunately, they hadn't caught her lurking either. She'd been careful to press herself against the building, hiding in the shadows as she attempted to spy on them. Compliments of her reporter's repertoire, I guessed.

Natalie had been hanging out at Parker's house when we'd previously seen her. Neither of us was sure whether she'd continued taking up residence there once his body had been recovered. What perplexed us was—other than Charlie and Natalie—Parker really had no other friends or immediate family. So who would have taken possession of his car so soon?

Manuel stopped by our table, an equally curious look spanning his face. "The margaritas were not to your liking?" Leah and I exchanged glances after looking at the empty pitcher in front of us.

"Manuel, what would give you that impression?" I asked, rocking it back and forth.

He shook his head and pointed to a large plastic cup, the type found at any convenience store, leaning against one of the table legs. In it was a watered-down version of the limey goodness from our previously full pitcher.

"Err, our friend had a hole in her glass?" Leah offered as the confused server picked up the cup and peered at the contents.

Hole in her facade was more like it. I wasn't sure whether I should have been relieved to learn Natalie wasn't a lush, or annoyed because she'd played us for ninnies. For Manuel's purposes, however, we simply shrugged and added a few extra dollars to the tab, hoping he would chalk it up to a bunch of silly girls letting off steam after work. He narrowed his gaze, but seemed appeased and thanked us for our patronage, though didn't mention looking forward to seeing us next time, as was typically his custom.

As he retreated, Leah grumbled under her breath, "Great, now he thinks we're either drunk or a bunch of Fruity Pebbles."

"After that carefully scripted act, why do you think she risked leaving the cup?"

"Who knows, but it does mean that Natalie fed us those details…on purpose."

"Girl's good—I'll give her that."

"Indeed. I never even saw her hand leave the table, much less realize she was spinning a tale even taller than Krystle's and Alexis' shoulder pads."

Rolling my eyes at her campy *Dynasty* reference, I tapped my chin. "Does make you wonder, doesn't it—with what other forms of deception is our girl-next-door acquainted?"

"Oh, come on, AJ. Faking drunk is a far cry from *Impale and Dump Your Boyfriend: A Modern Girl's Guide to Giving a Jerk the Literal Heave-Ho*." I winced at her choice of words, glad we were standing on the sidewalk waiting for our cab, safely out of Manuel's earshot.

"That's not what I'm saying. I think Natalie wanted to give us selective information with regards to Parker and Charlie. I have no idea why she felt the need to concoct such a farce. Maybe she felt guilty talking negatively about Parker?"

"I guess. You notice how she hasn't talked about him—I mean *really* talked about him—the way a girlfriend would? Not since that day at the lake, anyway. I don't know, it seems weird considering they'd been in a relationship for more than a couple of years."

"Maybe things had cooled down. Or, maybe it was just a relationship of convenience all along and it's her way of dealing with his death. We didn't spend much time with her after Parker was found. Maybe she's been going through all the phases of grief and we just haven't seen it."

"That's a lot of maybes," Leah commented. "One thing is for sure."

She had me intrigued. "What's that?"

She inhaled a deep breath. "The only way Charlie's getting out of this mess is if you and I figure out who killed Parker."

* * *

We contemplated the situation in silence on the cab ride home while Nicoh nestled between us—yes, there are pet-friendly cabs —his head on my lap and tail in Leah's, oblivious to the drama unfolding. Knowing Leah, she had already devised some sort of scheme in that devilish brain of hers. Before I had a chance to press her for details, my phone rang. Ramirez.

"AJ, I've got some news about Winslow Clark." I hadn't been expecting that but quickly told him I was putting him on speaker-phone so Leah could join us. "I talked to some friends at the FBI, who talked to their contacts, who in turn confirmed Clark and his father, Theodore Winslow, are in two separate, secured facilities. Both are in single-occupant cells for twenty-three hours a day— with one for exercise—under armed guard. Neither has had outside contact, other than with their court-appointed counsel, which they've both denounced. No incoming or outgoing mail. No visitors. No calls. Nothing. Time essentially stopped for them the minute they stepped into federal custody, meaning—"

"Neither was directly responsible for the messages," Leah finished.

"That is correct."

"Couldn't they have minions on the outside doing their dirty work, ones they were in contact with before they were captured and incarcerated?" she asked.

"Minions?" Despite the gravity of the conversation, I had to stifle a snort when I heard the confusion in Ramirez's voice.

"Yeah, minions. Haven't you heard of *Despicable Me*?" Leah asked, incredulous.

"Despicable...what? What are you talking about?" Ramirez's tone grew terse so I gestured for Leah to zip it, for all the good it did.

"Minions, Detective, as in flunkies, followers, groupies, cohorts—"

"Point taken, Leah," I growled.

"She does have a point." Ramirez added. "Just because Clark and his father claimed to have worked off the grid for all those years doesn't mean they did so alone. They could have built up a small following, a group of people to be their eyes and ears whenever and wherever they were needed."

"Sounds risky," I commented, "especially considering how paranoid and arrogant those two are. I'm not sure they'd trust just anyone with their dirty work."

"True enough," Ramirez replied, "but you'd be surprised what kind of people are out there on the fringe. Clark and Winslow may have found themselves a few true believers. Either one of them could easily incite a loyal following. Anyway, I've got another friend looking into the source of your messages. He may not be able to extract much, but for everyone's sanity it's worth a shot."

"Another FBI friend?"

"Let's just say a friend with connections."

I looked at Leah and shrugged. "So, in the meantime, is there anything you need us to do?"

"Just go about things as you normally would. The important thing is to not change your behavior, meaning don't purposely engage him. Don't reply to the texts. Let the voicemails run their course and forward whatever you get to me. Hopefully by tomorrow, we'll have more on him than we have today."

Leah scrunched her face. "I don't know, Detective. That advice sounds more reactive than proactive. Considering you and your friend are making AJ here a guinea pig, I'm not sure I like it." I voiced a similar opinion.

"Gals, please. Do not do anything rash. Let my guy look into it. If something comes up, you'll be the first to know. For once, please do what I ask." It was the non-detective part of him that was asking.

"Well, Leah, he did say please," I let out an exaggerated sigh for his benefit as we grinned at one another.

"You two," Ramirez growled.

Leah smirked at the phone. "Now that we've gotten Clark out of the way, we have a few interesting items of our own to share. AJ, why don't you tell the detective about your conversation with Charlie?"

I stared, unaware we'd decided to share, but had no recourse other than to shake my head, collect my thoughts and give Ramirez a quick rundown of the visit. Once finished, Leah jumped in and started telling him about cocktail hour with Natalie. I threw my hands up, beyond exasperation. She made no bones about laughing at me as she gave Ramirez a play-by-play of Natalie's bizarre behavior while masking her alcohol consumption.

After several moments of deafening silence, Ramirez spoke, "I know the way the two of you think, especially when you have your minds set on something. I can't begin to emphasize this enough—do not get involved in your own investigation—let TPD do their job. I'm warning you, if you interfere, I'll arrest you both myself.

"Besides, you're off-base about Natalie Ingram. She's got an iron-clad alibi and that's all I'm going to say about that. So leave it alone," he sighed into the phone. "I've got to get back to it. Stay out of trouble, both of you."

Even before we'd heard the connection break, we had no intention of following Ramirez's advice. Instead, we plotted the next steps of Operation Charlie. Sure, it was amateur hour and we knew it, but we also knew the cops had enough evidence to convince the County Attorney to lock Charlie away for the rest of his life, or worse.

Leah scribbled furiously on her trusty notepad. "We should see if we can get a look at the security videos from Charlie's building," she mumbled absently to herself, nibbling on a non-existent nail. She glanced up to catch me looking at her. "What?"

"Nothing," I replied, smiling warmly. "I'm just glad I have my partner-in-crime working with me on this."

"You know, I'm gonna remind you of that when Ramirez tosses us in lockup," she teased.

"Duly noted. Looking at the security footage is a good plan, provided TPD hasn't already confiscated all of it."

"Well, we know who to ask." Though dreading the conversation, we'd reluctantly agreed to have a chat with Arch. At the very least, we hoped he'd give us access to the information we needed. He was also on the list of partygoers, so we were technically killing two birds with one stone. Err, poor choice of words.

Anyway, considering Arch held more than a couple of the puzzle pieces we needed, a little visit to Charlie's assistant went straight to the top of our list.

Whether the world was ready for us or not, Operation Charlie was now underway.

* * *

Rather than calling ahead the next morning—no sense giving Arch an opportunity to escape—we checked in with Charlie's doorman, Stuart Klein.

Stu was a jovial guy, with a sharp wit and watchful eyes, cultivated from the years spent as an armored truck driver and security guard. He took his post at Charlie's building no less seriously. He was sweet and funny and knew how to make a girl blush, but if push came to shove, he wasn't someone you'd want to underestimate. He knew every trick in the book and could lay someone out flat before the devious thought had fully formed in their mind. I had often wondered how Charlie had managed to lure such a seasoned and loyal man.

Though Stu was several years Charlie's senior, he always referred to him as Mr. Wilson out of respect, whether Charlie deserved it or not. He was courteous to us as well and more than eager to watch Nicoh before Charlie allowed pets in the building. With more and more of his residents requiring companion-friendly accommodations, however, Charlie was forced to lift the ban, though his penthouse suite had been the final holdout. To this day, Nicoh was one of the few four-legged creatures to have graced the top floor, a feat that was five years in the making.

During that time, Stu and Nicoh developed quite a relationship. On the days I worked with Charlie—who knows why he needed a freelance photographer on call—Stu would share his lunch with Nicoh and tell him stories of the good old days, as though he was with his drinking buddies. Perhaps Stu took the opportunity to embellish a bit, whereas his human pals kept him in check. Either way, they were always excited to see one another, with Nicoh on his hind legs while Stu embraced him like a bear. It was endearing and a sight to see, considering Nicoh towered over the man by several inches. If Stu minded the dog slob Nicoh graced the top of his head with on each visit, he never complained.

Today was no different. Once reunited with his pal, Stu greeted us with a big smile. "Ms. Arianna, Ms. Leah, it's so nice to see you both, as always." He straightened his suit jacket and tie, tugging his cuffs down. "Terrible business about Mr. Wilson, just terrible."

"Actually, Stu, it's the reason we're here." Leah wagged her eyebrows at him conspiratorially. "We're planning on having a little…chat with Arch, to see if he remembers anything out of the ordinary the night of the White Party. And, since we're here, maybe we could ask you some questions, too?" It was always a plus to have a crack reporter on your team.

Stu nodded thoughtfully. "Mr. Wilson doesn't have many friends like you, that's for sure. If I can do something to help, then by all means, ask away. It's the least I can do."

"So you don't think he had any involvement in the murder, then?" Leah asked.

Stu gave her a sly look. "We both know Mr. Wilson, Ms. Leah, which means we both know he isn't capable of murder—not even the murder of someone as unscrupulous as Parker Harris. No, I doubt something as bawdy as cold-blooded murder would have entered his mind. Mr. Harris, on the other hand"—Stu sniffed in distaste—"would have been more amenable to something along those lines. Sorry, it's not respectful to speak ill of the dead." Leah and I nodded our understanding, though it wasn't the first time since Charlie had been arrested someone had made that observation about Parker's character.

"As for that night, I did see Mr. Harris and Ms. Ingram leave, both very alive and extremely tipsy, but neither of them returned. In fact, the only odd thing that occurred all evening was when Mr. Wilson stopped by my desk to say he was going out, but had misplaced his key card and indicated he would need me to buzz him back in.

"Like the other guests, he was a bit intoxicated so I offered to call him a taxi. He waved me off, saying he needed the fresh air and wanted to stretch his legs. As you know, he's not one for small talk nor does he go out of his way to be friendly, so I was surprised when he made a point of thanking me for my concern. In all the years I've worked for him, he's never thanked me once, so I was surprised by his sudden congeniality. In looking back, he seemed off his game—distracted, worried even."

"But not angry?" Leah prompted.

"Agitated maybe, but not angry—he rarely shows that kind of emotion. Tantrums...yes, but raging anger...no." We both nodded, quite familiar with Charlie's outbursts, which were more theatrical in nature than malicious or driven by heated emotion.

"What was he wearing when he left?" I asked.

Stu tapped his chin and chuckled. "He was wearing a white monkey suit—atrocious if you ask me—and a bit too retro for my taste." The suit both he and Parker had been wearing had indeed been retro, but it was a style that was back en vogue and both had likely known it. Whether they had planned on being triplets—with Arch in the mix—was still up in the air. Knowing Parker and Charlie, I thought not. In fact, I wouldn't have been surprised if Charlie's stylist had lost her job that night.

Stu continued. "Anyway, when I saw him, he was a bit more relaxed than usual. Shirt opened at the neck, but still very immaculate." I thought back to the only other time I had recently seen

Charlie so relaxed. It had been the morning of the party. He had been distracted then too. Something occurred to me.

"You said the neck of the shirt was open. Was he still wearing the tie?" Leah nodded, understanding the direction I was headed.

It took him longer to respond this time, "Yes, now that you mention it, he did have a tie on, hanging loose around his collar. Other than that, he looked like he was still in party mode, all the way down to his white shoes." He reached over and scratched Nicoh behind the ears.

"Was he carrying anything—like a wallet or keys?" Leah asked.

"Not that I could see, though his hands were in his trouser pockets most of the time. Of course, if he was going for a walk, I'd doubt he'd need car keys." Good point.

"Did he ever go to the garage this way?"

"No, he typically went directly from his elevator to the parking garage, so I rarely saw him." Stu squinted. "Ah, I see where you are going with this. You are trying to determine whether Mr. Wilson was attempting to create an alibi for himself the night of the party. That would be clever—very clever indeed."

Stu was right, but if we'd come to that conclusion, the police had likely done the same. Meaning, Leah and I would need to prove it hadn't been intentional—something forced Charlie off his game, causing him to be distracted, as Stu had indicated.

"What was Charlie like when he returned?" I asked.

Stuart shrugged. "He seemed the same."

"What about his clothes? Were they dirty? Disheveled in any way?"

"No, though it did seem like he had been running his hands through his hair. I know it always looks like that—you kids and your styles—but it was messier than usual." Again, I flashed back to the morning before the party, when Charlie had absently, and uncharacteristically, rubbed his hands through his hair.

"And his clothes?" Leah prompted.

"Except for the fact he wasn't wearing shoes or socks when he returned, there wasn't a spot on him."

"He was barefoot?" both Leah and I chimed at the same time, startling Stu.

"Sorry," Leah patted the man on the arm, we had been a bit shrill in our response. "You're saying he came back carrying his shoes?"

"No, he was barefoot all right, but his didn't have the shoes with him."

"Did you ask him about it?"

"I thought it was curious at the time, but it certainly wasn't my place to question him." He was right. Charlie wouldn't have taken kindly to being interrogated by his staff.

"Was he still wearing the tie?"

"That, I'm not sure about. The video should be able to confirm it one way or the other, though."

We nodded and turned our questioning back to Parker, though Stu had nothing out of the ordinary to report and his account of Parker's arrival and departure were the same as we'd previously heard. Natalie arrived early, waited for Parker and they went up to the penthouse together. What had happened to Parker once he'd left Natalie later that evening was anyone's guess.

"Did you talk to Natalie while she waited for Parker?" Leah asked.

"Yes, just small talk, mostly about her work. Turns out she volunteers at one of the hospitals where my wife works as respiratory therapist. Ms. Ingram knew my wife. Sweet girl, that one."

"Did she seem fidgety at all, or impatient? It was our understanding she and Parker chose to drive separately because she'd expected to be the one running late that evening."

Stu shook his head. "No, she didn't seem either. Said Mr. Harris had some last minute business meeting or something or other. Other than that, there's not much more to tell. Mr. Harris showed up and they took the elevator up to the penthouse. He was never very friendly." Stu scrunched his nose, clearly not a fan of the late Parker Harris. We nodded sympathetically. Parker hadn't been particularly cordial to anyone.

"And when they left?"

"Like I mentioned, lit but not wasted. I overheard Parker calling her a cab. She didn't seem totally thrilled about it. Not about the cab, but that he wasn't taking it with her. She was worried he might try to drive himself home. I overheard him say he wouldn't but she didn't seem convinced. I didn't actually see the cab arrive—it would've taken me too far away from my post —though I assumed she's taken it home and he…well, I guess we won't ever know." I glanced at Leah—that was one point we disagreed with Stu on—*someone* knew.

She swiftly changed the subject, "We understand there are several cameras positioned around the building."

Stu nodded. "Normally, I wouldn't share this type of information with anyone other than the police and that's only if they supply a warrant, but seeing how they've managed to get this whole thing backwards, I think Mr. Wilson would approve. Especially considering you're the only two who seem to care what happens to him and are interested in doing some real investigating."

"Thank you, Stu, though I'll be honest with you. I'm not sure what we're doing could technically be construed as 'investigating,' in anyone's book," I replied somberly.

Stu chuckled, waving off my comment. "Nonetheless, you're trying to do something positive for Mr. Wilson, which makes you the good guys…err, gals, in my book. Anyway, the cameras are currently placed here at the entrance, at the entrance to the elevator and throughout the parking garage."

"Charlie told me about the ones he recently installed in the penthouse," Leah added.

"Yup, he did that at my suggestion, right after he mentioned bringing his assistant back on. You know, for good measure." He winked but his expression was serious.

"You don't trust Arch?" I asked.

"It's not so much about trust as it is about putting Mr. Wilson's interests first. Now if you're asking me if I would personally trust the kid, the answer is no. Don't get me wrong, he appears harmless, but he's way too shifty for my liking. Typically, that doesn't mean anything by itself, but sometimes you just know to keep your eyes peeled when something feels hinky. You know what I mean?" We nodded that we did. "Anyway, if it had been me, I wouldn't have hired him back. Period. Now this happens and he's installed himself in the penthouse, doing who knows what. It doesn't sit right with me."

"Uh, you mean he's *living* in the penthouse?" Leah managed to ask as she did an Oscar-worthy job of masking her shock.

"Yup, he moved himself in the day the police took Mr. Wilson and hasn't been out since. My relief, Maynard, confirmed it."

I wondered what the heck Arch had been doing up there all this time. And more importantly, did Charlie know? "Wait…can't you see what he's up there doing using the cameras Charlie just installed?"

Stu shook his head. "Mr. Wilson wanted sole access to the penthouse's footage. Oh, his tech guy has access, too, but I don't know who *he* is. In fact, Mr. Wilson, the techie and I are probably the only ones, other than the two of you, who know about those cameras." Meaning TPD still hadn't gotten access to them, much less were even aware they existed.

Argh, had I known that, I would have asked Charlie when I'd seen him. Perhaps Leah and I could convince him to let someone —preferably us—monitor that feed in his absence? Certainly, he'd be able to see it was in his best interest once he learned Arch had been camping out in his penthouse, right? For now, all we could hope for was the next best thing.

"Stu, any chance we could have copies made of the footage you do have access to?" I asked.

"Sure, I can get you dups of the videos TPD took. No matter what people think of him, Mr. Wilson has always been doggedly thorough, and had the foresight to have second and third copies made and stored offsite. I'll make arrangements to have them brought over while you two are up chatting with Arch."

"You are truly a sweetheart, Stu. If you weren't already taken…" Leah gushed.

"Now, now, Ms. Leah, don't you let my wife hear you say that," the doorman teased. "She may just let you have me."

CHAPTER ELEVEN

Stu warned us Arch had access to the building's security feed, so we weren't surprised to find him waiting as we stepped off the elevator and into Charlie's penthouse. He'd probably been watching us from the comfort of his laptop all along. I hoped there was no audio, otherwise we were in for a short conversation. It did, however, make me wonder how secret the cameras *inside* the penthouse were—if Leah had found out about them, perhaps Arch had too? I fought the urge to look around but the instant he turned away, both Leah and I were craning our necks in awkward angles. Arch scowled when he swung back to face us, clearly inconvenienced by our intrusion.

"Why are you here?" His upper lip twitched, a cross between a smirk and a snarl. Billy Idol he was not.

Annoyed by his attitude, I quickly stepped toward him, closing the distance between us. The movement caught Arch off-guard and he staggered back a step as I continued to invade his space.

"Is that a rhetorical question, Arch?" My voice came out like sweet tea, thick and sugary, borderline diabetic. "Or are you just pretending to be a complete dolt? Because I'm pretty sure you already know the answer."

Leah and Nicoh had closed ranks and we faced him, three abreast, a united front. Or, more accurately, two cranky chicks and one ravenous canine, the latter of which was currently looking at Arch's legs like they were the last chicken wings on Earth. Temporarily subdued, Arch bowed his head in resignation.

"Now that we're all on the same page, we've just got one question for you. Are you going to help us get Charlie out of this mess, or what?" I crooked my eyebrow at him, a hint of malice in my tone.

After a moment, Arch sighed and to show his concession, shuffled to the open living room and motioned for us to sit. Leah nodded at me, but kept her poker face intact. We were both aware giving Arch any leeway would be a mistake. If we wanted compliance, we needed to maintain control of the situation, which in this case meant keeping the tension high.

Arch slumped into a modern, uncomfortable looking chair as far away from us as the space permitted. We selected our own seats and once settled, noticed he'd been keeping the penthouse tidy in Charlie's absence, just the way his boss would have liked it. The only addition to the stark decor was an enormous bouquet of vibrant purple orchids, artfully composed in a striking crystal vase.

Arch caught me admiring the display and elaborated, "I thought they might add a splash of color, improve the vibe... given all the negativity that's transpired the past few days." I nodded though I wasn't sure who, other than Arch, would have been around to enjoy them.

We sat for a few moments in awkward silence until Arch spoke. "In case you were wondering, I don't think Charlie killed Parker." Arch's statement may have effectively sliced through the tension, but it was his resolve that surprised me the most. "I don't have any proof and I'm betting neither of you do either. But we all know Charlie…and well, he couldn't have done it."

Pausing to survey our reactions, he exhaled deeply before continuing, "What I do know is Charlie let me go the night of the party immediately after the last guest left. He said the clean up could wait until later." He shrugged. "I was surprised. It was so unlike him to put things off. It had been a long day though, so I wasn't about to question him. As I got onto the elevator, he asked me to be in at my usual time. I didn't think anything more of it until he was arrested."

"What do you know about Charlie and Parker's relationship over the past few months?" Leah asked him casually.

"I assume you, like everyone else, noticed something was brewing between them at the White Party. I figured it had to be business-related, though recently it seemed like Charlie was trying to distance himself from Parker."

"Distance, such as…" I prompted.

"Charlie called Parker less, routinely ignored Parker's calls, even Parker himself. He avoided going to places and events where Parker would be and even went as far as having me tell Parker he wasn't here when he'd stop by. Stuff like that." He tapped his chin. "He did, however, talk to Natalie on occasion, even though he suspected Parker had put her up to it."

Leah snorted. "Parker had his girlfriend keeping tabs on Charlie? That's rich."

"Does seem pretty desperate, especially for Parker," I added, before turning to Arch. "When was the last time Parker came to see Charlie?"

"Hmm, it had to have been at least a couple of weeks before the party."

"And Charlie turned him away?"

"Actually, no. On that day, he agreed to see Parker. They went into the atrium and ten minutes later, Parker came back out, ignored me and left. Of course, that was nothing new. Parker always treated me like crap."

"Other than ignoring you, how did he appear as he was leaving?" I asked. "And how about Charlie, what was he like?"

"Hard to say with Parker, he was always annoyed about something. That day was no different. But like I said, he didn't speak to me. He wasn't bursting with joy, that's for sure." Arch shrugged. "Charlie was definitely more moody than usual after Parker's visit, but didn't say a word about it. Instead, he mumbled something about an errand and left. He didn't return by the time I had wrapped up for the day and when I arrived the following morning, he was back to his normal self. I'm sure you know what Charlie's 'normal' is like." He gave us a small, sad smile.

Honestly, I couldn't imagine working for Charlie full-time, much less as his assistant. Still, it was hard to sympathize with Arch, who was clearly reaping more from the situation than he was letting on. Mirroring my own thoughts, Leah rolled her eyes before changing the subject.

"What happened to the clothes Charlie wore the night of the White Party?"

"Err, I don't know. I assumed they went to the cleaners, as they normally did."

"You didn't handle that for Charlie?" I asked, genuinely curious. I certainly hadn't meant to imply anything and was surprised when Arch's eyes narrowed, letting a glimpse of his usual haughty attitude slip though.

"No, I did not *handle* Charlie's laundry. He had...has a service for that." He gritted through his teeth, barely managing to keep the snarkiness at bay.

Honestly, I hadn't intended to strike a nerve and had bigger fish to fry, so I quickly played it off. "Oh, right. Was it a scheduled laundry service?"

"Yeah, they came every day. I typically checked them in, collected the delivered items and handed the new ones off." Arch's feathers started to smooth and his talons were now safely retracted, though I had to bite my lip to keep from pointing out point that he actually did handle his boss' laundry.

Leah noted my amusement and intercepted, "So they came the day after the party to collect the previous day's clothes, which included the suit Charlie wore to the party?"

"I guess so, but they must have come early that day or maybe I was busy doing something else, because I never saw them."

"Did you ask Charlie about it?" Leah asked.

"No, by that time it was too late and everything happened so fast. All of sudden there were police everywhere. Then Charlie was arrested." He shook his head. "It was a nightmare. I forgot all about the laundry service after that, until you asked me just now. You think there's something there?"

"I doubt it," Leah replied. "We just wanted to cover our bases." We had bases? I raised an eyebrow at her and she shrugged in response, giving me a head nod to proceed.

"Who has access to the penthouse, and by access, I mean key cards, key codes or whatever it is you use?"

Arch nodded at my question. "It's a short list. Charlie, the doormen and I have key cards to the penthouse. Essentially, each resident has a set specifically for his or her condo, which also works at the building's exits and entrances. In addition to the key cards, each resident also has a unique key code to access the parking garage."

"So, you have a key code for the garage, too?" Leah asked.

"Me? No…why would I need a key code?"

"So you can park your car?"

"Oh," Arch laughed stiffly, "I don't own a car. I take the light rail to and from work."

"What do you do when Charlie needs you to run errands?" I excused myself to use the restroom, while Leah quickly added, "Oh sorry, I forgot. You don't do errands." I barely managed to contain my snickering.

"We have a car service if Charlie has tasks offsite." His tone indicated the question was bordering on the ridiculous. For once, I had to agree with him—she was actually trying to buy me some snoop time.

I peered into Charlie's room and found it to be as neat and orderly as it always was. No dust puppies here. As Arch prattled on, I moved down the hall and snuck a peek into the guest room and hit paydirt.

From all appearances, he had made himself quite comfortable in Charlie's absence and from the look of things, wasn't overly concerned with impromptu visits from Charlie's friends. Closets overflowed with clothes, while the bathroom countertop held dozens of hair care products and other miscellaneous toiletries. One thing was for sure, someone planned on staying for more than a few days. The rest of the room was as well-kept as the remainder of the penthouse. I quickly stepped into the hallway bathroom, ran the water and slipped back into the living room before my absence was noticed. If Arch suspected anything as I returned to my seat, he concealed it extremely well.

"Have you had any visitors since Charlie was arrested?"

"Other than Natalie and then Charlie's ex, the lawyer, the answer is no," He made no bones about repeatedly checking his watch. "I wouldn't have expected too many people. I don't mean to be rude…"

"Our apologies Arch, you've obviously got things to do, we'll let you get back to it." We'd probably gotten about as much out of him as we were going to. Besides, the details he hadn't elected to share were far more interesting.

"If we have any more questions, we'll know where to find you, won't we?" Leah laughed, but given the way Arch narrowed his eyes, I seriously doubted he found her amusing.

"Anyway, we'd best be going, Leah." I looked at her pointedly, before turning to Arch. "Thanks for your time. We appreciate it and I'm sure Charlie will too." He said nothing but followed us as I hauled Leah into the elevator, with Nicoh close on our heels. For once, my Alaskan Malamute was being more compliant than my BFF—go figure.

I gave Arch a finger wave, praying the doors would shut but Leah managed to get the last word in after all, "We'll let Charlie know you said hello." Arch's mouth tightened and as the elevator slid shut, he graced her with a long, hard look.

Apparently Arch wasn't the only one sporting a thistle in his paw. Nicoh huffed as we exited and made a beeline toward Stu's station, to the awaiting treats. Stu chuckled and after rewarding the grumbling beast—for what I had no clue—he provided us with DVDs of the security camera footage as promised. We waited until we were back at the car and safely tucked inside to discuss our conversation with Arch.

"Well, that went off without a hitch," Leah snarked.

"At least we didn't walk away empty-handed," I replied, a bit giddy about the discovery during my scouting mission. "Let's just say Arch has been taking full advantage of his boss' absence." I proceeded to share my observation of the guest room.

"Interesting…" she commented once I'd finished. "Do you think Charlie knows?"

"Are you kidding? I don't think Charlie would let his own mother stay, if she was still alive."

"Well, other than taking up residence, Arch wasn't much use for anything else," she grumbled.

I smirked. "On the contrary, my friend, not if you think about it in terms of what he didn't say."

"Ah, well, he never asked us a single question about Charlie."

"Exactly."

"Certainly a curious curiosity, if Nero Wolfe's Archie Goodwin ever had one."

A curious curiosity, indeed, no matter who was having it.

CHAPTER TWELVE

Leah and I were trying to determine out next move—watch the security camera videos or talk to Charlie, Natalie and the party attendees. Our decision was conveniently made for us with a single phone call. My chest tightened as my cell phone rang, registering another unavailable number. I cursed under my breath before answering, my voice sounding unusually sharp. Leah shot me a concerned look as I shook my head.

After a long moment of silence and another few where I stopped breathing, a familiar but somewhat grainy voice filled the other end of the connection, "AJ?"

I resumed breathing—it was definitely not my mystery texter or caller.

"Charlie, is that you?"

His reply was crackly, "I…I don't know how much time I have to talk. Can you come and see me?"

"Absolutely. In fact, Leah and I just left your penthouse and have some…things to discuss with you, too."

"Oh, ok…good, good. Yeah, please come…and bring her, too." The connection went dead.

The police station was only minutes away from Charlie's

building and upon entering for the third time, yet another desk sergeant greeted us, informing us we were on the list. I wondered if that was a good thing—given our recent track record, probably not.

"An officer will be up to collect you shortly. In the meantime, you will need to leave your canine with me."

After checking out the artillery strapped to his side, I wasn't about to dispute the issue. Instead, I patted Nicoh on the head and handed his lead to the sergeant. Nicoh was still miffed about the stint with Arch in Charlie's penthouse and happily complied with what he saw as a new source for potential snacks. As if on cue, the sergeant scruffed Nicoh under the chin and pulled a treat from a container behind his desk.

"You know," I commented dryly, "if you encourage him, you'll have to deal with him."

The sergeant laughed, a low rumble. "No worries. I've got three retired police dogs at home—all German Shepherds—I know the drill." I nodded, noticing how unusually quiet Leah suddenly was. I followed her gaze. Our police escort had arrived —Detective Jere Vargas. I smirked, this would be interesting.

"AJ...Leah..." the big man drawled, his eyes never leaving Leah, who was studying grout patterns on the floor. "You two ready to meet with Wilson?"

I nodded and gestured for him to lead the way. As we moved down the hallway, I noticed a spark of electricity in the air as Leah looked up at the detective shyly. Leah...shy? I stared at my friend, who had resorted to shuffling her Chuck Taylor's like a three-year-old as we moved into the conference room. It was arranged like the others with a simple set of table and chairs and of course, the two-way mirrors.

Fortunately, there was no time for embarrassing small talk, as a guard ushered Charlie in, a meaty hand clamped securely around his bicep. I barely contained a gasp. Charlie's appearance had changed dramatically in the hours since I had last seen him. This time, he was dressed in the jail-issued attire: an orange and white striped jumpsuit with canvas slippers. The ensemble was completed with wrist and leg irons, something I had not been prepared for. His hair, long devoid of styling products, hung limply as pieces strayed across his eyes while others danced beyond the tip of his nose. His usually tanned skin had a grayish cast, which under the fluorescent lights gave him a sallow, vitamin-deprived appearance. As he lifted his chin, I noticed his lips were pressed together in a firm, unforgiving line. His bangs shifted, exposing his eyes, rimmed with dark circles caused by sleep deprivation and filled with an unmistakable emotion —humiliation.

I stepped forward in an attempt to bridge the gap between us but the guard strong-armed me, briskly reminding me I was not to touch the prisoner. I held my hands up in apology before settling on the nearest bench. Leah gave the guard a hard stare but followed suit. What was that all about? Before I could ask, Charlie sat down across from us, hands and feet in awkward angles to accommodate his wieldy accessories.

We looked at one another in silence until Detective Vargas offered us privacy, noting the guard would be stationed just outside the door, should we need anything. I chuckled to myself as I translated it to "Don't try anything." Ha, as if we'd stage a jail break.

"Charlie...you look..." Once the three of us were alone, I found myself struggling for the right words. How do you tell someone like Charlie that he looked...well, like death?

He sensed my discomfort and elected to complete the thought himself, "Heinous? Barbaric? Like a complete hot mess?" He gave a small, bitter laugh. "Take your pick. I'm fortunate my accommodations lack mirrors."

Leah attempted to lighten the mood. "It seems pretty stingy to me. I'd think my tax dollars would at least warrant a cot, a bedpan, a wash basin and a mirror for primping. You know, the standard jailhouse accoutrement."

Charlie smiled thinly. "They don't want to risk anything that could be broken and used as a weapon on our fellow inmates, or on ourselves."

"Err...yeah, there's that, too," Leah balked as her face flushed. Clearly Charlie wasn't in the mood for witty banter. "So, how are you doing?"

He responded with a long, hooded look. Leah quickly recognized his annoyance and raised her hands in surrender. "Sorry, sorry, just trying to make conversation. Let's not forgot, you summoned us."

He nodded as his gaze traveled to his shackled hands. "The County Attorney is getting ready to formally charge me." He swallowed hard before continuing, "And I need your...help... with some things. Before that happens and before they move me...elsewhere."

"Do you need us to hire a lawyer?" I asked, reaching out but retracting my hand as I remembered the guard's admonishment.

"No, nothing like that. I've got that handled." He smiled wryly, making me wonder who he had retained. Maybe his ex? "Anyway, it seems as though the police and the County Attorney's Office think they've got enough evidence to move forward with first degree murder. They're going for the death penalty." His tone was more glum than distraught, as though telling us Aston Martin had stopped all production for the interminable future.

Leah must have been thinking the same. "Charlie Wilson, they're talking about the death penalty. How can you be so...so lackadaisical?"

Charlie rolled his eyes. "Gee, thanks for that info, Leah. Now that you've cleared things up, I can go back to my cell and watch the cement crack." Leah pursed her lips, not buying his bravado. "Sure, the death penalty or life in prison—either would be dire— if I was guilty."

"The proof they have must be pretty solid if they think they can move forward with formal charges," Leah replied.

"That's true. It's also the reason I asked you both here." He leaned forward, squinting at each of us conspiratorially. "I want you to figure out who killed Parker…and bring him to justice."

* * *

A resounding "no" echoed as we responded in tandem, empha- sizing the barrenness of the room. Making casual inquiries was one thing, conducting an actual investigation—on a murder case —was quite another. Had Charlie not received the memo? A conviction would mean his life, one way or the other.

"Charlie, we are not PIs," I gritted out, carefully enunciating each word.

"I don't care," he replied simply.

"We have friends—the Stanton brothers in L.A.—we could hire…professional help from professional investigators who know how to run an investigation. See a theme here, Charlie? And let's not forget the benefits associated with acquiring solid legal coun- sel." I looked at him squarely. I needed him to listen to me, to hear me.

He shook his head, adamant. "I've thought about it and it's what I want." He must not have liked the look that passed between us, because he tacked on his most sincere "please."

Leah rolled her eyes but nodded. I sighed and did the same. Though we had already done some initial snooping, we were offi- cially graduating to amateur sleuths. Nancy Drew lite, on our best day.

Obviously pleased, Charlie clasped his hands together as a small smile escaped. "Where do we start?"

"Whoa, hold up there, Chuck." Charlie bristled, precisely the reaction Leah had wanted. "We need to set some ground rules if we are going to do this...whatever *this* is."

I agreed. "First, you need to be more forthcoming with the details. A lot more, actually."

"What my friend is saying, Charlie"—Leah gritted out his name—"is that it's time you stop jerkying us around."

"You mean jerking," he replied dryly.

"I mean what I say," she snarked. "I'm the resident word smith, after all."

"What Leah is trying to say is that we need you to be absolutely truthful with us, about everything." I paused to glare at her. She was getting way too much pleasure from torturing Charlie. Even if he deserved it, we were wasting valuable time. Besides, we could prod him with a sharp stick after we got him out of this predicament.

"And we mean everything. If we ask, you answer—truthfully. If you balk, hedge or outright lie, all bets are off. Are we clear?"

Charlie worked his jaw and nodded, before turning to Leah. "To use your analogy, I will refrain from treating you like an old, tough, mangy side of bovine. Just don't blame me if you don't like everything you hear."

"Agreed. We may not like it, but we won't bail on you because of it," Leah replied.

"Ok, then," I clapped, "let's proceed. For starters, do you have any idea what the police have on you? Other than the stuff we already know about, of course."

"Honestly, no, not really," Charlie replied. "It could be anything at this point."

"We understand Natalie was here? What was that all about?" Leah was in reporter mode.

"Not sure, other than to offer her support, I guess," he tapped his chin, "though at one point, she suggested things would be easier if I plead guilty. Of course, she immediately laughed it off, chalking it up as an attempt at humor."

"Wow, that's an unusual way of going about it—kind of insensitive, if you ask me—and frankly, not something I'd expect from her. Did you get the impression she thought you were guilty?"

"She did just lose her boyfriend, you know," his tone was droll, "which might explain her odd behavior. But no, she doesn't think I'm guilty, or at least that's what she indicated, though I'm obviously not a very good judge of people. Present company excluded, of course."

"Any idea who's driving Parker's Audi these days, other than Natalie?" I asked, thinking back to Natalie's mystery ride.

"What? No, no one should be driving Parker's car. There isn't anyone else." He looked perplexed. "Are you sure it was Parker's car and just not one that looked like it? There are other Audi R8s out there."

I shook my head. "Mmm…no, not that many, not in that particular shade of blue, anyway,"

"Sure there is. In fact, Morgan has one, in the same color."

"Morgan, your ex-girlfriend, the lawyer, has an R8?" When he nodded, Leah added, "Ok…but I think I would have noticed a California license plate."

"No, she maintains a dual-residence. Her car is registered in Arizona."

"Ok…is there any reason Natalie and Morgan would be hanging out and Morgan would be acting as Natalie's designated driver?"

Charlie laughed. "Not likely. Morgan doesn't do anything that doesn't benefit Morgan. She wouldn't even offer taxi money to her best friend, much less be expected to be at someone else's beck and call." He shook his head. "Besides, they don't exactly run in the same circles. Morgan thinks Natalie is a dip. No, it must have been another Audi." I disagreed and from the look on Leah's face, she did too—it was too much of a coincidence.

I put the car in park for the time being, electing to move on to another topic. "On the night of the party, why didn't you take your key card when you left the penthouse to take a walk?"

"I don't know. I was distracted and must have misplaced it at some point during the day. It was stupid and so unlike me. I didn't realize it until after the party, but by then I was too tired to mess with it, so I had Stu let me back in." He chuckled softly. "I didn't think it was that big of a deal at the time."

Unfortunately, the police did think it was a big deal and believed Charlie had attempted to establish an alibi by engaging the doorman that night under false pretenses. One thing was for sure, Leah and I would be hard-pressed to prove otherwise without our own evidence. I gritted my teeth. We were so in over our heads.

"What happened to your shoes and tie after the walk?"

Charlie squinted, trying to remember. "My shoes got soaked when I tromped along the lake. Actually, given the amount of alcohol I had that night, I probably spent most of my walk off the pathway. I can't begin to tell you how bad of an idea that turned out to be." Neither of us replied. It had been a bad idea, probably the worst of his life, "When I came back, I went into the parking garage and placed the shoes under the Aston Martin to allow them to dry, along with the socks."

"Using your key code?" Leah prompted.

"Yes, the code is specific to me," he replied. I wondered if the police had checked the activity log for the parking garage and if so, if it meshed with what he was telling us.

Something else occurred to me. "Hang on a second, what about the tie?"

Charlie's expression immediately changed from puzzled to

concerned. "I hadn't realized it was missing. After Stu let me in, I went up and threw everything into the bag for the laundry service to pick up the following morning."

Stu hadn't been sure about the tie, either and yet Natalie had found one near the lake. Had it been Parker's? Or Charlie's? There was no sense pursuing the issue at this point—Charlie would likely never remember anyway, given the amount of alcohol he'd had—we'd need to rely on the security videos to fill in the blanks.

Thinking of the videos reminded me of something else. "You mentioned the penthouse cameras to Leah. Does Arch know about them?"

Charlie smiled thinly. "He knows about the cameras I want him to know about."

"Such as..." Leah was getting impatient with the brevity of his responses. I couldn't say I blamed her, time was of the essence.

"The cameras placed throughout the main portion of the building, including the entrance and parking garage."

"Not the cameras inside the penthouse?"

"Of course not," Charlie snarked, "that would defeat the purpose."

"Careful, Charlie Brown..." Leah snapped. "We didn't come here for your attitude." Charlie glared at her and opened his mouth to retort.

"Play nice, kids," I interjected. "What about audio?"

Charlie shook his head. "Currently, the penthouse's cameras are the only ones set up to capture sound."

"Can we get access to that feed? Stu was able to supply us with everything but—" I snapped my mouth shut, hoping I hadn't gotten the doorman into trouble.

Charlie waved his hand, apparently not concerned by my comment. "Certainly, I'll give you the name and number of my security expert. He's more of a computer and audio visual geek, but he's a genius with pretty much anything tech-related." As Leah jotted the information down, he added, "You didn't happen to check on the penthouse while you were there talking to Stu, did you? Not that I have any plants or pets, but I'm hoping the cops didn't make a total mess."

I gave Leah an uh-oh glance, which Charlie caught. There was no good time to tell him about the suspected penthouse squatter. He worked his jaw as we told him about Arch and the inhabited guest room.

"You want us to boot him?" Leah asked when we finished, sounding a tad too hopeful.

"No," Charlie replied slowly, thinking as he spoke, "this could actually work out to our advantage. It will allow us...you...to keep an eye on him, meaning you should contact my security guy sooner rather than later."

"Speaking of that, he's not going to give up the goods based on our say so." Leah had a good point.

"No, you'll have to give him the secret handshake, followed by a blood oath." Charlie chuckled at our horrified expressions. "Just give him your nickname, AJ," he winked at me, "that's the password."

I was too startled to respond before the guard entered, informing us the visit was over. As we parted ways, I turned and looked back at Charlie shuffling in the opposite direction under heavy-handed guidance.

"Charlie!" I shouted, causing the guard's perma-frown to deepen. "What is Natalie to you?"

Charlie glanced over his shoulder in surprise as his handler continued to propel him forward. "What?" he managed to sputter. "Natalie? Nothing—a friend, if that."

They disappeared through the double doors. If Charlie had

been prepared to elaborate, he'd lost his chance. I wondered if he had been relieved.

As we collected Nicoh from the desk sergeant, I realized Detective Vargas had not returned to escort us out. Given Leah's sour expression, she noticed as well. I started to comment, when I observed the sergeant was in an equally bitter mood.

"What's the matter?"

He thrust Nicoh's lead at me. "What's the matter? I left my sandwich on the desk to take a call. My back was turned...oh, I don't know...three seconds? I finished the call, went to eat my sandwich and...it...was...gone." It was all I could do not to giggle.

Leah opted to bat her baby blues. "Any chance the wind blew it away?"

I bit my tongue and shot her a pithy look before turning to the sergeant. "I'm so, so sorry. I usually chalk it up to hazard duty. Please let me buy you another lunch. We could run down to Mill Street and grab you another sandwich, or up to Oregano's on University?"

The sergeant shook his head and waved a hand, though I could tell he was still miffed. "I truly appreciate the offer, Miss. Honestly, I'm not mad your dog ate my lunch. It's that he inhaled it so fast, he didn't even bother to enjoy it." He wiggled a finger at Nicoh, whose tongue dangled happily as he scouted for dessert.

"Welcome to my world, Sergeant."

CHAPTER THIRTEEN

Running interference for Charlie was proving to be a lot more time-consuming than either Leah or I had imagined, we mused as we checked our missed messages.

One text in particular caught my eye: *YOU MIGHT BE ABLE TO SAVE YOUR FRIEND, ARIANNA, BUT WILL YOU BE ABLE TO SAVE YOURSELF?* Well…crap. Apparently this person wasn't a member of the Arianna Jackson fan club after all. I handed my cell to Leah after she tucked Nicoh into the back seat.

After reading it, her mouth formed a thin line. "Call Ramirez —now."

She drove as I dialed, putting my cell on speakerphone. He picked up on the first ring and after a few niceties, I filled him in on my latest mystery text.

"Darn it, AJ," he growled, once I had finished.

"Tell me about it. Was your contact able to come up with anything?"

"Not yet, other than our caller is into using throwaway phones."

"So what's AJ supposed to do in the meantime—wait until this guy escalates to anthrax-laced greeting cards?"

I patted my friend's knee. "I doubt anything like that is going to happen."

Ramirez's response surprised me, "Leah's right to be concerned. You're going to need to be more careful, watch your surroundings and if anything seems out of place—no matter how insignificant—call me." Though I couldn't see his face, his tone indicated he wasn't about to take "no" for an answer. "And, at least for a while, I'd like the two...three...of you to stick together, if at all possible. The more eyes we have on deck, the better."

"I have no idea what that means." Leah snorted. "So that's it, then? Just stick to AJ like glue, grow eyes in the back of our heads, attach a beacon to Nicoh and wait until this jerk rears his crazy head? For how long are we supposed to do this, anyway? Until we become crotchety old maids bickering about our bad 80s hair days?"

"Considering you're already pretty crabby, I guess all you'll need to contend with is your questionable hair choices over the years." I snickered under my breath as Ramirez teased my friend.

"Hey, wait just a minute—if you weren't a cop..."

"A homicide detective," I added helpfully.

"Whatever. I just wish there was something more proactive we could do," she conceded, but not before sticking her tongue out at me. "Since we've already got your ear, Detective Ramirez, we'd like to pick your brain about Charlie's case."

"I thought I asked you to stay out of it," his tone was no longer jovial. "Besides, why not hit up your TPD source, unless he's already shut you down, too?"

She made a face at the phone. "A girl's gotta keep her bases covered, no sense spreading myself too thin. Even a detective should understand that. Oh well, I just thought your poker buddy was keeping you in the loop. Guess I was wrong about that."

At Ramirez's grumbled response—I won't repeat it verbatim, other than to say it involved tossing a particular region of her anatomy into the brig—I quickly intercepted by highlighting our findings. I hoped sharing the information we'd discovered first might open the exchange of information. After a brief outline of our conversations with Stuart, Arch and Charlie, my gamble worked.

Ramirez was quiet for a moment before responding, "The Tempe boys have copies of the camera feed, though given the range of dates they're reviewing, I'm not sure how far they've gotten." His tone indicated he wasn't about to share what had been found to date, but I got the distinct impression from what he hadn't said TPD had found something. I hoped it wasn't more bad news for Charlie. Before I had the opportunity to comment, Ramirez abruptly ended the conversation, citing an urgent matter needing his attention.

"That was evasive," Leah commented as we stared at my cell phone. "Makes me glad we kept a few juicy details to ourselves."

"You don't suppose Vargas would be any more forthcoming, do you?"

"Heck no, I've already run that tab higher than even I'm comfortable doing. Pretty soon, he's going to want to cash in on some of that good will."

"So, you don't like him?" I was curious.

"It's not that I don't like Vargas...Jere...I just don't care for his baggage."

"Err, come again?"

"His ex. Baggage. Call her Samsonite, as in she doesn't fit well in the overhead bins."

"Ah," I nodded in understanding, though it wasn't like my friend to throw in the towel so easily. Girl typically liked the challenge, so it had to be something else. "He's still hung up on her?" I ventured a guess.

"No, it's that I *know* her."

"She's still around?"

She laughed harshly. "You could say that. She was one of my former editors at the paper and the primary reason I left. A jealous, vindictive boss tends to evaporate the creative juices." At my surprised look, she waved a hand. "Heck, I was ready for a change anyway."

I was floored. I thought she'd left the paper, given up her condo and moved in with me because she needed a fresh start after being kidnapped and nearly murdered by Winslow Clark. I'd had no idea one of her bosses had also been making her work life hell, simply because she could.

No, I couldn't imagine Leah losing the choice assignments she had worked so hard for or being forced to work in vile or unsafe locations. It was likely more than she could bear. And after she'd given up so much: security, control, piece of mind.

"Oh Leah, I'm so sorry. I didn't know."

She waved a hand at me. "You already had a lot of your own stuff to deal with—the death of your parents and your sister—you didn't need to deal with my crap, too. Besides, leaving that mess behind turned out to be the best and most profitable decision I ever made. Anyway, now you know why Detective Jere Vargas and I can never be more than friends. And a source of information, of course." She smiled and patted my leg. "Why don't we find out what those cameras captured? I'll bet watching the videos TPD has will even up that information playing field."

"And the videos *inside* the penthouse will put us a step ahead." We both giggled conspiratorially.

Darn, I knew we were best friends for a reason.

* * *

Tony Barbados, a.k.a. Tony B.—Charlie's security expert/audio video/computer geek extraordinaire—picked up on the first ring sounding harried and if I wasn't mistaken, more than a little paranoid. Fortunately, after explaining my reason for calling and giving him the secret handshake—my nickname, Ajax—Tony B. chilled as much as I imagined a guy on a Red Bull-fortified diet could muster. His voice fluctuated as he energetically explained how to go about accessing the video feed via my laptop. After a few dozen strokes, I was in. I thanked Tony B. repeatedly for his assistance, but he made noises into the phone that indicated he was more interested into getting back to whatever geeky evil genius types did.

After hanging up, I filled Leah in and suggested we make an afternoon out of watching the videos. This meant procuring the appropriate snacks. While Leah made popcorn—on the stove, of course—I started putting together a snack tray when the doorbell rang.

Upon peering through the keyhole, I was surprised to find Randy Newman—not *that* Randy Newman—my neighbor from around the corner looking back. Thanks to Nicoh's happy dance on my foot, I knew Randy had his Keeshond, Pandora, in tow and after a few howls and small yips were exchanged through the door, the two were united.

Though he'd originally retired at the ripe old age of thirty-eight, Randy had recently returned to the world of corporate law in a position that required moderate travel. We'd become acquainted while out walking our dogs in the neighborhood, as well as on the occasions when Pandora had escaped and made her way into my yard. As a result, we had become friendly to the point he felt comfortable leaving her in my care when his job took him out of town. I suspected it was the reason for his current visit.

Randy blushed as we joined Leah in the kitchen. I'd always believed that—much like Abe Stanton—he had a bit of a crush on her and had told her as much, though she vehemently denied it. Randy was definitely a nice, well-mannered guy and decent looking to boot, with sandy hair, deep tan and athletic build honed from years of tennis. Unfortunately, the only thing Randy loved more than his work was talking about it.

Needless to say, it was one of Leah's dating non-negotiables. I could hardly say I blamed her, though I did feel sorry for Randy. He had it bad for Leah and though he was normally a pretty talkative guy, became a rambling fool around our little spiky-haired pixie. And, after a few embarrassing episodes, he started clamping up whenever she was in the vicinity. Today, he was content with leaning against the counter, watching her make popcorn.

"So, are you heading out of town again, Randy?"

"Oh, yeah…sorry," he momentarily peeled his eyes from Leah's activity, exciting as it was, "it's kind of short notice, but one of my clients in Dallas needs some hand-holding."

"Say no more, I'd be happy to watch Pandora. Wouldn't we, Nicoh?" The two canines were doing their customary sniff-and-wag bit, oblivious to the humans in the room. I opened the sliding doors that lead to the backyard patio, "Out of the kitchen, you two. You can do…that…outside." They ran out in tandem, barking and nipping at each other's tails.

Randy left for the airport with a promise to call with his return plans, leaving Leah and I to finish our snack preparations. Once completed, we enthusiastically made our way to the living room to convene the video watching portion of our investigation. As it turned out, the security footage of Charlie's building was B-O-R-I-N-G. People came. People went. People did what people do. For hours, nothing out of the ordinary occurred or was even remotely interesting.

I realized I'd lost Leah when a small snore came from the section of the cushions where she'd burrowed, one hand still draped in the popcorn bowl. As I got up to move it, I almost missed a segment of video that showed Natalie entering the building. I noted the time on the feed—it was during the period I'd been in the penthouse setting up for the White Party. I watched as she exited, less than five minutes later.

I opened my laptop and logged into the penthouse's video links as Tony B. had directed. Several keystrokes later, I was looking at the entryway to Charlie's penthouse, a few minutes prior to the time indicated on the feed from the building. For a moment I felt kind of voyeuristic, but quickly pushed the squishy thought aside as Charlie appeared, moving quickly through the entryway and onto the elevator—likely on his way to the meeting he still wouldn't discuss. I had forgotten there was sound on this video and adjusted it a couple of levels above Leah's snores.

Less than fifteen minutes passed before Arch came into view and sat at his desk—whether he realized Charlie had left, I wasn't sure—and shortly after that, Natalie stepped off the elevator. I checked the timestamp on the video from the building's entrance —a little more than a minute has passed—the time it took to ride the elevator to the penthouse.

Natalie appraised Arch for a moment, her face devoid of its usual perkiness, and her pouty lips in a grim line. "Do you have what I came for, or what?" she snapped.

"I do…" Arch replied slowly, twirling his fingers in a circular pattern over the steel surface, his own expression smug. *What the heck?* I thought.

"I don't have all day." Natalie thrust out her hand expectantly.

"Before I hand this over, I want some assurances." He smiled coyly.

"Listen, you little freak," she gritted out, her features turning dark—hardly recognizable from the pretty, polite girl I knew. Her finger prodded his chest. "We had a deal, buddy. So either you give me what I came for—"

"Or what, Natalie?" Arch remained surprisingly calm, more amused than angered as he enunciated her name in an effort to taunt her.

"Or I let Charlie know what you've been up to." Her smile transformed into a sneer—neither had been attractive on her.

Arch shifted slightly, but smirked as they glared at one another. After a long moment, he slid something across the desk, which she easily palmed and placed into her monstrosity of a handbag. She spun on her heel and without looking back, called to him as she entered the elevator, "I was never here."

Arch replied, his voice sharp, "Just remember, we had a deal. I want no part of the rest of it."

Natalie turned, carefully inching cat-eye sunglasses up her nose, her eyes piercing his. As the elevator doors slid shut, her voice was barely a whisper, but the meaning was clear, "Oh, I remember, Archy Boy. I remember…everything."

CHAPTER FOURTEEN

I quickly rewound the tape and tried several dozen times to zoom in on whatever it was Arch had given her, but it was masked by their hands as it passed between them. It was so frustrating. I put a few choice expletives out into the universe loudly enough to wake Leah, who ended up knocking over the popcorn bowl I had removed from her slumbering clutches.

"Crap." She squinted, frowning as she tried to focus. "Did you drink all the margaritas, or what?"

I laughed so hard I snorted. "Wrong dream, Sunshine. No margaritas here."

Leah grumbled, throwing pillows, stray popcorn kernels, a few gummy bears and at least one Sour Patch Kid as she attempted to reposition herself on the couch.

After I managed to contain myself, I added, "Sorry, I interrupted your nap, but now that you're awake, I found something interesting on the video the morning before the party. Here, maybe I should just show you." I adjusted the videos to the same timestamp and once Leah gave me a nod, started them both.

The audio boomed, causing us to cover our ears in surprise.

"Why in the heck is that so darn loud?" Leah cried as I scrambled to adjust the audio.

"Because I was trying to hear over your snoring," I replied dryly.

"I do not snore. I have sinus issues." She sniffed indignantly while waving at me in a *let's get on with it* manner.

After a successful second attempt, we watched the scene between Natalie and Arch. When the elevator doors closed on Natalie's death glare, Leah stopped the recording. "And we thought Parker was the ruthless one. Any idea what that was?" she asked, pointing to the item that passed between them.

I shook my head. "Not a clue. I even tried to zoom in but it was too small and conveniently concealed."

"Are we sure that Arch doesn't know about that camera?"

"Charlie says no, but at this point I don't think we can afford to discount the possibility."

"How the heck do they even know each other? Like *that*, I mean."

"I have no idea, but whatever is going on certainly doesn't give you a warm fuzzy."

"Totally agree with you, but we're going to have to scrounge up more than that"—she gestured toward the screen—"to prove something mischievous is afoot."

"Let's hope we can find something of value on the remainder these videos, provided you can manage to stay awake." A piece of candy bounced off my head. "Just say 'no' to gummy bear abuse, Leah."

We returned our attention to the video, where nothing of interest occurred until after I'd finished my setup duties and left the penthouse. A short while later, Charlie's Aston Martin entered the parking garage and maneuvered into his space. Upon exiting the car, Charlie looked up at the camera and immediately pulled his cell phone from his pocket. After a brief call, all the parking garage feeds simultaneously went blank. I glanced at Leah—at least Charlie had been truthful about one thing—he'd definitely disabled the cameras.

Minutes later, he was visible on the penthouse feed as he exited the elevator, a healthy frown emerging as he saw Arch at his post.

"I've temporarily disabled the cameras in the parking garage as Senator Conrad requested, so he and his entourage may come and go unnoticed."

"Ok," Arch replied slowly, "doesn't that mean dismantling the security on your vehicles and the other resident's vehicles, too?"

"Yes," Charlie snapped, "there's nothing I can do about that. It had to be done, and now it is. That's all you need to know. Got it?" It wasn't a question. "Of course, if something happens to Conrad's car while it's in the structure, it's on him."

"Oh, I would think the senator has people to take care of stuff like that, don't you?" Arch replied in an attempt to be helpful. Of course, it had the opposite effect, as Charlie whirled on him.

Arch quickly nodded. "Of course he does. Then…why…why did he request to have the security cameras turned off?"

Both Leah and I blanched as Charlie's expression turned from irritated to irate. "Arch, I get the impression you are purposely trying to test my patience today. Bad idea." Arch backed up, just a little, though I doubted Charlie registered the movement, given the blackness of his mood. "The senator will be bringing some special…guests to the party. Guests that will be arriving with his entourage, but aren't to be seen accompanying him, if you get my meaning?" He spun on his heal and marched toward the kitchen.

I looked at Leah, even if Arch hadn't gotten it, we certainly had. If the rumors about former Senator Davis Conrad were true, they would be special *female* guests, other than his wife. It wasn't until we watched him watching Charlie's departure we realized Arch wasn't the stooge everyone thought him to be.

As he stared after his boss, a tiny smile escaped.

* * *

Considering Arch had just gotten his job back, you would have thought he'd avoid aggravating Charlie. Yet here he was, clearly putting his foot into it, and enjoying it. Charlie was wrong—Arch wasn't a nitwit. He was a manipulator. He'd played on Charlie's impatient, arrogant nature to get a rise out of him and possibly, some valuable information. The question was why? And for what purpose? While Arch had done a decent job of playing Charlie, he wasn't a murderer, much less the facilitator of one. Something told me whatever he was up to, it wasn't good.

The last scene had given us something to gnaw on, but it wasn't enough. We continued to watch as Arch went back to his duties, which consisted of organizing his sparsely-covered desk in an attempt to appear as though he was performing meaningful work. Amusing, but boring.

Not having to deal with the parking garage videos was certainly a plus, but even screening the others at a faster speed was time-consuming. At times, it was humorous—especially watching ourselves arrive for the party all decked out in white, tugging here and there, while bickering back and forth in double time. Once the guests finally started arriving for the White Party, however, we returned the playback to its normal speed, paying especially close attention to Natalie's arrival.

We couldn't read lips, though it appeared she had transformed back to her girl-next-door persona, making polite small talk with Stu while she waited for Parker. When he arrived several minutes later, Parker ignored the doorman while giving Natalie's ensemble a disapproving perusal. Natalie, however, seemed oblivious to his gaze—or had grown used to it—as she giggled and threaded her arm through his. Parker impatiently ushered her onto the elevator, which made me wonder if she was an exceptional actress, or genuinely happy to be in his company. My gut told me one thing while my gag reflux was threatening another.

Watching the rest of the party play out—including Charlie's snub of Parker—was surreal and frankly, a bit bizarre, especially when seeing your own reaction. You never look quite the way you imagined, do you?

I was also struck by the realization these were likely the last moments of Parker's life. It no longer mattered he'd spent it as an egotistical, self-serving jerk. It had been his life to live, good or bad. And yet, on this night, someone decided the ending of his story for him. In a few short hours, Parker would be dead. That alone was the most surreal, and sobering fact.

Charlie's ex, Morgan, entered the party next, looking every ounce as gorgeous as I remembered but…

"Leah, she never entered the building though the main entrance—she never passed Stuart!"

"What? I missed it." We reversed the playback and sure enough—prior to the point we had witnessed Morgan emerge from the elevator—she hadn't entered the building through the main entrance. She had come in another way.

"She's one of Senator Conrad's special guests," I whispered.

"No!" Leah pointed excitedly. "She *is* the senator's special guest." Moments after Morgan had passed through the entryway alone, the elevators reopened and the man himself stepped out… also very alone.

"Whoa, do you think Charlie knew…that his ex and the senator…and that was the reason he was so short with Arch?"

"I don't know, but I don't think it matters." I tapped my chin thoughtfully, "What matters is that *she* knew."

"Err, I don't follow," Leah crinkled her nose at me, "of course Morgan would know…"

"No, Leah, she knew the security cameras would be disabled

in the parking garage."

We continued watching in silence as the party droned on and people drank, cavorted and did what people generally do when they've imbibed too much. But other than some sidebar silliness that occurred when people thought no one was watching, nothing more of interest happened.

From our perspective, Morgan and the senator had limited to no interaction. When she eventually left the party, however, her escort left shortly after. As expected, neither made an exit through the front of the building. Instead, the elevator had taken each of them to the parking structure, where they were able to steal away unnoticed.

Leah and I had left the party by that time, along with several other guests. I strained to find a glimpse of Charlie among the partygoers, but wherever he was, the cameras were out of reach. My attention was drawn to Parker and Natalie leaving the party, then exiting the building minutes later. As they slipped into the night, I again reflected on the moment being the last record of his life.

It was a shame Charlie had dismantled the security cameras in the parking garage, a fact the police were likely having a field day with. And knowing Charlie as I did, he'd probably failed to mention the former senator's request, making their case stronger and his situation worse. Even if he had, I doubted Senator Conrad would have corroborated the claim. Charlie had gotten himself into a real pickle this time.

The party continued to wind down as guests left and Charlie finally came into view. I quickly realized he had been in the atrium, one of the few areas—along with the bedrooms and bathrooms—devoid of cameras. As he walked the last of the guests to the elevator and wished them good night, he seemed genuinely pleased as a small smile formed. It didn't quite reach his eyes, indicating his mind was elsewhere.

The smile evaporated as Arch appeared and while still facing the elevators, Charlie spoke to his assistant in a hushed, raspy voice, "Would you mind telling the staff they can go for now?"

"Are you sure? "Arch stammered, clearly taken aback by his boss' directive. "There's a lot of clean up to be done."

Charlie waved off his concern, his back still to his assistant. "It's fine. It all can be done…later. Can you coordinate that?" he asked quietly, while Arch nodded. As though sensing the affirmation, he added, "Thank you. After that, you should go ahead and take off, too. Get some rest. You'll be back soon enough."

Arch started to say something but must have thought better of it, silently returning to the kitchen to confer with the staff. When Charlie turned around, an undecipherable expression spanned his face, as he trudged toward master bedroom,

Arch and the others were gone by the time he emerged. His jacket was off and his tie loose as he looked around solemnly, reaching into the pocket of his slacks. Frowning, he reached into the other pocket, then muttered in frustration as he flipped off the remaining lights and entered the elevator. He reappeared on the building video as he stopped to talk with Stu before leaving through the front entrance.

He returned, over an hour later. As he and Stu had both indicated, he was neither wearing nor carrying his shoes. Also missing was the tie. And though he appeared even more tired than before, he looked just like the Charlie we'd seen leaving the building. There was no evidence—physical or otherwise—he'd been in a struggle, much less murdered his best friend.

We watched until he entered the penthouse and headed toward his bedroom before fast-forwarding to the point when Arch arrived to begin his workday a few short hours later, followed by the party cleanup crew.

At 9 a.m., Charlie emerged from his room with a laundry bag in hand just as an elderly man, dressed neatly in a short sleeve shirt and chinos exited the elevator. Few words were exchanged before the man left, laundry bag in hand. Arch was overseeing the cleanup crew in another part of the penthouse, which explained why he'd missed the transaction that morning.

After another hour of yawning and capturing nothing of value, we took a break to document a few of the questions we had accumulated to this point.

Question #1—What had Arch handed to Natalie? It was obvious Charlie had been missing his key card—was that it? If so, why had she taken it?

Question #2—What was going on between Arch and Natalie? How did they know one another (other than through Charlie)?

Question #3—Did they know who killed Parker? Or have any knowledge that might help Charlie?

Question #4—Morgan and the former senator had known the parking garage cameras would be disabled that evening. Had they shared that information with anyone?

Question #5—How did Parker end up in the parking garage? Natalie had taken a cab—leaving Parker to walk to his own car. Had he ever made it that far? What happened to him between the time Natalie left him and the time he was killed? Was he lured somehow? Had he already planned to meet someone?

Question #6—Why hadn't Natalie mentioned seeing his car when she went back to get hers?

Question #7—Could one person feasibly incapacitate, kill and dump someone Parker's size?

As expected, we had more questions than answers and of the people that could provide them, we weren't convinced they would. One thing was for sure, we weren't prepared to deal with Natalie. Not yet, anyway. She had been fairly unpredictable during our previous discussions and after what we'd seen of her in the video footage, maybe even a bit devious. No, before we dealt with her again, we'd need more ammunition. The same was true of Arch. As for Senator Conrad, good luck cracking that nut. We'd likely end up spending valuable time and yielding minimal results. Plus, we'd have to explain our knowledge of the dismantled camera, which would divulge information only Charlie should have known. That left Morgan, Charlie's ex and the former senator's mystery guest.

Unfortunately, tracking Morgan Thompson down turned out to be more difficult than we had anticipated. Upon calling the law firm in San Francisco where she served as a partner, we were promptly informed Morgan had recently taken a leave of absence to attend to a family matter and had not left a private number where she could be reached.

Leah managed to work her magic and after a few phone calls and a whole lot of grousing, was able to obtain what we believed to be Morgan's personal cell phone number. Of course, now that we had it, we couldn't exactly call her and ask her outright if she was Senator Davis Conrad's mistress. We needed information, not to confirm some seedy gossip, and decided the best way to go about it was on the pretense of locating character references to aid in Charlie's defense.

I was elected to make the call after losing the gummy bear toss—neither of us had any coins—and was surprised when Morgan picked up after two short rings, sounding breathless. Thinking I had gotten the wrong number or that Morgan had some interesting side business going, I considered hanging up when she quickly apologized, explaining she had a habit of answering phone calls during her daily run. I, too, apologized for my interruption and quickly detailed my reason for touching base with a few of Charlie's friends.

Morgan laughed harshly, clearly amused. "Charlie doesn't have *friends*, darling. He has acquisitions." She paused a moment before adding, "He's just lucky we live in the desert, otherwise he'd be hard-pressed to keep himself warm at night." I wasn't surprised by what she said, it was how she said it that spoke volumes, in the Encyclopedia Britannia kind of way. That and something else piqued my attention.

"So, you're living here now?"

She chuckled, her tone much lighter. "It's just an expression, darling. When you are born and raised in Phoenix, the Valley of the Sun is always part of you, no matter where your physical home resides." I quirked an eyebrow at Leah, currently biting her lip as she was forced to sit back and listen via speakerphone. "Besides, my parents still live here."

It was news to us. Neither of us had realized Morgan was from Arizona, much less from right in our own backyard. It was surprising that Charlie had never mentioned it. It was definitely worth looking into.

As Leah furiously jotted in her trusty notebook, Morgan and I made small talk about Charlie's party—carefully avoiding the topic of her escort for the evening—as well as Parker's death and the ongoing investigation. She didn't believe Charlie killed Parker, or had any involvement. When I asked if she could drum up any other likable candidates or possible motives, her mood darkened.

"Arianna, Charlie and Parker...are not good people. Charlie could have been killed, just as easily as Parker and no one would have cared, much less cried. Tears spill *because* of those two, not *for* them. As for motives, it would be easier to identify what wouldn't have been a motive. It's a short list." She sighed heavily before hanging up, leaving me to wonder if this was the tale of a scorned and bitter ex-girlfriend, or the reality of someone who'd experienced Charlie and Parker's world first hand.

Either way, it was clear that while Morgan believed Charlie was not responsible for killing Parker, in the end she felt they were both getting exactly what they deserved.

CHAPTER FIFTEEN

I'll admit, we didn't have much of a game plan after talking to Morgan, so I shouldn't have been surprised Leah's expression was one of horror when I placed a spontaneous call to Natalie the following afternoon. Something about my chat with Morgan had inspired me and sometimes, you've gotta trust your gut. I only hoped my instincts hadn't gotten confused by the overabundance of Sour Patch Kids currently rumbling around in my tummy.

"You just invited…Natalie…over…for drinks," Leah commented slowly, after I'd hung up. "Natalie."

I shrugged. "I guess we'd better move the potted plants."

Natalie promptly arrived an hour later. Seeing her fresh face and perky smile, it was hard to rationalize her snarling exchange with Arch as she hugged us and presented us with Costco-sized bottles of tequila and margarita mixer and enough limes to make me think she must have foraged someone's backyard tree. The girl came armed and ready.

Natalie moaned as she tested Leah's cilantro lime jalapeño hummus on a baby carrot and tried bribing her for the recipe as I fed Nicoh and Pandora and got them situated for the evening.

Though the two knew the routine, I had to scold their repeated attempts to inch closer to the activity in the living room.

Natalie giggled as she watched me giving Nicoh the stink-eye, "I've wanted to get together like this for so long."

"Get together, with us?" Leah asked curiously.

"Well, sure. We did all go to high school together and have mutual friends. We should have done this ages ago," she replied. We nodded and munched in silence, both of us contemplating the best way of approaching our questions now that we'd lured our guest here. We need not have worried, Natalie initiated the conversation for us.

"It's something about Charlie, huh?" I started to wonder if the girl was psychic as she casually settled into an overstuffed arm chair. "All that evidence. I hear the County Attorney is actually getting ready to formally charge him with murder one. It's all pretty crazy, if you ask me." I wondered where she was getting her inside information.

Apparently, Leah was thinking the same thing, "Huh, that's interesting. What have you heard?"

Natalie leaned forward, her eyes bright as she shared her scoop. "A friend of mine at the County Attorney's Office said they have evidence placing Charlie in the garage at the time Parker was impaled with Big Bess." I winced at her callous choice of phrasing. "Plus, Charlie's admitted to disabling the security cameras in the garage prior to the party. He made up some excuse about doing work on the Eldorado he didn't want recorded, then the car turns out to be the murder weapon. Kind of sloppy, if you ask me."

Leah and I nodded, even though we knew the real reason Charlie had dismantled those cameras, but until we could confirm who was to be trusted, we weren't sharing.

"Anyway, he claims he forgot to turn them back on, meaning

they were off during the party and therefore, during the time Parker conveniently wandered into the parking garage to meet his demise. I mean, who writes this stuff?

"Another thing—no one else had access to Big Bess. It's not like someone would take the time to hotwire an old car like that just so they could murder someone with it. Which didn't happen, by the way." Upon seeing our raised brows, Natalie elaborated, "My friend said the techs tested for that. The car was started with a key, which only one person had access to." She formed a "C" with her thumb and forefinger.

"Err, that all seems pretty circumstantial…" Leah started to comment but Natalie held up a finger.

"Oh, there's more, girlfriend. The shoe and tie I found at the lake were Charlie's…not Parker's, as I had originally thought, though they did dredge his up later. Yuck, I'd bet no amount of OxiClean would get those stains out." She appeared amused by her own rather insensitive joke, making me wonder if she'd changed her mind about Charlie's innocence. The way this conversation was going, it certainly seemed to be the case.

"What about Charlie's claim he placed them in the garage after his walk by the lake?" I asked, assuming her source had already shared whatever specifics the police had gathered.

"Oh, he was there all right, but it wasn't to deposit his shoes. A witness puts Charlie at the entrance of the parking garage during the time they've established Parker was murdered. She said he was cursing at the security panel."

"I thought Charlie turned the security cameras off in the parking garage?"

"The cameras yes, but not the entry keypad. You still had to have a code to get into the garage. Charlie was probably too drunk to remember his, or kept fat-fingering it, because it was the theatrics of his outburst that made him stand out to the woman," Natalie added.

"She's a resident in his building?" Leah asked hopefully.

"I'm not sure about that. All I know is she was out walking her dog."

"Walking her dog at that hour? Interesting," I commented with a sarcastic undertone that only Leah caught.

She rolled her eyes before turning to Natalie. "The friend at the County Attorney's Office you mentioned—the one who gave you the inside track on the investigation—it isn't Sherman, is it? Because some of the details—"

"Oh yes, you know him too?" Natalie seemed pleased by their shared acquaintance.

"Yes, Sherman's been quite helpful in the past, definitely a source you want to have in your bag of tricks," Leah tilted her head slightly as she replied, as though something had aroused her curiosity.

"You got that right," Natalie replied, eager to continue. "He also told me the security log corroborates the witness' account. Apparently, each person has their own unique key code and Charlie's was used at the time the witness puts him at the parking garage's entrance."

"Which puts him in the vicinity of the garage during the time they think Parker was killed," Leah groaned.

"Maybe Charlie gave the key code to someone else?" I thought of the arrangements he had made with Senator Conrad.

"Except he didn't," Natalie replied earnestly, "or at least he said he didn't. Besides, it hadn't been used since he disabled the cameras." My heart sank—Charlie had probably given the senator and his entourage other key codes to use that evening.

Natalie prattled on, "The video of his reentry into the building also fits within their timeframe of the crime. Meaning between the time he returned to the building without his tie and shoes and the witness placed him at the parking garage, Charlie had plenty of leeway to kill Parker in the garage, dump his body and the evidence in the lake." When finished, she opened her hands in apology but her vibe indicated otherwise.

"Hold up a minute, Natalie. Let's assume Charlie had the means and opportunity—what's his motive? We are talking about premeditation after all, which assumes Charlie had planned to kill Parker. Over what—a few lousy deals? Charlie would have been mad—yes. Inconvenienced—yes. But, murderous?" Natalie's expression told me she wasn't buying what I was selling, but honestly, I didn't care. It wasn't Natalie I needed to convince. "I don't know much about law, but I thought, at a minimum, it took means, motive and opportunity to prove someone guilty of first degree murder. In my book, this case isn't quite as open and shut as the County Attorney thinks. Or I don't know Charlie."

Leah nodded. "I agree with AJ. Their rationale just doesn't hold water and without motive, you've got a lopsided wagon."

Natalie stiffened, obviously feeling challenged, though it hadn't been our intention. We were just having a friendly get-together, right?

"I can't answer that. No one but Charlie can. Maybe the business stuff was bigger than we thought? Maybe there were… other…more far-reaching implications?" I shrugged at Leah. We had no idea where Natalie was going with that thought.

Sensing she'd lost us, Natalie waved a white paper towel. "Hey guys, enough of this heavy stuff, who's up for some tasty snacks?" After Leah and I quickly thrust our hands up in the air, a giggle broke through and Natalie relaxed, obviously pleased about the change in topic.

For the next several hours, we ate, gossiped and giggled. During a more raucous bout of laughter, Nicoh and Pandora used the distraction to slink in and nab stray crumbs, but their less than stealthy attempts made the outbursts even more boisterous. Leah took the opportunity to announce it was time to claim our *Real Housewives of Phoenix* taglines, starting us off with hers.

"People say I dig up dirt, but it just tells me they've got something to hide." She finished it off by pimping her best pucker face.

Though Natalie and I could barely contain ourselves, I managed to chime in, "Think of me as a modern day da Vinci—the lens is my canvas and with it, I create masterpieces." I got up and did a little jig, a cross between the Cabbage Patch and Churnin' Butter, putting the other two into further hysterics.

It was Natalie's turn. "People say I'm as sweet as apple pie, but honey don't you dare compare me to baked goods."

We continued to snort and squeal with girlish laughter until Nicoh howled at the top of his lungs, his way of imploring us to stop. Pandora wasn't sure what to make of the situation and took cover under a nearby coffee table. After we'd suitably calmed ourselves, I was able to coax her out and placed her gently on my lap while Nicoh looked on with concern and perhaps a bit of jealously. He'd never been much of a lap top. At ninety-eight pounds, go figure.

Natalie yawned, and after looking at her watch, announced she needed to get a move on. It was a school night for all of us. We offered to call her a cab but she waved us off, noting a girlfriend had dropped her off and was ready to pick her up at a moment's notice. She quickly hugged us, scratched both pups and was down the drive before we had the opportunity to walk her out.

Leah started to say something but I grabbed her arm, pulled her through the door and down the steps, carefully tucking in behind a hedge of bougainvilleas that lined the pathway. Prickly little suckers. A car door opened and we could hear Natalie's tinkling laugh. We peered around the shrub in time to see a familiar blue Audi slip into the night. Its license plate read 4JUSTIS. Charlie had been right—it wasn't Parker's car—though it could very well have belonged to a particular female attorney.

"That alone may have been an interesting culmination to the

evening's events," Leah thumbed in the direction of the Audi, "but Natalie's friend, Sherman, in the County Attorney's Office? Is *Lisa* Sherman…and I'm pretty sure she's still a girl."

CHAPTER SIXTEEN

Why had Natalie been so forthcoming, only to lie about the source of her information? And, if she lied about that, what else had she lied about? After another fitful night, I padded down the hall in my Powerpuff Girl slippers, grumpily noting the superhero powers hadn't started kicking in yet. I was barely recharged and ready to tackle those questions, not to mention the dozens of others Leah and I had somehow managed to accumulate.

I hoped Leah had a more restful night. Even Nicoh and Pandora had seemed content, gently snoozing side by side on his king-sized pet bed until they escaped to the outdoors during the early morning hours. I looked out the window and found them sunning themselves by the pool, belly-sides up. Quite a pair, those two. It would be hard to separate them when Randy returned from Dallas. It always was.

I carefully poured water into the Keurig, one of the many delightful treats Leah brought from her condo, and munched absently on a pretzel from the previous night's snackfest. It got me thinking about Natalie...and Morgan. Now that was an odd pair. Neither of them had anything in common. Then again, what

did I know? I'd been off-base about Natalie. Or, maybe Natalie
was just off as of late?

And, what did I know about Morgan, other than what Charlie
had told me, which was very little? How had she hooked up with
Davis Conrad? And why was she on leave? It obviously wasn't to
help Charlie with his defense. To my knowledge, she hadn't even
gone to see him since his arrest. Who was Morgan Thompson?

I sipped my coffee, effectively burning my tongue on the first
attempt as I called my friend, Stacy, at the bar association. We'd
met while volunteering at an animal rescue festival in North
Scottsdale years earlier and had been friends ever since. Not only
was she a fierce animal advocate, she also had an inside line on
the legal community. If anyone could get the goods on Morgan, it
was Stacy.

Stacy knew about Charlie's arrest and after a brief explanation
of what I needed, put me on hold. I assumed she was going to
provide me with a number for another contact, but when she
returned she gave me one better.

"As it turns out, Morgan is not exactly on a leave of
absence. She's been suspended from the firm and her partner-
ship placed under review for undisclosed disciplinary reasons.
All of this went down...let's see...about three weeks ago. I
would need to make a direct inquiry to get more specific
details."

"Nah, hold off on that. Leah and I don't need to be raising any
more red flags at this point. At least this tells us why she's not at
her job. Now I need to find out more about her background here
in Arizona."

Stacy snorted. "It shouldn't be too hard, given her family
connections."

"I don't follow."

"Geez, AJ. I thought you knew. Morgan's the daughter of the
former state senator, Davis Conrad." Wow, Nicoh could have

knocked me over with his tail. Morgan Thompson was Morgan Conrad. I certainly hadn't seen that one coming.

After I thanked Stacy and promised to treat her to lunch for her assistance, I immediately typed Morgan's name into the search engine on my trusty laptop. Why hadn't I thought of doing this before? There was more information than I ever wanted to know about Charlie's ex-girlfriend and her family.

Morgan had gone to a boarding school on the east coast—the same one her socialite mother, Cecilia Thompson, had attended before marrying a young attorney named Davis Conrad. Shortly after her father became a state senator, during Morgan's junior year in high school, she changed her name—perhaps to avoid the scrutiny that often followed children of public figures? If so, why choose her mother's maiden name? Perhaps it was preferable to be known as the daughter of a renowned socialite than one of a politician with questionable integrity? Regardless of her rationale, by the time Morgan headed off to Harvard, she was known as Morgan Thompson.

From all appearances, Morgan had gotten into the Ivy League on her own accord, excelled while she was there and graduated with honors. Her post-Harvard years were equally successful. She was the youngest person to make partner in the prestigious San Francisco law firm and until recently, had a stellar record.

Many of the online photos depicted the Conrad family on happy occasions—social and political outings, family get-together, even several with their brood of Scottish Terriers, all named after past or present Supreme Court Justices. I was squinting at a few pictures taken of Morgan and another familiar face at Harvard when Leah shuffled into the kitchen, hair standing on end, eyes puffy from sleep and too many salt-rimmed margaritas.

"What's up?" she murmured sleepily, grabbing my coffee cup and taking a long swig as I swung the laptop around to face her.

"Morgan was Greg's girlfriend before she dated Charlie." I pointed at the beaming couple, taken during happier times during their college days.

Leah sat the mug down with a clunk and stared at the screen. "Wow, small world. How come we never knew about this?"

She seemed miffed that such a juicy detail would have slipped her radar. I shrugged and filled her in on Morgan's background—including her famous family and subsequent name swap—and worked my way to her current career-botching snafu.

"So, I guess we now know the senator's guest was legit," I commented as Leah nibbled her lip.

"Do we?" Leah replied absently. "Do we know it was legit? If so, how come Charlie didn't know? And why all the secrecy?"

"What if Morgan hadn't been his intended guest? Maybe Morgan decided to accompany her dad after the arrangement to disable the security camera had been made."

"Or because the arrangement was made."

"Exactly."

"I may have a way to get some more background on Morgan, to find out the reason behind her suspension." She drained the last of my coffee and retreated to her room.

I groaned, not only was I out of coffee, I didn't want to know how she was going to get that information. Not one single drop.

I half-expected Leah to be napping when I checked on her a couple of hours later, but as I wiggled a fresh cup of joe through the partially opened doorway, a snicker emerged before the mug was snatched and the door thrown open. Leah's face beamed as she did a victory dance, the mug's contents precariously sloshing from side to side.

"Spill it before you actually do. What did you learn?" A mass of notepads was strewn about every surface. It was how she worked best, though given her lack of organizational skills, I marveled at her ability keep it all straight. Most of the time, I was convinced the notepads served as impressive-looking props while she stored all the pertinent goodies in her head.

"Well…" She loved drawing out the suspense. Of course, considering my best friend was more impatient than a canine at dinner time, the tension-building was typically short-lived. This time was no different. "Turns out Morgan's strong suit is not creative accounting. She's facing disciplinary sanctions— including disbarment and prosecution—for unauthorized utilization of the firm's funds."

"What the heck does that mean? Is that legalese for she embezzled from her firm?"

"Technically, she did use the funds without permission, but it was for a good cause." She bobbed her head in an attempt to convince me.

I wasn't buying—besides, when had she become such an advocate of Morgan's? Wasn't Charlie our priority? We certainly didn't have time to worry about Morgan's indiscretions and said as much.

"A good cause as in what—a big sale at Barney's?"

Leah chuckled. "That's what I thought, too. Turns out, Morgan possesses a quality her Harvard pals Charlie and Parker, not to mention that father of hers, don't. Loyalty. Especially where her mother is concerned."

"Senator Conrad's wife, Cecilia?"

Leah nodded. "She's been missing from the social scene for a while now, shortly after her husband's term ended. Apparently, she's been battling Huntington's—the Thompson family carries the gene."

I gasped. I didn't know much about it, but from what I'd heard, Huntington's was a cruel disease that wasted away nerve cells in the brain, causing rampant devastation to one's mind and body. Among the casualties were severely affected muscle and motor skills, along with dementia. Presently, there was also no known cure.

"She's currently in a private facility, the same one that cared for her sister, Morgan's aunt, until her death. Apparently, she'd had a long, excruciating battle with the same disease, which brings me to the reason behind Morgan's suspension." She paused to catch her breath. "From what I understand, the facility has been struggling to keep its head above water for a while now, like everyone during this economic downturn. The principals also made some unfortunate business decisions along the way and now they're faced with closing several facilities, including the one where Morgan's mother resides.

"Of course, the family can certainly afford to move her else-where, but think about the disruption, not to mention stress, it would cause her. And let's not forget about the other residents, many of whom are without the means to go elsewhere.

"Apparently, Morgan went to her father for assistance, but he refused to intervene because of the perception it would put out into the political universe. Favoritism...crap excuses like that."

I groaned. "Let me guess, Morgan took money from her law firm to keep her mother's facility in the black."

Leah nodded. "Just enough to keep things going, in small enough amounts to fly under the radar."

"How long did this go on?"

"Two years, give or take." Talk about modern day Robin Hood. Morgan certainly hadn't seemed suited for the role. "Any-way, her borrowing finally caught up with her. Or rather, her firm caught on. My source did intimate at least a couple of the other partners had been aware of Morgan's actions all along."

"Perhaps hoping she would put it back?"

"Yeah, something like that. Regardless, what Morgan did was

criminal. Her firm's desire to minimize the fallout is the main reason she's not in jail yet."

I laughed, though I wasn't feeling jovial. "I'm sure Senator Conrad feels the same way."

"That would be an affirmative."

"Where did you get this information, anyway?"

"You don't want to know."

"The rational side of me says no, but the other side that enjoys the sick fascination of knowing how you do the devious things you do? She's winning out."

"Ok, you asked, but don't say I didn't warn you," she teased as I pretended to cover my ears. "I found some juicy tidbits using the pictures you scrounged up on the Internet." She laughed at my doubtful glance. "Seriously, I jotted down the names of the people in the pictures with Morgan and created a roster of sorts. Turns out, she still keeps in touch with a couple of her law school buddies. One of them happens to work at the same law firm. In fact, he was grateful to Morgan because she helped bring him on board."

"And just like that"—I snapped my fingers—"he gave up dirt on Morgan?"

"He did…" she replied slowly, "after I told him in addition to the possible disbarment and prosecution she faced as a result of her issues with the firm, Morgan was also being looked at as an accessory in the murder of one of her childhood chums. One who also happened to be an alum."

I chuckled. "You are brutal—creative—but brutal."

Leah gave me her best evil genius laugh. "You'd be surprised what a guy would do to save a fair maiden."

"Oh yeah, totally getting that whole damsel in distress vibe off Morgan," I replied sarcastically, thinking of the conversation we'd recently had with her. She'd more likely reward the chivalry by shoving hot pokers into his eyes.

It did make me wonder about the dynamic between Morgan, Parker and Charlie once Greg had passed. To date, no one had been forthcoming about the nature of their relationships with one another and frankly, I was fed up with all the secrecy.

"Do me a favor?" Leah looked at me sideways, but nodded. "Keep an eye on Nicoh and Pandora. There's something I need to do," I looked at my watch, "sooner rather than later."

"Where are you going?" she asked.

"To have a little chat with Charlie. Before we go any further with this wild goose chase, I want to know exactly where we stand."

At this point, I wasn't sure of anything, other than there was a distinct possibility we'd been running around like chickens this whole time, while the murderer sat in jail.

CHAPTER SEVENTEEN

Charlie was even more pale this visit. Like vampire pale. It didn't occur to me until much later that it was due to his missed spray tan appointments. His demeanor was more upbeat on this visit, given that his minions were out there working hard to get him out of his current predicament. *Always someone there to clean up your mess for you, isn't there?* I grumbled, fully prepared to wipe the smile off his face. I figured there were only a couple of ways the conversation could go: A, Charlie would give me the information I wanted and I would return to being a good little minion or B, he'd continue to hold out on pertinent information, I'd punch him in the throat and we'd end up sharing a cell. I preferred option A, but was warming up to B.

"You have something?" his voice was hopeful as he searched my face.

"Leah and I have been doing some…research," I worked to keep both my tone and expression blank, "though honestly, we aren't exactly sure what we have, other than a crock filled with half-truths." Charlie's eyes widened. "You failed to mention that Morgan dated Greg first." Correct that—his eyes popped. He hadn't expected me to confront him. I waited expectantly for him to compose his thoughts.

"That was…a long time ago," he replied after a moment. "You know what happened."

"I know Greg died. They were together then?"

He nodded. "They dated off and on in high school and throughout college."

"So, they were obviously serious."

"Sure, as serious as Morgan gets."

"Well, golly gee, Charlie. She strikes me as someone who is as serious as say…murder." He balked. It was cruel but at least I had his attention. "You also knew about her mother's illness."

"She was diagnosed while we were dating. It wasn't the reason we stopped seeing each other, though."

"Do I want to know?"

"Morgan's always been a bit…intense, even when we were at Harvard."

"What about in high school? I was surprised I never knew her, much less knew she was the senator's daughter."

"The three of us knew her because of our parents. It was a society thing." He shrugged. "No reason you would have known her."

"Nice, Charlie, truly appreciate the condescending dig."

"I didn't mean it like that. You're just being difficult, you know what I meant."

"Getting back to Morgan—you mentioned her being intense. So you wouldn't be surprised if I told you she was currently suspended and facing possible disbarment." I quickly filled him in on Morgan's creative use of the firm's resources. I'm not sure what reaction I expected but Charlie's expression remained neutral as he eyed me silently. I decided to take a pass on that for the time-being. I had other ground to cover.

"Why did you dismantle the video before the party?"

He held my gaze for a moment before looking away. "It was at the senator's request."

I gestured for him elaborate and when he didn't respond immediately, I filled in the blanks. "He had a special guest that he was bringing to the party—one that would be present but not to be seen accompanying him."

Charlie's mouth dropped open. "How did you know?"

"Leah and I watched the videos, Charlie. We saw you in the parking garage before you dismantled the cameras and after, during your conversation with Arch."

"I don't understand. If you knew, they why did you..." His jaw clenched. "You wanted to see if I would lie." He sighed when I didn't respond, his pale, cracked lips pursing, "Senator Conrad likes to bring a friend with him. It wasn't the first time I've had to accommodate such a request." The way he said it led me to believe the former senator wasn't the only guest of Charlie's trying to conceal extracurricular activities.

"You ever know who the friends were?"

He shook his head. "It would be hard to tell. Many of my guests bring a plus one. And frankly, I don't care. It's good business." I assumed he meant having someone like David Conrad in his corner and wondered if it had been worth it.

"So, on the night of the party, it's safe to say you weren't aware which partygoer had accompanied the senator?"

"No idea."

"Would you be surprised to learn it was Morgan?"

"Right, he went to all that trouble so he could bring his daughter to the party." He frowned when I nodded. "That makes no sense—why would she sneak in—she already had an invite."

"I have no idea. You previously indicated she and Natalie weren't friends—what about Natalie and Arch, were they friendly?"

Charlie snorted. "No, definitely not."

"What do you know about Arch?"

"What kind of question is that? He's my assistant—it's not like he would have...hurt Parker..." I looked at him impatiently. He raised his hands in defeat, "Ok, ok...just answer the question." He blew out a long breath. "Honestly, not much. He lives in Mesa now. I think he used to live with his mom until she died a while back. I got the impression she'd been sick for some time, though I'm not familiar with the details. He never talked about it, but I overheard him talking to the hospice toward the end. `

"Then, when he came back to work for me, he told me he'd moved. Place must have been a dump in a pretty seedy area, because he constantly worried about going home, finding the place broken into and his belongings either gone or destroyed." He shook his head, disgusted, "I don't know how people can live like that."

"Not everyone is born with money, Charlie." He started to protest, but I stopped him, "Why did you rehire him, anyway?"

He grumbled. "Considering he's taken up residence in my absence—and hasn't bothered to visit once—I'm seriously starting to wonder the same thing. It was Natalie's idea. She made a pretty good case using that second chance nonsense. She can be surprisingly convincing when she wants to." Somehow, I didn't doubt that in the least.

The guard entered and told us our time was up. As he collected Charlie, I threw out on last question, "On the day of the White Party, where did you go from 12:30 to 6:40 p.m. while the rest of us were setting up?" Surely he couldn't deny it this time, knowing Leah and I had seen the video?

His eyes flashed with anger, surprising me. "Stay out of it, AJ. It has nothing to do with this, or with you." He turned on his heel and nodded to the guard, leaving me to stare at his back. As he marched through the doorway, he hesitated for a moment. "Not everyone deserves second chances."

* * *

As if my conversation with Charlie hadn't been enough of a treat, I had another one waiting when I exited the police station. I was brooding and would have normally missed her had it not been for her combative stance as she leaned against her Audi, arms crossed and foot tapping, irritation rippling from her like whitecaps. All six feet of her curvaceous figure were clad in black, from studded biker jacket to skin-hugging jeans to the knee-high riding boots with fierce-looking toeplates. Even her hair whipped angrily as the wind picked up, as if sensing a storm was brewing. If she'd been going for effect, it worked. Startled, I tripped over my size nine Chuck Taylors, barely catching myself before tumbling nose first into the sidewalk. If my reaction had amused her in the least, it failed to translate to her expression.

"The famous Arianna Jackson," Morgan's voice was husky as she slid aviators to the tip of her nose, her perusal overtly disapproving. "You're here visiting Charlie, I presume?" I didn't respond, more preoccupied with maintaining a safe distance.

"Don't bother answering that. I know you and your little blond-haired friend have been running around town asking questions, hoping to clear his good name. Well, even smart girls need some advice from time to time." Before I could reply, she cut the space between us until I could smell the combination of her musky perfume and cinnamony breath.

"Things are not always as they seem, Arianna. Sometimes it's better to leave them alone than it is to involve yourself in something you don't understand." I may have been mistaken, but it sounded more like a threat than friendly advice. Morgan stared at me, her eyes boring into mine and for a moment, I thought she would elaborate. Instead, she unceremoniously pushed her sunglasses up, turned on her heel and strode back to her car.

She was at the driver's door before I finally spoke, "And what about the truth, Morgan? Are we to leave it alone, too?" She paused just long enough I was convinced she would return to infringe upon my personal space.

She remained in place, though her mouth quirked. "I guess that depends upon whose truth you seek." She started to get into her Audi, effectively dismissing me.

I thumbed behind me. "It's about his truth. And Parker's. Don't you think they deserve that?"

Her lips curled into a snarl. "Deserve? Parker is a little beyond deserving anything. The truth is for the living, Arianna. And honestly, even if it revealed itself, I doubt you'd like the outcome." This time, she got in, revved the engine and left me standing there, sucking her fumes.

* * *

I returned home to find Leah sitting in the kitchen, pouring over her laptop while scribbling frantically on a notepad. Nicoh bounded to me with Pandora following close behind, tails wagging expectantly. I chuckled and scratched them both until Leah came up for air.

"Well, that's interesting," she replied after I finished filled her in on my latest conversation with Charlie, as well as the surprise appearance from Morgan. "What do you make of her advice?"

"Not sure. I wonder how she knew I would be there in the first place."

Leah shrugged. "Same way I know what I know." Right... inside information. One of these days, I'd need to expand my own network of confidential informants. I added it to my mental checklist, right after "get Charlie out of jail" and "find Parker's killer."

"I'm not saying your chats with Charlie and Morgan weren't enlightening, but do you wanna hear what I've got?" I sighed, but nodded. "Against my better judgment, I talked to Vargas…dum, dum, dum. Charlie's not the only one without a decent alibi for the time of Parker's murder."

"Mystery witness, notwithstanding."

"Right, right…but except for that witness, Arch, Morgan, Natalie and at least a dozen people were either at home alone or with someone who couldn't be forced to incriminate them. Meaning, we've got a whole list of people, other than Charlie, who had the opportunity to kill Parker and dump him afterward."

"Ok, that gives us other people with opportunity, big whoopee. Sorry, but that isn't a showstopper, Leah. The police already have that list and Charlie's still behind bars." I didn't want diminish her efforts, but that tidbit by itself got us nowhere. We needed less gristle and more meat. "What about motive?"

"Bear with me here. Some of the things Charlie told you meshed with what I just found out—for starters, Arch's mom."

"Charlie said she passed away. What does she have to do with this?"

"Well, I reached out into the information highway and found some juicy stuff on Senator Conrad's family—his wife, Cecilia, to be specific. Remember the sister with Huntington's?"

I snapped my fingers. "Right, the one that was in the same facility as Mrs. Conrad."

"That's the one. Before Arch's mom was Marie Underwood, she was Marie Thompson."

I blew out a low whistle. "Cecilia Conrad's sister. Morgan and Arch are cousins." Another puzzle piece found its way home.

Leah gave me a small, satisfied smile. "Hang on, Rockfish, I'm not done yet. When we met at Los Olivos, Natalie had come from volunteering at a long term care facility. She mentioned the funding she'd been working to obtain had finally come through."

"It's same facility where Mr. Thompson currently resides? So

Natalie knows Morgan's mother…and possibly knew Arch's as well?"

She nodded. "Likely, it's a small facility and Natalie's been volunteering there for years."

"Interesting, but other than providing a connection between Morgan, Natalie and Arch, it doesn't seem particularly…devious."

"Maybe not, but when you combine it with Natalie's bizarre behavior, her meeting with Arch and now Morgan's not-so-subtle threat, it means something."

I snorted. "Yeah, it mean three people who also know Charlie and Parker are all either related or connected in some way. It still doesn't scream motive for murder."

"Are you playing devil's advocate now, or just trying to be a buzz kill?" Leah was clearly incensed by my blasé attitude toward her research efforts.

"I'm not insinuating they're all coincidences, but we need something more concrete than the evidence the police currently have, including the witness who puts Charlie near the parking garage at the time of Parker's murder."

"Ugh, I knew I forgot to ask Vargas something. You mind?" I shook my head as she whipped out her cell phone and dialed. When Vargas answered, she put him on speakerphone.

"Hey Detective, Leah and AJ here, you have a few seconds for a couple of your favorite citizens?"

Vargas groaned. "Didn't I just talk to you? I do work, you know. Speaking of which, it would make my job a whole lot easier if a particular couple of Nancy Drew wannabes stopped mucking up the works on the Parker Harris case."

"First off," Leah retorted playfully, "we're more along the lines of Charlie's Angels—Charlie being, well Charlie, with me as Jill and AJ as Kelly." We heard Vargas snort on the other end of the connection. "Second, it isn't our job to make your job easier. It's our job to make sure you're *doing* your job, giving Charlie a fair shake, that type of thing. So for now, we'll let that whole mucking reference slide—if you agree to help us."

Vargas snorted. "Well, just so that we're clear. I'm not playing Bosley in this little fantasy. The two of you are going to get me into hot water for all the tips I've provided to your little side investigation."

"Hey, you'd better keep my good name out of that. Leah's been the one doing all the cajoling. I'm just an innocent bystander," I teased.

"That's not what I hear. The two of you—yes, I said two—are notorious for getting yourselves into all kinds of situations where you shouldn't have been sticking your noses in the first place." We both started to protest, but Vargas intervened. "So, getting back to the reason you called."

"Right, right, we know you've gone through the videos for the days surrounding the murder. What if we told you we'd been given access to the feed from the security cameras *inside* Charlie's penthouse and there were a few juicy morsels that would not only help your case, but might change your perspective on the murderer?"

Leah's query was met with silence. "Detective, you still with us?"

A grumble came from the other end of the extension. "I'm here. I'm just trying to decide whether I should go over there and arrest you both for obstruction. In case you two Nancy—err, Charlie's Angels weren't aware, it is a crime to withhold evidence pertinent to an ongoing investigation."

"Uh, consider what we've told you a peace offering?" I feebly countered.

Another grumble, or maybe it was a growl. "I'll get back to you on that. Meanwhile, I'll be there in ten. Do I need to tell you two to stay put?" He hung up before we could respond and fortu-

nately, before I had the opportunity to tell him I'd never figured
him for a Bosley type, anyway.

* * *

"Good going, *Jill*...you could have at least warned me you were
going to give up the goods. And, you didn't even get the scoop
on the witness, which was the purpose of the call." I threw my
hands up, actually kind of scared that Vargas would arrive in...
oh, nine minutes and counting now...with two pairs of handcuffs
in tow. Leah nodded silently, having arrived at a similar
conclusion.

When the doorbell rang in what seemed less than the ten
minutes Vargas had threatened, I hoped Leah had concocted a
solution in that spiky little head of hers. I contemplated hiding
out, but Nicoh and Pandora made enough noise to let the detective
know we were home. Sucking in a deep breath, I opened the door
to an intense-looking Detective Vargas. To my surprise, he had
brought backup.

Ramirez.

Undeterred, Leah cawed over my shoulder, "Oooh, Starsky
and Hutch ride again. Since when does PPD tag along with TPD,
anyway? You need special reinforcement on this one, Detective
Vargas?" And there she went, dashing all hope we'd be able to
talk our way out of this predicament.

"When TPD's poker game is interrupted by meddling busy-
bodies," Vargas snapped, stepping through the doorway as
Ramirez followed, his stature equally imposing and expression
consumed with barely-contained fury.

He caught me by surprise when he whispered in my ear as he
passed, "He was losing anyway."

I started to laugh but he put a finger to my lips and shook his
head before leveling me with look that catapulted a series of chills

down my spine and clearly communicated Leah and I wouldn't be getting off that easily.

"So, we're here to pick up those videos," Vargas' tone was all business as he glanced around.

"Well, had you not ended the conversation so abruptly, we could have saved you a trip and your poker game," Leah replied tersely, though Vargas looked unconvinced. "You access these videos through Internet links...you know...using a computer?"

"I know how to use a computer, Leah," Vargas snapped impatiently. "Let's see 'em." He gestured to the laptop she had left on the kitchen island, though his eyes were focused on the array of snacks still strewn about from the previous night. "Did we interrupt something?"

Leah blushed. "Natalie Ingram stopped by last night to share some information she had gotten about the investigation—inside information." She glanced warily at Vargas.

"Well, she certainly didn't get anything from me," he replied sharply. "I'm a one girl per investigation type of source."

Despite being furious, he managed to slip her a smoldering look before his brusque demeanor returned. It was my turn to blush and look away while Leah ignored him, pretending to focus on her laptop. Once she accessed the correct feed, she fast-forwarded to the interaction between Arch and Natalie before swiveling the laptop toward the detectives.

Though his irritation was just as palpable as Vargas', Ramirez had been surprisingly quiet to this point. "Interesting that Wilson never mentioned these cameras," he commented once they finished watching the feed, before turning his steely gaze on us.

Though I personally wanted to squirm my way out of the room, beyond the reach of its intensity, both Leah and I responded with tiny shrugs. Who knew why Charlie did half the things he did, or didn't do. Maybe he hadn't been sure what they'd find. One thing was certain, throughout the course of the investigation he hadn't gone out of his way to make things easier for the police, much less for himself.

I still wondered where he'd been all those hours prior to the party and why he was overtly evasive, if not hostile, when I'd brought it up. A bit too late, I realized I'd muttered that last bit out loud. Leah could only shake her head while both detectives stared at me. Vargas' gaze was a bit more scrutinizing than I liked, his midnight-colored eyes drilling into mine. I bit my lip, seriously hoping handcuffs and a ride in a smelly police cruiser weren't in my immediate future.

Fortunately, he glanced away. "We plan on finding out. Wilson contends he had several private business meetings that afternoon but up to this point, has refused to divulge who they were with. We know it wasn't Harris. We've located and interviewed the individuals he'd been with during that time and Wilson was not among those present."

I nodded. "Speaking of being present, the witness who placed Charlie at the parking garage, does she happen to live in his building?"

Vargas squinted. "It's funny you should ask. Off the record, no, she wasn't a resident, nor did she live at the address she provided. No one with that name did. We're still trying to track her down, but it appears she's in the wind."

I looked at Leah. We'd caught a break. The only witness placing Charlie at the scene had gone missing, or perhaps she'd never existed. Either way, the County Attorney's case was starting to crack. A few more whacks and maybe, just maybe, Leah and I would be able to break this nut wide open…meaning the two of us could turn out to be Charlie's angels. Stranger things have happened. Right?

CHAPTER EIGHTEEN

"We barely dodged a bullet with those two," Leah commented, a long moment passing as the detectives descended the steps. It felt like a staircase scene from a Hitchcock movie—long and agonizing.

"Yeah, but we learned the witness was bogus."

"True—" She was interrupted by the doorbell.

We looked at each other in horror. Surely the detective hadn't changed their minds about hauling us off in handcuffs? As we stood there silently debating about what to do, it rang again. And again. Pandora surprised us when she rushed toward it, barking and dancing on her hind legs. Considering the detectives would not have elicited that reaction, I motioned for Leah to open the door. Pandora's dad, Randy, stood there, a confused look on his face as he glanced over his shoulder.

"Was that...the police I saw leaving?"

"Um, yeah, they're friends of ours." Randy nodded skeptically.

Leah ushered him in, while I bolted out a bit too enthusiastically, "You're home early!"

He flushed, shifting from one foot to the other while tapping his cell phone against his thigh. "Err…about that. It turns out… I'm moving."

"Oh, wow. Like to Ahwatukee or something?" Leah asked.

"Err…no," Randy replied quietly, lowering his eyes, "to Dallas. The client I've been working with needs a bit more hand-holding than was originally thought. My firm has assigned me to oversee their account, indefinitely." He shrugged. "Essentially, that could mean three years or it could translate to something longer. I'll still keep the house here until we figure things out, but in the interim, they've set me up in a condo." He babbled, clearly excited about the new opportunity, but he'd lost me back at the whole "moving" part.

"So, you'd like for me to keep Pandora while you are out there?" I asked once he finished. Leah nodded, absently scratching both dogs while their tails beat against her legs.

"What? Oh no, I could never ask you to do that. I actually came back to get her and to pack a few necessities. I've got to head back by the end of the weekend—start the week fresh and all."

Randy searched our faces, hoping for approval. I hadn't had a chance to digest his news, so I wasn't sure what vibe I was giving him. Pandora wasn't mine, so I certainly couldn't say no. I looked into Nicoh's eyes, so brown and soft, his current happy expression and waggy tail. I knew losing his best gal pal would be tough. Pandora hadn't left his side and—sensing something was amiss—nudged the base of his ear with her muzzle, her own tail fluttering in short sporadic beats. I exhaled a deep breath, praying I could keep the waterworks at bay, at least until Randy departed.

"Congratulations, Randy. I mean that. We'll certainly miss you…both. I know Nicoh will miss his pal. Would you be able to bring her by before you leave on Sunday?"

He nodded and scruffed Nicoh under the chin. "Definitely. I

know it will be an adjustment for Ms. P., too, but we'll return every other month or so, so we'll be back before you know it."

I gave them both quick, fierce hugs and managed to see them out before a single tear broke free. Nicoh howled sadly. Leaning against the closed door, I let out a long breath and looked at Leah, who had been uncharacteristically quiet during Randy's visit. Her eyes were rimmed in red, mouth pursed as she too, fought the inevitable downpour.

* * *

My emotions were shot and brain mush as my body needled me with fatigue. I needed to keep moving—even if it was mindless busywork. After some less than stellar housecleaning, I mulled over my latest project, photographing a series of galleries that were part of the seasonal downtown art walk. The city's Chamber of Commerce was my client—and while the turnaround time was short—the paycheck was substantial and much-needed.

Unfortunately, my mind wandered as I read the specs. First, to the loved ones I'd lost and then to the ones I'd lost but never known. Though it had been no fault of my own, their absence still stung. In fact, it weighed on me more than I'd ever confess. Immediate on my mind were my two sets of parents—the first had raised me and the second had given me life—and my sister. I had never gotten the opportunity to meet the latter three and was left with a hole where they should have been and where so many questions remained unanswered. Leah and Nicoh were my family now, as were my close circle of friends—Ramirez, the Stanton brothers—even Charlie. If I'd learned anything over the past few years, most of us would protect the ones we cared for at any cost.

That's when it clicked. To this point, the police had assumed Parker had been murdered because of a bad business deal, that the motive had been simple greed. What if they were wrong? What if the reason had been more deeply rooted. Deeper than revenge or retribution? What if the choices Parker made had put him on a path, one that sealed his destiny? In making those choices, Parker had crossed a line that changed lives, divided families. Would that be enough reason to kill? If there was one thing I could be sure of —when it came to Parker Harris—you'd better believe it.

* * *

Grimacing, I placed the call, nibbling on a fingernail as I counted rings, convinced I would end up with voicemail.

"What do you want now, Jackson?" Vargas growled, picking up after five.

"It's nice to talk to you again too, Detective,"

"Whatever. What do you want? Keep in mind I'm trying to run an investigation here. So, unless you have more information, this isn't a two-way street. As it is, I'm sitting here—on my night off—watching video footage I received at the thirteenth hour."

"Actually, it's not even midnight yet." I tried my best to be helpful.

"You know, you two are lucky I didn't arrest you for with-holding evidence." Hadn't we already covered this ground? I decided not to stir that pot, the big guy wasn't in the best of moods. "I'm not sure the term 'thin ice' has any meaning to you." Vargas exhaled.

"I'm sorry, Detective. I'll preface this by saying I would like to avoid a private escort to the police station in your cruiser, but I do have a question."

He scoffed. "Ramirez warned me you were a pill." Ramirez had called me a pill? Truth be told, I hadn't previously been fond of the spitfire reference, but this took things to another level. At some point in the immediate future, Ramirez and I would need to have a little chat. "I don't have all day, Action Jackson."

"Err, yeah…sorry, got distracted. I'm curious about the missing witness. Did you talk to her personally?"

"No, she approached one of the patrolmen the day we pulled Harris from Tempe Town Lake. He was working the scene perimeter, manning the crowd, when she just showed up."

"So he has a description?"

"A rough one. It was crazy down there that day. Always is when we pull one out, draws the lookie loos like overfed pigeons." I heard papers shuffling. "Here it is. Margaret O'Connor. Late twenties to early thirties. Tall, between 5 feet 11 inches and 6 feet 1 inch. Wearing a black windbreaker, tennis shoes and black baseball cap that covered the majority of her hair, which he thought might have been reddish-brown. No description of her features. Apparently she was wearing sunglasses that covered the better part of her face. That's about it."

"What about the dog?"

"Yeah, what about it?"

"What did it look like?"

"Officer said it was small and black with pointy ears. Not being a dog person he wasn't sure about the breed." He paused to laugh. "He did note it was the type you'd expect to see wearing a red plaid sweater. It wasn't…wearing a sweater, that is, red or otherwise. Oh, and he heard her call it Ginsburg—odd name for a dog."

I shook my head, not odd at all. O'Connor and Ginsburg were both names of Supreme Court Justices.

Vargas knew I was on to something, but before he could threaten the handcuffs again, I feigned sleepiness and ended the conversation. For the next several minutes, I sat alone in the dark and thought, continuing to torture that fingernail in the process.

I went back to the beginning and thought about Charlie. And Parker. And Greg. I added Natalie, Morgan and Arch into the mix.

Six people.

Two were dead.

One by suicide.

One by murder.

One was in jail.

Three remained.

Linked by blood or by circumstance, all three had been less than truthful as of late. Whether it had been by omission or outright lie had no bearing. Each had guilty knowledge and more importantly, means, motive and opportunity. In the end all the deception, mistruths and subterfuge led to the same destination and the same conclusion.

One of them had murdered Parker.

CHAPTER NINETEEN

In hindsight, I suppose I should have called Vargas back, or Ramirez, at a minimum. I'd been warned by both about my continued involvement, yet even the threat of jail couldn't sway me. Unfortunately, selective listening wasn't my only flaw. I'd also inherited stubbornness from my parents. I hoped it wouldn't prove fatal.

I shook my head, time was running out and Charlie was about to be formally charged with murder. I had to trust my gut and forge ahead, no matter how harebrained my scheme might have been.

I wanted to tell Leah my plan, but when I snuck a peek into her room, only tufts of hair were visible from beneath the covers. Instead, I left her snoozing, justifying it as much-needed rest. Nicoh, too, was crashed, his large frame sprawled across the bed, head buried beneath a mass of pillows. My decision made, I left Leah a detailed note, glanced around and pulled the door shut, hoping I'd come back in one piece.

I cursed after finding the Mini low on gas and borrowed Leah's SUV, knowing she'd already be grumpy about missing out on the adventure. I made a mental note to pick up Starbucks on the way home as a peace offering and after glancing at the clock, hoped it would be open by the time I made my return trip.

Had I not been so engrossed in thought, I would have noticed the car following a good measure behind, especially considering I'd been through this scenario before. Given my past experiences, you'd think a girl would learn.

Traffic was limited, so I made good time across the cities and was pleased to find I had my choice of parking on the barren Tempe streets. Stu buzzed me in without question and after a brief conversation, I proceeded to the penthouse. I had checked the video feed before I'd left and while I had not seen him, I knew Arch was in there somewhere. It was dark when I entered, not surprising considering the hour, though I half-expected him to be playing The Legend of Zelda on Charlie's Wii while eating Doritos or some other greasy, color-injected snack on the pristine leather couches. My only guide through the space was the moon trickling through the skylights, causing me to narrowly miss a lamp as I shuffled along the walls. Someone had been moving things around in their boss' absence, I mused.

"What are you doing here?" Arch's voice came from the direction of the living room. After squinting for a moment, I was able to make out his silhouette, sitting alone in the darkness.

"I came to see you, of course." I chuckled in an effort to lighten the mood.

"No pet this time?" I couldn't see his face but his tone was glib.

My fingers found a light switch. Arch blinked even though the lighting was dim, indicating he'd been sitting like that for a while. He'd likely not slept recently either, as evidenced by his blood-shot eyes. Oddly enough, they defied an otherwise unruffled appearance. His hair was styled, face cleanly shaven and attire crisp. Had it not been for the circumstances, he looked ready to work or perhaps, to meet someone.

"You look tired, Arch. Not been sleeping well?" He shrugged and took a long drink from the cocktail glass he'd been clutching, draining the amber liquid until only ice cubes tinkled. As he placed it on the coffee table, I noticed the empty Maker's Mark bottle on its side.

"Hmm, guilty conscience, perhaps?"

His head snapped in my direction, though he averted his gaze. "My conscience is clear," he rasped.

I put my hands up in mock surrender. "Since I'm already here, care if I ask you a couple of questions then? He waved, indicating he didn't. "On the day of the White Party, what did you give Natalie?"

He squinted, his eyes meeting mine. "How did you know about that?" It was my turn to shrug and after scrutinizing me for a moment, he laughed. "Let me guess. Charlie's got this place geared up too," He shook his head, clearly not amused by the knowledge his boss had been keeping tabs on him.

"The key to Big Bess," he replied after a long pause.

I nodded. "Anything else?"

He chuckled. "Charlie's key card."

"Why did she say she wanted them?"

"Parker knew a friend of this classic car guy from California Charlie had talked about. Apparently he has his own show on the Speed channel?" I shook my head. I had no idea who or what he was referencing. "Anyway, Parker found out the car guy was going to be in town and thought it would be a hoot to have him detail Charlie's Eldorado. They needed the car keys to facilitate the surprise. She wanted the key card so that she could return the car keys in case I wasn't around when the guy finished." Was he serious?

"I'm not buying it, Arch. Even if that story was true, either Parker or Natalie could have returned the car keys while you were here. The party was that night. It wasn't like you were going anywhere before then. They certainly didn't need Charlie's key card for that."

"It was what she wanted. She didn't want to spoil the surprise if something didn't work out as planned." I'll bet she didn't.

"But you gave her more than those two items, didn't you? You gave her Charlie's code to parking garage as well." Though he tried to mask his surprise, his eye twitched.

"Why?" I pressed. This time he shrugged but didn't respond. "Ok, so when the police determined Parker had been killed that same day, in the parking garage, with the car whose keys you'd just handed off…that didn't seem suspect to you?"

"Natalie didn't have anything to do with that. It's just a coincidence."

"Right, a coincidence Charlie supposedly killed Parker using Big Bess, while Natalie was in possession of the only set of keys? 'Cause you can't be sure she ever returned them, can you?" I replied sarcastically. "Yeah, I'd say that was a real coincidence."

"I'm sure she had returned everything by then." The way he was defending her made me wonder if Arch had a thing for Natalie. After seeing how she'd treated him on the video, it was clear Arch didn't know much about women. "The police found them when they searched the penthouse, before they arrested Charlie." I shook my head. Copies could have been made and the originals returned during the party. It still didn't explain Charlie's missing key card.

Frustrated I wasn't getting anywhere with him, I changed tactics, "Did Natalie convince you to ask Charlie for your job back?"

"Why would she? I needed a job and Charlie hadn't filled mine yet, so I figured it was worth a shot. He doesn't stay mad long and frankly, the reason he severed our working relationship in the first place was bogus."

"So you'd be surprised if I told you she went to Charlie on your behalf and suggested it?"

He shook his head from side to side. "She wouldn't do that. Charlie asked me to come back because he needed me." *Asked?* Someone was seriously delusional. "In fact, he still needs me." I rest my case.

"All right, what about your cousin—what was her beef with Parker?"

He snorted. "Morgan? Everyone and everything pisses her off." At least he hadn't tried to deny their connection, though I could tell he was trying to figure out how I'd made it.

A sudden, satisfied twitch at the corner of Arch's mouth, followed by the slight shift of his eyes told me we were no longer alone in the penthouse. Natalie and Morgan had come to join our late night party. Someone had been keeping tabs on me.

"What? No margaritas?" Natalie appeared to be feeling particularly snotty.

She was dressed similarly to Morgan, still clad in the black ensemble from our previous confrontation. Maybe she was only allotted one death-eater costume per capital crime? I was about to comment, but decided sarcasm would be wasted on this crowd, even though it chafed me both were having such good hair days. I was sure my ponytail stood at all angles and could have afforded to have a pitchfork run through it, while Natalie's golden mane trailed down her back in a tidy braid and Morgan's auburn tresses billowed like flames. The breeze flowing through the open skylights only enhanced the effect.

Distracted by my hair envy, I had failed to notice both were also wearing gloves, and in Morgan's right hand clutched an equally fierce-looking piece of hardware. What surprised me more than the gun itself was that it wasn't aimed in my direction. Given his open-mouthed expression, I ventured a guess that Arch had noticed as well.

"You have a big mouth, cuz. You know that, don't you?"

Arch's eyes went wide. "What? I didn't tell her anything she didn't already know, I promise."

Morgan ignored his pleas, turning her black eyes toward me. "Natalie was convinced she could sway you and your little blond friend to side with us on this…matter. She lost that particular bet." She glanced at Natalie and laughed. "Pay up, Nat." Natalie pursed her lips in response.

"Side? What side is that?" I asked.

"Our side. Or Charlie's. I'm sorry to have to inform you that you picked the losing team, Arianna," Morgan's voice was husky.

"Why, because you have a gun?" My comment drew several annoyed glances.

"No, you simp. Because it's the right thing—the moral thing —to choose."

"Says the person holding the gun," I replied dryly.

Morgan threw her head back and laughed. "You are a feisty one. I'll give you that. No wonder Charlie keeps you around. You should take notes, Arch." Ignoring his seething looks, she turned back to me. "I'm guessing you want to know what's going on, which is why you chose the weakest link here." She wiggled the gun at Arch.

I nodded, no sense denying it now. Morgan lowered the gun and tapped it against her leg, while Natalie leaned against the wall, looking bored. Arch folded his arms and avoided looking at either of them, clearly enraged by his cousin's condescending jabs.

It was Natalie who spoke after a prolonged silence, "Parker and Charlie killed my brother. They killed Greg." Even Morgan stilled at the mention of his name.

"I thought Greg…committed suicide," I replied as quietly and gently as I could muster, but Morgan's head snapped in my direction, her eyes flashing.

"Because of Parker and Charlie...what they did to him...what they forced him to do."

Whatever had been stirring in Arch erupted as he launched himself at his cousin and slapped her hard across the face.

"Your precious Greg doesn't deserve your pity, you stupid cow! He was no better than they were. All three of them... killed...my mother, your aunt. It was their fault she died." Arch flopped into his chair while Morgan glared at him, a blotchy handprint forming on her face.

I thought she might be contemplating the advantages of shooting him, so I cleared my throat and attempted to diffuse the tension, "I'm sorry for your loss, I understand your mother had Huntington's before she passed?"

Arch nodded as he continued his stare down with Morgan. "She was in a private facility. Parker, Charlie *and* Greg were heavy into playing with the stock market—taking risks with other people's money—their usual modus operandi. She"—he dipped his head toward Morgan—"was dating Greg at the time and told him about a small group of investors representing various private healthcare facilities throughout the southwest. There's a large demand here for medical services due to the size and age of the population, as well as the type of transplants we attract from other states." I nodded, the term "snowbirds" popping into mind. "Greg took this information back to his cohorts, and they immediately concocted another money-making scheme the investors couldn't refuse. I mean, who would turn down the possibility of making millions, if not billions, within a relatively short time, if the risk was presented as being minimal?"

Morgan started to interject but Arch, with his renewed back-bone, cut her to the quick with a look. "I'm telling this part of the story, *cuz*." I noticed the rhythm of the gun tapping on her thigh had increased two-fold, but Morgan only nodded while Natalie looked on, her lips pressed into a tight line.

"As luck would have it...ha...what funny word. Luck." His laugh was harsh. "More like arrogance meets ignorance. Anyway, things went well, for a while. The boys made money. The investors made money. The facilities flourished. Everyone was happy. Until Parker got bored, as he inevitably would. He started dabbling on the side—the higher the risk, the better. It was all about living on the edge, being on the fringe. He was like an adrenaline junkie and money was his extreme sport. Only Parker wasn't playing with Monopoly money, or even his own. No, the real rush came from taking risks with *other* people's livelihood. And like any junkie, the high eventually wore off and when you're playing with real money, the consequences have devastating, life-altering affects. Investors couldn't honor their commitments. Their intended recipients were forced to either eliminate services and staff or close down entirely—leaving employees, patients, families and communities in peril. The facilities that were able to remain afloat did the best they could. And while I'm sure they would claim no one died as a result, patients were left to deteriorate without the benefit of services that would allow for appropriate diagnosis and treatment."

"People like your mother," I added, though Arch was lost in his thoughts and did not answer.

It was Morgan who responded, "She eventually died and of course, as Arch said, we couldn't prove it was because of the cutbacks. She was merely the result of her environment, they said, the victim of a ruthless disease. At the same time, my mother was already starting to show signs. We all will, someday." She stared out the window, her face unreadable.

I wondered what that must be like, to know your body was a ticking time bomb, and that one day you could wake up and not be...you? Regardless of what I thought about Morgan, no one deserved that.

"As Arch mentioned, I was dating Greg at the time," she gave

Natalie a sympathetic nod, the first compassionate gesture I'd seen her offer, "and despite what Arch *thinks*"—she shot him a less than endearing look—"Greg was devastated by Parker's actions—even pleading with Parker and Charlie, begging them to formulate a plan to replenish the funds—desperate to the point of utilizing his own money.

"Of course, Parker thought he was ridiculous and Charlie... well, by playing Switzerland, was essentially backing Parker, whether he would admit it to himself or not. The two of them went about doing what they always did when one game was over. They moved on to the next. In the meantime, Greg drove himself mad in his attempt to 'fix things,' as he would phrase it. It was just too much, too much devastation for one person to fix. 'Too much and too far gone,' he used to mumble near the end. Eventually, his conscience got the better of him..." her voice trailed off as she continued gazing out into the night.

Natalie's voice crackled, her throat dry, "He killed himself on the anniversary of Arch's mom's death." I withheld a gasp, I hadn't known that. "The three of them—Parker, Charlie and Greg —had only recently reconciled and in celebration, decided to road trip in Big Bess. The weather had been nice, so Charlie took the opportunity to get her out for a drive. I don't remember where they were ultimately headed, but their road trip took them into an area with mountainous, windy roads, hairpin turns and hair-raising drop-offs. At one point, they pulled off to look at the view. Parker and Charlie were joking back and forth about some nonsense and when they turned around, Greg launched himself over the guardrail using the tail end of Charlie's car. They tried to stop him but were too late. The last thing he said before he plunged to his death was 'Tell them I'm sorry...I tried to fix it, but it was just too far gone.'"

"I'm so sorry. I didn't know." No one had known the details surrounding Greg's suicide, which eerily mimicked that of my biological father, Martin. "I had a family member...pass...in a similar manner. I'm truly sorry."

Natalie nodded, her eyes glassy. "They retrieved his body eleven days later. It took them that long to...to get down to where he was." I nodded sadly. Martin's body had never been recovered. Never found. Honestly, I didn't know which would be worse. "Parker's actions not only ruined those facilities—indirectly or otherwise—he destroyed two families."

"So, all of this"—I waved my hand at the gun still tapping against Morgan's thigh—"is about revenge."

"Revenge?" Morgan seethed, her eyes piercing mine. "*This* is beyond revenge. Or retribution. *This* is about doing what's right."

"And two wrongs make a right in your book, I take." I replied flatly. "If that is the case, why punish Charlie?"

"'Why punish Charlie?' she asks," Morgan sneered. "I've given you way too much credit, Arianna. I didn't realize you were so ignorant to the ways of the world."

I shrugged, "Then educate me." The look I got in response told me not to toy with her. "I'm being serious, Morgan." She rolled her eyes, looking disgusted.

Instead, Natalie responded, "Charlie could have stopped Parker, yet he chose not to."

"So his inaction deemed him as culpable as Parker, and yielded him the same fate?" If Charlie got the death penalty, it essentially would be.

"Charlie *chose* his fate," Natalie clarified.

"It seems to me you've been manipulating things to suit your needs. And, if we're being completely honest here, that's not fate as much as it is—"

"Are you seriously trying to piss us off?" Morgan asked, incredulous that I would mess with a chick holding a loaded weapon.

I raised my hands in surrender. "Sorry, just trying to get some clarification. I'm still back at that 'beyond revenge or retribution' part of the conversation." I was rewarded with a slap upside the back of my head, compliments of the lovely Natalie. Not so girl-next-door after all.

"I warned you she had a smart mouth," Arch piped in. *Thanks, Arch,* I thought to myself. *I'll repay the favor by not telling you they're probably going to shoot you first.*

"Let's get a couple of things straight, shall we?" I noticed Morgan had repositioned the gun suspiciously close to my head. Perhaps I'd been hasty on my prior assessment? "From here on out, keep the commentary to yourself. Or you'll be eating jell-o through a straw." Though it could have been a good way to drop those M&M's binging pounds, it was probably not the time mention I preferred red raspberry jell-o over strawberry or cherry.

"Permission to ask you something, then?"

Natalie shook her head in annoyance, while Morgan looked amused by my gumption. "Charlie said you were a pain, but I had no idea." Considering Charlie annoys easily, I took that to be a compliment, as well as a thumbs-up to proceed.

"You dated Parker," I nodded at Natalie while Morgan scoffed. "Morgan, you dated Charlie. And you, Arch, work for him. Was all this an elaborate setup—an attempt to integrate your-selves into their world—to figure them out while learning their routines?"

Natalie clapped. "See Morgan, I told you she wasn't as dumb as she looks. Sorry AJ, but that hair?" She shot a finger pistol at my head—unnerving, to say the least. I made a note to have a chat with Paolo, my hair stylist, should I live to make it to my next appointment. "That and the company she keeps. Leah gives Kathy Griffin a run for her money in the talks-too-much cate-gory and is nowhere near as funny. If she didn't know so many people, I'd seriously consider dumping the broad. And that dog of yours, I'd ask the shelter you got him from for a refund. In the meantime, he could stand an air freshener and a breath mint."

It took everything in me not to throw her down and chop off the perky braid she was sporting. Insulting a girl's do was one thing, but insulting her best friend AND her dog pushed her right into WWE territory. Just as I channeled my inner John Cena with a Rock chaser, Natalie surprised me by responding.

"Getting back to your question—yes, the three of us became acquainted the day of my brother's funeral. Thanks for coming by the way. Greg always liked you. Despite the current circumstances, I can see why. You're a decent chick and unfortunately, loyal to a fault." I shrugged. It was what it was.

"Anyway, we installed Arch as Charlie's assistant. He was fresh out of college and needed a job, and as luck would have it, Charlie needed someone to help him oversee his day-to-day activities. He asked Parker for a referral and in turn, Parker asked me. Of course, I was happy to offer up Arch. Charlie never knew— and still doesn't—that he and Morgan are cousins."

"So the decision to kill Parker using Big Bess was because of Greg and the road trip?" Natalie nodded. It was sad that they chose to equate human life with an inanimate object, but Big Bess was the most important thing to Charlie and as they saw it, the best way to torture him.

"Arch, just to reconfirm, the day of the White Party you gave Charlie's car keys to Natalie, along with his penthouse key card and parking garage key code." When both Morgan and Natalie swiveled their heads toward him, I laughed. "Oh come on gals, we're way beyond establishing that. But how did you know Charlie would leave you alone long enough to facilitate the hand-off? You couldn't have known he would leave the penthouse that day, much less know when."

Arch shook his head. "I didn't. I certainly didn't expect him to leave during preparations for the White Party, but when he did, I called Natalie. She would have stopped by anyway, though this worked out to our advantage because we didn't have to concoct an excuse for her being there." I doubt this got him off the hook with Morgan and Natalie, who were both still looking at him with contempt.

"At some point, you gave the items to Morgan, didn't you, Natalie?" Both of them were noncommittal though given their body language, I could tell I was on the right track. "You arrived at the White Party first, with the former senator." I looked at Morgan, her face remained hard, unmoving. "Charlie wasn't aware you'd be your father's guest for the evening—he'd invited you separately and you'd accepted—so he had no way of knowing he'd be providing you with the access you needed to get in and out of the parking garage without being detected. So not only were the cameras disabled at the senator's request, you had both your father's and Charlie's key codes for the garage's entrance."

I shifted my attention to Natalie, who looked at me with an equally stony expression. "You…arrived before Parker, using your volunteer work at the hospital as an excuse to go to the party separately. I'm guessing this was because you need to ensure his car was still visible on the street the following day, another part of your ruse to make it appear as though he'd gone missing. Plus, you needed your own car so you and Morgan could get away cleanly after you dumped Parker into the lake.

"But something went wrong with the plan, didn't it?" I only had to look at one of them to know I'd hit a nerve. "As you were leaving the party, Parker unexpectedly called you a cab and rather than join you, he tucked you in and sent you on your merry way. You had to get to him before he left in his car and ruined everything, so you either called or texted Morgan, who was already lying in wait in the parking garage for you and Parker to arrive. And you"—I pointed at Morgan—"must have made up an excuse so your father would leave without you."

Morgan huffed, but replied, "Yes, Father and I left the party before Parker and Natalie, by design. Once in the garage, I told my father I had forgotten to tell Charlie something and would catch a cab later. My father, a hopeless romantic despite his extra-marital activities, saw it as an opportunity for Charlie and me to rekindle our relationship."

"Only Parker and Natalie weren't both along shortly. Natalie had originally planned to get Parker into the garage somehow so that the two of you could proceed with your plan. Instead, she was stuck in a cab halfway across town."

Morgan nodded, pacing the length of the sterile concrete floor, her boots echoing with each step. "After I got the text from Natalie, I had to improvise and intercept Parker before he made it to his car. So I jogged—in six inch heels, I might add—the four blocks to where he'd parked. Of course, he always had it way out in Timbuktu so it didn't get dings, and given that he and Charlie were at odds, I doubted he would have asked to park in the garage."

"Wait, how did you know where he parked?" I hated to inter-ject but I was truly curious.

Morgan didn't seem to mind. "Pure luck. Father and I passed Parker getting out of his car on the way to the party. He was going into a nearby sports bar." She glanced at Natalie, who bristled at the knowledge her boyfriend stopped off for a pint while she waited for him to escort her to the party. "I just figured he had hoofed it rather than risk moving his car and losing what he considered to be a prime parking spot."

Parker had been funny that way, though I wouldn't have been surprised if he had taken a cab from the sports bar to Char-lie's building, rather than walking the four blocks. She was lucky he hadn't done that after the party, given all the alcohol he'd imbibed. I wondered how she'd known that hadn't been the case.

As if reading my thoughts, Morgan added. "Parker told Natalie he needed some fresh air and was going to walk, which she relayed to me in the text. She was also able to verify his car was still parked where I'd last seen it because her taxi drove right past it."

"You're right, you certainly got lucky. So you caught up with Parker, how did you manage to get him back to the parking garage?"

Morgan rolled her eyes as she waved a hand over her curvy physique. If Natalie was peeved by Morgan's advances on her boyfriend, she made no show of it.

"Err…ok. So you…encouraged Parker to return to the parking garage with you, then what?"

Morgan laughed. "Parker was pretty wasted, so he was fairly…compliant. Once I got him in the garage, I just popped him with a little hypodermic filled with happy juice." At my raised eyebrow, she added, "A muscle relaxant with a bit of kick. Parker was on his lips in no time." Her laugh was harsh as she recalled the memory. "Meanwhile, there was no sense alerting the first cab driver by having him turn around, so once Natalie got home, she caught another cab from a different company back to parking garage and let herself in using Charlie's key code."

"And concocted the witness to account for the entry on the time log, thereby effectively putting Charlie at the garage at the time of the murder," I added.

The way his brows were drawn, Arch may have been lost but both Morgan and Natalie managed to look impressed. "How'd you figure that out?"

"It was the dog." I shrugged. "The officer at the scene remembers your witness, Margaret O'Connor, called her dog—a small black one with pointy ears that looked like it should be wearing a plaid sweater, as he described it—Ginsburg." Morgan frowned as I clarified for the others, "Morgan and her family have a habit of naming their Scottish Terriers after Supreme Court Justices. In this case, she threw the witness' last name into the mix." The last bit did nothing to improve Morgan's surly mood, given I now had a gun barrel pressed firmly against my right temple. "If I figured that out, so will the police."

Morgan snorted. "If by police, you mean Vargas, I doubt it. His thought processes are seriously impeded by his propensity for that blond tart you call a friend."

Arch shot his cousin a bemused look. "Sounds like someone is jealous, I didn't think the cop was your type."

"Shut up, lap dog. Don't forget you're still here at my convenience. You're lucky I didn't kill you when we were kids, which, by the way, was completely out of respect to your mother."

Morgan knew how hit below the belt, that was for sure. Arch glared, crossing his arms defiantly, but said nothing. Natalie, on the other hand, chuckled under breath and for a moment, I though Morgan might cut her down, too.

I cleared my throat. "I would have thought your inside source would have told you. Vargas already knows the witness was bogus. How long do you think it's going to take him to find a correlation between a haughty lawyer friend of Charlie's—one whose father happens to be former state senator—and a witness who fits the same general description and has a similar looking dog with the same name?"

"Real smooth, Morgan," Natalie smirked. "Perhaps you should have let the ding dong socialite manage the little details after all." As Morgan's lip curled into a nasty snarl, I realized it was not all giggles and matching friendship bracelets in the world of Morgan and Natalie. And given the smug look Natalie was tossing at Morgan, it had never been.

I stepped in before the hair-pulling could ensue, "Getting back to the parking garage. Natalie returns, then what?"

Morgan continued, "We fired up Big Bess using the keys Arch had supplied and after propping Parker up, we took turns backing into him." I blanched, as did Arch.

Morgan only shrugged. "Natalie wanted to run over him but logistically, puncturing him with the tailfins was much more... efficient." Double eww.

Natalie nodded in agreement. "Either way, it was messy. But at least..." she smiled, not in a pretty way, "we finally got to stick it to Parker." Morgan's boisterous laughter filled the room, as Natalie joined in. I shook my head, disgusted by what these two considered common ground.

"Ok. That's...interesting. How did you keep from damaging Charlie's car?"

Natalie clapped her hands. "Morgan found some mattresses in the garage's storage room still covered in heavy duty plastic. We placed them behind Parker to cushion the blows between the car and the block wall. It worked out great." Morgan nodded, clearly pleased with her creative use of bedding.

Arch wasn't as thrilled by this news, "Wait a minute, you used those mattresses from the storage room? I've been sleeping on Parker's...innards?" That would certainly teach him to ask before taking items that weren't his the next time around. I doubted he was thinking along those lines as his expression changed from exasperation to repulsion. I couldn't disagree as I fought to keep my own gag refluxes from engaging. Morgan and Natalie appeared bored and maybe even a bit annoyed by Arch's outburst.

After confirming Arch wouldn't projectile vomit on anyone, Morgan moved on, "Anyway, we'd had our fun with Parker, but were on a timetable and still had to clean up and deposit him else-where before the sun made its way over the horizon. We were just about finished—Parker was wrapped, Big Bess was wiped down, the mattresses stripped of their plastic and placed back into the storage room—when Charlie entered the garage."

Natalie giggled. "OMG, I was so freaked! Remember how we'd just finished pulling Parker out into the middle of the garage so we could transfer him to my car? I was so sure he'd see us."

Morgan nodded. "I know, we barely pulled Parker back into the shadows in time. Charlie was still drunk from the party, otherwise who knows what would have happened. We certainly hadn't expected him to go out for a walk at that hour." I wondered if the two of them had been stalking Charlie, but decided the real question was how long they'd been doing it.

"But, as it turned out, Charlie ended up leaving us with some parting gifts. His muddy shoes were enough of a treat, but when he accidentally dropped his tie? It was just icing on the cake. Of course, his access code was logged when he entered the garage, but the police erroneously assumed he'd returned to clean up after dumping Parker in the lake. We couldn't have planned it any better." Despite the near-misses, Morgan seemed smug while Natalie continued to giggle. I silently wished she had an off button.

"So, Charlie leaves. You collect his shoes and tie and Parker…and…" I gestured for them to continue.

Morgan scoffed. "Easy, Slick—we'd like the opportunity to revel in the moment."

Unless my ears were deceiving me, I was pretty sure I heard Arch mutter "psychos" under his breath. I might have agreed with him on that point, but wasn't about to form an alliance with him. I'd seen enough horror movies to know what happened to the third wheel. Before the end of the first act, they always ended up dead meat.

* * *

After the two took their requisite revelation time, whatever that entailed, Morgan proceeded, "Natalie ran back and grabbed her car, which we had prepped in advance to transport Parker. Once we had him tucked safely inside, I placed the earring Leah dropped during the party near Big Bess. From there, we drove along Tempe Town Lake until we found a pullout with a boat launch that wasn't occupied. It didn't take us long, considering the lake hours were enforced, so we were able to pull right up and dump him out."

"Is that when you disposed of Charlie's shoes and tie?" I asked.

Natalie chuckled. "We considered it, but were afraid riffraff would find them before the police did, so I waited until later." Of course, the search party—it had been Natalie's idea. She'd not only needed a way to distribute the evidence, but control when the items were found. The large bag had seemed out of place at the time, but now made sense. She had chosen it for its functionality.

Something else had been weighing on my mind. "Was Parker even dead when you dumped him in the water?" Ramirez had already confirmed the answer but I needed to know if *they* had known.

It didn't surprise me that it was Morgan who answered, "Does it matter?"

"It does to me."

She let out a deep breath and gave me a long, hard look. "You're going to have to learn to live with disappointment then, because I don't know. I was caught up in an adrenaline rush at the time. It never occurred to me to check."

Natalie nodded before focusing on her shoes. Neither one of them had expected the question. And now they were faced with the reality of their actions.

Morgan was thoughtful, before adding, "I can tell you he was unconscious the entire time, if that soothes your mind."

"It's not my mind that needs soothing."

"Then your soul should rest easy, because Parker's went dark the minute he killed my brother," Natalie jutted out her chin defiantly, the fact she wouldn't meet my eyes told me she was anything but.

"And my mom," Arch whispered.

I had almost forgotten he was still with us. Perhaps it was what Charlie liked about him, he was present without being seen or heard. Regardless of how limited the role he had played in Morgan and Natalie's twisted little drama, it still made him deadly in my book.

CHAPTER TWENTY

Despite the tension that filled the room, I felt my own emotion bubbling to the surface—anger. Oh yeah, I was mad. Don't get me wrong. I had no allusions why Morgan and Natalie had been so forthcoming with the details of Parker's murder. They intended to kill me and likely Arch as well. Since I had nothing to lose, I asked the question I had come for, one they had not yet answered. At least, not to my satisfaction. In the end, it was the only answer that mattered.

"Why?"

Morgan looked at me, flat, soulless eyes boring into mine, lips pulled into a tight unforgiving line. While she wasn't completely devoid of emotion, what consumed her far more disconcerting. Bitterness. After everything she'd done, she'd found no comfort. No solace.

It was Natalie who replied, "Why? Haven't we thoroughly—and I might add, graciously—explained that to you?" Apparently, her emotions hadn't quite evolved the way Morgan's had.

"No, you told me who, what, when, where and how, but you conveniently left out the answer to the most important question. In the beginning, Morgan said it wasn't for revenge. Or even retribution. However, based upon all of this," I motioned to the gun Morgan was still gripping though thankfully, was no longer pointed at my head, "it appears not to be far from the truth. Parker is dead, Charlie's life is over. One draws the obvious conclusion."

"Both made choices," Natalie gritted out, "choices, with consequences."

"So you keep saying." I shrugged.

"Surely you can understand? They acted with blatant disregard. People not only suffered, they died. What about Parker's and Charlie's consequences? Why did they get to go on living their lives? Don't you get it, AJ? Don't you understand?" She was almost pleading with me.

"I do," I replied, choosing my words carefully, "but there had to have been other, less drastic means?"

"Don't you think that I...that we tried? Do you think we would have started with the most extreme measures if we hadn't already exhausted all the others? What do you take us for—monsters?" I bit my lip and drew blood to prevent myself from blurting out a response.

"We approached Parker directly—Charlie too—to no avail. Then, we spent years...*years*...attempting to engage with law enforcement, lawyers, politicians, even the Federal Trade Commission. We researched, communicated, lobbied...anything and everything we could think of to intercept Parker and no one could help us.

"The worst thing about it, we weren't even close to shutting him down. Investing may have been second nature to Parker, but he was a genius when it came to the law—almost as good as Morgan." If the comparison to Parker agitated her, Morgan made no indication, other than to resume the tapping of the gun. "When it came to the law, he was always careful to color within the lines, even if that meant coloring on it, which is where he did his best work. So while we had a lot of sympathizers, the issues were moral in nature and therefore, outside the confines of the law."

"Then if murder was the solution, why not kill them both—you said they were both culpable, after all—why not rid the world of the entire albatross?"

Natalie considered my question for a moment. "Believe me, we talked about it, even gave it some serious consideration." She chuckled. "Charlie may have the Tin Man's version of a heart but at least he has one, which means he's capable of feeling emotion. That being said, we decided the best way to deal with him was to make him feel it, through fear, humiliation, loss. That's basically the only reason he's sitting in a jail cell right now, and not in the ground eating worm dirt with Parker."

I grimaced. "Charlie could still get the death penalty."

Natalie nodded, but it was Morgan who replied, "Even if it does come to that, he'll be incarcerated for years—someone as astute as Charlie could facilitate endless appeals—meaning he'll have plenty of time to reflect on the choices he made. And the ones he should have made."

Perhaps it was just me, but their logic seemed faulty. They had killed Parker because he was too evil and incarcerated Charlie because he had condoned it. Parker may be dead in the ground, but something couldn't help but make me wonder if Charlie hadn't been the one to get the raw end of the deal.

* * *

Something else bothered me.

"Why now? Why choose Charlie's White Party to eliminate Parker?"

Natalie threw her hands up. "Parker was back at it—messing with things that weren't his, refusing to listen to anyone's rationale. We could see where it was going to go."

"It was the reason Charlie and Parker were at odds near the end," I added.

Morgan nodded. "With the new federal regulations in place, things were tougher for Parker this time around. He needed Charlie's assistance and his high-powered contacts more than he ever had in the past. To his surprise, Charlie refused."

"Ok, but it seems like Parker would have been mad at Charlie, yet at the party, the animosity went the other direction." I thought about the looks that had passed between them and couldn't recall Charlie ever looking that enraged.

Natalie's laugh came out harsh. "Oh, Parker was plenty mad, but he was convinced Charlie would change his mind."

Morgan nodded. "In the interim, he identified another solution to his problem, one that ultimately undermined Charlie, and ended their friendship."

"So Charlie caught wind of this workaround?"

"Yup, that pretty much sums it up. It was just a matter of time —Parker had already gotten his mitts on what he needed—there would have been no stopping him."

Had I not been so distracted by the gun, which had begun dancing even more briskly against Morgan's thigh, I would have sensed the swift movement behind me.

"Get up," Natalie growled, her breath hot on my ear as she pressed something cool against the base of my neck.

Morgan's laugh was harsh as I gasped in surprise. She turned and rolled the atrium windows up, allowing a gust of warm air to flood the space. The nasty look she cast over her shoulder indicated she wasn't merely interested in taking in the nightly breeze. She nodded sharply at Natalie, who initiated an attempt to shove me toward the open window with her knees, but given the difference in our heights, ended up hitting me calf-level. I seized the opportunity to head butt her, effectively knocking her off balance, but failing to dislodge the weapon from her hand. Instead, the sudden movement caused her to fire what I had previously thought to be a gun. I flinched as it discharged, belatedly realizing I was no longer in its path, though found myself up close and personal with a fully-charged stun gun as Natalie liberated it into Arch's chest.

I momentarily found myself watching in fascinated silence as Arch screeched, "What the—" before dropping to floor, the charge rendering him unconscious.

Natalie looked at her hand in surprise, but was unable to regain her footing as I plowed into her with the best offensive tackle I could muster, which resulted in a satisfying "oomph" as she sprawled on the floor.

I managed to untangle myself from Natalie and stagger to my feet, only to have Morgan headlock me from behind. At this point I had no idea where the gun was, but rage and adrenaline surged as we struggled. Morgan and I were more evenly matched in height, though I was betting I had a few extra pounds on her that I planned to use to my advantage. There was no way I was going out that window.

Not alone, anyway.

I tried to remember the moves Ramirez had shown me. I don't recall him mentioning any specific hair-pulling techniques, but as Morgan's locks fell forward, I yanked a sizable section.

"Extensions, Morgan? Seriously?" I huffed as we knocked knees. "And you had the gall to insult my hair?"

"I'm sure it'll look better with your head cracked open on the pavement," she panted, spittle blasting my cheek.

"Well, if I'm going, you're going," I replied, serving up a pointy elbow to her ribcage as I worked to position my legs behind hers.

Morgan grunted but choked out a harsh laugh. "Not likely, but you should take comfort knowing that I'm going to gut your mangy canine once I'm done with you."

That did it. She'd gone too far. Fury raged through me as I launched myself backward, taking her with me. As we twisted and fell, Morgan's head clipped the corner of one of Charlie's solid steel sculptures and we landed with a thud, our bodies intertwined in a contorted heap. Dazed, I felt blood pooling in my mouth and warming my face. Morgan's blood. Her weight was stifling as I attempted to wiggle free. I had finally gotten to my knees and was spitting out blood when I heard the gun cock. Given her current temperament, I doubted Natalie was above shooting me in the back.

"Let's try this again," she wheezed. "Get up." Painfully, I complied and started to face her. "No, don't turn around. Move your skinny butt over to the window."

I glanced down at a prone Morgan. She still hadn't moved since our fall and now blood oozed from her wound, saturating her hair and streaking Charlie's concrete floor with color. I paused to check her pulse but Natalie snapped at me. I gave Morgan one last look as I shuffled forward slowly. No sense making this easy on her.

Out of the corner of my eye I saw a flash of movement, followed by various squeaks and scuffling sounds. I spared a glance behind me, convinced the last thing I would see was the barrel of a gun. Instead, I was rewarded with an awkward, rare grin from Arch as he pinned a squirming, furious Natalie with his arms.

My eyes went wide, looking for the gun.

"There, AJ, it's there!" Arch yelled excitedly, bobbing his head toward a spot on the floor, a few feet to the right of where he'd intercepted her.

After gingerly picking the weapon up, I trained it on Natalie, who continued thrashing about while directing obscenities at us, our various body parts, our family members and pretty much the entire human civilization. I considered offering her my supply of

Borax but frankly, she required more than I presently had on hand.

"Keep a firm hold on her, Arch. She's a deceptively slippery one."

"That she is, AJ. That she is."

Despite the gravity situation, when Natalie let out a small frustrated wail, it was all I could do not to laugh.

* * *

I called Ramirez with my free hand, briefly filled him in on the situation and asked him to have Vargas send in the cavalry. After a few choice expletives from his end, I asked him to call Leah as well. Exasperated, he hung up.

A short time later, several intense-looking police officers dressed in full combat gear engulfed the penthouse, led by one very large, extremely grumpy Detective Vargas.

I surrendered the weapon to the first officer who approached me. His was bigger, after all. Once the team secured the surroundings, Vargas called in the paramedics. I waved them off, quickly pointing at Morgan, who had only just begun to regain consciousness. I hadn't wanted to meet my fate with her on the pavement down below, but I didn't want her to die here, either. After a couple of medics gave Natalie and Arch the thumbs-up, they were handcuffed without incident.

"Time for us to have a little chat, AJ," Vargas' tone was steely, but as I glanced up at him, I noticed something else lingering in his expression—he was impressed.

I nodded, carefully easing myself into the nearest chair. For once, I didn't mind its lack of comfort. I gave him my account of the events that had transpired, while another officer took notes and asked occasional questions. Once satisfied they had what they needed, Vargas dismissed the officer. We sat side by side, quietly watching as his team worked around us, in the devastation that had once been Charlie's home.

"Will this be enough to help him?" I asked after a long moment.

"It may take a few days and a mountain of paperwork, thanks to you," he teased, "but I think charges will be dropped and he'll be released."

I nodded. "I'd like to see him. We have some…unfinished business."

"For you, AJ, that can be arranged." He chuckled, just as another officer ushered a solemn, handcuffed Arch past us.

"You're a better friend than he gives you credit for," Arch commented quietly.

I knew he meant Charlie, but was I? I thought about the times I'd openly questioned his innocence. I continued to watch as Vargas skillfully directed his team and the paramedics loaded a semi-conscious Morgan onto a stretcher. I smiled a bit as I thought about her reaction when she finally woke up, wearing a pretty little peek-a-boo hospital gown while handcuffed to the bed. Suddenly, I realized I wasn't alone.

"Ajax, you get yourself into the most…interesting predicaments."

Ramirez.

* * *

"Promise me you'll never leave your house again without back-up." Before I had a chance to protest, he smirked and pretended to contemplate something. "Never mind that, I've seen your backup. Next time, please call your boyfriend—"

"Oh my gosh, Leah. Is she totally freaking out? Is Nicoh ok? *Wait*…did he say 'boyfriend'?" Belatedly, I realized that last bit had inadvertently slipped out. Too bad there wasn't a good soap for that.

Ramirez only chuckled. "Calm down, she's fine, but a little miffed you left her out of your fun. And, just so that you know, you did butt-dial her a few times."

"I did what?" I felt around for my phone, realizing it had been in my back pocket when I had pulled it out to call Ramirez.

"There was so much commotion, she thought you and I were...rolling around...until she heard Morgan saying some nasty things about Nicoh, which is when she called Vargas. He was already en route when I called him."

I couldn't decide whether to blush or cheer, so I just nodded and pursed my lips. Rolling around? With Ramirez? I must have been making quite a face because I suddenly noticed Ramirez scrutinizing me.

"Err...Morgan did make some pretty awful threats against Nicoh and both she and Natalie had some nasty things to say about Leah, too."

My feeble attempt to cover was not lost on him, though he simply nodded. "Why don't we go and see them both."

As we made our way to the elevator, I whispered, "Do you think we can keep the whole butt-dialing incident to ourselves?"

CHAPTER TWENTY-ONE

It had been a moot point. Several officers chuckled—I swore a few others glanced at my behind—when we exited the building. I started to comment but was distracted by the high-pitched squeals coming from the direction of the crowd that had formed just beyond the building's perimeter. It could have come from only one source—Leah.

After breaking free from a portly officer who attempted to keep her at bay, I was mobbed by a force so strong, I needed Ramirez to keep me upright. Nicoh stood on his haunches, his front paws braced on my shoulders as he licked me chin to crown. Contrary to the comments Natalie had made, his breath was decent. Either that or I smelled pretty bad myself. I crossed my fingers, hoping for the prior, given the proximity I had just shared with Ramirez. Once Nicoh was satisfied I had been properly greeted, he lowered himself to the ground and chastised me with a low grumble. Leah stood cautiously to one side, watching us. One look at her tear-filled eyes and I tugged her into a fierce embrace.

"We've gotta stop doing this." She sniffled. "Between people trying to kill us at high altitudes, the daily dog cleansings and the sappy hugging and crying thing, we're never going to get any decent dates."

"Tell me about it."

* * *

"Thanks for filling her up with gas." I nodded at the Mini when we reached our respective vehicles.

"It was the least I could do, especially considering you left me behind," she replied dryly.

"Hey, I left a note," I pleaded, though she waved me off, meaning I would owe her margaritas and details later.

"When they were hauling Natalie out—nice handcuffs, by the way—she saw me in the crowd and yelled that she wanted to revise her quote."

"Her quote?" Ah, the *Real Housewives* taglines we had crafted a few nights earlier over girl talk. "Do I want to hear it?" Leah shrugged, so I gestured for her to continue.

"She said 'Life is about living with no regrets. I'd rather die doing the wrong thing for the right reasons than live wishing I'd had the courage to do them at all.'"

* * *

I emerged from my house a few days later only a bit more rested and a whole lot more bruised from my tumbles with Morgan and Natalie than I remembered being when I had gone in. I promised Leah and Ramirez I'd take it easy but things hadn't turned out quite that way. Nicoh had become increasingly restless without his gal pal and after repeated attempts to get Randy Newman on his cell phone, Leah had driven to his house, only to find it locked up tight and his car gone from the driveway. After chatting with a few of the neighbors, she returned to deliver the news. Randy and

Pandora had packed up and left for Dallas a few days early. I caught up with him a day or so after that, or I should say, he left a message on my home phone. He apologized, indicating he just wasn't one for tearful goodbyes.

Meanwhile, Nicoh was sullen and lacked his usual energy. I'm certainly no expert, but our animal friends seem to feel loss, too, perhaps even more so. It was heartbreaking to watch and though Leah and I tried our best to comfort him, he refused to eat, play with his toys or even sleep on my bed, much less his own. Instead he stayed by the front door, day after day, waiting for Pandora to return. Late at night, he would howl the same sorrowful, pained song.

When I finally chose to leave the house, I did so hesitantly. Nicoh usually accompanied me but showed no interest today. He sat at his post by the door and though his eyes remained closed, I knew he was not resting. As I left, I did not promise him I would return. If I had learned anything over the past several months, no matter how well-meaning our intentions might be, no one can guarantee that. Instead I patted him on the head, told him I loved him and as I pulled the front door shut, I knew at the very least, that much was true.

CHAPTER TWENTY-TWO

Charlie was waiting for me when I arrived at my favorite Starbucks, sipping a mug of cappuccino on the patio. We hugged awkwardly before I sat down across from him with my own iced caramel sauce latte. If he was surprised by the thick layers of caramel sauce that outweighed the balance of milk and coffee, he made no comment. He'd gained some of his color back, along with a few of the pounds he'd lost. He smiled at me, almost shyly, but the warmth didn't reach his eyes, their usual spark missing, replaced by a haunted sadness.

He squinted as though trying to place something. "You didn't bring Nicoh."

I shook my head. "He still not...doing well...with Pandora being gone."

"I'm sorry."

"Me too."

He reached across the table, just enough to encourage me to raise my eyes to meet his. "I'm sorry about more than just Nicoh, you know."

"I know you are, Charlie, but—"

"AJ, please let me finish. For once, the last word is going to be mine." I chuckled—where had I heard that before? I feigned shock, making him laugh. It sounded…and looked good on him. And so, we talked, or perhaps I should say Charlie talked and I listened, mostly. Either way, it was the longest conversation the two of us had in the twenty-plus years we had known one another. And it was a doozy. We talked about growing up as kids, going off to college, falling in love, falling out of love.

Turns out, he did care for Morgan. I couldn't bear to tell him the feeling had likely never been mutual, but I think somewhere deep inside, he'd already known. We talked about the crazy, fun times he spent with Greg and the sad ones, too. He confessed he'd kept Big Bess as a reminder, so he'd never forget the feeling of hopelessness and loss Greg's death had brought him. I'll admit I had completely misjudged him on that one. And finally, we talked about Parker—the good, the bad and the demons that had consumed him until the day he died.

And just when I thought Charlie had finished surprising me, he told me about the missing hours on the afternoon of the White Party, the ones he'd previously refused to discuss. I wasn't sure whether I should hug him or punch him when he revealed he'd been working with a private detective for several months, during which time the two of them had accumulated enough proof to put a stop to Parker's shenanigans. They planned on approaching the Attorney General the day after the party and met one final time that afternoon to ensure all their ducks were in a row. The next day came, however, and Parker went missing.

"Why didn't you present your evidence once they arrested you?"

He shook his head. "Parker was dead. Nothing good would have come from causing the few loved ones he had any more suffering. No, I had to find another way to show the police I wasn't guilty of his murder."

"Which is why you declined counsel?"

He nodded. "I couldn't risk them inadvertently finding out about my investigation."

I shook my head to show my understanding, but truthfully, had to wonder about Charlie's intentions. Just how selfless had his investigation been? Had he been trying to do the right thing by having Parker investigated? Or saving himself from an equal fate by shifting the focus off his own wrong-doings and onto those of his supposed best friend and business associate? One thing was for sure, being the one to present the evidence certainly had its benefits.

It also made me wonder—if Natalie and Morgan had known about Charlie's evidence, would it have spared Parker's life? Somehow, I doubted it. It was hard to ignore the irony, though. Had Charlie moved forward—even one day sooner—Parker would have likely spent the better part of his life in prison. Instead, he would forever be buried in a lonely grave. By altering his destiny, Morgan and Natalie also changed their own, and would now take his place, as they spent their days locked away.

If Charlie had known the outcome, would he have done things differently? With Charlie you just never knew. I shook my head—when had I gotten so cynical? I was about to give the notion a kick in the pants when Charlie snapped me out of my reverie.

"See you first thing tomorrow morning then, to photograph the progress being made on the penthouse remodel? Oh, before I forget, I'd prefer if you leave the dog at home—no sense getting sued when he gets under some construction worker's foot or his tail—"

Like I said, with Charlie you never knew. For the time being, I carefully tucked the cynic back in my pocket.

* * *

Things were only a bit less convoluted when it came to the others.

Arch pled to a lesser crime as part of a plea deal with the County Attorney and even so, would spend many years inside a prison cell. There was speculation Morgan and Natalie would receive the death penalty due to the heinous nature of the crime, as well as for the lack of remorse they'd shown to date.

In a very political move, Morgan's father distanced the Conrad family from the situation. It was rumored that given her fragile state, Cecilia Conrad had not been told of her daughter's complicity in the murder of Parker Harris. Instead she was led to believe Morgan was working abroad on behalf of her law firm to facilitate relations with various foreign entities. Natalie's family attended her initial arraignment, but as details of the crime continued to emerge, they were seen less and less at court proceedings and eventually disappeared altogether from the public eye.

No one acknowledged Charlie—unless you counted Leah and me—it was as though he never existed. Surprisingly, Charlie took it as a sign to close one chapter in his life and begin a new one. How that would work out for him was anyone's guess, only time would tell. At least he'd made the effort once the opportunity presented itself, which is more than I can say for most. Morgan and Natalie had wanted to punish him, leaving him humiliated, hopeless and alone. In the end, they had lost that bet on all counts, because for all their grand plans and schemes, there was one thing they hadn't counted on.

Me.

EPILOGUE

It was a perfect day for a picnic. One of those lazy southwestern days where the sun warms your shoulders as the gentle breeze lulls you to sleep. Ramirez had selected a remote location where the only sound was from a nearby fountain that burbled as plumes of water danced to a synchronized, yet silent symphony. At least that was the way I imagined it.

A blanket had been carefully smoothed across an even patch of ground. On top he had meticulously arranged a simple but mouth-watering picnic. Even Nicoh had recently come out of hiding to join us and was happily gnawing on a gargantuan-sized dog bone—peanut butter-flavored, of course.

Ramirez laughed, tugging on a long strand of my hair as I moaned over the first bite of the peanut butter and pickle sandwich he had made, just for me. It was only after I'd polished off one half and was well into the second I realized he'd been watching me.

"What?" I mumbled, my mouth still partially-full as I batted self-consciously at the tip of my nose. "Please do not tell me I've had peanut butter on my face this entire time?" When he chuckled and shook his head, I added, "Ok, you're totally amazed by my freakish, yet amazing peanut butter and pickle sandwich-eating abilities?"

Once again, he shook his head before taking a long sip of his iced tea. "Just trying to decide something."

Intrigued, I gently placed the sandwich on its wax paper wrapper. "Um…you and Vargas and your other poker buddies aren't going to start placing bets on how many of these babies I can put away, are you? Because I'll have you know, I have a very important professional reputation to uphold."

His voice was quiet when he replied, his eyes searching mine, "I was just wondering if you thought you could ever like me as much as you do those peanut butter and pickle sandwiches." A smile tugged the corner of his mouth, but there was a hint of seriousness in his eyes…and a question.

"Well…" I could feel the heat rising in my cheeks, "these are pretty good sandwiches."

"Uh huh."

"And you did make them."

"I did."

"I suppose…in time…I could like you both equally."

"Equally, as in fifty-fifty?"

"I might be able to manage that."

"Oh?"

"Just one thing though."

"What's that?"

"Don't think for a minute you can ply me with sandwiches to improve your odds."

"I wouldn't dream of it." He leaned closer, smiling.

I put a hand firmly on his chest. "I wasn't done yet."

"Oh? Sorry. What else?"

"Don't ever think about sharing your second peanut butter and pickle sandwich with anyone else."

"It's a deal." Our lips met just as his phone buzzed, causing us both to shift back in surprise.

"Better get that." I started to reach for the rest of my sandwich.

Ramirez smiled. "Still aren't sure about that fifty-fifty, are you?" Before I could answer, he stood and moved a short distance away to take the call.

"What are you looking at?" I grumbled at Nicoh, whose tongue flopped lazily as he zeroed in on my sandwich. Having missed his opportunity, he emitted his own rumble before crossing his paws, continuing the destruction of the monster bone.

Ramirez returned moments later, his happy mood gone.

"What?" I struggled to get out. "What is it?"

"That was my contact with the FBI."

"Ok..."

"Winslow Clark escaped from the federal prison where he was being held. They think he broke out three weeks ago."

"*Think?* Oh...no...no..." At least now I knew the identity of my mystery texter and caller, for whatever that was worth.

"It's worse, AJ."

"Just tell me, Ramirez. Please tell me. Is he...is he coming to get me?"

He shook his head, looking me straight in the eye. "He's already here."

I groaned.

Couldn't a peanut butter and pickle sandwich ever just be a peanut butter and pickle sandwich? I thought to myself as Nicoh engulfed the rest in one noisy bite.

Nope. Life is never that simple.

~ The End ~

BLOOD OF GEMINI

Mischievous Malamute Mystery Series Book 3

It was a perfect day for a picnic. One of those lazy southwestern days where the sun warms your shoulders as the gentle breeze lulls you to sleep. Ramirez had selected a remote location where the only sound was from a nearby fountain that burbled as plumes of water danced to a synchronized but silent symphony.

A blanket had been carefully smoothed across an even patch of ground. On top he had meticulously arranged a simple but mouth-watering meal. Even Nicoh was happily gnawing on a gargantuan-sized dog bone. Peanut butter-flavored, of course.

Ramirez laughed, tugging on a long strand of my hair as I moaned over the first bite of peanut butter and pickle sandwich he'd made, just for me. It was only after I'd polished off one half and was well into the second I realized he'd been watching me.

"What?" I mumbled, my mouth still partially full as I self-consciously batted the tip of my nose. "Do not tell me I've had peanut butter on my face this entire time." When he chuckled and shook his head, I added, "Okay, you're awed by my freakish, yet masterful sandwich-eating abilities?"

Once again, he shook his head. "Just trying to decide something."

Intrigued, I gently placed the sandwich on its wax paper wrapper. "Um…you and your poker buddies aren't going to start placing bets on how many of these babies I can put away, are you? Because I'll have you know, I have a very important professional reputation to uphold."

His voice was quiet when he replied, his eyes searching mine, "I was just wondering if you thought you could ever like me as much as you do those sandwiches." A smile tugged the corner of his mouth but there was a hint of seriousness in his eyes. And a question.

"Well…" I could feel the heat rising in my cheeks, "these are pretty good sandwiches."

"Uh huh."

"And you did make them."

"I did."

"I suppose…in time…I could like you both equally."

"Equally, as in fifty-fifty?"

"I might be able to manage that."

"Oh?"

"There's just one thing."

"What's that?"

"Don't think you can ply me with sandwiches to improve your odds."

"I wouldn't dream of it." He leaned closer, smiling.

I placed a hand firmly on his chest. "I wasn't done yet."

"Oh? Sorry. What else?"

"Don't ever think about sharing your sandwiches with anyone but me."

"It's a deal." Our lips met just as his phone buzzed, causing us both to shift back in surprise.

"Better get that." I started to reach for the remainder of the sandwich.

Ramirez smiled. "Still aren't sure about that fifty-fifty, are you?" Before I could answer, he stood and moved a short distance away to take the call.

"What are you looking at?" I grumbled at Nicoh, whose tongue flopped lazily as he zeroed in on my sandwich. Having missed his opportunity, he emitted his own rumble before crossing his paws, continuing his destruction of the monster bone.

Ramirez returned moments later, his happy mood gone.

"What?" I struggled to get out, nearly choking in the process. "What is it?"

"That was my contact with the FBI."

"Okay…"

"Winslow Clark escaped. Three weeks ago."

Horror washed over me as I digested the news. "Is he…is he coming to get me?"

He shook his head, looking me straight in the eye. "Worse. They believe he's already here."

Couldn't a peanut butter and pickle sandwich ever just be a peanut butter and pickle sandwich? I groaned as Nicoh engulfed the rest of my half in one noisy bite.

Nope. Life is never that simple.

CHAPTER ONE

"AJ, did you hear what I said?"

Oh, I'd heard him. Right up to the point he'd told me the monster who had killed my parents and sister was on the beeline express to yours truly—provided he hadn't already trained his sharp little eyes on me. I placed my bet on the latter. Clark was antsy to finish the job he'd failed to complete months earlier—to witness my last breath as he ended my existence in this world.

One might wonder what would make a twenty-something photographer so enticing. With Clark, it was all about exacting a revenge long overdue, though I had been responsible for no part. And yet, like my insatiable need for the elusive peanut butter and pickle concoction, Clark's need was rooted in the execution—the completion—of his mission. So he'd returned to destroy me.

Rather than serve myself up as a sitting duck or waste time formulating a response for Ramirez, I bid farewell to the picnic I'd barely started to share with the hunky detective. It only added to the irony that my ninety-eight pound Alaskan Malamute had already had his way with it. I hastily collected the remains; then bitterly snatched his dog bone and tossed it into my bag. I wasn't in the mood to talk about Clark or his current whereabouts, much less his agenda for me. All I cared about was getting out of the park and safely to my home.

Mind you, I had no intention of hiding from him. I simply needed time alone. Time to think. Perhaps I should have been frightened out of my gourd and maybe if I was honest with myself, somewhere deep down I was...frightened. For the moment, I had eclipsed the fear and replaced it with something far more visceral—rage.

It was not an emotion I revered but it was hard to forget the mark Clark had left in the wake of his previous visit. After killing my loved ones, he'd terrorized me and kidnapped my best friend. And now he had the audacity to return. I smirked, my lips forming a vicious snarl. This time, Clark had another thing coming. I wasn't going down without a fight and he sure as heck wouldn't be leaving with what he'd returned for...if he left at all.

Ramirez didn't need to be a mind reader or a detective to register my mood, or my intentions. "Let us—and the Feds— handle this, AJ. I promise, we'll get him," he yelled at my back after I'd rebuked his attempt to grab my arm.

I stormed on, muttering to myself, "That line's been over-played, Detective."

* * *

Camouflaged by a crop of trees, he observed their heated interaction. Once the cop returned from taking his phone call, their conversation had taken on a strained, agitated vibe, almost forcing him to smile.

Almost.

After all these years, he was one step closer to getting what he wanted. What he deserved. He wasn't about to get sidetracked now. Arianna had enjoyed her peace for long enough.

He looked at the old, tattered photograph—a memory of what

had been—promises of what could have been. Tracing the silhouettes with his thumb ignited emotions he'd long tucked away. He shook his head, setting the memories free. The past couldn't be altered or reversed, but the present and the future—that he could control.

And this time, no one—not even Arianna Jackson—would stop him.

CHAPTER TWO

Of course Ramirez was waiting for me when I got home, leaning against his police cruiser with his legs crossed. I gritted my teeth, hoping he hadn't violated any laws while zigzagging through the back streets of Phoenix. One of the perks of being a cop, I huffed to myself, biting my tongue in the process.

Ramirez smirked as he took in my sour welcome. "We hadn't finished our discussion or our picnic, for that matter."

"Winslow Clark makes for bad conversation, not to mention, poor digestion." Ramirez chuckled, forcing me to cock my head to one side. "I hardly think this is the appropriate time for your amusement, Detective."

"I didn't say it was." He continued to peruse my expression, lingering on my body language before frowning. "So we're reverting back to 'Detective' now, are we?"

I shifted under the weight of his scrutiny. "I don't make the rules, *Detective*, I just roll with them as they come."

"Says the girl hell-bent on going after a killer by herself."

I was irritated he had my number and managed to get my goat at the same time. Baaah. "I'd hardly be alone."

Ramirez snorted. "Oh yeah, drag your best friend and canine into it. That's worked out well for you in the past."

I didn't appreciate his haughty tone and threw a few less than ladylike adjectives out before adding, "If memory serves, we managed all right."

Immune to my colorful language, Ramirez shook his head. "And nearly got yourselves killed in the process. Next time, you may not be so lucky. Before you go bounding off like a woman obsessed, I suggest you give that some serious thought."

"I'll take your *suggestions* under advisement." Ramirez scowled but kept his thoughts and own bounty of adjectives to himself. "In the meantime, I'd still like to know how Clark managed to worm his miserable way out of round-the-clock monitoring in a facility supposedly locked down like the Loop 101 during rush hour." He nodded, noting my sarcasm was a special gift reserved for the Feds. There had been no love lost where they were concerned.

"And I would have gladly shared what I had learned, had you not shoved me off and stormed away." Summoning every ounce of maturity I could muster, I responded by sticking my tongue out. "Now that you've had your moment, can we go inside and finish our conversation?"

"Hmph...I don't suppose you'd have any of those sandwiches left, would you?"

Ramirez laughed and shook his head. "You'd have to ask Nicoh about that."

I looked at the massive canine, who was more interested in snapping at flies than the humans who had the audacity to ignore his presence. Catching one—a fly, not a human—he smacked his lips before moving on to the next.

Disgusted, I stomped into the house. "Never mind, I wasn't really that hungry anyway."

* * *

I offered Ramirez a beer but he declined, an indication the recent call had not only brought bad news, it had placed him back on duty. It also meant the longer he lingered around babysitting me, the more time it gave Clark to plot his evil deeds, so I gestured for him to begin.

Ramirez scruffed the back of his head, a gesture that suggested he was revisiting the information he'd received, if not editing it for my benefit. "Details are sketchy at best, though I'm sure they're trying to keep things close to the vest while they investigate. Initial rumblings point to an inside job."

"Ya think?" My tone might have come out a bit snottier than I'd intended but it mirrored my emotions.

Ramirez ignored it and continued, "In the meantime, they are supplying pertinent information to the appropriate agencies, but warning them to keep it under wraps from the media to prevent the public from panicking. Or impeding their ability to track his movements."

I grunted, unimpressed by the sparse details the Feds had collected to this point. It had been nearly three weeks since they'd misplaced Clark. Given all the state, local, foreign and probably extraterrestrial resources they had at their disposal, I would have expected something more promising than he was probably some-where in the state of Arizona.

Granted, it was a fairly large state but a fifty-mile radius would have been nice. I'm pretty sure my roommate, best friend and news hound extraordinaire, Leah Campbell, would have nailed down his geo-coordinates in a quarter of the time...unless... I looked at Ramirez and tried to gauge his BS meter. When his face revealed nothing, 1 should have remembered he was a skilled poker player.

"So they've got nothing. Clark could be on my doorstep in

two weeks, two days...or two minutes." Ramirez's silence provided my answer. Even without the benefit of their fancy technology and vast network of resources, I could have told them one thing was certain.

Clark would come.

* * *

Ramirez and I had nothing more to discuss, so I thanked him for the well-intentioned afternoon and saw him on his not-so-merry way before placing two quick calls. The first was to Leah, my partner-in-crime, urging her to come home when she could and the other to an acquaintance the two of us had met months earlier while trying to identify my twin sister Victoria's killer.

A former bureau chief with the *Chicago Tribune* twenty-plus years earlier, Mort Daniels had made more than a pet project of the field of genetic engineering. Specifically, projects related to the top two research facilities at the time: Alcore and GenTech. Alison Anders, a research assistant at Alcore, had been our biological mother and Martin Singer, a geneticist for Alcore's primary competitor, GenTech, our father. *Had* being the operative word in both cases.

Martin had also worked with another scientist, Theodore Winslow, on a human cloning project GenTech had tagged as Gemini, until they'd had a falling out. Quite literally. The result of that fallout had cost my biological parents their lives. But despite their deaths, Theodore held onto his grudge, ingraining his own share of entitlement—and revenge—into his son.

Though Leah and I hadn't known at the time, Mort Daniels' history lesson would soon place us on a collision course with that son, who had changed his name to Winslow Clark. The play on his father's name was intentional, as was murdering my sister and leaving her body in a dumpster behind my house at his father's behest. Now Clark was making his second run at doing the same to me. I intended to thwart his attempt, but needed to locate him first. Even though Mort had retired from the newspaper several years earlier—choosing to spend his days tending to his yard in Ahwatukee—Leah and I agreed, if anyone could get a line on Clark, Mort was our guy.

The elderly gentleman answered his phone after two rings and once we exchanged pleasantries, I dove into the purpose of my call. Once finished, my leg bounced in anticipation as I awaited his response.

"Clark didn't just walk out of a maximum security facility, pat the guard on the arm, thank him for an enchanting visit and disappear off into the sunset—in this case, the Valley of the Sun—he had help. Powerful help."

"The Feds think there was an inside connection. By 'powerful help' are we talking about prison staff…or the warden? Clark's shrink? Both?"

"Maybe." The way he drew it out told me he wasn't convinced. "I'd like to check on a few things. Mind if I get back to you in the morning?"

Despite my disappointment, I managed a courteous and even gracious response before ending the connection. As I stared at the cell phone in my hand, I contemplated the probability his efforts would yield the results I needed in time.

Clark was like a tsunami, a horrific monster that thrived on obliterating the unsuspecting innocents in its path. But unlike those who fell victim to its unforgiving, callous devastation, I had the benefit of anticipation. And knowledge. And while that advantage would mean looking into the monster's eyes as he mowed me down and choked out my final breath, I also had the benefit of something more. I was no victim. Nor was I innocent.

When I went down, I was taking the monster straight to Hell with me.

CHAPTER THREE

Not even the sight of Leah's spiky blonde locks bobbing from side to side improved my mood as I watched her jamming to the tunes filtering through her headphones while she belted out her own rendition of "Crazy Train." Fitting, I mused.

"Whaassup buttercup?" she drawled, taking in my bemused expression.

"Besides the fact you're butchering a classic, you mean? Perhaps you should consider lip-synching. Silently."

My best friend slowly removed the headphones and put her hands up in surrender. "Whoa. What's the matter with you? Someone replace your Lucky Charms with Shredded Wheat? Wait—Nicoh didn't eat all my Nutty Bars again, did he? If that furball so much as—"

"No, wisecracker. Two words: Winslow. Clark."

She nodded, letting out a low whistle as she plopped onto a kitchen stool. "I take it Mort couldn't help, then?"

"He said he wanted to look into a few things. In the meantime, I'm biding my time...festering. Clark could be anywhere right now, meaning he could strike at any moment. And we both know what he's capable of."

Leah pressed her eyes shut and shuddered, recalling the time she'd spent as Clark's captive—a ploy to elicit my attention and my compliance—though in the end his intention had been to kill us both.

"Hey—" I started to comfort my friend but she quickly waved me off.

"Let's not do this again, AJ." After everything that had gone down the past year—including the number of times we'd gotten ourselves into trouble or nearly killed—she was ready for the dramafest to stop. Period.

I couldn't disagree. It would be refreshing to go back to our normal lives, the ones that had been regularly scheduled and already in progress. Not that those lives had always been filled with puppies or an endless supply of gummy bears and margaritas but they'd been *our* lives.

A look passed between us—we both knew good and well—even if Clark was no longer a threat and there was no danger on the horizon, our lives would never be normal again. Somehow, I was okay with that, and given the calmness that washed over my usually impish, energetic friend, I knew, she too, had made peace with it. Her comment had not been one of pleading or evolved from a place of fear—it was a resolution.

We would not grant Clark another free pass.

* * *

Mort called shortly before 9 a.m. the following morning, as I was collecting my camera equipment for my first client and almost immediately, I noticed his tone was unusually curt.

"I was able to gather some information but I'd rather not discuss it over the phone. Can you meet?"

"Okay...I have a photo shoot at the Desert Botanical Garden

that will take the bulk of the morning but I can drop by your house after—"

"No, no..." Mort interjected, his voice sharp and impatient, borderline hostile, "that won't work. The Andean bear exhibit at the Phoenix Zoo—do you know it?"

I was surprised by his choice of location, which was just a quick shot up Galvin Parkway from the botanical garden.

"Yes, I know where that particular exhibit is located but—"

"Be there. 1 p.m."

I stared at my phone and had it not been for our previous interactions, would have called him out for his rude behavior. Now, he just had me worried.

"Alright... Is everything okay, Mort? I mean—"

"Not now, Arianna." The way he enunciated every word made it sound like he did so through gritted teeth. "Just be there at 1 p.m. And make sure you come alone."

The connection ended, leaving me confused and more than a little concerned for the retired newspaperman. The rumbling in my belly wasn't helping matters, though it could have just been the peanut M&Ms I'd had for breakfast, colliding like balls on a pool table.

Typically a warm, gentle man, Mort had been uncommonly harsh and commanding. Whatever he'd learned, it couldn't have been good. I called Leah, knowing she would be disappointed about his insistence I come alone, which also prevented Nicoh from accompanying me—definitely a curious curiosity.

"And here I thought old Mort liked me best." I pictured Leah pulling on the ends of her hair as the corners of her mouth turned down.

"Um, no...sorry. I think he actually likes Nicoh best."

My attempt at lightening the mood fell flat on its big fat face as Leah snorted into my ear. "Whatever, AJ, it certainly doesn't seem to be the case anymore, considering he's left his favorite out of the fun."

"Yeah, what do you make of that?"

"Who knows. You said he sounded irritable. Maybe he had to call in a few favors to get your information? I know I'd be pretty crabby if I had to call in *another* one for you," she grumbled. "In fact, if I had to count the number of unsavory things I've had to do to get your skinny hiney—"

"Is that right?" I was incensed she was taking Mort's request out on me by bringing up old dirt. "Well, I think we'll all benefit from finding out where Clark is, don't you?" Her silence told me she'd conceded the point—a rare occurrence. "So, if I'm going to tackle this meeting without the benefit of your expertise—how do you suggest I proceed?"

"Well..." she spoke slowly as her mind switched into reporter-mode, "if Mort wants to meet with you away from his home, alone, it means he's worried. Perhaps he believes he's given whomever he contacted reason to keep tabs on him, which would explain the need to meet at a public location."

"Okay, so he's being cautious."

"Or completely paranoid."

"Maybe...I think we need to operate under the assumption he has good reason to be concerned and take it at face value."

"Um...hello? What did you do with my best friend? Geez, AJ, when did you become such a cynic?"

"When Winslow Clark decided to claw his way out of Hell and set up shop in my backyard, that's when." As she scoffed in my ear, I added, "So that's all the sage advice you've got stored in your bag of tricks?"

"As if," she huffed, "just try to get him to tell you as many details as you can—who gave him the info, what and how they said it, how they know it, blah, blah, blah. And as a final tip—

record it all. Whatever *it* is, my gut's telling me something hinky is about to go down."

Hinky or not, I didn't need Leah's gastric intuitions to tell me the crazy train was on a collision course with yours truly.

* * *

I was glad to have my work to keep me occupied for the next several hours. I certainly couldn't afford to have my impending meeting with Mort distract me from my professional duties, or the payday it promised. I was fortunate to have had early success with my freelance photography business, which by no coincidence I'd named Mischievous Malamute—a result of a few awkward predicaments Nicoh had put me in at the beginning of my career. In hindsight, perhaps I should have reconsidered allowing him to accompany me to my shoots but after a few near-misses, snafus and a great many apologies, I'd continued to tote him with me from location to location. Or maybe it was vice-versa.

Needless to say, Nicoh was less than thrilled about being left behind and verbalized as much as I hauled my equipment from the house to the Mini. Of course, the howling and moaning increased two-fold as I backed out of the driveway. I cringed, thinking of the poor neighbors, who were likely hustling to their fallout shelters. One of these days, I'd probably receive a lovely note on my front door, compliments of the city, informing me of the various code violations I was infringing upon. Violating the strict noise ordinance and harboring wild animals without a permit would likely be the starters. Yup, Nicoh was gonna make me pay. Today, he'd probably howl until he was no longer able to hear the rumble of my tiny engine before heading into the back-yard to leave a special treat for my homecoming.

On a brighter note, my client was an absolute peach and things ran smoothly throughout the shoot, leaving me with time to spare. I grabbed a caffeinated beverage and reorganized my tote so that my cell phone would be in a prime recording position, as Leah had instructed. It would probably turn out to be overkill but considering we'd both gotten those gut feelings, a girl couldn't be too careful.

I gave the application a quick test to ensure the quality was good and that it wouldn't fall to the bottom of the bag when jostled. Sure, I could have just as easily put the darn thing in my back pocket but after a recent butt-dialing incident at my friend Charlie's penthouse, I was hesitant to place the phone on my person. There was no sense validating my cellularly challenged reputation. I grimaced at the recollection but as I paid the zoo's admission and proceeded to the Andean bear exhibit, my discomfort quickly evaporated as I recounted the childhood moments spent at this exhibit, hoping to catch a glimpse of the spectacled bears—aptly nicknamed for their unique facial markings.

As I reached the enclosure Mort had indicated, I wondered why—of all the exhibits the zoo had to offer—he had selected this exhibit? My stomach formed a volleyball-sized knot, sending signals to the rest of my body, along with an unnerving tingling sensation in the remainder of my extremities. I cursed, wishing I'd not encouraged the barista to be so liberal with the extra shots of espresso. I blew out a long breath and proceeded.

Mort's back was to me as I approached. The ground crunched under the weight of my shoes, causing him to turn. I squinted, taking in the man's features. My mind flashed to a photograph I'd seen while searching for clues related to my sister's murder. He had aged a few decades, given the crinkles at the corners of his dark eyes and slight loosening of skin across his angular jawline but he was a mirror image of one of the men in that photo—still retaining his ruggedly handsome looks and mop of hair, now laced with silver.

A man who was most definitely…not Mort Daniels.

"Hello, Arianna. My name is—"

"Martin."

Surprised by my acknowledgment, he rubbed his hands together, contemplating how to proceed now the cat was out of the bag. A long moment passed before he raised his head and looked me straight in the eye.

"Yes, Arianna. My name is Martin Singer. I am your father."

CHAPTER FOUR

Once I had absorbed the initial shock that Martin Singer was even alive, the hair on the back of my neck bristled at his brazen announcement.

"My *biological* father," I clarified. If the distinction bothered him, he gave no indication. "Yes, I've known about our…connection for a few months now, since the death of my twin sister—your other daughter—surely you heard about her murder?"

Martin bowed his head and said nothing but kept his eyes focused on me. I had the benefit of sunglasses and utilized them to their full advantage to observe him as well. The family resemblance was uncanny, especially around the mouth and nose and the way his eyebrows rose and fell when surprised.

"You look so much like her," he whispered. I nodded, knowing he was referencing Alison Anders, the woman who had given me life; then died a few short hours later. "I assume Ella favored her, too?"

I nodded at his reference to the name Victoria had been given at birth. "From the pictures I've seen of her, yes, very much so." Martin tilted his head and squinted in confusion—another gesture we had in common. My voice came out raspy, "I never knew

Victoria, Ella, when she was alive. I only became aware of her existence after she was murdered." I blew out a breath. "I was the one who found her." Martin's eyes widened at the revelation and when he started to respond, I waved off his sympathy.

"Why are you here, Martin?"

The empathy surrounding him rippled and faded at the harshness of my voice and he realized now was not the time for a family reunion. Though his eyes never left mine, he was silent for so long, I was compelled to fill the uncomfortable void.

"How do you know Mort Daniels? More importantly, why did he contact you, much less know *how* to contact you?" Martin smiled but this time, there was no warmth behind it and something clicked. "You were Mort's contact when he worked at the *Chicago Tribune*, back when he was doing research on Alcore and GenTech. *You* were his inside track." His expression revealed nothing but the shift in the energy surrounding us suggested I had nicked something. "Has he known you were alive this whole time? I personally would like to know how that transpired, by the way, in addition to finding out where you've been the past twenty-odd years? Winslow Clark said his dad pushed you off the Skyway Bridge in an attempt to make it look like suicide. And yet, decades later...here you are. Why? Why now?" As the questions poured out, my skin grew hot as my heartbeat doubled. I attempted another barrage but Martin put his hands up in surrender and chuckled in amusement.

"So much like Alison—so inquisitive, so darned smart..." his voice trailed off as he appeared to revel in some long lost memory. Finally, he shook his head, as though pushing away cobwebs. "But no, I wasn't Daniels' 'inside track' nor am I aware who that person is, or was." I wasn't buying his answer but waved my hand, urging him to continue. "Daniels made contact through a mutual acquaintance. I was notified once the urgency of your phone call had been assessed. He doesn't know I'm alive or that I was the person sent to meet you. He only knew you would be meeting with a resource that could assist you with your current…situation."

I thought about my conversation with Mort—how uncommonly abrupt he'd been—and wondered why he'd felt obligated to set me up for this meeting with an unknown and possibly dangerous stranger.

As though he'd been reading my mind, Martin nodded. "Our acquaintance is very well connected. I assure you, we mean you no harm. My deepest apologies for causing you distress but Mort had sworn to not reveal his source and was also assured your safety would be our primary concern." His explanation seemed dubious but I let it slide. "As for Winslow Clark, the story he told you was true. His father, Theodore Winslow, plotted my demise and lured me to the bridge but his execution—no pun intended— was severely lacking. He didn't stick around to verify the results. Thankfully, he was as sloppy with attempted murder as he was in his work, otherwise I wouldn't be standing here today. But that, my dear Arianna, is a story for another day. Today…today we must focus on the matter at hand: Winslow Clark. That answers the 'why' portion of your query. As for the 'why now'? Because it's time to destroy the monster I've created. Permanently."

* * *

I clucked my tongue at his confidence.

"I know you have many questions, Arianna. I have many of my own. Too many," his voice wavered and I caught a hint of moisture glistening in his eyes. Fortunately my emotions were masked behind sunglasses. "I do hope someday soon you will oblige me but today we do not have the benefit of time on our side. Winslow Clark is here, preparing to strike. For the time being, he must be the primary focus of our attentions. Having said that, I have a favor to ask." I nodded for him to proceed. "The only way I can ensure your safety and the safety of the ones you love is if you agree to leave town."

Oh, heck no. I told Martin as much and after unleashing the sailor on him, I wouldn't have been the least bit surprised if he'd whipped a bar of soap from his pocket. Instead, he offered a bemused expression. Exasperated, I released another round of expletives before slamming my fists onto my hips while tapping my foot.

This time, my efforts were rewarded with a small chuckle. "Forgive me, the similarities to your mother—to Alison— continue to amaze me."

"If I'm half as stubborn as you say she was, then you should know I have no intention of leaving town—leaving my loved ones behind—while I'm off taking a vaca, waiting for the freak show of a monsoon known as El Clark to pass through town. My town. Ain't gonna happen, Pops."

This time, Martin winced and I immediately felt a flush of regret for my callousness before remembering the man had conveniently elected to go missing for the majority of my life. When he said nothing, I added, "Besides, that would kind of defeat the purpose. I mean, Clark came to Phoenix to eliminate me. What purpose would leaving serve anyone?" I shrugged and waved my hands to emphasize the point. Apparently Martin was not one for dramatic flourishes and looked bored, if not a bit impatient. "He'd come looking for me, regardless of where I went, so there's no sense having him tear up the whole country in the process. Let's face it, he's not going to back down or crawl back into whatever hole he clawed his miserable way out of—not empty-handed, anyway."

"He will if he's offered something better."

I had to refrain from bursting out in laughter. "Something better? Like what? A front row seat on the maiden voyage of

Richard Branson's Virgin Galactic spacecraft?" This time I laughed but there was no humor in it and given the look on Martin's face, he clearly didn't appreciate my brand of sarcasm. "I seriously doubt Clark's willing to hang out with the gila monsters and javelinas here in the desert for that long."

Martin shook his head, still not amused. I wondered if Alison had bristled his fur to such an extent. Given the way I was feeling about the man at the present, I hoped her talents in that arena superseded mine. He squinted, regarding me and when he finally spoke, his expression was flat.

"He won't have to wait. He'll have me."

Score one for Martin—that certainly earned my attention.

"You? No offense, Martin but how do you interpret that as 'something better'? To my knowledge, Clark doesn't even know you're alive, much less would believe you were who you claim to be."

Though neither of us was feeling jovial, Martin offered a cryptic smile. "Oh, I believe I can make a pretty convincing argument."

Knowing Clark as I did, I snorted at Martin's bravado. "Okay...say he's got his DNA decoder ring handy and it confirms you're...you...why would he be satisfied with that exchange? And what's to say he won't take us both out anyway?"

"Because I have something he wants, Arianna. And when I present it to him, in all its glory, he'll want it so badly he'll do anything to finally have it in his possession."

"Err...not sure if you're familiar with Clark but unless you've got an in with Versace and Ferrari...with maybe a little Charlie Manson thrown in, I doubt he'll bite."

"Oh, I suspect he'll do a lot more than bite when he learns what I have to offer," Martin gave me a knowing look, "especially since it involves Gemini."

* * *

Martin could only be referring to one thing: the formulas to the human cloning project both Clark and his father had not only coveted, but killed for. Putting those babies in either of their hands, along with the scientist who'd created them was a dangerous, if not monstrous business.

Though strained, my voice found its way past my urge to vomit. "I'll admit, I don't know you very well, Martin, but you certainly don't strike me as crazy." Absently, I rechecked my math—perhaps my initial calculations were off? Was he crazy? There was only one way to find out. "Why would you suggest such a thing knowing what happened...the consequences...last time?"

"I promise you, it won't come to that."

"How can you make a promise like that?"

"Because I'm going to destroy them before it gets that far."

CHAPTER FIVE

I wasn't sure if he'd meant destroying the formulas—or the father and son killing team—but he didn't appear above entertaining both options.

Regardless, I didn't trust him and right now, placing some distance from the situation was starting to sound less hair-brained than when I had initially dredged it up, even if it had only been a few minutes earlier. Yeah, I realized time was a hot commodity where Clark was concerned but that nagging voice inside my skull told me it was worth the risk.

I had just learned my biological father was still alive, which was a lot to contend with and considering he hadn't made his presence known until now, I wasn't convinced he had done so merely out of concern for his daughter. It was far more plausible his reasons were self-serving, which made me question anything he'd said.

Adding another chestnut to that fire, Martin had asked me to keep our meeting private before we parted ways. I understood why he wouldn't want the masses knowing his current status—being presumed dead made one funny that way—but he caught me off-guard when he attempted to swear me to secrecy from everyone, including Leah. In the end, I might have made a few grunting noises that sounded like agreement but I wasn't going to let pseudo-Dad dictate anything to me. We'd only just met and in my book, blood neither earned nor guaranteed him that right.

* * *

I was so busy replaying my conversation with Martin, it took me a moment to register my neighbor Susie was walking a dog as I breezed on past with a distracted half-wave. It took me another moment to realize she didn't own a dog.

She was walking *my* dog.

I threw the Mini in reverse and cursed as she squealed in protest—the car's tires, not Susie.

Susie leaned in as I rolled down the window. "I'd keep the day job if I were you. You'd make a questionable valet and an even worse race car driver. Typically, the goal is to proceed that way." She thumbed in the opposite direction. "By the way, was just returning Nicoh to his yard."

"He thought he'd partake in another adventure, did he?" Content with his current handler, the canine ignored me—part of my payback for that morning.

In addition to the occasional passive-aggressive streak, Nicoh had become adept at creating escape routes now that his gal pal Pandora had moved to Dallas with her dad. I would find him sitting in her backyard, patiently awaiting her return. He would typically become belligerent when forced to return home, where he would give me the stink eye until mealtime rolled around.

Susie gave me a perplexed look. "No, your friend Clark— good looking boy, that one—said you were at a photo shoot that was running late and had asked him to run Nicoh home. It wasn't until he got here he realized you'd forgotten to give him your keys, so he came over to ask if I could watch Nicoh until you returned. I told him I had my own set and could do him one better. He was most appreciative and seemed like he was in a hurry to get back to the shoot." She waved a finger at me. "Say, you didn't tell me you'd expanded your business—hiring assistants and all—nice to hear you've been doing so well."

Though her story nearly made me barf on my shoes and throw various expletives out into the universe, I didn't want to alarm my neighbor. I doubted she'd take kindly to the revelation she'd spent face time with a cold-blooded killer. "Um yeah, business has been good. Clark's been a real lifesaver, though I wish he'd ease up on wearing the designer suits to work. I don't need my clients thinking I'm making so much bank I can afford to pay my associates that well, meaning I can also afford to give them some slack where my rates are concerned."

Susie laughed. "You know, I did wonder. Armani, wasn't it? Boy's a sharp dresser and a definite keeper." She wiggled her eyebrows at me suggestively.

"Err...yeah...sort of already taken but I'll let Clark know you appreciated his wardrobe when I see him again."

Susie giggled and after thanking her for watching Nicoh, coaxed the surly beast into the Mini and continued to the house. "So...Buster, what have you been up to in my absence, besides consorting with the enemy?"

Nicoh was uncharacteristically subdued. At first I figured he was still mopey about being left behind but when I looked into his eyes and watched his laborious gait, I noticed he was acting a bit punchy, like he'd been drugged. This time I allowed the expletives to fly as I checked him over. How else would Clark have gotten Nicoh's compliance, especially after he'd knocked Clark on his arse the last time we'd crossed paths?

I immediately called the vet and was relieved to learn he was on his house call rotation. After providing him with a truncated version of my suspicions, he agreed to swing by once he'd finished with his last patient.

I moved Nicoh into the house, where he collapsed into the corner of the living room. Moments after tucking himself into a tight circle, snores rumbled from the center of the mass.

My impatience got the better of me while waiting for the vet, so I searched for clues indicating how and where Clark had breached my homestead. At first glance, nothing seemed out of place in any of the rooms but when I walked the perimeter of the yard, I found an empty meat wrapper near the back gate. Bingo. I carefully collected it and placed it into a plastic baggie and was about to resume my search when I heard a vehicle pull into the drive. I trotted to the front of the house to find my vet pulling supplies from his van.

Ushering him into the living room, I offered what little I knew about Nicoh's afternoon and produced the baggie. The vet listened with interest as he checked Nicoh's vitals and asked about any vomiting or other side-effects. I indicated there had been none, other than Nicoh's extreme moodiness and unusual physical imbalance. After extracting a few blood samples, he provided follow-up instructions, took the baggie and assured me he would call once he had the results.

I walked him to his vehicle and nibbled on a fingernail while calling Leah. I wasn't prepared to deal with Ramirez or his reaction to Clark's invasion of my privacy and honestly, still had yet to decide what to do about mentioning Martin's sudden appearance. Leah would take whatever news I could throw at her and have advice to spare. Besides, I needed to ensure Clark hadn't paid her a little visit as well.

I suddenly realized I could hear her cell phone, only the

ringing wasn't isolated to my ear. It appeared to coming from somewhere…in the house. I quickly tracked the sound, taking a mental account as I went. Her SUV hadn't been in the driveway and there was no trail of keys, tote bag, laptop, etc. that typically followed her arrival. I squinted, revisiting anything that seemed out of order while searching for evidence Clark had been present. I shook my head in repulsion at the thought of him touching my things or rifling through my undie drawer, noting my fingers had started to go numb from gripping the phone. Impatient, I called again and when the ringing turned to voicemail, I honed in on the sound, throwing the door open to the room where it had led me.

My room.

I had given it a quick once-over when I arrived home and had seen nothing blatantly obvious but now I searched from a fresh perspective and found Leah's phone under my comforter. Thoroughly expecting a Sigourney Weaver *Copycat* moment—complete with ants and a bloody, severed finger—I squeezed my eyes closed and threw the bedding to the side with the force of an arm wrestler gunning toward victory. Sweat threatened to escape my brow as I opened one eye a slit to look at the offending —phone.

Just a phone.

I exhaled deeply and a bead of sweat trickled into my eyes, forcing me to blink rapidly while I attempted to confirm my discovery. Still, it was just a phone. I thumbed through the missed calls and noticed several since early that morning. Surely she hadn't left it behind or placed it under the covers of my bed. I ventured a guess as to who had done the honors, the list not particularly long.

Clark was really getting on my nerves. After breaking into my home, drugging my dog and hauling him around the neighborhood, he had managed to commandeer my best friend's phone. I quickly panned through her text messages to see if they might offer any explanation as to her whereabouts. My eyes settled on one in all caps from an unknown sender—addressed to me.

ARIANNA—IF I CAN GET THIS CLOSE—HOW LONG DO YOU THINK YOU HAVE?

My heart thudded against my chest as I bit my lip in an attempt to rein in the emotion that raged through me. Suddenly, I realized I was no longer alone in the room. I swiveled on one heel, prepared to throw my fists, arms, legs, phone…whatever, to ward off the unwelcome visitor…stopping short of my crazed onslaught as I took in the startled, wide-eyed expression of my roommate.

"Whoa! What's going on? And, hey…where'd you find my phone?"

I couldn't decide whether to flog my roomie, or shriek because she'd startled me, so I grabbed her and hugged her fiercely, until she mouthed, "Oww…" Relief washed over me as I released her and tears spilled down my cheeks.

"Hey, hey…are you okay?" She stuttered, surprised by the downpour, though perhaps it was the side-effects of having the oxygen squeezed out of her.

I stifled a last, small sob and wiped mascara-stained tears on the back of my hand before plopping on the bed. Leah followed suit and glanced at her phone, still clutched in my grasp and threatening to crack until the pressure. She reached for it but I shook my head.

"We need to talk."

She retracted her hand as though a jolt of electricity had shocked her and clamped her mouth into a thin line before nodding for me to proceed. After a few cleansing breaths, I quickly told her about my visit with Mort—who turned out to be Martin—and about finding Nicoh with Susie. I finished with Clark's intrusion.

"Have you contacted Ramirez?"

I shook my head. "I called you first. That's how I found your phone."

"Huh. I had it with me this morning but after my first interview, I noticed it was gone." I tilted my head, curious about what would separate my best friend from her favorite piece of technology. She caught the gesture and chuckled. "Part of my current research involves interviewing the head honchos at a local server farm, including the VPs of Data Center Operations and Infrastructure. Considering how tight their security is—you should see the crap I had to offer up just to get inside—I locked my cell phone and laptop in the trunk." I shrugged. She'd lost me at 'server farm.'

"Anyway, I didn't think about them again until I was at my second interview on the other side of town. I opened the trunk and bam...my laptop was there but my phone was missing. I figured I'd just gotten confused about having it on me before the first meeting—it was only a four shot espresso day, after all." I rolled my eyes, though I knew Leah didn't operate on all cylinders until she'd had twice that much. "Long story short, this was the first chance I had to come back to look for it. You mentioned Clark sent a text to my phone, addressed to you?" I nodded and handed her the phone. She scrolled through the messages and read—and reread—Clark's text.

"Kind of weird he didn't just send it to your phone. Huh, and it was sent at the same time I was in my first interview." It was also the same time I was meeting with Martin at the zoo. So knowing—and loathing Clark as I did—no, I did not think it was weird. Not. One. Bit. I told her as much.

"Sounds like someone's been keeping pretty close tabs on us," she replied.

"Well, except for the phone in the bed and drugging my dog, I guess we should be happy he's keeping a safe distance." Like sarcasm would help me keep my sanity.

Leah nodded and momentarily shifted the subject. "So Martin asked you to keep your meeting a secret—he obviously doesn't know you very well. He's just lucky Clark's not onto him."

I didn't believe in luck and neither did she. Martin had been adamant that Clark didn't know of his existence but it certainly seemed as though Clark was ahead of the game. Whatever game that was, was anybody's guess. With Clark, all bets were off. The bigger question was, was Clark the puppet master—as he liked to fancy himself—or a puppet doing his master's bidding?

My cell phone distracted me from that line of thought, so I put a mental bookmark in its place for later consideration. The number of the incoming call told me it was Nicoh's vet. I immediately put him on speakerphone, hoping he had the results of my slumbering beast's blood work, along with a positive prognosis.

"Looks to be nothing more than a light sedative typically used during outpatient surgery, though based upon Nicoh's reaction, he was administered enough for two dogs his size, which is amazing, considering he was still upright when you found him."

Though Clark's audacity made me livid, I managed to hold my temper. The good doctor need not be apprised of *all* the circumstances surrounding Nicoh's drugging. "Apparently, your pup has an iron will," he added.

"More like an iron gut," Leah retorted, causing the vet to chuckle, "much like his owner." More laughter erupted from the opposite end of the connection. I gave her the evil eye and followed it up with a solid punch to the arm.

"Would these sedatives have made Nicoh more…compliant? Perhaps more likely to venture out of his territory, or go with someone he didn't know?" Go with someone he didn't trust was more like it but again, I didn't need to alert the vet to an already complicated situation.

"Absolutely, and unless the person who drugged the meat was an expert in administering meds, he could have easily ended up with a different outcome on his hands," the vet replied, meaning Clark might have killed Nicoh.

I nearly growled out loud. Perhaps that had been his intention? I quickly thanked him and signed off before he could press me for additional details. I wondered if he would be obligated to report it to the authorities. I needed to keep Ramirez off my back for as long as possible and wondered how long I had if the vet did report it.

As it was, it would only be a matter of time before I had to fill Ramirez in on...everything but right now I needed time—without his coply intuition—to figure things out on my own. Leah seemed to be thinking the same thing and was tugging on the ends of her shorn locks.

"Other than the obvious drama, what's going on with you?"

She avoided my eyes. "I was supposed to meet Vargas tonight."

Jeremiah "Jere" Vargas was a homicide detective for the city of Tempe. He was also the ex-boyfriend of Erica Stone, the editor that had made Leah's life hell at her former place of employment and ultimately initiated her decision to leave her post. Erica was also the primary reason Leah's relationship with the cop never seemed to evolve past friendship. The publishing world was small and though Leah was both talented and successful, there was no need to give a jealous ex ammo for monkeying up the works.

At my raised brow, she quickly added, "For drinks."

I looked at her skeptically but saw her point. If the vet reported the incident with Nicoh, Vargas would certainly catch word of it, considering the veterinary hospital was located within his jurisdiction. And if Vargas knew, it wouldn't be long before his Tuesday night poker buddy Ramirez was alerted. After a few cocktails, he'd drill Leah for specifics and she'd end up spilling the beans about Clark. Worst case scenario, she'd also bring up Martin. Not good. Not good, at all.

"I should cancel. Our time will be better spent doing some recon around this place while keeping an eye on Nicoh."

"Aren't those typically one in the same?" She gave me a small smile. Apparently, my attempt at humor was not completely lost on her, despite her grim expression as she glanced around the room, as though Clark might pop out from beneath the bed. "Anyway, it's really up to you but I won't complain if you decide to stay. I can definitely see why you'd want to avoid having that conversation with Vargas. I'm having the same anxiety about Ramirez." Talk about tall, dark and imposing—especially when agitated; then times that by two—it wasn't pretty. "I know we'll have to deal with both of them sooner or later."

"Alex, I'll take the latter for two hundred." My friend replied dryly while dialing the detective's number. "Fortunately, he's in a team meeting, so I'll be able to leave him a message without getting into too many details." She crafted quite the tale—I would have settled on a headache-themed excuse—and after disconnecting, smugly shoved the phone into her pocket.

"Wow, you are way too good at making up excuses. Anyone ever tell you that?"

"Tricks of the trade, my sweet, tricks of the trade."

I gave her a sideways glance. "And just what trade might that be, sweet?" She scrunched her nose and stuck out her tongue, forcing me to chuckle. "Just saying, Leah. Perhaps you're taking these freelance assignments with the Stanton brothers a bit too literally. They did have you interviewing a few pros while tracking down the leader of that prostitution ring. Maybe you've picked up a few other things you'd like to share?"

She blushed at the mention of Abe and Elijah Stanton. She'd been doing research for them off and on since leaving the newspaper, after they had helped me uncover Clark's involvement in my sister's death. I had always believed that, like Vargas, Abe had a crush on her and that the feeling was mutual, despite her emphatic denials. It was one situation where she just wasn't quite as convincing. I suspected I knew the reason. She attempted to ignore me and though she made a show of straightening my comforter, the pink tips of her ears betrayed her.

"So, are we going to de-Clark this place, or what?" she asked.

I released a long, slow breath and nodded. I was more than ready to let the de-Clarking, disinfecting and exorcising begin.

* * *

Our first order of business was to check on Nicoh. He was sleeping so soundly Leah actually placed her smartphone under his nose for confirmation of life. Of course, she snatched it away after being rewarded with a dollop of doggie drool on her Swarovski-encrusted case. I could barely contain my laughter until we made it outside to perform our search for potential points of entry.

We quickly learned, given the density and prickliness of the oleanders, it didn't seem possible one could, much less would even want to attempt that feat, with or without a canine in tow. Sure, Clark could have tossed the tainted meat over the ten-foot hedge but scaling it or plunging through it didn't seem feasible. Still, we continued to work our way, foot by foot, along the perimeter and as we approached the trailer gate, found what appeared to be Clark's entry point.

I would have missed it entirely had it not be for the bolt that snagged my running pants. As I cursed my clumsiness, I noticed it appeared to be less tarnished than its counterparts and extended nearly an inch farther. But while the bolt was somewhat unusual, the wood panel it held in place revealed our gold nugget. After retrieving a wrench, I unscrewed each nut and bolt and once the board had been removed from the gate, Leah easily slipped between the wrought iron bars. I followed suit, considering I was more of a size match to Clark. Like my friend, I had room to spare, which meant Clark would have been able to pass through and coax a drugged Alaskan Malamute of Nicoh's girth between the bars.

After placing a quick call to a handyman I used from time to time, Leah and I attempted to secure the gate the best we could until he could install a more permanent solution. Less than satisfied with our efforts, we surveyed the yard again before retreating indoors, securing all windows, doors and doggie exits and setting the alarm. Of course, if Clark was still inside—say, lurking in the attic—we were hosed. Neither of us had the energy to venture up there to make that discovery, though it was tempting to fry up a smelly batch of liver and onions or sauerkraut to smoke him out. Unfortunately, we had neither on hand and elected to barricade ourselves in instead, meaning Clark would just have to stay put and suffer as we dusted off the karaoke machine.

Exhausted, we passed on croaking out our favorite 1980s tunes and opted for a movie night. After checking on Nicoh, we settled into the living room, popped in *To Catch A Thief* and pretended it kept our attention. It turned out to be a futile exercise, considering Leah obsessively checked her text messages while I chewed on an unwitting nail.

Leah almost cried out in relief when her phone rang but her expression went from one of excitement to another of puzzlement when she looked at the incoming number. She gasped as the caller spoke and her eyes widened in alarm. After a few murmured responses, she hung up, wringing the phone between clenched hands.

"Leah?" I shook her arm gently when she didn't respond. "What is it?"

It took her several seconds to reply as she struggled to find the words. "That was the managing editor from the newspaper. Erica was found dead in her home…murdered."

"Oh my!"

She shook her head. "That's not even the worst part. They think Vargas did it."

CHAPTER SIX

"What do you mean 'they think Vargas did it'? Isn't he at some cop-type meeting? You did just text him, right?"

"That was a while ago and he never responded." She shrugged but the hollowness of her voice was a dead giveaway. "Besides, they've initiated a statewide manhunt for him since then."

"Don't tell me you believe this foolishness?" When she said nothing, realization washed over me. "You actually think he might have murdered that woman." It was not a question and again, my friend failed to respond. "Leah Campbell, we *know* Vargas, he's our friend. And a good cop."

She whispered, as if saying the words betrayed their friendship, "But the police have evidence—skin under her nails and blood that isn't hers." She shuddered but waved me off when I went to comfort her. "She fought hard, AJ. Erica didn't want to die...like that." She wrapped her arms around herself. "And then the killer just left her there. Ran away like a coward and didn't even attempt to cover his crime."

I was surprised by her resignation. Leah? Distraught...yes. But throwing in the towel? I didn't think so. I took her by the shoulders and gave her a good shake until she met my eyes.

"The police have got it wrong, Leah. They have to. What you've just described sounds nothing like Vargas. He's a decent, hardworking cop, a loyal friend to not just you and me, but to Ramirez and a whole lotta other people out there."

Her mouthed turned downward. "Even the good guys have a breaking point."

All but exasperated, I replied through gritted teeth, "Not Vargas. Not like this. Blowing off steam...sure. But nothing...and no one would drive him to murder."

"Erica could." As her coloring grew paler and her expression more haunted, it became clear my friend had not finished relaying her horrifying tale. "There was also an altercation at the police station. Erica showed up, made a scene and heaved some gnarly threats at Vargas. Said she'd expose him for the dirty, lying cop he was and by the time she finished with him, she'd not only end his career but the careers of every cop in the department, all the way up to the Chief of Police. After that, things got kind of physical and it took four guys to keep Vargas under control, but not before he issued his own threat. In a matter of speaking, he vowed to rip her throat out for lying."

I shuddered. It was pretty graphic, even for Vargas. "It's just an expression, Leah, said in the heat of the moment. No one would fault him. Not after that."

She looked at me evenly. I had never seen my friend so flat, so devoid of emotion. Suddenly, a chill passed through my bones, like someone walking over my grave.

"You don't understand," her voice was nothing but a husky whisper, "Erica's throat had been sliced so savagely her trachea was severed. The killer also removed her tongue."

* * *

Before she could venture any farther, the doorbell forced us both to jump.

"What now?" I growled as I stalked to the front door and threw it wide. *No sense standing on civilities at this point in the game,* I muttered to myself.

Ramirez filled the doorway. Tension rolled from him in waves, only adding to state of unrest permeating my home.

"You've heard about Vargas." He offered no question, only a statement of fact as he absorbed my friend's grim demeanor. "How much do you know?"

"Leah had just gotten the call from her former editor. We've heard Vargas is your primary suspect but he's magically disappeared, and now there's a bounty on his head."

Ramirez snorted in disgust. "Not *my* primary suspect. And, check your facts. They don't put a bounty on heads in this century. It's considered barbaric—no matter who the murderer is."

I raised my hands in mock surrender. "So, other than to add another burr to our saddles, what brings you by, Detective?"

Ramirez ignored my sarcasm and directed his steely gaze at Leah. "I wanted to see if he's contacted you."

Not appreciating his attitude or the insinuation, she leapt from the couch and stomped until she was within centimeters of him. "What exactly is that supposed to mean? Are you implying that I helped Vargas escape? Or that I know his current whereabouts?" Ramirez said nothing, still eying her speculatively. "I see. Well, if that's the way you're going to play it, Detective, I need to know: are you asking as Vargas' friend? Or as a cop? And be careful how you answer that, because contrary to what you might think, they are not one in the same. And the wrong answer might just get your invite revoked until you've got the proper documentation to compel me to provide commentary for those questions."

Ramirez gave her a hard stare before responding, "Vargas and I have been friends longer than the two of you have been doing whatever it is you've been doing all these months. So I resent *your* implication that I would supersede the boundaries of jurisprudence by using my badge to elicit information against that friend." He shook his head and turned away from her. From us. I thought he was going to leave and moved to stop him when he spoke, his voice so low I had to lean forward to hear him. "I have to find him. Before they do."

I reached out and touched his arm but he wouldn't face us as he continued, "Jeremiah Vargas grew up in a broken home, watched his mother get beaten to death by her boyfriend and by the time he was nine, lived on the streets after being used as a meal ticket by not one, but three foster homes. Even after all he'd endured he never claimed to be a victim, or a product of his environment. He went into the military—served in Desert Storm—then came home and became a cop. All because he wanted to serve and protect those who couldn't fend for themselves. He would gladly put his life on the line to save another. So no, he wouldn't commit cold-blooded murder much less butcher anyone that way."

Leah spoke softly, not wanting to fracture an already unsteady balance of energy swirling throughout the room: anger, fear, remorse, sadness. "But after the incident at the station, surely you could see how they could have come to that conclusion. And then, there's the evidence—"

Ramirez swirled. "Wait, what 'incident'?"

Leah flinched at the sharpness of his tone but quickly filled him in on the scene that had occurred between Erica and Vargas and the unfortunate comments that followed. I moved closer to Ramirez, grasping his arm more firmly though I wasn't sure why. Nor did I understand how he had not been apprised of the confrontation when Leah's editor had already been privy to it. Once she'd finished, I said as much.

Looking a little gray around the gills, Leah looked at each of us before responding, "My editor didn't divulge that little tidbit. I was there when it happened."

* * *

Ramirez started to interject but Leah put up a hand, "I was there in an official capacity—doing some background for the Stantons—and Erica happened to be there, too, though I doubt she ever saw me. When she arrived, she was clearly on a mission. And while Vargas did snap at the end, no one would have blamed him. Erica was totally off-base and out of control—I'm sure every other person in the room was thinking the same thing."

"Only Vargas *said* it," I added.

"Yeah, and now this." Leah vigorously rubbed her hands through her hair and pressed her eyes shut. "I just can't believe…"

Ramirez squinted as he mulled over Leah's latest bombshell. "Leah's right—this is going to go from bad to worse if we don't find Vargas before they—the police do. I had hoped they'd find the evidence circumstantial—possibly planted by the real killer—but that combined with this very public altercation…and the fact Vargas is nowhere to be found…" He shook his head, still not able to fathom his friend and fellow officer could have facilitated such an atrocity. "I can't get any more involved than I already am, especially not when what I'm proposing is contrary to what the department is implementing. We do, however, have a short list of friends who can."

Leah and I both nodded, drawing on his conclusion—the Stanton brothers could do what Ramirez couldn't—reach beyond the boundaries of the towering wall of blue.

"If we could get them on board, focus their energy on tracking Vargas down—preferably before my guys got to him—that would allow me to focus on the evidence," Ramirez commented to himself.

"What exactly was this evidence?" I asked but Leah shook her head in a manner that indicated I didn't really want to know.

Ramirez didn't catch the gesture and commented absently, "His blood from the struggle—she put up quite a fight—and his hunting knife."

Finally, he glanced up to see my horrified expression. "Sorry, I thought Leah had probably already filled you in."

I shook my head. "So...the knife...it was the one used to...uh..."

"Carve out Erica's tongue," Leah finished, belatedly noting her choice of words had caused me to wince. "Where did they find it, anyway?"

"In her apartment." I couldn't help but notice the brevity of Ramirez's response.

"How original. And so like a cop," Leah replied dryly. Apparently, Ramirez's arrival had put the spit back into her fire. "What, did the killer wrap it in plastic and put it in the freezer for safe-keeping?"

Ramirez leveled a stony glare before deflating her sarcasm balloon. "Nope. They found it in her dog's stomach."

CHAPTER SEVEN

I barely managed to keep myself from upchucking on Ramirez's boots—though I noted he had moved a few steps away from both of us after divulging that fun factoid—and changed the subject.

"So, you'll see about getting the Stantons involved?" Both of us nodded, though I assumed he thought Leah would be making the call. "By the way, where's Nicoh?" Ramirez looked around, used to his pal venturing onto the scene when he arrived.

"Err...I'll be making that call now." Leah raised her phone and made an animated show of dialing while escaping to her room. Ramirez's eyes narrowed and I felt them zero in, expectantly awaiting a response.

"Um, yeah, about that..." I found myself wringing my hands as I led him to the corner where Nicoh was sprawled on his side, snoring softly as drool glazed the floor. "We had a bit of excitement earlier." I told him about Clark's visit and how he'd lured Nicoh out of the yard and left him with Susie under the ruse of bringing him home early from a photo shoot at my request. When I reached the vet's diagnosis, I looked up to find him with arms crossed. It also appeared the heels of his boots were making nice divots in the hard wood floor, as he worked to contain his anger.

"Just when were you planning on telling me, Ajax?" Uh oh, out came the nickname, spoken through gritted teeth—never a good sign.

"Well—"

Ramirez put a hand up to stop me. "Let me guess, you avoided calling me about Clark's break-in, but calling the police in general was never a consideration, was it?" I felt like a chastised five-year-old who about to be banished to the corner for snagging cookies out the jar without asking.

I didn't have a chance to plead my case—as thin as it was—because Leah bounded into the room, sporting a satisfied look. "The Stanton boys are on board. They'll drive over from L.A. tomorrow morning. In the meantime, they'll put the word out about Vargas and start some intel. Discreetly, of course."

"Good. I'd appreciate it if you—or they—kept me in the loop." I noticed Ramirez addressed her, refusing to acknowledge my presence now that he'd finished chewing me out. Leah nodded, sensing the tension in the room and started to say something when his cell phone buzzed. Ramirez looked at it and frowned. "Gotta run, duty calls. We'll finish this later."

He briefly directed his gaze at me and I saw disappointment, mixed with frustration. Before I could speak, he strode out of the house without looking back.

"Probably a good thing you failed to mention this." Leah wiggled her phone at me, referencing the text message from Clark.

"Listening in, were we? I figured he already had enough on his plate." I glanced at the space Ramirez once filled. "Besides, even if you hadn't managed to trounce your way into our conversation, I probably wouldn't have made it that far. You saw the look on his face."

She nodded and tapped her chin. "Yeah, funny how you seem to have that effect on the men in your life."

I sniffed. "Not all men, just the homicide detectives." She shivered at the thought of Vargas and I immediately regretted the words no matter how innocent they had been. "We'll find him, Leah, and bring him home." Again, she nodded but there was no conviction behind it. Her mind had returned to the dark place where our friend was considered a dangerous fugitive. A savage killer. "In the meantime, there's a call I need to make and someone I need to see." Leah looked at me with curiosity. "I need to see a guy who knows a guy," I replied in my best gangster accent.

"I have absolutely no idea what that means."

"Neither do I." I shrugged, causing her to laugh. It was a small concession, given the circumstances. I gave her a quick hug before she headed for her room then reached for my phone.

The fact was...I did know what it meant.

And I was betting Martin did too.

* * *

The following morning, I found him sitting alone on a worn bench near the duck pond at the park a few blocks from my house. As I approached, my gaze shifted to the movement that had captured his attention. It was a young couple, perhaps in their early twenties, coaxing a toddler to venture to the edge of the pond's bank, where several baby ducks were happily playing while the mama duck looked on. The tiny girl clutched a piece of bread that easily filled the span of her hand, despite her daddy's insistence that it was okay to release it to the duckling's care. The mama duck posed no threat but given their similarities in size, it was easy to see the child was more fearful of the repercussions from her than she was of feeding the babies.

Finally, she opened her fingers just enough to prompt the ducklings to waddle over to retrieve her offering. One nudged her toe for an additional morsel, making the toddler giggle and clap with delight. I looked at Martin and found a smile eclipsing his face. Though his eyes crinkled at the corners, the simple gesture made him seem youthful, giving me a glimpse into the man he had once been.

Not wanting to spoil the moment, I put my head down to avoid his eyes and approached. He stood and when I finally raised my head, saw his smile was still present.

"Lovely, isn't it?"

"The park? The city takes pride in maintaining it. Fortunately, this is just one of many it has to offer." His smile slipped when he thought I hadn't captured his meaning.

"Yes, that too." He looked longingly at the family, still laughing as the little girl gently patted the top of her new friend's heads under the mama duck's watchful eye.

I looked at the family, a happy memory forming as I thought of my own parents. I had been that child once, long ago. Martin hadn't had the benefit of such a memory, with me or my sister, Victoria. I wondered what he saw when looked at the child. Did he see me…us…and long for what might have been with Alison? Of the years—and people—he'd lost? Or was it something deeper? A lifetime of loneliness and heartbreak? Whatever had brought him to me now couldn't be resurrected in a lifetime of those moments.

And still, here he was.

"Why did you come, Martin?"

"Why did I come? Because you asked me to, Arianna—"

I shook my head. "No, Martin, I mean, why did you come out of hiding after all these years? Why now?"

He appraised me, pressing his lips together as he struggled to find words for the questions he wasn't prepared to answer.

"You're asking why I didn't come when I could have done something to save your sister," he murmured.

"Maybe, though I guess we'll never know," I replied.

He sighed. "I've spent a lifetime hiding. Sometimes even fooling myself into thinking it's been because of Clark, or his father but truthfully, I've been running. Running from myself. Running from choices I made. And perhaps, others I didn't or wouldn't make. I guess after I found out about Victoria, I could no longer allow my mistakes to become my children's—my remaining child's—burdens."

"Mistakes?"

"Gemini, Theodore Winslow, my association with Alison…" He trailed off, his eyes wandering to the small family.

His choice of words struck me as odd. "You didn't love her?"

"Alison? Of course I loved her. But if I hadn't been so adamant about my work, the project, perhaps she'd still…" Despite the years that had passed, finishing the thought was still too raw for him.

"You know what they say about hindsight, Martin."

"I guess the same could be said about saving Victoria," he replied somberly.

"True. But you still haven't answered my question."

"No, I suppose I haven't."

"Are you looking for absolution?"

He laughed and shook his head, amused by my forthrightness. "No, nothing as simple as that—nor would I ask it of you, daughter."

I ignored the familial reference. "That remains to be seen. In the meantime, I came here to discuss another matter." I told him of Clark's visit to my home and his abduction and poisoning of Nicoh.

When I finished Martin quietly uttered, "I'm assuming you still won't entertain my request to leave town for the duration?"

I leveled a glance that effectively closed the book on that

question before responding, "No, I actually have something more urgent to contend with."

He frowned. "Something more important than Clark?"

"One of my friends is in trouble. Serious trouble. Missing, actually."

"Is it the Tempe Homicide Detective…Vargas, I believe is his name?"

I nodded. "I don't have many friends but yes, he's one of the good guys…and I'm really hoping we'll find him soon."

"I understand. And I hope everything works out," he replied.

"Are you talking about me, or yourself?"

He regarded me for a moment but did not break my gaze. "Do what you need to help your friend. I'll reach out to my network to find a solution for dealing with Clark."

Normally, I would have snickered at his mention of a "solution"—ever the scientist he was—as though Clark was a mere puzzle that could be solved by concocting an elaborate formula in his lab. Now his second comment about having outside help piqued my interest.

"Your network?" I asked.

This time, Martin's eyes failed to reach mine. "For now, the less you know the better."

"Better for me? Or for you?"

He chuckled, shaking his head. "Point taken. You're more like your mother—like Alison—than I could have imagined."

"Yeah, well, from what I hear about Victoria, we would have made quite the trio."

Martin nodded solemnly. "I don't doubt that for a minute. Alison would have been proud, you know."

I dismissed his comment. I only had Martin's word for it and while he was probably onto something, we'd never know for sure.

"Ever thought about having your own?" Martin tipped his head in the direction of the family.

"Oh sure, that's what I have Nicoh and Leah for," I replied dryly.

Martin laughed. It was a hearty, joyous sound, tainted by a hint of sadness. "While I'm sure both your canine and best friend can be a handful at times, it's not exactly what I meant."

I shrugged. I didn't know Martin well enough to get all chatty about personal details, though it did make me reflect on the fact that my attempts at wrangling a stubborn, demanding Alaskan Malamute often exceeded the bounds of my maternal instincts.

After wrapping up the conversation, I left him sitting on the bench, where he resumed his quiet observation of the small family. Perhaps he was pondering what life might have brought him, had he selected another path. I wondered if he would he ever find the answers he sought.

As I turned away, I realized he'd never fully provided me with the reason behind his sudden appearance. Then again, perhaps the answer to that question was just as much of a mystery to him as the answers to his own.

* * *

Regardless of the life or moral crises Martin was facing—or my feelings toward him at moment—I had no choice other than to leave the proper care and handling of the Clark situation in his hands. Clark, after all, wasn't a gently simmering pot you placed on the back burner while you went about your business. He was more like the kettle that had been overfilled and now was vomiting scalding water over everything within its reach.

Presently, I had a bigger kettle to boil—finding my friend Vargas and bringing him home. Hopefully, unscalded and in one piece. I pursed my lips at the thought, until I realized there was a figure leaning against my Mini Cooper.

"Is there something you've been meaning to tell me, Ajax?"

CHAPTER EIGHT

"It's apparent that you followed me, Ramirez. The question is why?"

"What's apparent is that my spidey senses, as you like to call them, weren't far off the mark when I got the impression you were holding out on me. I'll ask you again, is there something you forgot to tell me?"

"Are you asking me as a cop? Or as my boyfriend?"

"Depends. Who's your friend?" Ramirez nodded in the direction of the bench, forcing my heart to thud against my chest. He didn't know who Martin was and I needed to keep it that way.

"Jealous, Ramirez? He's a prospective *client*." I held up a hand to keep him from interjecting, though he'd made no motion to do so. Okay, I was crap for ad-libbing. Oh heck, where was Leah when I needed her?

"Being a *professional* photographer, don't you usually meet the client at his place of business?"

"Not that it's any of your business but he's from out of town." Not a lie.

"Okay then, what about a portfolio? I'd assume he'd want to

see your work before he hired you? And, I didn't see you taking any notes."

"That's why I have a *professional* website, Detective—so that prospective clients can browse through my previous projects, see the companies I've worked with and their testimonials—and hey, I even have client list so that they can make direct inquires. Geesh, this is starting to sound like an interrogation!" I threw my hands up and exhaled a long, frustrated breath. Ramirez didn't appear to buy my sudden flair for the dramatic. "As for the 'notes,' that's why we professionals carry these." I sarcastically wiggled my smartphone under his nose. "It's called technology, Detective. You might try coming out of the cave once in a while and sniffing around before clobbering a gal over the head."

Ramirez uttered something he should have had his mouth washed out for before adding, "If you're trying to tell me I need to evolve, AJ, you're going about it in a very snarly manner."

I huffed out a harsh laugh. "*I'm* being snarly?"

"You know, I can tell I'm not getting anywhere with you. It appears your roommate's tendencies to circumvent the truth are wearing off on you."

"Seriously? First you have the audacity to follow me, accuse me of doing something unsavory and then call Leah, my best friend of twenty-plus years, a liar? To my face? You have some nerve, buddy. And you're certainly not winning any Eagle badges, or whatever it is you neo-man types aspire to…" I turned on my heel and marched as quickly as my thirty-six inch legs would allow, hoping he would not follow.

He didn't, though his retort was more damaging, "You're actions are simply proving my point, Ajax. I can tell you're dodging me."

I marched on, muttering under my breath. "Yeah, well maybe someone's got his panties twisted because his detection and interrogation skills are on the fritz and he's got the relationship acumen of a baboon."

Behind me, I heard Ramirez blow out an exasperated sigh.

Then again, maybe I'd erroneously said that last bit a little too loud.

* * *

By the time I got home, a black Ferrari—in all its luxurious and shimmering glory—filled my driveway—an indication the Stanton brothers had arrived. Early. I sighed as I got out and patted my Mini on her top.

"No worries, old girl, I'm not replacing you today, though you're welcome to make nice with the pretty pony." I hoped my reassurance would keep her jealousy under control and ensure she started for me on my next go-around. She was fairly feisty that way and prone to fits when she observed me salivating over other chassis.

Unfortunately, a temperamental chariot was the least of my concerns, as was overanalyzing my squabble with Ramirez. I had enough on my plate with Clark's reappearance, Nicoh's poisoning, Vargas' issues, Erica's murder…and of course, Martin. I bit my lip to hold back tears before entering. Muffled voices came from the kitchen and as I rounded the corner, found Leah, Abe and Elijah hunched over what appeared to be a kitchen-turned-command-post. Maps, diagrams and paperwork were taped or strewn across every surface. Cupboards bore colorful topographic maps, flip charts and several official-looking documents. Had I really been gone that long?

I watched them from the doorway, talking in hushed voices, pointing at various points on the map. Leah absently twirled a red pen in her hair and nodded as the brothers took turns explaining the various highlighted portions of the geography, until something wet nudged my hand, nearly making me shriek.

Nicoh's soft brown eyes gleamed as his tail beat in a slow, leisurely wag. I smiled and kneeled to nuzzle my face into his warm neck, thankful he had come back to me. Though he still seemed to be recovering from the effects of the poisoning, as he leaned his sturdy frame into me, his heartbeat was strong and his demeanor was…Nicoh-like. I scratched him gently behind the ears and was rewarded with a low whoo-woo of approval, before he nudged me again.

"Hey, stranger," the older brother, Abe, drawled.

Hugs were forthcoming as I gave the Stantons a quick once-over. Neither had changed a bit since I had last seen them and both were still just as easy on the eyes. At six feet three inches, both towered over Leah—their angular features and tanned skin striking in a masculine, rugged way. Abe's hair was masterful as ever, with artfully gelled spikes jutting in every direction, a perfect complement to his all black ensemble. Elijah, the younger of the two, let his sun-bleached waves carelessly brush his shoulders while the front fell into his eyes. His casual appearance ended with the preppy, buttoned-down shirt he'd paired with expensive jeans and Italian loafers.

"How's Anna doing?" Their right hand gal, Anna Goodwin, had become a close friend since she and the Stantons first worked on my sister's case. A looker in her own right, she had brains and a fierce kick to boot. Needless to say, she kept those boys on track. And in line.

"Good, good…working on wedding plans while keeping the business running. Girl's definitely a multi-tasker." Anna had recently gotten engaged to a rising L.A. film producer and earned her own private investigator's license.

"Well, you tell her we're happy to come over and help out whenever she needs us."

"Yeah, right. Just what we need—all three of you casing the streets of L.A.," Elijah teased.

"Oh, we're not going to case the streets, silly, we're simply going to borrow the company credit card and go shopping on Rodeo, in your car," Leah retorted, not bothering to hide her smugness. "And, of course, that will be followed by the most outrageous bachelorette party you've ever seen."

I nodded. "You know what they say…what happens in…"

Abe threw up his hands, "Okay, okay! Enough already! I can't handle the torture." Everyone laughed until one of the charts came loose from the cupboard and collapsed onto the floor—a grim reminder of the task that had reunited us.

"We set up shop. Hope you don't mind?" Elijah's voice was pensive as he retrieved the fallen chart.

"No, not at all," I replied. "Our kitchen is yours to use. Not much cooking goes on in here, anyway."

Abe scratched his head. "Err…well, we might have strayed. We're just mapping things out in here. That's the evidence collection area." He pointed toward the living room.

"Oh?" My curiosity got the better of me and before he had a chance to issue a warning, I ran smack-dab into a massive white board filled with crime scene photos. And Erica. Dead. "Oh my!"

"AJ, I am so sorry!" Abe stammered.

I diverted my gaze from the colorful images but one imprinted on my mind. Even in death, Erica's eyes were wide with shock. Combined with the gaping hole that had once been her mouth, it bore an eerie resemblance to Munch's *The Scream*. Abe rushed to pull the photo down but I shook my head.

"It's okay, guys. It just caught me off-guard. She…she was alive when that…happened to her?" It came out in a squeak.

"Afraid so," Elijah replied, eying me skeptically. "Are you sure you don't want us to pull these down or cover them, at a minimum?"

I shook my head. "I'm okay, really. How did you get them so quickly?"

Elijah looked at me, clearly confused. "Ramirez didn't tell you he'd gotten them to us?"

Now I was confused. "You've spoken to him, already? Leah and I just talked to him ourselves, when he asked us to get you involved."

Both crinkled their brows and Abe responded, "Um, no, Ramirez actually contacted us before Leah did. Right after they found Erica. We thought you knew."

I glanced at Leah. It certainly seemed as though we weren't the only ones holding back information. If that wasn't the pot calling the kettle—Abe cleared his throat, interrupting my thoughts.

"I did just see Ramirez a few minutes ago but it was on another...matter," I grumbled.

Leah's eyes went wide as she realized Ramirez had seen me at my meeting with Martin. "AJ, would you mind taking a look at my eye—in the other room—where the light is brighter? There's something in it."

Smooth, Leah, real smooth.

"I thought you girls only went to fix your faces in groups when you were in public?" Abe teased.

"Who said anything about needing to fix our faces, Stanton? We're simply going elsewhere so that we can talk about the two of you behind your backs," Leah retorted. "In the meantime, why don't you continue getting organized—we've got a lot of work ahead of us." She ushered me into her room with Nicoh in close pursuit. I was surprised by the latter until I realized she had two candy bars sticking out of her back pocket.

"Saving a snack for later, are we?"

She absently checked her pocket. "Oh, shoot, I wondered where I had put these. Those boys tend to overfeed the d-o-g."

"Why are we spelling?" I asked.

"He's been particularly alert since he's come back around and now that we have guests, he seems to be more persuasive than usual."

I sniffed. "You're overestimating his abilities, Leah."

"Whatever, the d-o-g's eaten like a p-i-g ever since those two have arrived." She waved a hand. "Anywhoo, what gives?"

I quickly filled her in on my meeting with Martin and the events that transpired with Ramirez immediately following.

She gasped in surprise. "So he doesn't know about Martin? Didn't he recognize him?"

"How could he, Leah? We're the only ones who've ever seen the pictures, much less know he's still among the land of the living."

"And, Martin? I forgot to ask earlier but he looks…well, does he look like you?" She slapped herself upside the head. "Of course he looks like you. Does he look good? And, I don't mean that in a creepy I-want-to-know-if-your-dad-is-a-hottie sort of way."

"No, you just want to know in a guy-whose-been-dead-for-over-two-decades sort of way."

"Exactly."

I shrugged. "I guess. I wasn't really there to bond."

"Well, of course not. You hardly know the guy," she huffed.

"I don't know him at all, Leah. And right now, I don't know that I want to."

"Whatever. At least he's taking care of Clark while we work on this other…issue."

"He's got to find him first," I countered.

"Sounds like a familiar dilemma." Meaning Vargas. "You think Martin will come through?"

I shrugged. "Don't know. At least it will allow us to focus on

Vargas. Of course, we'll still have to watch our backs in the meantime."

"Err…about that…"

I swiveled my head to look at her. "What…about that?"

"Ramirez asked Abe and Elijah to keep an eye on us."

"Big surprise there. He obviously doesn't think we can manage to stay of out trouble. Then again, they'll be off looking for Vargas, so they can't be here watching us day and night," I replied.

"Uh, that's exactly what he instructed them to do." I raised an eyebrow. "They're moving in with us."

CHAPTER NINE

Before I could formulate a G-rated response, Abe knocked on the door and poked his head in. "Everything okay in there?" We nodded and moved back into the kitchen. "I take it Leah told you about Ramirez's suggestion?"

"Sounds more like a directive than a suggestion," I replied.

"If you're not cool with it, we can certainly stay out in the car," Elijah offered, sounding mildly amused.

"Oh sure, and fill that lovely machine with boy stink?" Leah scrunched up her nose.

"Boy stink?" Abe asked.

"Don't even get me started—"

I waved my hands, indicating a cease fire. "It's fine, guys. No problem. I'm sure we can make it work. It might even be to our advantage." When Leah wiggled her eyebrows, I quickly added, "I meant having the evidence, maps and all of us in one place could be beneficial for brainstorming and in coordinating our efforts."

"So, we're ready to proceed, then?" Once everyone had given Abe a single nod, he clapped his brother on the back. "Let's do it. Time is wasting away and Vargas certainly needs friends out there looking for him and clearing his name. Speaking of which, Leah, I meant to ask you, did you happen to work with Grace Turner?"

"Erica's assistant? Sure. Grace was at the paper before I started. Why?"

"Would you be willing to have a chat with her—see if she has a short list of people who had it in for Erica?"

Leah snorted. "Not to be disrespectful but that list ain't going to be short."

"That's what we've been hearing," Abe replied, looking less than pleased.

"And you thought she might be more willing to share the goods with a person she's already familiar with," I added.

"Yeah, and she might have a better idea of how to narrow that list down." Elijah looked at Leah. "What do you think?"

"Certainly worth a try. Of course, you do realize"—Leah tapped her chin—"Grace's probably already earned her place at the very top of that list."

* * *

Leah filled me in on our way to the girl's apartment in downtown Phoenix. We'd left Abe and Elijah with Nicoh so they could continue reviewing the documents Ramirez had provided. Hopefully, they'd also be able to identify acquaintances to shed more light on Vargas' possible whereabouts, as well as the situation with his ex. Given Leah's pursed lips, it wasn't something she was ready to tackle on her own.

I interrupted whatever negative thoughts she was chewing on, "So Grace worked for Erica before you joined the paper?"

"Grace was actually an associate editor before Erica was hired and would have been a shoe-in for the lead editorial position had Erica not used her assets to work her way into it. And I don't mean the brainy type."

"You're saying she blackmailed her way into the editor's seat?" I asked.

"Pretty much what happens when you have evidence placing your boss in some compromising situations, including ones that you're personally privy to," she replied dryly.

"Yuck, sounds like Erica was a piece of work. Didn't even think that sort of thing flew these days with all the human resource policies."

Leah laughed. "Oh, you'd be surprised. It happens more than people think. People like Erica have just gotten more creative about it. And the Internet, social media and smartphone apps make it a lot easier to capture and disseminate incriminating information. So yeah, Erica not only got the brass ring, she skipped all the other rings to get it."

"And bypassed Grace and others along the way? That *is* going to be a long list."

"You've got that right, my friend. There certainly won't be any love lost there," Leah replied.

I shook my head. "It's not the love part I'm worried about."

Grace lived in a modest apartment complex in a recently revitalized section of the downtown area. It took her a few moments to register the visitor was a former co-worker when she opened the door but after the initial surprise passed, she pulled Leah into a quick hug. As she ushered us in, I noted Grace was pretty in a natural way. Her sun-kissed hair was cut into an angled bob that was longer in the front and ended at her chin. Her eyes were a luminous hazel and despite being puffy and red from crying, were warm and inviting. She was thin but athletically muscular. Leah mentioned she had been a former long distance track runner in college and hiked either Camelback or Papago Mountains on her days off.

She motioned toward the small living room that was just off the kitchenette and the two of us sat on a tan microfiber loveseat while she chose its matching chair.

"Sorry, I don't have anything but water to offer you but I can make a mean glass with ice?" We both indicated we were fine. "I guess you've probably heard about Erica?" If there had been any resentment between them, it certainly wasn't apparent. Grace appeared more miserable than elated.

Leah nodded. "We came by to make sure you were doing okay and see if there was anything we could do for you."

"You were always so sweet, Leah. Even now, despite the fact we no longer work together, you are the only one who ever consistently remembers my birthday." She turned to me. "Leah brings me African Violets every year. And somehow manages to find Peanut Butter Frangos. Both are my absolute favorite, though I'll never know how you learned that."

Leah wiggled a finger. "Not telling, my friend. Trade secrets." She used her thumb and forefinger to fabricate a locking movement across her lips and then tossed it over her shoulder.

Grace chuckled easily but the laughter was gone just as quickly. "I think there were a lot more secrets being tucked away than anyone ever imagined."

"You're referring to Erica." I let Leah take the lead. Though I'd seen Grace on occasion when visiting Leah at her former workplace, we were no more than passing acquaintances.

Grace nodded. "Despite her overtures to move up the ladder, she kept stuff pretty close to the vest and had irons in every fire. Everyone else's fire." She smiled but it wasn't one that emitted a great deal of fond memories of her boss.

"Sounds like the Erica I knew and loathed." Leah scrunched

up her nose, thinking about her own interactions with the editor. "Anyone top your list of suspects?"

Grace snickered. "I see your mind still works like an investigative reporter's. Unfortunately, I think people would be scratching, clawing and outright clamoring over one another to be at the front of that list. It's like they say, it would be simpler and quicker to identify who *wouldn't* be on it. The police department, media, etc. tend to like her ex, Jeremiah Vargas, though I have doubts where he is concerned. Then again, the timing of his disappearance doesn't make any sense." She shook her head, as baffled as we were. "Of course, Detective Ramirez, Vargas' poker-playing buddy, is currently spinning his own theory."

"So…who does Ramirez like for it?" I asked, causing Leah to roll her eyes. Apparently, I hadn't come off quite as nonchalant as I'd anticipated.

"Ramirez has his fan favorite, all right." Grace was less than pleased, given the downward turn of her mouth and the sour undertone. "Me."

"What?" both Leah and I exclaimed, loud enough to rattle the glasses in her cupboard.

Leah offered a quick apology before continuing, "Why the heck would he think that?"

"I don't have a credible alibi. I was here alone and no one tends to see me come or go. Of course, there are other reasons: Erica was promoted to a job I had actually worked for, her treatment of me, the book deal—"

"Whoa…whoa…whoa…hold up the truck. What book deal?" It was definitely news to Leah.

Grace snapped her fingers. "Oh, right. I forgot you weren't around by the time that opportunity popped into her lap. Actually, if memory serves, it was shortly after you resigned. But no matter, like most of Erica's side projects, she kept the important details buttoned up, even from me. She'd wave me off when I pressed her, convinced she was the only one capable of getting the real story—she even bragged she could make it a bestseller."

"Huh. I take it this wasn't Erica's usual fictionalized take on reality, spun as the truth?" Leah asked.

Grace laughed harshly. "She did have a unique…flair for wordsmithing when it came to sensationalizing an ordinary, run-of-the-mill situation, didn't she?" Grace turned to me. "Erica could…and would…make your average ninety-year-old grand-mother look like a lying, scheming, adultering con artist."

"Nice chick," I replied dryly.

"That she was." Grace shook her head.

"So, getting back to this book, what was it about?" Leah asked.

Grace smiled. "Ah, it was an oldie but goodie and something right out of a science fiction novel. Remember when scientists cloned that sheep named Dolly back in the late 1990s?"

Leah looked at me and suddenly my stomach felt like it was doing backflips. "Um, yeah, we're not much for science—fiction or otherwise—but we're both familiar with the story." I nodded, unable to offer without launching my latte.

"Anyway, it turns out there was another group of scientists who had been working on a similar project years earlier. Only, they weren't interested in cloning farm animals."

I knew how this story went. Leah slid me a warning glance. We needed to get as much out of Grace as we could without adding our own distractions into the mix. Fortunately, Grace was so wrapped up in telling the story she was oblivious to my attempts at preventing the latte, now shaken, from making an appearance.

"They were cloning humans," she concluded.

"Wow," was all we could manage.

"Yeah, there's even proof the experiments were successful. To this day, there are probably a handful of cloned humans out there somewhere." She inhaled a deep breath. "We could walk by one every day and not even realize it. Isn't that something?"

"Err…yeah. And you're saying this guy was willing to give information like that to Erica? Don't you find that a bit strange? I mean, if she was supposed to dig up details to run an article, or even a series of articles, that's one thing. But trusting her to write a *book*? Why?" Leah was breathless and a little more than exasperated. I couldn't say I blamed her.

Grace shrugged. "Strange? Yes and no. Yes, considering he knew of Erica's body of work he'd still choose her. But they knew one another from the days she worked for him as a copywriter back east. He needed an unbiased source to put a stamp on the book, so he agreed to supply her with the necessary resources, evidence…whatever she needed to make it happen."

"Meaning if Erica had made it public—"

"She would have been worth a few bucks. It would have also put her in the kind of spotlight she'd always wanted," Grace responded.

"Front and center of the entire world." Grace nodded. Clearly, she and Leah had known and understood Erica for who and what she was. "And her death…"

"Would have been construed as…timely, to certain individuals," Grace finished Leah's thought, pressing her lips together in a tight line.

"You mentioned Ramirez liked you for her murder?" Leah asked.

"Because I would have been a likely shoe-in for her position," Grace replied.

Leah nodded. "And as her assistant, you'd also be a suitable replacement for writing the book."

"Given I did much of her research, yes. Erica was just a vessel to put it out into the universe—one that could be replaced." She scrunched her face. "Sorry, that was really insensitive. I meant her death wouldn't have prevented it from being written."

"So the editorial position combined with the possibility of becoming the author of a bestselling novel…"

"Only compounded my lack of an alibi and put me right at the top of Detective Ramirez's list of suspects," Grace replied, her expression tight. "Funny thing is, on any other night, I would have been at the office or at Erica's pulling an all-nighter."

"Why was that night different?" I asked.

"She said she had an important meeting with her contact on the book and sent me home."

"Did you ever know who this contact was?" Leah prodded.

Grace shook her head. "Oh yeah, he was her former bureau chief when she worked at the *Chicago Tribune*."

I gogged while Leah managed to stutter, "Erica worked at the *Chicago Tribune*?"

"Back in the early days, yeah. She claims she'd made quite an impression on him but we all know what that meant in Erica's world. Anyway, word has it he helped her get on the staff there but retired shortly after. In fact, he lives here in Arizona now…in Ahwatukee."

This time, I groaned out loud, making Grace pause. Fortunately, Leah, always the quick thinker, jumped in, "She had some bad sushi earlier." I nodded, while trying my best not to kick her. Like I said, she was a quick thinker. I didn't say she was tactful.

My heart thudded as my stomach threatened to stage a protest. "So…this contact, does he have a name?"

Grace looked at me curiously, perhaps wondering why I was so interested. Still she offered me the benefit of a response.

"Sure, his name is Mort Daniels."

CHAPTER TEN

"Well, that was interesting," Leah commented after we'd said our goodbyes to Grace with the agreement we'd be in touch.

"Yah, think?" I replied, feeling no less nauseous, though the latte seemed to be temporarily taking a siesta. "I mean, what are the odds?"

"The bigger question is why now? And did it have any correlation whatsoever to Erica's death?"

"At this point I have no idea."

"Mort didn't mention anything to you?" Leah asked.

"You mean between Clark's B&E, poisoning my dog, Vargas being accused of murder and oh yeah, the surprise visit by Bio Pop?"

Leah chuckled. "Is that like a Blow-Pop?"

"Might as well be. It's leaving a nasty taste in my mouth."

"So, I take that as a 'no' on Mort?"

"Honey, I doubt I gave Mort the time to divulge that bit of information—though it would have been nice to know my life as a science fiction guinea pig was about to be exposed to the world." I groaned; then jabbed a finger at my best friend. "But don't you dare mention it. Next thing you know, *I'll* be at the top of Ramirez's crap list."

"I thought you already were." Point taken.

"Anyway…" I gritted my teeth. "No, I've only talked to Mort briefly—on the phone—after that we were supposed to meet at the zoo."

"Only Bio Pop shows up instead."

"Exactly."

"Then perhaps we need to pay our friend Mort a little visit," Leah suggested.

"I'm down with that. Let's do it before someone else does."

"Given our history, I doubt we'd get that lucky." If she only knew how true that would turn out being.

$$* * *$$

We were silent on the trip to Ahwatukee as we mulled over the information Grace had provided. I found myself wondering just how much she had known about her boss' new project. While it was clear Erica had been very bright and more than capable of handling her own research and writing, she'd delegate whatever would allow her to pursue other more fruitful activities. She was definitely greedy and power hungry, which by no means suggested she'd deserved to be murdered, though it might have explained why she had been mutilated in the manner she had. Had her tongue been extracted to shut her up? To serve as a warning to others? Or both?

We parked in front of Mort's home, which in my book was more of an estate. He had planted annuals around the perimeter since our last visit, along with a combination of succulents and blooming varietals, which added a pop of color to the desert surroundings.

The driveway was empty, though his car could have easily

been tucked in the garage. After ringing the doorbell several times and walking around the side to take a peek—without success—it was clear he was elsewhere. We cursed the fact we had not thought to call ahead. He typically welcomed our visits and would not have expected us to breach the subject of Erica or the book.

Perhaps I was naive but I hadn't thought he would have considered such a move and until I heard it straight from the horse's mouth, I was giving him the benefit of the doubt. It could have simply been a collaboration on a fictionalized version of the project. Erica could have concocted the tell-all aspect to suit her own interests.

Unfortunately, the Sour Patch kid doing the trampoline in my stomach was telling me this collaboration was much more than a work of fiction and the truth would be far more profitable.

For someone.

I was letting the hamster run the wheel in my head when I heard a thump, followed by a squeak. Realizing it wasn't Mr. Hamster taking a dive, I looked over my shoulder to find Leah sprawled across one of Mort's newly planted flower beds.

"Leah! What the heck?"

"A little hand here? I just trashed my new Kate Spade boots."

I reached over and yanked her up with both hands. Moist dirt and a few stray petals covered her knees and the tips of her boots, but other than a bruised ego, she didn't look any worse for the wear. "That's what you get for tromping through Mort's landscaping. See those flagstones there? That's called a pathway. Perhaps you should try using it."

"Alright, Ms. Smart Alec. I really appreciate your concern. Do you know how long I had to save up to buy these boots?"

"You got them on eBay."

"Yeah, well, I was forced to give my keyboard and my manicure a workout on that auction. I'm still convinced there were ringers bidding."

"Whatever. Can we get on with it? We're bordering on trespassing here."

Leah sniffed. "It's not my fault he put that viney crap there. It practically reached out and grabbed me."

I pointed at the cell phone peering from beneath the fleshy succulents. "I don't suppose that could have anything to do with your face plant?"

My friend's cheeks flushed. "I was not texting! And even if I had been, I am perfectly capable of walking and chewing gum at the same time."

"My point exactly," I replied evenly, receiving an exasperated huff in return.

"I'm just saying Mort shouldn't be putting those things so close to the walkway. They don't go with the whole cactus theme anyway." She kicked at the mud, frowning as it landed on her boots.

"You should probably leave the landscaping to Mort," I replied as I bent down to retrieve her phone. She was correct, though. The plants, whatever they were, seemed an odd choice with the other mix of foliage and plant life.

Then again, given my black thumb, I probably needed to take my own advice.

* * *

Abe took one look at us as we entered the Stanton's command station. "Playing in the mud, were we?"

"You can shut up now, Stanton. I need to go wash up," Leah retorted, flipping her non-existent locks over her shoulder as she spun on her heel and marched away.

"Maybe you should put a little elbow grease into cleaning up that attitude," he called after her, his voice playful.

Leah huffed in annoyance. "You could use your own spit

shine, buddy."

He watched her stomp down the hall and slam the bathroom door. "I do like a little spit-fire."

I glanced at Elijah and we both snickered. Grumpy boots or not, Abe had it bad for my best friend. When not flicking mud off her pride, she had been a bit flirty with him, too, despite her on and off thing with Vargas. Thinking of the missing detective wiped the smile off my face.

Elijah took note and quickly changed the subject. "So, we did a bit of recon while you were gone. Took inventory of your alarm system, beefed up the motion sensors, added a couple more cameras…"

"Please tell me there aren't any trip wires?"

"No trip wires but we surrounded the back of the property with about fifteen feet of barbed wire."

"You didn't."

Elijah shook his head and chuckled. "Why don't Abe and I run you through the new mods and show you how to use the updated alarm system."

"Err…you probably should mention the minor construction, too," Elijah added.

I groaned. "What 'minor construction'?"

Elijah shook his head at his older brother. Clearly, they hadn't managed to craft a plan for springing this delightful news on me. "Well, before we could add the new equipment, we had to make a few modifications to your office to allow for the monitoring console—"

"Monitoring console? What do you think this is—the Pentagon?"

"Come on, is that all you think we can manage? We're more on the level of an octagon." Abe flashed a knowing smile at his brother, who offered me a cheesy grin and a double thumbs-up.

"Maybe you'd better just show me," I grumbled.

"You want to wait for Leah?" Elijah asked. "We don't need her tripping things up."

That was an understatement. "Perhaps we'd better make sure she's not wearing those darn boots. I don't need the swat team swarming my compound."

"I do like those boots," Abe teased; then added, "besides, it would probably just be the bomb squad."

I continued to grumble until Leah emerged from the bathroom, mud-free, though one look at her pursed lips indicated her demeanor was still favoring the prickly side. Our new security setup was going to be a real hit.

I quickly filled her in before the boys led us outside for a summary of their enhancements. For the most part, everything was strategically placed and hidden from view. It was a bit surreal to think my home, which had once been my parent's little slice of paradise, needed such an elaborate system. But thanks to the return of Clark, it was best to be on the safe side. And besides, I trusted the Stantons, so who better to secure my home and our livelihood?

It wasn't until I saw the new monitoring console that I began to worry about the bill.

I took a deep breath as we entered what had once been my father's office. Except for a few additions here and there, including a new computer and some camera equipment, it was exactly as he had left it just over two years earlier—the day he and my mother never returned home. I was pleased to see the Stantons had taken this into consideration and at first glance, didn't notice the difference.

Abe noticed my confusion and nodded toward the walk-in closet, where my father had kept a few file cabinets and a small safe. Both Leah and I gasped when he opened the door. One wall had been replaced with state-of-the-art monitors and a tablet. Views of the house's exterior and interior could be seen from every angle and though they'd been careful not to invade the more private spaces of the home, it would be hard not to make a move without having the camera's eye on us.

"Cool, huh?" Elijah asked, looking fairly pleased with himself.

"Kind of...overwhelming." Concerned filled the Stanton's faces as they misread my astonishment for disapproval. I quickly dispelled their worry. "Oh, yes! It's cool! There's just so...much."

"We can certainly taper it back. It's all customizable to your preferences." Elijah picked up the tablet and outlined the system's features.

"And we can set various alarms from here, too?" Leah looked on, equally amazed by the complexity of the system.

"Yes, and we can also install apps on your cell phones, so you can make adjustments from there, set the alarm, check status and even monitor activity," Elijah replied.

"Hmm, this could help clear up those missing cookies." I nodded at Nicoh, who was the prime suspect in a rash of late-night cookie-nappings. Realizing all eyes were on him, he let out a low rumble and sauntered out of the room. Apparently we had insulted his sensibilities.

Leah laughed and pointed at one of the monitors. "I swear he just checked the kitchen counter when he went by."

Sure enough, Nicoh perched his head on the "cookie counter," inhaled a deep sniff, grumbled and moved to his pet bed, where he positioned himself with his back to the camera.

"I guess we got his goat." I offered a bleating sound, causing laughter to fill the room.

After a few more instructions, we moved on to more pressing matters, filling Abe and Elijah in on our chat with Grace and our strikeout at Mort's.

When we finished, they glanced at one another before Abe replied, "Your friend Grace is being less than honest about her involvement in the book project. At the very least, she's down-playing it."

"Spill, Stanton. At this point, I'm more concerned about finding Vargas and clearing his name than protecting Grace." Leah could be pretty direct when she wanted.

Abe nodded and continued, "With Anna's help we asked around, made a few inquiries…essentially, Grace's been sharing —though gloating may be a better word for it—details about the book deal." He blew out a long breath before proceeding, "A couple of weeks ago, she was out celebrating, had a few too many martinis during reverse happy hour and ended up chatting up the bartender at this joint downtown."

Leah rolled her eyes, clearly not convinced Grace was doing anything underhanded, and certainly not at some 'joint.'

Elijah raised a hand and picked up for his brother, "The bartender indicated Grace's boss had pissed her off about some-thing. Whatever it was, she never told him. Anyway, it must have been quite a brewhaha because the bartender said Grace bragged about contacting Mort directly to schedule a meeting—sans Erica —where she divulged her involvement in writing and researching the book. She even went as far as supplying him with proof. In a nutshell, Grace wanted Erica thrown to the curb and demanded whatever concessions Erica had been promised. We're still trying to find out how far it had gotten but according to Grace's rants to the bartender, it was just a matter of time before it was a done deal and Erica got the boot." Leah winced at the reference, the emotional wounds from her damaged Kate Spade's still fresh.

"Wow, pretty ballsy for such a little thing," I murmured. It was hard to imagine Grace undercutting someone so callously, but the bartender certainly couldn't have had that knowledge if at least part of it weren't true.

Leah nodded. "Knowing Erica, who could blame Grace? I wonder what her tipping point was?"

Abe shook his head. "We're still trying to figure that one out, though it must have been something pretty drastic. From what the bartender said, she was going after Erica's editorial position next."

"Certainly an interesting turn of events," Leah replied, "but it also shows someone other than Vargas had the means and motive to kill Erica."

"But if Grace was going to get the brass ring in the end, why murder Erica?" I countered. "Wouldn't she want Erica to witness her own downfall? And why would she bother with secret meetings if she already had proof to back up her claims?"

"Getting her ducks in a row? Or using it as a diversion? Trying to make it appear as though she had no reason to kill Erica?" Leah threw her hands in the air. "I don't know, maybe the deal fell through or Erica caught wind of it and intervened."

"Gosh, and here I thought you liked Grace," I replied sarcastically.

"I do, but if she's up to her neck in this and framed Vargas for it, then all bets are off."

I nodded. "We've got a ton of blanks to fill in before with can even connect Point A with Point B, though. What about the presence of Vargas' knife at the scene?"

Leah waved her hand. "Bah, the knife could have been circumstantial, placed there after the fact to make Vargas look guilty."

"By Grace?" I asked, my tone incredulous.

"Whoever, all I'm saying is that the *possibility* is there."

Abe interjected our volley, "Little problem with that theory. You didn't give us a chance to tell you that Ramirez called. Vargas' blood was all over the crime scene. And given the quantity identified as being distinctly his and not Erica's, it's clear he didn't get away unscathed." He released a long breath before continuing, "In fact, he could be mortally wounded."

CHAPTER ELEVEN

"Mortally wounded...as in dying?" I gasped, while Leah looked mortified.

"According to the evidence at the scene and span of the blood, Erica didn't go down easily. She probably fought her attacker for several minutes before she was subdued."

"Don't you mean killed?" I asked.

Elijah shook his head, looking me straight in the eye. "She was still alive when her tongue was removed. Her throat was slit after the fact, almost to the point of beheading."

As horrific and vicious as the last moments of Erica's life had been, of one thing I was certain: there was no way Jeremiah Vargas was capable of cold-blooded murder.

For once, I was thankful Martin was tracking Clark so I could focus my attention on Vargas. I would have to check in with Bio Pop sooner or later, but thanks to the Stanton's quick work, I would hopefully prevent Clark from getting into my home or hurting my dog again.

At least Nicoh had recovered, though it shouldn't have happened in the first place—much like having to lie to Ramirez about Martin. Ugh, Ramirez—I bristled, realizing I hadn't spoken to him since I'd walked away at the park. Just one more thing I would have to deal with sooner or later.

I snapped out of my reverie to find Abe, Elijah and Leah in the midst of formulating our plan of attack. Abe and Elijah would follow up on Anna's conversation with the bartender and hopefully once in person, attempt to elicit a few more details than he'd elaborated on over the phone. It was too bad they couldn't have sent Anna in person—she would have had the guy eating out her hand the moment she crossed the bar's threshold.

They would also see if Ramirez had any updates on the investigation; then reach out to their network for possible leads on Vargas or friends inclined to assist him.

Leah and I would place another visit to Grace and then continue on to the newspaper to chat up Leah's former co-workers. Hopefully they would be able to shed more light on the contentious relationship between Erica and Grace and offer additional insights surrounding the book deal.

We'd also try to reconnect with Mort—surely the elderly gentleman would have returned home by now? If we knew anything about him, he was dedicated to his landscaping endeavors. One couldn't fault him for that. At least it kept him occupied during his retirement. I wondered what would keep us moving through ours. Then again, it would be nice to believe we would even make it that far.

If the last couple of years were any indication, we were in big trouble.

* * *

Upon receiving Grace's voicemail, we continued on to the newspaper. After checking in at the front desk for visitor's badges, we were escorted to Leah's old floor by a very large, imposing security guard. Vibrant chatter filled the open workspace. Cubicles had long been replaced by half walls to encourage collaboration. Staffers scurried about like mice in a maze—their cheese being a deadline met and the editor's approval. Disapproval meant a return trip through the maze for a rewrite, humiliation or possibly starvation. No cheese would often mean no job. It was a tough business but once again, technology had changed the way publishers did business and ultimately, the way the news was crafted and disseminated. It was a hard road, often walked barefoot on broken glass. Without the benefit of one's cheese.

Several hugs, high fives and cheers abounded as Leah quickly made the rounds. We didn't have much time, so we had to zone in on a few key people to get the details we wanted, stopping when we reached a desk whose occupant—a freakishly tall, pencil-thin man with John Lennon-style glasses and a mop of red hair— raised a finger to indicate he would be with us once he'd concluded his phone call.

He was rather cute in an I-want-to-take-the-puppy-home kind of way and had it not been for his direct and forthright manner in dealing with the individual on the other end of the connection, I would have taken him for someone who endured getting his cheeks pinched and hair mussed on a regular basis.

From his side of the conversation, it was clear what topic he was fielding. "As I've already told you, Phillip, we're fully cooperating with the authorities on the matter, as is our policy. Having said that, it is also within that policy to refrain from divulging details that could be pertinent to the ongoing investigation or that may inhibit or prevent the future arrest and prosecution of the individual or individuals—" A squawk emitted from the receiver before the man responded by slamming the phone back onto its base. "It's one thing to report the news…quite…something else… to be part of it."

"Tough day, Darrell?" Leah asked as the man bounced up and hugged her. He was twice her height, so I withheld a giggle as she spoke to his belly button. Catching me mid-snicker, Leah backed out of the hug and introduced us, "Darrell Petrie, this is my best friend, Arianna Jackson. Darrell's an associate editor on the crime beat. We go way back…" She waved her hand.

"Ah, the elusive AJ." He gave me a knowing smile and squeezed my arm. I had no idea what stories he'd heard about me and noticed my friend did not have the good graces to look even remotely embarrassed.

I decided to give her a break and played along. "One and the same but don't let my looks fool you. I can kick some serious boo-teh when I need to."

"Oh…*I know.*" I inadvertently gasped when I realized Darrell might have been a bit smitten, given his goofy, lopsided smile and quick wink.

Of course, Leah couldn't help but snicker, before adding, "Yes, your notoriety precedes you, Ajax. Anywhoo…Darrell, we came to pick your brain, so get your eyeballs off my BFF's assets. At least until we're done interrogating you. After that, I'll let AJ decide what she wants to do with you."

"Mmm hmm, I like that." He plopped into his chair and gestured toward two spares in the next workspace.

Once we pulled them around and huddled in his tight quarters, Leah proceeded. "So, I know you told *Phillip* you were required to keep your lip buttoned but I'm here now…so spill your guts, Big D. What's your take on Erica's murder?"

"You know, I miss your directness, LeeLee." *LeeLee?* I snorted and was rewarded with a sharp pinch on my thigh. I refused to look down, hoping that it had come from LeeLee and not Big D. "Are you sure you don't want to come back now that the witch has melted?"

"Pretty harsh, even for you, D. And no, I'm still not interested, even if that broomstick has been laid to rest. I've moved on to greener pastures."

He clucked his tongue. "It does appear our boss has moved on to a…toastier climate. Couldn't have happened to a nicer…witch. Anyway, not to be disrespectful the dead—or Erica—but she probably crossed one too many lines and it finally bit her in the behind. You know what they say about karma."

Leah nodded. "Indeed I do, Big D, indeed I do. But, *who*, D? I need names."

He laughed. "You don't ask for much, do you?" She gave him a bored look. "Oh…gosh…just the same ones you've probably got rattling around in your melon. If you take the ex-boyfriend off the table—none of us have our money on him." When Leah raised her eyebrow, he waved his hand at her. "Come on, I know you two have a thing going and I'm not shining you on to get on your good side, but seriously? I don't think killing her would have made it onto his radar, no matter what the cops think or the evidence they have. Sure, it looks a little hinky that he skipped out—a lot hinky, actually—but let's put that on hold for a second and look at the real facts.

"After Vargas dumped Erica, he got as far away from her as a man can muster without a restraining order. He'd moved on. Besides, she was more interested in accumulating things than chasing them: money, power, men, prominence…whatever. The chase had to be worth the effort. Even if that hadn't been the case, there is no way Vargas would have inserted himself back into that drama, much less have risked his career and livelihood on her."

Leah waved her hands. "Okay, okay! You're preaching to the choir. Enough about Vargas—any other fan favorites?"

Darrell nodded. "Sure. Like I said before, my list probably jives with yours. And, as I'm sure you're aware, the possibilities are endless. Other editors, associate editors, reporters, staff, politicians, law enforcement, the grocery store clerk, her laundromat owner, her tanning salon owner, her stylist—"

"Dude, I get the picture," Leah interjected. "Anyone and everyone and everyone's dog had a motive. What about Grace?"

Darrell frowned. "What about her?"

"Anything about her working relationship with Erica change in the past few weeks or months? Anything that would indicate it was *her* line Erica crossed?"

His eyes widened. "Gracie? Our girl's no saint but she'd put up with so much for so long. If the bough hadn't broken yet, it wasn't ever going to."

Leah twirled her hair in an attempt to appear nonchalant. "So there were no rumblings about Grace wanting Erica's job? Or about any new projects?"

Darrell threw his head back and snorted out a harsh laugh. "Everyone wanted Erica's job at one point or another. Present company included. As for new projects—not that I'm aware of..." He squinted at her. "Why? What is it you've heard?"

"Nuh uh...buddy, don't try to out-maneuver the pro. I'm merely here on a fact-finding mission—posing a few routine questions."

He wasn't convinced. "Riiight, but nope, still no idea. However, if you believe there's something to it, why don't you ask her yourself?" He gestured over his shoulder, toward one of the offices that bordered the main workspace.

"Grace's *here*?"

Darrell shrugged. "Yeah, she's in Erica's office." When Leah looked at him questioningly, he added, "She's been temporarily assigned as Erica's replacement. Looks like she's the one moving on to greener pastures."

I'm not sure what I expected but Erica's office was something... else. The twenty-foot by twenty-foot space was garishly decorated, making it look like someone had barfed on top of a splatter paint machine—you know, the ones you sometimes see street vendors use to attract small crowds to their spun art? One would think they would eventually go the way of the Pet Rock, but I digress.

The office was a shrine dedicated to its owner, complete with a Warhol-style Marilyn Monroe—of Erica. Trophies loaded the shelves but I doubted Erica had been the one who had earned them, regardless of the name etched on the base. Another large photo of Erica sat on the armoire behind the desk, so anyone seated facing her would be staring at two of her. It was a bit unnerving, if not disturbing. Even in death, Erica appeared to have her beady little eyes on everyone and everything.

I certainly didn't think we'd find Grace doing a victory dance or handing out glasses of celebratory champagne but as we gently knocked on the door and peered in, I was surprised to find her so frazzled. We watched in silence while she desperately scribbled on various papers and checked them against several computer monitors. Traces of sweat were visible through her thin tunic as she muttered to herself.

Leah spoke quietly to avoid startling her, "Grace?"

It took her a moment to look up and when she did, another to register who we were. "Hey. Twice in one day. I'm not sure if I should be flattered. Or paranoid."

Leah played it off. "Oh, we came by to say hi to Darrell—long time no see and all. We're surprised to see you here, though. Are you sure you're up to it?"

Grace slumped in her chair. "Honestly? No, not really, but the world keeps moving no matter who dies, which means the news does too. The editor in chief called me after you left and begged me to come in using excuses like 'we're short-handed' and 'crap's really hitting the fan'... yada yada..."

"Because of Erica?"

She shrugged. "Partially. We've got people all over the place —including Darrell—fielding calls about her death but as the publisher preaches, 'We still have news to deliver, deadlines to meet and competitors to beat.'"

"Darrell mentioned you were assigned her post?" Leah asked.

She waved a hand. "Temporarily. They probably felt sorry for me and tossed a coin. I doubt it will last very long before a permanent replacement is assigned."

"You don't want the position, then?"

"Doesn't really matter what I want. Sure, it would be nice. But it's not very realistic. There are others already in line equally deserving and probably more suited for it."

"Huh. Well, if I can put in a good word, let me know," Leah replied.

"Don't trouble yourself. Like I said, it was more of a sympathy play on the publisher's part."

My friend chuckled. "I doubt that, Grace. You're good at what you do. And given the opportunity—the right opportunity, without all the drama attached—you'd make a fine editor."

"It's nice of you to say. If that time comes, be prepared. I'll be coaxing you back." We all laughed, despite the cloud that permeated the room. "So, what else is on your mind?"

Leah looked at her curiously and Grace laughed harder. "Oh, come on, Leah, you've got that look. I worked with you long enough to recognize when you're on the warpath. I'm not buying the whole 'visiting Darrell' bit. You haven't come to our office once since you left. Suddenly it occurs to you to come to my home for a visit and now you're here. And before you try to convince me otherwise, it doesn't bum me out in the least that you have an agenda. I was aware of it the first time you stopped by— so let's have it." She gestured for us to sit.

We did and Leah, as per usual Leah, took the direct approach.

"We've come across an individual who claims you were writing Erica's book."

Grace frowned. "What individual?"

Leah snorted. "Does it really matter? Is it true, Grace? Were you ghostwriting Erica's book for her?"

Grace's scowl deepened as she stared at Leah. After a moment, she got up and closed the door.

"This doesn't leave the room." She pointed a warning finger at each of us.

Leah shrugged. "Nothing's going to come from me but it will come out, Grace. In fact, part of it is already out there."

Grace crossed her arms. "So I guess I should prepare for additional interrogations, then? And what do you consider this, my prep run?"

Leah put her hands up in surrender. "Whoa, we didn't come here to put you on notice. We're simply trying to find our friend and clear his name. So if that means asking tough questions along the way and you're on the receiving end? Well, I'm sorry for it. But if I've already gathered this information, the cops will eventually do the same. Either way, Erica's real killer will be exposed."

Grace scoffed. "And you think I'm a likely candidate because someone told you I was writing her book for her?"

Leah shook her head. "Didn't say that. But if I drew that conclusion then the cops might, too."

"And I suppose if I don't give you the answers you want, you'll go to them and tell them about this 'information' you've stumbled across?"

"Again, didn't say that. And no. Even though it would help remove some pressure from Vargas, we wouldn't do that to you. Not unless the crumbs lead directly from the cookie jar to you." Grace shot Leah a look that insinuated she was less than amused. "So, enlighten us. We're probably the only ones in the position— and with the inclination—to help you."

"You've got a real way about you, Leah." Grace shook her head, looking more amused than angry. "I just never thought I'd be on this side of it. Okay, here's the deal. Yes, I was collaborating—Erica's word, not mine—with her on the book, even though she was more than capable of doing the work herself." Leah pursed her lips, apparently doubtful but Grace shook her head. "She was quite a talented writer and researcher when she wasn't obsessed with delegating. She'd just gotten lazy and wasn't willing to do the legwork." This time her laugh was filled with disgust and years of frustration. "And why should she, when she had me? Let's just say it got old. Fast."

"If you didn't want to collaborate, why'd you do it?" Leah asked.

Grace looked at my friend, her expression incredulous. "Hello, you met Erica, right? I needed to keep my job."

Leah shrugged. "But this wasn't part of the job."

"No, but as you are well aware, Erica got whatever she wanted. She could have made things difficult for me. Don't tell me you weren't affected by her manipulations, Leah. I know you left because of those crappy and usually dangerous assignments she forced you to work. You had other options. I do not. I have other responsibilities and can't afford to lose my job or branch out on my own, as you've done."

"What responsibilities?" Leah pressed.

"They are none of your concern, so drop it." Grace gritted her teeth and flashed Leah a look of warning.

Leah shook her head. "Sorry, Grace, like I mentioned before, if I was able to get this information, it's only a matter of time before the police do, too. And while you may not go to the head of their list of suspects, they'll dig so deep you'll start preferring daily root canals to the havoc they'll wreak on whatever 'responsibilities' you think you have."

Waves of contempt rolled from Grace as she shot to her feet. "You're a real—"

"Pill? Yeah, I hear that a lot. Just ask AJ." She thumbed in my direction. "But we're in a better position to *help* you if you *tell* us what's going on. The whole story. The whole enchilada. The whole rotten tomato—"

"All right, all right. Got it! Geesh!" Grace collapsed back into her chair and threw her hands up. "My responsibilities are not as self-serving as you're thinking. I'm doing this for my daughter."

We both blinked. I didn't know Grace well but certainly hadn't seen any evidence of a child in her tiny apartment.

"Your daughter?" Leah asked.

"When I was sixteen, I was a handful. Partying, a few recreational drugs…you know…the usual rebellious teen crap. I also had a penchant for bad boys. I hooked up with one, got myself knocked up and found myself kicked out of the house. I roomed with a friend, cleaned up for a short while, had the baby and life was good. I had a plan…you know? I had finished high school, gotten really good grades and even had a scholarship to the University of Arizona all lined up.

"Enter hottie bad boy baby daddy. I went off the rails again, went back to my old tricks…partying, clubbing. Still thought I was being a pretty good mom, though. Always found a babysitter. Made sure she was clean, fed and loved.

"But then, one night, my old habits kicked me in the butt. Woke up screaming in a hospital room with IVs hanging out of my arms and a whole lotta people I didn't know poking and prodding me. From what they told me, I gave myself a nice case of alcohol poisoning after drinking an entire bottle of Jack and chasing it with about twelve Red Bulls and at least three Jager Bombers. Somehow, I managed to top that off with a nice display of theatrics, followed by an award-winning face plant. Anyway, half the club either saw me, or captured my fine moment on their cell phones. Next thing I knew, I was out of the hospital, out of a place to live and minus a child. Child Protective Services came and collected her from the babysitter while I was still unconscious in the hospital. The father's parents found out—he was a lawyer and she was a nurse—and they took me to court and were awarded temporary custody.

"I went to rehab, got sober and still lost custody of my daughter. That was nine years ago. Sure, I catch glimpses of her but she doesn't even remember me, much less know I exist. I've been sober ever since, even went back to college, earned both bachelor's and master's degrees in journalism and really tried to put my life back together.

"Then, shortly after Erica got the book deal, I found out my ex's parents were moving to Florida. Both have retired and are planning on making a permanent home there. If that happens, I'll never get to see her. I've saved my pennies and put away enough to give my daughter a good life but I'm not rich. Not like they are, anyway. I needed a way to quickly make more." Grace absently shook her head.

"So you thought you'd approach Mort, show him proof you'd done the work and secure a cushy deal for yourself?" Leah asked.

Grace grimaced at my friend's bluntness but still offered a response, "Erica had boasted the story was worth six figures easily…seven if it really took off."

"But if you couldn't afford to lose your job, why would you even take the risk? If your plan backfired…" Leah drew a line across her throat, wincing only after she took in our horrified expressions. "Ooof…sorry, a little too close to the collar?"

"Geesh, Leah, try to contain yourself—a woman is dead," I growled.

She started to respond but Grace interjected, "I was desperate but I wasn't greedy. I didn't expect to take the deal away from

Erica. I simply wanted what was fair—a share of the deal. I was the one doing the work, after all."

"Regardless, Erica would have viewed it as the ultimate betrayal," Leah replied.

"Again, it was worth the risk at the time. Only Mort Daniels knew about it."

Leah snorted. "Yeah, and everyone at that joint you frequent. Let's talk risky…"

Grace looked at her in confusion. "I didn't—"

"Come on, Grace. You were seen tossing back martinis, spouting all the juicy details. Gloating. The bartender confirmed it."

From the look on her face, she'd taken the comment as though we'd passed judgment on her.

Maybe we had.

"I wasn't drinking. I wasn't gloating. And I certainly wasn't blabbing my business. But yes, I did tell one person—one person —in that bar." Grace got up, threw the door open and glared at us over her shoulder. Before storming out, she heaved a last piece of venom. "For the record…that lousy bartender? He happens to be the father of my child."

CHAPTER TWELVE

"That went smoothly. Good going, Leah. Anyone else's heart you want to rip out today?"

I should have known better than to ask.

"Nah, I leave the organ-ripping to the killer. Is the tongue even an organ?" she replied, causing me to blanch and fake-wretch. "Whatever, AJ. My tactics got us the information we came for, didn't they?"

"Not sure where they got us—other than they confirmed she wrote the book and probably didn't kill Erica. Point being, I hope it was worth losing a friend over."

"Grace? She'll be okay, I'll—"

"What? Buy her African Violets and Peanut Butter Frangos with a 'Sorry I was a giant boob' card attached?" I interjected.

"No, wisecracker, Grace will be fine. She has a temper like a redhead but she'll cool down soon. I'll talk to her tomorrow. For now, let's say goodbye to the other redhead and blow this popsicle stand."

"Don't you mean looney bin?"

"Like I said."

After the fun-filled conversation with Grace, we made the

rounds and chatted up a few other people but didn't get any more out of that exercise than we'd already known. No one liked Erica. No one was surprised she was dead. And frankly, except for the fact it added fodder to the newsreel, no one cared.

* * *

As we ventured to Mort's Ahwatukee neighborhood, Leah appeared to be mulling over the mysteries of the world, given the way she tortured the ends of her hair.

"Penny for your thoughts?" I asked.

"No, but I'd kill for a frappuccino."

"Extra whip?" I teased.

"Heck, I'd lick someone else's Starbuck's cup just to taste the remnants," she huffed.

I shot her a sideways glance. "After we get through this, we really need to have a little chat about that. In the meantime, let's see where we can get with Mort and then I'm buying."

"Promise?" Her face brightened at the thought.

I rolled my eyes. We might need to have that chat sooner than later. For the time-being, it would have to wait.

"Hey, you're driving, I'm buying."

"I like your style."

"I'll remind you of that when we get done with Mort." It came out more of a grumble than I'd intended.

"Troubling, isn't it?" she asked.

"Oh what, the fact he's putting my life story on display?" I replied, feeling the hairs on the back of my neck bristling.

"Yeah, and the fact he never seemed eager to put the story out into the universe before."

I nodded. "Maybe he needed the money. Or maybe he felt he had a moral obligation. Either way, I would have appreciated the courtesy of a heads-up."

She sighed. "One would have thought. Then again, he did ask Erica to write his book."

"It sure seems like it would have been more trouble than it was worth," I replied.

"No doubt, it certainly seems hinky to me."

"Which part?" I asked, though I agreed with her assessment.

"How the offer to write his book just sort of fell into her lap."

I nodded. "I'm curious to find out about that, too. I'm not convinced he was as impressed by her skill set as Grace had implied."

"We'll certainly find out when we finally track Mort down."

"*If* we finally track Mort down," I replied somberly.

"Way to keep your chin up, Ajax."

"Whatever, Leah, just saying."

She nodded and neither of us spoke again until we exited the freeway and wove our way through the various streets leading to Mort's neighborhood.

"Huh." Leah tilted her head, as though finally realizing calculus wasn't her strong suit. "It just occurred to me—this is not only Mort's neighborhood—it's Erica's, too."

"No way, really?" I swiveled my head, taking in the surroundings. I'd known Erica had done well for herself, but was surprised to learn it extended to living in such an exclusive area.

"Yeah, I'd totally forgotten she lived over here. You don't mind if I take a little detour, do you?"

"Be my guest. Now you've got me curious. Aren't you surprised she could afford this neighborhood?"

She shot me a look. "We're talking Erica, AJ. Anything is possible." She slowed as we approached a modest ranch house, tucked among the generous estates and custom-built homes. "Who the heck do you think that is?"

I squinted in the direction she was pointing. In front of Erica's house was a dark blue suburban with heavily tinted windows.

"No idea. Are those even legal?"

Leah snorted, "I doubt it, but then neither is that license plate." She was right—the plate was conveniently obscured by a cover.

"Suspicious." And way too coincidental. "You thinking what I'm thinking?" I nodded toward the suburban as it eased away from the curb.

"Oh, did you want me to take pursuit?" Leah wiggled her brows at me.

"Hurry, before they get away!" I growled, waving at the suburban, which had disappeared around the corner.

Leah rolled her eyes in an "as if" gesture before stomping on gas, surging us forward. I'd give her credit for knowing how to make that tennis shoe-sized vehicle fly, even if it meant we weren't always on all four wheels. Unfortunately, this time around, it appeared the extra ooomph hadn't helped. The suburban was nowhere in sight.

At least not in front of us.

We both craned our necks at the sound of the massive engine barreling down on Leah's tail end.

"Where the heck did he come from? Punch it, Scottie—the Clingons are in hot pursuit!" I shouted as the suburban continued to close the gap.

I hoped the "objects are larger than they appear" sticker on the side mirror was wrong, otherwise the loaded missile had already locked in and was prepared to strike in less than a millisecond.

"I'm doing my best, Captain! Any faster and she's gonna blow!" I prepared for impact as Leah screeched, "Son of a—"

She turned the wheel hard, causing us to skid as we hit the sandy shoulder. Panicking, she over-corrected, sending us into a spin that finally ended in an abrupt halt, just inches from landing us in a drainage ditch. As we performed a quick sanity check, the suburban whisked past, disappearing around the next corner.

Leah shot me a look that said we weren't to speak of the incident again.

I nodded and patted her on the arm. "Way to save the ship. And crew, Mr. Scott."

"Aye, Captain, all in a day's work."

* * *

If coming inches from ending up face down in a stinky sewage ditch wasn't punishment enough, it turned out Mort was still MIA. We returned home, exhausted and empty-handed, only to find Ramirez's police cruiser parked next to the Ferrari.

"Oh joy, this should be fun," Leah muttered under her breath.

"I am so not prepared to deal with this." I placed my forehead against the dashboard, which was surprisingly cool despite the workout the SUV had just been given. I contemplated staying in that position. Indefinitely.

"Then don't deal with him."

"What do you propose I do, stay out here all day?" She raised an eyebrow. I did sound a bit too hopeful.

Leah shrugged. "Ignore him, I do."

"You do not."

"Yup. I've developed a knack for pretending to be interested in what he's saying, especially when he gets that lecturing tone."

"I know the one you mean," I replied.

"Anyway, I like to pretend his is mouth moving but no words are coming out." She made a flapping gesture with her fingers.

"He doesn't even sound like Charlie Brown's teacher?"

"Nope, in my head, he's the strong, silent type." She quickly added, "He doesn't need to know any of that.

"No, I suppose not," I replied.

"I suggest you give it a try."

"Maybe I should."

I had finally summoned the nerve to get out of the SUV when Ramirez emerged from the house. I sucked in a deep breath as his eyes pierced mine. He stood that way for a long moment before thrusting his sunglasses on; then turned his back, got into the cruiser and pulled away.

"Um, that seemed a bit...abrupt." Leah released a breath, which made me realize I had been holding my own.

"I guess. Maybe it's foreshadowing," I replied.

She looked at the dust Ramirez had left as he departed. "A sign of things to come?"

"Or the beginning of the end."

* * *

Thankfully, Abe and Elijah were more sociable than Ramirez had been and if they had sensed any discontent on anyone's part—including Ramirez's—they certainly didn't acknowledge it. Instead, both seemed eager to share their news but encouraged us to divulge our recent findings first—being ladies and all. Ha, did we have those boys snowed or what? Then again, perhaps their mama had brought them up right. Personally, my bet was on the latter.

We proceeded to give them a play-by-play of our outing, starting with our visit to the newspaper, which resulted in our second meeting with Grace. Neither seemed surprised to learn she had been ghostwriting Erica's book. It was Grace's relationship with the bartender that got their investigative juices flowing.

"So, the bartender, Darian Hopkins, is Grace's ex-boyfriend?" Abe asked.

"Well, not so much boyfriend. It was more of an unfortunate hookup situation," Leah replied.

"Friends with benefits, then," Elijah clarified.

"Friends with benefits...with child," I added.

"So that gives us a common denominator." Abe appeared to be contemplating this new thread.

"That about sums it up," I confirmed. "Grace has no contact with the child due to some legal mumbo-jumbo, which she was trying to appeal. And now the grandparents are moving out of the state."

"Out of Grace's reach?" Abe asked.

I nodded. "It would be a difficult reach. Florida."

"So, the grandparents are retiring. Downsizing. Whatever." Abe thought aloud, "And they're taking the child with them." He turned to us. "Did you get the impression they were doing so on purpose? Perhaps they were aware Grace was planning to take them to court and decided to make a preemptive strike before she had a chance to do so?"

"Hard to say," I replied. "Grace didn't mention any preemptive maneuvering on the grandparent's part. Besides, she'd made her intentions pretty clear years ago, once she'd gotten her life back on track. Killing Erica would only derail those plans."

"What did Bartender Darian have to say?" Leah asked.

"Nothing, he didn't show up for work today and didn't call in either. His boss was steamed. In fact, when we identified ourselves as private investigators, he offered to pay us to track him down." Abe chuckled. "Of course, we declined but he was still agitated enough to share Darian's address without being asked for it." He referenced a piece of paper from his pocket. "It's an apartment on Pecos Road in Chandler."

"And when you got to the address?" My voice sounded more hopeful than I felt.

"Gone, according to the next door neighbor," Abe replied.

"Let me guess, this was right after he had his little phone chat with Anna?" Leah confirmed. When Abe nodded, she shook her own head in frustration. "Kind of a coincidence, don't you think?" I shot my friend a look—there were no such things as coincidences.

"It now appears we have three individuals who are MIA." I held up my fingers and counted. "One: Vargas. Two: Darian. Three: Mort."

"Mort Daniels is missing?" Abe and Elijah both asked at once.

I held up my hand and offered clarification, "Not so much missing," I shot a look at Leah and she shrugged, "as evasive."

We took turns filling them in on our failure to locate Mort and the attempted tail on the suspicious-looking suburban at Erica's. Of course, we left out the part where we nearly wrecked. No need to make ourselves look like amateurs, right?

"Did you get the suburban's license plate?" Abe asked when we finished.

I gave him a scribbled list of possibilities, explaining how the license plate cover had impeded our view.

"How about the state?" Elijah prompted. After Leah and I both shrugged, he added, "Even a front license plate might help narrow things down."

I replied, thinking about my glances in the rearview mirror, "Arizona doesn't require one but even if there had been one, it could have been obscured by a cover, too."

"And you didn't see the occupants because the window were tinted," Elijah confirmed, frowning after Leah and I shook our heads.

"Don't tell me this entire day has been a bust," Leah growled at no one in particular.

It was Abe who replied, "We did manage to track down several of Vargas' friends, family and co-workers, and while none of them have heard a peep, we were able to come up with a pretty extensive list of places he might go if he was in trouble. None of them expected him to reach out, so wherever he's gone, he's gone there alone."

"Probably didn't want to drag anyone into this mess with him," Leah murmured, just loud enough for me—and no one else —to hear. I gave her hand a quick squeeze and she nodded somberly.

Elijah continued, "Anyway, we have no reason to believe anyone was lying. In fact, all offered assistance if more bodies were needed to search the various locations."

"Err...Elijah...can we refrain from talking about bodies?" I asked quietly.

"Oh geez, just a turn of phrase...warm bodies, of course." We shook our heads, indicating that it wasn't much of an improvement. "Sorry. Resources. Helping hands."

Leah was eager to change the subject. "So, you'll let us know when you start looking into these locations? We'd like to take our fair share of the list."

Abe nodded. "We were planning to start when Ramirez stopped by. He basically confirmed what we'd already learned: Vargas hasn't made any contact to date, nor has he used his credit cards, cell phone or returned home since the incident."

Elijah continued, "They were, however, able to identify another source of blood at the crime scene. While Ramirez indicated they were still waiting on results to see if it matched anyone in the system, he did confirm the individual had lost more blood than Vargas, but less than Erica before she expired."

Leah's hand flew to her mouth. "But if Vargas could be mortally wounded, then this person..."

"Is in really bad shape," Abe replied, his tone dark.

"Have they been able to recreate the scene to determine the order of events as they transpired or identify who did what to whom?" I asked.

"Ramirez said they're working on it day and night. It doesn't help that Erica's dog spent an entire day in the apartment with her. Crime scene is pretty...contaminated," Elijah replied, causing me to shudder as I glanced at the white boards.

Abe continued, picking up several documents, "Ramirez did manage to obtain a copy of Erica's cell phone records. Guess who the last call was from, just an hour before they believe she was attacked?"

"No idea...Elvis?" Leah offered, her mind still reeling.

"Close...Mort Daniels. He called her via his cell phone, talked to her for about eight and a half minutes—"

"Wait a minute—Mort doesn't have a cell phone," I interjected.

"I'm just telling you what Ramirez said the investigating team found. They retrieved Erica's cell phone records, came across the last incoming call and pulled those records, which turned out to be one of the numbers associated with his wireless account," Abe replied.

"Mort has multiple cell phones?" I asked, still perplexed by the fact he had one.

Abe shrugged. "According to these printouts Ramirez shared —on the sly—he's got one...two....six?"

"Six cell phone numbers? Leah doesn't even have that many." My comment was rewarded with an indignant scoff.

Elijah squinted at the printouts his brother was holding. "Didn't you mention both Erica and Mort lived in the same area?"

"Yeah, both live in the Ahwatukee Foothills," Leah replied.

"And despite the proximity of their homes, their signals are transmitted from different towers?" Elijah asked.

I snorted. "Uh, have you seen the metro area? There are towers everywhere—buildings, mountains, churches, dog houses."

"Thanks AJ, I get the picture," Elijah replied, still focused on the printouts. "On the night of Erica's murder, Mort was not only the last person to talk to her when she was alive. He was also within the vicinity of her house."

Silence filled the room. It could mean something. Or it could mean nothing.

One thing was certain. Until the police could get their hands on evidence proving someone other than Vargas had murdered and mutilated Erica, he would continue to be the primary focus of their investigation. Given his injuries, every day we were unable to locate him could mean minutes sheared off his life. Unless we caught a break, time was the ultimate enemy.

I hoped, for Vargas' sake, the sand hadn't already sifted through the hourglass.

CHAPTER THIRTEEN

Now that we had Mort's list of cell phone numbers, we had to decide if we should use any of them. After much discussion, the consensus was no. While it might have yielded us faster results, in the long run we still didn't know exactly how involved he was. I was having a hard time convincing myself that the sweet, grandfatherly man could have been connected to such a heinous crime. Given his age and physical stature, he certainly could not have done so alone. Still, he'd never suggested an interest in turning the Gemini project into a book. I wondered how Martin would take that news.

Martin!

I was mentally chastising myself for not checking in with him sooner when I heard Leah's banter with Abe.

"By the way, you never said—how is Mort even remotely close to Elvis?" Leah had taken his bait. Hook. Line. And sinker.

"Well, just like Elvis, according to the two of you, it appears Mort has 'left the building.'"

If Leah wasn't sorry she asked I knew I was.

In the end, we decided to call Mort before venturing to his home again. I wasn't surprised to receive his voicemail and after a bit of coaching from Abe, Elijah and Leah, did my best to craft a message that would elicit a return call. Let's just say, I didn't share my whole package of mint Oreos but I left enough crumbs to leave him wanting his own cookie.

We proceeded to review the list of locations Vargas' friends and family had supplied, grouping them by location so they could be searched quickly by the assigned team. The four of us would tackle the locations in the metro Phoenix area, allowing us to maintain proximity to the home base. Law enforcement already had the borders covered, so Vargas' friends would take the rest of the state, breaking them into quadrants. It was still a lot of ground to cover, considering a resourceful man like Vargas could safely remain under the radar for an extended period. The question was...if he was innocent, why would he need to?

I hoped we'd have answers before it was too late.

We were all busy collecting whatever we needed to make our necessary rounds when Abe pulled me to the side.

"Say AJ, when Ramirez was here, Elijah and I got the sense there was some tension between the two of you. He didn't mention anything and normally I wouldn't pry but if it's because we're staying here—at your house—we could certainly make alternative arrangements."

I flushed at his mention of Ramirez. Tension? Oh yeah. But not for the reason Abe was thinking. I couldn't easily explain Martin's sudden arrival, much less my meeting with him or what I had asked him to do while I concentrated on Vargas. I had already told Leah—against Martin's wishes—and hoped I wouldn't live to regret it. Her life was already in grave danger due to her association with me and her previous encounters with Clark. This time around, he may try to rectify his earlier misstep, when he had failed to kill us both. Strike that—at some point, he would make an attempt. Unfortunately, he was good at biding his time—

exceptional really—and there was no way of knowing when he would pounce.

Enter Martin. I hoped my request would yield an outcome worthy of the price I would have to pay when it came to my fractured relationships. I assigned a plural because I was convinced that by the time all was said and done and the truth came out, like Ramirez, the Stantons would harbor resentment and disappointment for my failure to confide in them.

Abe peered at me intently, awaiting an answer. I cleared my throat but the lump that was Ramirez remained, making my voice gravely. "Not to worry, Abe. It's an entirely separate matter we'll address once this is finished. I do appreciate your concern, though." I chuckled. "Besides, he's the one who suggested you keep an eye on me. He wouldn't have expected you to do any less." I gave him a quick hug and though he nodded, he didn't look convinced. I quickly added, "And believe me, you guys are more like a buffer between what he's facing with Vargas and my ordeal with Clark."

"Crap, AJ, I hope you don't feel as though we'd forgotten about Clark—"

I put a hand up to stop him. "In this whole crappy scenario, we can be certain of one thing and one thing alone—Clark *is* out there. And yeah, sooner or later he'll pop his head out and we'll let the mongoose bite it off. In the meantime, I can't spend my life worrying about what he may or may not do to me. We need to focus on finding Vargas. Preferably alive."

I realized Leah and Elijah had joined us and much like his brother, Elijah didn't appear convinced Clark could be taken down quickly or that my issues with Ramirez would be resolved easily. Both looked at Leah for confirmation but thankfully, she did a fabulous job of making it appear as though she was none the wiser.

Abe surveyed me for a moment before responding, "Okay

then. We could always make the security room into an extended panic room and lock the three of you in. That would certainly take a load off Ramirez's mind, knowing you were all safely tucked in and out of danger."

"Rather than out causing it," Elijah added.

I laughed and punched him on the arm. "Nice try but I think not. Though, now that you mention it, a panic room may come in handy—with the caveat the locks are on the inside—to keep all you bad boys out."

Both laughed. "Sure, sure, we'll get right on that," Abe replied.

"We may just hold you to that, Stanton," Leah added.

"I'm counting on it." He wiggled his eyebrows at her, causing her to blush before she took her turn at punching his arm. He feigned injury and limped out of the room.

When they were safely out of earshot, outside packing up their car, she whispered, "You really need to get Martin on the horn, touch base and make sure that he doesn't blow us out of the water. All this covert stuff is making me itchy."

I cast a doubtful look in her direction. "I thought you lived for this stuff. Isn't it part of the standard reporter repertoire?"

She threw a hand to her chest, pretending to be offended. "I'm anything but standard. And, my problem isn't with actual spy stuff—it's remembering who knows what."

"So basically, remembering when to keep your mouth shut." She smirked and stuck her tongue out at me. "But yes, I was thinking the same thing. Though I doubt he'll be making a spectacle of himself, or us, for that matter. His goal is to fly under the radar, not *be* the radar."

"More and more that seems to be our job," Leah sighed.

"Tell me about it."

* * *

We waited until the rumble of the Ferrari faded to call Martin, placing it on speaker with the strict directive Leah was to remain on her best behavior—meaning not seen, nor heard. Anything above a peep would result in a month-long ban on junk food *and* margaritas, even though she protested at first, claiming the agreement was damaging to her physical, psychological and emotional well-being.

Martin picked up on the first ring. "Arianna, this is a surprise."

"Uh, I wanted to touch base. Also to let you know there have been some other...developments."

"I see..." His voice was low, as if he was somewhere he did not wish to be overheard. "Are you alone?"

"Yes." I winced when there was a pause. Apparently, I was pretty bad at this lying stuff.

"I'd prefer not to talk over the phone. Can you meet me at the same place we met last time?" he asked.

"Yes, I'll come now. But I'll need to be brief. There are other...matters I need to attend to."

"I understand. It won't take long," Martin replied. I started to hang up when he added, "And you might as well bring your friend Leah along."

Before I could respond, he disconnected.

Leah's eyes were wide. "I swear I didn't make a sound!" When she misconstrued my head-shaking, she threw her head back in agony and wailed, "I shouldn't be punished for this. It's not right. How could he have known? Don't tell me he's got people watching us too!"

Maybe I was paranoid but given the way our lives had changed over the last several months, anything was possible, if not probable.

* * *

There was no little family at the park to entertain us this time around as Leah, Nicoh and I made our way to the bench in the park. Once again, Martin was already waiting, only this time he stood as we approached. I made brief introductions and after Martin gave Nicoh a few scratches on the head, he gestured for us to walk with him.

"You said there have been some developments since we last talked?" he asked.

Given the frown that formed when I relayed the details surrounding Mort's book deal with Erica, he had not been aware nor was pleased by the news. At the same time, he didn't appear terribly surprised, either.

I said as much.

"It wasn't going to remain a secret forever, Arianna. At some point, the public was going to find out, whether it was Mort or someone else associated with the project. What's troubling is the proximity in timing of the book deal, Clark's arrival and now, this girl's death."

"You think Clark is involved?" The thought had crossed my mind but I'd set it aside, thinking I was simply grasping for the longest straw.

He shook his head. "I don't know. It might actually work to his and Theodore's benefit if the details surrounding the project were to come out."

"How so?" I asked.

"Clark and his father might try to use the project to cast blame elsewhere, to use it as a distraction for their own crimes."

Leah's coughed out a laugh. "Seriously? Kind of like those kids who kill and then claim they were products of their environment?"

"Not exactly but as long as the details surrounding Gemini are kept under wraps, the original benefactors can continue to fly safely under the radar. If, however, Clark and his father use what they know to save their own hides, well…" he opened his hands, inviting us to draw our own conclusions.

"That's kinda sick thinking, Marty." Leah looked as though she'd eaten sauerkraut.

I attempted to get a handle on Martin's logic. "You're saying Clark is seen as a liability to these benefactors? That he basically already has a target—one that has nothing to do with law enforcement—on his back?"

"Knowledge is power, Arianna."

"So, if the information were to come out, say in a book and not from Clark or his father…"

Martin finished my thought, "Then the people who brought Gemini to fruition would be at a greater risk of being exposed, given the source would likely be considered more credible and unbiased. Ultimately, the same people could also be held responsible for letting the project get out of control."

"It would have also placed Mort and Erica in extreme danger," I added. "One thing I don't get—surely you're not insinuating Clark and his father would use this little revelation as a means of getting away with the crimes they've committed over the last twenty-plus years?" I thought of my parents, my sister, my birth mother and countless others. Leah looked equally mortified.

Martin put a hand on my arm, a calming gesture a father might make. "I wouldn't go quite that far. If that were the case, why wouldn't they have shown their hands already—divulged what they knew once they were captured?"

Leah was having none of it. "Who knows half the reasons Clark and his father do the things they do—perhaps they were biding their time. Getting the most bang for their bucket list. I don't know, Marty. But what I'm saying is that it's within the realm of possibility. Clark and his father could use what they know to get away with murder." These were all things Martin could not possibly know for certain much less guarantee.

Still, he remained calm, shaking his head as she continued her animated pontifications. "To people like Clark and Theodore, it's more about vindication. Justice has no hand in their game."

"Spoken like a man who knows," Leah muttered. If Martin had heard her, he ignored her comment.

"What about you, Martin?" I asked.

He was taken aback by my question, or perhaps my forthrightness. "What about me?"

I looked him straight in the eye. "What do you get out of this?"

He thought for a long moment, his gaze never leaving mine. "Either way, I will get closure."

Leah wasn't buying either. "So for now, you're hedging your bets. Surely, you have a preference, if the scale could be tipped?"

He broke my gaze to meet hers. "My preference would be to keep the information under wraps until it can be evaluated by the appropriate and responsible parties. Without boundaries and parameters, the information is a time bomb waiting to be detonated. If it were to find its way into the wrong hands..."

Leah didn't appear to be impressed by his answer. If anything, she thought he was grandstanding for my benefit. "Huh. Are you shooting this from the hip, Marty? Or do you have a bloodhound with his nose to the ground?"

He seemed amused by her directness, his mouth quirking at the corner, yet his tone was serious. "My opinions are mine and mine alone. They are not based on certain knowledge but more from inference, based on decades of analysis, introspection and reasoned conclusions." I looked at Leah and shrugged. Spoken like a true scientist. As he looked at us, realization dawned and disappointment filled his eyes, "You're thinking it also gives me a motive to kill the deal, so to speak?"

"If you've drawn that conclusion, then others likely will, too," I replied.

"Except others are not aware I exist."

"Not yet, anyway."

It wasn't a threat but like Martin, we had drawn our own conclusions. The opinions were ours and there was someone out there, other than the two of us, who could reveal his identity and confirm his existence in the land of the living. Martin may have gone off the bridge that day but today he was very much in front of us, in living color. And we weren't the only two with the benefit of this knowledge. Others also knew—Grant wasn't buried in Grant's tomb.

If we'd jarred him, it didn't make its way to his face, or his body language. "For now my focus is keeping you safe." He nodded at Leah and Nicoh. "I don't want you losing any more than you already have."

I nodded. "I appreciate that, Martin."

He looked at his shoes and kicked at a clump of dirt in the grass. "It's the least I can do, after all these years."

I changed the subject, uncomfortable with this daddy and daughter moment. Apparently, it was none too soon for Leah either, who looked as though she'd spent some time in the rhubarb patch. "So, has there been any movement on Clark's part?"

"We haven't pinpointed him to an exact location but we have identified places he's been over the past several days, so the team is looking at patterns. As I'm sure you're painfully aware, Clark doesn't do anything without a reason."

"So we've got patterns to look forward to, huh? Sounds really promising, Marty," Leah's tone implied she still hadn't gotten the rhubarb out of her mouth.

Martin looked grim. Apparently, he thought his news on Clark would ease our minds, if not elicit a more positive response.

"Unfortunately, right now, I can't tell you any more than that without jeopardizing the team working on this."

Leah snorted, crossing her arms, "'Jeopardizing the team'? We can somewhat appreciate that but geez, Marty, keeping us in the dark isn't exactly making us any safer. Or preparing us for when Clark strikes."

I nodded, the optimum word being 'when.'

"My associates will not allow him to get that close. Not again, anyway."

"But how—wait a minute, do your 'associates' have us under surveillance? Are you following us?" I gritted my teeth.

"Yeah, Marty, been driving any oversized SUVs lately? Driving us off the road? Is that your definition of safety?" Leah added.

Martin squinted, confused by her questions but still offered a reply, "Things are being monitored from a safe distance. You won't even be aware of their presence—no matter where they are." I looked at Leah. Like that cleared things up.

"Great, guess I'd better stop that nude sunbathing," Leah retorted. "So, do you have anything else for us?"

By this point, Martin looked completely exasperated. Clearly he wasn't skilled in the art of dealing with sassy twenty-somethings.

He shook his head. "Nothing as concrete as a smoking gun—"

"Who cares about the smoking gun, Marty?" Leah interrupted. "We'd rather have Clark delivered with an apple in his mouth."

"I will be in contact when we have him in our sights." Before Martin disappeared into the night, he turned, an ominous expression crossing his face. "Just for future reference, Ms. Campbell, once we have Clark, would you prefer him skewered or sautéed?"

CHAPTER FOURTEEN

"It's not that I don't like him, Leah, I just don't know him. And I certainly don't trust him." We had returned to Leah's SUV and were perusing our list of locations to scout for Vargas.

"That makes two of us, sister."

"No, I'm pretty sure you just don't like him."

Leah absently chewed her thumbnail. "Probably true. Guy doesn't give off a warm and fuzzy vibe."

"He's not a puppy, Leah."

"Not even close. He's too shifty for puppydom." I motioned for her to continue, having drawn a similar conclusion. "His body language is closed off—crossed arms, the way he positioned himself when he talked to us and his intermittent use of eye contact."

"At least he made eye contact," I commented.

"Yeah, but only when he wanted to get his point across, when he wanted to make sure we believed him."

"You're saying he was selling us a line of bullpucky?" I asked.

She shrugged. "Half-truths at a minimum. I'm sure parts were true."

"Yeah, like the parts that would lend credibility to the other not-so-true parts."

"You picked up on it too, I take?" My friend surveyed me. "No, I can definitely see that you don't trust him. I had to wonder…"

"Wonder…what?" I asked.

"If you were just saying it to convince yourself you shouldn't trust him."

"Are you suggesting I am reverse-psychologizing myself?"

"Maybe. You're a good person, AJ. You give people the benefit of the doubt. You think they are good and decent, until they prove otherwise. And even then, you believe they have a few redeeming qualities."

"You make me sound like a sap. Do you think I'm being naive?"

She shook her head. "You just see the world from a more positive perspective. Less jaded. With Martin, you are being more cautious than usual but it troubles you doing so. Perhaps you feel you owe him some sort of concessions?"

"Concessions? For what? Being my biological father?"

"That's part of it," she replied, her tone softening and her voice quiet. "I think you feel sorry for him."

"Feel sorry…for Martin?"

She nodded. "For the life you think he's given up."

I frowned. Perhaps Leah was right. Maybe I felt badly for the things he had lost: his work, the woman he said he loved, his children and ultimately, his identity. For nearly thirty years, Martin Singer did not exist, except for the name shared on a lonely, forgotten grave.

There I went again, falling into my old trap, letting my guard down. I thought about what Leah had said and decided to put myself first for a change. This time, I reflected on what *I* had lost:

my parents, my twin sister and the opportunity to have a relationship with her.

I would have liked to include my biological mother, Alison Anders and perhaps once, Martin, too, but you can never really lose something you didn't have to begin with. When it came to Alison, I never would. Perhaps in time, I would get to know and understand Martin, but when I thought about the time he'd spent hiding, never revealing himself, I had to wonder why. Perhaps I was fooling myself into believing it had been a form of sacrifice? Perhaps, in reality, it had been a choice—much like choosing to make an appearance in my life now—and there was more to his agenda.

Something struck me. "You said I feel sorry for the life I *think* he's given up?"

"Like I said, you're being particularly cautious. Something deep down beyond your gut, deep in your soul knows he's not being entirely truthful, that he didn't just suddenly show up out of the blue to have some precious daddy-daughter time or to swoop in on his white horse to save the day."

She was right about the gnawing feeling of discontent I had when it came to Martin. He hadn't returned solely for the benefit of a reunion or even to intercept Clark. What if the reason he had come out of hiding was much simpler? Had I been over-thinking it all along? What if the real reason Martin rose from the grave was to beat Clark to the punchline? What if Martin had come out of hiding...for me?

Leah interrupted my thoughts. "By the way, Ajax, you still owe me junk food and margaritas."

* * *

Eight hours, six iced caramel sauce lattes, four bags of gummy bears and three sets of tired paws later, we trudged back into the house, our list of potential Vargas sightings a bust. Not even a stray morsel indicated he had even been there, much less had been seen in the vicinity since the time of the murder.

"Do you think it's odd that we haven't heard anything from Clark since his initial handiwork? Not even a vague text message with an extremely poor use of punctuation and grammar?" Leah asked as she plopped onto the sofa.

I collapsed into a nearby chair and tugged the scrunchy holding my ponytail, which had been giving me a headache since noon. "Funny…no. Strange…yes. Does make me feel a bit itchy, though. It's like you never know when the other shoe's gonna drop with him." Leah dropped hers onto the floor, resulting in a resounding thump.

"Honestly, I wouldn't mind adding him to the missing list," she replied.

I nodded. "Only if we could exchange that sicko for one of the others we're not able to currently locate."

"Agreed. My vote would be for Vargas. I am really worried we won't find him in time, especially given his injuries…whatever they are." I knew it had been hard for her to admit that out loud. Neither of us had wanted to think about Vargas…alone… hurt…possibly dying. It was much easier focusing on finding him. Alive.

We heard more than one vehicle rumble into the driveway and Abe and Elijah entered shortly after, with Ramirez in tow. Given their wrinkled shirts, the sleep-deprived shadows under their eyes and their grumpy dispositions, whatever news they had to offer didn't appear to be promising.

Abe was the first to confirm our suspicions, as he and his brother plunked on either side of Leah. "We got nada, please tell me you two gals came up with something better?"

Leah repositioned herself, jockeying for more room between the two brothers. "Does zilch trump nada?"

"It does not." Elijah frowned, his tone revealing the depth of his weariness. "You've got to be kidding me. We've been all over this city. How does one man bury himself that far underground without leaving any breadcrumbs?"

I directed the conversation to Ramirez, who had remained standing since his arrival. "How about you, Detective, you got any news for us?" Though I hadn't more than glanced in his direction, I could feel his eyes on me. Disconcerting to say the least.

"It would be a wasted effort, supplying anything of value to you two delinquents." His eyes flashed and I swore under my breath as the temperature of the room spiraled.

Leah glared at Ramirez. "Just who are you calling 'delinquents,' Detective? I thought we were all on the same side?"

Ramirez's penetrating gaze finally moved to her as he replied. "We are. It's the way you two—three, if you count Nicoh—go about things I'm questioning."

"Our way works just fine, thank you very much." Leah crossed her arms in defiance.

A smirk danced across the corner of his mouth. "Oh? And just what juicy tidbits have you managed to drum up since I last saw you?"

"Like I told Abe here…zilch. Nothing. Nada," she replied.

"Thanks for making my point for me," he replied.

Leah started to argue. "No, Detective your *point* would be made if we'd actually found something. Not finding anything doesn't count."

Ramirez shook his head, only slightly more amused. "That's some messed up logic. So what's your point?"

Leah threw her hands up. "Hey don't look at me! You're the one who's counting points here."

This nonsensical banter—no matter whose point I saw—was getting us nowhere, so I changed the subject. "Did anyone manage to find the owner of the suburban?"

Ramirez eyes narrowed. "What suburban?"

Leah waved her hands, annoyed. "The navy one parked outside Erica's. We couldn't get a license plate because it was covered by one of those thingies."

"Thingies?" Ramirez asked, frowning.

"Here at the Jackson household, we like to think of them as license plate covers," I clarified.

"Why is this the first time I'm hearing about it?" He took turns glowering at us while grinding his teeth.

"Right after it happened, you were too busy peeling out of our driveway." I referenced his visit—or lack thereof—earlier in the day.

"I wasn't peeling out of anything. I was on the clock and had to get back to work," he snapped as he turned to Abe and Elijah. "Why didn't you tell me about it?" When Elijah started to respond, Ramirez impatiently waved him off and addressed me. "Getting back to this suburban...what have you got?"

I shrugged. "It was just your typical navy suburban. Except for the license plate cover which blocked most of the number, there wasn't anything out of the ordinary, though the windows were tinted pretty heavily, too." Ramirez nodded in a way that meant he was confirming something he already knew. "Why so curious about it?"

His eyes met mine, their intensity unnerving. "Because a vehicle exactly like the one you just described went missing from the Tempe Police Department's impound lot."

"Went missing?" Leah asked.

Ramirez nodded. "Shortly after the altercation in the police station."

"The one between Erica and Vargas," I confirmed.

"That's the only altercation I'm aware of," Ramirez's voice was challenging. This time, I didn't check to see where his glare had landed, but one could venture a guess.

I didn't appreciate his tone but let it slide. "Okay, connect the dots, Detective, I'm not a mind reader. Certainly you guys have video surveillance at your impound lots?"

"We do. And we've reviewed it and the person who last checked it out was clearly visible."

"Err...I hate to break it to you, Ramirez, but if you already know who checked it out, then it's technically not missing." My response came out a bit snappier than I had intended.

Ramirez shook his head. "The person who checked it out also went missing shortly after."

Vargas.

Dots A and B connected, he proceeded, "The vehicle was confiscated as part of a drug bust and placed in the impound lot with others that resembled the suburban you saw at Erica's. Vargas doesn't work narcotics so the vehicle would have had no prior association to him. Anyway, the theory is that he researched the vehicles impounded, picked the most vanilla, checked it out under false pretenses—for a stakeout, whatever—then used it to facilitate not only the crime but his getaway."

"So the vehicle was seen at Erica's around the time of her murder?" Abe had been so quiet I had forgotten he was still there. Perhaps once a cop, always a cop. I tended to forget that. Like Ramirez, law enforcement had been part of his past.

Ramirez nodded. "By a neighbor of Erica's. Of course, some would like to believe Vargas' acquisition of the vehicle shows premeditation—that he needed something other than his own ride to commit the crime and allow enough time for a clean getaway." I bit my lip. I had already provoked Ramirez enough, but if the vehicle would eventually be traced back to the impound lot—and to Vargas—why would he have taken the risk? It was not a detail a seasoned detective would overlook.

I elected not to poke the angry bear. "What do you believe, Detective?"

"Honestly, I think he intended to use the vehicle for a case he was working on. I can't divulge the details of an open investigation, other than to say it merited some discrete surveillance a vehicle like the one he checked out would have offered. Unfortunately, it doesn't matter what I, or anyone else, chooses to believe. It comes down to what we can prove. Right now, the best proof is Vargas himself," he replied and for the first time, I saw the beginning of a crack in his armor and the uncertainty that overwhelmed him.

"I'm not sure I agree," I commented and immediately felt the intensity of six pairs of eyes on me. "I mean, we've got to find Vargas before the police do especially considering his wounds, but we don't physically need him to prove anything. At a minimum, we just need to find evidence that contradicts their theory or casts reasonable doubt on it. The next best thing would be evidence proving someone else killed Erica. And the icing on the cake? *That* would be finding Vargas and bringing him home…safely."

"Quite a speech, Ajax," Ramirez replied after a long moment, "but you're absolutely right—perhaps we…I need to change my perspective. Not that we shouldn't continue looking for Vargas, but we should also focus on finding evidence that would help clear him. Maybe then, he'd be able to come out of hiding."

None of us wanted to say it on the heels of my rah rah speech, but the looks that passed throughout the room indicated we were all thinking the same thing: we hoped Vargas still possessed the ability to come out of hiding.

We spent the next several minutes rehashing what we'd learned. While none of us believed Grace killed her boss—now including Ramirez—when the police had learned she'd contacted Mort about the book deal, they were forced to take a closer look at the editor's assistant. If she hadn't murdered Erica directly, she had the means, motive and opportunity to conspire with the person who had. Of course, in their book, that person was still Jere Vargas.

Their newest theory was that Grace—having undergone years of emotional abuse and setbacks in her career and family life—discovered an opportunity to have the last laugh, at Erica's expense. She'd found an ally in Vargas and together they had gotten revenge on the person who had interfered in both their lives one too many times. I didn't know Grace all that well, but from what I had learned about her and what I knew to be true about Vargas and his character—the theory was based more on trying to make fictitious pieces fit a puzzle than meeting any factual certainty.

No one brought up Clark but the topic did venture in the direction of Mort Daniels, whose name had come up in conjunction with the book deal with Erica and again when Grace had made her play. Ramirez quickly assured me the police were not aware of the nature of the book and indicated what few details they did have led them to believe it was a work of fiction. Until they spoke directly to Mort, there was no way to confirm otherwise.

While Abe, Elijah and Leah were busy referencing their notes and updating the white boards, I took the opportunity to clear the air with Ramirez.

"Can we talk?" I gestured to the patio.

An uncomfortable silence filled the air, long after we'd sat on opposing lounge chairs, the distance between us as stifling and unforgiving as his gaze.

I cleared my voice. "I'm sorry." It came out in a raspy whisper.

"Sorry for what?" His eyes never left mine but his tone conveyed a hint of distrust I would never have dreamed I could have been responsible for creating.

I broke his gaze and stared at my hands, clasped tightly in my lap. "Sorry for all this. For Vargas… For Clark…" I paused, my voice cracking. "For us…"

I didn't dare venture a glance, fearing I would not be able to handle what I saw and was surprised when he moved to my side and pulled my hands into his.

"You don't need to be sorry for Vargas or Clark. Those situations were not your doing and certainly not within your control. We have a good team here and there are still boys in blue who believe in Vargas' innocence. Like you said, if we can put our heads together and focus on the evidence, perhaps we can clear his name and bring him home. As for Clark, we've got people on the streets looking for him, the security system is amped up here and you, Leah and Nicoh have skilled babysitters…" I shot him a look and found a small smile gracing his lips. But even in his teasing, the smile did not reach his eyes. He looked weary. And sad.

"And us?" I prompted.

He shook his head. "I'm not sure, AJ. Every time we seem to make progress, something gets in the way…some sort of barrier. And while I believe you're sorry, I don't think you know what you're really sorry for."

"Are you saying *I'm* the barrier?"

He nodded. "For as trusting as you are of people—the blind faith you put into others—you don't put the same level of trust in yourself. So while you think the best of others, when it comes to you, the opposite is true. You expect to let others down, to the point you not only anticipate but accept it. In the end, you force yourself to ignore anything that could allow you to believe otherwise."

I hadn't ever really thought of myself in that way but as I reviewed the recent events in my life, I could see his perspective. Perhaps subconsciously, I blamed myself for my parents' death—though I had no control over the way I'd come into this world—my life had led to the ending of theirs. Victoria's, too…

had she not come looking for me...to warn me, she would have been spared. These were the things that haunted my dreams at night, the things that gave me sweats and woke me up scream-ing. The blackened hand that clawed and scratched in an attempt to reach me...perhaps it hadn't been Death? Perhaps it was guilt. My guilt. My hand, scorched by the wrongs I had subcon-sciously taken credit or accepted responsibility for. Perhaps it was the reason I'd refused to tell Ramirez about Martin, fearing my burdens would become his and ultimately, lead to his demise.

I knew Ramirez would eventually forgive me but until I accepted and addressed it myself, he would not forgive my decep-tion. Meaning, we could not be.

I swallowed, the realization sobering. The inherent problem-solver inside wanted to fix it. But this was not a wound a Band-Aid would heal. It would take time to absolve myself from the guilt; to trust myself. I looked at Ramirez's sad expression as he gently rubbed his rough thumbs over my clasped hands and knew what small step I needed take.

I moved my hands over his and squeezed them gently, until he raised his eyes to mine. "I need to tell you something about the man in the park—" Before I could utter another syllable, his cell phone's shrill ringtone forced us both to jump.

"I need to get this." I nodded and Ramirez stepped out of earshot before answering.

The conversation appeared tense as he listened to the caller, given the way his muscles strained against his shirt. Several minutes passed before he spoke, too low for me to hear. After he ended the call, he stared up at Camelback Mountain. I wondered if he wished he were there, perched on her highest peak, away from the insanity and troubles of the world below.

Finally, I couldn't bear the silence any longer and went to his side. Gently touching his arm, I whispered, "Is everything okay?"

Mentally kicking myself—of course it wasn't—I started to add some clever quip when he beat me to the punchline.

He turned to me, his face grim. "They found Mort—"

"What? That's great news—"

Ramirez cut me off with a single shake of his head, gazing back at the mountain in the distance before responding, "Mort Daniels is dead."

CHAPTER FIFTEEN

"No...no...no...that can't be right. I just talked to him." The words came out sounding mechanical as I realized another person in my life—and a potential lead that could have helped Vargas—had slipped away. Accepting the reality that the gentle man I had known was gone was entirely a different matter.

"No, AJ. Not unless you talked to...a dead man," Ramirez replied, his voice so quiet I could barely hear it over the thoughts racing through my head. "Daniels has been dead for a while."

Before Ramirez could continue, I led him back to the living room where Abe, Elijah and Leah looked at us expectantly—perhaps hoping we had worked out our differences—until the detective dashed those hopes as he shared the news of Mort's death.

"His body was found in a remote section of the desert, between Marana and Tucson. You might remember the discovery being mentioned on the news?" Leah and I nodded, still numb with shock. It had been hard to forget.

The local television and radio stations had been buzzing for at least a week, having gotten their hands on some fresh meat or in this case, a not-so-fresh corpse. "Who was this person?" filled the news stream, where members of each outlet took best-guesses and offered conjectures. At the time it was considered big news—until the next story came along. In this case, updates on the body in desert were quickly replaced with the capture of a woman who habitually targeted mall spas, where she received Botox injections and then ditched before paying her tab. Big news, indeed.

According to Ramirez, the degradation of the skeletal remains had made its identification more challenging, so the results had only recently been confirmed. No one had reported Mort Daniels missing, so until now, there would have been no reason to think the body could have been his.

It did raise the question—if the man in the desert had been identified as Mort—who had I spoken to just one day earlier? And then there was Erica, who had known Mort longer than any of us and up until the time of her death, had been working with him on the book. His absence certainly would not have gone unnoticed, nor would his replacement by an impostor.

Even though the police considered Grace a possible suspect, we agreed that she might be able to shed some light on the situation, considering she'd recently been in contact with Mort, too. Leah quickly placed a call to her former colleague. As expected, she was still at the newspaper, toiling away and harried under her new responsibilities. Once Leah managed to smooth things over from our previous meeting—using their mutual shock over Mort's death as an icebreaker—Grace agreed to answer a few additional questions and allowed Leah to place her on speakerphone so the three of us could converse.

"Well, at least it clears up a few things," Grace huffed. We could hear shuffling paper in the background as she attempted to multi-task. Apparently, it wasn't working out too well for her, because a few mumbled curse words managed to escape immediately following a solid thud.

"Err, everything okay, Grace?" Leah raised an eyebrow and I shrugged in response.

Grace cursed again before replying, "Noooo…I just knocked my iPad off the desk. Actually it was on the chair and the notebook fell of the desk, hitting the iPad—" I made a motion to Leah to circle the cattle before Grace wandered completely off the prairie.

"You were saying Mort's death clears up a few things up?" my friend prompted.

"Well, just that I haven't been able to get ahold of him for days." More shuffling ensued from her end, followed by more muttering, followed by more cursing. Obviously, the girl was a little distracted.

"Um, Grace, what exactly do you know about Mort's death?" I asked, looking at Leah. We both assumed that—working at a newspaper—she'd already been privy to more information than we were currently working with.

"Oh, just that he'd been found dead out in the desert. Some of the other editors and reporters were talking about it but I've been so darn busy—between answering questions from cops, fielding phone calls from yahoos, keeping up with the investigation and ongoing manhunt and all Erica's other duties—I haven't had time to breath, much less catch up on it. I assumed he went hiking, got dehydrated, fell. Why? What have you heard?"

We waited for her to actually take that breath before dropping the anvil on her, ACME style.

"Mort's been dead for weeks, Grace," Leah replied, her voice much quieter and calmer than she appeared, given her constant fidgeting.

"Are you trying to convince me I've been communicating with a dead man?" Grace asked after Leah filled her in on the specifics.

"Oh, I am quite sure you were communicating with a living person, it just wasn't Mort Daniels," Leah replied.

Grace snorted. "Are you kidding me? Don't you think Erica, of all people, would have recognized her former bureau chief?"

"Perhaps…" I gave it a moment to sink in. Erica may have been murdered because she *hadn't* recognized the man and could have pegged him for the impostor he was. Eliminate the problem to perpetuate the lie. Who else besides Erica could identify Mort? "When was the last time you remember meeting with Mort?"

It took Grace a moment to respond—we'd hit her with a lot and she was justifiably confused. "What? Met him? I never actually *met* Mort in person. All communications were done by phone and text but email seemed to be his preferred method."

"Surely Erica had met with him? Talked to him on the phone?" Leah asked.

"Oh, yeah, definitely. Especially at the beginning, when they were hammering out the book deal, deciding who would do what —discussing numbers, signing contracts, things of that nature."

"When was that…the beginning?" Leah asked.

"Oh, let's see. It's been several months now, back at the start of the year." We heard her shuffling papers. "Of course, in the weeks before her death, she was furious because he repeatedly missed their meetings, wouldn't return phone calls, barely returned emails or texts." I looked at Leah. That didn't sound like Mort at all. "She finally got so riled up she decided to track him down and have it out with him in person."

"So, how did that turn out for her?" Leah asked.

Grace's voice was barely a whisper when she replied, "It was the same meeting she scheduled with him the night she…was murdered. I guess we'll never know, will we?"

Then again, I think we already did.

CHAPTER SIXTEEN

"So neither Erica nor Grace saw this person posing as Daniels?" Ramirez clarified, once we'd finished our conversation.

Leah shook her head. "Grace said Erica had talked to the real Mort Daniels both in person and on the phone and from the dates she could remember, it would have shortly before his death. After that, Erica couldn't get him to return her calls and was barely communicating with him via email."

"Grace, too," I added, "though she'd never met Mort—either one of them—in person." Something occurred to me. "Didn't she mention she had at least *talked* to him? Which means Mort would have been replaced by the impostor by then."

"You're absolutely right. Of course, maybe it's not surprising this fake Mort—or Mork, as I like to call him—wouldn't want to talk to, much less be seen by someone who could out him for the lying, conniving, faker—"

"Mork?" Ramirez interjected.

"Fake plus Mort equals Mork." Leah waved her hands, impatient with having to explain what she believed to be common sense.

Ramirez shook his head and slid a look at Abe and Elijah that suggested my friend had fallen off her pogo stick and bonked her head one too many times.

"Allriiiight...*Mork* took a risk calling Grace. We'd be lucky if he left a voicemail—risky and stupid—but is it possible she recorded their conversation? And the text messages and emails— any chance she would have saved them? I can get ahold of Erica's —hopefully pre-Mork and post-Mort, but it would be helpful to have Grace's as well," Ramirez replied.

"Oh, I'd bet a good bottle of hair detangler she recorded their conversations." Leah stopped when she noticed the men's confused expressions. "I'm saying I would have recorded them. Old habits die hard with reporters."

I cleared my voice. "What are you thinking, Detective?"

"Patterns," Abe replied for him. "He's looking at patterns and clues surrounding the impostor."

Ramirez nodded. "Abe's right. Mork will slip up and give us something. So, yes, it would be helpful to have the voicemail in case we needed to make a match. You two think she'll cooperate?"

"Does Nicoh like to howl at the power company man?" Leah nodded at me.

"The gas company man, too," I replied.

"Don't forget the phone man," Leah countered.

I laughed. "Oooh, especially when he's up on that pole...like eighty feet up—"

Ramirez voice boomed, "Enough you two! I have no idea what that means and I'm not sure I want to."

"It means if it shifts the focus off Grace and places it onto someone else, then I'm sure she'll be more than willing to give us...give you whatever she's got."

Ramirez sighed. "Sometimes having conversations with the two of you can be challenging and more trouble than it's worth."

"Hey buddy, what's that supposed to mean?" Leah snapped.

"It means, why can't you just say what you mean?" Ramirez replied.

"I think we just did," she huffed.

Ramirez shook his head. "Without the shenanigans, innuendos and secrecy."

This time, my cheeks grew warm—he wasn't talking about whether we could get Grace's cooperation. It wasn't my fault I hadn't been able to finish telling him about Martin. I rocked back and forth on my Chucks, noting the shoelaces could use a good washing, when thankfully, Leah responded.

"We'll make the call, Detective. In the meantime, you said you were going to see what else you could learn about Mort's death? You never did say *how* he died."

"I didn't. Because I didn't know then. And now I do," Ramirez replied.

Leah looked at me. "And he said talking to us was challenging."

Ramirez leveled an icy glare at the group. "His throat was slit, the trachea severed." He refused to look away as he delivered the rest, "And though it was missing, there was evidence his tongue had been forcibly removed."

* * *

Leah and I were uncharacteristically quiet as Ramirez continued. Though the specifics were still being pieced together, Mort had been bludgeoned several times before his throat was slit and tongue extracted. His body had then been dumped, far enough off the beaten path for the desert scavengers to easily feast in solitude and where human foot traffic would not normally have been an issue. Mort's killer hadn't accounted for the possibility that hikers would venture deep into the desert in search of various rocks and other treasures. Mort's remains had not been the type of trophy they had intended to add to their collection, nor had their discovery likely been part of the killer's plan.

I did a mental breakdown. To date we had two dead; one—possibly two—missing, two prime suspects and one unidentified impostor. Erica and Mort had been killed in the same manner and despite the fact they had worked together in the past, the only thing linking them recently was the book. I wondered how many others had been aware of the proposed tell-all, and if Erica and Mort had been eliminated to keep their mouths shut. Or as a warning to others.

This led to Vargas and Grace. While both had motive to kill Erica, Vargas hadn't even known Mort. Grace would have only benefited if Mort were still alive. Why set up two people—who previously had no connection—when they would likely be cleared once Erica's murder was linked to Mort's? What were the killer's motivations? To squash the book deal? If so, why eliminate *both* Erica and Mort? Had one of them seen something? Or posed some other risk?

And then there was the bartender, Darian. It was too soon to tell if he was really missing or simply trying to stay off the cop's radar for a different reason. Grace had made him seem like a bad boy. Perhaps once he'd thrown her under the bus, he belatedly realized his words bore meaning and to ensure their validity, the police would need to look into the background of the man who'd spoken them. Maybe he had a few of his own things to hide. Unfortunately, until we found him, it didn't help us clear Grace or Vargas.

And who was this impostor? Though he had quietly stepped into another man's shoes, it did not seal his fate as the murderer. At the very least, however, he did have knowledge of the circum-stances surrounding the life and death of the man he was hired to or had volunteered to portray. I silently vowed to uncover his level of complicity and expose the truth—no matter what that truth revealed.

Processing the parts and pieces made my head hurt and didn't even take the outliers into consideration—the issues that had no bearing on the murder investigation. It wasn't as though I needed a full-blown migraine but Clark had been uncharacteristically quiet after poisoning Nicoh. It made me antsy, knowing he was out there somewhere…waiting…watching. I hoped Martin would deliver some positive news soon.

I winced, thinking about Martin. Of course, Ramirez chose that moment to glance in my direction and once he'd latched onto my guilty expression, I knew there was no way I was sidestepping the conversation a second time.

"Can we talk for a minute?" I asked him quietly but found everyone, including Ramirez, looking at me. "Err…Ramirez. I wanted to talk to Ramirez. Alone."

Leah looked mortified as she realized what I intended to do but I interjected before she could stage a protest. "Not now, Leah." She gave me a look of concern as I took Ramirez's hand and led him to the patio; then scurried to the kitchen so that Abe and Elijah couldn't press her for details.

"What's this all about, AJ?" Ramirez asked after we'd been sitting on the bench near the pool in silence for a short while. "You wanted to talk to me but haven't said a word, or looked at me after insisting we come out here."

"I know there's a lot going on with Vargas, the murder investigation and all—"

"AJ, relax. Just tell me what's going on. Is this about our fight at the park? Because I can assure you, it's the furthest thing from my mind right now."

I waved a hand. "No, it's more than that. I have to get this off my chest. Like now. Wait, did you think that was a fight? 'Cause I didn't really think of it as much of a fight as a difference of opinion—"

"AJ, stop it!" Ramirez's voice was stern but when I looked at him, there was no heat behind the words. Only concern. "Stop babbling and use your words!"

I chuckled at the *Must Love Dogs* reference—a romantic comedy I had recently forced him to watch. And despite that it fell into his chick flick category, as a fellow John Cusack fan, he seemed to enjoy himself and even commented it hadn't been all that bad. Of course, that was after he inadvertently noted Diane Lane looked hot. I couldn't deny him that, as long as I got to be his leading lady.

"It's not about the fight in the park, specifically..." While Ramirez waited patiently, I fidgeted. Sure, I'd committed to telling him about Martin but I'd never really mapped out *how* I would do it. Not that I needed an outline with bullet points but a general plan to keep it in the ballpark probably would have been warranted. I sighed, hindsight was so overrated. I clenched my hands until a couple of fingers went numb; then took a deep breath and prepared for the worst. "It's about the man who I was there to see."

"Your client?" There was skepticism in his voice.

Just let me get through this, I told myself.

"Not my client. It's a personal matter. Between me and this... man." Err, bad choice of words.

"Okay..." This time, Ramirez sounded wary, just enough so that I looked up and saw something I hadn't expected—jealousy.

"Oh...oh...it's nothing like that. Honestly." Ramirez cleared his throat, indicating he was not buying. "Seriously, Ramirez... Jonah. What I'm about to tell you is probably the hardest thing I've ever had to say and even as I'm telling you, I'm not sure I fully believe, much less can comprehend it myself."

"Do you love him?" Ramirez's voice was earnest.

"What? Love him? No, though I suppose I should…" I gritted my teeth, realizing I needed those bullet points more than I'd thought.

"How long has this been going on?" This time, his tone cast a chill over the warm evening.

"How long has *what* been going on?" I slapped the side of my head in frustration. "I'm not cheating on you, Ramirez!"

"If you say so." He shrugged, a failed attempt to dismiss me.

I shot to my feet and placed my face millimeters from his. "I'm not saying anything!"

"Oh, you've said quite a lot without actually saying it, AJ. You have quite a knack for it." He started to rise but I pushed him back down. The gesture surprised him but not as much as the volume of my voice.

"I'm not in love with this man! And I'm certainly not having an affair with him!" I belted out. "He's my father, you bobble-headed baboon!" If I'd been concerned about letting Martin's livelihood out of the bag, the entire neighborhood—including my houseguests—had now been informed.

Ramirez looked incredulous. "Your father, Richard Jackson? That's not only ridiculous, it's impossible."

I shook my head. "Not my adopted dad, my biological one. Martin Singer."

"Now I know you've gone off the deep end, Ajax. He's been dead for nearly as long as you've been alive." Under different circumstances he might have been amused but now he was just plain angry, thinking I had fabricated an atrocious lie to cover up an affair.

I winced. "Not quite. He went missing less than two weeks after my sister and I were born."

"Went missing? If I remember correctly, he took a trip off the Skyway Bridge in Chicago, compliments of Theodore Winslow." His sarcasm was not lost on me, especially when he offered a belligerent snort to further his point—quite unnecessary, in my opinion. "I'm sorry, AJ, but I don't have time for this. I seriously thought you were a different person. A genuine person. But between you and your roommate, you cook up more shenanigans than the Three Stooges, Lucy, Ethyl and Steve-O combined. I just don't have the time or energy for all this drama. Grow up, AJ—or at the very least—try to live in the real world. Because right now, that's where I need to…have to live. My friend is out there… dying…and I just can't…I won't deal with this right now." His verbal purge apparently concluded, he crossed his arms and huffed out a long breath.

"Sufficiently calmed, Mr. Maturity? Done with your discharge of insults?" Though his demeanor didn't change, his pinched expression indicated he hadn't prepared for my redress. And frankly, given our distinctive bull-headed natures, I was glad to have the advantage, no matter how long I was able to hang onto it. Ramirez had crossed a line, no matter how invisible it was. He'd cut deeply enough it could not be buffed out or thrown under the rug. I needed to call him to that carpet. Now. "Let me give *you* a dose of reality, Detective. My reality.

"Two days ago, I called Mort Daniels—or at the time the man I believed was Mort Daniels—to see if he had heard any rumblings about Winslow Clark. At the time, Mort was abrupt, distracted, but said he would get back to me. The next morning he did, and we agreed to meet at the Zoo, near the spectacled bear exhibit. When I got there, Mort was not, but another man was. Though he had aged twenty years, I recognized him from pictures I had acquired from Mort as being my biological father, Martin Singer." I took a moment to catch my breath and collect my thoughts, but did not give Ramirez the concession of even a glance. "He confirmed his identity and though he has not told me how he escaped death, he did indicate he was forced to go into hiding, for the safety of his newborn twins. For Victoria and I. He only came out into the open because he had received word Winslow Clark had escaped from the FBI facility and was on the warpath for me. He came to offer his assistance—"

"'His assistance'? AJ, are you listening to yourself?" Not the reaction I had expected from Ramirez. Cool as tempered steel.

"Perhaps you're the one who should be listening...no...checking...yourself, Mr. Hotshot Hotdog Detective! You don't even know Martin."

"*Martin*? So, you're on a first name basis with a man who claims to be your father, after a couple of *Terms of Endearment*-filled moments?"

"For the record, it was three visits and he doesn't just *claim* to be my biological father, Ramirez. I've seen the pictures. I've seen the proof. He looks a lot like me, down to my sharp little eyes!"

"Huh, I thought you said your favored your mother," he replied smugly.

"Why are you being so difficult?" I managed to grit out. "The man came to help me find Clark and has made some serious progress, which is a lot more than I can say about you and your cop friends!"

"Low blow, Ajax, low blow." Ramirez's eyes narrowed. "You know I've been trying to deal with that, in addition to this murder investigation, which happens to involve one of my best friends."

My laugh came out harsh. "Then you should appreciate the fact that someone else has offered to step in and offer a life jacket so you can focus your attention on finding Vargas and apprehending the real killer!"

"Appreciate what? Vigilante justice? Your father is a scientist...was a scientist, AJ. What is he doing, using a microscope to find Clark? And oh...just how did he find out about Clark in the first place? Oh, that's right! Mort Daniels, the impostor, informed him. Yeah, that makes it all seem okay. One has to wonder how he plays into this? Oh, but you're too busy *appreci-*

ating Martin's efforts." Ramirez ended by emitting a healthy snort.

I chose to ignore it, as well as the comment regarding Mort for the moment because frankly, I wanted to ask Martin the very same thing. The other comments, however, were not getting past my radar.

"Oh my, look who's talking about low blows and maturity levels, Ramirez." I shook a finger. "Shame on you. For your edification…yes, my biological father was *merely* a scientist. And while that may not mean much in the garbanzo-sized brain you're walking around with, others considered him a great scientist for his time. A revered scientific mind—"

Ramirez snort cut me off. "More like a *twisted* mind…"

It was my turn to cut in. "At least he makes good on his promises. Meanwhile, what are you batting?" I formed a goose egg with my thumb and forefinger, spun on my heel and walked away. I flung the slider door open. Before stomping in, I turned to face him and threw my last bit of venom, "And for the record, Detective Ramirez—that twisted mind? It made me."

CHAPTER SEVENTEEN

Ramirez certainly hadn't won any brownie points. As I stormed in the house and slammed the slider shut with a satisfying thud, it was clear everyone in the surrounding counties had heard our volatile exchange. In fact, I was more than a bit surprised Nicoh hadn't begun howling, though it pleased me immensely when Ramirez entered a short time later and my canine companion pressed himself against me, serving as my stoic protector. Ramirez reached out a hand for him to sniff but Nicoh sensed my anger, thrust his head and shoulders higher and ignored the offering.

Meanwhile, Abe, Elijah and Leah attempted to make a show of reviewing various notes, spreadsheets and laptops, though I could feel the heat of their stares on my back.

"We're not finished having this discussion," Ramirez uttered roughly as he passed.

I snorted and muttered my own snarl, "On the contrary. I don't think we ever *started* a discussion. You listened to a few words, drew a conclusion and then passed judgment. Before hearing all the facts. Not very coply of you, Detective."

Ramirez sighed, his voice slightly less tense, "AJ, *please.* I'm merely looking out for you. You don't know a thing about this man. And yet you seem so eager to take everything he says at face value."

I shook my head. "I never said that."

"No, but it's the vibe you give when you talk about him. You defend him at the first sign of resistance. You've met with him on more than one occasion but it's the first time you've bothered to mention him. Yet, I know you've told Leah. Don't bother denying it, I can read her face, too." Ramirez looked exhausted as he opened his hands in resignation. "Why didn't you just tell me that day in the park?"

"He asked me not to, for safety reasons."

He retracted his outstretched hands as he worked to contain his anger. "Uh huh, there you have it, because 'he asked you not to.' " His emphatic use of finger quotes—my gesture—was not appreciated.

I crossed my arms and tapped my Chucks impatiently. "Are you going to parrot everything I say, or do you have a point?"

"The point is—I am a public safety officer, AJ. But more than that—I am your friend—your boyfriend when you allow me to be," he replied through gritted teeth, causing a flutter of paper shuffling behind me. Can you say awkward? Ramirez remained unaffected. "So while this stranger asks you not to talk about him to anyone, you run and tell Leah but don't trust me enough to bother mentioning it, even after I'd asked you point blank?"

I pressed my lips together in defiance. Frankly, I didn't like having to justify my actions under pressure. Still, I offered him the courtesy of a reply. "Honestly? I felt like you were checking up on me. I don't know, Ramirez, sometimes it feels like you're the one who doesn't trust me." More harried paper-shuffling arose from the peanut gallery.

Ramirez ignored them, his tone solemn. "I was worried about

you because Clark was on the loose. No sooner than I told you to stay put—off you ran."

"It actually took me a day to get the meeting with Mort, err… Martin. But people knew where I was." I waved in the direction of Leah and noticed she was trying hard not to appear interested in our conversation.

Ramirez shook his head and again, anger and frustration boiled to the surface. "The point is, Arianna—*I* didn't know. You didn't tell *me*."

"Well, apparently I didn't need to tell you because you knew where I was all along," I replied.

"Argh—you are so frustrating," Ramirez growled. For a moment, I wondered if he considered sending me to my room, or worse, giving me a good spanking. Under different circumstances, I might have enjoyed the latter but given his mood and present company, reserved my comments on that topic for another day.

Instead, I decided Ramirez needed to take a handful of the blame. "Oh, and you're quite the communications champion your-self. You know what, Ramirez? Why can't you just concede that you got jealous over something you thought you saw, mad because I didn't do what you told me and outraged because I told my best friend of twenty years before I even considered telling you? Oh and by the way, I told her because she's not so judgy and when she says she's helping me, she really does."

"She's right, I really do," Leah piped in, despite both Stanton's attempts at shushing her.

"Shut up and mind your own business, Leah," both Ramirez and I snarled.

"Geez…just trying to help a girl out…I'll let you two…get back to it," she murmured.

We ignored her and continued to glare in a silent standoff until Ramirez finally broke it, "You're missing the point, AJ. You're so blinded by the shiny new toy you're not seeing its sharp little edges."

I threw my head back and released a harsh laugh. "The shiny toy being Martin, I presume."

"The man managed to stay in hiding for over twenty years, AJ. *Twenty years*." He enunciated the words to ensure I understood his warning. "He didn't show up to save your sister, so why did he suddenly choose to show up now? If you think it was to help you with your Clark problem, you are not only naive—you're fooling yourself into believing something that isn't real. Rather than asking yourself *how* he's going to save you from Clark, you should be asking *why*."

Ramirez left without as much as a head nod to anyone. Despite his accusations, he had made a valid point. Or two. The first of which was that Martin had been notified about Clark by the impostor. How did he know where to find Martin? How did they know one another? Had Martin actually known the real Mort Daniels? Before I could wade through the myriad of thoughts forming, a hand was on my arm.

"You okay?" I turned to face my best friend. Her eyes were filled with concern and tiny mouth formed an unhealthy frown as she absently stroked Nicoh's back.

"Okay with what part? The part where I got into it with Ramirez? The part where my biological father is alive and kicking after twenty-plus years? The part where the man we thought was Mort Daniels may or may not have been involved in the real Mort Daniels' death? Or the part where our friend Vargas is mortally wounded, missing and being hunted like an eighteen-point buck during deer season?" Winded and a bit light-headed, I finally took in a deep breath.

Leah looked at me carefully before responding, "I meant the part where Ramirez walked out."

"It seems to be a theme of ours lately." Leah nodded but said nothing. I noticed Abe and Elijah had been purposely quiet, pretending to work on their white boards. "So, what did I miss?"

"Hey, welcome back." Elijah made a feeble attempt at sounding cheerful. Odd comment considering it was my house and I'd just been outside, not on holiday in the south of France. "We've just been reviewing our notes, looking for different angles. While you were out...err, talking to Ramirez, the three of us contacted Grace again to see if we could have access to her email, texts and any phone recordings with Mork and she agreed to collect the emails and send them over." It reminded me Ramirez had said he'd try to get his hands on Erica's and hoped our tiff hadn't changed his mind about sharing his findings with us.

"What about the phone recordings and text messages? At the very least it would be nice to use those recordings to confirm Grace and I had talked to the same individual."

"No go. As Leah had suspected, she did record their conversations but her phone went missing shortly before Erica's death," Abe replied.

I groaned. "Went missing? Don't you mean stolen?" Realization dawned and I groaned again, thrusting my fists in the air in utter frustration. "Which means her text messages are gone, too," I didn't need verbal confirmation. The looks that crossed their faces told me what I had said was true. "Wait! What about her cellular carrier—the backups they keep—surely she could access them that way?"

Elijah dashed my hopes. "Nope. She already tried that and their system sustained some sort of hiccup that wiped her data from the server. All of them."

"Convenient. And let me guess—only Grace's data was affected during this hiccup?"

"They couldn't confirm it, for confidentiality purposes, yada yada," Abe replied, his tone matching the disappointment we all felt.

"Seems like their confidentiality went out the window when their system suffered a glitch," I replied. "Perhaps they could benefit from a little security tune-up, compliments of Stanton Investigations."

Both laughed, though the amusement was short-lived as I recapped what I had just learned, "So, we have a second 'missing' phone in a matter of days, which leaves us without a recording of Mork's voice or text messages. Please tell me the emails contained a glass slipper?"

"Not a chance," Leah replied as she handed me the printouts. "It's all pretty much boilerplate stuff that could have been copied and pasted from anywhere. Guy likes his Caps Lock key though." She scrunched her nose, clearly not a fan of reading her correspondence in all capital letters. I didn't blame her, I loathed it myself. "Grace mentioned his texts were much the same way, in all caps with minimum word usage. She said it gave her the impression he wasn't a fan of electronic messaging." Or perhaps, it was simply a means of preventing anything from being inadvertently divulged about himself? Vernacular or tone in written correspondence can often tell you a lot about a person. Regardless, the missing phone was just icing on the cake, for someone.

Frustration turned to anger as I thought about the heinous, cruel murders and the single thing that tied them together—the book. A book, according to Grace, that outlined every detail of the Gemini project.

But who would resort to murder? Who also possessed the means, method, motive and sadistic predisposition to carry it out?

I could think of one person. A devil in sheep's clothing if one placed eyes on him because like the impostor, his appearance and demeanor outwardly masked the evilness that enveloped his soul like tar and allowed him to suck the life force from unsuspecting victims at will—without remorse or concession.

As I thought about it, the individual I had in mind had the annoying tendency of typing threatening correspondence in all caps. Lately, he had a penchant for stealing cell phones that didn't belong to him to aid in his nefarious activities. This same individual had broken out of prison, threatened my security and harmed my dog. He also lived to torture my psyche, nearly as much as he wanted me dead.

Winslow Clark.

CHAPTER EIGHTEEN

As I wove through the various threads of this revelation—no matter how loosely based in fact they were—I was suddenly very, very worried. Martin suggested Clark and his father could have benefitted from the book. Whether he was mistaken or trying to convince me otherwise remained to be seen but it did raise several questions. Was Clark working with Mork? Had he orchestrated Clark's escape? Was Mork a ruthless killer like Clark and his father or simply a pawn in their game—a minion convinced to aid in their cause? Or was he complicit in the murders of Erica and Mort—an equivocal deliverer of death?

Had Vargas come into contact with them or done something that made him a threat? Or like Grace, simply a means to an end? I shuddered, not wanting to tread that path, which told me that Vargas was also very disposable.

I lifted my head and was met with grim faces as I realized I'd mumbled that last bit out loud. Against my better judgment I shared the director's cut of my thoughts, only to be met with a myriad of expressions—disbelief, skepticism and alarm.

"Okay, let's say Mork has been working with Clark, do you

think he's providing him a hideout—a way to keep off law enforcement's radar?" Elijah asked when I had finished.

"I suppose it's possible," I murmured. It would also explain why Martin and his team had only been able to determine where Clark had been, but just shy of identifying where he was at any given moment. Clark would have had resources to help him elude not only law enforcement, but anyone else on the lookout for the escaped killer. Something else occurred to me. "That blue suburban we saw at Erica's. It could have been Clark. Or Mork. Or both."

Leah nodded. "It would also place both of them at Erica's' house on at least one occasion, if not a prior." She shuddered at the possibility Clark had been involved. None of us wanted to think about what that could mean for Vargas.

"Do you think we could get into Mort's house to look around?" I asked of no one in particular.

"I assume the police have already gone over the house with a fine-toothed comb, now that Mort Daniels has been officially identified," Abe replied.

He was probably right but I wasn't prepared to give up—not before I started, anyway. "Maybe they missed something. They weren't looking at the situation from the same perspective." Perhaps we'd see something relevant they wouldn't know was pertinent or even something meant just for me.

"She's got a point." Elijah nodded at his elder brother. "You think we'd be able to get inside, now that they're done?"

"What about a police escort?" Leah offered, giving me an apologetic glance.

Abe nodded. "I'll see what I can do." He excused himself to make the call. If our request was granted, I crossed my fingers Ramirez would send another detective in his place.

My hopes were thwarted as Abe returned, looking mildly amused as he glanced in my direction. "He'll meet us there first thing in the morning." Fabulous. I loved it when a plan came together.

Leah squeezed my arm. "Are you sure you want to do this?" Her eyes were pleading—pleading for me to be honest with her. And with myself. Only Leah could understand the depths of the betrayal I felt in keeping secrets from Ramirez. That secret being Martin.

I shrugged and sighed. "It's not like I have a choice. Besides, it was my idea."

She gave me a quick hug. "Then let's go wrangle up some bad guys."

* * *

The next morning, we convoyed over to Mort's. Nicoh and I tucked into the Mini, Elijah in the Ferrari, followed by Abe and Leah in her SUV. Why we needed three vehicles was beyond me but Leah winked, indicating she wanted to have a little chat with the older Stanton brother. While I didn't think the timing was right for one of her romantic interludes—her other boy toy being our primary concern—I could hardly throw a hissy, considering I'd recently had my own relationship sidebar.

After arriving at Mort's, we walked the perimeter as we waited for Ramirez, Leah grumbling all the while. "Last time I was here, those darn vines reached out and tackled me to the ground!"

"And nearly ruined your Kate Spade boots," I added.

"Those viney rooty things are nasty!" She huffed, still peeved about the incident.

Abe and Elijah looked left and right; then back at us. "What vines? All I see is a bunch of bushes." Elijah made a barrel shape with his hands, as if we needed a lesson in shrubbery at the moment.

"'What vines?' I'll show you what vines." Exasperated, she marched toward the side of the house where the travesty had occurred.

As the troop followed in close pursuit, an indescribable odor filled the air.

"Whew! It really stinks back here!" My eyes started watering from the intensity.

Leah paused, scrunching her nose. "Yeah, what *is* that?"

"How would I know?" I shrugged. "Probably a form of weird plant food or dirt Mort was using."

"Yeah? Well it sure doesn't smell like dirt," Leah muttered.

"Well, the sooner we do this, the sooner we can move away from it," Abe snipped. Apparently, he took no pleasure in the eau de toilette Mort had selected, either. "Where's this vine thing?"

"Duh, dude. It's right here." Leah rooted around with her foot but quickly pulled away, squealing when she found it covered in mucky grime, "Ewwww!"

"That's what you get," Elijah replied dryly.

"What the heck did I do?" Leah growled and was about to take the offending shoe off and toss at his smart mouth when Abe interrupted them both.

"Err…guys? Those aren't vines…or roots." He dropped to his knees and started working the ground with his bare hands. Elijah squinted before quickly joining his brother.

Leah and I looked at one another, unsure if we should follow suit, or call the men with the little white jackets.

"Um…Abe? Elijah? What are you doing?" I whispered, though I doubted I would have interrupted their manic search. That's when I noticed Nicoh had engaged in his own digging frenzy, dirt and grime covering his muzzle and paws as he attacked the earth, looking like a bear going after a tasty snack. Then again, thinking about the peanut butter fudge brownies Leah and I devoured last week, we may have been placed in that category on occasion, too. "Nicoh!"

"Let him be, AJ. He's on the right track," Abe said, his voice filled with excitement. "See here?"

Hands and nails filthy from digging, he pointed to a section of the ground he and Elijah had managed to clear. What Leah had mistaken for a vine was a worn piece of rope, threaded through a series of thick iron hooks. The ground below them wasn't dirt, but a large wooden door.

My mind did a mad dash back in time. I'd seen something similar years ago, when my parents had visited friends on their farm on the eastern side of Washington State. It had been used as an underground storage space—a root cellar, I believed they had called it. I remembered it had taken two of us—children of eight or nine years at the time—to lift the trap-like door from the earth using the roped-handle. Once were able to maintain enough leverage to toss it to one side, it revealed a steep set of uneven stairs.

Undaunted in our youth, we had descended the rickety steps and were rewarded with a cool, dark haven. It had been filled with the garden's bounty as far as the eye could see which served as the family's food surplus. Of course, my imagination ran a little wilder back then but my recollection yielded a treasure-chest filled with burlap bags and wooden crates overflowing with more varieties of potatoes, carrots, onions, squash, beets and other root vegetables than I had ever seen in my young life. Though dry and safe from the elements, the harvest smelled as fresh and earthy as it had the day it was picked.

Setting up forts framed with empty crates and draped in burlap, we had played in our secluded fortress from sun-up to sundown when our parents collected us for supper. We did so hesitantly, rising with the sun the next day to fabricate a new adventure, more elaborate than the one before. It had been a wondrous time to be a child at play, while our parent had looked on in amused silence. Perhaps they had been a bit envious, too, remembering their own carefree days of summers long past.

I let the memory drift. A more sobering task was at hand as I contemplated the uses for a root cellar in an urban neighborhood in the southwest. Suddenly I found myself on the ground. Leah followed and the five of us worked side-by-side, scraping and scratching at the dirt.

Several minutes later, we sat back on our haunches, sweaty, dirty, panting and marveling at our discovery—a pair of four-foot by six-foot doors. Abe's suspicion had been correct—Nicoh had been on the right path. The section he'd cleared had revealed the handles for the double doors, latched together by the same vine-like rope that was threaded through the rest of the iron eye-hooks. But it was not the door that had drawn the canine's attention. It was the vile, noxious stench that enveloped every gasp of fresh air that remained.

My eyes continued watering and I fought the urge to vomit. The others looked equally distressed and Leah's color shifted from pink to a grayish-green as she pressed the back of a filthy hand to her mouth to suppress a gag.

"What died?" she finally managed to choke out.

From the looks we gave one another, we hoped it was a matter of what…and not *who*.

CHAPTER NINETEEN

"Do you think we should call Ramirez?" I asked quietly, surprised by my own suggestion.

"He should be here soon." Abe brushed grime from his watch.

"I think we should look." Leah's voice was shaky.

"I agree." I threw my vote in but it lacked conviction.

"Elijah?" Abe prompted his brother, who gave a single head nod. "All right then, let's do this." He hefted himself from a squatted position before offering us each a hand.

"Any chance we could get him to pull this thing open?" Leah nodded at Nicoh, who sat off to the side of the cellar door, still panting and silently observing the stupid humans contemplating opening the gates to Hell.

"Not on your life," I replied, immediately regretting my choice of words.

"I'll do it," Elijah offered, trying to put on his best game face.

"*We'll* do it," his brother countered.

"Alrighty, then. What can we do?" Leah asked, with faked enthusiasm.

Abe look at each of us skeptically before replying, "Stand back. And be prepared to—"

"Wretch?" Leah offered.

"I was going to say hold your breath," Abe replied.

"I was thinking run," I added.

"That might be good, too." Abe turned to his brother. "On the count of three?"

As the countdown began, I braced myself for the worst but ended up looking like I was posing for the Heisman trophy. Leah wrapped her arms tightly around her core and absently bit her nails until she realized they were thick with the same grime permeating from beneath the wood and iron. The look on her face indicated she would have vomited on her shoes, had she not been so anxious to see beyond the cellar's doors.

The hinges moaned from the stress of being awoken as Abe and Elijah each hefted a panel. Once open, they immediately backed away and covered their faces. The stench slapped me in the face, forcing me hack out a brutal cough. I attempted wiping my mouth on a clean section of shirt but none remained, so I distracted myself from the disgusting taste by rummaging in my pocket for the tiny LED travel light I had remembered to grab from the Mini.

"I know it's not much but maybe it'll help." I waved the two-inch light, trying to sound positive, until I realized its beam only extended to the tip of my shoes.

Unimpressed with my Eddie Bauer point-of-sale impulse splurge, Abe grunted. "I've got a Maglite in the Ferrari."

Leah glanced skeptically in his direction. "Wonder where the heck he manages to keep it in that thing?"

"Says the girl who drives an SUV the size of a tennis shoe from Baby Gap," I replied.

"Huh, this coming from the girl who drives a Mini Coop while carrying ninety-eight pound canine on her lap," she retorted.

"I don't *carry* him on my lap. He sits on the front passenger seat."

She scoffed. "Ha! You've proved my point."

"Ladies, please!" Abe presented not one, but two Maglites. Speechless, Leah could only shrug after he'd handed her one.

We all crept toward the edge of our discovery—noses covered, armed with Maglites and a muddy, less than fresh-smelling canine—and peered into the gaping hole. Blackness filled the void, despite the flashlights. All that was visible from our vantage point was a set of wooden stairs that offered nothing more than a twenty-foot plunge to whatever morbidity awaited us.

"Oh my, that is…awful!" Leah attempted to reposition her hoodie so that it doubled as a mask.

"Awful doesn't even begin to cover it," I managed to choke out from beneath my shirt.

Even Nicoh rethought his curiosity and moved away to observe from a distance. I gave him a look and he returned a guttural whoo-woo. I took it as his final warning.

Abe was the first to attempt the descent. Despite the size of the opening, the stairs were narrow, not more than eighteen inches and lacked any supporting handrail or sidewall. Grasping the edge of the door to brace himself until he could no longer reach, he carefully made his way from one step to the next, checking his footing to ensure they were sturdy while using the Maglite to investigate his surroundings. He hadn't quite reached the bottom when we heard him suck in a deep breath.

"Abe? What is it?" Leah's voice cracked.

Abe continued down the steps, until he was out of view before answering, "Bro, I'll think you'd better call Ramirez. Tell him to bring his team."

"Abe?" Elijah's brow furrowed in concern.

"Just do it!" Abe snapped, causing his brother to recoil as he fumbled in his pockets in search of his phone.

"Here, use mine," I offered.

Elijah gave me a nod of thanks as he took the phone and moved toward the street to make the call. Leah, meanwhile, had perched near the top of the stairs and appeared to be weighing the pros and cons of what she was about to do. Before I could stop her, she skidded down the first half-dozen steps until she lost her balance and slipped, crashing at the bottom with a bone-crunching thud.

"Leah!" Mortified, I chased after her and barely avoided the same fate as I leapt over her and nearly collided with—

"Oh, oh!" I screeched as I came within inches of a faceless mass.

I scrambled backward but the soft dirt made the footing uneven, causing me to stumble as I struggled to keep from pitching forward. Abe caught me but dropped his Maglite in the process. It rolled to a stop at the feet of the body, illuminating the space and casting eerie shadows on our ghastly surroundings. Only the shadows weren't playing tricks.

The deceased was propped against the left-hand corner of the cellar and had it not been the sizable hole where his face had been, one would have assumed he was sleeping. The figure was male in stature, approximately six feet three inches with broad shoulders, thick arms, torso and legs, given the way his shirt and blue jeans stretched against his once taut frame. Dark cropped hair in a military cut covered what remained of his head.

Blood stained the walls, splattering every surface and transforming the clay-like dirt into the murky reddish-brown of a rusted-out car. Only this was not a vehicle, it was a dungeon for this person, whose warden had used him to create a gruesome Jackson Pollock imitation.

I tried hard not to notice the details but they stained every surface and oozed from every crevice, coating even my shoes and hands. I shuddered, all too familiar with the horrors of violence.

Of death. Of the toll it took on the human body. I tried averting my eye, focusing instead on the man's shoes. As I scrutinized the black lace-up Doc Marten boots, recognition made my heart skip a beat.

I looked at Leah to confirm she hadn't been hurt during the fall and found her on her knees, one hand clasped to her mouth. "Those boots," she whispered as I went to her side and wrapped my arms around her, as though it would shield her from the truth.

Abe and Elijah, still taking their own horrified assessment, looked at us in confusion, "The boots?" Elijah peered at the dead man's feet. One pant leg had risen up, exposing an empty holster strapped to his calf, its leather sheath empty where a knife had once been secured.

"Leah gives him…gave him crap about them. He got them in England when he was in the military and wore them every day since. She teased him that one day…" I stifled a sob and felt Leah's hot tears on my arms, "that one day he'd be buried in them." The last words came out in a whisper.

After a long moment, Abe broke the silence, "You think this is…"

"Vargas," Leah's whisper came out crackly as I hugged her fiercely, perhaps to offer her comfort or to distract my own emotions from surfacing.

I knew if I started crying, I would never stop. I was sick of losing people too soon. And while we're never prepared to lose anyone, I certainly never thought, no matter his current circumstances, the burly detective with his quick wit and undeniable presence could be reduced to this. Why Vargas? I cursed the earth his killer walked.

My thoughts were interrupted by the sound of approaching vehicles. I helped Leah to her feet and made sure she was steady enough to manage the stairs on her own. As the four of us emerged from the cellar, Nicoh waited quietly at the top, his position undisturbed. Despite the distance we'd put between ourselves and the hellish scene, the air to my lungs still felt constricted, as though death was suffocating me as punishment for being alive. The grim faces of the others told me they were feeling much the same: confused, heartsick…devastated.

I watched Ramirez approach with at least four other officers I didn't recognize in tow. The news would cause his world to come crashing down, too.

"What do we have here?" He developed a healthy frown as he surveyed each of our faces, his nose crinkling as he took in the smell.

"It's bad, Detective Ramirez," I said, showing incredible restraint in my attempt to be respectful of his position in front of his team.

He nodded toward the open cellar. "We obviously have remains down there, am I correct?"

As Abe and Elijah took turns answering Ramirez questions, I quietly stepped to the side and gave Leah's arm a reassuring squeeze. Her misery was palpable as she resumed chewing on a nail, ignoring the filth and grime. I knew she was thinking about Vargas and the last thing she'd said to him. I ventured a small glance at Ramirez and wondered what his last conversation had been with his friend. The Stantons had not yet revealed that detail and I knew no amount of preparation—no matter how tough the cop or the person—would soften the blow. Anxiety built as they walked through our steps—how we'd come to find the root cellar, our clearing of the area and descending into its depth—to our discovery of the body.

There was no reason for Ramirez to assume we knew the person's identity, especially considering the condition we'd found him in, so before anyone had a chance to tell him, he assigned tasks to his team and each dispersed in a flurry of activity, leaving him to enter the cellar first. I attempted to insert myself between him and the opening and nearly tumbled into the hole. Ramirez grabbed my arms and started a familiar lecture when I cut him off.

"There's something else you need to know, Detective. Something you need to be prepared for."

He glanced at me, less than amused, "I've seen a dead body or two in my day, AJ."

"I know, I know...just let me catch my breath."

"AJ," he growled, "not now."

"Please," I pleaded, garnering a look of concern from the sturdy detective who was still clutching my arm. "It's different when you know the person." It came out a whisper. "Believe me."

"You know who it is? I thought the victim's face was missing?"

"It is, but there were other...identifiers."

"Such as..." This time, I had his interest.

"His boots. His Doc Marten boots," I whispered. "As you well know, he notoriously fell under the category of 'never leaves home without them'...until now."

A look of surprise crossed his face. "You're not saying..."

I nodded, looking away...away from Ramirez. Away from the pit where our friend had taken his last breath, where his life had been robbed from him. "I'm sorry, Ramirez." It was all I could manage. And, if I hadn't previously thought a guy his size could move that fast, I was now a believer as he effortlessly skimmed the steps, skipping two at a time.

I started after him but was given a stern "Don't" by both Abe and Elijah, as the latter used his arm to hold me back. "Let him be."

"But..." I countered.

"AJ, trust us on this one," Abe replied.

For what seemed like a lifetime, there was nothing but silence. I could not bear to peer down at Ramirez. The time that passed before he emerged was excruciating. Though he did a stellar job of remaining stoic, he nodded in our direction before quietly relaying the information to each of his team members. Every one of them had known and worked with Vargas, so I couldn't imagine what they must be feeling. I only knew how I felt.

And it hurt like hell.

* * *

We gave our statements to one of Ramirez's team members—an officer whose name I don't remember—while the rest of the team worked. Long after we were told by another officer we were free to go, but elected to stand off at a safe distance until the body was removed.

Why we chose to stay, I had no idea. Perhaps to offer Ramirez moral support, even though he'd managed to maintain a cool exterior as he skillfully orchestrated the investigation. I admired his ability to remain professional and wondered if Vargas being his friend made it that much more important. Still, I thought it must be hard to separate the two and my heart went out to him.

Hours passed before a team of three artfully maneuvered the steps—careful in the way they handled their fellow officer—before placing him on a gurney for transport to the Medical Examiner's van. I could not bring myself to look at the body bag much less accept it would be the last time I would ever see Vargas —my memory of him now tarnished by blood and bone and the smell of decay. And death. My gaze found Ramirez and was surprised to find him looking back.

Before I could interpret his current expression, he waved us over then asked one of the Medical Examiner's assistants to wait before loading Vargas into the van. I wasn't sure what Ramirez had in mind and was glad Vargas' prone frame was covered, masking his violent disfigurement from view.

"I wanted to share something with you." I shuddered, perhaps

I had been wrong. Surely Ramirez wouldn't subject us to this sort of cruelty and force us to view our dead friend again? Leah gasped and clutched my arm as we inched forward. I'll give credit to Abe and Elijah though. Their expressions remained unchanged as we huddled around the gurney.

Once he was sure he had our attention, Ramirez continued, "I take it none of you actually touched the body?" The circulation in my arm dropped a notch under Leah's death grip as a revolted frown covered her face. I didn't dare tell him how close I'd come to sitting on Vargas' lap and frankly, didn't relish reliving the visual. After each of us shook our heads, Ramirez nodded. "Good answer. Then it's not surprising you didn't see this."

He raised a corner of the sheet, exposing Vargas' right arm. As he carefully peeled back the sleeve of the t-shirt, exposing the muscled bicep, a blueish-black mark appeared.

"What is that…a bruise?" Leah asked.

Ramirez shook his head. "Look closer."

Collectively, we leaned toward the gurney and stared at the marking. It wasn't a bruise at all, but a tattoo. Inked in a rudimentary fashion, the lines were jagged and uneven, weathered by sun…and time. As I squinted, allowing the details of the design to emerge, a single word formed. A name.

Grace.

CHAPTER TWENTY

"It's not him! It's not Jere," Leah breathed, squeezing my hand as a collective sigh of relief was released.

"I don't think so," Ramirez replied and while I could tell he was happy the body was not his friend's, it was still a very dead body. Meaning it told only a portion of the story.

"It could be Grace's ex, Darian," Leah added.

"We have to wait until the Medical Examiner's official report is released for confirmation." Despite the boilerplate law enforcement response, Ramirez offered a single head-nod.

A barrage of questions erupted as we absorbed the new information. Was it a coincidence Darian's build and features were similar to Vargas'? I personally didn't think so and though no one made a comment to that effect, we were left to wonder why he was wearing Vargas' boots. How had he crossed paths with the killer? Was he a decoy—meant to put us on the wrong track—or another means to an end?

More importantly, if this wasn't Vargas, where was he?

* * *

As our little convoy made its way home, I realized we'd never gotten to look inside Mort's house for clues. And now that it was an official crime scene, we probably never would.

We had left Ramirez with his team, still directing the flurry of activity. Though he'd agreed to stop by later, his presence would be for our friend Vargas and for our commitment to finding him and bringing him home. If, along the way, we pieced together the puzzle of this wandering tale, then justice would come full circle. But after that, I wasn't sure where Ramirez and I went. I'd broken his trust and he'd damaged my soul when he questioned my loyalty and called me naive. In the end, whether we came to a common ground, or if we failed miserably and came to an impasse, one thing was certain—I'd either lose my biological father, or I'd lose him.

I shook my head to clear the cobwebs but only managed to make it worse. Realizing I hadn't eaten in hours—and no one else had either—I called Leah before making a quick detour to Oregano's for pizzas.

Upon hearing my plan, she nearly drooled in my ear. "Oooh, Abe and Elijah will love you for that. You know it's their favorite when they're in town. Can't get a pie like that in La La Land." It was the most cheerful she'd been in a long while, now reenergized by the prospect Vargas was still alive.

"A little dough and cheese are a pretty wimpy offering, considering everything they've done to help us find Vargas. Who knew it would go to this extent or amount to so much drama."

"Somehow I don't think you're simply talking about Vargas."

"No, I suppose I'm not," I replied as my thoughts drifted to Clark; then to Martin and of course, Ramirez.

I let out an audible sigh.

"Want me to pick up a few refreshing adult beverages to pair with our tasty offering?" she asked. "Perhaps that would take your mind off the good, the bad and the ugly. I'll let you decide who is what."

Sometimes, it was hard to distinguish one from the other, I thought wryly. "Eh, better make it a round of Starbuck's—I have a feeling it's going to be a long night—and we don't need anything dulling our senses." In hindsight, perhaps there were parts I needed to forget altogether.

* * *

As expected, the Stanton brothers were both surprised and ecstatic after I arrived home with my haul, which included a couple of pizzookies—peanut butter chocolate chip pizza cookies, topped vanilla bean ice cream—for dessert if they remained on their best behavior.

I fed Nicoh while the others cleared a space in the living room for our working dinner. Despite licking his bowl clean, the temptation of stray pizza toppings was too great as he stealthily inched his way closer, making Leah his first victim. She squealed in horror as he snatched her piece. Of course, it was Nicoh who got the surprise when he realized she had added a few condiments to her slice. Unfortunately, one of them happened to be a healthy dose of Smoked Chipotle Tabasco.

We laughed as he snuffed, sneezed and made his best pucker-pooch face. "It serves you right, you thieving wretch." She jabbed a fork in his direction before returning to survey the remaining pizza options.

"So, rough day," I breached the topic we'd been chewing over in silence.

"Yeah, though I'm thrilled Vargas wasn't the one we found in that hole, we certainly managed to stumble upon on an entirely different can of worms," Elijah mumbled as he stuffed a pizza bone into his mouth.

"It definitely feels like we're back to square one," Abe replied.

"Were we ever off square one?" Leah countered. "If it was even a square to begin with—it sure feels more like a circle to me."

"I don't know. Let's look at this objectively." I placed the remainder of my slice safely out the reach of Nicoh's tongue before moving to the white boards. "We have three murders: Mort, Erica and Darian. The thing that ties the first two together is the book—a tell-all about the Gemini cloning project. We need to identify who has the most to gain by preventing its publication. It's obvious they'll do whatever it takes."

"So, why get Vargas and Grace involved?" Elijah asked.

"They were simply pawns, used to divert suspicion or cause misdirection," I replied. "And whether the real killer intended to make it appear as though one of them masterminded it or they collaborated as equal partners, it provided the police with viable suspects to focus their attention on.

"The killer selected them—singled them out—because each had a connection to Erica. Anyone doing a bit of quick research could have learned about her contentious relationship with Vargas and her undermining of Grace's career and personal life.

"That brings us to Grace's ex, Darian. It's too much of a stretch he just happened to match Vargas' physical description."

"I agree. Perhaps it was a way to throw more suspicion onto Grace or prevent her from continuing the book," Leah suggested. "But what I don't get is how the killer missed the tattoo."

I shrugged. "Maybe he didn't miss it. Maybe he just didn't care. Or didn't expect the body to be found as soon as it was, figuring decomp would take care of it."

"So what exactly is the killer doing with Vargas, then?" Elijah asked.

"I don't know but I'm pretty sure Vargas plays a role in the killer's end game," I replied.

"Which is what, exactly?" Abe posed a good question.

I thought for a moment before responding, "No idea but I have a feeling this impostor—whether he's a killer or not—has an insight into whatever it is. And who's responsible."

"How we find him?" Leah asked. "The real Daniels has been identified so his cover is blown. And now that the body has been found under the house he's been occupying, he certainly can't stick around."

I waved her off. "Not to worry, I think I know someone who can help track him down."

CHAPTER TWENTY-ONE

Martin didn't seem surprised by my call but when I shared its purpose, his tone was serious. "You told Detective Ramirez I was your father?"

"Well, technically, he already knew you were my biological father but I did mention you were the person I had met in the park. Meaning, he's now aware you are alive."

"I see." He took care in formulating his response. "I thought we had an agreement, Arianna. It was, after all, for your own safety."

I sighed at his attempted reprimand. "No Martin, you made a suggestion…a recommendation…whatever. I went along with it for as long as I could. At great cost, I might add. I certainly hope you can appreciate the effort I made until it was no longer within my power to withhold the information from him." I thought about Ramirez's face that day. The frustration. The disappointment. The betrayal he'd tried to hide when he'd known I was lying. "He followed me to the park, Martin. If I hadn't told him, he would have learned your secret some other way. And you may not have liked what he managed to unearth. He's very persistent when he wants to find the truth."

"I only wish—"

I cut him off. It was not a subject I cared to rehash. "Martin, it's too late for that. Dog's outgrown the doghouse. Move on. You're not really on Ramirez's radar at the moment. He's got more pressing things to deal with."

"Oh? There have been additional developments?"

"You could say that." I told him about finding the body at Mort's house.

He was quiet for a moment as he digested my news. "You were right to call me. Where can we meet?"

We agreed on a nearby dog park. Nicoh had been cooped up for days and his jaunt about the neighborhood with Clark didn't count as exercise. A trip to the dog park would give us both a much needed reprieve.

I thought I had made decent time and was going to use the extra minutes to review the old GenTech files Mort had given me months earlier but once again, Martin had arrived ahead of us.

His attention was on a pair of pups playfully nipping at one another in an energized mixture of whimsy and camaraderie. I wished things could be as effortless for us.

"Hello, Martin."

"Hello, my dear. And Nicoh." He bent to give Nicoh a generous round of scratches before I released him to join the pups. The two younger dogs welcomed him into their group and soon the three engaged in a game of tag.

While I kept an eye on Nicoh, Martin got down to business, or at the very least, what had been at the forefront of his mind. "You're quite sure the dead man found in the cellar was not your detective friend?"

"Vargas? No, we're fairly certain it wasn't." I told him about the tattoo and the missing bartender, who had also been the father of Grace's child.

"Interesting." Martin squinted as he mulled over the details.

I shifted topics. "Had you ever met Mort Daniels?"

"The newspaper reporter?" He shook his head but a gnawing feeling in my gut told me he wasn't being completely truthful.

"So you wouldn't have known he'd been replaced by an impostor—if you'd never met or talked to him, that is," I confirmed.

Martin turned to face me. This time, his reaction struck me as genuine. "When my associates need to get in touch with me, they contact me on a special phone. I believe you kids call them burners?" I shrugged, not familiar with the vernacular, perhaps indicating I was no longer in the group defined as "you kids." "Anyway, a woman contacted me—part of the arrangement with my associates. We never know who, or when. We just know that sooner or later, a call will come."

"I don't understand. How did you know she was legit? That someone didn't infiltrate your group of associates and give false information in an attempt to draw you out?"

He shook his head. "It doesn't work like that. We're very careful. There is a rotating call list. A sequence of calls must be made. Each person gives a code to the next and the recipient must return the correct code, otherwise the connection is broken. Once I supplied the correct information, the woman gave me a message that roughly translated to 'your daughter needs you' and so I showed up."

"Just like that?" It was a bit too loose for my taste.

Martin looked at the dogs and shrugged. "I had no reason to doubt her and after losing Victoria, I couldn't afford not to come."

His response gave me that same unsettled feeling I'd had earlier. Something about the way he'd relayed the information seemed contrived. Rehearsed. Martin was a scientist, after all. I doubted covert ops were part of his daily repertoire. Then again, the man had been underground for over twenty years. It did make me wonder about these associates. How could a dead man not know who was helping him? Or vice versa?

"So you're telling me you had no idea I'd called Mort Daniels and in turn, he managed to get through to you?" When he shook his head again, I added, "Sounds like you need a better set of associates, 'cause it sure seems like you've got a rat in the haystack." Again, he shrugged. "You are awfully calm for someone who's just been outed and probably has a target on his back."

"It's been part of my plan all along," he replied flatly.

"Geez, Martin." His lack of affect was driving me nuts. "Do you have a death wish or something?"

"Not at all. This new information could work to our advantage. It means we're getting close." He offered me a knowing look.

"So now you think Clark's prison break, his subsequent arrival here and the deaths are connected?" I asked because he hadn't been so sure before.

"Now I'm convinced they're connected," Martin replied.

"Do you think Clark is the killer?"

"I can't provide a definitive answer but if he didn't kill these people, he knows who did. Besides, I doubt he broke himself out of prison."

"So he has a team of associates, too, wouldn't you say?" I prodded.

"It's a definite possibility."

"How do you know your associates aren't his associates as well?" This gave Martin pause, the furrow in his brow deepening. "Do you have any idea who the impostor could be?"

"No, but it appears he's involved, too." I was disappointed by his response though perhaps I had expected too much.

"It does appear to be the case," I replied, "which means we no longer have the luxury of assuming he's an innocent bystander, hired to act as a stand-in for Mort Daniels. His hands are definitely dirty. So he's either being paid quite a lot or his motivations run as deep as Clark's." Even as I said it, the words gave me no comfort, realizing we were dealing with a person just as evil as Winslow Clark. "Let's assume this has to do with the book project Erica and Mort had in the works. Who would benefit from the project getting canned?"

"Currently?" Martin blew out an extended breath. "Any number of people."

"Then let's make a go at the short list. Could any of them be a part of your team?"

"I can't tell you that." He looked away, pressing his lips into a tight, unforgiving line.

"Because you don't know? Or won't tell me?"

"A bit of both, perhaps. That, and the unnecessary risk. To you and everyone else involved."

"You make them sound like a very serious bunch, Martin."

"Deadly serious, Arianna." His response sent a chill through my body as I saw of glimpse of a man I didn't know slip through the façade.

"Are you involved in criminal activity, Martin?" He laughed as the chill retreated and his calm demeanor returned. Still, he didn't answer. "Detective Ramirez thinks I should be suspicious about you and your sudden appearance."

"I couldn't argue with his assessment or blame him for it, either." The look he leveled on me—and held—indicated the conversation was not up for further discussion.

I dropped it and moved on, "Getting back to Clark. Any updates?"

He shook his head and sighed. "Much the same. We've been able to track where he's been, but not where he is currently."

"Why do you think he's been so quiet? I mean, it's not like I enjoy his cryptic text messages or having him break into my home to assault my dog." I glanced at Nicoh, who appeared to have recovered without any long-lasting effects, given the way he ran, chased and cavorted with the other dogs.

"I'm not sure you'll appreciate my thoughts on that."

I opened my hands. "I've got nothing, Martin. Try me."

"Well, based upon what I know about him—and knowing the same thing held true for his father—it can only mean one thing." I gave him a prompt to expound. "The quiet calm we're experiencing? It means he's busy plotting his end game."

I had drawn the same conclusion but had to ask, "How do you know?"

"Because it's what I would do."

* * *

When Martin spoke again, his tone was sad as he looked into the distance. "When Theodore pushed me off the bridge, every fragment of the life I had known went with me. And when I miraculously survived and decided to go underground, there was no turning back. It meant leaving no breadcrumbs and nothing to indicate I had been anything but a blip on the screen for a moment in time."

"But you left me behind. And Victoria. Along with our secrets."

"Yes, when I survived, it was my only choice. You see it now, don't you, Arianna?" His voice, as well as the sadness in his eyes, pleaded for me to believe him and somehow find it in my heart to forgive him for the choices he'd made. For abandoning us. "I only did what I thought was best. I had no idea the lengths Theodore would go or that he would foster the same hatred and resentment in his son—the need for vengeance and retribution. Resurrecting myself from the dead was the only way."

"The only way?" I shook my head. "The only way...what?"

"To end this," he raised his hands in frustration, "once and for all."

"But *I* have what they want, Martin." I pounded a fist to my chest. "*I* alone have the chips."

"True…" his voice was slow and calm. He'd given this a great deal of thought. "But I can offer them something you can't."

"Something more than the chips? And me dead?" I asked, incredulous. "What more could they want?"

"Oh, there's always more, Arianna."

"So when you said it was part of your plan all along…"

"I plan on offering them the icing on the cake, so to speak. What I'd be offering them…is me."

Perhaps Martin was ready to seal—or reseal—his fate, but I didn't need him prodding mine in the same direction. "And you think once they have you, they won't need me?" I shook my head. "How, Martin? I have the information."

"As do I, my dear." He tapped the side of his head, offering me a small smile, which did nothing to bolster my confidence.

"You know *everything* that's on those chips?"

He shrugged, shoving his hands into his pockets. "I know enough to make them believe I do."

"Surely you realize you're making yourself a pawn?" I was beyond exasperated and it was all I could do to not give him a good, solid shaking. "Once they get what they need, they'll kill you." Of that, I was quite certain. Then, they'd hurt everyone I'd ever cared about. Or worse. They'd make me witness it before putting me out of my own misery. This plan was sounding worse by the minute.

"It won't ever get that far, Arianna," he replied. "There are… people…who will want them dealt with."

I held no affection for Clark but the tone in Martin's voice suggested these people wanted to do a little more than have a friendly chat with Clark and his minions. "Dealt with, as in killed?" my voice crackled, as if merely speaking the words would put things—bad things—into motion. "And these people— they are your *associates*?" I raised an eyebrow.

He chuckled, realizing the conclusion I had drawn. "They are not vigilantes, Arianna. Think of them as a group of concerned citizens—individuals with the means to monitor certain types of situations and react accordingly." Another chill ripped through me as the crap-meter amped up a notch.

For now, I'd play along. "Like a neighborhood watch?"

Martin nodded. "Only on a broader scale with better connections. And funding."

"Care to share the MVPs on this team?"

"That's all you need to know."

"For now? Or forever?" I pressed.

He shook his head, putting out a hand to stop me. "That's all I can tell you."

"Alrighty then…" I was getting nowhere with the 'who' of this conversation, I needed to change tactics with him and focus on the 'what.' "You still haven't told me what you're intentions are with Clark and his cohorts? Will you…will your associates kill them?"

"Would it bother you if they did?" He raised an eyebrow at me. "After everything they have done?"

I was weary of the runaround. "Just answer the question, Martin."

He sighed. "It wouldn't be our intention, Arianna, but Clark's already chosen his path."

My laugh came out harsh. "Yeah, well, up to this point his path seems to be interfering with mine."

"And yet you worry how he will be treated in the end." It was Martin's turn to lay on the sarcasm. I gave him credit—he was pretty good at it. Perhaps I was more like him than I'd wanted to believe. The thought nearly gave me a rash.

"Not worried. I'd just like to know what type of people we're dealing with here. What type of people *you're* dealing with."

His eyes crinkled and the corner of his mouth turned up. Frankly, it annoyed me he was getting any entertainment value out of this conversation. "Why, Arianna? Are you concerned your father is into something corrupt?"

"My biological father, Martin." I corrected. The smile quickly dropped from his face. "And my concern runs more along the lines of the company you keep."

"I see." Oh, I doubted he did. Even if he'd caught a glimpse of what I was thinking, he'd not even touched the tip of the iceberg. He was still safely standing on the shore looking at the world through binoculars.

"Just so we're clear." I pointed a finger at him and called Nicoh to my side. Winded from the energetic play with his new friends, he came reluctantly but allowed me to clip his lead. "I'm all for taking Clark and his cohorts down but we do this by the book or we don't do it at all. If you or any member of your secret club takes them out, or makes them go poof, I will unleash Ramirez and his team on you like a pack of rabid dogs. Whether you're my *father* or not."

CHAPTER TWENTY-TWO

Once again, Martin had been evasive and I'd only managed to confirm things I'd already ventured a best-guess at, though it had been intriguing to learn in the years since his supposed death, Martin had made acquaintances with some very powerful, motivated individuals. Not knowing his level of involvement with them concerned me. While I knew Clark's end game, how could I be sure the one Martin's associates were playing wasn't the same?

It irritated me to admit Ramirez might have been on the money when he called me out on my naivety where Martin was concerned. Of course, when I pulled up to my house and found his police cruiser in the driveway, I decided I wasn't prepared to allow him to gloat. I looked at Nicoh, who'd slobbered all over the front seat, dashboard and console in his attempt to cool down after a hard hour of play. Seeing Ramirez's vehicle gave him a second wind and he grumbled a low moan of impatience as I collected my belongings, along with my wits and prepared for the confrontation.

Nicoh trotted into the house, while I took more time than usual to scale the stairs and greet my housemate and our guests, who were gathered in the living room, engrossed in something

Ramirez was relaying. He paused when I entered and scrutinized my expression.

"How'd it go?" he asked wryly.

I shot a glance at Leah. "You told him?"

"Don't look at me," she huffed. "The man's got super spidey senses. When he arrived and you were the only one MIA, he drew his own conclusions."

"I suppose…considering you're here…you had someone follow me." I could not face him but felt the heat of his gaze.

"I did not," he replied, his tone even. "Leah was correct, I drew my own conclusions and she didn't deny it."

"I didn't utter a single word, Detective," Leah replied indignantly, rose to her feet and placed curled fists on her hips.

"It wasn't what you said, Leah, it's what you didn't say. Your body language betrayed you."

"You keep your eyes off my body…language, Detective," she growled. "You are so on my crap list."

Ramirez appeared only mildly amused. "You mean you've downgraded me? I would have assumed I was on some sort of other unsavory list of yours by now."

"That's her department. Talk to her." She hooked a thumb in my direction.

"My lists are currently not up for discussion," I retorted, "but now that you're all here, I have a few other things I'd like to share. Of course, you could go first if you like, Detective?"

"Oh…no, no…you're house, you've got the floor. I'm dying to hear what you've learned."

He pursed his lips as I mustered my best teacher voice before detailing my conversation with Martin. I concluded with a few final thoughts on the subject, including my curiosity surrounding the identity of Martin's cohorts.

Ramirez's mouth twitched. "I hope you urged Martin to let the authorities handle this matter. That any interference by outside individuals, whether attempting to track, capture, detain Clark, or otherwise—"

I felt a lecture coming on and faked a yawn before cutting Ramirez off, "Would result in being charged with obstruction of justice. I know the drill, Detective. And yes, I did mention it to him but..."

"But?" Ramirez prompted.

"Martin's a big boy and not my concern. Whatever lines he crosses are all on him."

"Hmm, changing your tune on the old man, are you?"

Ramirez dangled the licorice rope in front of me but for once, I managed to keep my sweet tooth under wraps, moving the conversation elsewhere. "You came here for a reason, didn't you, Detective?"

My directness earned me a tight smile and an uncomfortable shifting of seats from Abe and Elijah.

"The Detective had just started sharing his latest fashion tips." Thank goodness for Leah, who always managed to make the awkward moments less awkward. Less awkward for me, anyway.

"So, what does this Fashion Policeman have to say for himself?" I crooked an eyebrow at Ramirez, who was not even remotely amused.

"I can boil my couture tips and tricks down to one word, Ladies—handcuffs." Belatedly, he realized he'd stepped into it, as Leah gave him a ferocious growl.

"Oh, Detective! You know all the right things to say to a lady." She winked and blew him a kiss.

Temporarily flustered, Ramirez coughed. "I might have used the term 'ladies' a bit loosely." He must have been tired otherwise our usual shtick wouldn't have ruffled his feathers so easily. I ventured a glance at Leah and found her grinning unabashedly. "Now that we've gotten that out of the way, I do have a few points of interest. First, I was able to obtain Erica's text and email conversations with

Daniels." He gave me a sideways glance. "What? You thought I'd forgotten?" Shaking my head, I gestured for him to proceed.

"Much like Grace's, they are in all caps and fairly nondescript. That is—until we dug up the correspondence before Daniels went missing. Here, see for yourselves." He pulled a few sheets of paper from an accordion-style file folder and spread them across the coffee table.

We crowded around the pages and based upon the diction and depth of details after Leah read a few of the threads aloud, it was plain to see a different author had crafted this email than the one who had pieced together the blocky, nondescript correspondence.

"To confirm, the *Chicago Tribune* supplied us with samples Daniels had written when he served as the bureau chief." Ramirez laid a few more sheets in front of us. Clearly, Erica's original correspondence had been with the real Mort Daniels.

"No wonder she was so agitated. Not only was she unable to get a face-to-face with him, but his written correspondence had gone from outlining the book and providing all the nitty-gritting details—to nada." Leah pointed at the radically different correspondence.

"If Erica put two and two together, maybe she tripped the impostor up or threatened to expose him in some way. Suddenly, the cat's out of the bag and bye-bye Erica." Several heads nodded in agreement.

Even Ramirez seemed mildly intrigued. "Too rough around the edges to be a working theory but it does have some teeth to it."

Leah supplied her two cents. "It sounds like something Erica would have done. She wouldn't have passed up an opportunity to make another person look bad. No matter how much she needed them."

"Unfortunately, it could have been her downfall," I added.

Leah looked thoughtful. "Especially if she started poking around."

I nodded. "She would have gone from cash cow-ess to a liability, though chances are she already was one. A liability, that is. But perhaps she served a greater purpose as long as she was alive." Having worked with the gal, Leah looked doubtful.

"Maybe they needed to find out what she knew," Elijah offered.

"Or maybe they needed her to *tell* them what she knew?" I suggested.

"Meaning, something they weren't already aware of?" Leah worked the idea like Silly Putty in her mind.

"You don't think Erica knew about Martin, do you?" Abe piped in.

"If that were the case, wouldn't it mean Mort Daniels also knew and was likely the one who told her?" Elijah countered.

"It's very likely." Leah was warming up to the idea. "AJ, what if that inside source Mort mentioned really was Martin?"

"I honestly don't know. Martin denied it when I brought it up. You have to consider what was at stake for him at the time. Not just the project but his relationship with Alison. Plus there was her pregnancy to consider. He would have been burning the candle at both ends."

"Maybe he's just that good of an actor." Up to this point, Ramirez had been quietly watching our banter.

"Yeah, AJ, he's played dead exceptionally well for over twenty years," Elijah replied.

"That is true." I was reminded of the undercurrents that washed over me each time I had spoken to him. I couldn't deny Martin had been less than honest, but about which parts?

"Of course, one thing we've got to remember, if Erica knew about Martin then Grace could have known, too," Abe added.

I shook my head, out of my league when it came to those two. "I don't know…Leah?"

She tapped her chin. "Interesting point but if Erica thought certain details could be of potential value, she would have withheld them from Grace until she'd gotten everything from them she could. That means she would have still been hanging onto them when she died. It does present another item for consideration. If Erica had known about Martin then she could have also known about you." Her eyes were wide with excitement. "And if she had identified other players, she could have been sitting on a gold mine."

I was thinking more of a land mine but didn't say it, leaving Ramirez to interject, "We can certainly follow-up with Grace but for the time-being, let's work under the assumption Erica knew something more about the Gemini project—something that got her killed. We can agree the book deal drew the players out, but there would have been other ways for interested parties to have put the nix on it. They wouldn't have had to murder three people to do it." He nodded toward our white board, where pictures of the victims were displayed. "There has to be something more to the story that would not only draw Clark out, but whoever else had a stake in the game." Ramirez moved away from the board and began pacing. "At the end of the day, those stakes have resulted in three dead people, one that's missing and others—including Grace and everyone in this room—that are in potential danger."

The room was unusually quiet for several minutes, minus the sounds of Nicoh gnawing on a rawhide bone before Ramirez continued, "On a separate note, the crime lab came back with some interesting results on one of the sources of blood found at Erica's house."

"Please tell me the initial findings were wrong and it wasn't Vargas'?" Leah pressed her eyes shut.

"While the third source has yet to be identified, some of the blood found at the scene was Vargas'. But unlike Erica's, neither his nor the unknown source were fresh," he replied.

Leah opened one eye and squinted at him. "Err…what do you mean they weren't fresh? Are you saying they've got rotten blood?"

Ramirez shook his head. "It means the blood had been extracted then frozen before it was distributed throughout the house—*after* Erica's murder."

"Which means the blood is circumstantial and could have been placed there by Erica's assailant," I offered. "What about Vargas' knife? It certainly seems plausible if one piece of evidence was placed at the scene, then others could have been to, doesn't it?"

Ramirez nodded. "We can hope law enforcement, the prosecutors, etc. will come to the same conclusion. Unfortunately, we still don't know where he is, or who that third source of blood belongs to. And like you, they're running out of leads."

"At this point we're holding out for a miracle, considering every trail has dried up," Elijah replied.

"A miracle would be Vargas coming home on his own, in one piece," Leah replied. Everyone nodded in agreement. While Ramirez's news was better than we had expected, it wasn't the ace we needed.

I shifted the conversation away from Vargas. "What about the bartender, Darian—was he just collateral damage—another means to distract the cops? If so, why was the killer so sloppy with the tattoo?"

Ramirez ground his teeth, incensed by the level of subterfuge the criminals were willing—and arrogant enough—to attempt. "It certainly helped he was of the same size and build and had similar features to Vargas. I'm sure the intent was to slow us down. As for the tattoo, it could have just been an oversight, or the killer thought he had more time to remove it."

"Or the body would decay to a point it wouldn't matter," I added.

"That too," Ramirez replied.

"What about Mort's house? We never did make our way inside after the business with the cellar." I shuddered. "Were there any more surprises found there? Any other hidey-holes?" Leah's coloring turned a lovely puce. Even though I had been the one to pose the question, I also fought the urge to dry-heave.

Ramirez shook his head in disappointment. "Nada. It had been cleaned. As in Mr. Clean."

That caught Leah's interest and returned her coloring to a more healthy shade. "Oh! A professional?" Of course, she also had a bit of a crush on Mr. Clean, despite the fact he never inspired her to do any actual cleaning.

"Would be my guess," Ramirez replied. "They are using ground-penetrating radars on the rest of the property but at last check, hadn't come across any other disturbances in the ground."

"I assume by 'disturbances' you are referring to underground death chambers?" Leah asked.

"That would be correct. And no other bodies." Another gag reflex went into overdrive.

"Well, for Vargas' sake, I'm glad to hear it, though I'm also disappointed the contents of the house yielded nothing," I replied. "Are you sure we can't go inside to see if there's something the crime scene techs missed?" Ramirez shook his head in the negative.

I was tempted to use the opportunity to point out there wouldn't have been any crime scene had it not been for our discovery, but was interrupted by the doorbell. I started to move toward it but Ramirez used his forearm to stop me.

"Hold on, AJ. Let me." He moved out of the living room

toward the front door. He hadn't given instructions otherwise, so I slipped in behind him with Nicoh on my left flank, serving as my wingman.

I heard a surprised "Oh!" as Ramirez opened the door.

After peering through the crook in his arm, I managed to squeak out my own response before receiving a glare reminding me I had been told to stay put. "Grace?"

"AJ?" Her eyes were wide as she attempted to capture a glimpse of me around Ramirez's massive frame.

Ignoring Ramirez's hard stare, I pretended he was merely an obstruction and elbowed him in the side. "Come on you big lug, don't just stand there. Let the girl in." Ramirez squinted as he formulated an appropriate retort. Considering the company, he thought better of it and stepped aside.

"Come on in, Grace. You already know Detective Ramirez but I'll introduce you to the others," I gestured toward the living room, where Leah gave her a quick hug as I introduced her to Abe and Elijah. "So, what can we do for you?"

"Oh, it's what I can do for you. I came to deliver a message to you, AJ." She looked from me to the others. I nodded, giving her the go-ahead to relay it in their presence. "A man contacted me at the office—said his name was Martin. Nothing else, just Martin. When I pressed him, he said you'd know who he was?"

I nodded. "You could say in a manner of speaking, I know Martin better than most." Ramirez's gaze pierced mine, his expression unreadable.

If Grace noticed, she made no mention. "Okay, then. Martin said it was urgent I deliver the message in person immediately— that it could mean life or death," she paused, looking at me with curiosity before continuing. "He wanted me to tell you he'd made good on his word and had tracked down the information you discussed. After doing so, he was able to make a trade for the item you've been looking for." I kept my expression neutral for the benefit of the others while my stomach did flip-flops. "He also said to tell you to expect a text message with the location of that item." I bit my lip. What had Martin gone and done now?

Grace shook her head. "Not that I understood a word of what he said, but the last part of the conversation really had me scratching my head. Before signing off, he apologized for the loss of my ex-husband and said if he'd done anything to perpetuate the situation, it hadn't been his intention." She squinted at me. "Any idea what he meant by that?"

My stomach sank as I realized Grace was not yet aware Darian had been found at Mort's. No one did, as the body had yet to be officially identified by the Medical Examiner's office. Martin only knew because I had told him and inadvertently assumed they had been married.

"Sorry, my...Martin assumed you were married." I glanced at the others. How were we going to tell her the father of her child was on a slab in the ME's office, missing most of his face after being held captive in an underground dungeon? Ramirez gave me a single head shake, indicating I was not to go there. Leah saw it and pursed her lips. Like me, she believed Grace had a right to know. I looked at Grace and found her watching our silent exchange with growing curiosity.

When none of us elaborated, she tossed in her own shocker, "Yeah, well, actually, I *was* married to Darian."

"You...were married...to Darian." My tone was flat. How could this have slipped our radar? I glanced at Leah, who shrugged, not having been aware of this bombshell either.

Grace gave a small wave and chuckled. "Oh, most people didn't know. We ran off to Vegas over one Labor Day weekend— this was before I got pregnant. His parents made us get it annulled once we got back. So the 'marriage' lasted all of six minutes. We were stupid kids, yada yada. Surprised your friend Martin even knew about it." As I looked around the room, it was clear she wasn't the only one curious how Martin had managed to obtain that little detail. "So, I hate to make this about me, but why would he think Darian was dead?"

"Err…about that. Maybe you should sit." I gestured to the couch, avoiding eye contact with Ramirez as I sat beside her and after Leah followed suit, we took turns telling her about our trip to Mort's, finding the root cellar and the body of man who bore the tattoo "Grace."

She took the news remarkably well and her response was as telling as it was surprising, "Honestly, I wouldn't wish something like that on anyone—I almost hate to say it—but for people like Erica and Darian, when you start dancing in the Devil's playground, at some point, he's gonna start collecting a cover charge."

I couldn't disagree with her. Only in my world, the Devil sends his minions to do the dirty work.

CHAPTER TWENTY-THREE

Heading off any further discussion, Ramirez called for a patrolman to escort Grace back to her office. She was relieved when we suggested the officer stay with her while she worked, but reluctant about missing an opportunity to press me for more details surrounding the cryptic message she'd been asked to deliver. Unfortunately, as much as I liked Grace, I wasn't prepared to divulge my relationship with Martin or the specifics of the item he had referenced—if not for her own safety, then for the rest of ours.

Once she was safely on her way, Ramirez turned to me. "I'd like to know what Martin meant."

"So would I," Abe added.

If I could have rolled my eyes without drawing attention I would have. I'd known I wasn't going to dodge this line of questioning forever. "Martin suggested offering himself to Clark so he would leave me alone. Personally, I think it's a stupid plan." I shrugged.

"He shouldn't be attempting anything in the first place," Ramirez growled.

"I'm not going to argue with you, Detective, but what do you expect me to do about it? Like I told you before, Martin's a big boy." This time I did roll my eyes. The sneer I received for my effort told me it was not appreciated.

"What do you think he meant about returning the item you were looking for?" I shrugged, hoping that would suffice but Ramirez was dogged. "You said Martin's associates had been able to track Clark but hadn't nailed down his location?"

"Yup, that's what he told me." Ramirez jingled his handcuffs, apparently in no mood for brevity.

"Then how did he manage to make contact in such a short time?" He gritted his teeth.

I released an exasperated breath. "I don't know, Ramirez. Maybe rather than worrying about where Clark was, he concentrated on where he'd been." The last bit made him look like he gulped down a glass of sour milk.

"Perhaps you should try calling him." It wasn't a suggestion.

I shook my head, suddenly aware of the others carefully watching our volley. "I don't think so, Ramirez. If Martin went to the trouble of asking Grace to deliver the message, we should stick to his plan and wait for the text."

"What do you guys make of that, anyway?" Leah asked. "Don't you think it was pretty risky for him to contact her using Grace? And why?"

Something made me wonder if it wasn't to ensure all the players were safe before he put his plan in motion. Made sense, considering Ramirez had provided security for Grace and the rest of us were already together. I wondered how Martin knew Ramirez would be with us to do so. I shook my head at my own stupidity—Martin had his associates watching Ramirez, too.

It was difficult keeping all the players straight, especially considering I didn't know who any of them were. Or how many there were. Remembering what I had said to Martin about the rat in the haystack, it also made it difficult to figure out which side they were on. What if there weren't any sides? What if there were only pawns to be traded? Everything had a price. And a cost. Something to be gained and something to be lost.

Suddenly, I knew what Martin had done.

"Oh, Martin…no…" I muttered, more loudly than I had anticipated, drawing a round of stares. "I know what he's trading."

Before I could explain, my cell phone alerted me to an incoming text message, the sender unknown.

Four sets of eyes were on me as I read it aloud, "Look outside."

"And?" Leah prompted.

I shook my head, my voice coming out a whisper, "There's nothing more." But there wouldn't be, would there…unless…

Surprising everyone, I ran to the front door and like one of those bumbling idiots fresh out of a campy horror movie, threw it open and raced out, ignoring Ramirez's warning growl behind me. Heavy footsteps told me he wasn't far behind. Not to be deterred, I ran down the steps, toward the end of the driveway. Even his shocking display of profanity did not distract me. If I made it through this day, I'd make him pay for it later.

"AJ!" Ramirez yelled as I broke into a full sprint, running toward what, I had no idea.

I only hoped I looked more like an Olympic runner barreling to the finish line than a bad imitation of Steve Martin in *The Jerk*. Had it been Leah, she would have taken either scenario as long as her hair looked good while she was doing it. I chuckled, amused by the thoughts I used to distract my mind until they caught up with my body.

And that's when I saw it. A giant mass covered in burlap and bound together by thick rope, just beyond the shrubs at the end of the driveway, where the pavement met the street. Had I not known better, it looked as though I had received an oversized shipment of Idaho potatoes.

Panicked, but filled with enough adrenaline to fuel a race car at the Daytona 500, I crossed the mental finish line and dropped to my knees, tearing at the knots with my bare hand in an attempt to work them free. Before I could finish the first, Ramirez was next me and together we tore at the restraints. Abe and Elijah joined us while Leah clung to an agitated Nicoh. It was hard to ignore the dark stains that mottled the material and the smell that permeated from within. I could hear my heart beating as sweat trickled down my face. I tried not to focus on the horror in front of me. Work the knots, I silently chanted to myself. Don't look at the blood. Work the knots.

After several minutes of getting nowhere fast, Ramirez broke from the group, ran to his cruiser and pulled a utility knife. Tossing his phone to Leah as he passed, he shouted for her to call 9-1-1. I moved back as he worked the knife against the rope, fraying it until it snapped. Free of restraints, we scrambled to uncover the burlap-covered heap.

Leah released an ear-splitting scream when a lump of bloodied flesh was revealed. An arm. I moved toward what I assumed would be the head and flipped back a section of material, bracing myself for the worst. Still, horror washed over me and I let out a horrified wail when I digested what had once been a ruggedly handsome face.

Vargas' eyes were swollen shut and a flap of skin had been ripped from his cheek, exposing bone. His lips were cracked and dried with blood, partially from dehydration, partially from the assault. As we removed the remainder of the material, we found him bound in a fetal position, secured with more rope. Ramirez carefully worked the bindings while I gently pulled them away from Vargas' skin, wincing as flesh peeled.

"They're bound so deep," I murmured, my voice shaky.

Ramirez's voice comforted me as he whispered in my ear. "Just take it easy, AJ. You're doing fine." As I removed the last binding, Abe and Elijah helped us roll Vargas onto his back. It was all I could do not to survey his wounds, bleeding through torn cotton and denim. Several bones appeared to be skewed at odd angles and his bare feet showed signs of disjointed, if not broken bones.

I tore my gaze from Vargas' unmoving form, pressing my head on his chest, not caring whether I became coated in the same blood, sweat, grime and muck. I could barely hear it but it was there—a tiny, frail rhythm of heartbeats.

"He's breathing." My lip quivered and tears streamed down my face as the emotion I'd been withholding washed over me. I let them fall. Their heat burned my cheeks and still, I welcomed them. "Call 9-1-1!"

"Already done!" Leah shouted. Her eyes glinted with tears and hope. She quickly dabbed them away. "Backup's on the way, too, Ramirez."

The detective nodded as he assessed the damage. Vargas had been badly beaten. Angry cuts lashed every piece of flesh that was exposed and his clothing was reduced to bloody shreds. He was filthy and given the musty, rotting odor that rolled from him, it was clear he'd been cooped up for a while. I was betting he'd been in Mort's cellar at some point.

Looking at all the blood, I began to wonder if perhaps some of it wasn't Vargas', but the dead bartender's. I shuddered, my eyes drifting to meet Ramirez's. If I'd hoped for comfort, he was fresh out, his eyes black and fists clenched as he thought of the monster he would seek out, whatever the cost.

The driveway soon swarmed with activity, as both law enforcement and medical assistance arrived. After giving my statement and ensuring Vargas was being well cared for, I firmly grasped Nicoh's lead and treaded up the street, away from the sounds. Away from the nightmares.

"Just going around the block. In need some…fresh air," I

shouted over my shoulder, refusing to look back at my friend's haunted, sullen faces when they called to me, as though the path ahead would offer an escape from what I'd left behind.

When would I ever learn?

No sooner than I had cleared the end of the block, my cell phone buzzed. I half-expected another adjective-filled reprimand from Ramirez.

"I'm still within line-of-sight, Detective. Surely you can see my ponytail bouncing?" I tried keeping my tone even but came off sounding more irritated than I had intended.

"Now that's an offer I've definitely been looking forward to," the voice oozed into my ear, like a vat of slugs. Only this slug had a name.

Clark.

"What do you want?" I avoided turning around—no need to put the others on alert—instead using my peripheral vision to peer from side to side.

Clark huffed, "What? No friendly kiss hello? At the very least I would have expected you to ask about the moldy prison bologna on white."

I snorted, processed animal parts—ridden with mold or otherwise—were too good for the likes of him. "A lot of people are looking for you, Clark."

"By people, I assume you mean Ramirez?" It was his turn to emit an amused snort.

I shrugged, as though he could see me. "And others."

He laughed, that same annoying sound I remembered so well. "If you're referring to Ramirez's porky friends, it looks like they have their hands full with other matters."

"I thought you were too busy breaking out of prison and ruining lives to care about the police, Clark? Maybe you're the one who's gone all soft and doughy?"

He laughed, the sound grated on my already impatient nerves.

"I have missed you, Arianna Jackson. But then again, you weren't really talking about Ramirez and the doughboy set, were you? You were referencing your dear old dad and his wiley friends."

My tone was flat, I would concede nothing. "My father is dead, Clark. My mother, too, thanks to your handiwork."

"Come on Arianna, did you really forget who you were dealing with? Stop babbling. That's not the daddy I was talking about, and you know it."

"If you say so."

"I say Marty and his friends are too darn slow. And old. It's probably time for me to put Papa Bear out of commission. He's been a bad boy for far too long. And honestly, I'd thought you'd be pleased, Arianna."

I kept my tone neutral. Clark had always been quite a braggart and loved to talk. If I was going to have to hose slime out of my ear for a month having to listen to this annoying piece of shoe gum, I might as well get something useful out of it. "Pleased about what?"

"Pleased he was dead, obliterated, once and for all. He didn't save your sister, after all. And his presence will only ensure your demise." His tone turned congenial, almost pleasant, "Why not help me? We could team up, take him down together."

I laughed harshly. "What? Like the Wonder Twins? I think I'll pass. But, for the sake of old times, let's say you're right about Martin Singer…"

A snort pierced my eardrum. "Give me a break, Arianna, we've already established that."

"Perhaps you had. Getting back to your…offer. What do you care about an old man?"

He scoffed. "I could care less if he had ceased to exist as originally planned the day he plunged off that bridge."

"The day your father helped him off the bridge," I clarified, just to be sure we kept the playing field even. Not that I was a huge advocate of Martin's but the events of that day on the bridge had been no fault of his own.

"'Helped'...now *that's* an interesting way to phrase it. And interesting you would have drawn that conclusion. Perhaps I've underestimated you?" I had no clue what he was mumbling about. Then again, Clark was like that when he was full of himself. In my experience, that tended to be most of the time.

"So, if you could care less about whether he 'ceased to exist,' then why are we talking about him? Why do you care what he does? Or with who?"

"Knowledge is power, Arianna. And those with the power..."

I feigned a yawn. Geez, where I had I heard that before? "Been staying up late watching too many of those self-empowerment infomercials again, I see."

"Fine, Arianna," Clark was annoyed, his tone flat, "let's get down to business. Martin has something I want. Something he took from me and my father. And now that he's popped out of his gopher hole, I expect him to return it." He paused for a moment before continuing, "Of course, in using you to draw him out, I had no idea I'd end up getting a two-for-one."

"Go on," I prompted.

"I figured I'd have to use you as collateral but then Martin showed up and offered me a better deal."

"I'm still listening, Clark."

"Turns out, Daddy wanted to make good with his little girl, so instead of making a trade for you—the trade I'd assumed it would take—"

"He made it for Vargas."

"Now *that's* Daddy's girl." I heard a clapping sound in the background and wished I could force my fist through the receiver. Perhaps Apple could work that into an application and call it the iSlug.

"And now that you've got your copsicle back, I'm calling in another favor."

"From me?" I couldn't wait to hear this proposal.

"If you don't want to lose another parent, you'll give me what I want."

I groaned inwardly. He could mean only one thing: the chips. Martin had served himself up to save my friend, thinking the knowledge he had would suffice. Instead, he'd signed both of our death warrants.

"How much time do I have to decide?"

Clark snorted, "If that cop reaches the ER and I don't see your shining face, it's bye bye Marty."

"But, they're already gone, Clark. There *is* no time." I raked my hand through my hair, my mind racing.

"That's why I always come prepared, Arianna." This time, the voice I heard wasn't in my ear.

It was behind me.

As I turned, something was pressed into my back and as I fell to the ground, Nicoh let out an unearthly whine.

As darkness swelled around me, I pleaded with my captor, "Please don't kill my dog."

I was rewarded with a cruel, unforgiving laugh.

CHAPTER TWENTY-FOUR

Despite feeling like I'd been hit by a Humvee, I found nothing bound or broken when I awoke on an unforgiving concrete surface. The pinprick of light overhead did little to illuminate my surroundings but after hitting my head, realized I had propped myself in the corner of two wood-paneled walls. I jerked as something touched my right shoulder. Looking up, I found it belonged to the handle of a broom, hanging alongside several other gardening tools. The area smelled musty, a combination of old dirt and fertilizer.

Searching for my cell phone, I wasn't surprised to find it missing. I hoped Clark hadn't ditched it. Or worse, was using it. I bristled at the thought of that jerk racking up minutes. I looked at the broom and made a mental note. It might just come in handy.

The sound of breathing told me I wasn't alone. I felt the ground and came into contact with something furry and long—a tail. Familiarity washed over me as I found Nicoh's chest. The rise and fall was shallow but he was alive. I moved to his muzzle and found his breath warm and tongue damp as it lolled against my hand. Relief washed over me—my brave boy had been spared.

"I love you, Nicoh," I whispered, before leaning back on my haunches and cautiously rising to my feet.

I didn't get far before ramming my shins into various unmovable objects. Sucking in a deep breath and collecting every ounce of superpower I could muster, I counted the steps I had taken. If my calculations were correct, the open space I had traveled was roughly sixty by ninety feet.

Now if I could only see my surroundings. The flashlight app on my phone certainly would have come in handy but that was long gone. I couldn't reach the light source but it appeared to filter in from the outside. I knew it hadn't been light out when Clark had accosted me. Had I been out of commission for that long? Something about the way it fluoresced struck me. It was similar to the lights on the security cameras the Stantons had just installed. Horror washed over me as I realized I was being filmed. The thought of Clark watching me was both revolting and maddening.

I grabbed the broom handle and jabbed at the spot, which yielded me nothing. I half-expected Clark to come on via intercom—channeling his best *Wizard of Oz* voice—but the beady eye continued to stare. I flipped the broom over so that the bristle side was up and offered a sneer before positioning it over the light.

After taking an inventory of the other gardening tools left at my disposal, I decided Rake and Shovel were my new best friends. Not that I had anything against the hoe—despite the fact they always seemed to get the bad rap and ended up on the raw end of the deal—I selected the shovel as it suited my current needs and continued to survey my surroundings, limited as they were.

I had yet to locate an entrance to the space and selected the wall—or what I assumed to be a wall—farthest from where I had started. Inching forward, I used Mr. Shovel as my tour guide to unmovable objects. I soon found the expedition to be a fruitless one, not having determined where the door was, much less a suitable escape route. I returned to the corner and plopped down to contemplate my next plan of attack, which entailed whapping the business-end of Mr. Shovel against the wall housing my new besties. The sound...echoed.

After giving my new friend a pat on the head for good behavior, I began rapping my knuckles against various sections of the wall. Finding it hollow, I moved to the other side of the corner and was rewarded with the same result. Was it possible I was somewhere someone could hear me?

Like a crazed lunatic, I yelled for assistance while using my weight to bang Mr. Shovel against every surface within reach. Suddenly, the ground shifted. Only, it wasn't the ground. It was the walls. Moving. Up. Light filtered in, illuminating my feet and ankles as they creaked upward. I grabbed Hoe and Rake and together with Mr. Shovel, we flattened ourselves on the ground, preparing for whatever awaited us.

I squinted as my eyes adjusted to the harsh fluorescence. My escape route quickly evaporated into another wrong turn as I took in the smug expression of the form looming in the distance. Scrambling to my feet, I dropped Hoe and Rake in the process, but managed to secure a firm grip on trusty Mr. Shovel. I looked for cover but Clark had already spotted me. He perused me from head to toe in way that made me want to gag and punch him in the throat.

I took the opportunity to survey him in kind, noting his tousled locks were blonder than they had previously been, which made his ocean-colored eyes even more piercing. His attire was also uncommonly casual. I hadn't thought a black t-shirt and Levis would have occurred to him. Of course, the last time I'd seen him, he'd been sporting a designer suit belonging to another one of his victims—his brother.

"Tell Paolo I love the new do." Clark preened like a peacock when he noticed I was squinting at his perfect highlights.

"What did you do to him?" My voice cracked from dehydration but the tone was clear. If he dared harm a follicle on Paolo's perfectly gelled hair, I would rip Clark's blonde strands out one by one. And fully enjoy it. Didn't he know how hard it was to find a decent stylist in this town?

Clark clucked, dismissing me with a hand. "Not to worry, Paolo's still Lord of the Salon, overcharging clients for his services and up-selling them with unnecessary product." He shook his head in disgust, while I snorted. "By the way, Arianna, looks like those ends are due for a bit of a trim. Too bad I informed Lord Paolo you would be otherwise occupied. Indefinitely." He tapped his chin. "Of course, perhaps he thought you and I were off to have ourselves a little tryst."

I snorted in disgust. "Not even if you dipped me into a fryer and made me into a deep-fried mushroom."

"That could be arranged, my dear," Clark replied, his smile laced with malice.

"Where are we?" Looking around, I noticed several old projector parts and film reels. Remnants of cameras and light casings had been tossed into piles, while more faux walls and risers were haphazardly strewn in every direction.

"Old public television station," Clark's tone was congenial, as though we were old friends. We were not. "Went out of business many years ago. My father bought it 'as is' in an auction sometime after that, figuring the space would come in handy."

"Handy for a safe house," I replied. No wonder Martin and his team had a hard time tracking him down. If memory served, a few of the old stations had been located in warehouse districts scattered throughout the metropolitan Phoenix area, meaning we could literally be anywhere.

"Homey, isn't it?" Clark waved his hand like a game show

hostess presenting the latest prizes. "Your guest accommodations were the home and garden set. I thought you'd see the humor in it, given the lack of green thumb at your own abode."

I ignored his last quip, no matter how on the mark he might have been. "I would have thought the Phoenician or the Biltmore, the Scottsdale Princess at the very least, to be more your speed."

Clark laughed. "Shows how little you truly know about me, Arianna. I adapt. Like a chameleon."

"More like you spread, like a bad rash," I muttered.

"Getting down to insults already?" Clark wiggled a finger at me.

I shrugged. It was what it was. "How did you manage to snatch me away from the others?"

He snorted, as though the answer was obvious. "Getting you away was easy. Your detective boy toy was distracted with other priorities." He tapped his chin. "How does that make you feel? Always playing second fiddle?" he asked coyly, attempting to get a rise out of me. We had played this game before and it was getting stale. Clark had that effect on me, like a hangnail or a kink in the neck after a bad night's sleep. Only this particular kink never goes away.

"Ramirez was taking care of his friend, no thanks to you. Why did you have to drag Vargas into it, anyway? Erica, I could understand—but why him?"

Clark snickered, amused by my earnest query. "Always putting the cart before the horse, Arianna. When will you learn?"

I bowed my head, keeping my tone as even and as genuine as I could muster, "Educate me then." I swiveled the shovel on its head as I slowly made my way back to my two other besties. I promised to give up gummy worms for a year if Clark didn't notice my retreat. Sour Patch Kids, if I lived.

Clark hummed a few bars of Dr. John's "Right Place, Wrong Time" in response, causing me to groan. I had once enjoyed that song. Now I would need therapy every time I heard it. I cleared my throat, hoping to distract the bile that was creeping its way up, as well as force Clark back to the present. Or at least into his own body.

"Ah, where were we?" Clark smiled, taking in my discomfort. "You were asking why Vargas was such an enticing…guinea pig. No pun intended." He put a finger to his lips, tapping it. "Actually, a pig is a pig no matter the jig."

I gave him a dry look. He wasn't Dr. John by a long shot. But Dr. Seuss? Not even in the same ballpark.

"Vargas was merely…a happy coincidence." He looked thoughtful. On him, it was downright creepy. I used it as an opportunity to shimmy back toward Hoe and Rake. "Don't think I'm not seeing that, Arianna." He laughed but as his eyes met mine, a chill went up my spine. "Creating a statewide manhunt for a cop had not been on my bucket list but wow…those metro police of yours, they really take the ball and run, don't they? I merely put the bait under their noses and they were off like starved rats. Of course, it would have been thrilling to see that outcome, had they managed to catch him." He chuckled; then sighed, disappointed at having missed the opportunity.

"Why break onto my property, drug Nicoh and steal Leah's cell phone?" I asked. "Why go to all the trouble?"

"Trouble? That was child's play. I simply wanted to let you know I was around. Everywhere. Watching. That I could get to you and those you cared about. Any time. Any place. Though I should have disposed of that pesky neighbor of yours. Susie, is it? Annoying old bird. Attractive, yes, but a little on the dry side for my taste." He snorted out a laugh.

"So, why am I here?" I asked through gritted teeth.

"That should be fairly obvious," he replied. "I want those chips, of course." Taking in my look, he snickered. "What? Did you think Marty's offer—to exchange himself for the formulas—

would suffice? I'm surprised even you believed his line of bull. As if the formulas alone would have been worth all this effort." He gestured to the surroundings.

I blinked, unsure of what to make of his comment. "If not the formulas, what?"

Clark shifted off the riser and bent to grab what appeared to be a power brick with switches. "Why don't you ask Daddy Dearest yourself?" He flipped a switch on the device and a spotlight lit the area a hundred or so feet to my left. Its harsh light fell on one thing.

Martin.

I gasped. Though disheveled, he didn't appear to be harmed. It was the contraption he was rigged to that had me panicking. Martin's frame had been used to lift the fabricated home and garden set, judging by the pulleys that lead to his waist and ankles. A second set of pulleys circled his neck and while they hung loosely on the ground, one look at the controller told me it was how Clark had managed to keep him under control. Any warning from Martin could have been deadly, for all of us.

"What have you done, Martin? I told you this wouldn't work."

"Hush, Arianna," Martin's voice was gruff as he shot me a look that could have singed my eyebrows.

Clark was clearly enjoying the reunion. "What's the matter, Marty? Baby girl's got your number? Apparently, she isn't the only one. You're losing your edge, old man."

"I have nothing to say to you." Martin sounded as angry as I'd ever heard him, which wasn't all that often. Still, from what little I knew of the man, he didn't have the patience to deal with Clark's animated behavior. It was one way I was a chip off the old block. Unfortunately, he was no better at hiding his emotions and Clark quickly saw Martin held little regard for his antics.

"Oh? Perhaps you'd prefer chatting with an old friend?" Clark snarled, using his controller to tighten the reins. Martin's face reddened at the pressure against his neck, leaving Clark to chortle in delight. I started to cry out in protest but something in Martin's eyes willed me to stop. Clark ignored us and made a call on an ancient walkie talkie he'd pulled from his back pocket.

When he saw me eyeballing it, he shrugged. "Place is a fortress. Even I can't find most of the entrances and exits." The grin forming at the corner of his mouth said otherwise.

A door creaked behind me. I squinted as our new visitor made his way through the quagmire of props. Finally, the stranger emerged from the darkness. As my mind caught up with my eyes, my heart chimed in with a sharp jolt, causing me to gasp.

Clark bowed. "Hello, Father."

CHAPTER TWENTY-FIVE

The moment he entered, Theodore Winslow's steely gaze trained on Martin and the two appeared to be in a mental stare down. Nicoh took the opportunity to sit upright, looking a little drunk and discombobulated from whatever concoction Clark had popped him with. Though it was hard to dislike the man any more than I already did, the abuse he continued to inflict upon my canine companion reserved him a very special spot in Hell. My mental meanderings were distracted by Theodore, who swiftly moved toward Nicoh and began securing him roughly.

"Hey! There's no need for that!" Theodore ignored me, using a rope to tie Nicoh to a nearby pallet. Nicoh howled and thrashed but in his sluggish condition was no match for the man's deft handiwork. After ensuring Nicoh was restrained, Theodore stood and started making his way toward me. I backed up a few inches, nearly stumbling in the process. After miraculously catching my balance, I grinned at the three men and feigned as much enthusiasm as I could muster. "So, who's going to make the introductions?"

Clark snickered until his father gave him a sharp look. It was easy to see Clark was on a short leash with the older man. This could prove interesting, if not beneficial. One look at Martin told me he had surmised the same thing.

"I believe you are well aware of who is who," Theodore replied after a long moment, though the blackness in his eyes told me formal introductions were off the table "It's been a long time, Martin." Theodore studied his former colleague. "Time has been good to you."

"Doesn't appear you're any worse for the wear either, Theodore." Though Martin kept his tone congenial, the look he returned was anything but.

Theodore snorted. "Times could certainly have been better." To this, Martin said nothing and the two continued to glare at one another.

"I can imagine this is a far cry from the good old days at GenTech," I muttered sarcastically, drawing an angry look from Theodore.

"What would you know about it?" he snarled.

"Err, I simply meant—"

"Arianna, I think it's best if you let Theodore and I handle this." Martin attempted to chastise me but if I let the two of them continue their silent standoff, we'd soon be as dusty as the equipment in this place.

So I did what I always do when given advice I don't care for. I ignored it. "Getting back to my original question, Clark," I glanced at him, his eyes still fixated on his father and Martin. "Why am I...are we here? It's certainly not to hold a multiple family reunion. I didn't even have time to bake a pie or whip up a batch of my famous potato salad. Though, in hindsight, it probably wouldn't have fared well under these conditions with the mayo and all—"

Theodore cut me off, "Though she has difficulty staying on point, much less getting to it, she reminds me of Alison." He looked at me with something just past the wrong side of creepy

—admiration.

"She is a lot like Alison, despite her upbringing." I didn't care much for Martin's tone, or his innuendo.

"My upbringing, which is absolutely no business of yours, was just fine. As for my shortcomings in getting to the point, the three of you have been sidestepping it quite nicely. So let's get down to it, boys. Why are we here and what do you want?"

"Definitely like Alison," Theodore murmured, with more affection in his voice than my gag-meter allowed. Martin must have felt the same, given the look he shot at Theodore. Clark looked strangely befuddled, perhaps not used to being the odd man out. "We're here, Arianna, to conclude old business. Clean the slate of old debts." I shook my head in disgust—these guys held onto old baggage for way too long. "Martin took something that belonged to me...belonged to all of us, really."

"When you say 'all of us,' are you referring to the proverbial us or something else?" I asked.

"I mean the other scientists at GenTech, as well as to the world at large, Arianna," Theodore replied. "Technology that would have revolutionized the way we look at human life, at evolution and the universal gene pool." I felt a yawn coming on and kicked myself for failing to ask for the Wikipedia version.

Fortunately, Martin interrupted what was quickly becoming a lecture, "It's easy to allow the truth to be blurred by time, Theodore, but the fact of the matter remains—I didn't steal Gemini. I was saving it from being manipulated and corrupted by wanton greed and fantastical visions of a superhuman race. You and I both know the pressures we were under—even to get meager funding—the hoops we had to jump through, the promises we were forced to make and eventually the results we would have been expected to produce." Martin shook his head, despite his former colleague's attempt to interject. "No, Theo, when you're honest with yourself—when you dig deep and find the truth you once knew—you will realize I did what was best for everyone."

"You did what was best for *you*, Martin. You didn't even bother consulting me. We were colleagues…friends even at one point." Clark blanched at his father's admission, not having considered the enemy he'd known since birth had once been an ally to his father.

"No, Theo. I saw what you were doing. Knew what you were up to when you hushed the others in the corridors or in the lab late at night when you thought I was with Alison. The greed had gotten to you. I could see it in your eyes—the promise of fame and adulation in the scientific community. The promise of power."

"And a fat bank account," Clark added, receiving a wicked glare from his father. "Seriously, Father! This…man took everything you worked for and ran—"

"Silence, Winslow! I do not need you to tell me what he's taken. Or what it has cost me." Theodore turned to Martin. "It wasn't what you thought, Martin, it wasn't like that at all, especially not after we had formulated the plan…that day at the bridge—"

Martin cut him off sharply, surprising us all by the venom in his voice. Had Theodore been about to reveal something he hadn't want me to know? "It's a moot point now, isn't it Theo? So, now that you've got me here, let's finish this."

It was my turn to interrupt. I wasn't as eager to rush to my death. "Whoa, guys! Before we get down to your business"—I didn't really want to know what that entailed, given the lengths Clark and his father had gone to over the past several months —"could I pose a few questions? You know, just for my own edification? It's not going to matter in the end but I'd like to clear a few of the things rattling around in my brain."

Martin started to speak but Theodore raised a hand. "I think the girl deserves some answers. She's been made a pawn in this, though none of it was her doing." Some might have thought the man had a soft side but his unforgiving sneer and the black vaults of his eyes told me Theodore had no soul. I wondered what he had to gain by drawing out the game. I looked at Martin, his expression grim and caught a glimpse of something he hadn't intended for me to see.

Fear.

Now Theodore really had me curious. What would terrify Martin more than his own death? Realization washed over me.

The truth.

I clutched the handle of Mr. Shovel and managed to get within a foot or two from Hoe and Rake then posed my questions before Theodore could change his mind.

"So…Mr. Winslow—"

"*Dr. Winslow*." Theodore sniffed, giving me a look of impatience. I glanced at Martin, who rolled his eyes.

"Err, my apologies, *Dr. Winslow*. It's obvious the Feds did not arrest you in Florida. So who is sitting in that prison cell on your behalf?"

It was Clark who answered, though his father looked less than pleased. "It was just some vagrant I found in our travels who looked a bit like Father. He was whacked out on drugs at the time, until Father and I took him in, got him sober and provided him with food, clothes and a roof over his head…" I wanted to gag, both of them looked as though they remembered the time fondly, believing they had actually helped another human being out of the kindness of their cold, dead hearts.

"And let me guess, he was so appreciative, he agreed to become one of your minions…one of your precious flock," I commented dryly.

"You can call it what you want." Theodore could have cared less about my opinion, much less convincing someone like me of his methods. I was beneath him. And for the time-being, he was just toying with me. "The man was most appreciative of our offerings and once he was able to become a productive member of society—"

"You forced him to repay your generosity by setting him up to take the fall for you?" I interjected.

Theodore didn't appreciate being interrupted nor questioned and from his sharp look, certainly was not accustomed to it. "I was going to say, he knew a sacrifice had to be made to support the cause. He was a willing participant."

I snorted. "Your cause? Exactly what cause is this? You brainwashed him, like you did the person who helped break your son out of prison."

"Friends of the cause are very loyal." Nothing I said appeared to affect or deter him. "Winslow was being held for crimes he had no control over."

I quirked an eyebrow. "You're not suggesting he had no control over killing my parents?"

Theodore shook his head and gave me a look one would garner on a simpleton. "I assure you, he did not have anything to do with killing Alison. And, as you can see, Martin is quite alive and well."

I gritted my teeth. Had it not been for the circumstances—and my need to ferret the truth out of these two—I would have allowed Mr. Shovel to give him a free tooth adjustment. "Those are not the parents I am talking about, Dr. Winslow. And I think you know it." Theodore responded by pursing his lips. "As for assessing guilt, he admitted to killing them. And the pilot of the plane. And Victoria, my sister. As well as her parents. Oh, and there was his brother—" Theodore blinked in surprise. "Oh, what? *Winslow* didn't share that little tidbit with you?" I laughed, my tone rough as Clark started to speak.

Theodore raised a hand. "That was an unfortunate hiking accident. As for the others…the evidence was fabricated by the police to make my son look guilty."

"Oh? And just how do you explain his confession?"

"Coercion, by the same incompetent fools," Theodore sniffed.

"I meant his confession to *me*." My patience was wearing thin with this dog and pony show.

Still, Theodore shook off the notion. "A misunderstanding, Clark was under extreme pressure. You threatened him."

I threw back my head and laughed. "Wow. You are delusional, aren't you? Clark was certainly right when he said you'd lost your marbles."

"I said no such thing!" Clark's face reddened as his father cast him a murderous glare.

I waved a hand. "Whatever, I digress…so this homeless guy *volunteers* to take your place in prison. Months later, some of the other appreciative members of your cause break Junior out. Just how did you manage to facilitate that?"

Theodore sniffed. "We have eyes and ears everywhere and when I put out the request, things happen. Our network of friends is vast. And that's all I am willing to divulge. Certainly you can appreciate the anonymity of one's confidants, Martin?" He slid a coy glance in his former colleague's direction. Martin looked away, causing Theodore to chuckle. "Still holding it close to the vest, I see. You'd think after all this time, all that I've—"

"Arianna still has questions that need answering, Theodore," Martin's sharp tone made us turn and look at him but whatever burr Theodore had put in his craw, the emotion did not reach his face. It occurred to me Martin was trying to direct the conversation away from himself. I wondered why it mattered.

I wasn't thrilled with Martin's attempt at misdirection and hoped I'd have an opportunity to get to the bottom of it later. Of course, I wasn't exactly getting the answers I needed from Theodore and Clark either.

"Err…yeah, thanks, Martin." He nodded, an awkward movement given his current predicament. I turned to Theodore, his appraising look still on Martin as though deciding something. "Did you know Mort Daniels before you took over his life?"

Theodore's gaze never left Martin but he appeared thoughtful. "I never met Daniels personally but others at GenTech had, and all were aware he was collecting information about the cloning projects at GenTech and Alcore. After he retired and moved here, we kept an eye on him and eventually, he seemed to have dropped it altogether."

"It was his pet project though, wasn't it?" I asked.

"Oh yes, that part was true but he'd been out of the game for so long…"

I picked up as he hesitated, eager for him to proceed. "So you were caught off-guard when he contacted Erica Stone and began discussing a tell-all about Gemini. Why do you think he became so interested again, after all those years?"

"You really don't know, do you?" I shook my head and Theodore shot Martin an annoyed glance. "It was your sister, Victoria. She'd done her own research and when she came across his name, she contacted him to compare notes and determine whether he could lend anything to what she'd already learned."

"But that was long before she came here—before your son murdered her and left her for me to find." I glared at Clark, who was contently picking at his manicure.

"Victoria and Mort had never met in person prior to that, all their correspondence was done by phone or email. After he contacted that…woman about the book, we knew he wasn't going to let things rest," Theodore replied.

"And that's when you knew you had to intervene," I added.

"As I mentioned, we'd been keeping an eye on him for years. We knew his routines, his daily patterns and things of that nature.

All we had to do was find a suitable replacement, tie up loose ends and the situation would have been under control."

"You appointed yourself as this 'suitable replacement.' Isn't that a bit of a coincidence?" I asked.

Theodore shrugged. "We were of the same body structure, same general coloring and after studying his mannerisms, dying my hair, adding colored contacts, along with a few other modifications, I easily slipped into his role."

"So by tying up loose ends, you mean Erica—someone who would have known you were an impostor and realized the subterfuge sooner or later."

"Yes, the people Mort Daniels was associated with had to be dealt with, along with other matters."

"Did these other matters include his research?"

Theodore nodded. "We had to get our hands on it to understand the full extent of what we were dealing with."

"After you found out, he was removed from the picture —permanently."

"Another accident…" He glared when I clucked my tongue, a reminder of the mutilation Mort and Erica had endured before their *accidents*.

"Huh, there sure are a lot of accidents around you two, Theodore. Must be terrible, to be part of such an accident-prone family?"

Theodore slid a look at Clark, whose lips curled into a small snarl. Apparently, they had no more love lost for their own family than they did anyone else's. What a pair.

"Yours appears to be no less accident prone, Arianna. Perhaps you should ask yourself the same question." I ignored Clark's comment, returning my attention to his father.

"So you took on Mort's persona in the interim. What went wrong? What suddenly made Erica a liability? A loose end?"

"That girl was a nuisance from the start and far more clever than anticipated. We'd done our research on her, too, but she was a more formidable opponent than we'd initially given her credit for. Once her mind was set on something, her greed fed her tenacity, which drove her persistence," Theodore replied.

"The way you talk about her, she sounds more like a promising recruit for your cause than someone who needed to be eliminated." I added a thick layer of sarcasm to Theodore's admiration sandwich.

He pursed his lips. "I take it you didn't know Erica Stone very well."

I shrugged. "I knew enough, my best friend used to work for her."

"Then you should understand Erica was her *own* cause. When she didn't get exactly what she wanted precisely when she wanted it, she became—"

"Like you said, a nuisance. So, why not just make sure she had the information she needed—edited, of course—and send her on her merry way? Certainly there were ways to fulfill her demands?"

Theodore shook his head. "It was never going to be that easy. She got snoopy and managed to catch of glimpse of me, as Mort, and once she'd seen the GenTech photos…"

"Erica put the pieces together and the gig was finally up. Erica not only recognized you as the impostor but realized you weren't where you were supposed to be—in your comfy prison cell. And when she confronted you about it, she'd finally worn out her welcome and her usefulness," I replied.

"Her usefulness?" Theodore quirked a brow at me.

"Surely before you eliminated her, you wanted to find out exactly how much she knew about the project, beyond whatever Mort had shared with her? She was a journalist after all, and despite the fact she manipulated others into doing her bidding, she wouldn't have merely taken Mort at his word, nor would she have trusted she'd gotten the full story from him. Erica may have been many things but she was thorough, too. She wasn't about to put her name on a book without having all the facts. And I mean *all* the facts. Enough to blow the public's socks off and perhaps even blow a few of you guys out of the water, especially when she realized who you really were." I glanced around the room, both Martin and Clark seemed less than interested, though given the twitch at the corner of Martin's mouth, he wasn't pleased with the way things were going. Why was that, exactly? "Anyway, you decided she had to be…contained. Before she got out of the Tupperware and ran off with the lid. I hate it when those things go missing."

Theodore looked confused by my analogy but shrugged it off. "Something like that."

"So rather than paying her off or asking her to join your little club"—both Theodore and his son snorted in disgust—"you agreed to meet her, only you surprised her by showing up at her house—where you extracted the threat. Quite literally. A bit barbaric but I guess it got the point across." My comments were met with bland stares and oblique silence. "Convenient, too, after Vargas had already threatened to rip out her tongue a few hours prior, in full view of at least a dozen of his co-workers. Though I have to ask, if you went to the trouble of eliminating Erica—weren't you concerned Grace Turner might do the same thing? Considering she was doing the lion's share of Erica's work on the book, she could have easily obtained the same information Erica had. Even with Erica out of the way, she could have been equally dangerous." While I knew Erica had likely kept certain details to herself, including the juicy morsels that could have given her leverage and a fatter payday, I wanted to hear Theodore's rationale.

He shook his head. "Grace had other factors that made her…pliable."

"You mean made her a likable scapegoat." Might as well call a spade a spade.

"Perhaps it seems that way but her situation, particularly the one involving the custody of her child, definitely made her more manageable." I hoped he wasn't alluding to hurting a child, had things not worked out so fortuitously. Who was I kidding—this was Theodore Winslow and his son we were talking about.

"Especially once her ex out of the way," I replied wryly.

Theodore ignored the tone but looked thoughtful at the notion. "It probably relieved a huge burden off her mind." Even up to this point, I noticed he never fully accepted responsibility for murdering the bartender, much less Erica. Perhaps another tactic —plausible deniability—if he didn't say the words, it wasn't true.

Or was there another reason?

"However, despite being more manageable, you also succeeded in making Grace a suspect in the murder of her boss," I added.

"A backup in case the detective didn't work out." Clark belatedly realized he had spoken out of turn when his father glazed him with a stare reserved for dog crap on the bottom of one's shoe.

"How did you get to Vargas? Or the bartender? Did you know about Vargas' altercation with Erica at the police station, or was that just another happy coincidence?" I asked.

"There's no such thing as coincidences, Arianna. Like I said before, we have eyes and ears everywhere. While Vargas could have been easily manipulated—to get him where we wanted when we wanted—the altercation certainly put him right in the middle of the action."

"Meaning the evidence you fabricated in Erica's apartment." Theodore shrugged. "Cat's got your tongue? Sorry, no pun intended. Let me elaborate for you. You commandeered Vargas' suburban after rendering him unconscious, extracted his blood, froze it for later, dribbled some across the crime scene—added in a bit of Darian's for good measure—then used Vargas' knife to do the deed. But you also went to the effort of making us believe he was dead—using Darian as a body double—despite keeping him alive. Why? And don't tell me Junior here got squeamish about killing a cop." Clark responded with a grin so rabid, he looked like he could have gnawed on a raw T-bone.

"He was useful for other reasons," Theodore replied, ignoring his son's fervor at the mention of murdering a cop.

"To distract Ramirez and draw me out?"

"Among other things, which I am not prepared to discuss," Theodore replied, his tone flat.

"Okay, let's talk about the bartender then. Was he just a diversion, or part of a greater plan?" I asked.

"I thought we had already discussed his level of participation." Theodore was clearly bored.

Tough gummy bears.

"To keep Grace pliable? Nope, not buying it, Doc. If that were the case, the Clark Bar here wouldn't have done such a bang-up job of blowing a hole in Darian's distinguishing features." Theodore leveled a glare at his son that had me wondering if he wasn't considering a shorter leash for Junior. Nothing like the present. "Yeah, nice job, Clark. Considering Darian's size and build was similar to Vargas', you could have kept the police in the dark for a while, had it not been for the tattoo."

"What tattoo?" Gotcha. Clark's voice almost squeaked, like the wooly chew man toy Nicoh destroyed at PetsMart during our last visit. If only Nicoh could do the same to Clark. Then again, wiping that annoying smirk off Clark's face?

Priceless.

I played it off, waving a hand at him. "Ah, never mind that now. How else do you think they would have been able to identify him so quickly?" I released an obnoxious snort. "Getting sloppy, Junior."

"Stop calling me that, you wench!" The spittle from his outburst landed on my cheek. Where was a wet-nap when you needed one?

I moved my hand in a calm-down gesture. "Hey now, there's no need to get rude just because I've got your number. Besides, only Leah gets to call me that but for future reference, the correct title is Margarita Wench."

"Shut up!" He was at a full-boil now, dropping the controller and advancing on me like a raging bull.

Theodore quickly interceded, stepping between the two of us. "Enough, Winslow! I don't recall inviting your commentary."

"I didn't realize I needed permission," his son spat. Future father and son baseball games were obviously out of the question.

I glanced at Martin and found him staring intently at me. As Clark and his father exchanged a mental battle of wills, he nodded ever so slightly in the direction of Nicoh before mouthing a single word. My eyes widened in surprise as I looked at Nicoh's contraption—awkward and cumbersome—but not unmovable. I gave Martin a small nod of understanding.

All I needed to do was create a distraction.

"Sorry to break up the family squabble but why exactly are we all here again? I'm still not totally clear." Both father and son turned to face me, their looks venomous. Oops, perhaps I shouldn't have interrupted family time?

Clark snorted. "See, Father? I told you she wasn't all that bright. That cow of a sister of hers got all the brains."

"How dare you talk ill of the dead, Junior, my sister was not a cow," I glared at him and enunciated each word through gritted teeth. "And I may not be the brightest color in the crayon box but I'm also not the person who botched the murder of an innocent man." Clark started toward me, but his father placed a firm hand on his chest to prevent him from throttling me. "Anyway, it was my understanding Martin made a trade, fair and square. Detective Vargas for himself. Seems like someone reneged on that deal, Dr. Winslow. I get that you've had Junior here keeping tabs on me, breaking into my house, poisoning my dog." Theodore frowned at Clark then looked at Nicoh. "Oh, you weren't aware of that part? Whatever. I'm assuming you were trying to draw Martin out by hazing me. But why do you even need me or the chips when you already have Martin?"

Clark stepped toward Martin and snickered. "Come on Marty, why don't you do the honors of telling her?"

I shrugged. "Tell me what? What is it Martin is supposed to be telling me?"

Theodore looked at his old colleague and shook his head in disappointment. "She really doesn't know, does she?" Martin pursed his lips.

"I knew the old man was holding out," Clark growled. "Some things never change, huh, Father?"

"No, son, it appears they do not." Theodore scowled at Martin.

Clark continued, "Just using her as bait, while pretending to be long last daddy come to save the day—"

"Shut up!" Martin's eyes suddenly went wild as he spat out the words. "Ignore them, Arianna. Typical rantings of madmen."

Clark turned to me, his voice earnest, "Have I ever lied to you, Arianna?" I tilted my head. Clark had a point, if you over-looked the whole killing part—which I didn't—he'd technically never lied. Several months ago, he had said he would kill me. And here he was. Again. I gave him credit for persistence. He certainly had Martin rattled.

"Would someone…anyone, like to tell me what's going on here?" I looked from Theodore to Clark to Martin, challenging any one of them to do the deed.

It was Clark stepped to the plate, whether the action had been warranted or not. "Seems like Daddy Dearest hasn't told you the truth about the chips he implanted in you and your sister."

"If you're talking about the formulas for Gemini it's old news, Clark," I replied, unimpressed.

"That's rich." Clark appeared to be the only one amused by my comment, given the way Theodore and Martin were launching visual daggers at one another.

I gripped the handle of Mr. Shovel in frustration. As usual, Clark could never just get to the point. Everything was a production. All part of his little drama. "If you've got something to say, then spill it. This song and dance should have been left in the 1980s," I growled. Nicoh wasn't the only one who could show teeth when needed.

Clark scoffed, "A ten-year-old could have reproduced those formulas."

"Yeah, well, a lot of ten-year-olds are smarter than most adults I know. So, other than the formulas, what exactly are we talking about?"

"Oh, I'm sure Marty will concur what's on those chips is far more valuable than some outdated formulas." Clark laughed. "Just as I'm sure he knew the minute he implanted them, he'd sealed your fate." When I didn't respond, he added, "Look what happened to Victoria."

"Oh, no, you can't put that blame on anyone but yourself, Clark. Not your father. Not Martin. Not your secret club members. *You* brutalized and beat her to a pulp. And dumped her like trash." My voice sounded foreign, if not a bit crazed.

The venom I wanted to unleash on him had risen to the surface, refusing to stay tucked where I had buried it for months. I feared it made me too much like the monster standing before me. Too much like his father. And perhaps, much too much like Martin. All of them repulsed me. Human lives were flesh and blood with thoughts, emotions and souls. Not playthings to be manipulated or destroyed simply because it suited their needs. Clark may not have been the worst of them but he was part of the environment these men had created.

"Tell him, Dr. Winslow. Victoria would have been more useful alive than eating worm dirt. Had he not acted so hastily, so savagely…like the selfish, spoiled, undisciplined little boy he's always been, you probably would have already had the chips by now." I stared straight at Theodore and had my answer.

Though soulless, his eyes could not lie.

Clark saw the truth, too, and suddenly his life came unraveled. And just my luck, it did so…right on me.

CHAPTER TWENTY-SIX

Clark converged with such momentum and sheer rage even Theodore couldn't prevent him from launching into me, knocking me to the ground. I heard Martin call out and Nicoh howl but Clark was a wild man, quickly regaining his balance and rewarding me with a hard kick to the gut. Followed by another to my ribs.

A scream echoed. It took a few seconds to comprehend it had been mine. There was shuffling, scraping and yelling but the thumping of my heartbeat was the only sound I recognized as pain surged through every nerve. Clark was unrelenting and only after the fourth kick—this one landing squarely on my right kidney—Theodore managed to corral his frenzied son in an awkward bear hug.

"That's payback for your friend Leah." Clark was breathless from the energy he'd exerted as he struggled to free himself from his father's grasp. I was surprised the elder man was able to detain him for as long as he had, though perhaps having a son like Clark required a stronger arm than most. "I've waited quite a while to dish out that punishment and considering she's not here, you make a suitable stand-in. Not quite as satisfying I might add, but still delicious." He laughed before hawking a spitball at me.

"You kick like a little girl, Clark," I huffed. "And spit like one, too." Blood oozed from my mouth as I snorted, dripping rivulets onto the ground. Clark struggled and cursed under his father's weight but Theodore maintained his grip. For the moment, I was thankful, if not a bit impressed.

Suddenly, I registered movement off to the right.

Martin.

In Clark's zeal, he'd left the controller on the riser just within Martin's reach. During our altercation, Martin had managed to unhook himself. His wrists were still bound with a threaded bike lock but the slack allowed him to move each arm separately. He yelled my name and upon catching my eye, glanced at Nicoh.

I turned to the canine and belted out the word Martin had mouthed to me earlier, "Mush, Nicoh, mush!"

Theodore had inadvertently created a crude sled when he'd attached Nicoh's lead and mid-section to the pallet and now the canine's ears perked as he used his weight to shift the platform. Gaining momentum, despite the slickness of the concrete floor, he heaved the contraption forward—toward our captors.

Too bad Theodore and Clark had treated us poorly, I mused, as Nicoh got his revenge and pounced upon both men, using the full force of an Alaskan Malamute followed by the makeshift dog sled. Clark took the brunt of the blow and was thrown to the ground upon impact, his head connecting with the concrete in a satisfying thump. Theodore was knocked off balance, which allowed Martin to charge in from behind. Using the extra span of bike lock chain as a noose, he pulled it taut against the other man's windpipe. Theodore gasped as his hands scratched and clawed at Martin's head. Martin used the man's imbalance to take him to the ground, subduing him with the chain. Theodore emitted a sickening, burbling rasp as he struggled for air and finally slipped into unconsciousness. Martin continued to apply pressure, his demeanor unnervingly calm, as though the act brought him peace.

I forced myself to look away and screamed in horror. Nicoh was lying on his side partially covered by the riser. After colliding with Clark and his father, he had landed on the rake, now embedded into his side. Blood wept from the wound as I strained to listen for signs of life. Tears surged from my eyes when I heard the muffled gurgling of his labored breathing.

I wanted to comfort him but Clark was conscious and despite being woozy from the impact, still looked murderous as he snarled at the wreckage and the prone canine. Fighting through the pain, I struggled to my hands and knees while holding a hand against my injured ribs, as though the effort would meld them back into place. Mr. Shovel had managed to get himself stuck under the mess but I spotted Hoe and as I struggled to my feet, ripped it from beneath the rubble, stalking toward Clark.

He was panting and bleeding from the back of his head, as well as from the other injuries to his chest and midsection. Blood spittles erupted from his mouth as he laughed at me, amused by the girl with the gardening tool bearing down on him.

"Given the way you look right now, I'd say I won this round, Arianna."

I snorted but quickly had to fight the urge to react to the pain the gesture caused. "This is hardly a competition, Clark."

"Don't you get it? Life *is* a competition. Every day we fight to cheat death."

I shook my head. "No one cheats death, Clark."

"Ah, but that's where you are wrong, every day we live—we may be fighting the inevitable—but our survival means we've won." He hadn't struck me as a glass-half-full kind of guy but I went with it.

"Even though we lose in the end." This time, I posed no question.

"Only if you see death as a loss." Clark shrugged awkwardly, wincing from his injuries. I was happy to see he wasn't impervious to the pain.

"And you don't?" I asked.

"It depends on what you do with the time you have—the battles you've won, the challenges you've overcome—"

Who was this guy? Tony Robbins' evil twin? "The number of lives you take and are able to get away with?" I replied sarcastically.

Clark ignored my tone. "My life is my own to live. I make my own challenges and rewards and therefore, my own victory over death."

"But you interfere with other's battles and challenges in doing so. Your victories actually destroy their opportunities and their lives," I replied through gritted teeth.

"They have the same opportunities to survive, they just choose a safer path," he huffed, indignant he had to explain what seemed to be common sense for him. A dark comedy was more like it. Or a satire.

"So you're saying it's their own fault they didn't cheat death longer?" I scoffed.

Clark shrugged. "They made choices that put them on a losing path."

"Or perhaps just a collision course with a sociopath," I replied dryly. My attitude, or lack of agreement was not lost on him but he would not allow it to dissuade him. His ego and delusions of grandeur were too great, eclipsing even those of his father's. Would Papa Smurf have approved of his son's little soapbox moment? Or would he have realized it for it was? He'd created a monster that had no bounds. And no loyalty. Clark would eventually kill his own father, if the notion appealed to him or suited his needs.

"We all do what we have to—to survive. And to achieve victory, there must also be sacrifice," Clark replied.

"But the blood is not yours, Clark."

"Isn't it?" he growled. "You don't think I've made sacrifices?"

I gave him a single head shake. "Not unless these 'sacrifices' were a means to satisfy your ends."

"And *that's* why it's a competition, Arianna. In the end, it all comes down to life or death. Who possess the strength and the will to do what it takes." Every conversation with this guy was circular. The point he missed was in cheating death, he had also cheated life. At some point, that scale would have to be balanced. "Just out of curiosity, are you going to do anything with that gardening tool? Or are you just going to stand there and bleed all over me?"

"In a hurry, Clark?" I inched Hoe closer to his throat, so it had a front row seat to his carotid artery. "No worries. Where you're going—or should I say, going back to—you'll have plenty of time to pontificate how great of a player you've been in the game of life. You can even throw a few tea parties with your prison buddies to celebrate those victories. You are, after all, already familiar with all the activities they enjoy doing. Maybe you'll even find a few like-minded individuals to play Scrabble with. Or better yet, Twister." I grinned and when the taste of blood filled my mouth, I was happy to share my hideous smile.

Clark's lips curled into a snarl. "I'll twist your scrawny neck if you don't shut up." Hmmm, hit a nerve, did I? As if reading my thoughts, he managed to contain himself long enough to grit out, "All your incessant chirping interrupts me from deciding how to eliminate you. Permanently." His smile cracked the mercury right out of the creep-meter.

"Oh?" I toyed with Hoe, using Clark's neck for balance. "I thought you *needed* me, Clark. Martin, too? And, why was that again? You started telling me when—well, when Martin kicked Daddy's keister." Speaking of Martin, he'd been noticeably silent after wrangling with Theodore, which had me worried. "Been pretty quiet over there Martin, you doing okay?" I didn't dare take my eyes off Clark.

Martin replied, his voice weary, "Just trying to maintain control over here…"

He started to say something else but Clark surprised me by grabbing the back of my leg, forcing me off-balance and plunging me forward, along with Hoe. A sickening crunch echoed through the warehouse and Clark's eyes went wide as he gasped and gurgled, crimson spewing from the freshly made crevasse that had been his throat, coating me like a shawl as I made my downward journey. My battered frame connected with his, forcing the air from my lungs until there was nothing but blackness and silence.

I captured a final glimpse of Clark as consciousness eluded me. It turned out I had been wrong.

The hoe hadn't gotten the raw end of the deal after all.

CHAPTER TWENTY-SEVEN

Time had no relevance.

No hours.

No minutes.

No seconds.

Subliminal blips on the screen, only they weren't persuading me to buy cars, cologne, liquor…or love.

They were random glimpses.

Of Life.

And Death.

Glimpses of Clark's horrified expression as Death won the final match.

Glimpses of Martin, speaking soft and low. Brushing bloody, sweaty hair from my eyes. Squeezing my hand. Whispering my name.

Glimpses of activity. Commotion. Screeching. Crashing. Footsteps in a frenzied shuffle—like runners escaping a stampede of angry, charging bulls—followed by obscure voices. When had I been transported to a death metal concert?

One voice in the distance—a child's lullaby in comparison—familiar but worried.

Ramirez.

Time, sound and sight intertwined until I welcomed the blackness that beckoned me and offered the solace I sought. Still, something tugged at the back of my mind, begging me to return. I pushed it away, not wanting to remember.

As darkness took my hand, a persistent nudge made its last attempt and the memory slipped through. In it, a sickening crunch. A man's frame slumped, his neck contorted. And though the life behind them had extinguished, even in death, his soulless eyes stared on.

* * *

Hospitals.

Does anyone enjoy visiting them, much less waking up in one? I hadn't been given much choice in the matter, thanks to Clark's assault. While my stomach and kidneys were still mad and not at all shy about telling me just how they felt, my two cracked ribs—now known as Death Wishbone 1 and 2—were a constant reminder of the importance of playing nice in the school yard. Or not. Then again, Clark had probably never spent much time mastering that art.

Faces swarmed around me like faded watercolors. I could not move my arms but could feel the warmth of others enclosing my hand. My throat was dry and lips were cracked. Someone dribbled a bit of liquid into my mouth, like a small bird fetching a worm or tiny insect from its mother's beak. I pressed my lips together and winced as they chafed.

A small chuckle erupted to my right. "You'll get used to it." I exerted a great deal of effort turning my head and found my ears had not deceived me.

Vargas looked like a cross between a zombified soldier of death and one of Dr. Frankenstein's rejects, with a bad case of road rash tossed in. My head was swimming as I took in the road map of stitches and surgical tape that did little to mask the angry gashes and bruises that had once been his face.

"I really hope I'm not looking in a mirror," I rasped, drawing a round of chuckles from the others in the room, which included Leah, Abe, Elijah and Grace.

"Nah, this stuff's not for amateurs," Vargas teased, grunting as he shifted uncomfortably in his wheelchair. I noticed it was his hand that held my right. Except for the IVs, it was hard to tell where his began and mine ended, the bandages barely patching together skin and bone. I started to retort but felt a squeeze on my left.

"He's right you know." Despite her beaming smile, I saw the worry in my best friend's eyes as she took me in. "This time, anyway." She reached across and squeezed Vargas' free hand, resting on the edge of the bed. An unexpected look of tenderness passed between them.

Abe patted my leg. "Glad to have you back with us, Ajax. For a while there, we thought you were gone for good this time."

"Of course there was no way we were going to let you leave us with that unruly canine of yours," Elijah added, winking at me.

"Nicoh..." My heart and stomach did simultaneous flip-flops as I remembered the last time I had seen my big boy. "He...he... saved me..." I stuttered, tears welling in my eyes.

Leah clutched my hand. "He's gonna be okay, AJ. The rake did some damage but the vet got in there in time, did his magic and patched him up. And while he's currently mad about being poked and prodded, he'll be back to a hundred percent in no time."

I attempted to nod but the movement made me woozy. "I wasn't sure..." I replied quietly. "He was so still..." Again, tears burbled as the memory surfaced.

"Of course, it will be a while before he's eating cookies off the counter or chasing Mrs. Grimley's cat out of the bushes," Leah offered me a quick wink and smiled, "which means you and I'll will have to step up and do our part...on the cookies, anyway."

I chuckled but the sound didn't translate as I'd expected and the group worked hard not to wince.

"Hey Grace, is that you over there?" She looked less disheveled than the last time I had last seen her—in her smart red business suit and heels—hair pulled into a sleek up-do. The bags had diminished from beneath her eyes and her pale pallor was now flushed with a healthy pink.

She stepped forward and placed a small stuffed dog on my bed. "Hey you...I know it's not the same as having Nicoh here but I thought this little guy was a reasonable facsimile and could keep you company until you get out."

"How are you?" I asked after relaying my thanks.

"You're the one in the hospital and yet you're asking how I'm doing?" She chuckled, shaking her head. "I came to thank you."

"Thank me?"

"If you...and Leah...and well, all of you hadn't gotten involved..." She looked down. "Let's just say, things could have gotten messy."

"The police would have eventually figured everything out," I replied.

"Maybe, but it was you. You wouldn't let it go and now the monsters who killed Erica and Darian and Mort Daniels. And kidnapped Detective Vargas"—she looked shyly at the detective —"have been identified. And gotten what they were due." I inadvertently shuddered and looked away—if she'd known what I'd done, would she have felt the same? "Anyway, I wanted to thank you. And I don't want to seem morbid but something positive did come out of all this." She paused, a tiny smile forming at the corner of her mouth. "My ex's parents—the ones who have custody of my daughter? Well, since Darian's death, they've reached out to me and we've really had a chance to sit down and talk about things. And while we're not there yet, we're talking about visits, possibly shared custody. Anyway, it's promising."

"That is wonderful, Grace. I'm truly happy for you." If something good could come out of this tragedy and the mess Clark and his father had created, then Grace should definitely be on the list of people to benefit. "How about work?"

"I'm still filling Erica's position until they find a permanent candidate," Grace replied.

"You'd be a fine replacement." Leah patted her former co-worker on the arm.

"Oh, I don't know about that. It would be strange." Grace shook her head.

"At least give it some consideration," I added and everyone nodded in agreement. "In the meantime, what's going to happen with the book?"

Her eyes perked up at the mention of it but she patted my leg. "I've taken up enough of your time, AJ. There are a lot of people here who want to see you. Besides, we can talk about that later." She gave me a hurried wink and after thanking me again, made her exit.

"What do you suppose that was all about?" Elijah asked.

I slid a glance at Leah. "Who knows," I replied, changing the subject as I perused one face to the next. "So what else have I missed?"

"Err, you should probably talk to Detective Ramirez about that." I could only stare at my friend—typically the first to divulge every juicy detail—as she shifted uncomfortably.

"For once, the voice of reason." I hadn't realized he'd been in the room until the group parted and suddenly there he stood, arms crossed, leaning casually against the door jamb.

"Come in and join the fun, Ramirez," I managed to scratch

out, while the peanut gallery barely managed to withhold their chuckles.

"Actually, why don't we leave you two to talk?" Abe nodded at his brother, before leaning down to kiss me on the forehead.

"Yeah, we've got to get back before Anna completely takes over," Elijah replied.

"I hate to tell you this but I think she already has." I laughed.

"True, true," Elijah sighed but his smile was wide. "She sends her best. By the way that obnoxious display of roses was her doing, though we managed to deliver them."

"Uh, huh. Girl's definitely got taste. And class. Tell her thank you and I hope to see you all soon."

"You'd better behave yourself. She still expects you in L.A. to help with the wedding plans. She wants her photographer to be in top form, after all," Abe teased.

"Like I said, girl's got good taste." Both Stantons laughed and shook hands with Ramirez and Vargas before leaving.

Leah released my hand and shifted off the bed. "Ready to go, gimpy?" She looked at Vargas, who mocked-growled. The guy was completely smitten with my best friend.

He squeezed my hand as she maneuvered his wheelchair. "You take it easy, Ajax." As Leah rolled him away, I had a feeling he was talking about more than nursing my wounds.

Ramirez remained in place long after Leah and Vargas retreated down the corridor to his room, tossing insults back and forth all the while, just like old times. I tried to laugh but the movement caused me to wince and though I fought to hide the pain it inflicted, the detective's sharp eyes missed nothing.

"Smarts, doesn't it?"

"Just getting used to all this gift-wrapping." I gestured toward the bandages and IVs.

"Still, must have been a rude awakening to find yourself in this condition." His tone was sarcastic but his gaze was more than a little intense. "I have to wonder what you were thinking, running off like that?"

"What?" I scoffed. "You think it was part of my grand plan to get blindsided by Clark; then beaten to a pulp?" I wanted to throw my head back and have a good laugh—show him how ridiculous that notion was—but my injuries had other ideas.

"Your actions suggest you have a death wish. Do you?" He searched my eyes.

I squinted. "What exactly are you getting at?"

"Things around you tend to die." When I grimaced, he raised a hand to clarify. "Or at least, that's your perception. I honestly don't know, perhaps you don't feel like you deserve to live, because they didn't? That somehow, their lives were more important and that you're not worthy of being the last one standing?" He shrugged; then began to pace. "Why else would you take the risks you do? Certainly not for the sport of it."

I thought back to my last conversation with him. "No, Ramirez, I do not have a death wish. But I also don't like seeing my friends and family hurt. Or worse. There's already been so much loss."

He raised an eyebrow. "And so it's Ajax in her Wonder Woman suit and lasso, off in her invisible jet on a solo mission to take down all forces of evil?"

"Actually, I'd like to think of myself as a grown-up version of a Powerpuff Girl armed with my Chemical X, high ponytail, mischievous Alaskan Malamute and spunky best friend."

Exasperated, Ramirez shook his head. Clearly, he didn't watch the Cartoon Network. "Chemical X or not, you take risks—absurd risks—which could end up not only hurting you but the people who love you." I bowed my head so he couldn't see the tears welling. "What would Leah do without you? You're the only family she's got. And Nicoh?"

"And you?" His silence spoke volumes and when he would

not meet my gaze, I changed the subject. "All this heavy stuff is making my brain hurt. Would you mind if we discussed what happened when Clark snatched me? And perhaps you could fill me in on what happened...after? I'm a bit fuzzy on some of it." Boy was I.

I yawned and suddenly, the biggest peanut butter fudge shake couldn't have kept me awake. Perhaps this impromptu sleepiness was some form of subconscious avoidance technique. Whatever it was, within a few short minutes, despite my attempts to keep my eyes open I lapsed into that dream land, where only happy memories awaited me.

Ramirez was waiting when I woke, sitting in a corner chair, reading a *People* magazine.

"Catching up on the latest gossip, are we?"

Ramirez smirked at me over the top of the well-endowed celebrity gracing the front cover. He looked as though sleep was a thing that existed in the past, his eyes tired but still alert.

"As if I know who half these people are. Or care. What was I supposed to do? You fell asleep. One might draw the conclusion it had to do with the company."

I yawned, wishing I could scratch the itch on my nose but the IVs had other plans. "Nah, it was nice everyone could make it. They certainly didn't need to—"

He put the magazine down and stood but remained at a safe distance. "I wasn't talking about everyone, AJ."

"Urrr...what was it we were talking about before I zonked out?"

Ramirez ignored my side-step. "You were going to fill me in on what occurred after we found Vargas."

"Right. So what have I already told you? "

He shook his head. "Not much. At least not much more than your constant reference to the 'ho.' " He smirked, using his index fingers for emphasis.

I chuckled. "The hoe is not a person, Ramirez. It's a gardening tool." He shook his head in disbelief. "What? You've never worked with garden tools before?"

Ramirez grunted out a harsh laugh. "I know what a hoe is, AJ. The question is, what does it have to do with anything?"

My face flushed and my stomach stirred with what could only be described as a flurry of bumblebees as I remembered the look on Clark's face. And the flood of crimson. "The hoe killed...I killed Clark."

"No, AJ. He was killed in an accident." An accident? This was news to me. Ramirez caught my surprise and elaborated, "An entire set from the abandoned television station landed on him."

I shook my head and winced. "That's not what killed him, Ramirez. Believe me, I got him with the hoe first. He was... spurting blood...everywhere." I started shaking and though Ramirez moved to comfort me, he stopped short when I waved him off. The walls were already closing in without having him dote over me.

He sighed. "I'm sorry, AJ, but there was no hoe at the scene. At least not when we got there."

"That's impossible," I whispered, my mind reeling through the events. I was sure it wasn't playing tricks. I hadn't dreamt the whole thing.

Ramirez evaluated my expression. "Maybe you'd better start at the beginning." He patted the foot of the bed, careful not to venture closer. "Just take your time and please breathe, will you?"

I shook my head, giving him a small smile and once I'd drawn a few cleansing breathes—with extreme discomfort—I told my tale, top to bottom, left to right, front to back. Just the facts, ma'am. When I finished, he was quiet for a long while. Too long, even for a cop.

"Say something," I whispered.

He rubbed his chin as he carefully formulated his response.

"All right. There appears to be several…inconsistencies between what you have just told me and what we found when we arrived on the scene."

"I'm sure Martin corroborated what I told you." I shrugged. "He saw the same things I did."

Ramirez shook his head. "That's the thing, AJ, Martin's one of those inconsistencies."

I raised my head off the pillow. "Come again?"

"Martin wasn't at the warehouse when we arrived."

"How did you know where to find me?"

"I received an anonymous call. A man told me where to find you and Nicoh and hung up." When I raised an eyebrow, Ramirez elaborated. "He called you both by name."

"And you're thinking it was Martin." It wasn't a question. He shrugged, noncommittal, causing me to sigh. "Tell me what you found. Did you see Clark snatch me?"

"I saw you get thrown into a black Escalade. Leah had gone with Vargas to the hospital, so Abe, Elijah and I took pursuit. We temporarily lost sight of it as we weaved in and out of an industrial park and after we spotted it again, we realized the driver had used the distraction to swap out vehicles." I wondered how they'd known it had been a decoy and Ramirez did not disappoint. "Plates were the same but the first vehicle had a trailer hitch with a crease in the bumper molding. Anyway, we eventually lost that one, too and had to assume they'd snuck into one of the warehouses."

"And once you lost them—what? You waited to get the call?"

"No, we didn't just wait until we got the call," he growled. Apparently, the detective was feeling a bit touchy despite the fact I hadn't intended for the comment to have been taken that way. "We went back to your house and looked for clues. I talked to the other officers, neighbors, etc. to see if they had noticed anything suspicious but they hadn't. Your neighbor Susie is horrified now that she knows what really happened to Nicoh and that she chatted it up with a ruthless killer." Words couldn't remove that image from my mind, though the look Ramirez tossed me came pretty darn close.

"What? I certainly didn't tell her. Nicoh is like a teenager at a Justin Bieber concert when it comes to her homemade doggie treats, not to mention she's one of the best neighbors a person could have. Do you think I'd want her moving on account of my penchant for attracting the unwanted attentions of murderous psychos?" Ramirez nearly broke his jaw chewing that one over before I quickly added, "Present company excluded, of course."

He waved it off. "Not you. I think Leah let it slip but she wouldn't confirm when we asked her. Did pretty much the same circle dance you tend to do, though."

"I learned it from her," I replied, pleased by the level of smugness I'd managed to conjure.

"I'd believe that," he replied, though his expression suggested I'd been a willing participant. "Getting back your question. We got the call and when we arrived at the abandoned warehouse, you and Nicoh were out front. No one else. We were checking you out—Nicoh still had the rake embedded in his side—when we heard the crash. I had called for backup while we were en route, along with a couple of ambulances but they hadn't arrived yet, so Abe, Elijah and I went in. Place was a booby-trapped maze. We were surprised the whole place didn't come falling in on us."

"I'm sure old Theo had something to do with that—it probably made purchasing the property all the more worth his while."

"I don't doubt the booby-trapping part—the place was a dump to begin with—but Theodore Winslow didn't own it. In fact, had it not become a crime scene, it was slated to be torn down by the real owner within a few months."

"Huh." Clark had lied to me after all. "Guess you guys

wouldn't have found us had it not be for that anonymous caller."
Another testament to how close I'd come to death's door.

Ramirez ignored my comment. "We made our way through
that minefield of a television junkyard until we found Theodore
and his son. It appeared as though the rigging from one of the sets
gave way while both were underneath."

I reconstructed where we'd been positioned during those last
few moments. It was possible both men had been in the vicinity
when the structure fell. But crushed? Improbable. Certainly not
without some serious staging. "Were they…dead?" I managed to
squeak out.

Ramirez nodded. "Both sustained massive trauma when the
structure collapsed, obliterating Theodore Winslow's windpipe
and severing his son's head." Despite what the evidence
suggested, I was still convinced I had inflicted Clark's fatal
wound. What happened afterward just ensured he stayed that way.
"Of course, we need wait for the official report but…" he
shrugged, the facts being what they were, before taking in my
impassive expression. "You're still thinking about the hoe."

"Yeah, that…and other things." I had yet to mention the
memory I had before slipping into darkness.

"You care to share these 'other things' with me, AJ?" Ramirez
searched my eyes and for a moment, I was afraid they would
betray me.

I looked at my hands. "I don't know. Just images mostly.
There was so much going on and I was out of it at the end. I
certainly don't remember leaving the building." He nodded, not
completely convinced. "And considering Nicoh was injured and I
didn't have much in the way of defense other than a hoe and a
shovel, our odds of getting out of there unscathed were slim."

"AJ, there was no shovel, either."

I snorted. "Surely you're not suggesting Martin took the hoe
and shovel, but left the rake?"

"He saved Nicoh's life when he left the rake in place. Nicoh would have bled out if Martin had removed it."

"You realize how ridiculous this sounds, don't you? Martin, who was probably injured himself, not only manages to get me out but Nicoh out as well, with a rake impaled in his side. He then reenters the building, repositions Clark and Winslow, releases the mechanism holding the set in place and then has the wherewithal to remove evidence?" I huffed.

Ramirez heard me out before speaking. "It's not all that ridiculous. Not if Martin was trying to protect you by ensuring you were in the clear. You did handle the shovel too, did you not?" My expression was a dead giveaway. "I thought so. Sure does seem like Martin's going out of his way for you, AJ. Now why do you suppose that is?"

I shrugged, not really wanting to have this discussion, though I did wonder where Martin had put the tools, given the time frame. And, how had he known where to put them. Or better yet, where to put them so the police wouldn't find them. When I looked up, I found Ramirez studying me and tried my best to remain nonchalant. "No idea. Making up for lost time, I suppose. Plus, he thinks it's his fault Theodore and Clark came after me in the first place as a ploy to draw him out."

Ramirez wasn't convinced. "A convenient response, especially when you're the one with the chips everyone's hot for."

"Are you suggesting he wants the chips for himself and with the other two out of the way, things have worked out quite nicely for him?"

He shrugged. "I know you've been contemplating whether to hand the chips over to him but you should think long and hard before doing so. In fact, I would advise against it. It could be to your own detriment. You're safer with them than without."

I snorted, gesturing to my current predicament. "Yeah, real safe, Ramirez. Real safe." He pursed his lips. "Did it ever occur to you Martin might be the only one who can ensure the information on the chips is safe from people like Clark or Theodore? Or whoever they were working with?"

He didn't respond immediately but something I'd said had gotten under his saddle. "There's something else I wanted to tell you—about Vargas. When he was held captive down in that pit, he was forced to watch Darian's execution."

I gasped as horror rolled through me. "Clark forced him to watch—"

Ramirez shook his head. "It wasn't Clark. Or Theodore."

"There's a third man," I inadvertently uttered.

"Looks that way." It wasn't what he'd said but the way he'd said it.

"What? Don't tell me you think it was Martin?" He continued to work his jaw, providing me with my answer. "You actually think he could have been in cahoots…with them?" My voice went up a perilous octave. Ramirez raised a hand, encouraging me to tone it down before the hospital staff brought in a crash cart.

"I think Martin knows more than he's letting on—that his connection to Theodore and his son was more involved than any of us realized—and that it was in his best interest to have them out of the way. I believe they were a means to an end and you were the tool he needed to facilitate that end. I have nothing linking him directly—whether he personally executed Mort, Erica or Darian—but indirectly, I doubt his intentions were as innocent as saving his daughter."

"What about the others Clark and Theodore were working with?"

"There's no proof there was anyone else, AJ. Just as there is no proof Martin had any associates helping him. How do you know it wasn't just the three of them all along and when Martin saw an opportunity to double-cross the others?" Ramirez paused, allowing me to draw my own conclusions.

I felt my face reddening in fury, though several of the same questions had been swirling around in my brain and gnawing at my gut. "I can't believe you can so easily come to this conclusion, Ramirez. Even after he traded himself for Vargas and saved Nicoh. And me."

"From where I sit, it changes nothing. Regardless of what he's done as of late, I still don't trust him." He shook his head. There would be no reasoning with him and when it came to Martin we were at an impasse. He must have been reading my thoughts or perhaps, I had been wearing my emotions like a comfortable, old pair of Chuck Taylors. "Anyway, you should draw your own conclusions about Martin."

I quirked an eyebrow. "Are you assuming I haven't?"

"I think you're still on the fence. Your mind is telling you one thing, your gut another and your heart…" his voice trailed off as his eyes took in the sunset from the limited view of my hospital window, as though he wished he could be anywhere—anywhere but here.

I urged him to finish his thought. "What does my heart say?"

"Your heart says…" he paused, shaking his head and when he finally replied, his voice was filled with sadness and disappointment, "it doesn't really matter anymore." He turned away, placing a hand on the door.

My lip trembled. I wanted to call out to him, to beg him to take it back. Once again, tears emerged and I couldn't speak. Ramirez did it for me but they weren't the words I'd hoped for.

"And AJ? You're going to need to repeat what you just told me—leaving nothing out and I mean nothing, including the part about Martin—to Detective Chavez." He easily slipped back into his detective role, like a suit of armor that had been custom-designed. It pained me to realize he found solace in it and not in our relationship. It was, in effect, his escape from it.

"Your partner?" I managed to choke out.

Despite the shakiness of my voice, Ramirez still would not turn to face me. "He's waiting outside to take your formal statement. And a piece of friendly advice: if Martin contacts you in any way, you need to encourage him to come to the station, as well as contact Detective Chavez immediately."

"You're not staying?" I asked, my voice hopeful.

"No, AJ, I've done all I can," he paused, his voice barely a whisper and for a moment I thought he would continue. Instead, he silently opened the door and walked out of my life.

At that moment, I realized while my fractured ribs would eventually mend, the piece of my heart I'd reserved for Ramirez had shattered forever.

CHAPTER TWENTY-EIGHT

Once my story had been told and told again, I cried myself to sleep. It was something I hadn't done since my parents died. The tears scorched my cheeks but I welcomed their pleasant diversion from the bitter, savage chill that nipped at my bones.

When I dreamt, it wasn't of the horrors I'd witnessed or the pain I now felt. It was of sunshine kisses…of smiling faces…and laughter. Images filtered by on a hazy cloud, like random snapshots in a photo album. The past danced with the present and mingled with unrecognizable fragments. The future, perhaps? All I knew was that I felt safe and as long as I stayed, nothing would threaten to steal my warmth, ever again.

Something told me I couldn't stay locked in my cocoon forever and once the images had melted away, I emerged from my sanctuary. Feeling a familiar hand clutching my own, my heart did a little pitter patter.

"Ramirez?" I let a yawn escape as my eyes fluttered to adjust to the darkness of the room.

"No, sweetheart, he's gone." My heartbeat slowed in disappointment.

"Martin?" My throat was rough from sleep and tears long cried out.

"Yes, my darling…" His face was hidden by the shadows but his voice was gentle and soothing. "Why don't you have a sip of water?" I felt the cup against my lips and though it was room temperature, I shook off a chill.

"Where have you been, Martin?"

"I tried to get here sooner but that detective of yours is quite persistent, as are your friends—who waited tirelessly for you to awaken."

"You were here, then?"

"At a safe distance but yes, always near."

"How did you manage—"

"The duty nurse stepped away."

"I had to tell them everything, Martin," my voice cracked as I muffled a sob.

Martin patted my hand, his voice reassuring, "Of course you did, my darling."

"Why didn't you stay? They don't believe me. At least, not about everything."

"In due time, they will."

"But, Martin…they need to know…you saved me."

"No AJ, you saved yourself. I merely moved you and Nicoh out of harm's way."

"You saved his life by not removing the rake."

"Because he's important to you," his tone was earnest.

"He is…very, very important." My voice cracked, thinking of my big beast. I wanted nothing more than to scratch his muzzle and tell him I loved him. Had I told him I loved him that day? I swallowed hard and turned to where Martin sat, wishing I could see his face. "Did you kill him, Martin? Did you kill Theodore?" I sucked in a deep breath. "After I killed…after the struggle with Clark, I thought I heard…"

Martin cut me off, his voice firm but gentle, "Theodore died a long time ago, Arianna."

"I know the two of you shared quite a history." Recalling the scene at the warehouse, neither father nor son had appeared to be surprised by Martin's sudden manifestation or that he looked so fresh after being dead for nearly three decades. There was also Martin's lack of venom when interacting with the man he'd supposedly not seen in all those years—the same man who'd murdered the mother of his newborns and had attempted his own demise. In fact, Martin had been quick—too quick—to shut Theodore and his son down. "He even alluded to circumstances surrounding that history—they both did—though they never quite managed to divulge any specific details." And now the only man left standing who could reveal those details was sitting before me. Silent. One was left to wonder why. "Did he help you disappear, Martin? Is that what he was trying to tell me? Is that how he knew you were alive?"

Martin sighed, his voice weary. "It's not that simple, Arianna."

"The truth never is, Martin."

"Theodore and Clark were bad men—men with no conscience, no souls."

"What kind of man are you, Martin?"

It took him a moment but he finally answered. The strain in his voice told me it pained him to do so, "One who has seen and done too many things to recall what it was once like to differentiate black from white."

"The Gray Man." My response bore no judgment, merely an observation. A conclusion.

He chuckled. "So it would seem."

"Does the Gray Man's inability to differentiate the black from the white also give him the capacity to murder innocents?"

"By innocents, I assume you mean Erica Stone and the bartender?" he asked, his tone contemplative.

I nodded. "And Mort Daniels."

"Even the Gray Man…even I have limits, Arianna. While I may have traipsed across one line or the other, I am not without morals, or without a soul."

"So the answer is no?"

"The answer is no."

"On all the above?" This time, there was only silence. As usual, there was no clear-cut answer with him and while I believed he had not killed Erica, Mort or Darian, I wasn't convinced he hadn't had knowledge that would have spared them. With Martin, it seemed as though there were always contingencies —truths within the truths. He'd kept things close to the vest for so long he probably couldn't remember what those were.

"You were never really going to tell me about yourself, were you, Martin?" I'd known the answer before I'd asked.

"Some things are better left alone, just as they are, which sometimes means leaving them in the past," he replied.

"I am part of that past," I countered.

"I said *some* things, Arianna."

"Does that include the chips? You've been awfully careful not to ask me about them," I hesitated, "but you want them, don't you?"

"Unfortunately, Mort Daniels brought the Gemini project back into the limelight, sharing it with Erica and perhaps even this girl, Grace," his displeasure was palpable as he bit out the words, "which now makes it extremely dangerous for you to have them."

"So, I assume you want me to hand them over. To you," I replied dryly.

"It would be your decision," he replied, "but it would be for your own safety. And for the safety of the ones you care for."

"Some decision," I responded.

He chuckled again. "The tough ones—the ones that mean something—always are. The rest…"

"Just fodder?"

"Exactly."

I nodded. "May I have some time to think about it?"

"Of course," he replied and if he was disappointed, his voice didn't betray him.

"A couple things have been puzzling me—how did you know about Vargas?"

He might have been a skilled actor but his confusion sounded sincere. "I'm not sure I understand what you mean?"

"Back when I told you about my friend who was in trouble and missing, you asked if it was the Tempe Homicide Detective, despite the fact I hadn't mentioned it was a *cop* friend. It could have just as easily been Leah, or another friend altogether."

"Surely I heard it on the news." His tone wasn't as convincing this time around.

I shook my head, though he probably couldn't see me either. "No, Martin. The police had just started searching for Vargas. The news media hadn't even been alerted much less associated him with Erica's murder."

"Oh? I'm not sure, then. Why do you ask?" I noticed he had released my hand. If only I could see his face.

"Just something Ramirez said," I replied, nonchalant. "Vargas was forced to watch as Darian, the bartender, was shot…executed. I assumed it had been Clark but Vargas insisted it was neither Clark nor his father, but a third man."

"Huh…I had no idea." A tiny tremor filtered in, but was gone just as quickly.

I clucked my tongue. "No, of course you didn't. But then, now that I think about it, Clark never mentioned it. And if I've learned anything about Clark, he wouldn't pass up an opportunity to blab about his feats. As for old Theo doing the deed? From what I saw, he would not have done his own dirty work when he had a son that was so proficient at it." I shrugged. "Anyway, I guess we'll just have to assume it was one of their minions, who managed to escape into the sunset."

"Looks that way." His voice was now devoid of emotion—the switch had been flipped into the off position—apparently, the father-daughter session was over. I wasn't going to get answers to any of the other questions either—like how he'd finally managed to track down and make contact with Theodore or his son, or how he'd known Grace had been married to Darian. Not today, anyway. "I hear the nurse coming back. We'll talk more about this later? Once you're out of the hospital, of course. In the meantime, you'll give some serious thought to what we discussed regarding the chips?"

"You can count on it, Martin."

Martin slipped out as silently as he had entered, leaving me to contemplate the truth behind the truth.

And the foundation of lies it had been built on.

EPILOGUE

I was released from the hospital a few days later and of course, assigned to a regiment that required limited movement. For once, I decided obedience was in my best interest. I'd like to think Ramirez would have been both proud and probably a bit amused by the state of affairs in my household. Leah had brought Nicoh home from the vet with strict instructions which included the threat of an e-collar, should he choose to deviate from them. In the end, we were both vying for prime real estate on the couch while Leah served as our surly nursemaid.

Honestly, she didn't seem to mind, as it allowed her to unleash her bossy streak. Plus, with her manning the snacks, it meant she got to pick her favorites. At one particularly cantankerous moment, she threatened to bring out the cocktail weanies and while that might have had Nicoh salivating, I opted for being a good little patient. Though I'll admit, I did fantasize about getting even with her one day.

As we'd settled in one night, I noticed she had a mildly amused look about her.

"Spill it," I growled, praying Spam Surprise wasn't on the menu. Again.

She did her best to maintain a poker face—even using Nicoh to distract me—but he was immersed in his own bowl of popcorn and could not be bothered with the absurdities of humans, so all she received for her efforts was a disgusted canine snort.

"Abe and Elijah left us a special little parting gift." I motioned for her to continue before I became part of the couch. "All right, all right! They made a few tiny 'modifications' to the security room."

I groaned, whenever she used finger quotes for emphasis, I knew we were in trouble. "How tiny?"

"They converted it into a small panic room. Of sorts." She winced, as though I would risk tossing my box of Junior Mints at her. "I'll give you a tour once you've gotten the clear to give the couch back its cushion."

I smirked at her as she prattled on about the Stanton brother's architectural prowess in regards to security—at least, that's what I hoped she was talking about—in addition to the various benefits of having such a feature. I couldn't deny I was intrigued by the concept, but was more curious about the intention.

Had Abe and Elijah designed a panic room to keep the baddies out? Or to keep us in?

Apparently, my reputation as a trouble magnet had continued to precede me but before I had a chance to ponder another one of life's little mysteries, my phone tinked at the sound of an incoming text message.

From Martin.

Have you made a decision?

My thoughts drifted to the information I had received earlier that day. Before I gave Martin an answer, I'd needed to know why the chips were so important. If they were worth killing and dying for, would they be safe in Martin's hands? Or in the hands of his unknown associates?

I had to be sure, once and for all, so that morning I had

contacted the geekiest person I'd known—a computer, audio visual and security expert who went by the alias Tony B. After swearing him to secrecy, I had relayed all the sordid details surrounding the Gemini project, including the ones involving Victoria and me. When I finished, he was eerily silent.

"Tony?"

"I'm here, just calculating the likelihood—given your track record—that you're going to get both of us killed if I do this."

"Oh, is there an app for that?"

Tony snorted. "Yeah, I wrote it."

"Give it to me straight, what are my…our odds?"

"Less just say they are not in our favor and leave it at that."

"I didn't need an app to tell me that," I joked.

"It never hurts to know what you're facing though," he replied, "even when writing your own death warrant."

"Hmm…a realist. Always good to have one on the team." He was silent. As a self-proclaimed hermit—I'd never actually met him in person—I doubted he'd want to be associated with anyone's team, whether going to his death or not. "Anyway, you want me to messenger these over?"

"Same place," he replied. "And AJ?"

"Yeah, Tony?"

"I may be a genius but I'm not a miracle worker. Nor am I a super hero. So, even if I'm able to extract something off these suckers, I can't save your bacon once the information is out there."

"It's okay, Tony, you do your geeky best, take care of your own bacon and leave the super hero stuff to me." A snort reverberated in my ear, followed by the sound of a dial tone.

It turned out Tony B. was both a genius and a miracle worker, as he got back to me within hours of taking delivery of messengered package. He wasn't one for bursts of emotion but his findings warranted a bit more than he managed to exude.

"You're not going to like this," were his first words.

"It can't be any worse than what I've already cooked up. It's like Sauerkraut Sunday back in the day at the Jackson household —you knew it was coming but you could never escape the stench." My analogy was met with awkward silence. "Just give it to me straight, Tony."

"It was pretty simple getting the data if you had both chips. Each chip contained a code needed to unlock the information on the other. You just had to do it in the right sequence." Much like Martin's arrangement when he contacted his associates. Clever? Or paranoid? "Once paired together, I was able to access the comprehensive data."

"So, one's like the table of contents and the other contains the chapters?"

"A bit more complex than that but generally speaking, you're in the ballpark." His tone indicated I wasn't even in the same time zone. "Anyway, the chips contained the formulas for the project— as you'd expected—along with the dates, times, names of bene-factors, patients and donors, including details about the off-spring and their adoptive parents. Quite a dossier on your family tree, in case you're interested."

"Err…yeah, maybe later. Surely there was something…more? Something worth killing for?"

"I believe I just mentioned it."

"Come again?"

Perhaps it was the connection but I was pretty sure I heard a head-slap. "The names, AJ. It all comes down to the list of names."

"The benefactors? The donors? The children? The adoptive parents?"

"*All* of them, AJ. The list is quite a doozy. You'll never guess whose names popped up." This time, Tony B. sounded almost human.

"Do I really want to know?"

"Oh, I think you'll find it very…educational."

"Go on…"

"Two of the products of Gemini turned out to be local boys. The first is your pal, Jeremiah Vargas, and the second, Congressman Bob Fenton." I gasped. What were the odds? The congressman was married to Ramirez's ex, Serena. Vargas was his best friend. "And that's not even the best part—they're brothers."

Too speechless to respond, Tony B. took it as a sign to proceed and continued to rattle off other several high profile names—politicians, entertainers, athletes—even a few miscreants, including a recently decommissioned drug czar, as in dead. Most of them had more than enough reason to ensure Erica's book never saw the light of day. Some even had the means to guarantee it. And just when I thought things were starting to get complicated, Tony B. graciously tossed in another wrinkle.

"Of course, this is where it gets *really* interesting." Good old Tony B., always saving the beast for last. "Turns out the benefactors had a board of directors, for lack of a better term. Anyway, the Chairman of the Board, so to speak, was also the scientist who spearheaded the consortium—someone whose name I think you're more than a little familiar with…" His revelation sent the world toppling off its axis, where it landed squarely on the right toe of my favorite vintage Chucks.

"Earth to AJ! Have you even been listening to a word I've said?" Leah's exasperated expression told me I'd missed out on more than a few pertinent details involving the Stanton's modifications while I'd taken that mental sidebar to revisit my conversation with Tony B.

I sighed and looked at Martin's message one last time, before flipping the phone over and shoving it out of the way with the toe of my injured foot.

Leah looked at me curiously, having seen the message from where she was sitting. "Aren't you going to respond to that?"

I nabbed the remaining gummy worm just as Nicoh's tongue was zeroing in, popping it in my mouth with a satisfied grin.

"I believe I just did."

~ The End ~

ABOUT HARLEY

Harley Christensen lives in Phoenix, Arizona with her significant other and their mischievous motley crew of rescue dogs (aka the "kids").

When not at her laptop, Christensen is an avid hockey fan and lover of all things margarita. It's also rumored she's never met a green chile or jalapeño she didn't like, regardless of whether it liked her back.

For more information on the author and her books, please visit her at www.mischievousmalamute.com.

Made in the USA
Lexington, KY
08 August 2019